A Robert Silverberg
Omnibus

A Robert Silverberg
Omnibus
THE MAN IN THE MAZE
NIGHTWINGS
DOWNWARD TO THE
EARTH

ROBERT SILVERBERG

HARPER & ROW, PUBLISHERS, New York

Cambridge, Hagerstown, Philadelphia, San Francisco

1817 London, Mexico City, São Paulo, Sydney

Library of Congress Cataloging in Publication Data

Silverberg, Robert.
  A Robert Silverberg omnibus.
  CONTENTS: The man in the maze.—Nightwings.—Downward to the Earth.
  1. Science fiction, American. I. Title.
PS3569.I472A6 1981   813'.54   80-8232
ISBN 0-06-014047-X

81 82 83 84 85 10 9 8 7 6 5 4 3 2 1

Contents

Introduction

These three novels date from the most fertile period of my career, the late 1960s, when wonders brimmed to overflow in my mind and novels came pouring in splendid excess from my fingers. Not only these three but also *The Masks of Time*, *To Live Again*, *Thorns*, *Tower of Glass*, and *Son of Man* issued forth all in one mighty rush. After that it all became much more difficult, and for a while it became impossible, for me to write fiction. The storytelling impulse returned eventually, but I suspect that never again will I startle the world with so many books so swiftly. Which is all right with me; all I ask of myself is that I write well, not that I write with freakish abundance, and my main goal is to give pleasure to my readers through the satisfying practice of my art and craft, not to win a place in the *Guinness Book of World Records*. Still, it does amaze me how readily those novels of the late 1960s came.

Why I should have been so productive then I have no real idea. Of course, I was younger then: everybody was. The young have more energy than the—well, not quite as young—and they have more to prove, more to make known to the world. Paradoxically, too, they seem to feel time's winged chariot hurrying on in a way that older people have learned to ignore. I was in my early thirties when I wrote these novels, and the thirties, for a writer, seem to be a time of peak creative energy, I know not why. Painters and composers and poets often do their best work in late middle age, if they are lucky enough to have a late middle age; but writers surge early. Dickens, by the age of 37, had *David Copperfield*, *The Pickwick Papers*, *Oliver Twist*, and *Barnaby Rudge* behind him, among much else. Faulkner, at 35, had already done *The Sound and the Fury*, *As I Lay Dying*, *Light in August*, and *Sanctuary*. Hemingway's key work was accomplished in his twenties and early thirties, and he was only 42 when he wrote *For Whom the Bell Tolls*, after which he accomplished relatively little.

In science fiction there is a remarkable correlation between youth and creativity. Some honorable exceptions exist, writers like Ursula Le Guin, Gene Wolfe, and James Tiptree, who were only beginning their careers at an age when most in their field were essentially finished with theirs, and yet went on to great things beyond 40. But the novels for which Isaac Asimov is famous were written between the ages of 22 and 33. Theodore Sturgeon's classic *More Than Human* appeared when he was 35, amid a great burst of other wondrous stories. Arthur Clarke had achieved *Childhood's End*, *Against the Fall of Night*, and *Sands of Mars* by the same age. The two great novels of Alfred Bester were written before he reached 43. Robert Sheckley's phenomenal flow of short stories emerged in his late twenties. Philip K. Dick, Poul Anderson, Philip José Farmer, Walter M. Miller, Jr., and many others had accomplished their basic work by the time they reached 40. (Most of these writers, of course, have gone on to do excellent work in their later years, and we also have the sterling example before us of Robert A. Heinlein, who after hitting the customary burst of creative vitality between the ages of 32 and 35 had a second such spurt a decade and a half later. But in general it seems that a writer and especially a sciencefiction writer has his time of greatest intensity when he is young.)

The earliest of the three novels reprinted in this omnibus is *The Man in the Maze*, which I wrote in the autumn of 1967. The snarling, alienated protagonist, caught in a tragic and hopeless predicament, was then a fairly uncommon sort of figure for science fiction, though a few perceptive readers did notice his true literary ancestry in the *Philoctetes* of Sophocles. (I learned much of what I know about constructing plots from a careful study of Greek tragedy in my undergraduate days, and from time to time I pay tribute to my masters by borrowing one of their narrative situations.) I think it is one of my strongest books. It attracted little attention when it first appeared, no awards nominations or instant elevation to the pantheon of s-f classics, but it has remained in print constantly for a decade and a half, has been translated into eight languages, and periodically almost gets turned into a film, so the audience has evidently come to agree with my appraisal of it.

There never were audience difficulties with *Nightwings*, which I began a few months later. Probably it is the most popular book I wrote before *Lord Valentine's Castle*, and from the beginning of its career it has been well received. The first of the three sections that constitute the novel was written in March of 1968, at one of the darkest times in my life, just after the fire that wrecked the magnificent house I had when I lived in New York. Living in improvised rented quarters, working on an unfamiliar typewriter in a strange and uncomfortable place, numb with the exhaustion of coping for weeks with a major catastrophe, I somehow found the energy to invent and set on paper the romantic and colorful opening section in just a few days—a bizarre and by now implausible summoning of mysterious strength. That opening section, as an independent item, went on to win a Hugo award and to miss a Nebula by just a few votes. When I wrote it, I had no idea I was beginning a novel; sleepwalker that I was in those days, I was happy enough to have 20,000 coherent words written. But a week or so later I realized that the rest of the story needed telling, and I produced the second part in April of 1968, the third in June. The two sequels also were award nominees, although—since they had less independent life of their own—they failed to win any trophies. Weaving the three into a single novel took little effort, and the book appeared in 1969. It has had many editions since then.

Downward to the Earth is a product of 1969, my next to last year of really unfettered productivity. The fatigue of the fire and its aftermath was passing from me now; I had moved back into my rebuilt house, unaware that I would soon sell it and move to California; and the books that had flooded from me during the past few years were at last gaining the sort of attention that encourages a writer to go on. In February of 1969 I visited the great game parks of East Africa, and there, seeing the enormous surviving herds of zebras and wildebeests and gazelles, while at the same time experiencing the realities of post-Colonial African politics, I had the notion of a science-fiction novel, set in a time of diminishing imperialist exploitation, in which the real heroes were the elephants. The transcendental element in my work, which is somewhat visible in *Man in the Maze* and rather more conspicuous in *Nightwings*, now came to play a major role also. Oddly, despite all these ambitious concepts, the actual novel that emerged displeased me greatly at first—thus illustrating the adage that a writer is the last person to trust in the evaluation of that writer's work. I'm not sure what it was then that I didn't like about *Downward to the Earth*, but I seem to be the only reader who found fault with it, for it was warmly received by the magazine editor who serialized it and the book editor who published the complete version, and by the readers, who gave it the usual award nominations, and when I went back and read the thing myself a couple of years later I was delighted with it too. As I am, I shamefully admit, with the other two novels in this volume. As I hope you will be, now that all three are brought together for the first time in permanent form.

Robert Silverberg
Oakland, California
July, 1980

THE MAN IN THE MAZE

one

Muller knew the maze quite well by this time. He understood its snares and its delusions, its pitfalls, its deadly traps. He had lived within it for nine years. That was long enough to come to terms with the maze, if not with the situation that had driven him to take refuge within it.

He still moved warily. Three or four times already he had learned that his knowledge of the maze, although adequate and workable, was not wholly complete. At least once he had come right to the edge of destruction, pulling back only by some improbable bit of luck just before the unexpected fountaining of an energy flare sent a stream of raw power boiling across his path. Muller had charted that flare, and fifty others; but as he moved through the city-sized labyrinth he knew there was no guarantee that he would not meet an uncharted one.

Overhead the sky was darkening; the deep, rich green of late afternoon was giving way to the black of night. Muller paused a moment in his hunting to look up at the pattern of the stars. Even that was becoming familiar now. He had chosen his own constellations on this desolate world, searching the heavens for arrangements of brightness that suited his peculiarly harsh and bitter taste. Now they appeared: the Dagger, the Back, the Shaft, the Ape, the Toad. In the forehead of the Ape flickered the small grubby star that Muller believed was the sun of Earth. He was not sure, because he had destroyed his chart tank after landing here somehow, though, he felt that that minor fireball must be Sol. The same dim star formed the left eye of the Toad. There were times when Muller told himself that Sol would not be visible in the sky of this world ninety light-years from Earth, but at other times he was quite convinced. Beyond the Toad lay the constellation that Muller had named Libra, the Scales. Of course, this set of scales was badly out of balance.

Three small moons glittered here. The air was thin but breathable; Muller had long ago ceased to notice that it had too much nitrogen, not enough oxygen. It was a little short on carbon dioxide, too, and one effect of that was that he hardly ever seemed to yawn. That did not trouble him. Gripping the butt of his gun tightly, he walked slowly through the alien city in search of his dinner. This too was part of a fixed routine. He had six months' supply of food stored in a radiation locker half a kilometer away, but yet each night he went hunting so that he could replace at once whatever he drew from his cache. It was a way of devouring the time. And he needed that cache, undepleted, against the day when the maze might cripple or paralyze him. His keen eyes scanned the angled streets ahead. About him rose the walls, screens, traps and confusions of the maze within which he lived. He breathed deeply. He put each foot firmly down before lifting the other. He looked in all directions. The triple moonlight analyzed and dissected his shadow, splitting it into reduplicated images that danced and sprawled before him.

The mass detector mounted over his left ear emitted a high-pitched sound. That told Muller that it had picked up the thermals of an animal in the 50-100 kilogram range. He had the detector programmed to scan in three horizons, of which this was the middle one, the food-beast range. The detector would also report to him on the proximity of 10-20 kilogram creatures—the teeth-beast range—and on the emanations of beasts over 500 kilograms—the big-beast range. The small ones had a way of going quickly for the throat, and the great ones were careless tramplers; Muller hunted those in between and avoided the others.

Now he crouched, readying his weapon. The animals that wandered the maze here on Lemnos could be slain without stratagem; they kept watch on one another, but even after all the years of Muller's presence among them they had not learned that he was predatory. Not in several million years had an intelligent life-form done any hunting on this planet, evidently, and Muller had been potting them nightly without teaching them a thing about the nature of mankind. His only concern in hunting was to strike from a secure, well-surveyed point so that in his concentration on his prey he would not fall victim to some more dangerous creature. With the kickstaff mounted on the heel of his left boot he probed the wall behind him, making certain that it would not open and engulf him. It was solid. Good. Muller edged himself backward until his back touched the cool, polished stone. His left knee rested on the faintly yielding pavement. He sighted along the barrel of his gun. He was safe. He could wait. Perhaps three minutes went by. The mass detector continued to whine, indicating that the beast was remaining within a hundred-meter radius; the pitch rose slightly from moment to moment as the thermals grew stronger. Muller was in no hurry. He was at one side of a vast plaza bordered by glassy curving partitions, and anything that emerged from those gleaming crescents would be an easy shot. Muller was hunting tonight in Zone E of the maze, the fifth sector out from the heart, and one of the most dangerous. He rarely went past the relatively innocuous Zone D, but some daredevil mood had prodded him into E this evening. Since finding his way into the maze he had never risked G or H again at all, and had been as far out as F only twice. He came to E perhaps five times a year.

To his right the converging lines of a shadow appeared, jutting from one of the curving glassy walls. The song of the mass detector reached into the upper end of the pitch spectrum for an animal of this size. The smallest moon, Atropos, swinging giddily through the sky, changed the shadow pattern; the lines no longer converged, but now one bar of blackness cut across the other two. The shadow of a snout, Miller knew. An instant later he saw his victim. The animal was the size of a large dog, gray of muzzle and tawny of body, hump-shouldered, ugly, spectacularly carnivorous. For his first few years here Muller had avoided hunting the carnivores, thinking that their meat would not be tasty. He had gone instead after the local equivalent of cows and sheep—mild-mannered ungulates which drifted blithely through the maze cropping the grasses in the garden places. Only when that bland meat palled did he go after one of the fanged, clawed creatures that harvested the herbivores, and to his surprise their flesh was excellent. He watched the animal emerge into the plaza. Its long snout twitched. Muller could hear the sniffing sounds from where he crouched. But the scent of man meant nothing to this beast.

Confidently, swaggeringly, the carnivore strode across the sleek pavement of the plaza, its unretracted claws clicking and scraping. Muller fined his beam down to needle aperture and took thoughtful aim, sighting now on the hump, now on the hindquarters. The gun was proximity-responsive and would score a hit automatically, but Muller always keyed in the manual sighting. He and the gun had different goals—the gun was concerned with killing, Muller with eating; and it was easier to do his own aiming than to try to convince the weapon that a bolt through the tender, juicy hump would deprive him of the tastiest cut. The gun, seeking the simplest target, would lance through that hump to the spine and bring the beast down: Muller favored more finesse.

He chose a target six inches forward from the hump: the place where the spine entered the skull. One shot did it. The animal toppled heavily. Muller went toward it as rapidly as he dared, checking every footfall. Quickly he carved away the inessentials—limbs, head, belly—and sprayed a seal around the raw slab of flesh he cut from the hump. He sliced a hefty steak from the hindquarters, too, and strapped both parcels to his shoulders. Then he swung around, searching for the zigzagging road that was the only safe entry to the core of the maze. In less than an hour he could be at his lair in the heart of Zone A.

He was halfway across the plaza when he heard an unfamiliar sound.

Pausing, he looked back. Three small loping creatures were heading toward the carcass he had abandoned. But the scrabbling of the scavengers was not what he had heard. Was the maze preparing some new deviltry? It had been a low rumbling sound overlaid by a hoarse throb in the middle frequencies, too prolonged to be the roaring of one of the large animals. It was a sound Muller had not heard before.

No: a sound he had not heard *here* before. It registered

somewhere in his memory banks. He searched. The sound was familiar. That double boom, slowly dopplering into the distance—what was it?

He placed its position. The sound had come from over his right shoulder, so it seemed. Muller looked there and saw only the triple cascade of the maze's secondary wall, rising in tier upon glittering amber tier. Above that wall? He saw the star-brightened sky: the Ape, the Toad, the Scales.

Muller remembered the sound now.

A ship; a starship, cutting out of warp onto ion drive to make a planetary landing. The boom of the expellers, the throb of the deceleration tubes, passing over the city. It was a sound he had not heard in nine years, since his self-exile on Lemnos had begun. So he was having visitors. Casual intruders, or had he been traced? What did they want? Anger blazed through him. He had had enough of them and their world. Why did they have to trouble him here? Muller stood braced, legs apart, a segment of his mind searching as always for perils even while he glared toward the probable landing point of the ship. He wanted nothing to do with Earth or Earthmen. He glowered at the faint point of light in the eye of the Toad, in the forehead of the Ape.

They would not reach him, he decided.

They would die in the maze, and their bones would join the million-year accumulation that lay strewn in the outer corridors.

And if they succeeded in entering, as he had done—

Well, then they would have to contend with him. They would not find that pleasant. Muller smiled grimly, adjusted the meat on his back, and returned his full concentration to the job of penetrating the maze. Soon he was within Zone C, and safe. He reached his lair. He stowed his meat. He prepared his dinner. Pain hammered at his skull. After nine years he was no longer alone on this world. They had soiled his solitude. Once again, Muller felt betrayed. He wanted nothing more from Earth than privacy, now; and even that they would not give him. But they would suffer if they managed to reach him within the maze. If.

The ship had erupted from warp a little late, almost in the outer fringes of Lemnos' atmosphere. Charles Boardman disliked that. He demanded the highest possible standards of performance from himself, and expected everyone about him to keep to the same standards. Especially pilots.

Concealing his irritation, Boardman thumbed the screen to life and the cabin wall blossomed with a vivid image of the planet below. Scarcely any clouds swathed its surface; he had a clear view through the atmosphere. In the midst of a broad plain was a series of corrugations that were sharply outlined even at a height of a hundred kilometers. Boardman turned to the young man beside him and said, "There you are, Ned. The labyrinth of Lemnos. And Dick Muller right in the middle of it!"

Ned Rawlins pursed his lips. "So big? It must be hundreds of kilometers across!"

"What you're seeing is the outer embankment. The maze itself is surrounded by a concentric ring of earthen walls five meters high and nearly a thousand kilometers in outer circumference. But—"

"Yes, I know," Rawlins burst in. Almost immediately he turned bright red, with that appealing innocence that Boardman found so charming and soon would be trying to put to use. "I'm sorry, Charles, I didn't mean to interrupt."

"Quite all right. What did you want to ask?"

"That dark spot within the outer walls—is that the city itself?"

Boardman nodded. "That's the inner maze. Twenty, thirty kilometers in diameter—and God knows how many millions of years old. That's where we'll find Muller."

"If we can get inside."

"*When* we get inside."

"Yes. Yes. Of course. *When* we get inside," Rawlins corrected, reddening again. He flashed a quick, earnest smile. "There's no chance we won't find the entrance, is there?"

"Muller did," said Boardman quietly. "He's in there."

"But he's the first who got inside. Everyone else who tried has failed. So why will we—"

"There weren't many who tried," Boardman said. "Those who did weren't equipped for the problem. We'll manage, Ned. We'll manage. We have to. Relax, now, and enjoy the landing."

The ship swung toward the planet—going down much too rapidly, Boardman thought, oppressed by the strains of deceleration. He hated travel, and he hated the moment of landing worst of all. But this was a trip he could not have avoided. He eased back in the webfoam cradle and blanked out the screen. Ned Rawlins was still upright, eyes glowing with excitement. How wonderful to be young, Boardman thought, not sure whether he meant to be sarcastic or not. Certainly the boy was strong and healthy—and cleverer than he sometimes seemed. A likely lad, as they would have said a few centuries ago. Boardman could not remember having been that sort of young man himself. He had the feeling of having always been on the brink of middle age—shrewd, calculating, well organized. He was eighty, now, with almost half his lifetime behind him, and yet in honest self-appraisal he could not bring himself to believe that his personality had changed in any essential way since he had turned twenty. He had learned techniques, the craft of managing men; he was wiser now; but he was not qualitatively different. Young Ned Rawlins, though, was going to be another person entirely sixty-odd years from now, and very little of the callow boy in the next cradle would survive. Boardman suspected, not happily, that this very mission would be the crucible in which Ned's innocence was blasted from him.

Boardman closed his eyes as the ship entered its final landing maneuvers. He felt gravity clawing at his aging flesh. Down. Down. Down. How many planetfalls had he made, loathing every one? The diplomatic life was a restless one. Christmas on Mars, Easter on one of the Centaurine worlds, the midyear feast celebrated on a stinking planet of Rigel—and now this trip, the most complex of all. Man was not made to flash from star to star like this, Boardman thought. I have lost my sense of a universe. They say this is the richest era of human existence; but I think a man can be richer in knowing every atom of a single golden island in a blue sea than by spending his days striding among all the worlds.

He knew that his face was distorted by the pull of Lemnos as the ship plunged planetward. There were heavy fleshy jowls about his throat, and pockets of extra meat here and there about his body, giving him a soft, pampered look. With little effort Boardman could have had himself streamlined to the fashionably sleek appearance of a modern man; this was an era when men a century and a quarter old could look like striplings, if they cared to. Early in his career Boardman had chosen to simulate authentic aging. Call it an investment; what he forfeited in chic he gained in status. His business was selling advice to governments, and governments preferred not to buy their counsel from men who looked like boys. Boardman had looked fifty-five years old for the last forty years, and he expected to retain that look of strong, vigorous early middle age at least another half a century. Later, he would allow time to work on him again when he entered the final phase of his career. He would take on the whitened hair and shrunken cheek of a man of eighty, and pose as Nestor rather than as Ulysses. At the moment it was professionally useful to look only slightly out of trim, as he did.

He was a short man, though he was so stocky that he easily dominated any group at a conference table. His powerful shoulders, deep chest, and long arms would have been better suited to a giant. When he stood up Boardman revealed himself as of less than middle height, but sitting down he was awesome. He found that feature useful too, and had never considered altering it. An extremely tall man is better suited to command than to advise, and Boardman had never had the wish to command; he preferred a more subtle exercise of power. But a short man who looks big at a table can control empires. The business of empires is transacted sitting down.

He had the look of authority. His chin was strong, his nose thick and blunt and forceful, his lips both firm and sensuous, his eyebrows immense and shaggy, black strips of fur sprouting from a massive forehead that might have awed a Neanderthal. He wore his hair long and coarse. Three rings gleamed on his fingers, one a gyroscope of platinum and rubies with dull-hued inlays of U-238. His taste in clothing was severe and conservative, running to heavy fabrics and almost medieval cuts. In another epoch he might have been well cast as a worldly cardinal or as an ambitious prime minister; he would have been important in any court at any time. He was important now. The price of Boardman's importance, though, was the turmoil of travel. Soon he would land on another strange planet, where the air would smell wrong, the gravity would be just a shade too strong, and the sun's hue would not be right. Boardman scowled. How much longer would the landing take?

He looked at Ned Rawlins. Twenty-two, twenty-three years old, something like that: the picture of naive young manhood, although Boardman knew that Ned was old enough to have learned more than he seemed to show. Tall, conventionally handsome without the aid of cosmetic surgery; fair hair, blue eyes, wide, mobile lips, flawless teeth. He was the son of a communications theorist, now dead, who had been one of Richard Muller's closest friends. Boardman was counting on that connection to carry them a good distance in the delicate transactions ahead.

Rawlins said, "Are you uncomfortable, Charles?"

"I'll live. We'll be down soon."

"The landing seems so slow, doesn't it?"

"Another minute now," Boardman said.

The boy's face looked scarcely stretched by the forces acting upon them. His left cheek was drawn down slightly, that was all. It was weird to see the semblance of a sneer on that shining visage.

"Here we come now," Boardman muttered, and closed his eyes again.

The ship closed the last gap between itself and the ground. The expellers cut out; the deceleration tubes snarled their last. There was the final awkward moment of uncertainty, then steadiness, the landing jacks gripping firmly, the roar of landing silenced. We are here, Boardman thought. Now for the maze. Now for Mr. Richard Muller. Now to see if he's become any less horrible in the past nine years. Maybe he's just like everyone else, by now. If he is, Boardman told himself, God help us all.

Ned Rawlins had not traveled much. He had visited only five worlds, and three of them were in the mother system. When he was ten, his father had taken him on a summer tour of Mars. Two years later he had seen Venus and Mercury. As his graduation present at sixteen he had gone extrasolar as far as Alpha Centauri IV, and three years after that he had made the melancholy trip to the Rigel system to bring home his father's body after the accident.

It wasn't much of a travel record at a time when the warp drive made getting from one cluster to another not much more difficult than going from Europe to Australia, Rawlins knew. But he had time to do his jaunting later on, when he began getting his diplomatic assignments. To hear Charles Boardman tell it, the joys of travel palled pretty fast, anyway, and running around the universe became just another chore. Rawlins made allowances for the jaded attitude of a man nearly four times his own age, but he suspected that Boardman was telling the truth.

Let the jadedness come. Right now Ned Rawlins was walking an alien world for the sixth time in his life, and he loved it. The ship was docked on the big plain that surrounded Muller's maze; the outer embankments of the maze itself lay a hundred kilometers to the southeast. It was the middle of the night on this side of Lemnos. The planet had a thirty-hour day and a twenty-month year; it was early autumn in this hemisphere, and the air was chilly. Rawlins stepped away from the ship. The crewmen were unloading the extruders that would build their camp. Charles Boardman stood to one side, wrapped in a thick fur garment and buried in an introspective mood so deep that Rawlins did not dare go near him. Rawlins' attitude toward Boardman was one of mingled awe and terror. He knew that the man was a cynical old bastard, but despite that it was impossible to feel anything but admiration for him. Boardman, Rawlins knew, was an authentic great man. He hadn't met many. His own father had been one, perhaps. Dick Muller had been another; but of course Rawlins hadn't been much more than twelve years old when Muller got into the hideous mess that had shattered his life. Well, to have known three such men in one short lifetime was a privilege indeed, Rawlins told himself. He wished that his own career would turn out half as impressively as Boardman's had. Of course he didn't have Boardman's foxiness, and hoped he never would. But he had other characteristics—a nobility of soul, in a way—which Boardman lacked. I can be of service in my own style, Rawlins thought, and then wondered if that was a naive hope.

He filled his lungs with alien air. He stared at a sky swarming with strange stars, and looked futilely for some familiar pattern. A frosty wind ripped across the plain. This planet seemed forlorn, desolate, empty. He had read about Lemnos in school: one of the abandoned ancient planets of an unknown alien race, lifeless for a thousand centuries. Nothing remained of its people except fossilized bones and shreds of artifacts—and the maze. Their deadly labyrinth ringed a city of the dead that seemed almost untouched by time.

Archaeologists had scanned the city from the air, probing it with sensors and curdling in frustration, unable to enter it safely. The first dozen expeditions to Lemnos had failed to find a way into the maze; every man who entered had perished, a victim of the hidden traps so cleverly planted in the outer zones. The last attempt to get inside had been made some fifty years ago. Then Richard Muller had come here, looking for a place to hide from mankind, and somehow he had found the route.

Rawlins wondered if they would succeed in making contact with Muller. He wondered, too, how many of the men he had journeyed with would die before they got into the maze. He did not consider the possibility of his own death. At his age, death was still something that happened to other people. But some of the men now working to set up their camp would be dead in a few days.

While he thought about that an animal appeared, padding out from behind a sandy hummock a short distance from him. Rawlins regarded the alien beast curiously. It looked a little like a big cat, but its claws did not retract and its mouth was full of greenish fangs. Luminous stripes gave its lean sides a gaudy hue. Rawlins could not see what use such a glowing hide would be to a predator, unless it used the radiance as a kind of bait.

The animal came within a dozen meters of Rawlins, peered at him without any sign of real interest, then turned gracefully and trotted toward the ship. The combination of strange beauty, power, and menace that the animal presented was an attractive one.

It was approaching Boardman now. And Boardman was drawing a weapon.

"No!" Rawlins found himself yelling. "Don't kill it, Charles! It only wants to look at us—!"

Boardman fired.

The animal leaped, convulsed in mid-air, and fell back with its limbs outspread. Rawlins rushed up, numb with shock. There hadn't been any need for the killing, he thought. The beast was just scouting us out. What a filthy thing to do!

He blurted angrily, "Couldn't you have waited a minute, Charles? Maybe it would have gone away by itself! Why—"

Boardman smiled. He beckoned to a crewman, who squirted a spray net over the fallen animal. The beast stirred groggily as the crewman hauled it toward the ship. Softly Boardman said, "All I did was stun it, Ned. We're going to write off part of the budget for this trip against the account of the federal zoo. Did you think I was all that triggerhappy?"

Rawlins suddenly felt very small and foolish. "Well— not really. That is—"

"Forget it. No, don't forget it. Don't forget anything. Take a lesson from it: collect all the data before shouting nonsense."

"But if I had waited, and you really had killed it—"

"Then you'd have learned something ugly about me at the expense of one animal life. You'd have the useful fact that I'm provoked to murderousness by anything strange with sharp teeth. Instead all you did was make a loud noise. If I had meant to kill, your shout wouldn't have changed my intention. It might have ruined my aim, that's all, and left me at the mercy of an angry wounded beast. So bide your time, Ned. Evaluate. It's better sometimes to let a thing happen than to play your own hand too quickly." Boardman winked. "Am I offending you, Ned? Making you feel like an idiot with my little lecture?"

"Of course not, Charles. I wouldn't pretend that I don't have plenty to learn."

"And you're willing to learn it from me, even if I'm an infuriating old scoundrel?"

"Charles, I—"

"I'm sorry, Ned. I shouldn't be teasing you. You were right to try to stop me from killing that animal. It wasn't your fault that you misunderstood what I was doing. In your place I'd have acted just the way you did."

"You mean I shouldn't have bided my time and collected all the data when you pulled the stungun?" Rawlins asked, baffled.

"Probably not."

"You're contradicting yourself, Charles."

"It's my privilege to be inconsistent," Boardman said. "My stock in trade, even." He laughed heartily. "Get a good night's sleep tonight. Tomorrow we'll fly over the maze and map it a little, and then we'll start sending men in. I figure we'll be talking to Muller within a week."

"Do you think he'll be willing to cooperate?"

A cloud passed over Boardman's heavy features. "He won't be at first. He'll be so full of bitterness that he'll be spitting poison. After all, we're the ones who cast him out. Why should he want to help Earth now? But he'll come around, Ned, because fundamentally he's a man of honor, and that's something that never changes no matter how sick and lonely and anguished a man gets. Not even hatred can corrode real honor. You know that, Ned, because you're that sort of person yourself. Even I am, in my own way. A man of honor. We'll work on Muller. We'll get him to come out of that damned maze and help us."

"I hope you're right, Charles." Rawlins hesitated. "And what will it be like for us, confronting him? I mean, considering his sickness—the way he affects others—"

"It'll be bad. Very bad."

"You saw him, didn't you, after it happened?"

"Yes. Many times."

Rawlins said, "I can't really imagine what it's like to be next to a man and feel his whole soul spilling out over you. That's what happens when you're with Muller, isn't it?"

"It's like stepping into a bath of acid," said Boardman heavily. "You can get used to it, but you never like it. You feel fire all over your skin. The ugliness, the terrors, the greeds, the sicknesses—they spout from him like a fountain of muck."

"And Muller's a man of honor . . . a decent man."

"He was, yes." Boardman looked toward the distant maze. "Thank God for that. But it's a sobering thought, isn't it, Ned? If a first-rate man like Dick Muller has all that garbage inside his brain, what do you think ordinary people are like in there? The squashed-down people with the squashed-down lives? Give them the same kind of curse Muller has and they'd be like beacons of flame, burning up every mind within light-years."

"But Muller's had nine years to stew in his misery," Rawlins said. "What if it's impossible to get near him now? What if the stuff he radiates is so strong that we won't be able to stand it?"

"We'll stand it," Boardman said.

two

Within the maze, Muller studied his situation and contemplated his options. In the milky green recesses of the viewing tank he could see the ship and the plastic domes that had sprouted beside it, and the tiny figures of men moving about. He wished now that he had been able to find the fine control on the viewing tank; the images he received were badly out of focus. But he considered himself lucky to have the use of the tank at all. Many of the ancient instruments in this city had become useless long ago through the decay of some vital part. A surprising number had endured the eons unharmed, a tribute to the technical skill of their makers; but of these, Muller had been able to discover the function of only a few, and he operated those imperfectly.

He watched the blurred figures of his fellow humans working busily and wondered what new torment they were preparing for him.

He had tried to leave no clues to his whereabouts when he fled from Earth. He had come here in a rented ship, filing a deceptive flight plan by way of Sigma Draconis. During his warp trip, of course, he had had to pass six monitor stations; but he had given each one a simulated great-circle galactic route record, carefully designed to be as misleading as possible.

A routine comparison check of all the monitor stations would reveal that Muller's successive announcements of location added up to nonsense, but he had gambled that he would manage to complete his flight and vanish before they ran one of the regular checks. Evidently he had won that gamble, for no interceptor ships had come after him.

Emerging from warp in the vicinity of Lemnos, he had carried out one final evasive maneuver by leaving his ship in a parking orbit and descending by drop-capsule. A disruptor bomb, preprogrammed, had blasted the ship to molecules and sent the fragments traveling on a billion conflicting orbits through the universe. It would take a fancy computer indeed to calculate a probably nexus of source for those! The bomb was designed to provide fifty false vectors per square meter of explosion surface, a virtual guarantee that no tracer could possibly be effective within a finite span of time. Muller needed only a very short finite span—say, sixty years. He had been close to sixty when he left Earth. Normally, he could expect at least another century of vigorous life; but, cut off from medical service, doctoring himself with a cheap diagnostat, he'd be doing well to last into his eleventh or twelfth decade. Sixty years of solitude and a peaceful, private death, that was all he asked. But now his privacy was interrupted after only nine years.

Had they really traced him somehow?

Muller decided that they had not. For one thing, he had taken every conceivable antitracking precaution. For another, they had no motive for following him. He was no fugitive who had to be brought back to justice. He was simply a man with a loathsome affliction, an abomination in the sight of his fellow mortals, and doubtless Earth felt itself well rid of him. He was a shame and a reproach to them, a welling fount of guilt and grief, a prod to the planetary conscience. The kindest thing he could do for his own kind was to remove himself from their midst, and he had done that as thoroughly as he could. They would hardly make an effort to come looking for someone so odious to them.

Who were these intruders, then?

Archaeologists, he suspected. The ruined city of Lemnos still held a magnetic, fatal fascination for them—for everyone. Muller had hoped that the risks of the maze would continue to keep men away. It had been discovered over a century earlier, but before his arrival there had been a period of many years in which Lemnos was shunned. For good reason: Muller had many times seen the corpses of those who had tried and failed to enter the maze. He himself had come here partly out of a suicidal wish to join the roster of victims, partly out of overriding curiosity to get within and solve the secret of the labyrinth, and partly out of the knowledge that if he did penetrate he was not likely to suffer many invasions of his privacy. Now he was within; but intruders had come.

They will not enter, Muller told himself.

Snugly established at the core of the maze, he had command of enough sensing devices to follow, however vaguely, the progress of any living creatures outside. Thus he could trace the wanderings from zone to zone of the animals that were his prey, and also those of the great beasts who offered danger. To a limited degree he could control the snares of the maze, which normally were nothing more than passive traps but which could be employed aggressively, under the right conditions, against some enemy. More than once Muller had dumped an elephantine carnivore into a subterranean pit as it charged inward through Zone D. He asked himself if he would use those defenses against human beings if they penetrated that far, and had no answer. He did not really hate his own species; he just preferred to be left alone, in what passed for peace.

He eyed the screens. He occupied a squat hexagonal cell—apparently one of the housing units in the inner city—which was equipped with a wall of viewing tanks. It had taken him more than a year to find out which parts of the maze corresponded to the images on the screens; but by patiently posting markers he had matched the dim images to the glossy reality. The six lowest screens along the wall showed him pictures of areas in Zones A through F; the cameras, or whatever they were, swiveled through 180° arcs, enabling the hidden mysterious eyes to patrol the entire region around each of the zone entrances. Since only one entrance provided safe access to the zone within, all others being lethal, the screens effectively allowed Muller to watch the inward progress of any prowler. It did not matter what was taking place at any of the false entrances. Those who persisted there would die.

Screens seven through ten, in the upper bank, relayed images that apparently came from Zones G and H, the outermost, largest and deadliest zones of the maze. Muller had not wanted to go to the trouble of returning to those zones to check his theory in detail; he was satisfied that the screens were pickups from points in the outer zones, and it was not worth risking those zones again to find out more accurately where the pickups were mounted. As for the eleventh and twelfth screens, they obviously showed views of the plain outside the maze altogether—the plain now occupied by a newly-arrived starship from Earth.

Few of the other devices left by the ancient builders of the maze were as informative. Mounted on a dais in the center of the city's central plaza, shielded by a crystal vault, was a twelve-sided stone the color of ruby, in whose depths a mechanism like an intricate shutter ticked and pulsed. Muller suspected it was some sort of clock, keyed to a nuclear oscillation and sounding out the units of time its makers employed. Periodically the stone underwent temporary changes: its face turned cloudy, deepened in hue to blue or even black, swung on its mounting. Muller's careful record-keeping had not yet told him the meaning of those changes. He could not even analyze the periodicity. The metamorphoses were not random, but the pattern they followed was beyond his comprehension.

At the eight corners of the plaza were metallic spikes, smoothly tapering to heights of some twenty feet. Throughout the cycle of the year these spikes revolved, so they were calendars, it seemed, moving on hidden bearings. Muller knew that they made one complete revolution in each thirty-month turning of Lemnos about its somber orange primary, but he suspected some deeper purpose for these gleaming pylons. Searching for it occupied much of his time.

Spaced neatly in the streets of Zone A were cages with bars hewn from an alabaster-like rock. Muller could see no way of opening these cages; yet twice during his years here he had awakened to find the bars withdrawn into the stone pavement, and the cages gaping wide. The first time they had remained open for three days; then the bars had returned to their positions while he slept, sliding into place and showing no seam where they could have parted. When the cages opened again, a few years later, Muller watched them constantly to find the secret of their mechanism. But on the fourth night he dozed just long enough to miss the closing again.

Equally mysterious was the aqueduct. Around the length of Zone B ran a closed trough, perhaps of onyx, with angular spigots placed at fifty-meter intervals. When any sort of vessel, even a cupped hand, was placed beneath a spigot it yielded pure water. But when he attempted to poke a finger into one of the spigots he found no opening, nor could he see any even while the water was coming forth; it was as though the fluid issued through a permeable plug of stone, and Muller found it hard to accept that. He welcomed the water, though.

It surprised him that so much of the city should have survived. Archaeologists had concluded, from a study of the artifacts and skeletons found on Lemnos outside the maze, that there had been no intelligent life here for upward of a million years—perhaps, five or six million. Muller was only an amateur archaeologist, but he had had enough field experience to know the effects of the passing of time. The fossils in the plain were clearly ancient, and the stratification of the city's outer walls showed that the labyrinth was contemporary with those fossils.

Yet most of the city, supposedly built before the evolution of mankind on Earth, appeared untouched by the ages. The dry weather could account in part for that; there were no storms here, and rain had not fallen since Muller's arrival. But wind and wind-blown sand could carve walls and pavements over a million years, and there was no sign of such carving here. Nor had sand accumulated in the open streets of the city. Muller knew why. Hidden pumps collected all debris, keeping everything spotless. He had gathered handfuls of soil from the garden plots, scattering little trails here and there. Within minutes the driblets of soil had begun to slither across the polished pavement, vanishing into slots that opened briefly and closed again at the intersection of buildings and ground.

Evidently beneath the city lay a network of inconceivable machinery—imperishable caretaker devices that guarded the city against the tooth of time. Muller had not been able to reach that network, though. He lacked the equipment for breaching the pavement; it seemed invulnerable at all points. With improvised tools he had begun to dig in the garden areas, hoping to reach the subcity that way, but though he had driven one pit more than a dozen feet and another even deeper he had come upon no signs of anything below but more soil. The hidden guardians had to be there, however: the instruments that operated the viewing tanks, swept the streets, repaired the mason-ry, and controlled the murderous traps that studded the outer zones of the labyrinth.

It was hard to imagine a race that could build a city of this sort—a city designed to last millions of years. It was harder still to imagine how they could have vanished. Assuming that the fossils found in the burial yards outside the walls were those of the builders—not necessarily a safe assumption—this city had been put together by burly humanoids a meter and a half tall, immensely thick through the chest and shoulders, with long cunning fingers, eight to the hand, and short double-jointed legs.

They were gone from the known worlds of the uni-verse, and nothing like them had been found in any other system; perhaps they had withdrawn to some far galaxy yet unvisited by man. Or, possibly, they had been a non-spacegoing race that evolved and perished right here on Lemnos, leaving this city as their only monument.

The rest of the planet was without trace of habitation although burial grounds had been discovered in a dimin-ishing series radiating outward a thousand kilometers from the maze. Maybe the years had eroded all their cities except this one. Maybe this, which could have sheltered perhaps a million beings, had been their only city. There was no clue to their disappearance. The devilish ingenuity of the maze argued that in their last days they had been harassed by enemies and had retreated within this tricky fortress; but Muller knew that this hypothesis too was a speculation. For all he was aware, the maze represented nothing more than an outburst of cultural paranoia and had no relation to the actual existence of an external threat.

Had they been invaded by beings for whom the maze posed no problems, and had they been slaughtered in their own sleek streets, and had the mechanical wardens swept away the bones? No way of knowing. They were gone. Muller, entering their city, had found it silent, desolate, as if it had never sheltered life; an automatic city, sterile, flawless. Only beasts occupied it. They had had a million years to find their way through the maze and take posses-sion. Muller had counted some two dozen species of mammals in all sizes from rat-equivalent to elephant-equivalent. There were grazers who munched on the city's gardens, and hunters who fed on the herbivores, and the ecological balance seemed perfect. The city in the maze was like unto Isaiah's Babylon: wild beasts of the desert shall lie there; and their houses shall be full of doleful creatures; and owls shall dwell there, and satyrs shall dance there.

The city was his now. He had the rest of his lifetime to probe its mysteries.

There had been others who had come here, and not all of them had been human. Entering the maze, Muller had been treated to the sight of those who had failed to go the route. He had sighted a score of human skeletons in Zones H, G, and F. Three men had made it to E, and one to D. Muller had expected to see their bones; but what took him off guard was the collection of alien bones. In H and G he had seen the remains of great dragon-like creatures, still clad in the shreds of spacesuits. Some day curiosity might triumph over fear and he might go back out there for a second look at them. Closer to the core lay an assortment of life-forms, mostly humanoid but veering from the standard structure. How long ago they had come here, Muller could not guess; even in this dry climate, would exposed skeletons last more than a few centuries? The galactic litter was a sobering reminder of something Muller already adequately knew: that despite the experience of man's first two centuries of extrasolar travel, in which no living intelligent alien race was encountered, the universe was full of other forms of life, and sooner or later man would meet them. The boneyard on Lemnos contained relics of at least a dozen different races. It flattered Muller's ego to know that he alone, apparently, had reached the heart of the maze; but it did not cheer him to think of the diversity of peoples in the universe. He had already had his fill of galactics.

The inconsistency of finding the litter of bones within the maze did not strike him for several years. The mechanisms of the city, he knew, cleaned relentlessly, tidying up everything from particles of dust to the bones of the animals on whom he fed. Yet the skeletons of would-be invaders of the maze were allowed to remain where they lay. Why the violation of neatness? Why cart away the corpse of a dead elephant-like beast that had blundered into a power snare, and leave the remains of a dead dragon killed by the same snare? Because the dragon wore protective clothing, and so was sapient? Sapient corpses were deliberately allowed to remain, Muller realized.

As warnings. ABANDON ALL HOPE, YE WHO ENTER HERE.

Those skeletons were part of the psychological warfare waged against all intruders by this mindless, deathless, diabolical city. They were reminders of the perils that lurked everywhere. How the guardian drew the subtle distinction between bodies that should be left in situ and those that should be swept away, Muller did not know; but he was convinced that the distinction was real.

He watched his screens. He eyed the tiny figures moving about the ship on the plain.

Let them come in, he thought. The city hasn't had a victim in years. It'll take care of them. I'm safe where I am.

And, he knew, that even if by some miracle they managed to reach him, they would not remain long. His own special malady would drive them away. They might be clever enough to defeat the maze, but they could not endure the affliction that made Richard Muller intolerable to his own species.

"Go away," Muller said aloud.

He heard the whirr of rotors, and stepped from his dwelling to see a dark shadow traverse the plaza. They were scouting the maze from the air. Quickly he went indoors, then smiled at his own impulse to hide. They could detect him, of course, wherever he was. Their screens would tell them that a human being inhabited the labyrinth. And then, naturally, they would in their astonishment try to make contact with him although they would not be aware of his identity. After that—

Muller stiffened as a sudden overwhelming desire blazed through him. To have them come to him. To talk to men again. To break his isolation.

He *wanted* them here.

Only for an instant. After the momentary breakthrough of loneliness came the return of rationality—the chilling awareness of what it would be like to face his kind again. No, he thought. Keep out! Or die in the maze. Keep out. Keep out. Keep out.

2

"Right down there," Boardman said. "That's where he must be, eh, Ned? You can see the glow on the face of the tank. We're picking up the right mass, the right density, the right everything. One live man, and it's got to be Muller."

"At the heart of the maze," said Rawlins. "So he really did it!"

"Somehow." Boardman peered into the viewing tank. From a height of a couple of kilometers the structure of the inner city was clear. He could make out eight distinct zones, each with its characteristic style of architecture; its plazas and promenades; its angling walls; its tangle of streets swirling in dizzyingly alien patterns. The zones were concentric, fanning out from a broad plaza at the heart of it all, and the scoutplane's mass detector had located Muller in a row of low buildings just to the east of the plaza. What Boardman failed to make out was any obvious passage linking zone to zone. There was no shortage of blind alleys, but even from the air the true route was not apparent; what was it like trying to work inward on the ground?

It was all but impossible, Boardman knew. The master data banks in the ship held the accounts of those early explorers who had tried it and failed. Boardman had brought with him every scrap of information on the penetration of the maze, and none of it was very encouraging except the one puzzling but incontrovertible datum that Richard Muller had managed to get inside.

Rawlins said, "This is going to sound naive, I know, Charles. But why don't we just come down from here and land the scoutplane in the middle of that central plaza?"

"Let me show you," said Boardman.

He spoke a command. A robot drone probe detached itself from the belly of the plane and streaked toward the city. Boardman and Rawlins followed the flight of the blunt gray metal projectile until it was only a few score meters above the tops of the buildings. Through its faceted eye they had a sharp view of the city, revealing the intricate texture of much of the stonework. Suddenly the drone probe vanished. There was a burst of incandescence, a puff a greenish smoke—and then nothing at all.

Boardman nodded. "Nothing's changed. There's still a protective field over the whole thing. It volatilizes anything that tries to get through."

"So even a bird that comes too close—"

"There are no birds on Lemnos."

"Raindrops, then. Whatever falls on the city—"

"Lemnos gets no rain," said Boardman sourly. "At least not on this continent. The only thing that field keeps out is strangers. We've known it since the first expedition. Some brave men found out about that field the hard way."

"Didn't they try a drone probe first?"

Smiling, Boardman said, "When you find a dead city in the middle of a desert on a dead world you don't expect to be blown up if you land inside it. It's a forgivable sort of mistake—except that Lemnos doesn't forgive mistakes." He gestured, and the plane dropped lower, following the orbit of the outer walls for a moment. Then it rose and hovered over the heart of the city while photographs were being taken. The wrong-colored sunlight glistened off a hall of mirrors. Boardman felt curdled weariness in his chest. They overflew the city again and again, marking off a preprogrammed observation pattern, and he discovered he was wishing irritably that a shaft of sudden light would rise from those mirrors and incinerate them on the next pass to save him the trouble of carrying out this assignment. He had lost his taste for detailwork, and too many fine details stood between him and his purpose here. They said that impatience was a mark of youth, that old men could craftily spin their webs and plot their schemes in serenity, but somehow Boardman found himself longing rashly for a quick consummation to this job. Send some sort of drone scuttling through the maze on metal tracks to seize Muller and drag him out. Tell the man what was wanted of him and make him agree to do it. Then take off for Earth, quickly, quickly. The mood passed. Boardman felt foxy again. ˎ

Captain Hosteen, who would be conducting the actual entry attempt, came aft to pay his respects. Hosteen was a short, thick-framed man with a flat nose and coppery skin; he wore his uniform as though he felt it was all going to slip off his left shoulder at any moment. But he was a good man, Boardman knew, and ready to sacrifice a score of lives, including his own, to get into that maze.

Hosteen flicked a glance from the screen to Boardman's face and said, "Learning anything?"

"Nothing new. We have a job."

"Want to go down again?"

"Might as well," Boardman said. He looked at Rawlins. "Unless you have anything else you'd like to check, Ned?"

"Me? Oh, no—no. That is—well, I wonder if we need to go into the maze at all. I mean, if we could lure Muller out somehow, talk to him outside the city—"

"No."

"Wouldn't it work?"

"No," said Boardman emphatically. "Item one, Muller wouldn't come out if we asked him. He's a misanthrope. Remember? He buried himself here to get away from humanity. Why should he socialize with us? Item two, we couldn't invite him outside without letting him know too much about what we want from him. In this deal, Ned, we need to hoard our resources of strategy, not toss them away in our first move."

"I don't understand what you mean."

Patiently Boardman said, "Suppose we used your approach. What would you say to Muller to make him come out?"

"Why—that we're here from Earth to ask him if he'll help us in a time of system-wide crisis. That we've encountered a race of alien beings with whom we're unable to communicate, and that it's absolutely necessary that we break through to them in a hurry, and that he alone can do the trick. We—" Rawlins stopped, as though the fatuity of his own words had broken through to him. Color mounted in his cheeks. He said in a hoarse voice, "Muller isn't going to give a damn for those arguments, is he?"

"No, Ned. Earth sent him before a bunch of aliens once before, and they ruined him. He isn't about to try it again."

"Then how are we going to make him help us?"

"By playing on his sense of honor. But at the moment that's not the problem we're talking about. We're discussing how to get him out of his sanctuary in there. Now, you were suggesting that we set up a speaker and tell him exactly what we want from him, and then wait for him to waltz out and pledge to do his best for good old Earth. Right?"

"I guess so."

"But it won't work. Therefore we've got to get inside the maze ourselves, win Muller's trust, and persuade him to cooperate. And to do that we have to keep quiet about the real situation until we've eased him out of his suspicions."

A look of newborn wariness appeared on Rawlins' face. "What are we going to tell him, then, Charles?"

"Not *we*. You."

"What am I going to tell him, then?"

Boardman sighed. "Lies, Ned. A pack of lies."

3

They had come equipped for solving the problem of the maze. The ship's brain, of course, was a first-class computer, and it carried the details of all previous Earth-based attempts to enter the city. Except one, and unfortunately that had been the only successful one. But records of past failures have their uses. The ship's data banks had plenty of mobile extensions: airborne and groundborne drone probes, spy-eyes, sensor batteries, and more. Before any human life was risked on the maze Boardman and Hosteen would try the whole mechanical array. Mechanicals were expendable, anyway; the ship carried a set of templates, and it would be no trouble to replicate all devices destroyed. But a point would come at which the drone probes had to give way to men: the aim was to gather as much information as possible for those men to use.

Never before had anyone tried to crack the maze this way. The early explorers had simply gone walking in, unsuspecting, and had perished. Their successors had known enough of the story to avoid the more obvious traps, and to some extent had been aided by sophisticated sensory devices, but this was the first attempt to run a detailed survey before entering. No one was overly confident that the technique would let them in unscathed, but it was the best way to approach the problem.

The overflights on the first day had given everybody a good visual image of the maze. Strictly speaking, it hadn't been necessary for them to leave the ground; they could have watched big-screen relays from the comfort of their camp and gained a decent idea of the conformation below, letting airborne probes do all the work. But Boardman had insisted. The mind registers things one way when it picks them off a relay screen, and another when the sensory impressions are flooding in straight from the source. Now they all had seen the city from the air, and had seen what the guardians of the maze could do to a drone probe that ventured into the protective field overlying the city.

Rawlins had suggested the possibility that there might be a null spot in that protective field. Toward late afternoon they checked it out by loading a probe with metal pellets and stationing it fifty meters above the highest point of the maze. Scanner eyes recorded the action as the drone slowly turned, spewing the pellets one at a time into preselected one-square-meter boxes above the city. Each in turn was incinerated as it fell. They were able to calculate that the thickness of the safety field varied with distance from the center of the maze; it was only about two meters deep above the inner zones, much deeper at the outer rim, forming an invisible cup over the city. But there were no null spots; the field was continuous. Hosteen tested the notion that the field was capable of overstrain by having the probe reloaded with pellets which were catapulted simultaneously into each of the test rectangles. The field dealt with them all, creating for a moment a single pucker of flame above the city.

At the expense of a few mole probes they found out that reaching the city through a tunnel was equally impossible. The moles burrowed into the coarse sandy soil outside the outer walls, chewed themselves passageways fifty meters down, and nosed upward again when they were beneath the maze. They were destroyed by the safety field while still twenty meters below ground level. A try at burrowing in right at the base of the embankments also failed; the field went straight down, apparently, all around the city.

A power technician offered to rig an interference pylon to drain the energy of the field. It didn't work. The pylon, a hundred meters tall, sucked in power from all over the planet; blue lightning leaped and hissed along its accumulator bank, but it had no effect on the safety field. They reversed the pylon and sent a million kilowatts shooting into the city, hoping to short the field. The field drank everything and seemed ready for more. No one had any rational theory to explain the field's power source. "It must tap the planet's own energy of rotation," the technician who had rigged the pylon said, and then, realizing he hadn't contributed anything useful, he looked away and began to snap orders into the handmike he carried.

Three days of similar researches demonstrated that the city was invulnerable to intrusion from above or below.

"There's only one way in," said Hosteen, "and that's on foot, through the main gate."

"If the people in the city really wanted to be safe," Rawlins asked, "why did they leave even a gate open?"

"Maybe they wanted to go in and out themselves, Ned," said Boardman quietly. "Or maybe they wanted to give invaders a sporting chance. Hosteen, shall we send some probes inside?"

The morning was gray. Clouds the color of wood smoke stained the sky; it looked almost as if rain were on the way. A harsh wind knifed the soil from the plain and sent it slicing into their faces. Behind the veil of clouds lay the sun, a flat orange disk that seemed to have been pasted into the sky. It seemed only slightly larger than Sol as seen from Earth, though it was less than half as distant. Lemnos' sun was a gloomy M dwarf, cool and weary, an old star circled by a dozen old planets. Lemnos, the innermost, was the only one that had ever sustained life; the others were frigid and dead, beyond the range of the sun's feeble rays, frozen from core to atmosphere. It was a sleepy system with so little angular momentum that even the innermost planet dawdled along in a thirty-month orbit; the three zippy moons of Lemnos, darting on crisscrossing tracks a few thousand kilometers overhead, were flagrantly out of keeping with the prevailing mood of these worlds.

Ned Rawlins felt a chill at his heart as he stood beside the data terminal a thousand meters from the outer embankment of the maze, watching his shipmates marshalling their probes and instruments. Not even dead pockmarked Mars had depressed him like this, for Mars was a world that had never lived at all, while here life had been and had moved onward. This world was a house of the dead. In Thebes, once, he had entered the tomb of Pharaoh's vizier, five thousand years gone, and while the others in his group had eyed the gay murals with their glowing scenes of white-garbed figures punting on the Nile, he had looked toward the cool stone floor where a dead beetle lay, clawed feet upraised on a tiny mound of dust. For him Egypt would always be that stiffened beetle in the dust; for him Lemnos was likely to be autumn winds and scoured plains and a silent city. He wondered how anyone as gifted, as full of life and energy and human warmth as Dick Muller, could ever have been willing to maroon himself inside that dismal maze.

Then he remembered what had happened to Muller on Beta Hydri IV, and conceded that even a man like Muller might very well have good reasons for coming to rest on a world like this, in a city like this. Lemnos offered the perfect escape: an Earthlike world, uninhabited, where he was almost guaranteed freedom from human company. And we're here to flush him out and drag him away. Rawlins scowled. Dirty dirty dirty, he thought. The old thing about the ends and the means. Across the way Rawlins could see the blocky figure of Charles Boardman standing in front of the big data terminal, waving his arms this way and that to direct the men fanning out near the walls of the city. He began to understand that he had let Boardman dragoon him into a nasty adventure. The glib old devil hadn't gone into details, back on Earth, about the exact methods by which they were going to win Muller's cooperation. Boardman had made it sound like some kind of shining crusade. Instead it was going to be a dirty trick. Boardman never went into the details of anything before he had to, as Rawlins was beginning to see.

Rule one: hoard your resources of strategy. Never tip your hand. And so here I am, part of the conspiracy.

Hosteen and Boardman had deployed a dozen drones at the various entrances to the inner part of the maze. It was already clear that the only safe way into the city was through the northeastern gate; but they had drones to spare, and they wanted all the data they could gather. The terminal Rawlins was watching flashed a partial diagram of the maze on the screen—the section immediately in front of him—and gave him a good long time to study its loops and coils, its zigzags and twists. It was his special responsibility to follow the progress of the drone through this sector. Each of the other drones was being monitored both by computer and by human observer, while Boardman and Hosteen were at the master terminal watching the progress of the entire operation all at once.

"Send them in," Boardman said.

Hosteen gave the command, and the drones rolled forward through the city's gates. Looking now through the eyes of the squat mobile probe, Rawlins got his first view of what lay in Zone H of the maze. He saw a scalloped wall of what looked like puckered blue porcelain undulating away to the left, and a barrier of metallic threads dangling from a thick stone slab to the other side. The drone skirted the threads, which tinkled and quivered in delicate response to the disturbance of the thin air; it moved to the base of the porcelain wall, and followed it at an inward-sloping angle for perhaps twenty meters. There the wall curved abruptly back on itself, forming a sort of chamber open at the top. The last time anyone had entered the maze this way—on the fourth expedition— two men had passed that open chamber; one had remained outside and was destroyed, the other had gone inside and was spared. The drone entered the chamber. A moment later a beam of pure red light lanced from the center of a mosaic decoration on the wall and swept over the area immediately outside the chamber.

Boardman's voice came to Rawlins through the speaker taped to his ear. "We lost four of the probes the moment they went through their gates. That's exactly as expected. How's yours doing?"

"Following the plan," said Rawlins. "So far, it's okay."

"You ought to lose it within six minutes of entry. What's your elapsed time now?"

"Two minutes fifteen."

The drone was out of the chamber now and shuttling quickly through the place where the light-beam had flashed. Rawlins keyed in olfactory and got the smell of scorched air, lots of ozone. The path divided ahead. To one side was a single-span bridge of stone, arching over what looked like a pit of flame; to the other was a jumbled pile of cyclopean blocks resting precariously edge to edge. The bridge seemed far more inviting, but the drone immediately turned away from it and began to pick its way over the jumbled blocks. Rawlins asked it why, and it relayed the information that the "bridge" wasn't there at all; it was a projection beamed from scanners mounted beneath the facing piers. Requesting a simulation of an approach anyway, Rawlins got a picture of the probe walking out onto the pier and stepping unsuspectingly through the solid-looking bridge to lose its balance; and as the simulated probe struggled to regain its equilibrium, the pier tipped forward and shucked it into the fiery pit. Cute, Rawlins thought, and shuddered.

Meanwhile the real probe had clambered over the blocks and was coming down the other side, unharmed. Three minutes and eight seconds had gone by. A stretch of straight road here turned out to be as safe as it looked. It was flanked on both sides by windowless towers a hundred meters high, made of some iridescent mineral, sleek and oily-surfaced, that flashed shimmering moire patterns as the drone hurried along. At the beginning of the fourth minute the probe skirted bright grillwork like interlocking teeth, and sidestepped an umbrella-shaped piledriver that descended with crushing force. Eighty seconds later it stepped around a tiltblock that opened into a yawning abyss, deftly eluded a quintet of tetrahedal blades that sheared upward out of the pavement, and emerged onto a sliding walkway that carried it quickly forward for exactly forty seconds more.

All this had been traversed long ago by a Terran explorer named Cartissant, since deceased. He had dictated a detailed record of his experiences within the maze. He had lasted five minutes and thirty seconds, and his mistake had come in not getting off the walkway by the forty-first second. Those who had been monitoring him outside, back then, could not say what had happened to him after that.

As his drone left the walkway, Rawlins asked for another simulation and saw a quick dramatization of the computer's best guess: the walkway opened to engulf its passenger at that point. The probe, meanwhile, was going swiftly toward what looked like the exit from this outermost zone of the maze. Beyond lay a well-lit, cheerful-looking plaza ringed with drifting blobs of a pearly glowing substance.

Rawlins said, "I'm into the seventh minute, and we're still going, Charles. There seems to be a door into Zone G just ahead. Maybe you ought to cut in and monitor my screen."

"If you last two more minutes, I will," Boardman said.

The probe paused just outside the inner gate. Warily it switched on its gravitron and accumulated a ball of energy with a mass equivalent to its own. It thrust the energy ball through the doorway. Nothing happened. The probe, satisfied, trundled toward the door itself. As it passed through, the sides of the door abruptly crashed together like the jaws of a mighty press, destroying the probe. Rawlins' screen went dark. Quickly he cut in one of the overhead probes; it beamed him a shot of his probe lying on the far side of the door, flattened into a two-dimensional mock-up of itself. A human being caught in that same trap would have been crushed to powder, Rawlins realized.

"My probe's been knocked out," he reported to Boardman. "Six minutes and forty seconds."

"As expected," came the reply. "We've got only two probes left. Switch over and watch."

The master diagram appeared on Rawlins' screen: a simplified and stylized light-pen picture of the entire maze as viewed from above. A small X had been placed wherever a probe had been destroyed. Rawlins found, after some searching, the path his own drone had taken, with the X marked between the zone boundaries at the place of the clashing door. It seemed to him that the drone had penetrated farther than most of the others, but he had to smile at the childish pride the discovery brought him.

Anyhow, two of the probes were still moving inward. One was actually inside the second zone of the maze, and the other was cruising through a passageway that gave access to that inner ring.

The diagram vanished and Rawlins saw the maze as it looked through the pickup of one of the drones. Almost daintily, the man-high pillar of metal made its way through the baroque intricacies of the maze, past a golden pillar that beamed a twanging melody in a strange key, past a pool of light, past a web of glittering metal spokes, past spiky heaps of bleached bones. Rawlins had only glancing views of the bones as the drone moved on, but he was sure that few were human relics. This place was a galactic graveyard for the bold.

Excitement built in him as the probe went on and on. He was so thoroughly wedded to it now that it was as if he were inside the maze, avoiding one deathtrap after another, and he felt a sense of triumph as minutes mounted. Fourteen had elapsed now. This second level of the maze was not so cluttered as the first; there were spacious avenues here, handsome colonnades, long radiating passages leading from the main path. He relaxed; he felt pride in the drone's agility and in the keenness of its sensory devices. The shock was immense and stinging when a paving-block upended itself unexpectedly and dumped the probe down a long chute to a place where the gears of a giant mill turned eagerly.

They had not expected that probe to get so far, anyway. The probe the others were watching was the one that had come in via the main gate—the safe gate. The slim fund of information accumulated at the price of many lives had guided that probe past all its perils, and now it was well within Zone G, and almost to the edge of F. Thus far, everything had gone as expected; the drone's experiences had matched those of them who had tackled this route on earlier expeditions. It followed their way exactly, turning here, dodging there, and it was eighteen minutes into the maze without incident.

"All right," Boardman said. "This is where Mortenson died, isn't it?"

"Yes," Hosteen answered. "The last thing he said was

that he was standing by that little pyramid, and then he was cut off."

"This is where we start gaining new information, then. All we've learned so far is that our records are accurate. This is the way in. But from here on—"

The probe, lacking a guidance pattern, now moved much more slowly, hesitating at every step to extend its network of data-gathering devices in all directions. It looked for hidden doors, for concealed openings in the pavement, for projectors, lasers, mass-detectors, power sources. It fed back to the central data banks all that it learned, thus adding to the store of information with each centimeter conquered.

It conquered, altogether, twenty-three meters. As the probe passed the small pyramid it scanned the broken body of the explorer Mortenson, lost at this point 72 years earlier. It relayed the news that Mortenson had been seized by a pressure-sensitive mangle activated by an unwary footstep too close to the pyramid. Beyond, it avoided two minor traps before failing to safeguard itself from a distortion screen that baffled its sensors and left it vulnerable to the descent of a pulverizing piston.

"The next one through will have to cut off all its inputs until it's past that point," Hosteen muttered. "Running through blindfolded—well, we'll manage."

"Maybe a man would do better than a machine there," said Boardman. "We don't know if that screen would muddle a man the way it did a batch of sensors."

"We're not yet ready to run a man in there," Hosteen pointed out.

Boardman agreed—none too graciously, Rawlins thought, listening to the interchange. The screen brightened again; a new drone probe was coming through. Hosteen had ordered a second wave of the machines to pick through the labyrinth, following what was now known to be the one safe access route, and several of them were at the eighteen-minute point where the deadly pyramid was located. Hosteen sent one ahead, and posted the others to keep watch. The lead probe came within range of the distortion screen and cut out its sensors; it heaved tipsily for a moment, lacking any way to get its bearings, but in a moment it was stable. It was deprived now of contact with its surroundings, and so it paid no heed to the siren song of the distortion screen, which had misled its predecessor into coming within range of the pulverizing piston. The phalanx of drones watching the scene was all outside the reach of the distorter's mischief, and fed a clear, true picture to the computer, which matched it with the fatal path of the last probe and plotted a route that skirted the dangerous piston. Moments later the blind probe began to move, guided now by inner impulses. Lacking all environmental feedback it was entirely a captive of the computer, which nudged it along in a series of tiny prods until it was safely around the hazard. On the far side, the sensors were switched on again. To check the procedure, Hosteen sent a second drone through, likewise blinded and moving entirely on internal guidance. It made it. Then he tried a third probe with its sensors on and under the influence of the distortion screen. The computer attempted to direct it along the safe path, but the probe, bedeviled by the faulty information coming through the distorter, tugged itself furiously to the side and was smashed.

"All right," Hosteen said. "If we can get a machine past it, we can get a man past it. He closes his eyes, and the computer calculates his motions step by step. We'll manage."

The lead probe began to move again. It got seventeen meters past the place of the distorter before it was nailed by a silvery grillwork that abruptly thrust up a pair of electrodes and cut loose with a bath of flame. Rawlins watched bleakly as the next probe avoided that obstacle and shortly fell victim to another. Plenty of probes waited patiently for their turn to press forward.

And soon men will be going in there too, Rawlins thought. *We'll* be going in there.

He shut off his data terminal and walked across to Boardman.

"How does it look so far?" he asked.

"Rough, but not impossible," Boardman said. "It can't be this tough all the way in."

"And if it is?"

"We won't run out of probes. We'll chart the whole

maze until we know where all the danger points are, and then we'll start trying it ourselves."

Rawlins said, "Are *you* going to go in there, Charles?"

"Of course. So are you."

"With what odds on coming out?"

"Good ones," said Boardman. "Otherwise I doubt that I'd tackle it. Oh, it's a dangerous trip, Ned, but don't overestimate it. We've just begun to test that maze. We'll know it well enough in a few days more."

Rawlins considered that a moment. "Muller didn't have any probes," he said finally. "How did he survive that stuff?"

"I'm not sure," Boardman murmured. "I suppose he's just a naturally lucky man."

three

Within the maze Muller watched the proceedings on his dim screens. They were sending some sort of robots in, he saw. The robots were getting chewed up quite badly, but each successive wave of them seemed to reach deeper into the labyrinth. Trial and error had led the intruders to the correct route through Zone H and well onward into G. Muller was prepared to defend himself if the robots reached the inner zones. Meanwhile he remained calm at the center of it all, going about his daily pursuits.

In the mornings he spent a good deal of the time thinking over his past. There had been other worlds in other years, springtimes, warmer seasons than this; soft eyes looking into his eyes, hands against his hands, smiles, laughter, shining floors, and elegant figures moving through arched doorways. He had married twice. Both times the arrangements had been terminated peacefully after a decent span of years. He had traveled widely. He had dealt with ministers and kings. In his nostrils was the scent of a hundred planets strung across the sky. We make only a small blaze, and then we go out; but in his springtime and his summer he had burned brightly enough, and he did not feel he had earned this sullen, joyless autumn.

The city took care of him, after its fashion. He had a place to dwell—thousands of places; he moved from time to time for the sake of changing the view. All the houses were empty boxes. He had made a bed for himself of animal hides stuffed with scraped fur; he had fashioned a chair from sinews and skin; he needed little else. The city gave him water. Wild animals roamed here in such quantity that he would never lack for food so long as he was strong enough to hunt. From Earth he had brought with him certain basic items. He had three cubes of books and one of music; they made a stack less than a meter high and could nourish his soul for all the years that remained to him. He had some woman cubes. He had a small recorder into which he sometimes dictated memoirs. He had a sketchpad. He had weapons and a mass detector. He had a diagnostat with a regenerating medical supply. It was enough.

He ate regularly. He slept well. He had no quarrels with his conscience. He had come almost to be content with his fate. One nurses bitterness only so long before one grows a cyst around the place from which the poison spews.

He blamed no one now for what had happened to him. His own hungers had brought him to this. He had tried to devour the universe; he had aspired to the condition of a god; and some implacable guiding force had hurled him down from his high place, hurled him down and smashed him, left him to crawl off to this dead world to knit his broken soul as best he could.

The way stations on his journey to this place were well known to him. At eighteen, lying naked under the stars with warmth against him, he had boasted of his lofty ambitions. At twenty-five he had begun to realize them. Before he was forty he had visited a hundred worlds, and was famous in thirty systems. A decade later he had had his delusions of statesmanship. And at the age of fifty· three he had let Charles Boardman talk him into undertaking the mission to Beta Hydri IV.

That year he was on holiday in the Tau Ceti system, a dozen light-years from home. Marduk, the fourth world, had been designed as a pleasure planet for the mining men who were engaged in stripping her sister worlds of a fortune in reactive metals. Muller had no liking for the way those planets were being plundered, but that did not prevent him from seeking relaxation on Marduk. It was nearly a seasonless world, which rode upright in its orbital plane; four continents of unending springtime bathed by a tranquil shallow sea. The sea was green, the land vegetation had a faint bluish tinge, and the air had a little of the sparkle of young champagne. They had somehow made the planet into a counterfeit of Earth—Earth as it might have been in a more innocent time—all parks and meadows and cheery inns; it was a restful world whose challenges were purely synthetic. The giant fish in the seas always wearied and let themselves be played. The snow-capped mountains looked treacherous, even for climbers in gravitron boots, but no one had been lost on them yet. The beasts with which the forests were stocked were tall at the withers and snorted as they charged, but they were not as fierce as they looked. In principle, Muller disapproved of such places. But he had had enough adventure for a while, and he had come to Marduk for a few weeks of phony peace, accompanied by a girl he had met the year before and twenty light-years away.

Her name was Marta. She was tall, slim, with large dark eyes fashionably rimmed with red, and lustrous blue hair that brushed her smooth shoulders. She looked about twenty, but of course she might just as well have been ninety and on her third shape-up; you never could tell about anyone, and especially not about a woman. But somehow Muller suspected that she was genuinely young. It wasn't her litheness, her coltish agility—those are commodities that can be purchased—but some subtle quality of enthusiasm, of true girlishness that, he liked to think, was no surgical product. Whether power-swimming or tree-floating or blowdart hunting or making love, Marta seemed so totally engaged in her pleasures that they surely were relatively new to her.

Muller did not care to investigate such things too deeply. She was wealthy, Earthborn, had no visible family ties, and went where she pleased. On a sudden impulse he had phoned her and asked her to meet him on Marduk; and she had come willingly, no questions asked. She was not awed to be sharing a hotel suite with Richard Muller. Clearly she knew who he was, but the aura of fame that surrounded him was unimportant to her. What mattered was what he said to her, how he held her, what they did together; and not the accomplishments he had accumulated at other times.

They stayed at a hotel that was a spire of brilliance a thousand meters high, thrusting needle-straight out of a valley overlooking a glassy oval lake. Their rooms were two hundred floors up, and they dined in a rooftop eyrie reached by gravitron disk, and during the day all the pleasures of Marduk lay spread out before them. He was with her for a week, uninterrupted. The weather was perfect. Her small cool breasts fit nicely into his cupped palms; her long slender legs encircled him pleasantly, and at the highest moments she drove her heels into his calves with sudden delicious fervor. On the eighth day Charles Boardman arrived on Marduk, hired a suite half a continent away, and invited Muller to pay a call on him.

"I'm on vacation," Muller told him.

"Give me half a day of it."

"I'm not alone, Charles."

"I know that. Bring her along. We'll take a ride. It's an important matter."

"I came here to escape important matters."

"There's never any escape, Dick. You know that. You are what you are, and we need you. Will you come?"

"Damn you," Muller said mildly.

In the morning he and Marta flew by quickboat to Boardman's hotel. Muller remembered the journey as vividly as though it had taken place last month and not almost fifteen years before. They soared above the continental divide, skimming the snowy summits of the mountains by so slim a margin that they could see the magnificent long-horned figure of a goatish rock-skipper capering across the gleaming rivers of ice: two metric tons of muscle and bone, an improbable colossus of the peaks, the costliest prey Marduk had to offer. Some men did not earn in a lifetime what it cost to buy a license to hunt rock-skipper. To Muller it seemed that even that price was too low.

They circled the mighty beast three times and streaked off into the lake country, the lowlands beyond the mountain range where a chain of diamond-bright pools girdled the fat waist of the continent, and by midday they were landed at the edge of a velvety forest of evergreens. Boardman had rented the hotel's master suite, all screens and trickery. He grasped Muller's wrist in salute, and embraced Marta with unabashed lechery. She seemed distant and restrained in Boardman's arms; quite obviously she regarded the visit as so much time lost.

"Are you hungry?" Boardman asked. "Lunch first, talk later!"

He served drinks in his suite: an amber wine out of goblets made from blue rock crystal mined on Ganymede.

Then they boarded a dining capsule and left the hotel to tour the forests and lakes while they ate. Lunch glided from its container and rolled toward them as they lounged in pneumochairs before a wraparound window. Crisp salad, grilled native fish, imported vegetables; a grated Centaurine cheese to sprinkle; flasks of cold rice beer; a rich, thick, spicy green liqueur afterward. Completely passive, sealed in their moving capsule, they accepted food and drink and scenery, breathed the sparkling air pumped in from outside, watched gaudy birds flutter past them and lose themselves in the soft, drooping needles of the thickly-packed conifers of the woods. Boardman had carefully staged all this to create a mood, but his efforts were wasted, Muller knew. He could not be lulled this easily. He might take whatever job Boardman offered, but not because he had been fooled into false unwariness.

Marta was bored. She showed it by the detached response she gave to Boardman's inquiring lustful glances. The shimmering daywrap she wore was designed to reveal; as its long-chained molecules slid kaleidoscopically through their path of patterns they yielded quick, frank glimpses of thighs and breasts, of belly and loins, of hips and buttocks. Boardman appreciated the display and seemed ready to capitalize on Marta's apparent availability, but she ignored his unvoiced overtures entirely. Muller was amused by that. Boardman was not.

After lunch the capsule halted by the side of a jewel-like lake, deep and clear. The wall opened, and Boardman said, "Perhaps the young lady would like to swim while we get the dull business talk out of the way?"

"A fine idea," Marta said in a flat voice.

Arising, she touched the disrobing snap at her shoulder and let her garment slither to her ankles. Boardman made a great show of catching it up and putting it on a storage rack. She smiled mechanically at him, turned, walked down to the edge of the lake, a nude tawny figure whose tapering back and gently rounded rump were dappled by the sunlight slipping through the trees. For a moment she paused, shin-deep in the water; then she sprang forward and sliced the breast of the lake with strong steady strokes.

Boardman said, "She's quite lovely, Dick. Who is she?"

"A girl. Rather young, I think."

"Younger than your usual sort, I'd say. Also somewhat spoiled. Known her long?"

"Since last year, Charles. Interested?"

"Naturally."

"I'll tell her that," Muller said. "Some other time."

Boardman gave him a Buddha-smile and gestured toward the liquor console. Muller shook his head. Marta was backstroking in the lake, the rosy tips of her breasts just visible above the serene surface. The two men eyed one another. They appeared to be of the same age, mid-fifties; Boardman fleshy and graying and strong-looking, Muller lean and graying and strong-looking. Seated, they seemed of the same height, too. The appearances were deceptive: Boardman was a generation older, Muller half a foot taller. They had known each other for thirty years.

In a way, they were in the same line of work—both part of the corps of nonadministrative personnel that served to hold the structure of human society together across the sprawl of the galaxy. Neither held any official rank. They shared a readiness to serve, a desire to make their gifts useful to mankind; and Muller respected Boardman for the way he had used those gifts during a long and impressive career, though he could not say that he liked the older man. He knew that Boardman was shrewd, unscrupulous, and dedicated to human welfare—and the combination of dedication and unscrupulousness is always a dangerous one.

Boardman drew a vision cube from a pocket of his tunic and put it on the table before Muller. It rested there like a counter in some intricate game, six or seven centimeters along each face, soft yellow against the polished black marble face of the table. "Plug it in," Boardman invited, "the viewer's beside you."

Muller slipped the cube into the receptor slot. From the center of the table there arose a larger cube, nearly a meter across. Images flowered on its faces. Muller saw a cloud-wrapped planet, soft gray in tone, it could have been Venus. The view deepened and streaks of dark red appeared in the gray. Not Venus, then. The recording eye pierced the cloud layer and revealed an unfamiliar, not very Earthlike planet. The soil looked moist and spongy, and rubbery trees that looked like giant toadstools thrust upward from it. It was hard to judge relative sizes, but they looked big. Their pale trunks were coarse with shredded fibers, and curved like bows between ground and crown. Saucerlike growths shielded the trees at their bases, ringing them for about a fifth of their height. Above were neither branches nor leaves, only wide flat caps whose undersurfaces were mottled by corrugated processes. As Muller watched, three alien figures came strolling through the somber grove. They were elongated, almost spidery, with clusters of eight or ten jointed limbs depending from their narrow shoulders. Their heads were tapered and rimmed with eyes. Their nostrils were vertical slits flush against the skin. Their mouths opened at the sides. They walked upright on elegant legs that terminated in small globe-like pedestals instead of feet. Though they were nude except for probably ornamental strips of fabric tied between their first and second wrists, Muller was unable to detect signs either of reproductive apparatus or of mammalian functions. Their skins were unpigmented, sharing the prevailing grayness of this gray world, and were coarse in texture, with a scaly overlay of small diamond-shaped ridges.

With wonderful grace the three figures approached three of the giant toadstools and scaled them until each stood atop the uppermost saucerlike projection of a tree. Out of the cluster of limbs came one arm that seemed specially adapted; unlike the others, which were equipped with five tendril-shaped fingers arranged in a circlet, this limb ended in a needle-sharp organ. It plunged easily and deeply into the soft rubbery trunk of the tree on which its owner stood. A long moment passed, as if the aliens were draining sap from the trees. Then they climbed down and resumed their stroll, outwardly unchanged.

One of them paused, bent, peered closely at the ground. It scooped up the eye that had been witnessing its activities. The image grew chaotic; Muller guessed that the eye was being passed from hand to hand. Suddenly there was darkness. The eye had been destroyed. The cube was played out.

After a moment of troubled silence Muller said, "They look very convincing."

"They ought to be. They're real."

"Was this taken by some sort of extragalactic probe?"

"No," Boardman said. "In our own galaxy."

"Beta Hydri IV, then?"

"Yes."

Muller repressed a shiver. "May I play it again, Charles?"

"Of course."

He activated the cube a second time. Again the eye made the descent through the cloud layer; again it observed the rubbery trees; again the trio of aliens appeared, took nourishment from the trees, noticed the eye, destroyed it. Muller studied the images with cold fascination. He had never looked upon living sapient beings of another creation before. No one had, so far as he knew, until now.

The images faded from the cube.

Boardman said, "That was taken less than a month ago. We parked a drone ship fifty thousand kilometers up and dropped roughly a thousand eyes on Beta Hydri IV. At least half of them went straight to the bottom of the ocean. Most landed in uninhabited or uninteresting places. This is the only one that actually showed us a clear view of the aliens."

"Why has it been decided to break our quarantine of this planet?"

Boardman slowly let out his breath. "We think it's time we got in touch with them, Dick. We've been sniffing around them for ten years and we haven't said hello yet. That isn't neighborly. And since the Hydrans and ourselves are the only intelligent races in this whole damned galaxy—unless something's hiding somewhere unlikely—we've come to the belief that we ought to commence friendly relations."

"I don't find your coyness very appealing," Muller said bluntly. "A full-scale council decision was taken after close to a year of debate, and it was voted to leave the Hydrans alone for at least a century—unless they showed some sign of going into space. Who reversed that decision, and why, and when?"

Boardman smiled his crafty smile. But Muller knew that the only way to avoid being drawn into his web was to take a frontal approach. Slowly Boardman said, "I didn't mean to seem deceptive, Dick. The decision was reversed by a council session eight months ago, while you were out Rigel way."

"And the reason?"

"One of the extragalactic probes came back with convincing evidence that there's at least one highly intelligent and quite superior species in one of our neighboring clusters."

"Where?"

"It doesn't matter, Dick. Pardon me, but I won't tell you at this time."

"All right."

"Let's just say that from what we know of them now, they're much more than we can handle. They've got a galactic drive, and we can reasonably expect them to come visiting us one of these centuries—and when they do, we'll have a problem. So it's been voted to open contact with Beta Hydri IV ahead of schedule, by way of insurance against that day."

"You mean," Muller said, "that we want to make sure we're on good terms with the other race of our own galaxy before the extragalactics show up?"

"Exactly."

"I'll take that drink now," said Muller.

Boardman gestured. Muller tapped out a potent combination on the console, downed it quickly, ordered another. Suddenly he had a great deal to digest. He looked away from Boardman, picking up the vision cube and fingering it as though it were a sacred relic.

For a couple of centuries man had explored the stars without finding a trace of a rival. There were plenty of planets, and many of them were potentially habitable, and a surprising number were Earthlike to four or five places. That much had been expected. The sky is full of main-sequence suns, with a good many of the F-type and G-type stars most likely to support life. The process of planetogenesis is nothing remarkable, and most of those suns had complements of five to a dozen worlds, some of which were of the right size and mass and density slots to permit the retention of atmosphere and the convenient evolution of life, and a number of those worlds were situated within the orbital zone where they were best able to avoid extremes of temperature. So life abounded and the galaxy was a zoologist's delight.

But in his helter-skelter expansion out of his own system man had found only the traces of former intelligent species. Beasts laired in the ruins of unimaginably ancient civilizations. The most spectacular ancient site was the maze of Lemnos; but other worlds too had their stumps of cities, their weathered foundations, their burial grounds and strewn potsherds. Space became an archaeologist's delight, too. The collectors of alien animals and the collectors of alien relics were kept busy. Whole new scientific specialities burst into being. Societies that had vanished before the Pyramids had been conceived now underwent reconstruction.

A curious blight of extinction had come upon all the galaxy's other intelligent races, though. Evidently they had flourished so long ago that not even their decadent children survived; they were one with Nineveh and Tyre, blotted out, cut off. Careful scrutiny showed that the youngest of the dozen or so known extrasolar intelligent cultures had perished eighty thousand years earlier.

The galaxy is wide; and man kept on looking, drawn to find his stellar companions by some perverse mixture of curiosity and dread. Though the warp drive provided speedy transport to all points within the universe, neither available personnel nor available ships could cope with the immensity of the surveying tasks. Several centuries after his intrusion into the galaxy, man was still making discoveries, some of them quite close to home. The star Beta Hydri had seven planets; and on the fourth was another sapient species.

There were no landings. The possibility of such a discovery had been examined well in advance, and plans had been drawn to avoid a blundering trespass of unpredictable consequences. The survey of Beta Hydri IV had been carried out from beyond its cloud layer. Cunning devices had measured the activity behind that tantalizing gray mask. Hydran energy production was known to a tolerance of a few million kilowatt hours; Hydran urban districts had been mapped, and their population density estimated; the level of Hydran industrial development had been calculated by a study of thermal radiations. There was an aggressive, growing, potent civilization down there, probably comparable in technical level to late twentieth-century Earth. There was only one significant difference: the Hydrans had not begun to enter space. That was the fault of the cloud layer. A race that never has seen the stars is not likely to show much desire to reach them.

Muller had been privy to the frantic conferences that followed the discovery of the Hydrans. He knew the reasons why they had been placed under quarantine, and he realized that only much more urgent reasons had resulted in the lifting of that quarantine. Unsure of its ability to handle a relationship with nonhuman beings, Earth had wisely chosen to keep away from the Hydrans for a while longer; but now all that was changed.

"What happens now?" Muller asked. "An expedition?"

"Yes."

"How soon?"

"Within the next year, I'd say."

Muller tensed. "Under whose leadership?"

"Perhaps yours, Dick."

"Why 'perhaps'?"

"You might not want it."

"When I was eighteen," Muller said, "I was with a girl out in the woods on Earth, in the California forest preserve, and we made love, and it wasn't exactly my first time but the first time it worked out in any kind of proper way, and afterward we were lying on our backs looking up at the stars and I told her I was going to go out and walk around among them. And she said, Oh, Dick, how wonderful, but of course it wasn't anything special I was saying. Any kid that age says it when he looks up at the stars. And I told her that I was going to discover things out in space, that men were going to remember me the way they remember Columbus and Magellan and the early astronauts and all. I said I was going to be right in the front of whatever was happening, that I was going to move through the stars like a god. I was very eloquent. I went on like that for about ten minutes, until we were both carried away by the wonder of it all, and I turned to her and she pulled me down on top of her and I turned my backside to the stars and worked hard to nail her to the Earth, and that was the night I grew my ambitions." He laughed. "There are things we can say at eighteen that we can't say again."

"There are things we can do at eighteeen that we can't do again either," said Boardman. "Well, Dick? You're past fifty now, right? You've walked in the stars. Do you feel like a god?"

"Sometimes."

"Do you want to go to Beta Hydri IV?"

"You know I do."

"Alone?"

Muller felt the ground give way before him, and abruptly it seemed to him that he was taking his first spacewalk again, falling freely toward all the universe. *"Alone?"*

"We've programmed the whole thing and concluded that to send a bunch of men down there at this point would be a mistake. The Hydrans haven't responded very well to our eye probes. You saw that: they picked the eye up and smashed it. We can't begin to fathom their psychologies, because we've never been up against alien minds before. But we feel that the safest thing—both in terms of potential manpower loss and in terms of impact on their society—is to send a single ambassador down there to them—one man, coming in peace, a shrewd, strong man who has been tested under a variety of stress situations and who will develop ways of initiating contact. That man may find himself chopped to shreds thirty seconds after making contact. On the other hand, if he survives he'll have accomplished something utterly unique in human history. It's your option."

It was irresistible. Mankind's ambassador to the Hydrans! To go alone, to walk alien soil and extend humanity's first greeting to cosmic neighbors—

It was his ticket to immortality. It would write his name forever on the stars.

"How do you figure the chances of survival?" Muller asked.

"The computation is one chance in sixty-five of coming out whole, Dick. Considering that it's not an Earth-type planet to any great degree, you'll need a life-support system. And you may get a chilly reception. One in sixty-five."

"Not too bad."

"I'd never accept such odds myself," Boardman said, grinning.

"No, but I might." He drained his glass. To carry it off meant imperishable fame. To fail, to be slain by the Hydrans, even that was not so dreadful. He had lived well. There were worse fates than to die bearing mankind's banner to a strange world. That throbbing pride of his, that hunger for glory, that childlike craving for renown that he had never outgrown, drove him to it. The odds were not too bad.

Marta reappeared. She was wet from her swim, her nude body glossy, her hair plastered to the slender column of her neck. Her breasts were heaving rapidly, little cones of flesh tipped by puckered pink nipples. She might have been a leggy fourteen-year-old, Muller thought, looking at her narrow hips, her lean thighs. Boardman tossed her a drier. She thumbed it and stepped into its yellow field, making one complete turn. She took her garment from the rack and covered herself unhurriedly. "That was great," she said. Her eyes met Muller's for the first time since her return. "Dick, what's the matter with you? You look wide open—stunned. Are you all right?"

"Fine."

"What happened?"

"Mr. Boardman's made a proposition."

"You can tell her about it, Dick. We don't plan to keep it a secret. There'll be a galaxy-wide announcement right away."

"There's going to be a landing on Beta Hydri IV," Muller said in a thick voice. "One man. Me. How will it work, Charles? A ship in a parking orbit, and then I go down in a powered drop-capsule equipped for return?"

"Yes."

Marta said. "It's insane, Dick. Don't do it. You'll regret it forever."

"It's a quick death if things don't work out, Marta. I've taken worse risks before."

"No. Look, sometimes I think I've got a little precog. I see things ahead, Dick." She laughed nervously, her pose of cool sophistication abruptly shattering. "If you go there, I don't think you'll die. But I don't exactly think you'll live, either. Say you won't go. Say it, Dick!"

"You never officially accepted the proposition," Boardman pointed out.

"I know," Muller said. He got to his feet, nearly reaching the low roof of the dining capsule, and walked toward Marta, and put his arms around her, remembering that other girl so long ago under the California sky, remembering that wild surge of power that had come upon him as he swung over from the blaze of the stars to the warm, yielding flesh and the parting thighs beneath him. He held Marta firmly. She looked at him in horror. He kissed the tip of her nose and the lobe of her left ear. She shrank away from him, stumbled, nearly plunged into Boardman's lap. Boardman caught her and held her. Muller said, "You know what the answer has to be."

That afternoon one of the robot probes reached Zone F. They still had a distance to go; but it would not be long, Muller knew, before they were at the heart of the maze.

four

"There he is," Rawlins said. "At last!"

Via the drone probe's eyes he stared at the man in the maze. Muller leaned casually against a wall, arms folded; a big weatherbeaten man with a harsh chin and a massive wedge-shaped nose. He did not seem at all alarmed by the presence of the drone.

Rawlins cut in the audio pickup and heard Muller say, "Hello, robot. Why are you bothering me?"

The probe, of course, did not reply. Neither did Rawlins, who could have piped a message through the drone. He stood by the data terminal, crouching a little for a better view. His weary eyes throbbed. It had taken them nine local-time days to get one of their probes all the way through the maze to the center. The effort had cost them close to a hundred probes; each inward extension of the safe route by twenty meters or so had required the expenditure of one of the robots. Still, that wasn't so bad, considering that the number of wrong choices in the maze was close to infinite. Through luck, the inspired use of the ship's brain, and a sturdy battery of sensory devices, they had managed to avoid all the obvious traps and most of the cleverer ones. And now they were in the center.

Rawlins felt exhausted. He had been up all night monitoring this critical phase, the penetration of Zone A. Hosteen had gone to sleep. So, finally, had Boardman. A few of the crewmen were still on duty here and aboard the ship, but Rawlins was the only member of the civilian complement still awake.

He wondered if the discovery of Muller had been supposed to take place during his stint. Probably not. Boardman wouldn't want to risk blowing things by letting a novice handle the big moment. Well, too bad. They had left him on duty, and he had moved his probe a few meters inward, and now he was looking right at Muller.

He searched for signs of the man's inner torment.

They weren't obvious. Muller had lived here alone for so many years—wouldn't that have done something to his soul? And that other thing, the prank the Hydrans had played on him—surely that too would have registered on his face. So far as Rawlins could tell, it hadn't.

Oh, he looked sad around the eyes, and his lips were compressed in a taut, tense line. But Rawlins had been expecting something more dramatic, something romantic, some mirror of agony on that face. Instead he saw only the craggy, indifferent, almost insensitive-looking features of a tough, durable man in late middle age. Muller had gone gray, and his clothing was a little ragged; he looked worn and frayed himself. But that was only to be expected of a man who had been living this kind of exile for nine years. Rawlins wanted something more, something picturesque, a gaunt, bitter face, eyes dark with misery.

"What do you want?" Muller asked the probe. "Who sent you? Why don't you go away?"

Rawlins did not dare to answer. He had no idea of the gambit Boardman had in mind at this point. Brusquely he keyed the probe to freeze and sped away toward the dome where Boardman slept.

Boardman was sleeping under a canopy of life-sustaining devices. He was, after all, at least eighty years old—though he certainly didn't look it—and one way to keep from looking it was to plug one self into one's sustainers every night. Rawlins was a trifle embarrassed to intrude on the old man when he was enmeshed in his paraphernalia this way. Strapped to Boardman's forehead were a couple of meningeal electrodes that guaranteed a proper and healthy progression through the levels of sleep, thus washing the mind of the day's fatigue poisons. An ultrasonic drawcock filtered dregs and debris from Boardman's arteries. Hormone flow was regulated by the ornate webwork hovering above his chest. The whole business was linked to and directed by the ship's brain. Within the elaborate life system Boardman looked unreal and waxy. His breathing was slow and regular; his soft lips were slack; his cheeks seemed puffy and loose-fleshed. Boardman's eyeballs were moving rapidly beneath the lids; a sign of dreaming, of upper sleep. Could he be awakened safely now?

Rawlins feared to risk it. Not directly, anyway. He ducked out of the room and activated the terminal just outside. "Take a dream to Charles Boardman," Rawlins said. "Tell him we found Muller. Tell him he's got to wake up right away. Say, Charles, Charles, wake up, we need you. Got it?"

"Acknowledged," said the ship's brain.

The impulse leaped from dome to ship, was translated into response-directed form, and returned to the dome. Rawlins' message seeped into Boardman's mind through the electrodes on his forehead. Feeling pleased with himself, Rawlins entered the old man's sleeproom once again and waited.

Boardman stirred. His hands formed claws and scraped gently at the machinery in whose embrace he lay.

"Muller—" he muttered.

His eyes opened. For a moment he did not see. But the waking process had begun, and the life system jolted his metabolism sufficiently to get him functioning again. "Ned?" he said hoarsely. "What are you doing here? I dreamed that—"

"It wasn't a dream, Charles. I programmed it for you. We got through to Zone A. We found Muller."

Boardman undid the life system and sat up instantly, alert, aware. "What time is it?"

"Dawn's just breaking."

"And how long ago did you find him?"

"Perhaps fifteen minutes. I froze the probe, and came right to you. But I didn't want to rush you awake, so—"

"All right. All right." Boardman had swung out of bed, now. He staggered a little as he got to his feet. He wasn't yet at his daytime vigor, Rawlins realized; his real age was showing. He found an excuse to look away, studying the life system to avoid having to see the meaty folds of Boardman's body.

When I'm his age, Rawlins thought, I'll make sure I get regular shape-ups. It isn't a matter of vanity, really. It's just courtesy to other people. We don't have to look old if we don't want to look old. Why offend?

"Let's go," Boardman said. "Unfreeze that probe. I want to see him right away."

Using the terminal in the hall, Rawlins brought the probe back to life. The screen showed them Zone A of the maze, cozier-looking than the outer reaches. Muller was not in view. "Turn the audio on one way," Boardman said.

"It is."

"Where'd he go?"

"Must have walked out of sight range," Rawlins said. He moved the probe in a standing circle, taking in a broad sweep of low cubical houses, high-rising archways, and tiered walls. A small cat-like animal scampered by, but there was no sign of Muller.

"He was right over there," Rawlins insisted unhappily. "He—"

"All right. He didn't have to stay in one place while you were waking me up. Walk the probe around."

Rawlins activated the drone and started it in a slow cruising exploration of the street. Instinctively he was cautious, expecting to find more traps at any moment, though he told himself a couple of times that the builders of the maze would surely not have loaded their own inner quarters with perils. Muller abruptly stepped out of a windowless building and planted himself in front of the probe.

"Again," he said. "Back to life, are you? Why don't you speak up? What's your ship? Who sent you?"

"Should we answer?" Rawlins asked.

"No."

Boardman's face was pressed almost against the screen. He pushed Rawlins' hands from the controls and went to work on the fine tuning until Muller was sharply in focus. Boardman kept the probe moving, sliding around in front of Muller, as though trying to hold the man's attention and prevent him from wandering off again.

In a low voice Boardman said, "That's frightening. The look on his face—"

"I thought he looked pretty calm."

"What do you know? I *remember* that man. Ned, that's a face out of hell. His cheekbones are twice as sharp as they used to be. His eyes are awful. You see the way his mouth turns down—on the left side? He might even have had a light stroke. But he's lasted well enough, I suppose."

Baffled, Rawlins searched for the signs of Muller's passion. He had missed them before, and he missed them now. But of course he had no real recollection of the way Muller was supposed to look. And Boardman, naturally, would be far more expert than he at reading character.

"It won't be simple; getting him out of there," Boardman said. "He'll want to stay. But we need him, Ned. We need him."

Muller, keeping pace with the drone, said in a deep gruff voice, "You've got thirty seconds to state your purpose here. Then you'd better turn around and get going back the way you came."

"Won't you talk to him?" Rawlins asked. "He'll wreck the probe!"

"Let him," said Boardman. "The first person who talks to him is going to be flesh and blood, and he's going to be standing face to face with him. That's the only way it can be. This has to be a courtship, Ned. We can't do it through the speakers of a probe."

"Ten seconds," said Muller.

He reached into his pocket and came out with a glossy black metal globe the size of an apple, with a small square window on one side. Rawlins had never seen anything like it before. Perhaps it was some alien weapon Muller had found in this city, he decided, for swiftly Muller raised the globe and aimed the window at the face of the drone probe.

The screen went dark.

"Looks like we've lost another probe," Rawlins said.

Boardman nodded. "Yes. The last probe we're going to lose. Now we start losing men."

2

The time had come to risk human lives in the maze. It was inevitable, and Boardman regretted it, the way he regretted paying taxes or growing old or voiding waste matter or feeling the pull of strong gravity. Taxes, aging, excretion, and gravity were all permanent aspects of the human condition, though, however much all four had been alleviated by modern scientific progress. So was the risk of death. They had made good use of the drone probes here, and had probably saved a dozen lives that way; but now lives were almost surely going to be lost anyhow. Boardman grieved over that, but not for long and not very deeply. He had been asking men to risk their lives for decades, and many of them had died. He was ready to risk his own, at the right time and in the right cause.

The maze now was thoroughly mapped. The ship's brain held a detailed picture of the inward route, with all the known pitfalls charted, and Boardman was confident that he could send drones in with a ninety-five per cent probability of getting them to Zone A unharmed. Whether a man could cover that same route with equal safety was what remained to be seen. Even with the computer whispering hints to him every step of the way, a man filtering information through a fallible, fatigue-prone human brain might not quite see things the same way as a lathe-turned probe, and perhaps would make compensations of his own in the course that would prove fatal. So the data they had gathered had to be tested carefully before he or Ned Rawlins ventured inside.

There were volunteers to take care of that.

They knew they were likely to die. No one had tried to pretend otherwise to them, and they would have it no other way. It had been put to them that it was important for humanity to bring Richard Muller voluntarily out of that maze, and that it could best be accomplished by having specific human beings—Charles Boardman and Ned Rawlins—speak to Muller in person, and that since Boardman and Rawlins were nonreplaceable units it was necessary for others to explore the route ahead of them. Very well. The explorers were ready, knowing that they were expendable. They also knew that it might even be helpful for the first few of them to die. Each death brought new information; successful traversals of the inward route brought none, at this point.

They drew lots for the job.

The man chosen to go first was a lieutenant named Burke, who looked fairly young and probably was, since military men rarely went in for shape-ups until they were in the top echelons. He was a short, sturdy, dark-haired man who acted as if he could be replaced from a template aboard the ship, which was not the case.

"When I find Muller," Burke said—he did not say *if*—"I tell him I'm an archaeologist. Right? And that if he doesn't mind, I'd like some of my friends to come inside also?"

"Yes," said Boardman. "And remember, the less you say to him in the way of professional-sounding noises, the less suspicious he's going to be."

Burke was not going to live long enough to say anything to Richard Muller, and all of them knew it. But he waved goodbye jauntily, somewhat stagily, and strode into the maze. Through a backpack he was connected with the ship's brain. The computer would relay his marching orders to him, and would show the watchers in the camp exactly what was happening to him.

He moved smartly and smoothly past the terrors of Zone H. He lacked the array of detection devices that had helped the probes find the pivot-mounted slabs and the deathpits beneath, the hidden energy flares, the clashing teeth set in doorways, and all the other nightmares; but he had something much more useful riding with him: the accumulated knowledge of those nightmares, gathered through the expenditure of a lot of probes that had failed to notice them. Boardman, watching his screen, saw the by now familiar pillars and spokes and escarpments, the airy bridges, the heaps of bones, the occasional debris of a drone probe. Silently he urged Burke on, knowing that in not too many days he would have to travel this route himself. Boardman wondered how much Burke's life meant to Burke.

Burke took nearly forty minutes to pass from Zone H to Zone G. He showed no sign of elation as he negotiated the passageway; G, they all knew, was nearly as tough as H. But so far the guidance system was working well. Burke was executing a sort of grim ballet, dancing around the obstacles, counting his steps, now leaping, now turning sideways, now straining to step over some treacherous strip of pavement. He was progressing nicely. But the computer was unable to warn him about the small toothy creature awaiting atop a gilded ledge forty meters inside Zone G. It was no part of the maze's design.

It was a random menace, transacting business on its own account. Burke carried only a record of past experiences in this realm.

The animal was no bigger than a very large cat, but its fangs were long and its claws were quick. The eye in Burke's backpack saw it as it leaped—but by then it was too late. Burke, half-warned, half-turned and reached for his weapon with the beast already on his shoulders and scrambling for his throat.

The jaws opened astonishingly wide. The computer's eye relayed an anatomical touch Boardman could well have done without: within the outer row of needle-sharp teeth was an inner one, and a third one inside that, perhaps for better chewing of the prey or perhaps just a couple of sets of replacements in case outer teeth were broken off. The effect was one of a forest of jagged fangs. A moment later the jaws closed.

Burke tumbled to the ground, clutching at his attacker. A trickle of blood spurted. Man and beast rolled over twice, tripped some secret waiting relay, and were engulfed in a gust of oily smoke. When the air was clear again neither of them was in view.

Boardman said a little later, "There's something to keep in mind. The animals wouldn't bother attacking a probe. We'll have to carry mass detectors and travel in teams."

That was how they worked it the next time. It was a stiff price to pay for the knowledge, but now they realized they had to deal with the wild beasts as well as with the cunning of ancient engineers. Two men named Marshall and Petrocelli, armed, went together into the maze, looking in all directions. No animal could come near them without telltaling its thermal output into the infrared pickups of the mass detectors they carried. They shot four animals, one of them immense, and had no trouble otherwise.

Deep within Zone G they came to the place where the distortion screen made a mockery of all information-gathering devices.

How did the screen work, Boardman wondered? He knew of Earth-made distorters that operated directly on the senses, taking perfectly proper sensory messages and scrambling them within the brain to destroy all one-to-one correlations. But this screen had to be different. It could not attack the nervous system of a drone probe, for the drones had no nervous systems in any meaningful sense of that term, and their eyes gave accurate reports of what they saw. Somehow what the drones had seen—and what they had reported to the computer—bore no relation to the real geometry of the maze at that point. Other drones, posted beyond the range of the screen, had given entirely different and much more reliable accounts of the terrain. So the thing must work on some direct optical principle, operating on the environment itself, rearranging it, blurring perspective, subtly shifting and concealing the outlines of things, transforming normal configurations into bafflement. Any sight organ within reach of the screen's effect would obtain a wholly convincing and perfectly incorrect image of the area, whether or not it had a mind to be tinkered with. That was quite interesting, Boardman thought. Perhaps later the mechanisms of this place could be studied and mastered. Later.

It was impossible for him to know what shape the maze had taken for Marshall and Petrocelli as they succumbed to the screen. Unlike the drone probes, which relayed exact accounts of everything that passed through their eyes, the two men were not directly hooked to the computer and could not transmit their visual images to the screen. The best they could do was describe what they saw. It did not match the images sent back by the probe eyes mounted on their backpacks, nor did it match the genuine configurations apparent from outside the screen's range.

They did as the computer said. They walked forward even where their own eyes told them that vast abysses lay in their path. They crouched to wriggle through a tunnel whose roof was bright with the suspended blades of guillotines. The tunnel did not exist. "Any minute I expect one of those blades to fall and chop me in half," Petrocelli said. There were no blades. At the end of the tunnel they obediently moved to the left, toward a massive flail that lashed the ground in vicious swipes. There was no flail. Reluctantly they did not set foot on a plumply upholstered walkway that appeared to lead out of the region of the screen. The walkway was imaginary; they had no way of seeing the pit of acid that actually was there.

"It would be better if they simply closed their eyes," Boardman said. "The way the drones went through—minus all visuals."

"They claim it's too scary to do it like that," said Hosteen.

"Which is better—to have no visual information, or to have the wrong information?" Boardman asked. "They could follow the computer's orders just as well with their eyes closed. And there'd be no chance that—"

Petrocelli screamed. On the split screen Boardman saw the real configuration—a flat, innocuous strip of road—and the screen-distorted one relayed by the backpack eyes—a sudden geyser of flame erupting at their feet.

"Stand where you are!" Hosteen bellowed. "It isn't real!"

Petrocelli, one foot high in the air, brought it back into place with a wrenching effort. Marshall's reaction time was slower. He had been whirling to escape the eruption when Hosteen had called to him, and he turned to the left before he halted. He was a dozen centimeters too far out of the safe road. A coil of bright metal flicked out of a block of stone and wrapped itself about his ankles. It cut through the bone without difficulty. Marshall toppled and a flashing golden bar stapled him to a wall.

Without looking back, Petrocelli passed through the column of flame unharmed, stumbled forward ten paces, and came to a halt, safe beyond the effective range of the distortion screen. "Dave?" he said hoarsely. "Dave, are you all right?"

"He stepped off the path," said Boardman. "It was a quick finish."

"What do you want me to do?"

"Stay put, Petrocelli. Get calm and don't try to go anywhere. I'm sending Chesterfield and Walker in after you. Wait right where you are."

Petrocelli was trembling. Boardman asked the ship's brain to give him a needle, and the backpack swiftly eased him with a soothing injection. Still rigid, unwilling to turn toward his impaled companion, Petrocelli stood quite still, awaiting the others.

It took Chesterfield and Walker close to an hour to reach the place of the distortion screen, and nearly fifteen minutes to shuffle through the few square meters the screen controlled. They did it with their eyes closed, and they didn't like that at all: but the phantoms of the maze could not frighten blind men, and in time Chesterfield and Walker were beyond their grasp. Petrocelli was much calmer by then. Warily, the three continued toward the heart of the maze.

Something would have to be done, Boardman thought, about recovering Marshall's body. Some other time, though.

3

The longest days of Ned Rawlins' life had been those spent on the journey to Rigel, four years before, to fetch his father's body. These days now were longer. To stand before a screen, to watch brave men die, to feel every nerve screaming for relief hour after hour after hour—

But they were winning the battle of the maze. Fourteen men had entered it so far. Four were dead. Walker and Petrocelli had made camp in Zone E; five more men had set up a relief base in F; three others were currently edging past the distortion screen in G and soon would join them. The worst was over for these. It was clear from the probe work that the curve of danger dropped off sharply past Zone F, and that there were practically no hazards at all in the three inner zones. With E and F virtually conquered, it should not be difficult to break through to those central zones where Muller, impassive and uncommunicating, lurked and waited.

Rawlins thought that he knew the maze completely by now. Vicariously he had entered it more than a hundred times; first through the eyes of the probes, then through the relays from the crewmen. At night in feverish dreams he saw its dark patterns, its curving walls and sinuous towers. Locked in his own skull he somehow made the circuit of that labyrinth, kissing death a thousand times. He and Boardman would be the beneficiaries of hard-won experience when their turns came to go inside.

Their turns were coming near.

On a chill morning under an iron sky he stood with Boardman just outside the maze, by the upsloping embankment of soil that rimmed the outer flange of the city. In the short weeks they had been here, the year had dimmed almost startlingly toward whatever winter this planet had. Sunlight lasted only six hours a day now, out of the twenty; two hours of pale twilight followed, and dawns were thin and prolonged. The whirling moons danced constantly in the sky, playing twisting games with shadows.

Rawlins, by this time, was almost eager to test the dangers of the maze. There was a hollowness in his gut, a yearning born of impatience and embarrassment. He had waited, peering into screens, while other men, some hardly older than himself, gambled their lives to get inside. It seemed to him that he had spent all his life waiting for the cue to take the center of the stage.

On the screen, they watched Muller moving at the heart of the maze. The hovering probes kept constant check on him, marking his peregrinations with a shifting line on the master chart. Muller had not left Zone A since the time he encountered the drone; but he changed positions daily in the labyrinth, migrating from house to house as though he feared to sleep in the same one twice. Boardman had taken care not to let him have any contact with them since the encounter with the drone. It often seemed to Rawlins that Boardman was stalking some rare and fragile beast.

Tapping the screen, Boardman said, "This afternoon we go inside, Ned. We'll spend the night in the main camp. Tomorrow you move forward to join Walker and Petrocelli in E. The day after that you go on alone toward the middle and find Muller."

"Why are you going inside the maze, Charles?"

"To help you."

"You could keep in touch with me from out here," said Rawlins. "You don't need to risk yourself."

Boardman tugged thoughtfully at his dewlap. "What I'm doing is calculated for minimum risk this way."

"How?"

"If you get into problems," Boardman said, "I'll need to go to you and give you assistance. I'd rather wait in Zone

F, if I'm needed, than have to come rushing in suddenly from the outside through the most dangerous part of the maze. You see what I'm telling you? I can get to you quickly from F without much danger. But not from here."

"What kind of problems?"

"Stubbornness from Muller. He's got no reason to cooperate with us, and he's not an easy man to deal with. I remember him in those months after he came back from Beta Hydri IV. We had no peace with him. He was never actually level-tempered before, but afterward he was a volcano. Mind you, Ned, I don't judge him for it. He's got a right to be furious with the universe. But he's troublesome. He's a bird of ill omen. Just to go near him brings bad luck. You'll have your hands full."

"Why don't you come with me, then?"

"Impossible," Boardman said. "It would ruin everything if he even knew I was on this planet. I'm the man who sent him to the Hydrans, don't forget. I'm the one who in effect marooned him on Lemnos. I think he might kill me if he saw me again."

Rawlins recoiled from that idea. "No. He hasn't become that barbaric."

"You don't know him. What he was. What he's become."

"If he's as full of demons as you say, how am I ever going to win his trust?"

"Go to him. Look guileless and trustworthy. You don't have to practice that, Ned. You've got a naturally innocent face. Tell him you're here on an archaeological mission. Don't let him know that we realized he was here all along. Say that the first you knew was when our probe stumbled into him—that you recognized him, from the days when he and your father were friends."

"I'm to mention my father, then?"

"By all means. Tell him who you are. It's the only way. Tell him that your father's dead, and that this is your first expedition to space. Work on his sympathies, Ned. Dig for the paternal in him."

Rawlins shook his head. "Don't get angry with me, Charles, but I've got to tell you that I don't like any of this. These lies."

"Lies?" Boardman's eyes blazed. "Lies to say that

you're your father's son? That this is your first expedition?"

"That I'm an archaeologist?"

Boardman shrugged. "Would you rather tell him that you came here as part of a search mission looking for Richard Muller? Will that help win his trust? Think about our purpose, Ned."

"Yes. Ends and means. I know."

"Do you, really?"

"We're here to win Muller's cooperation because we think that he alone can save us from a terrible menace," Rawlins said stolidly, unfeelingly, flatly. "Therefore we must take any approach necessary to gain that cooperation."

"Yes. And I wish you wouldn't smirk when you say it."

"I'm sorry, Charles. But I feel so damned queasy about deceiving him."

"We need him."

"Yes. But a man who's suffered so much already—"

"We need him."

"All right, Charles."

"I need you, too," Boardman said. "If I could do this myself, I would. But if he saw me, he'd finish me. In his eyes I'm a monster. It's the same with anyone else connected with his past career. But you're different. He might be able to trust you. You're young, you look so damned virtuous, and you're the son of a good friend of his. You can get through to him."

"And fill him up with lies so we can trick him."

Boardman closed his eyes. He seemed to be containing himself with an effort.

"Stop it, Ned."

"Go on. Tell me what I do after I've introduced myself."

"Build a friendship with him. Take your time about it. Make him come to depend on your visits."

"What if I can't stand being with him?"

"Conceal it. That's the hardest part, I know."

"The hardest part is the lying, Charles."

"Whatever you say. Anyhow, show that you can tolerate his company. Make the effort. Chat with him. Make it clear to him that you're stealing time from your scientific work—that the villainous bastards who are running your expedition don't want you to have anything to do with him, but that you're drawn to him by love and pity and won't let him interfere. Tell him all about yourself, your ambitions, your love life, your hobbies, whatever you want. Run off at the mouth. It'll reinforce the image of the naive kid."

"Do I mention the galactics?" Rawlins asked.

"Not obtrusively. Work them in somewhere by way of bringing him up to date on current events. But don't tell him too much. Certainly don't tell him of the threat they pose. Or a word about the need we have for him, you understand. If he gets the idea that he's being used, we're finished."

"How will I get him to leave the maze, if I don't tell him why we want him?"

"Let that part pass for now," Boardman said. "I'll coach you in the next phase after you've succeeded in getting him to trust you."

"The translation," Rawlins said, "is that you're going to put such a whopper in my mouth that you don't even dare tell me now what it is for fear I'll throw up my hands and quit."

"Ned—"

"I'm sorry. But—look, Charles, why do we have to *trick* him out? Why can't we just say that humanity needs him, and force him to come out?"

"Do you think that's morally superior to tricking him out?"

"It's cleaner, somehow. I hate all this dirty plotting and scheming. I'd much rather help knock him cold and haul him from the maze than have to go through what you've planned. I'd be willing to help take him by force—because we really do need him. We've got enough men to do it."

"We don't," Boardman said. "We can't force him out. That's the whole point. It's too risky. He might find some way to kill himself the moment we tried to grab him."

"A stungun," said Rawlins. "I could do it, even. Just get within range and gun him down, and then we carry him out of the maze, and when he wakes up we explain—"

Boardman vehemently shook his head. "He's had nine

years to figure out that maze. We don't know what tricks he's learned or what defensive traps he's planted. While he's in there I don't dare take any kind of offensive action against him. He's too valuable to risk. For all we know he's programmed the whole place to blow up if someone pulls a gun on him. He's got to come out of that labyrinth of his own free will, Ned, and that means we have to trick him with false promises. I know it stinks. The whole universe stinks, sometimes. Haven't you discovered that yet?"

"It doesn't *have* to stink!" Rawlins said sharply, his voice rising. "Is that the lesson you've learned in all those years? The universe doesn't stink. Man stinks! And he does it by voluntary choice because he'd rather stink than smell sweet! We don't *have* to lie. We don't *have* to cheat. We could opt for honor and decency and—" Rawlins stopped abruptly. In a different tone he said, "I sound young as hell to you, don't I, Charles?"

"You're entitled to make mistakes," Boardman said. "That's what being young is for."

"You genuinely believe and know that there's a cosmic malevolence in the workings of the universe?"

Boardman touched the tips of his thick, short fingers together. "I wouldn't put it that way. There's no personal power of darkness running things, any more than there's a personal power of good. The universe is a big impersonal machine. As it functons it tends to put stress on some of its minor parts, and those parts wear out, and the universe doesn't give a damn about that, because it can generate replacements. There's nothing immoral about wearing out parts, but you have to admit that from the point of view of the part under stress it's a stinking deal. It happened that two small parts of the universe clashed when we dropped Dick Muller onto the planet of the Hydrans. We had to put him there because it's our nature to find out things, and they did what they did to him because the universe puts stress on its parts, and the result was that Dick Muller came away from Beta Hydri IV in bad shape. He was drawn into the machinery of the universe and got ground up. Now we're having a second clash of parts, equally inevitable, and we have to feed Muller through the machine a second time. He's likely to be chewed again—which stinks—and in order to push him into a position where that can happen, you and I have to stain our souls a little—which also stinks—and yet we have absolutely no choice in the matter. If we don't compromise ourselves and trick Dick Muller, we may be setting in motion a new spin of the machine that will destroy all of humanity—and that would stink even worse. I'm asking you to do an unpleasant thing for a decent motive. You don't want to do it, and I understand how you feel, but I'm trying to get you to see that your personal moral code isn't always the highest factor. In wartime, a soldier shoots to kill because the universe imposes that situation on him. It may be an unjust war, and that might be his brother in the ship he's aiming at, but the war is real and he has his role."

"Where's the room for free will in this mechanical universe of yours, Charles?"

"There isn't any. That's why I say the universe stinks."

"We have no freedom at all?"

"The freedom to wriggle a little on the hook."

"Have you felt this way all your life?"

"Most of it," Boardman said.

"When you were my age?"

"Even earlier."

Rawlins looked away. "I think you're all wrong, but I'm not going to waste breath trying to tell you so. I don't have the words. I don't have the arguments. And you wouldn't listen anyway."

"I'm afraid I wouldn't, Ned. But we can discuss this some other time. Say, twenty years from now. Is it a date?"

Trying to grin, Rawlins said, "Sure. If I haven't killed myself from guilt over this."

"You won't."

"How am I suppose to live with myself after I've pulled Dick Muller out of his shell?"

"Wait and see. You'll discover that you did the right thing, in context. Or the least wrong thing, anyhow. Believe me, Ned. Just now you may feel that your soul will forever be corroded by this job, but it won't happen that way."

"We'll see," said Rawlins quietly. Boardman seemed

more slippery than ever when he was in this avuncular mood. To die in the maze, Rawlins thought, was the only way to avoid getting trapped in these moral ambiguities; and the moment he hatched the thought, he abolished it in horror. He stared at the screen. "Let's go inside," he said. "I'm tired of waiting."

five

Muller saw them coming closer, and did not understand why he was so calm about it. He had destroyed that robot, yes, and after that they had stopped sending in robots. But his viewing tanks showed him the men camping in the outer levels. He could not see their faces clearly. He could not see what they were doing out there. He counted about a dozen of them, give or take two or three; some were settled in Zone E, and a somewhat larger group in F. Muller had seen a few of them die in the outer zones.

He had ways of attacking. He could, if he cared to, flood Zone E with backup from the aqueduct. He had done that once, by accident, and it had taken the city almost a full day to clean things up. He recalled how, during the flood, Zone E had been sealed off, bulkheaded to keep the water from spilling out. If the intruders did not drown in the first rush, they would certainly blunder in alarm into some of the traps. Muller could do other things, too, to keep them from getting to the inner city.

Yet he did nothing. He knew that at the heart of his inaction was a hunger to break his years of isolation. Much as he hated them, much as he feared them, much as he dreaded the puncturing of his privacy, Muller allowed the men to work their way toward him. A meeting now was inevitable. They knew he was here. (Did they know who he was?) They would find him, to their sorrow and to his. He would learn whether in his long exile he had been purged of his affliction so that he was fit for human company again. But Muller already was sure of the answer to that.

He had spent part of a year among the Hydrans; and then, seeing that he was accomplishing nothing, he entered his powered drop-capsule, rode it into the heavens, and, repossessed his orbiting ship. If the Hydrans had a mythology, he would become part of it.

Within his ship Muller went through the operations that would return him to Earth. As he notified the ship's brain of his presence, he caught sight of himself in the burnished metal plate of the input bank and it frightened him, a little. The Hydrans did not use mirrors. Muller saw deep new lines etched on his face, which did not bother him, and he saw a strangeness in his eyes, which did. The muscles are tense, he told himself. He finished programming his return and then went to the medic chamber and ordered a forty-db drop in his neural level along with a hot bath and a thorough massage. When he came out, his eyes still looked strange; and he had sprouted a facial tic, besides. He got rid of the tic easily enough, but he could do nothing about his eyes.

The eyes have no expression, Muller told himself. It's the lids that do the work. My eyelids are strained from living in the breathing suit so long. I'll be all right. It was a rough few months, but now I'll be all right.

The ship gulped power from the nearest designated donor star. The ship's rotors whirled along the axes of warp, and Muller, along with his plastic and metal container, was hurled out of the universe on one of the shortcut routes. Even in warp, a certain amount of absolute time loss is experienced as the ship zips through the stitch in the continuum. Muller read, slept, listened to music, and played a woman cube when the need got great. He told himself that the stiffness was going out of his facial expression, but he might need a mild shape-up when he got to Earth. This jaunt had put a few years on him.

He had no work to do. The ship duly popped from warp within the prescribed limits, 100,000 kilometers out from Earth, and colored lights flashed on his communications board as the nearest traffic station signalled for his bearings. Muller instructed the ship to deal with the traffic station.

"Match velocities with us, Mr. Muller, and we'll send a pilot aboard to get you to Earth," the traffic controller said.

Muller's ship took care of it. The coppery globe of the

traffic station appeared in sight. It floated just ahead of Muller for a while, but gradually his ship drew abreast of it.

"We have a relay message for you from Earth," the controller said. "Charles Boardman calling."

"Go ahead," said Muller.

Boardman's face filled the screen. He looked pink and newly-buffed, quite healthy, well rested. He smiled and put his hand forward. "Dick," he said. "God, it's great to see you!"

Muller activated tactile and put his hand on Boardman's wrist through the screen. "Hello, Charles. One in sixty-five, eh? Well, I'm back."

"Should I tell Marta?"

"Marta," Muller said, thinking for a moment. Yes. The blue-haired wench with the swivel hips and the sharp heels. "Yes. Tell Marta. It would be nice if she met me when I landed. Woman cubes aren't all that thrilling."

Boardman gave him a you-said-a-mouthful-boy kind of laugh. Then he changed gears abruptly and said, "How did it go?"

"Poorly."

"You made contact, though?"

"I found the Hydrans, yes. They didn't kill me."

"Were they hostile?"

"They didn't kill me."

"Yes, but—"

"I'm alive, Charles." Muller felt the tic beginning again. "I didn't learn their language. I can't tell you if they approved of me. They seemed quite interested. They studied me closely for a long time. They didn't say a word."

"What are they, telepaths?"

"I can't tell you that, Charles."

Boardman was silent for a while. "What did they do to you, Dick?"

"Nothing."

"That isn't so."

"What you're seeing is travel fatigue," Muller said. "I'm in good shape, just a little stretched in the nerve. I want to breathe real air and drink some real beer and taste real meat, and I'd like to have some company in bed, and I'll be as good as ever. And then maybe I'll suggest some ways of making contact with the Hydrans."

"How's the gain on your broadcast system, Dick?"

"Huh?"

"You're coming across too loud," said Boardman.

"Blame it on the relay station. Jesus, Charles. What does the gain on my system have to do with anything?"

"I'm not sure," Boardman said. "I'm just trying to find out why you're shouting at me."

"I'm not shouting." Muller shouted.

Soon after that they broke contact. Muller had word from the traffic station that they were ready to send a pilot aboard. He got the hatch ready, and let the man in. The pilot was a very blond young man with hawklike features and pale skin. As soon as he unhelmeted he said, "My name is Les Christiansen, Mr. Muller, and I want to tell you that it's an honor and a privilege for me to be the pilot for the first man to visit an alien race. I hope I'm not breaking security when I say that I'd love to know a little about it while we're descending. I mean, this is sort of a moment in history, me being the first to see you in person since you're back, and if it's not an intrusion I'd be grateful if you'd tell me just some of the—highlights—of your—of—"

"I guess I can tell you a little," Muller said affably. "First, did you see the cube of the Hydrans? I know it was supposed to be shown, and—"

"You mind if I sit down a second, Mr. Muller?"

"Go ahead. You saw them, then, the tall skinny things with all the arms—"

"I feel very woozy," said Christiansen. "I don't know what's happening." His face was crimson, suddenly, and beads of sweat glistened on his forehead. "I think I must be getting sick. I—you know, this shouldn't be happening —" The pilot crumpled into a webfoam cradle and huddled there, shivering, covering his head with his hands. Muller, his voice still rusty from the long silences of his mission, hesitated helplessly. Finally he reached down to take the man's elbow and guide him toward the medic chamber. Christiansen whirled away as if touched by fiery metal. The motion pulled him off balance and sent him into a heap on the cabin floor. He rose to his knees and wriggled until he was as far away from Muller as it was possible to get. In a strangled voice he said, "Where is it?"

"That door here."

Christiansen rushed for it, sealed himself in, and rattled the door to make sure of it. Muller, astonished, heard retching sounds, and then something that could have been a series of dry sobs. He was about to signal the traffic station that the pilot was sick, when the door opened a little and Christiansen said in a muffled voice, "Would you hand me my helmet, Mr. Muller?"

Muller gave it to him.

"I'm going to have to go back to my station, Mr. Muller."

"I'm sorry you reacted this way. Christ, I hope I'm not carrying some kind of contagion."

"I'm not sick. I just feel—lousy." Christiansen fastened the helmet in place. "I don't understand. But I want to curl up and cry. Please let me go, Mr. Muller. It—I—that is—it's terrible. That's what I feel!" He rushed into the hatch. In bewilderment Muller watched him cross the void to the nearby traffic station.

He got on the radio. "You better not send another pilot over just yet," Muller told the controller. "Christiansen folded up with instant plague as soon as he took his helmet off. I may be carrying something. Let's check it out."

The controller, looking troubled, agreed. He asked Muller to go to his medic chamber, set up the diagnostat, and transmit its report. A little while later the solemn chocolate-hued face of the station's medical officer appeared on Muller's screen and said, "This is very odd, Mr. Muller."

"What is?"

"I've run your diagnostat transmission through our machine. No unusual symptoms. I've also put Christiansen through the works without learning anything. He feels fine now, he says. He told me that an acute depression hit him the moment he saw you, and it deepened in a hurry to a sort of metabolic paralysis. That is, he felt so gloomy that he could hardly function."

"Is he prone to these attacks?"

"Never," the medic replied. "I'd like to check this out myself. May I come over?"

The medic didn't curl up with the miseries as Christiansen had done. But he didn't stay long, either, and when he left his face was glossy with tears. He looked as baffled as Muller. When the new pilot appeared twenty minutes later, he kept his suit on as he programmed the ship for planetary descent. Sitting rigidly upright at his controls, his back turned to Muller, he said nothing, scarcely acknowledged Muller's presence. As required by law, he brought the ship down until its drive system was in the grip of a groundside landing regulator, and took his leave. Muller saw the man's face, tense, sweat-shiny, tight-lipped. The pilot nodded curtly, and went through the hatch. I must have a very bad smell, Muller thought, if he could smell it through his suit like that.

The landing was routine.

At the starport he cleared Immigration quickly. It took only half an hour for Earth to decide that he was acceptable; and Muller, who had passed through these computer banks hundreds of times before, figured that that was close to the record. He had feared that the giant starport diagnostat would detect whatever malady he carried that his own equipment and the traffic station medic had failed to find; but he passed through the bowels of the machine, letting it bounce sonics off his kidneys, and extract some molecules of his various bodily fluids, and at length he emerged without the ringing of bells and the flashing of warning lights. *Approved.* He spoke to the Customs machine. Where from, traveler? Where bound? *Approved.* His papers were in order. A slit in the wall widened into a doorway and he stepped through, to confront another human being for the first time since his landing.

Boardman had come to meet him. Marta was with him. A thick brown robe shot through with dull metal enfolded Boardman; he seemed weighted down with rings, and his brooding eyebrows were thick as dark tropical moss. Marta's hair was short and sea-green; she had silvered her eyes and gilded the slender column of her throat, so that she looked like some jeweled statuette of herself. Remembering her wet and naked from the crystalline lake, Muller disapproved of these changes. He doubted that they had been made for his benefit. Boardman, he knew, liked his women ornate; it was probable that they had been bedding in his absence. Muller would have been surprised and even a little shaken if they had not.

Boardman's hand encircled Muller's wrist in a firm greeting that incredibly turned flabby within seconds. The hand slipped away even before Muller could return the embrace. "It's good to see you, Dick," Boardman said without conviction, stepping back a couple of paces. His cheeks seemed to sag as though under heavy gravitational stress. Marta slipped between them and pressed herself against him. Muller seized her, touching her shoulder-blades and running his hands swiftly down to her lean buttocks. He did not kiss her. Her eyes were dazzling as he looked within them and felt himself lost in rebounding mirror images. Her nostrils flared. Through her thin flesh he felt muscles bridling. She was trying to get free of him. "Dick," she whispered. "I've prayed for you every night. You don't know how I've missed you." She struggled harder. He moved his hands to her haunches and pushed inward so fiercely that he could imagine her pelvic cage yielding and flexing. His legs were trembling, and he feared that if he let go of her, she would fall. She turned her head to one side. He put his cheek against her delicate ear. "Dick," she murmured, "I feel so strange—so glad to see you that I'm all tangled up inside—let go, Dick, I feel queasy somehow—"

Yes. Yes. Of course. He released her.

Boardman, sweating, nervous, mopped at his face, jabbed himself with some soothing drug, fidgeted, paced. Muller had never seen him look this way before. "Suppose I let the two of you have some time together, eh?" Boardman suggested, his voice coming out half an octave too high. "The weather's been getting to me, Dick. I'll talk with you tomorrow. Your accommodations are all arranged." Boardman fled. Now Muller felt panic rising.

"Where do we go?" he asked.

"There's a transport pod outside. We have a room at the Starport Inn. Do you have luggage?"

"It's still aboard the ship," Muller answered. "It can wait."

Marta was chewing at the corner of her lower lip. He took her by the hand and they rode the slidewalk out of the terminal room to the transportation pods. Go on, he thought. Tell me that you don't feel well. Tell me that mysteriously you've come down with something in the last ten minutes.

"Why did you cut your hair?" he asked.

"It's a woman's right. Don't you like it this way?"

"Not as much." They entered the pod. "Longer, bluer, it was like the sea on a stormy day." The pod shot off on a bath of quicksilver. She kept far to her side, hunched against the hatch. "And the makeup, too. I'm sorry, Marta. I wish I could like it."

"I was prettying for your homecoming."

"Why are you doing that with your lip?"

"What am I doing?"

"Nothing," he said. "Here we are. The room is booked already?"

"In your name, yes."

They went in. He put his hand on the registration plate. It flashed green and they headed for the liftshaft. The inn began in the fifth sublevel of the starport and went down for fifty levels; their room was near the bottom. Choice location, he thought. The bridal suite, maybe. They stepped into a room with kaleidoscopic hangings and a wide bed with all accessories. The roomglow was tactfully dim. Muller thought of months of woman cubes and a savage throbbing rose in his groin. He knew he had no need to explain any of that to Marta. She moved past him, into the personal room, and was in there a long while. Muller undressed.

She came out nude. All the tricky makeup was gone, and her hair was blue again.

"Like the sea," she said. "I'm sorry I couldn't grow it back in there. The room wasn't programmed for it."

"It's much better now," he told her.

They were ten meters apart. She stood at an angle to him, and he studied the contours of her frail but tough form, the small upjutting breasts, the boyish buttocks, the elegant thighs.

"The Hydrans," he said, "have either five sexes or none, I'm not sure which. That's a measure of how well I got to know them while I was there. However they do it, I think people have more fun. Why are you standing over there, Marta?"

Silently she came toward him. He put one arm around her shoulders and cupped his other hand over one of her breasts. At other times when he did that he felt the nipple pebble-hard with desire against his hand. Not now. She quivered a little, like a shy mare wanting to bolt. He put his lips to her lips, and they were dry, taut, hostile. When he ran his hand along the fine line of her jaw she seemed to shudder. He drew her down and they sat side by side on the bed. Her hand reached for him, almost unwillingly. He saw the pain in her eyes.

She rolled away from him, her head snapping back hard onto the pillow, and he watched her face writhe with some barely suppressed agony. Then she took his hands in hers and tugged him toward her. Her knees came up and her thighs opened.

"Take me, Dick," she said stagily. "Right now!"

"What's the hurry?"

She tried to force him onto her, into her. He wasn't having it that way. He pulled free of her and sat up. She was crimson to the shoulders, and tears glistened on her face. He knew as much of the truth now as he needed to know, but he had to ask.

"Tell me what's wrong, Marta."

"I don't know."

"You're acting like you're sick."

"I think I am."

"When did you start feeling ill?"

"I—oh, Dick, why all these questions? Please, love, come close."

"You don't want me to. Not really. You're being kind."

"I'm—trying to make you happy, Dick. It—it hurts so much—so—much."

"What does?"

She wouldn't answer. She gestured wantonly and tugged at him again. He sprang from the bed.

"Dick, Dick, I warned you not to go! I said I had some precog. And that other things could happen to you there besides getting killed."

"Tell me what hurts you."

"I can't. I—don't know."

"That's a lie."

"When did it start?"

"This morning. When I got up."

"That's another lie. I have to have the truth!"

"Make love to me, Dick. I can't wait much longer. I—"

"You what?"

"Can't—stand—"

"Can't stand what?"

"Nothing. Nothing." She was off the bed too, rubbing against him, a cat in heat, shivering, muscles leaping in her face, eyes wild.

He caught her wrists and ground the bones together.

"Tell me what it is you can't stand much longer, Marta."

She gasped. He squeezed harder. She swung back, head lolling, breasts thrust toward the ceiling. Her body was oiled now with sweat. Her nakedness maddened and inflamed him.

"Tell me," he said. "You can't stand—"

"—being near you," she said.

six

Within the maze the air was somehow warmer and sweeter. The walls must cut off the winds, Rawlins thought. He walked carefully, listening to the voice at his ear.

Turn left . . . three paces . . . put your right foot beside the black stripe on the pavement . . . pivot . . . turn left . . . four paces . . . ninety-degree turn to the right . . . immediately make a ninety-degree turn to the right again.

It was like a children's street game—step on a crack, break your mother's back. The stakes were higher here, though. He moved cautiously, feeling death nipping at his heels. What sort of people would build a place like this? Ahead an energy flare spurted across the path. The computer called off the timing for him. *One, two, three, four, five, GO!* Rawlins went.

Safe.

On the far side he halted flatfooted, and looked back. Boardman was keeping pace with him, unslowed by age. Boardman waved and winked. He went through the patterns, too. *One, two, three, four, five, GO!* Boardman crossed the place of the energy flare.

"Should we stop here for a while?" Rawlins asked.

"Don't be patronizing to the old man, Ned. Keep moving. I'm not tired yet."

"We have a tough one up ahead."

"Let's take it, then."

Rawlins could not help looking at the bones. Dry skeletons ages old, and some bodies that were not old at all. Beings of many races had perished here.

What if I die in the next ten minutes?

Bright lights were flashing now, on and off many times a second. Boardman, five meters behind him, became an eerie figure moving in disconnected strides. Rawlins passed his own hand before his face to see the jerky movements.

It was as though every other fraction of a second had simply been punched out of his awareness.

The computer told him: *Walk ten paces and halt. One. Two. Three. Walk ten paces and halt. One. Two. Three. Walk ten paces and halt. One. Two. Three. Proceed quickly to end of ramp.*

Rawlins could not remember what would happen to him if he failed to keep to the proper timing. Here in Zone H the nightmares were so thick that he could not keep them straight in his mind. Was this the place where a ton of stone fell on the unwary? Where the walls came together? Where a cobweb-dainty bridge delivered victims to a lake of fire?

His estimated lifespan at this point was two hundred five years. He wanted to have most of those years. I am too uncomplicated to die yet, Ned Rawlins thought.

He danced to the computer's tune, past the lake of fire, past the clashing walls.

2

Something with long teeth perched on the lintel of the door ahead. Carefully Charles Boardman unslung the gun from his backpack and cut in the proximity-responsive target finder. He keyed it for thirty kilograms of mass and downward, at fifty meters. "I've got it," he told Rawlins, and fired.

The energy bolt splashed against the wall. Streaks of shimmering green sprouted along the rich purple. The beast leaped, limbs outstretched in a final agony, and fell. From somewhere came three small scavengers that began to rip it to pieces.

Boardman chuckled. It didn't take much skill to hunt with proximity-responsives, he had to admit. But it was a long time since he had hunted at all. When he was thirty, he had spent a long week in the Sahara Preserve as the youngest of a party of eight businessmen and government consultants on a hunt. He had done it for the political usefulness of making the trip. He had hated it all: the steaming air in his nostrils, the blaze of the sun, the tawny beasts dead against the sand, the boasting, the wanton slaughter. At thirty one is not very tolerant of the mindless sports of the middle-aged. Yet he had stayed, because he thought it would be useful to him to become friendly with these men. It *had* been useful. He had never gone hunting again. But this was different, even with proximity-responsives. This was no sport.

3

Images played on a golden screen bracketed to a wall near the inner end of Zone H. Rawlins saw his father's face take form, coalesce with an underlying pattern of bars and crosses, burst into flame. The screen was externally primed; what it showed was in the eye of the beholder. The drones, passing this point, had seen only the blank screen. Rawlins watched the image of a girl appear. Maribeth Chambers, sixteen years old, sophomore in Our Lady of Mercies High School, Rockford, Illinois. Maribeth Chambers smiled shyly and began to remove her clothes. Her hair was silken and soft, a cloud of gold; her eyes were blue, her lips were full and moist. She unhinged her breast-binders and revealed two firm upthrust white globes tipped with dots of flame. They were high and close together, as though no gravity worked on them, and the valley between them was six inches deep and a sixteenth of an inch in breadth. Maribeth Chambers blushed and bared the lower half of her body. She wore small garnets set in the dimples just above her plump pink buttocks. A crucifix of ivory dangled from a golden chain around her hips. Rawlins tried not to look at the screen. The computer directed his feet; he shuffled along obediently.

"I am the Resurrection and the Life," said Maribeth Chambers in a husky, passionate voice.

She beckoned with the tips of three fingers. She gave him a bedroom wink. She crooned sweet obscenities.

Step around in back here, big boy! Let me show you a good time. . . .

She giggled. She wriggled. She heaved her shoulders and made her breasts ring like tolling bells.

Her skin turned deep green. Her eyes slid about in her face. Her lower lip stretched forth like a shovel. Her thighs began to melt. Patterns of flame danced on the screen. Rawlins heard deep throbbing ponderous chords from an invisible organ. He listened to the whispering of the brain that guided him and went past the screen unharmed.

4

The screen showed abstract patterns: a geometry of power, rigid marching lines and frozen figures. Charles Boardman paused to admire it for a moment. Then he moved on.

5

A forest of whirling knives near the inner border of Zone H.

6

The heat grew strangely intense. One had to tiptoe over the pavement. This was troublesome because none who had passed this way before had experienced it. Did the route vary? Could the city introduce variations? How hot would it get? Where would the zone of warmth end? Did cold lie beyond? Would they live to reach Zone E? Was Richard Muller doing this to prevent them from entering?

7

Maybe he recognizes Boardman and is trying to kill him. There is that possibility. Muller has every reason to hate Boardman, and he has had no chance to undergo social adjustment. Maybe I should move faster and open some space between Boardman and myself. It seems to be getting hotter. On the other hand, he would accuse me of being cowardly. And disloyal.

Maribeth Chambers would never have done those things.

Do nuns still shave their heads?

8

Boardman found the distortion screen deep inside Zone G perhaps the worst of all. He was not afraid of the dangers; Marshall was the only man who had failed to get past the screen safely. He was afraid of entering a place where the evidence of his senses did not correspond to the real universe. Boardman depended on his senses. He was wearing his third set of retinas. You can make no meaningful evaluations of the universe without the confidence that you are seeing it clearly.

Now he was within the field of the distortion screen.

Parallel lines met here. The triangular figures emblazoned on the moist, quivering walls were constructed entirely of obtuse angles. A river ran sideways through the valley. The stars were quite close, and the moons orbited one another.

What we now must do is close our eyes and not be deceived.

Left foot. Right foot. Left foot. Right foot. Move to the left slightly—slide your foot. More. More. A trifle more. Back toward the right. That's it. Start walking again.

Forbidden fruit tempted him. All his life he had tried hard to see clearly. The lure of distortions was irresistible. Boardman halted, planting each foot firmly. If you hope to get out of this, he told himself, you will keep your eyes closed. If you open your eyes you will be misled and go to your death. You have no right to die foolishly here after so many men have struggled so hard to teach you how to survive.

Boardman remained quite still. The silent voice of the computer, sounding a little waspish, tried to prod him on.

"Wait," said Boardman quietly. "I can look around a little if I don't move. That's the important thing, *not to move*. You can't get into trouble if you don't move."

The ship's brain reminded him of the geyser of flame that had sent Marshall to his death.

Boardman opened his eyes.

He was careful not to move. All about him he saw the negation of geometry. This was the inside of the Klein bottle, looking out. Disgust rose like a green column within him.

You are eighty years old and you know how the universe should look. Close your eyes now, C.B. Close your eyes and move along. You're taking undue risks.

First he sought Ned Rawlins. The boy was twenty meters ahead of him, shuffling slowly past the screen. Eyes closed? Of course. All of them. Ned was an obedient boy. Or a frightened one. He wants to live through this, and he'd rather not see how the universe looks through a distortion screen. I'd like to have had a son like that. But I'd have changed him by this time.

Boardman began to lift his right leg, checked himself, reimplanted it on the pavement. Just ahead, pulsations of golden light leaped in the air, taking now the form of a swan, now the form of a tree. Ned Rawlins' left shoulder rose too high. His back was humped. One leg moved forward and the other moved backward. Through golden mists Boardman saw the corpse of Marshall stapled to the wall. Marshall's eyes were wide open. Were there no bacteria of decay on Lemnos? Looking into those eyes Boardman saw his own curving reflection, all nose, no mouth. He closed his eyes.

The computer, relieved, directed him onward.

9

A sea of blood. A cup of lymph.

10

To die, not having loved—

11

This is the gateway to Zone F. I am now leaving death's other kingdom. Where is my passport? Do I need a visa? I have nothing to declare. Nothing. Nothing. Nothing.

3

A chill wind blowing out of tomorrow.

7

The boys camped in F were supposed to come out and meet us and lead us through. I hope they don't bother. We can make it without them. We just have to get past the screen, and we're all right.

5

I've dreamed this route so often. And now I hate it, even though it's beautiful. You have to admit that: it's beautiful. And probably it looks most beautiful just before it kills you.

3

Maribeth's thighs have small puckers in the flesh. She will be fat before she's thirty.

10

You do all sorts of things in a career. I could have stopped long ago. I have never read Rousseau. I have not had time for Donne. I know nothing of Kant. If I live I will read them now. I make this vow, being of sound mind and body and eighty years of age, I Ned Rawlins will I Richard Muller will read I will I I I will read I Charles Boardman

13

14

On the far side of the gateway Rawlins stopped short and asked the computer if it was safe for him to squat down and rest. The brain said that it was. Gingerly, Rawlins lowered himself, rocked on his heels a moment, touched his knee to the cool pebble-textured pavement. He looked back. Behind him, colossal blocks of stone, set without mortar and fitted to a perfect truing, were piled fifty meters high, flanking a tall narrow aperture through which the solid form of Charles Boardman now was passing. Boardman looked sweaty and flustered. Rawlins found that fascinating. He had never seen the old man's smugness pierced before. But they had never come through this maze before, either.

Rawlins himself was none too steady. Metabolic poisons boiled in the tubes and channels of his body. He was drenched with perspiration so thoroughly that his clothing was working overtime to get rid of it, distilling the moisture and volatilizing the substratum of chemical compounds. It was too early to rejoice. Brewster had died here in Zone F, thinking that his troubles were over once he got past the dangers of G. Well, they were.

"Resting?" Boardman asked. His voice came out thin and unfocussed.

"Why not? I've been working hard, Charles." Rawlins grinned unconvincingly. "So have you. The computer says it's safe to stay here a while. I'll make room."

Boardman came alongside and squatted. Rawlins had to steady him as he balanced before kneeling.

Rawlins said, "Muller came this way alone and made it."

"Muller was always an extraordinary man."

"How do you think he did it?"

"Why don't you ask him?"

"I mean to," Rawlins said. "Perhaps by this time tomorrow I'll be talking to him."

"Perhaps. We should go on now."

"If you say so."

"They'll be coming out to meet us soon. They should have fixes on us by now. We must be showing up on their mass detectors. Up, Ned. Up."

They stood. Once again Rawlins led the way.

In Zone F things were less cluttered but also less attractive. The prevailing mood of the architecture was taut, with a fussy line that generated a tension of mismatched objects. Though he knew that traps were fewer here, Rawlins still had the sensation that the ground was likely to open beneath him at any given moment. The air was cooler here. It had the same sharp taste as the air on the open plain. At each of the street intersections rose immense concrete tubs in which jagged, feathery plants were standing.

"Which is the worst part for you so far?" Rawlins asked.

"The distortion screen," said Boardman.

"That wasn't so bad—unless you feel peculiar about walking through stuff this dangerous with your eyes closed. You know, one of those little tigers could have jumped us then, and we wouldn't have known about it until we felt the teeth in us."

"I peeked," said Boardman.

"In the distortion zone?"

"Just for a moment. I couldn't resist it, Ned. I won't try to describe what I saw, but it was one of the strangest experiences of my life."

Rawlins smiled. He wanted to congratulate Boardman on having done something silly and dangerous and human, but he didn't dare. He said, "What did you do? Just stand still and peek and then move on? Did you have any close escapes?"

"Once. I forgot myself and started to take a step, but I didn't follow through. I kept my feet planted and looked around."

"Maybe I'll try that on the way out," Rawlins said. "Just one little look can't hurt."

"How do you know the screen's effective in the other direction?"

Rawlins frowned. "I never considered that. We haven't tried to go *outward* through the maze yet. Suppose it's altogether different coming out? We don't have charts for that direction. What if we all get clipped coming out?"

"We'll use the probes again," said Boardman. "Don't worry about that. When we're ready to go out, we'll bring a bunch of drones to the camp in Zone F here and check the exit route the same way we checked the entry route."

After a while Rawlins said, "Why should there be any traps on the outward route, anyway? That means the builders of the maze were locking themselves in as well as locking enemies out. Why would they do that?"

"Who knows, Ned? They were aliens."

"Aliens. Yes."

15

Boardman remembered that the conversation was incomplete. He tried to be affable. They were comrades in the face of danger. He said, "And which has been the worst place for you so far?"

"That other screen farther back," Rawlins said. "The one that shows you all the nasty, crawling stuff inside your own mind."

"Which screen is that?"

"Toward the inside of Zone H. It was a golden screen, fastened to a high wall with metal strips. I looked at it and saw my father, for a couple of seconds. And then I saw a girl I once knew, a girl who became a nun. On the screen she was taking her clothes off. I guess that reveals something about my unconscious, eh? Like a pit of snakes. But whose isn't?"

"I didn't see any such things."

"You couldn't miss it. It was—oh, about fifty meters after the place where you shot the first animal. A little to your left, halfway up the wall, a rectangular screen—a trapezoidal screen, really, with bright white metal borders, and colors moving on it, shapes—"

"Yes. That one. Geometrical shapes."

"I saw Maribeth getting undressed," Rawlins said, sounding confused. "And you saw geometrical shapes?"

16

Zone F could be deadly too. A small pearly blister in the ground opened and a stream of gleaming pellets rolled out. They flowed toward Rawlins. They move with the malevolent determination of a stream of hungry soldier ants. They stung the flesh. He trampled a number of them, but in his annoyance and fervor he almost came too close to a suddenly flashing blue light. He kicked three pellets toward the light and they melted.

17

Boardman had already had much more than enough.

18

Their elapsed time out from the entrance to the maze was only one hour and forty-eight minutes, although it seemed much longer than that. The route through Zone F led into a pink-walled room where jets of steam blew up from concealed vents. At the far end of the room was an irising slot. If you did not step through it with perfect timing, you would be crushed. The slot gave access to a long low-vaulted passageway, oppressively warm and close, whose walls were blood-red in color and pulsated sickeningly. Beyond the passageway was an open plaza in which six slabs of white metal stood on end like waiting swords. A fountain hurled water a hundred meters into the air. Flanking the plaza were three towers with many windows, all of different sizes. Prismatic spotlights played against the windows. No windows were broken. On the steps of one of the towers lay the articulated skeleton of a creature close to ten meters long. The bubble of what was undoubtedly a space helmet covered its skull.

19

Alton, Antonelli, Cameron, Greenfield, and Stein constituted the Zone F camp, the relief base for the forward group. Antonelli and Stein went back to the plaza in the middle of F and found Rawlins and Boardman there.

"It's just a short way on," Stein said. "Would you like to rest a few minutes, Mr. Boardman?"

Boardman glowered. They went on.

Antonelli said, "Davis, Ottavio, and Reynolds passed on to E this morning when Alton, Cameron, and Greenfield reached us. Petrocelli and Walker are reconnoitering along the inner edge of E and looking a little way into D. They say it looks a lot better in there."

"I'll flay them if they go in," Boardman said.

Antonelli smiled worriedly.

The relief base consisted of a pair of extrusion domes side by side in a little open spot at the edge of a garden. The site had been thoroughly researched and no surprises were expected. Rawlins entered one of the domes and took his shoes off. Cameron handed him a cleanser. Greenfield gave him a food pack. Rawlins felt ill at ease among these men. They had not had the opportunities in life that had been given him. They did not have proper educations. They would not live as long, even if they avoided all of the dangers to which they were exposed. None of them had blond hair or blue eyes, and probably they could not afford to get shape-ups that would give them those qualifications. And yet they seemed happy. Perhaps it was because they never had to stop to confront the moral implications of luring Richard Muller out of the maze.

Boardman came into the dome. It amazed Rawlins how

durable and tireless the old man was. Boardman said, laughing, "Tell Captain Hosteen he lost his bet. We made it."

"What bet?" asked Antonelli.

Greenfield said, "We think that Muller must be tracking us somehow. His movements have been very regular. He's occupying the back quadrant of Zone A, as far from the entrance as possible—if the entrance is the one he uses—and he swings around in a little arc balancing the advance party."

Boardman said, "Hosteen gave three to one we wouldn't get here. I heard him." To Cameron, who was a communications technician, Boardman said, "Do you think it's possible that Muller is using some kind of scanning system?"

"It's altogether likely."

"Good enough to see faces?"

"Maybe some of the time. We really can't be sure. He's had a lot of time to learn how to use this maze, sir."

"If he sees my face," said Boardman, "we might as well just go home without bothering. I never thought he might be scanning us. Who's got the thermoplastics? I need a new face fast."

20

He did not try to explain. But when he was finished he had a long sharp nose, lean, downcurving lips, and a witch's chin. It was not an attractive face. But it was not the face of Charles Boardman either.

21

After a night of unsound sleep Rawlins prepared himself to go on to the advance camp in Zone E. Boardman would not be going with him, but they would be in direct contact at all times now. Boardman would see what Rawlins saw, and hear what Rawlins heard. And in a tiny voice Boardman would be able to convey instructions to him.

The morning was dry and wintry. They tested the communications circuits. Rawlins stepped out of the dome and walked ten paces, standing alone looking inward and watching the orange glow of daylight on the pockmarked porcelain-like walls before him. The walls were deep black against the lustrous green of the sky.

Boardman said, "Lift your right hand if you hear me, Ned."

Rawlins lifted his right hand.

"Now speak to me."

"Where did you say Richard Muller was born?"

"On Earth. I hear you very well."

"Where on Earth?"

"The North American Directorate, somewhere."

"I'm from there," Rawlins said.

"Yes, I know. I think Muller is from the western part of the continent. I can't be sure. I've spent only a very little time on Earth, Ned, and I can't remember the geography. If it's important, I can have the ship look it up."

"Maybe later," said Rawlins. "Should I get started now?"

"Listen to me, first. We've been very busy getting ourselves inside this place, and I don't want you to forget that everything we've done up to this point has been a preliminary to our real purpose. We're here for Muller, remember."

"Would I forget?"

"We've been preoccupied with matters of personal survival. That can tend to blur your perspective: whether you yourself, individually, live or die. Now we take a larger view. What Richard Muller has, whether it's a gift or a curse, is of high potential value and it's your job to gain use of it, Ned. The fate of galaxies lies on what happens in the next few days between you and Muller. Eons will be reshaped. Billions yet unborn will have their lives altered for good or ill by the events at hand."

"You sound absolutely serious, Charles."

"I absolutely am. Sometimes there comes a moment when all the booming foolish inflated words mean something, and this is one of those moments. You're standing at a crossroads in galactic history. And therefore, Ned, you're going to go in there and lie and cheat and perjure and connive, and I expect that your conscience is going to be very sore for a while, and you'll hate yourself extravagantly for it, and eventually you'll realize that you've done a deed of heroism. The test of your communications equipment is now ended. Get back inside here and let's ready you to march."

22

He went alone only a short distance this time. Stein and Alton accompanied him as far as the gateway to Zone E. There were no incidents. They pointed in the right direction, and he passed through a pinwheeling shower of coruscating azure sparks to enter the austere funereal zone beyond. As he negotiated the uphill ramp of the entrance, he caught sight of a socket mounted in an upright stone column. Within the darkness of the socket was something mobile and gleaming that could have been an eye.

"I think I've found part of Muller's scanning system," Rawlins reported. "There's a thing watching me in the wall."

"Cover it with your spray," Boardman suggested.

"I think he'd interpret that as a hostile act. Why would an archaeologist mutilate a feature like that?"

"Yes. A point. Proceed."

There was less of an air of menace about Zone E. It was made up of dark, tightly-compacted low buildings which clung together like bothered turtles. Rawlins could see different topography ahead, high walls, and a shining tower. Each of the zones was so different from all the others that he began to think they had been built at different times: a core of residential sectors, and then a gradual accretion of trap-laden outer rings as the enemies grew more troublesome. It was the sort of thought an archaeologist might have; he filed it for use.

He walked a little way, and saw the shadowy figure of Walker coming toward him. Walker was lean, dour, cool. He claimed to have been married several times to the same wife. He was about forty, a career man.

"Glad you made it, Rawlins. Go easy there on your left. That wall is hinged."

"Everything all right here?"

"More or less. We lost Petrocelli about an hour ago."

Rawlins stiffened. "This zone is supposed to be safe!"

"It isn't. It's riskier than F, and nearly as bad as G. We underestimated it when we were using the probes. There's no real reason why the zones *have* to get safer toward the middle, is there? This is one of the worst."

"To lull us," Rawlins suggested. "False security."

"You bet. Come on, now. Follow me and don't use your brain too much. There's no value in originality in here. You go the way the path goes, or you don't go anywhere."

Rawlins followed. He saw no apparent danger, but he jumped where Walker jumped, and detoured where Walker detoured. Not too far on lay the inner camp. He found Davis, Ottavio, and Reynolds there, and also the upper half of Petrocelli. "We're awaiting burial orders," said Ottavio. Below the waist there was nothing left. "Hosteen's going to tell us to bring him out, I bet."

"Cover him, at least," Rawlins told him.

"You going on into D today?" Walker asked.

"I may as well."

"We'll tell you what to avoid. It's new. That's where Petrocelli got it, right near the entrance to D, maybe five meters this side. You trip a field of some kind and it cuts you in half. The drones didn't trip it at all."

"Suppose it cuts everything in half that goes by?" Rawlins asked. "Except drones."

"It didn't cut Muller," Walker said. "It won't cut you if you step around it. We'll show you how."

"And beyond?"

"That's all up to you."

23

ᵇoardman said, "If you're tired, stay here for the night."

"I'd rather go on."

"You'll be going alone, Ned. Why not be rested?"

"Ask the brain for a reading on me. See where my fatigue level is. I'm ready to go onward."

Boardman checked. They were doing full telemetry on Rawlins; they knew his pulse rate, respiration count, hormone levels, and many more intimate things. The computer saw no reason why Rawlins could not continue without pausing.

"All right," said Boardman, "go on."

"I'm about to enter Zone D, Charles. This is where Petrocelli got it. I see the tripline—very subtle, very well hidden. Here I go past it. Yes. Ye-es. This is Zone D. I'm stopping and letting the brain get my bearings for me. Zone D looks a little cozier than E. The crossing shouldn't take long."

24

The auburn flames that guarded Zone C were frauds.

25

Rawlins said softly, "Tell the galaxies that their fate is in good hands. I should find Muller in fifteen minutes."

seven

Muller had often been alone for long periods. In drawing up the contract for his first marriage he had insisted on a withdrawal clause, the standard one; and Lorayn had not objected, for she knew that his work might occasionally take him to places where she would not or could not go. During the eight years of that marriage he had enforced the clause three times for a total of four years.

When they let the contract run out, Muller's absences were not really a contributing factor. He had learned in those years that he could stand solitude, and even that he thrived on it in a strange way. We develop everything in solitude except character, Stendhal had written; Muller was not sure of that but, in any case, his character had been fully formed before he began accepting assignments that took him unaccompanied to empty dangerous worlds. He had volunteered for those assignments. In a different sense he had volunteered to immure himself on Lemnos, and this exile was more painful to him than those other absences. Yet he got along. His own adaptability astonished and frightened him. He had not thought he could shed his social nature so easily. The sexual part was difficult, but not as difficult as he had imagined it would be; and the rest—the stimulation of debate, the change of surroundings, the interplay of personalities—had somehow ceased quickly to matter. He had enough cubes to keep him diverted, and enough challenges surviving in this maze. And memories.

He could summon remembered scenes from a hundred worlds. Man sprawled everywhere, planting the seed of Earth on colonies of a thousand stars. Delta Pavonis VI, for example: twenty light-years out, and rapidly going strange. They called the planet Loki, which struck Muller as a whopping misnomer, for Loki was agile, shrewd, slight of build, and the settlers on Loki, fifty years isolated from Earth, went in for a cult of artificial obesity through glucostatic regulation. Muller had visited them a decade before his ill-starred Beta Hydri journey. It was essentially a troubleshooting mission to a planet that had lost touch with its mother world. He remembered a warm planet, habitable only in a narrow temperate belt. Passing through walls of green jungle bordering a black river; watching beasts with jeweled eyes jostling on the swampy banks; coming at last to the settlement, where sweaty Buddhas weighing a few hundred kilograms apiece sat in stately meditation before thatched huts. He had never seen so much flesh per cubic meter before. The Lokites meddled with their peripheral glucoreceptors to induce accumulation of body fat. It was a useless adaptation, unrelated to any problem of their environment; they simply liked to be huge. Muller recalled arms that looked like thighs, thighs that looked like pillars, bellies that curved and recurved in triumphant excess.

They had hospitably offered a woman to the spy from Earth. For Muller, it was a lesson in cultural relativity; for there were in the village two or three women who, although bulky enough, were scrawny by local standards and so approximated the norm of Muller's own background. The Lokites did not give him any of these women, these pitiful underdeveloped hundred-kilogram wrecks, for it would have been a breach of manners to let a guest have a subpar companion. Instead they treated him to a blonde colossus with breasts like cannonballs and buttocks that were continents of quivering meat.

It was, at any rate, unforgettable.

There were so many other worlds. He had been a tireless voyager. To such men as Boardman he left the subtleties of political manipulation; Muller could be subtle enough, almost statesmanlike when he had to be, but he thought of himself more as an explorer than as a diplomat. He had shivered in methane lakes, had fried in post-Saharan deserts, had followed nomadic settlers across a purple plain in quest of their strayed arthropodic cattle. He had been shipwrecked by computer failure on airless worlds. He had seen the coppery cliffs of Damballa, ninety kilometers high. He had taken a swim in the gravity lake of Mordred. He had slept beside a multicolored brook under a sky blazing with a trio of suns, and he had walked the crystal bridges of Procyon XIV. He had few regrets.

Now, huddled at the heart of his maze, he watched the screens and waited for the stranger to find him. A weapon, small and cool, nestled in his hand.

2

The afternoon unrolled swiftly. Rawlins began to think that he would have done better to listen to Boardman and spend a night in camp before going on to seek Muller. At least three hours of deepsleep to comb his mind of tension—a quick dip under the sleep wire, always useful. Well, he hadn't bothered. Now there was no opportunity. His sensors told him that Muller was just ahead.

Questions of morality and questions of ordinary courage suddenly troubled him.

He had never done anything significant before. He had studied, he had performed routine tasks in Boardman's office, he had now and then handled a slightly sensitive matter. But he had always believed that his real career still was yet to open; that all this was preliminary. That sense of a future beginning was still with him, but it was time to admit that he was on the spot. This was no training simulation. Here he stood, tall and blond and young and stubborn and ambitious, at the verge of an action which—and Charles Boardman had not been altogether hypocritical about that—might well influence the course of coming history.

Ping.

He looked about. The sensors had spoken. Out of the shadows ahead emerged the figure of a man. Muller.

They faced each other across a gap of twenty meters. Rawlins had remembered Muller as a giant and was surprised to see now that they were about the same height, both of them just over two meters high. Muller was dressed in a dark glossy wrap, and in this light at this hour his face was a study in conflicting planes and jutting prominences, all peaks and valleys.

In Muller's hand lay the apple-sized device with which he had destroyed the probe.

Boardman's voice buzzed in Rawlins' ear. "Get closer to him. Smile. Look shy and uncertain and friendly, and *very* concerned. And keep your hands where he can see them at all times."

Rawlins obeyed. He wondered when he would begin to feel the effects of being this close to Muller. He found it hard to take his eyes from the shiny globe that rested like a grenade in Muller's hand. When he was ten meters away he started to pick up the emanation from Muller. Yes. That must certainly be it. He decided that he would be able to tolerate it if he came no closer.

Muller said, *"What do you—"*

The words came out as a raucous shriek. Muller stopped, cheeks flaming, and seemed to be adjusting the gears of his larynx. Rawlins chewed the corner of his lip. He felt an uncontrollable twitching in one eyelid. Harsh breathing was coming over the audio line from Boardman.

Muller began again. "What do you want from me?" he said, this time in his true voice, deep, crackling with suppressed rage.

"Just to talk. Honestly. I don't want to cause any trouble for you, Mr. Muller."

"You know me!"

"Of course I do. Everyone knows Richard Muller. I mean, you were *the* galactic hero when I was going to school. We did reports on you. Essays about you. We—"

"Get out of here!" The shriek again.

"—and Stephen Rawlins was my father. I knew you, Mr. Muller."

The dark apple was rising. The small square window was facing him. Rawlins remembered how the relay from the drone probe had suddenly ceased.

"Stephen Rawlins?" The apple descended.

"My father." Rawlins' left leg seemed to be turning to water. Volatilized sweat drifted in a cloud about his shoulders. He was getting the outpouring from Muller more strongly now, as though it took a few minutes to tune to his wavelength. Now Rawlins felt the torrent of anguish, the sadness, the sense of yawning abysses sundering calm meadows. "I met you long ago," Rawlins said. "You had just come back from—let's see, it was 82 Eridani, I think, you were all tanned and windburned—I think I was eight years old, and you picked me up and threw me, only you weren't used to Earthnorm gravity and you threw me too hard, and I hit the ceiling and began to cry, and you gave me something to make me stop, a little bead that changed colors—"

Muller's hands were limp at his sides. The apple had disappeared into his garment.

He said tautly, "What was your name? Fred, Ted, Ed—that's it. Yes. Ed. Edward Rawlins."

"They started calling me Ned a little later on. So you remember me, then?"

"A little. I remember your father a lot better." Muller turned away and coughed. His hand slipped into his pocket. He raised his head and the descending sun glittered weirdly against his face, staining it deep orange. He made a quick edgy gesture with one finger. "Go away, Ned. Tell your friends that I don't want to be bothered. I'm a very sick man, and I want to be alone."

"Sick?"

"Sick with a mysterious inward rot of the soul. Look, Ned, you're a fine handsome boy, and I love your father dearly, if any of this is true, and I don't want you hanging around me. You'll regret it. I don't mean that as a threat, just as a statement of fact. Go away. Far away."

"Stand your ground," Boardman told him. "Get closer. Right in, where it hurts."

Rawlins took a wary step, thinking of the globe in Muller's pocket and seeing from those eyes that the man was not necessarily rational. He diminished the distance between them by ten per cent. The impact of the emanation seemed to double.

He said, "Please don't chase me away, Mr. Muller. I just want to be friendly. My father would never have forgiven me if he could have found out that I met you here, like this, and didn't try to help you at all."

"*Would have? Could have found out?* What happened to your father?"

"Dead."

"When? Where?"

"Four years ago, Rigel XXII. He was helping to set up a tight-beam network connecting the Rigel worlds. There was an amplifier accident. The focus was inverted. He got the whole beam."

"Jesus. He was still young!"

"He would have been fifty in a month. We were going to come out and visit him and give him a surprise party. Instead I came out by myself to bring his body back."

Muller's face softened. Some of the torment ebbed from his eyes. His lips became more mobile. It was as though someone else's grief had momentarily taken him from his own.

"Get closer to him," Boardman ordered.

Another step; and then, since Muller did not seem to notice, another. Rawlins sensed heat: not real but psychical, a furnace-blast of directionless emotion. He shivered in awe. He had never really believed in any essential way that the story of what the Hydrans had done to Richard Muller was true. He was too sharply limited by his father's heritage of pragmatism. If you can't duplicate it in the laboratory, it isn't real. If you can't graph it, it isn't real. If there's no circuitry, it isn't real. How could a human being possibly be redesigned to broadcast his own emotions? No circuitry could handle such a function. But Rawlins felt the fringes of that broadcast.

Muller said, "What are you doing on Lemnos, boy?"

"I'm an archaeologist." The lie came awkwardly. "This is my first field trip. We're trying to carry out a thorough examination of the maze."

"The maze happens to be someone's home. You're intruding."

Rawlins faltered.

"Tell him you didn't know he was here," Boardman prompted.

"We didn't realize that anyone was here," said Rawlins. "We had no way of knowing that—"

"You sent your damned robots in, didn't you? Once you found someone here—someone you knew damned well wouldn't want to have any company—"

"I don't understand," Rawlins said. "We had the impression you were wrecked here. We wanted to offer our help."

How easily I do this, he told himself!

Muller scowled. "You don't know why I'm here?"

"I'm afraid not."

"You wouldn't, I guess. You were too young. But the others—once they saw my face, they should have known. Why didn't they tell you? Your robot relayed my face, didn't it? You knew who it was in here. And they didn't tell you a thing?"

"I really don't understand—"

"Come close!" Muller bellowed.

Rawlins felt himself gliding forward, though he was unaware of taking individual steps. Abruptly he was face to face with Muller, conscious of the man's massive frame, his furrowed brow, his fixed, staring, angry eyes. Muller's immense hand pounced on Rawlins' wrist. Rawlins rocked, stunned by the impact, drenched with a despair so vast that it seemed to engulf whole universes. He tried not to stagger.

"Now get away from me!" Muller cried harshly. "Go on! Out of here! *Out!*"

Rawlins did not move.

Muller howled a curse and ran ponderously into a low glassy-walled building whose windows, opaque, were like blind eyes. The door closed, sealing without a perceptible opening. Rawlins sucked in breath and fought for his balance. His forehead throbbed as if something behind it were struggling to burst free.

"Stay where you are," said Boardman. "Let him get over his tantrum. Everything's going well."

3

Muller crouched behind the door. Sweat rolled down his sides. A chill swept him. He wrapped his arms about himself so tightly that his ribs complained.

He had not meant to handle the intruder that way at all.

A few words of conversation; a blunt request for privacy; then, if the man would not go away, the destructor globe. So Muller had planned. But he had hesitated. He had spoken too much and learned too much. Stephen Rawlins' son? A party of archaeologists out there? The boy had hardly seemed affected by the radiation except at very close range. Was it losing its power with the years? Muller fought to collect himself and to analyze his hostility. Why so fearful? Why so eager to cling to solitude? He had nothing to fear from Earthmen; they, not he, were the sufferers in any contact he had with them. It was understandable that they would recoil from his presence. But there was no reason for him to withdraw like this except out of some paralyzing diffidence, the encrusted inflexibilities of nine years of isolation. Had it come to that—a love of solitude for its own sake? Was he a hermit? His original pretense was that he had come here out of consideration for his fellow men, that he was unwilling to inflict the painful ugliness that was himself upon them. But the boy had wanted to be friendly and helpful. Why flee? Why react so churlishly?

Slowly Muller rose and undid the door. He stepped outside. Night had fallen with winter's swiftness; the sky was black, and the moons seared across it. The boy was still standing in the plaza, looking a little dazed. The biggest moon, Clotho, bathed him in golden light so that his curling hair seemed to sparkle with inner flame. His face was very pale, with sharply accentuated cheekbones. His blue eyes gleamed in shock, like those of one who has been slapped.

Muller advanced, uncertain of his tactics. He felt like some great half-rusted machine called into action after too many years of neglect. "Ned?" he said. "Look, Ned, I want to tell you that I'm sorry. You've got to understand, I'm not used to people. Not—used—to—*people.*"

"It's all right, Mr. Muller. I realize it's been rough for you."

"Dick. Call me Dick." Muller raised both hands and spread them as if trying to cup moonbeams. He felt terribly cold. On the wall beyond the plaza small animal shapes leaped and danced. Muller said, "I've come to love my privacy. You can even cherish cancer if you get into the right frame of mind. Look, you ought to realize something. I came here deliberately. It wasn't any shipwreck. I picked out the one place in the universe where I was least likely to be disturbed, and hid myself inside it.

But, of course, you had to come with your tricky robots and find the way in."

"If you don't want me here, I'll go," Rawlins said.

"Maybe that's best for both of us. No. Wait. Stay. Is it very bad, being this close to me?"

"It isn't exactly comfortable," said Rawlins. "But it isn't as bad as—as—well, I don't know. From this distance I just feel a little depressed."

"You know why?" Muller asked. "From the way you talk, I think you do, Ned. You're only pretending not to know what happened to me on Beta Hydri IV."

Rawlins colored. "Well, I remember a little bit, I guess. They operated on your mind?"

"Yes, that's right. What you're feeling, Ned, that's me, my goddam soul leaking into the air. You're picking up the flow of neural current, straight from the top of my skull. Isn't it lovely? Try coming a little closer . . . that's it." Rawlins halted. "There," Muller said, "now it's stronger. You're getting a better dose. Now recall what it was like when you were standing right here. That wasn't so pleasant, was it? From ten meters away you can take it. From one meter away it's intolerable. Can you imagine holding a woman in your arms while you give off a mental stink like that? You can't make love from ten meters away. At least, *I* can't. Let's sit down, Ned. It's safe here. I've got detectors rigged in case any of the nastier animals come in, and there aren't any traps in this zone. Sit." He lowered himself to the smooth milky-white stone floor, the alien marble that made this plaza so sleek. Rawlins, after an instant of deliberation, slipped lithely into the lotus position a dozen meters away.

Muller said, "How old are you, Ned?"

"Twenty-three."

"Married?"

A shy grin. "Afraid not."

"Got a girl?"

"There was one, a liaison contract. We voided it when I took on this job."

"Ah. Any girls in this expedition?"

"Only woman cubes," said Rawlins.

"They aren't much good, are they, Ned?"

"Not really. We could have brought a few women along, but—"

"But what?"

"Too dangerous. The maze—"

"How many men have you lost so far?" Muller asked.

"Five, I think. I'd like to know the sort of people who'd build a thing like this. It must have taken five hundred years of planning to make it so devilish."

Muller said, "More. This was the grand creative triumph of their race, I believe. Their masterpiece, their monument. They must have been proud of this murderous place. It summed up the whole essence of their philosophy—kill the stranger."

"Are you just speculating, or have you found some clues to their cultural outlook?"

"The only clue I have to their cultural outlook is all around us. But I'm an expert on alien psychology, Ned. I know more about it than any other human being, because I'm the only one who ever said hello to an alien race. Kill the stranger: it's the law of the universe. And if you don't kill him, at least screw him up a little."

"We aren't like that," Rawlins said. "We don't show instinctive hostility to—"

"Crap."

"But—"

Muller said, "If an alien starship ever landed on one of our planets we'd quarantine it and imprison the crew and interrogate them to destruction. Whatever good manners we may have learned grow out of decadence and complacency. We pretend that we're too noble to hate strangers, but we have the politeness of weakness. Take the Hydrans. A substantial faction within our government was in favor of generating fusion in their cloud layer and giving their system an extra sun—*before* sending an emissary to scout them."

"No."

"They were overruled, and an emissary was sent, and the Hydrans wasted him. Me." An idea struck Muller suddenly. Appalled, he said, "What's happened between us and the Hydrans in the last nine years? Any contact? War?"

"Nothing," said Rawlins. "We've kept away."

"Are you telling me the truth, or did we wipe the bastards out? God knows I wouldn't mind that, but yet it wasn't their fault they did this to me. They were reacting in a standard xenophobic way. Ned, has there been a war with them?"

"No. I swear it."

Muller relaxed. After a moment he said, "All right. I won't ask you to fill me in on all the other news developments. I don't really give a damn. How long are you people staying on Lemnos?"

"We don't know yet. A few weeks, I suppose. We haven't even really begun to explore the maze. And then there's the area outside. We want to run correlations on the work of earlier archaeologists, and—"

"And you'll be here for a while. Are the others going to come into the center of the maze?"

Rawlins moistened his lips. "They sent me ahead to establish a working relationship with you. We don't have any plan yet. It all depends on you. We don't want to impose on you. So if you don't want us to work here—"

"I don't," Muller told him crisply. "Tell that to your friends. In fifty or sixty years I'll be dead, and they can sniff around here then. But while I'm here I don't want them bothering me. Let them work in the outer four or five zones. If any of them sets foot in A, B, or C, I'll kill him. I can do that, Ned."

"What about me—am I welcome?"

"Occasionally. I can't predict my moods. If you want to talk to me, come around and see. And if I tell you to get the hell out, Ned, then get the hell out. Clear?"

Rawlins grinned sunnily. "Clear." He got to his feet. Muller, unwilling to have the boy standing over him, rose also. Rawlins took a few steps toward him.

Muller said, "Where are you going?"

"I hate having to talk at this distance, to shout like this. I can get a little closer to you, can't I?"

Instantly suspicious, Muller replied, "Are you some kind of masochist?"

"Sorry, no."

"Well, I'm no sadist either. I don't want you near me."

"It's really not that unpleasant—Dick."

"You're lying. You hate it like all the others. I'm like a leper, boy, and if you're queer for leprosy I feel sorry for you, but don't come any closer. It embarrasses me to see other people suffer on my account."

Rawlins stopped. "Whatever you say. Look, Dick, I don't want to cause troubles for you. I'm just trying to be friendly and helpful. If doing that in some way makes you uncomfortable—well, just say so, and I'll do something else. It doesn't do me any good to make things worse for you."

"That came out pretty muddled, boy. What is it you want from me, anyhow?"

"Nothing."

"Why not leave me alone?"

"You're a human being, and you've been alone here for a long time. It's my natural impulse to offer companionship. Does that sound too dumb?"

Muller shrugged. "I'm not much of a companion. Maybe you ought to take all your sweet Christian impulses and go away. There's no way you can help me, Ned. You can only hurt me by reminding me of all I can no longer have or know." Stiffening, Muller looked past the tall young man toward the shadowy figures cavorting along the walls. He was hungry, and this was the hour to begin hunting for his dinner. He said brusquely, "Son, I think my patience is running out again. Time for you to leave."

"All right. Can I come back tomorrow, though?"

"Maybe. Maybe."

The boy smiled ingenuously. "Thanks for letting me talk to you, Dick. I'll be back."

4

By troublesome moonlight Rawlins made his way out of Zone A. The voice of the ship's brain guided him back over the path he had taken inward, and now and then, in the safest spots, Boardman used the override. "You've made a good start," Boardman said. "It's a plus that he tolerated you at all. How do you feel?"

"Lousy, Charles."

"Because of the close contact with him?"

"Because I'm doing something filthy."

"Stop that, Ned. If I'm going to have to pump you full of moral reassurance every time you set out—"

"I'll do my job," said Rawlins, "but I don't have to like it." He edged over a spring-loaded stone block that was capable of hurling him from a precipice if he applied his weight the wrong way. A small toothy animal snickered at him as he crossed. On the far side, Rawlins prodded the wall in a yielding place and won admission to Zone B. He glanced at the lintel and saw the recessed slot of the visual pickup and smiled into it, just in case Muller was watching him withdraw.

He saw now why Muller had chosen to maroon himself here. Under similar circumstances he might have done the same thing. Or worse. Muller carried, thanks to the Hydrans, a deformity of the soul in an era when deformity was obsolete. It was an esthetic crime to lack a limb or an eye or a nose; these things were easily repaired, and one owed it to one's fellow man to get a shape-up and obliterate troublesome imperfections. To inflict one's flaws on society was clearly an antisocial act.

But no shape-up surgeon could do a cosmetic job on what Muller had. The only cure was separation from society. A weaker man would have chosen death: Muller had picked exile.

Rawlins still throbbed with the impact of that brief moment of direct contact. For an instant he had received from Muller a formless incoherent emanation of raw emotion, the inner self spilling out involuntarily and wordlessly. The flow of uncontrollable innerness was painful and depressing to receive.

It was not true telepathy that the Hydrans had given him. Muller could not "read" minds, nor could he communicate his thoughts to others. What came forth was this gush of self: a torrent of raw despair, a river of regrets and sorrows, all the sewage of a soul. He could not hold it back. For that eternal moment Rawlins had been bathed in it; the rest of the time he had merely picked up a vague and general sense of distress.

He could generate his own concretenesses out of that

raw flow. Muller's sorrows were not unique to himself; what he offered was nothing more than an awareness of the punishments the universe devises for its inhabitants. At that moment Rawlins had felt that he was tuned to every discord in creation: the missed chances, the failed loves, the hasty words, the unfair griefs, the hungers, the greeds, the lusts, the knife of envy, the acid of frustration, the fang of time, the death of small insects in winter, the tears of things. He had known aging, loss, impotence, fury, helplessness, loneliness, desolation, self-contempt, and madness. It was a silent shriek of cosmic anger.

Are we all like that? He wondered. Is the same broadcast coming from me, and from Boardman, and from my mother, and from the girl I used to love? Do we walk about like beacons fixed to a frequency we can't receive? Thank God, then. That's a song too painful to hear.

Boardman said, "Wake up, Ned. Stop brooding and watch out for trouble. You're almost in Zone C now."

"Charles, how did you feel the first time you came close to Muller?"

"We'll discuss that later."

"Did you feel as if you knew what human beings were all about for the first time?"

"I said we'll discuss—"

"Let me say what I want to say, Charles. I'm not in any danger here. I just looked into a man's soul, and I'm shaken by it. But—listen, Charles—he isn't really like that. He's a *good* man. That stuff he radiates, it's just noise. It's a kind of sludge that doesn't tell you a real thing about Dick Muller. It's noise we aren't meant to hear, and the signal's altogether different—like when you open an amplifier up to the stars, full blast, and you get that rasping of the spectrum, you know, and some of the most beautiful stars give you the most terrible noises, but that's just an amplifier response, it has nothing to do with the quality of the star itself, it—it—"

"*Ned.*"

"I'm sorry, Charles."

"Get back to camp. We all agree that Dick Muller's a fine human being. That's why we need him. We need you, too, so shut your mouth and watch your step. Easy, now.

Calm. Calm. Calm. What's that animal on your left? Hurry along, Ned. But stay calm. That's the way, son. Calm."

eight

When they met again the next morning it was easier for both of them. Rawlins, having slept well under the sleep wire, went to the heart of the maze and found Muller standing beside a tall flat-sided spike of dark metal at the edge of the great plaza.

"What do you make of this?" Muller asked conversationally as Rawlins approached. "There are eight of these, one at each corner. I've been watching them for years. They turn. Look here." Muller pointed to one face of the pylon. Rawlins came close, and when he was ten meters away he picked up Muller's emanation. Nevertheless, he forced himself to go closer. He had not been so close yesterday except in that one chilling moment when Muller had seized him and pulled him near.

"You see this?" Muller asked, tapping the spike.

"A mark."

"It took me close to six months to cut it. I used a sliver from the crystalline outcropping set in that wall yonder. Every day for an hour or two I'd scrape away, until there was a visible mark in the metal. I've been watching that mark. In the course of one local year it turns all the way around. So the spikes are moving. You can't see it, but they do. They're some kind of calendars."

"Do they—can you—have you ever—"

"You aren't making sense, boy."

"I'm sorry." Rawlins backed away, trying hard to hide the impact of Muller's nearness. He was flushed and shaken. At five meters the effect was not so agonizing, and he stayed there, making an effort, telling himself that he was developing a tolerance for it.

"You were saying?"

"Is this the only one you've been watching?"

"I've scratched a few of the others. I'm convinced that they all turn. I haven't found the mechanism. Underneath this city, you know, there's some kind of fantastic brain. It's millions of years old, but it still works. Perhaps it's some sort of liquid metal with cognition elements floating in it. It turns these pylons and runs the water supply and cleans the streets."

"And operates the traps."

"And operates the traps," Muller said. "But I haven't been able to find a sign of it. I've done some digging here and there, but I find only dirt below. Maybe you archaeologist bastards will locate the city's brain. Eh? Any clues?"

"I don't think so," said Rawlins.

"You don't sound very definite."

"I'm not. I haven't taken part in any of the work within the city." Rawlins smiled shyly. The quick facial movement annoyed him and drew reproof from Boardman, who pointed out over the monitor circuit that the shy smile always announced an upcoming lie and that it wouldn't be long before Muller caught on. Rawlins said, "Most of the time I was outside the city, directing the entry operations. And then when I got in, I came right in here. So I don't know what the others may have discovered so far. If anything."

"Are they going to rip up the streets?" Muller asked.

"I don't think so. We don't dig so much any more. We use scanners and sensors and probe beams." Glibly, impressed with his own improvisations, he went on headlong. "Archaeology used to be destructive, of course. To find out what was under a pyramid we had to take the pyramid apart. But now we can do a lot with probes. That's the new school, you understand, looking into the ground without digging, and thus preserving the monuments of the past for—"

"On one of the planets of Epsilon Indi," said Muller, "a team of archaeologists completely dismantled an ancient alien burial pavilion about fifteen years ago, and then found it impossible to put the thing back together because they couldn't comprehend the structural integrity of the building. When they tried, it fell apart and was a total loss. I happened to see the ruins a few months later. You know the case, of course."

Rawlins didn't. He said, reddening, "Well, there are always bunglers in any discipline—"

"I hope there are none here. I don't want the maze damaged. Not that there's much chance of that. The maze defends itself quite well." Muller strolled casually away from the pylon. Rawlins eased as the distance between them grew, but Boardman warned him to follow. The tactics for damping Muller's mistrust included a deliberate and rigorous self-exposure to the emotion field. Muller was not looking back, and said, half to himself, "The cages are closed again."

"Cages?"

"Look down there—into that street branching out of the plaza."

Rawlins saw an alcove against a building wall. Rising from the ground were a dozen or more curving bars of white stone that disappeared into the wall at a height of about four meters, forming a kind of cage. He could see a second such cage farther down the street.

Muller said, "There are about twenty of them, arranged symmetrically in the streets off the plaza. Three times since I've been here the cages have opened. Those bars slide into the street, somehow, and disappear. The third time was two nights ago. I've never seen the cages either open or close, and I've missed it again."

"What do you think the cages were used for?" Rawlins asked.

"To hold dangerous beasts. Or captured enemies. What else would you use a cage for?"

"And when they open now—"

"The city's still trying to serve its people. There are enemies in the outer zones. The cages are ready in case any of the enemies are captured."

"You mean us?"

"Yes. Enemies." Muller's eyes glittered with sudden paranoid fury; it was alarming how easily he slipped from rational discourse to that cold blaze. *"Homo sapiens.* The most dangerous, the most ruthless, the most despicable beast in the universe!"

"You say it as if you believe it."

"I do."

"Come on," Rawlins said. "You devoted your life to serving mankind. You can't possibly believe—"

"I devoted my life," said Muller slowly, "to serving

Richard Muller." He swung around so that he faced Rawlins squarely. They were only six or seven meters apart. The emanation seemed almost as strong as though they were nose to nose. Muller said, "I gave less of a damn for humanity than you might think, boy. I saw the stars, and I wanted them. I aspired after the condition of a deity. One world wasn't enough for me. I was hungry to have them all. So I built a career that would take me to the stars. I risked my life a thousand times. I endured fantastic extremes of temperature. I rotted my lungs with crazy gases, and had to be rebuilt from the inside out. I ate foods that would sicken you to hear about. Kids like you worshipped me and wrote essays about my selfless dedication to man, my tireless quest for knowledge. Let me get you straight on that. I'm about as selfless as Columbus and Magellan and Marco Polo. They were great explorers, yes, but they also looked for a fat profit. The profit I wanted was in here. I wanted to stand a hundred kilometers high. I wanted golden statues of me on a thousand worlds. You know poetry? Fame is the spur. That last infirmity of noble mind. Milton. Do you know your Greeks, too? When a man overreaches himself, the gods cast him down. It's called *hybris*. I had a bad case of it. When I dropped through the clouds to visit the Hydrans, I felt like a god. Christ, I *was* a god. And when I left, up through the clouds again. To the Hydrans I'm a god, all right. I thought it then: I'm in their myths, they'll always tell my story. The mutilated god. The martyred god. The being who came down among them and made them so uncomfortable that they had to fix him. But—"

"The cage—"

"Let me finish!" Muller rapped. "You see, the truth is, I wasn't a god, only a rotten mortal human being who had delusions of godhood, and the real gods saw to it that I learned my lesson. They decided to remind me of the hairy beast inside the plastic clothing. To call my attention to the animal brain under the lofty cranium. So they arranged it for the Hydrans to perform a clever little surgical trick on my brain, one of their specialties, I guess. I don't know if the Hydrans were being malicious for the hell of it or whether they were genuinely trying to cure me of a defect, my inability to let my emotions get out to them. Aliens. You figure them out. But they did their little job. And then I came back to Earth. Hero and leper all at once. Stand near me and you get sick. Why? It reminds you that *you're* an animal too, because you get a full dose of me. So we go round and round in our endless feedback. You hate me because you learn things about your own soul by getting near me. And I hate you because you must draw back from me. What I am, you see, is a plague carrier, and the plague I carry is the truth. My message is that it's a lucky thing for humanity that we're shut up each in his own skull. Because if we had even a little drop of telepathy, even the blurry nonverbal thing I've got, we'd be unable to stand each other. Human society would be impossible. The Hydrans can reach right into each other's mind, and they seem to like it. But we can't. And that's why I say that man must be the most despicable beast in the whole universe. He can't even take the reek of his own kind, soul to soul!"

Rawlins said, "The cage seems to be opening."

"What? Let me look!" Muller came jostling forward. Unable to step aside rapidly enough, Rawlins received the brunt of the emanation. It was not as painful this time. Images of autumn came to him: withered leaves, dying flowers, a dusty wind, early twilight. More regret than anguish over the shortness of life, the necessity of the condition. Meanwhile Muller, oblivious, was peering intently at the alabaster bars of the cage.

"It's withdrawn by several centimeters already. Why didn't you tell me?"

"I tried to. But you weren't listening."

"No. No. My damned soliloquizing." Muller chuckled. "Ned, I've been waiting years to see this. The cage actually in motion! Look how smoothly it moves, gliding into the ground. This is strange, Ned. It's never opened twice the same year before, and here it's opening for the second time this week."

"Maybe you've just failed to notice a lot of the other openings," Rawlins suggested. "While you slept, maybe—"

"I doubt it. Look at that!"

"Why do you think it's doing it right now?"

"Enemies all around," said Muller. "The city accepts

me as a native by now. I've been here so long. But it must be trying to get you into a cage. The enemy. Man."

The cage was fully open now. There was no sign of the bars except the row of small openings in the pavement.

Rawlins said, "Have you ever tried to put anything in the cages? Animals?"

"Yes. I dragged a big dead beast inside one. Nothing happened. Then I caught some live little ones. Nothing happened." He frowned. "I once thought of stepping into the cage myself to see if it would close automatically when it sensed a live human being. But I didn't. When you're alone, you don't try experiments like that." He paused a moment, "How would *you* like to help me in a little experiment right now, eh, Ned?"

Rawlins caught his breath. The thin air abruptly seemed like fire in his lungs.

Muller said quietly, "Just step across into the alcove and wait a minute or so. See if the cage closes on you. That would be important to know."

"And if it does," Rawlins said, not taking him seriously, "do you have a key to let me out?"

"I have a few weapons. We can always blast you out by lasing the bars."

"That's destructive. You warned me not to destroy anything here."

"Sometimes you destroy in order to learn. Go on, Ned. Step into the alcove."

Muller's voice grew flat and strange. He was standing in an odd expectant half-crouch, hands at his sides, fingertips bent inward toward his thighs. As though he's going to throw me into the cage himself, Rawlins thought.

Boardman said quietly in Rawlins' ear, "Do as he says, Ned. Get into the cage. Show him that you trust him."

I trust *him,* Rawlins told himself, but I don't trust that cage.

He had uncomfortable visions of the floor of the cage dropping out as soon as the bars were in place: of himself dumped into some underground vat of acid or lake of fire. The disposal pit for trapped enemies. What assurance do I have that it isn't like that?

"Do it, Ned," Boardman murmured.

It was a grand, crazy gesture. Rawlins stepped over the row of small openings and stood with his back to the wall. Almost at once the curving bars rose from the ground and locked themselves seamlessly into place above his head. The floor seemed stable. No death-rays lashed out at him. His worst fears were not realized; but he was a prisoner.

"Fascinating," Muller said. "It must scan for intelligence. When I tried with animals, nothing happened. Dead or alive. What do you make of that, Ned?"

"I'm very glad to have helped your resarch. I'd be happier if you'd let me out now."

"I can't control the movements of the bars."

"You said you'd lase them open."

"But why be destructive so fast? Let's wait, shall we? Perhaps the bars will open again of their own accord. You're perfectly safe in there. I'll bring you food, if you have to eat. Will your people miss you if you're not back by nightfall?"

"I'll send a message to them," said Rawlins glumly. "But I hope that I'm out by then."

"Stay cool," Boardman advised. "If necessary, we can get you out of that ourselves. It's important to humor Muller in everything you can until you've got real rapport with him. If you hear me, touch your right hand to your chin."

Rawlins touched his right hand to his chin.

Muller said, "That was pretty brave of you, Ned. Or stupid. I'm sometimes not sure if there's a distinction. But I'm grateful, anyway. I had to know about those cages."

"Glad to have been of assistance. You see, human beings aren't all that monstrous."

"Not consciously. It's the sludge inside that's ugly. Here, let me remind you." He approached the cage and put his hands on the smooth bars, white as bone. Rawlins felt the emanation intensify. "That's what's under the skull. I've never really felt it myself, of course. I extrapolate it from the responses of others. It must be foul."

"I could get used to it," Rawlins said. He sat down crosslegged. "Did you make any attempt to have it undone when you returned to Earth from Beta Hydri IV?"

"I talked to the shape-up boys. They couldn't begin to figure out what changes had been made in my neural flow, and so they couldn't begin to figure out how to fix things. Nice?"

"How long did you stay?"

"A few months. Long enough to discover that there wasn't one human being I knew who didn't turn green after a few minutes of close exposure to me. I started to stew in self-pity, and in self-loathing, which is about the same thing. I was going to kill myself, you know, to put the world out of its misery."

Rawlins said, "I don't believe that. Some men just aren't capable of suicide. You're one who isn't."

"So I discovered, and thank you. I didn't kill myself, you notice. I tried some fancy drugs, and then I tried drink, and then I tried living dangerously. And at the end of it I was still alive. I was in and out of four neuropsychiatric wards in a single month. I tried wearing a padded lead helmet to shield the thought radiations. It was like trying to catch neutrinos in a bucket. I caused a panic in a licensed house on Venus. All the girls stampeded out stark naked once the screaming began." Muller spat. "You know, I could always take society or leave it. When I was among people I was happy, I was cordial, I had the social graces. I wasn't a slick sunny article like you, all overflowing with kindness and nobility, but I interacted with others. I related, I got along. Then I could go on a trip for a year and a half and not see or speak to anyone, and that was all right too. But once I found out that I was shut off from society for good, I discovered that I had needed it after all. But that's over. I outgrew the need, boy. I can spend a hundred years alone and never miss one soul. I've trained myself to see humanity as humanity sees me—something sickening, a damp hunkering crippled thing best avoided. To hell with you all. I don't owe any of you anything, love included. I have no obligations. I could leave you to rot in that cage, Ned, and never feel upset about it. I could pass that cage twice a day and smile at your skull. It isn't that I hate you, either you personally or the whole galaxy full of your kind. It's simply that I despise you. You're nothing to me. Less than nothing. You're dirt. I know you now, and you know me."

"You speak as if you belong to an alien race," Rawlins said in wonder.

"No. I belong to the human race. I'm the most human being there is, because I'm the only one who can't hide his humanity. You feel it? You pick up the ugliness? What's inside me is also inside you. Go to the Hydrans and they'll help you liberate it, and then people will run from you as they run from me. I speak for man. I tell the truth. I'm the skull beneath the face, boy. I'm the hidden intestines. I'm all the garbage we pretend isn't there, all the filthy animal stuff, the lusts, the little hates, the sicknesses, the envies. And I'm the one who posed as a god. *Hybris*. I was reminded of what I really am."

Rawlins said quietly, "Why did you decide to come to Lemnos?"

"A man named Charles Boardman put the idea into my head."

Rawlins recoiled in surprise at the mention of the name.

Muller said, "You know him?"

"Well, yes. Of course. He—he's a very important man in the government."

"You might say that. It was Boardman who sent me to Beta Hydri IV, you know? Oh, he didn't trick me into it, he didn't have to persuade me in any of his slippery ways. He knew me well enough. He simply played on my ambitions. There's a world there with aliens on it, he said, and we want a man to visit it. Probably a suicide mission, but it would be man's first contact with another intelligent species, and are you interested? So of course I went. He knew I couldn't resist something like that. And afterward, when I came back *this* way, he tried to duck me a while—either because he couldn't abide being near me or because he couldn't abide his own guilt. And finally I caught up with him and I said, look at me, Charles, this is how I am now, where can I go, what shall I do? I got up close to him. This far away. His face changed color. He had to take pills. I could see the nausea in his eyes. And he reminded me about the maze on Lemnos."

"Why?"

"He offered it as a place to hide. I don't know if he was being kind or cruel. I suppose he thought I'd be killed on my way into the maze—a decent finish for my sort of chap, or at any rate better than taking a gulp of carniphage and melting down a sewer. But of course I told Boardman I wouldn't think of it. I wanted to cover my trail. I blew up and insisted that the last thing in the world I'd do was come here. Then I spent a month on the skids in Under New Orleans, and when I surfaced again I rented a ship and came here. Using maximum diversionary tactics to insure that nobody found out my true destination. Boardman was right. This was the place to come."

Rawlins said, "How did you get inside the maze?"

"Through sheer bad luck."

"*Bad* luck?"

"I was trying to die in a blaze of glory," said Muller. "I didn't give a damn if I survived the maze or not. I just plunged right in and headed for the middle."

"I can't believe that!"

"Well, it's true, more or less. The trouble was, Ned, I'm a survival type. It's an innate gift, maybe even something paranormal. I have unusual reflexes. I have a kind of sixth sense, as they say. Also my urge to stay alive is well developed. Besides that, I had mass detectors and some other useful equipment. So I came into the maze, and whenever I saw a corpse lying about I looked a little sharper than usual, and I stopped and rested when I felt my visualization of the place beginning to waver. I fully expected to be killed in Zone H. I *wanted* it. But it was my luck to make it where everybody else failed because I didn't care one way or the other, I suppose. The element of tension was removed. I moved like a cat, everything twitching at once, and I got past the tough parts of the maze somehow, much to my disappointment, and here I am."

"Have you ever gone outside it?"

"No. Now and then I go as far as Zone E, where your friends are. Twice I've been to F. Mostly I remain in the three inner zones. I've furnished things quite nicely for myself. I have a radiation locker for my meat supply, and a building I use as my library, and a place where I keep my woman cubes, and I do some taxidermy in one of the other buildings. I hunt quite a lot, also. And I examine the maze and try to analyze its workings. I've dictated several cubes of memoirs on my findings. I bet you archaeologist fellows would love to run through those cubes."

"I'm sure we'd learn a great deal from them," Rawlins said.

"I know you would. I'd destroy them before I'd let any of you see them. Are you getting hungry, boy?"

"A little."

"Don't go away. I'll bring you some lunch."

Muller strode toward the nearby buildings and disappeared. Rawlins said quietly, "This is awful, Charles. He's obviously out of his mind."

"Don't be sure of it," Boardman replied. "No doubt nine years of isolation can have effects on a man's stability, and Muller wasn't all that stable the last time I saw him. But he may be playing a game with you—pretending to be crazy to test your good faith."

"And if he isn't?"

"In terms of what we want from him, it doesn't matter in the slightest if he's insane. It might even help."

"I don't understand that."

"You don't need to," said Boardman evenly. "Just relax. You're doing fine so far."

Muller returned, carrying a platter of meat and a handsome crystal beaker of water. "Best I can offer," he said, pushing a chunk of meat between the bars. "A local beast. You eat solid food, don't you?"

"Yes."

"At your age, I guess you would. What did you say you were, twenty-five?"

"Twenty-three."

"That's even worse." Muller gave him the water. It had an agreeable flavor, or lack of flavor. Muller sat quietly before the cage, eating. Rawlins noticed that the effect of his emanation no longer seemed so disturbing, even at a range of less than five meters. Obviously one builds a tolerance to it, he thought. If one wants to make the attempt.

Rawlins said, after a while, "Would you come out and meet my companions in a few days?"

"Absolutely not."

"They'd be eager to talk to you."

"I have no interest in talking to them. I'd sooner talk to wild beasts."

"You talk to me," Rawlins pointed out.

"For the novelty of it. And because your father was a good friend. And because, as human beings go, boy, you're reasonably acceptable. But I don't want to be thrust into any miscellaneous mass of bug-eyed archaeologists."

"Possibly meet two or three of them," Rawlins suggested. "Get used to the idea of being among people again."

"*No.*"

"I don't see—"

Muller cut him off. "Wait a minute. *Why* should I get used to the idea of being among people again?"

Rawlins said uneasily, "Well, because there are people here, because it's not a good idea to get too isolated from—"

"Are you planning some sort of trick? Are you going to catch me and pull me out of this maze? Come on, come on, boy, what's in back of that little mind of yours? What motive do you have for softening me up for human contact?"

Rawlins faltered. In the awkward silence Boardman spoke quickly, supplying the guile he lacked, prompting him. Rawlins listened and did his best.

He said, "You're making me out to be a real schemer, Dick. But I swear to you I've got nothing sinister in mind. I admit I've been softening you up a little, jollying you, trying to make friends with you, and I guess I'd better tell you why."

"I guess you'd better!"

"It's for the archaeological survey's sake. We can spend only a few weeks here. You've been here—what is it, nine years? You know so much about this place, Dick, and I think it's unfair of you to keep it to yourself. So what I was hoping, I guess, was that I could get you to ease up, first become friendly with me, and then maybe come to

Zone E, talk to the others, answer their questions, explain what you know about the maze—"

"*Unfair* to keep it to myself?"

"Well, yes. To hide knowledge is a sin."

"Is it fair of mankind to call me unclean, and run away from me?"

"That's a different matter," Rawlins said. "It's beyond all fairness. It's a condition you have—an unfortunate condition that you didn't deserve, and everyone is quite sorry that it came upon you, but on the other hand, you surely must realize that from the viewpoint of other human beings it's rather difficult to take a detached attitude toward your—your—"

"Toward my stink," Muller supplied. "All right. It's rather difficult to stand my presence. Therefore I willingly refrain from inflicting it upon your friends. Get it out of your head that I'm going to speak to them or sip tea with them or have anything at all to do with them. I have separated myself from the human race and I stay separated. And it's irrelevant that I've granted you the privilege of bothering me. Also, while I'm instructing you, I want to remind you that my unfortunate condition was not undeserved. I earned it by poking my nose into places where I didn't belong, and by thinking I was superhuman for being able to go to such places. *Hybris.* I told you the word."

Boardman continued to instruct him. Rawlins, with the sour taste of lies on his tongue, went on, "I can't blame you for being bitter, Dick. But I still think it isn't right for you to withhold information from us. I mean, look back on your own exploring days. If you landed on a planet, and someone had vital information you had come to find, wouldn't you make every effort to get that information— even though the other person had certain private problems which—"

"I'm sorry," said Muller frostily, "I'm beyond caring," and he walked away, leaving Rawlins alone in the cage with two chunks of meat and the nearly empty beaker of water.

When Muller was out of sight Boardman said, "He's a touchy one, all right. But I didn't expect sweetness from him. You're getting to him, Ned. You're just the right mixture of guile and naivete."

"And I'm in a cage."

"That's no problem. We can send a drone to release you if the cage doesn't open by itself soon."

"Muller isn't going to work out," Rawlins murmured. "He's full of hate. It trickles out of him everywhere. We'll never get him to cooperate. I've never seen such hate in one man."

"You don't know what hate is," said Boardman. "And neither does he. I tell you everything is moving well. There are bound to be some setbacks, but the fact that he's talking to you at all is the important thing. He doesn't *want* to be full of hate. Give him half a chance to get off his frozen position and he will."

"When will you send the probe to release me?"

"Later," said Boardman. "If we have to."

Muller did not return. The afternoon grew darker and the air became chilly. Rawlins huddled uncomfortably in the cage. He tried to imagine this city when it had been alive, when this cage had been used to display prisoners captured in the maze. In the eye of his mind he saw a throng of the city-builders, short and thick, with dense coppery fur and greenish skin, swinging their long arms and pointing toward the cage. And in the cage huddled a thing like a giant scorpion, with waxy claws that scratched at the stone paving blocks, and fiery eyes, and a savage tail that awaited anyone who came too close. Harsh music sounded through the city. Alien laughter. The warm musky reek of the city-builders. Children spitting at the thing in the cage. Their spittle like flame. Bright moonlight, dancing shadows. A trapped creature, hideous and malevolent, lonely for its own kind, its hive on a world of Alphecca or Markab, where tailed waxy things moved in shining tunnels. For days the city-builders came, mocked, reproached. The creature in the cage grew sick of their massive bodies and their intertwining spidery fingers, of their flat faces and ugly tusks. And a day came when the floor of the maze gave way, for they were tired of the outworlder captive, and down he went, tail lashing furiously, down into a pit of knives.

It was night. Rawlins had not heard from Boardman for several hours. He had not seen Muller since early afternoon. Animals were prowling the plaza, mostly small ones, all teeth and claws. Rawlins had come unarmed today. He was ready to trample on any beast that slipped between the bars of his cage.

Hunger and cold assailed him. He searched the darkness for Muller. This had ceased to be a joke.

"Can you hear me?" he said to Boardman.

"We're going to get you out soon."

"Yes, but *when?*"

"We sent a probe in, Ned."

"It shouldn't take more than fifteen minutes for a probe to reach me. These zones aren't hazardous."

Boardman paused. "Muller intercepted the probe and destroyed it an hour ago."

"Why didn't you tell me that?"

"We're sending several drones at once," Boardman told him. "Muller's bound to overlook at least one of them. Everything's perfectly all right, Ned. You're in no danger."

"Until something happens," Rawlins said gloomily.

But he did not press the point. Cold, hungry, he slouched against the wall and waited. He saw a small lithe beast stalk and kill a much bigger animal a hundred meters away in the plaza. He watched scavengers scurrying in to rip away slabs of bloody meat. He listened to the sounds of rending and tearing. His view was partially obstructed, and he craned his neck to search for the drone probe that would set him free. No probe appeared.

He felt like a sacrificial victim, staked out for the kill.

The scavengers had finished their work. They came padding across the plaza toward him—little weasel-shaped beasts with big tapering heads and paddle-shaped paws from which yellow recurving claws protruded. Their eyes were red in yellow fields. They studied him with interest, solemnly, thoughtfully. Blood, thick and purplish, was smeared over their muzzles.

They drew nearer. A long narrow snout intruded between two bars of his cage. Rawlins kicked at it. The snout withdrew. To his left, another jutted through. Then there were three snouts.

And then the scavengers began slipping into the cage on all sides.

nine

Boardman had established a comfortable little nest for himself in the Zone F camp. At his age he offered no apologies. He had never been a Spartan, and now, as the price he exacted for making these strenuous and risky journeys, he carried his pleasures around with him. Drones had fetched his belongings from the ship. Under the milky-white curve of the extrusion dome he had carved a private sector with radiant heating, glow-drapes, a gravity suppressor, even a liquor console. Brandy and other delights were never far away. He slept on a soft inflatable mattress covered with a thick red quilt inlaid with heater strands. He knew that the other men in the camp, getting along on far less, bore him no resentment. They expected Charles Boardman to live well wherever he was.

Greenfield entered. "We've lost another drone, sir," he said crisply. "That leaves three in the inner zones."

Boardman flipped the ignition cap on a cigar. He sucked fumes a moment, crossed and uncrossed his legs, exhaled, smiled. "Is Muller going to get those too?"

"I'm afraid so. He knows the access routes better than we do. He's covering them all."

"And you haven't sent any drones in through routes we haven't charted?"

"Two, sir. Lost them both."

"Umm. We'd better send out a great many probes at once, then, and hope we can slip at least one of them past Muller. That boy is getting annoyed at being caged. Change the program, will you? The brain can manage diversionary tactics, if it's told. Say, twenty probes entering simultaneously."

"We have only three left," Greenfield said.

Boardman bit convulsively into his cigar. "Three here in the camp, or three altogether?"

"Three in camp. Five more outside the maze. They're working their way inward now."

"Who allowed this to happen? Call Hosteen! Get those templates working! I want fifty drones built by morning! No, make it eighty! Of all the stupidity, Greenfield!"

"Yes, sir."

"Get out!"

"Yes, sir."

Boardman puffed furiously. He dialed for brandy, the thick, rich, viscous stuff made by the Prolepticalist Fathers on Deneb XIII. The situation was growing infuriating. He knocked back half a snifter of the brandy, gasped, filled the glass again. He knew that he was in danger of losing his perspective—the worst of sins. The delicacy of this assignment was getting to him. All these mincing steps, the tiny complications, the painstaking edgings toward and away from the goal. Rawlins in the cage. Rawlins and his moral qualms. Muller and his neurotic world-outlook. The little beasts that nipped at your heels here and thoughtfully eyed your throat. The traps these demons had built. And the waiting extragalactics, saucereyed, radio-sensed, to whom even a Charles Boardman was no more than an insensate vegetable. Doom overhanging all. Irritably Boardman stubbed out his cigar, and immediately stared at its unfinished length in astonishment. The ignition cap would not work a second time. He leaned forward, got a beam of infrared from the room generator, and kindled it once more, puffing energetically until it was lit. With a petulant gesture of his hand Boardman reactivated his communication link with Ned Rawlins.

The screen showed him moonlight, curving bars, and small furry snouts bristling with teeth.

"Ned?" he said. "Charles here. We're getting you those drones, boy. We'll have you out of that stupid cage in five minutes, do you hear, five minutes!"

2

Rawlins was very busy.

It seemed almost funny. There was no end to the supply of the little beasts. They came nosing through the bars two and three at a time, weasels, ferrets, minks, stoats, whatever they were, all teeth and eyes. But they were scavengers, not killers. God knew what drew them to the cage. They clustered about him, brushing his ankles with their coarse fur, pawing him, slicing through his skin with their claws, biting his shins.

He trampled them. He learned very quickly that a booted foot placed just behind the head could snap a spinal column quickly and effectively. Then, with a swift kick, he could sweep his victim into a corner of the cage, where others would pounce upon it at once. Cannibals, too. Rawlins developed a rhythm of it. Turn, stomp, kick. Turn, stomp, kick. Turn, stomp, kick. Crunch. Crunch. Crunch.

They were cutting him up badly, though.

For the first five minutes he scarcely had time to pause for breath. Turn. Stomp. Kick. He took care of at least twenty of them in that time. Against the far side of the cage a heap of ragged little corpses had risen, with their comrades nosing around hunting for the tender morsels. At last a moment came when all the scavengers currently inside the cage were busy with their fallen cohorts, and no more lurked outside. Rawlins had a momentary respite. He seized a bar with one hand and lifted his left leg to examine the miscellany of cuts, scratches, and bites. Do they give a posthumous Stellar Cross if you die of galactic rabies, he wondered? His leg was bloody from the knee down, and the wounds, though not deep, were hot and painful. Suddenly he discovered why the scavengers had come to him. While he paused he had time to inhale, and he smelled the ripe fragrance of rotting meat. He could almost visualize it: a great bestial corpse, split open at the belly to expose red sticky organs, big black flies circling overhead, perhaps a maggot or two circumnavigating the mound of flesh—

Nothing was rotting in here. The dead scavengers hadn't had time to go bad; little was left of most of them but picked bones by now anyway.

Rawlins realized that it must be some sensory delusion: an olfactory trap touched off by the cage, evidently. The cage was broadcasting the stink of decay. Why? Obviously to lure that pack of little weasels inside. A refined form of torture. He wondered if Muller had somehow been behind it, going off to a nearby control center to set up the scent. He had no further time for contemplation. A fresh battalion of beasts was scurrying across the plaza toward the cage. These looked slightly larger, although not so large that they would not fit between the bars, and their fangs had an ugly gleam in the moonlight. Rawlins hastily stomped three of the snuffling, gorging cannibals still alive in his cage and, in a wondrous burst of inspiration, stuffed them through the bars, giving them a wristflip that tossed them eight or ten meters outside the cage. Good. The newcomers halted, skidding, and began at once to pounce on the twitching and not quite dead bodies that landed before them. Only a few of the scavengers bothered to enter the cage, and these came spaced widely enough so that Rawlins had a chance to trample each in turn and toss it out to feed the onrushing horde. At that rate, he thought, if only new ones would stop coming he could get rid of them all.

New ones finally did stop coming. He had killed seventy or eighty by this time. The stink of raw blood overlaid the synthetic stench of rot; his legs ached from all the carnage, and his brain was orbiting dizzyingly. But at length the night grew peaceful once more. Bodies, some clad in fur, some just a framework of bone, lay strewn in a wide arc before the cage. A thick, deep-hued puddle of mingled bloods spread over a dozen square meters. The last few survivors, stuffed on their gluttony, had gone slinking away without even trying to harass the occupant of the cage. Weary, drained, close to laughter and close to tears, Rawlins clung to the bars and did not look down at his throbbing blood-soaked legs. He felt the fire rising in them. He imagined alien microorganisms launching their argosies in his bloodstream. A bloated purpling corpse by morning, a martyr to Charles Boardman's over-reaching deviousness. What an idiot's move to step into the cage! What a doltish way to win Muller's trust!

Yet the cage had its uses, Rawlins realized suddenly.

Three bulky brutes paraded toward him from different directions. They had the stride of lions, but the swinishness of boars: low-slung sharp-backed creatures, 100 kilograms or so, with long pyramidal heads, slavering thin-lipped mouths, and tiny squinting eyes arranged in two sets of two on either side just in front their ragged droopy ears. Curving tusks jutted down and intersected smaller and sharper canine teeth that rose from powerful jaws. The trio of uglies inspected one another suspiciously, and performed a complex series of loping movements which neatly demonstrated the three-body problem as they executed circular interlocking trots by way of staking out territory. They rooted about a bit in the heap of scavenger corpses, but clearly they were no scavengers themselves; they were looking for living meat, and their disdain for the broken cannibalized little bodies was evident. When they had completed their inspection they swung about to stare at Rawlins, standing at a three-quarters-profile angle so that each of them had one pair of eyes looking at him straight on. Rawlins was grateful for the security of his cage. He would not care to be outside, unprotected and exhausted, with these three cruising the city for their dinner.

At that moment, of course, the bars of the cage silently began to retract.

3

Muller, arriving just then, took in the whole scene. He paused only briefly to admire the seductive vanishing of the cage into the recessed slots. He contemplated the three hungry pigs and the dazed, bloody form of Rawlins standing suddenly exposed before them. "Get down!" Muller yelled.

Rawlins got down by taking four running steps to the left, slipping on the blood-slicked pavement, and skidding into a heap of small cadavers at the edge of the street. In the same moment Muller fired, not bothering with keying in the manual sighting since these were not edible animals. Three quick bolts brought the pigs down. They did not move again. Muller started to go to Rawlins, but then one of the robots from the camp in Zone F appeared, gliding cheerfully toward them. Muller cursed softly. He pulled the destructor globe from his pocket and aimed the window at the robot. The probe turned a mindless blank face at him as he fired.

The robot disintegrated. Rawlins had managed to get up. "You shouldn't have blasted it," he said woozily. "It was just coming to help."

"No help was needed," said Muller. "Can you walk?"

"I think so."

"How badly are you hurt?"

"I've been chewed on, that's all. It isn't as bad as it looks."

"Come with me," Muller said. Already more scavengers were filing through the plaza, drawn by the mysterious telegraphy of blood. Small, toothy things were getting down to serious work on the trio of fallen boars. Rawlins looked unsteady; he seemed to be talking to himself. Forgetting his own emanation, Muller seized him by the arm. Rawlins winced and twitched away, and then, as if repenting the appearance of rudeness, gave Muller his arm again. They crossed the plaza together. Rawlins was shaking, and Muller did not know whether he was more disturbed by his narrow escape or by the jangling propinquity of an unshielded mind.

"In here," Muller said roughly.

They stepped into the hexagonal cell where he kept his diagnostat. Muller sealed the door, and Rawlins sank down limply on the bare floor. His blond hair was pasted by perspiration to his forehead. His eyes were moving jerkily, the pupils dilated.

Muller said, "How long were you under attack?"

"Fifteen, twenty minutes. I don't know. There must have been fifty or a hundred of them. I kept breaking their backs. A quick crunching sound, you know, like splitting twigs. And then the cage went away." Rawlins laughed wildly. "That was the best part. I had just finished smashing up all those little bastards and was catching my breath, and then the three big monsters came along, and so naturally the cage vanished and—"

"Easy," Muller said, "you're talking so fast I can't follow everything. Can you get those boots off?"

"What's left of them."

"Yes. Get them off and we'll patch those legs of yours. Lemnos has no shortage of infectious bacteria. And protozoa, and for all I know algae and trypanosomes, and more."

Rawlins picked at the catches. "Can you help me? I'm afraid that I can't—"

"You won't like it if I come any closer," Muller warned.

"To hell with that!"

Muller shrugged. He approached Rawlins and manipulated the broken and bent snaps of the boots. The metal chasing was scarred by tiny teeth; so were the boots themselves, and so were the legs. In a few moments Rawlins was out of his boots and leggings. He lay stretched out on the floor, grimacing and trying to look heroic. His legs were in bad shape, though none of the wounds seemed really serious; it was just that there were so many of them. Muller got the diagnostat going. The lamps glowed and the receptor slot beckoned.

"It's an old model," Rawlins said. "I'm not sure what to do."

"Stick your legs in front of the scanner."

Rawlins swiveled about. A blue light played on his wounds. In the bowels of the diagnostat things chuttered and clicked. A swab came forth on a jointed arm and ran deftly and lightly up his left leg to a point just above the knee. The machine engulfed the bloody swab and began to digest it back to its component molecules while a second swab emerged to clean Rawlins' other leg. Rawlins bit his lip. He was getting a coagulant as well as a cleanser so that when the swabs had done their work all blood was gone and the shallow gouges and rips were revealed. It still looked pretty bad, Muller thought, though not as grim as before.

The diagnostat produced an ultrasonic node and injected a golden fluid into Rawlins' rump. Pain-damper, Muller guessed. A second injection, deep amber, was probably some kind of all-purpose antibiotic to ward off infection. Rawlins grew visibly less tense. Now a variety of arms sprang forward from various sectors of the device, inspecting Rawlins' lesions in detail and scanning them for necessary repairs. There was a humming sound and three sharp clicks. Then the diagnostat began to seal the wounds, clamping them firmly.

"Lie still," Muller told him. "You'll be all right in a couple of minutes."

"You shouldn't be doing this," said Rawlins. "We have our own medical supplies back in camp. You must be running short on necessities. All you had to do was let the drone probe take me back to my camp, and—"

"I don't want those robots crawling around in here. And the diagnostat has at least a fifty-year supply of usefuls. I don't get sick often. It can synthesize most of what it's ever going to need for me. So long as I feed it protoplasm from time to time, it can do the rest."

"At least let us send you replacements for some of the rare drugs."

"Not necessary. No charity wanted. Ah! There, it's done with you. Probably you won't even have scars."

The machine released Rawlins, who swung away from it and looked up at Muller. The wildness was gone from the boy's face now. Muller lounged against the wall, rubbing his shoulderblades against the angle where two faces of the hexagon met, and said, "I didn't think that you'd be attacked by beasts or I wouldn't have left you alone so long. You aren't armed?"

"No."

"Scavengers don't bother living things. What made them go after you?"

"The cage did," Rawlins said. "It began to broadcast the smell of rotting flesh. A lure. Suddenly they were crawling all over me. I thought they'd eat me alive."

Muller grinned. "Interesting. So the cage is programmed as a trap too. We get some useful information out of your little predicament, then. I can't tell you how interested I am in those cages. In every part of this weird environment of mine. The aqueduct. The calendar pylons. The streetcleaning apparatus. I'm grateful to you for helping me learn a little."

"I know someone else who has that attitude," said Rawlins. "That it doesn't matter what the risk or cost so long as you collect some useful data out of the experience. Board—"

He cut the word short with a crisp biting gesture.

"Who?"

"Bordoni," Rawlins said. "Emilio Bordoni, my epistemology professor at college. He gave this marvelous course. Actually it was applied hermeneutics, a course in how to learn."

"That's heuristics," said Muller.

"Are you sure? I have a distinct impression—"

"It's wrong," said Muller. "You're talking to an authority. Hermeneutics is the art of interpretation. Originally Scriptural interpretation but now applying to all communications functions. Your father would have known that. My mission to the Hydrans was an experiment in applied hermeneutics. It wasn't successful."

"Heuristics. Hermeneutics." Rawlins laughed. "Well, anyway, I'm glad to have helped you learn something about the cages. My heuristic good deed. Am I excused from the next round?"

"I suppose," Muller said. Somehow an odd feeling of good will had come over him. He had almost forgotten how pleasant it was to be able to help another person. Or to enjoy lazy, irrelevant conversation. He said, "Do you drink, Ned?"

"Alcoholic beverages?"

"So I mean."

"In moderation."

"This is our local liqueur," said Muller. "It's produced by gnomes somewhere in the bowels of the planet." He produced a delicate flask and two wide-mouthed goblets. Carefully he tipped about twenty centiliters into each goblet. "I get this in Zone C," he explained, handing Rawlins his drink. "It rises from a fountain. It really ought to be labeled DRINK ME, I guess."

Gingerly Rawlins tasted it. "Strong!"

"About sixty per cent alcohol, yes. Lord knows what the rest of it is, or how it's synthesized or why. I simply accept it. I like the way it manages to be both sweet and gingery at the same time. Its terribly intoxicating, of course. It's intended as another trap, I suppose. You get happily drunk—and then the maze gets you." He raised his goblet amiably. "Cheers!"

"Cheers!"

They laughed at the archaic toast and drank.

Careful, Dickie, Muller told himself. You're getting downright sociable with this boy. Remember where you

are. And why. What kind of ogre are you, acting this way?
"May I take some of this back to camp with me?"
Rawlins asked.

"I suppose so. Why?"

"There's a man there who'd appreciate it. He's a gourmet of sorts. He's traveling with a liquor console that dispenses a hundred different drinks, I imagine, from about forty different worlds. I can't even remember the names."

"Anything from Marduk?" Muller asked. "The Deneb worlds? Rigel?"

"I really can't be sure. I mean, I enjoy drinking, but I'm no connoisseur."

"Perhaps this friend of yours would be willing to exchange—" Muller stopped. "No. No. Forget I said that. I'm not getting into any deals."

"You could come back to camp with me," said Rawlins. "He'd give you the run of the console, I'm sure."

"Very subtle of you. No." Muller glowered at his liqueur. "I won't be eased into it, Ned. I don't want anything to do with the others."

"I'm sorry you feel that way."

"Another drink?"

"No. I'll have to start getting back to camp now. It's late. I wasn't supposed to spend the whole day here, and I'll catch hell for not doing my share of the work."

"You were in the cage most of the day. They can't blame you for that."

"They might. They were complaining a little yesterday. I don't think they want me to visit you."

Muller felt a sudden tightness within.

Rawlins went on, "After the way I kicked away a day's work today I wouldn't be surprised if they refused to let me come in here again. They'll be pretty stuffy about it. I mean, considering that you don't seem very cooperative, they'll regard it as wasted time for me to be paying calls on you when I could be manning the equipment in Zone E or F." Rawlins finished his drink and got to his feet, grunting a little. He looked down at his bare legs. The diagnostat had covered the wounds with a nutrient spray, flesh-colored; it was almost impossible to tell that his skin had been broken anywhere. Stiffly, he pulled his tattered leggings on. "I won't bother with the boots," he said. "They're in bad shape, and it won't be pleasant trying to get them on. I suppose I can get back to camp barefoot."

"The pavement is very smooth," Muller said.

"You'll give me some of that liqueur for my friend?"

Silently Muller extended the flask, half full.

Rawlins clipped it to his belt. "It was an interesting day. I hope I can come again."

4

Boardman said, as Rawlins limped back toward Zone E, "How are your legs?"

"Tired. They're healing fast. I'll be all right."

"Be careful not to drop that flask."

"Don't worry, Charles. I have it well fastened. I wouldn't deprive you of the experience."

"Ned, listen to me, we did try to get the drones to you. I was watching every terrible minute of it when those animals were attacking you. But there was nothing we could do. Muller was intercepting our probes and knocking them out."

"All right," Rawlins said.

"He's clearly unstable. He wasn't going to let one of those drones into the inner zones."

"All right, Charles, I survived."

Boardman could not let go of it. "It occurred to me that if we hadn't tried to send the drones at all, you would have been better off, Ned. The drones kept Muller busy for a long while. He might have gone back to your cage instead. Let you out. Or killed the animals. He—" Halting, Boardman quirked his lips and denounced himself inwardly for maundering. A sign of age. He felt the folds of flesh at his belly. He needed another shape-up. Bring his age forward to an apparent sixty or so, while actually cutting the physiological deterioration back to biological fifty. Older outside than within. A façade of shrewdness to hide shrewdness.

He said, after a long while, "It seems you and Muller

are quite good friends now. I'm pleased. It's coming to be time for you to tempt him out."

"How do I do that?"

"Promise him a cure," Boardman said.

ten

They met again on the third day afterward, at midday in Zone B. Muller seemed relieved to see him, which was the idea. Rawlins came diagonally across the oval ball-court, or whatever it was, that lay between two snub-nosed dark blue towers, and Muller nodded. "How are your legs?"

"Doing fine."

"And your friend—he liked the liqueur?"

"He loved it," Rawlins said, thinking of the glow in Boardman's foxy eyes. "He sends back your flask with some special brandy in it and hopes you'll treat him to a second round."

Muller eyed the flask as Rawlins held it forth. "He can go to hell," Muller said coolly. "I won't get into any trades. If you give me that flask I'll smash it."

"Why?"

"Give it here, and I'll show you. No. Wait. Wait. I won't. Here, let me have it."

Rawlins surrendered it. Muller cradled the lovely flask tenderly in both hands, activated the cap, and put it to his lips. "You devils," he said in a soft voice. "What is this, from the monastery on Deneb XIII?"

"He didn't say. He just said you'd like it."

"Devils. Temptations. It's a trade, damn you! But only this once. If you show up here again with more liqueur—anything—the elixir of the gods—anything, I'll refuse it. Where have you been all week, anyway?"

"Working. I told you they frowned on my coming to see you."

He missed me, Rawlins thought. Charles is right: I'm getting to him. Why does he have to be such a difficult character?

"Where are they excavating?" Muller asked.

"They aren't excavating at all. They're using sonic

probes at the border between Zones E and F, trying to determine the chronology—whether the whole maze was built at once, or in accretive layers out from the middle. What's your opinion, Dick?"

"Go to hell. No free archaeology out of me!" Muller sipped the brandy again. "You're standing pretty close to me, aren't you?"

"Four or five meters, I guess."

"You were closer when you gave me the brandy. Why didn't you look sick? Didn't you feel the effect?"

"I felt it, yes."

"And hid your feelings like the good stoic you are?"

Shrugging, Rawlins said genially, "I guess the effect loses impact on repeated exposure. It's still pretty strong, but not the way it was for me the first day. Have you ever noticed that happening with someone else?"

"There were no repeated exposures with anyone else," said Muller. "Come over here, boy. See the sights. This is my water supply. Quite elegant. This black pipe runs right around Zone B. Onyx, I guess. Semiprecious. Handsome, at any rate." Muller knelt and stroked the aqueduct. "There's a pumping system. Brings up water from some underground aquifer, maybe a thousand kilometers down, I don't know. This planet doesn't have any surface water, does it?"

"It has oceans."

"Aside from—well, whatever. Over here, you see, here's one of the spigots. Every fifty meters. As far as I can tell it's the water supply for the entire city, right here, so perhaps the builders didn't need much water. It couldn't have been very important if they set things up like this. No conduits that I've found. No real plumbing. Thirsty?"

"Not really."

Muller cupped his hand under the ornately engraved spigot, a thing of concentric ridges. Water gushed. Muller took a few quick gulps; the flow ceased the moment the hand was removed from the area below the spigot. A scanning system of some kind, Rawlins thought. Clever. How had it lasted all these millions of years?

"Drink," Muller said. "You may get thirsty later on."

"I can't stay long." But he drank anyway. Afterward they walked into Zone A, an easy stroll. The cages had closed again; Rawlins saw several of them, and shuddered. He would try no such experiments today. They found benches, slabs of polished stone that curled at the ends into facing seats intended for some species very much broader in the buttock than the usual *H. sapiens*. Sitting like this they could talk at a distance, Rawlins feeling only mild discomfort from Muller's emanation, and yet there was no sensation of separation.

Muller was in a talkative mood.

The conversation was fitful, dissolving every now and then into an acid spray of anger or self-pity, but most of the time Muller remained calm and even charming—an older man clearly enjoying the company of a younger one, the two of them exchanging opinions, experiences, scraps of philosophy. Muller spoke a good deal about his early career, the planets he had seen, the delicate negotiations on behalf of Earth with the frequently prickly colony-worlds. He mentioned Boardman's name quite often; Rawlins kept his face studiously blank. Muller's attitude toward Boardman seemed to be one of deep admiration shot through with furious loathing. He could not forgive Boardman, apparently, for having played on his own weaknesses in getting him to go to the Hydrans. Not a rational attitude, Rawlins thought. Given Muller's trait of overweening curiosity, he would have fought for that assignment, Boardman or no, risks or no.

"And what about you?" Muller asked finally. "You're brighter than you pretend to be. Hampered a little by your shyness, but plenty of brains, carefully hidden behind college-boy virtues. What do you want for yourself, Ned? What does archaeology give you?"

Rawlins looked him straight in the eyes. "A chance to recapture a million pasts. I'm as greedy as you are. I want to know how things happened, how they got this way. Not just on Earth or in the System. Everywhere."

"Well spoken!"

I thought so too, Rawlins thought, hoping Boardman was pleased by his newfound eloquence.

He said, "I suppose I could have gone in for diplomatic service, the way you did. Instead I chose this. I think it'll work out. There's so much to discover, here and everywhere else. We've only begun to look."

"The ring of dedication is in your voice."

"I suppose."

"I like to hear that sound. It reminds me of the way I used to talk."

Rawlins said, "Just so you don't think I'm hopelessly pure I ought to say that it's personal curiosity that moves me on, more than abstract love of knowledge."

"Understandable. Forgivable. We're not too different, really. Allowing for forty-odd years between us. Don't worry so much about your motives, Ned. Go to the stars, see, do. Enjoy. Eventually life will smash you, the way it's smashed me, but that's far off. Sometime, never, who knows? Forget about that."

"I'll try," Rawlins said.

He felt the warmth of the man now, the reaching out of genuine sympathies. There was still that carrier wave of nightmare, though, the unending broadcast out of the mucky depths of the soul, attenuated at this distance but unmistakable. Imprisoned by his pity, Rawlins hesitated to say what it now was time to say. Boardman prodded him irritably. "Go *on,* boy! Slip it in!"

"You look very far away," Muller said.

"Just thinking how—how sad it is that you won't trust us at all, that you have such a negative attitude toward humanity."

"I come by it honestly."

"You don't need to spend the rest of your life in this maze, though. There's a way out."

"Garbage."

"Listen to me," Rawlins said. He took a deep breath and flashed his quick, transparent grin. "I talked about your case to our expedition medic. He's studied neurosurgery. He knew all about you. He says there's now a way to fix what you have. Recently developed, the last couple of years. It—shuts off the broadcast, Dick. He said I should tell you. We'll take you back to Earth. For the operation, Dick. The operation. The cure."

2

The sharp glittering barbed word came swimming along on the breast of a torrent of bland sounds and speared him in the gut. *Cure!* He stared. There was reverberation from the looming dark buildings. *Cure. Cure. Cure.* Muller felt the poisonous temptation gnawing at his liver. "No," he said. "That's garbage. A cure's impossible."

"How can you be so sure?"

"I know."

"Science progresses in nine years. They understand how the brain works, now. Its electrical nature. What they did, they built a tremendous simulation in one of the lunar labs—oh, a few years ago, and they ran it all through from start to finish. As a matter of fact I'm sure they're desperate to have you back, because you prove all their theories. In your present condition. And by operating on you, reversing your broadcast, they'll demonstrate that they were right. All you have to do is come back with us."

Muller methodically popped his knuckles. "Why didn't you mention this earlier?"

"I didn't know a thing about it."

"Of course."

"Really. We didn't expect to be finding you here, you realize. At first nobody was too sure who you were, why you were here. I explained it. And then the medic remembered that there was this treatment. What's wrong—don't you believe me?"

"You look so angelic," Muller said. "Those sweet blue eyes and that golden hair. What's your game, Ned? Why are you reeling off all this nonsense?"

Rawlins reddened. "It isn't nonsense!"

"I don't believe you. And I don't believe in your cure."

"It's your privilege. But you'll be the loser if—"

"Don't threaten me!"

"I'm sorry."

There was a long, sticky silence.

Muller revolved a maze of thoughts. To leave Lemnos? To have the curse lifted? To hold a woman in his arms again? Breasts like fire against his skin? Lips? Thighs? To rebuild his career. To reach across the heavens once more? To shuck nine years of anguish? To believe? To go? To submit?

"No," he said carefully. "There is no cure for what I have."

"You keep saying that. But you can't know."

"It doesn't fit the pattern. I believe in destiny, boy. In compensating tragedy. In the overthrow of the proud. The gods don't deal out temporary tragedies. They don't take back their punishments after a few years. Oedipus didn't get his eyes back. Or his mother. They didn't let Prometheus off his rock. They—"

"You aren't living a Greek play," Rawlins told him. "This is the real world. The patterns don't always fall neatly. Maybe the gods have decided that you've suffered enough. And so long as we're having a literary discussion— they forgave Orestes, didn't they? So why isn't nine years here enough for you?"

"*Is* there a cure?"

"The medic says there is."

"I think you're lying to me, boy."

Rawlins glanced away. "What do I have to gain by lying?"

"I can't guess."

"All right, I'm lying," Rawlins said brusquely. "There's no way to help you. Let's talk about something else. Why don't you show me the fountain where that liqueur rises?"

"It's in Zone C," said Muller. "I don't feel like going there just now. Why did you tell me that story if it wasn't true?"

"I said we'd change the subject."

"Let's assume for the moment that it *is* true," Muller persisted. "That if I go back to Earth I can be cured. I want to let you know that I'm not interested, not even with a guarantee. I've seen Earthmen in their true nature. They kicked me when I was down. Not sporting, Ned. They stink. They reek. They gloried in what had happened to me."

"That isn't so!"

"What do you know? You were a child. Even more then than now. They treated me as filth because I showed them what was inside themselves. A mirror for their dirty souls. Why should I go back to them now? Why do I need them? Worms. Pigs. I saw them as they really are, those few

months I was on Earth after Beta Hydri IV. The look
in the eyes, the nervous smile as they back away from
me. Yes, Mr. Muller. Of course, Mr. Muller. Just don't
come too close, Mr. Muller. Boy, come by here some
time at night and let me show you the constellations
as seen from Lemnos. I've given them my own names.
There's the Dagger, a long keen one. It's about to be thrust
into the Back. Then there's the Shaft. And you can see the
Ape, too, and the Toad. They interlock. The same star is
in the forehead of the Ape and the left eye of the Toad.
That star is Sol, my friend. An ugly little yellow star, the
color of thin vomit. Whose planets are populated by ugly
little people who have spread like trickling urine over the
whole universe."

"Can I say something that might offend you?" Rawlins
asked.

"You can't offend me. But you can try."

"I think your outlook is distorted. You've lost your
perspective, all these years here."

"No. I've learned how to see for the first time."

"You're blaming humanity for being human. It's not
easy to accept someone like you. If you were sitting here
in my place, and I in yours, you'd understand that. It
hurts to be near you. *It hurts.* Right now I feel pain in
every nerve. If I came closer I'd feel like crying. You
can't expect people to adjust quickly to somebody like
that. Not even your loved ones could—"

"I had no loved ones."

"You were married."

"Terminated."

"Liaisons, then."

"They couldn't stand me when I came back."

"Friends?"

"They ran," Muller said. "On all six legs they scuttled
away from me."

"You didn't give them time."

"Time enough."

"No," Rawlins persisted. He shifted about uneasily on
the chair. "Now I'm going to say something that will
really hurt you, Dick. I'm sorry, but I have to. What
you're telling me is the kind of stuff I heard in college.
Sophomore cynicism. The world is despicable, you say.

Evil, evil, evil. You've seen the true nature of mankind, and you don't want to have anything to do with mankind ever again. Everybody talks that way at eighteen. But it's a phase that passes. We get over the confusions of being eighteen, and we see that the world is a pretty decent place, that people try to do their best, that we're imperfect but not loathsome—"

"An eighteen-year-old has no right to those opinions. I do. I come by my hatreds the hard way."

"But why cling to them? You seem to be glorying in your own misery. Break loose! Shake it off! Come back to Earth with us and forget the past. Or at least forgive."

"No forgetting. No forgiving." Muller scowled. A tremor of fear shook him, and he shivered. What if this were true? A genuine cure? Leave Lemnos? He was a trifle embarrassed. The boy had scored a palpable hit with that line about sophomore cynicism. It was. Am I really such a misanthrope? A pose. He forced me to adopt it. Polemic reasons. Now I choke on my own stubbornness. But there's no cure. The boy's transparent; he's lying, though I don't know why. He wants to trap me, to get me aboard that ship of theirs. What if it's true? Why not go back? Muller could supply his own answers. It was the fear that held him. To see Earth's billions. To enter the stream of life. Nine years on a desert island and he dreaded to return. He slipped into a pit of depression, recognizing hard truths. The man who would be a god was just a pitiful neurotic now, clinging to his isolation, spitting defiance at a possible rescuer. Sad, Muller thought. Very sad.

Rawlins said, "I can feel the flavor of your thoughts changing."

"You *can?*"

"Nothing specific. But you were angry and bitter before. Now I'm getting something—wistful."

"No one ever told me he could detect meanings," Muller said in wonder. "No one ever said much. Only that it was painful to be near me. Disgusting."

"Why did you go wistful just then, though? If you did. Thinking of Earth?"

"Maybe I was." Muller hastily patched the sudden gap in his armor. His face darkened. He clenched his jaws. He stood up and deliberately approached Rawlins, watching the young man struggling to hide his real feelings of discomfort. Muller said, "I think you'd better get about your archaeologizing now, Ned. Your friends will be angry again."

"I still have some time."

"No, you don't. Go!"

3

Against Charles Boardman's express orders, Rawlins insisted on returning all the way to the Zone F camp that evening. The pretext was that Rawlins had to deliver the new flask of liqueur which he had finally been able to wheedle out of Muller. Boardman wanted one of the other men to pick up the flask, sparing Rawlins from the risks of Zone F's snares. Rawlins needed the direct contact, though. He was badly shaken. His resolve was sagging.

He found Boardman at dinner. A polished dining-board of dark wood mortised with light woods sat before him. Out of elegant stoneware he ate candied fruits, brandied vegetables, meat extracts, pungent juices. A carafe of wine of a deep olive hue was near his fleshy hand. Mysterious pills of several types rested in the shallow pits of an oblong block of black glass; from time to time Boardman popped one into his mouth. Rawlins stood at the sector opening for a long while before Boardman appeared to notice him.

"I told you not to come here, Ned," the old man said finally.

"Muller sends you this." Rawlins put the flask down beside the carafe of wine.

"We could have talked without this visit."

"I'm tired of that. I needed to see you." Boardman left him standing and did not interrupt his meal. "Charles, I don't think I can keep up the pretense with him."

"You did a excellent job today," said Boardman, sipping his wine. "Quite convincing."

"Yes, I'm learning how to tell lies. But what's the use? You heard him. Mankind disgusts him. He's not going to cooperate once we get him out of the maze."

"He isn't sincere. You said it yourself, Ned. Cheap sophomore cynicism. The man loves mankind. That's why he's so bitter—because his love has turned sour in his mouth. But it hasn't turned to hate. Not really."

"You weren't there, Charles. You weren't talking to him."

"I watched. I listened. And I've known Dick Muller for forty-odd years."

"The last nine years are the ones that count. They've twisted him." Rawlins bent into a crouch to get on Boardman's level. Boardman nudged a candied pear onto his fork, equalized gravity, and flipped it idly toward his mouth. He's intentionally ignoring me, Rawlins thought. He said, "Charles, be serious. I've gone in there and told Muller some monstrous lies. I've offered him a completely fraudulent cure, and he threw it back in my face."

"Saying he didn't believe it existed. But he *does* believe, Ned. He's simply afraid to come out of hiding."

"Please. Listen. Assume he does come to believe me. Assume he leaves the maze and puts himself in our hands. Then what? Who gets the job of telling him that there isn't any cure, that we've tricked him shamelessly, that we merely want him to be our ambassador again, to visit a bunch of aliens twenty times as strange and fifty times as deadly as the ones that ruined his life? *I'm* not going to break that news to him!"

"You won't have to, Ned. I'll be the one."

"And how will he react? Are you simply expecting him to smile and bow and say, very clever, Charles, you've done it again? To yield and do whatever you want? No. He couldn't possibly. You can get him out of the maze, maybe, but the very methods you use for getting him out make it inconceivable that he can be of any use to you once he *is* out."

"That isn't necessarily true," said Boardman calmly.

"Will you explain the tactics you propose to use, then, once you've informed him that the cure is a lie and that there's a dangerous new job he has to undertake?"

"I prefer not to discuss future strategy now."

"I resign," Rawlins said.

Boardman had been expecting something like that. A noble gesture; a moment of headstrong defiance; a rush of virtue to the brain. Abandoning now his studied detachment, he looked up, his eyes locking firmly on Rawlins'. Yes, there was strength there. Yes, determination. But not guile. Not yet.

Quietly Boardman said, "You resign? After all your talk of service to mankind? We need you, Ned. You're the indispensable man, our link to Muller."

"My dedication to mankind includes a dedication to Dick Muller," Rawlins said stiffly. "He's part of mankind, whether he thinks so or not. I've already committed a considerable crime against him. If you won't let me in on the rest of this scheme, I'm damned if I'll have any part in it."

"I admire your convictions."

"My resignation still stands."

"I even agree with your position," said Boardman. "I'm not proud of what we must do here. I see it as part of historical necessity—the need for an occasional betrayal for the greater good. I have a conscience too, Ned, an eighty-year-old conscience, very well developed. It doesn't atrophy with age. We just learn to live with its complaints, that's all."

"How are you going to get Muller to cooperate? Drug him? Torture him? Brainblast him?"

"None of those."

"What, then? I'm serious, Charles. My role in this job ends right here unless I know what's ahead."

Boardman coughed, drained his wine, ate a peach, took three pills in quick succession. Rawlins' rebellion had been inevitable, and he was prepared for it, and yet he was annoyed that it had come. Now was the time for calculated risks. He said, "I see that it's time to drop the pretenses, then, Ned. I'll tell you what's in store for Dick Muller—but I want you to consider it within the framework of the larger position. Don't forget that the little game we've been playing on this planet isn't simply a matter of private moral postures. At the risk of sounding pretentious, I have to remind you that mankind's fate is at stake."

"I'm listening, Charles."

"Very well. Dick Muller must go to our extragalactic friends and convince them that human beings are indeed an intelligent species. Agreed? He alone is capable of doing this, because of his unique inability to cloak his thoughts."

"Agreed."

"Now, it isn't necessary to convince the aliens that we're good people, or that we're honorable people, or that we're lovable people. Simply that we have minds and can think. That we feel, that we sense, that we are something other than clever machines. For our purposes, it doesn't matter *what* emotions Dick Muller is radiating so long as he's radiating something."

"I begin to see."

"Therefore, once he's out of the maze we can tell him what his assignment is to be. No doubt he'll get angry at our trickery. But beyond his anger he may see where his duty lies. I hope so. You seem to think he won't. But it makes no difference, Ned. He won't be given an option once he leaves his sanctuary. He'll be taken to the aliens and handed over to them to make contact. It's brutal, I know. But necessary."

"His cooperation is irrelevant, then," said Rawlins slowly. "He'll just be dumped. Like a sack."

"A *thinking* sack. As our friends out there will learn."

"I—"

"No, Ned. Don't say anything now. I know what you're thinking. You hate the scheme. You have to. I hate it myself. Just go off, now, and think it over. Examine it from all sides before you come to a decision. If you want out tomorrow, let me know and we'll carry on somehow without you, but promise me you'll sleep on it, first. Yes? This is no time for a snap judgment."

Rawlins' face was pale a moment. Then color flooded into it. He clamped his lips. Boardman smiled benignly. Rawlins clenched his fists, squinted, turned, hastily went out.

A calculated risk.

Boardman took another pill. Then he reached for the

flask Muller had sent him. He poured a little. Sweet, gingery, strong. An excellent liqueur. He let it rest a while on his tongue.

eleven

Muller had almost come to like the Hydrans. What he remembered most clearly and most favorably about them was their grace of motion. They seemed virtually to float. The strangeness of their bodies had never bothered him much; he was fond of saying that one did not need to go far from Earth to find the grotesque. Giraffes. Lobsters. Sea anemones. Squids. Camels. Look objectively at a camel and ask yourself what is less strange about its body than about a Hydran's.

He had landed in a damp, dreary part of the planet, a little to the north of its equator, on an amoeboid continent occupied by a dozen large quasicities, each spread out over several thousand square kilometers. His life-support system, specially designed for this mission, was little more than a thin filtration sheet that clung to him like a second skin. It fed air to him through a thousand dialysis plaques. He moved easily if not comfortably within it.

He walked for an hour through a forest of the giant toadstool-like trees before he came upon any of the natives. The trees ran to heights of several hundred meters; perhaps the gravity, five-eighths Earthnorm, had something to do with that. Their curving trunks did not look sturdy. He suspected that an external woody layer no thicker than a fingertip surrounded a broad core of soggy pulp. The cap-like crowns of the trees met in a nearly continuous canopy overhead, cutting almost all light from the forest floor. Since the planet's cloud layer permitted only a hazy pearl-colored glow to come through, and even that was intercepted by the trees, a maroon darkness prevailed below.

When he encountered the aliens he was surprised to find that they were about three meters tall. Not since childhood had he felt so diminished; he stood ringed by them, straining upward to meet their eyes. Now it was time for his exercise in applied hermeneutics. In a quiet voice he said, "My name is Richard Muller. I come in friendship from the peoples of the Terran Cultural Sphere."

Of course they could not understand that. But they remained motionless. He imagined that their expressions were not unfriendly.

Dropping to his knees, Muller traced the Pythagorean Theorem in the soft moist soil.

He looked up. He smiled. "A basic concept of geometry. A universal pattern of thought."

Their vertical slitlike nostrils flickered slightly. They inclined their heads. He imagined that they were exchanging thoughtful glances. With eyes in a circlet entirely around their heads, they did not need to change posture to do that.

"Let me display some further tokens of our kinship," Muller said to them.

He sketched a line on the ground. A short distance from it he sketched a pair of lines. At a greater distance he drew three lines. He filled in the signs. $1 + 11 = 111$.

"Yes?" he said. "We call it addition."

The jointed limbs swayed. Two of his listeners touched arms. Muller remembered how they had obliterated the spying eye as soon as they had discovered it, not hesitating even to examine it. He had been prepared for the same reaction. Instead they were listening. A promising sign. He stood up and pointed to his marks on the ground.

"Your turn," he said. He spoke quite loudly. He smiled quite broadly. "Show me that you understand. Speak to me in the universal language of mathematics."

No response at first.

He pointed again. He gestured at his symbols, then extended his hand, palm upraised, to the nearest Hydran.

After a long pause one of the other Hydrans moved fluidly forward and let one of its globe-like foot-pedestals hover over the lines in the soil. The leg moved lightly and the lines vanished as the alien smoothed the soil.

"All right," said Muller. "Now you draw something."

The Hydran returned to its place in the circle.

"Very well," Muller said. "There's another universal language. I hope this doesn't offend your ears." He drew a soprano recorder from his pocket and put it between his lips. Playing through the filtration sheet was cumbersome. He caught breath and played a diatonic scale. Their limbs fluttered a bit. They could hear, then, or at any rate could sense vibrations. He shifted to the minor, and gave them another diatonic scale. He tried a chromatic scale. They looked a trifle more agitated. Good for you, he thought. Connoisseurs. Perhaps the whole-tone scale is more in keeping with the cloudiness of this planet, he decided. He played both of them, and gave them a bit of Debussy for good measure.

"Does that get to you?" he asked.

They appeared to be conferring.

They walked away from him.

He tried to follow. He was unable to keep up, and soon he lost sight of them in the dark, misty forest; but he persevered, and found them clustered, as if waiting for him, farther on. When he neared them they began to move again. In this way they led him, by fits and starts, into their city.

He subsisted on synthetics. Chemical analysis showed that it would be unwise to try local foods.

He drew the Pythagorean Theorem many times. He sketched a variety of arithmetical processes. He played Schönberg and Bach. He constructed equilateral triangles. He ventured into solid geometry. He sang. He spoke French, Russian, and Mandarin, as well as English, to show them the diversity of human tongues. He displayed a chart of the periodic table. After six months he still knew nothing more about the workings of their minds than he had an hour before landing. They tolerated his presence, but they said nothing to him; and when they communicated with one another it was mainly in quick, evanescent gestures, touches of the hand, flickers of the nostrils. They had a spoken language, it seemed, but it was so soft and breathy that he could not begin to distinguish words or even syllables. He recorded whatever he heard, of course.

Eventually they wearied of him and came for him.

He slept.

He did not discover until much later what had been done to him while he slept.

2

He was eighteen years old, naked under the California stars. The sky was ablaze. He felt he could reach for the stars and pluck them from the heavens.

To be a god. To possess the universe.

He turned to her. Her body was cool and slender, slightly tense. He cupped her breasts. He let his hand move across her flat belly. She shivered a little. "Dick," she said. "Oh." To be a god, he thought. He kissed her lightly, and then not lightly. "Wait," she said. "I'm not ready." He waited. He helped her get ready, or did the things he thought would help her get ready, and shortly she began to gasp. She spoke his name again. How many stars can a man visit in one lifetime? If each star has an average of twelve planets, and there are one hundred million stars within a galactic globe X light-years in diameter.... Her thighs opened. His eyes closed. He felt soft old pine needles against his knees and elbows. She was not his first, but the first that counted. As the lightning ripped through his brain he was dimly aware of her response, tentative, halting, then suddenly vigorous. The intensity of it frightened him, but only for a moment, and he rode with her to the end.

To be a god must be something like this.

They rolled over. He pointed to the stars and called off their names for her, getting half of them wrong, but she did not need to know that. He shared his dreams with her. Later they made love a second time, and it was even better.

He hoped it would rain at midnight, so they could dance in the rain, but the sky was clear. They went swimming instead, and came out shivering, laughing. When he took her home she washed down her pill with Chartreuse. He told her that he loved her.

They exchanged Christmas cards for several years.

3

The eighth world of Alpha Centauri B was a gas giant, with a low-density core and gravity not much more troublesome than that of Earth. Muller had honeymooned there the second time. It was partly a business trip, for there were troubles with the colonists on the sixth planet; they were talking of setting up a whirlpool effect that would suck away most of the eighth world's highly useful atmosphere to use as raw materials.

Muller's conferences with the locals went fairly well. He persuaded them to accept a quota system for their atmospheric grabs, and even won their praise for the little lesson in interplanetary morality he had administered. Afterward he and Nola were government guests for a holiday on the eighth world. Nola, unlike Lorayn, was the traveling sort. She would be accompanying him on many of his voyages.

Wearing support suits, they swam in an icy methane lake. They ran laughing along ammonia coasts. Nola was as tall as he, with powerful legs, dark red hair, green eyes. They embraced in a warm room of one-way windows overhanging a forlorn sea that stretched for hundreds of thousands of kilometers.

"For always," she said.

"Yes. For always."

Before the week ended they quarreled bitterly. But it was only a game; for the more fiercely they quarreled, the more passionate was the reconciliation. For a while. Later they stopped bothering to quarrel. When the option in the marriage contract came up, neither of them wanted to renew. Afterward, as his reputation grew, he sometimes received friendly letters from her. He had tried to see her when he returned from Beta Hydri IV to Earth. Nola, he thought, would help him in his troubles. She of all people would not turn away from him. For old times' sake.

But she was vacationing on Vesta with her seventh husband. Muller found that out from her fifth husband. He had been her third. He did not call her. He began to see there was no point in it.

4

The surgeon said, "I'm sorry, Mr. Muller. There's nothing we can do for you. I wouldn't want to raise false hopes. We've graphed your whole neural network. We can't find the sites of alteration. I'm terribly sorry."

5

He had had nine years to sharpen his memories. He had filled a few cubes with reminiscences, but that had mainly been in the early years of his exile, when he worried about having his past drift away to be lost in fog. He discovered that the memories grew keener with age. Perhaps it was training. He could summon sights, sounds, tastes, odors. He could reconstruct whole conversations convincingly. He was able to quote the full texts of several treaties he had negotiated. He could name England's kings in sequence from first to last, William I through William VII. He remembered the names of the girls whose bodies he had known.

He admitted to himself that, given the chance, he would go back. Everything else had been pretense and bluster. He had fooled neither Ned Rawlins nor himself, he knew. The contempt he felt for mankind was real, but not the wish to remain isolated. He waited eagerly for Rawlins to return. While he waited he drank several goblets of the city's liqueur; he went on a killing spree, nervously gunning down animals he could not possibly consume in a year's time; he conducted intricate dialogues with himself; he dreamed of Earth.

6

Rawlins was running. Muller, standing a hundred meters deep in Zone C, saw him come striding through the entrance, breathless, flushed.

"You shouldn't run in here," Muller said, "not even in the safer zones. There's absolutely no telling—"

Rawlins sprawled down beside a flanged limestone tub, gripping its sides and sucking air. "Get me a drink, will you?" he gasped. "That liqueur of yours—"

"Are you all right?"

"No."

Muller went to the fountain nearby and filled a handy flask with the sharp liqueur. Rawlins did not wince at all as Muller drew near to give it to him. He seemed altogether unaware of Muller's emanation. Greedily, sloppily, he emptied the flask, letting driblets of the gleaming fluid roll down his chin and on his clothes. Then he closed his eyes a moment.

"You look awful," Muller said. "As though you've just been raped, I'd say."

"I have."

"What's the trouble?"

"Wait. Let me get my breath. I ran all the way from Zone F."

"You're lucky to be alive, then."

"Perhaps."

"Another drink?"

"No," said Rawlins. "Not just yet."

Muller studied him, perplexed. The change was striking and unsettling, and mere fatigue could not account for it all. Rawlins was bloodshot, flushed, puffy-faced; his facial muscles were tightly knit; his eyes moved randomly, seeking and not finding. Drunk? Sick? Drugged?

Rawlins said nothing.

After a long moment Muller said, just to fill the vacuum of silence, "I've done a lot of thinking about our last conversation. I've decided that I was acting like a damned fool. All that cheap misanthropy I was dishing up." Muller knelt and tried to peer into the younger man's shifting eyes. "Look here, Ned, I want to take it all back. I'm willing to return to Earth for treatment. Even if the treatment's experimental, I'll chance it. I mean, the worst that can happen is that it won't cure me, and—"

"There's no treatment," said Rawlins dully.

"No—treatment . . ."

"No treatment. None. It was all a lie."

"Yes. Of course."

"You said so yourself," Rawlins reminded him. "You didn't believe a word of what I was saying. Remember?"

"A lie."

"You didn't understand why I was saying it, but you said it was nonsense. You told me I was lying. You wondered what I had to gain by lying. I *was* lying, Dick."

"Lying."

"Yes."

"But I've changed my mind," said Muller softly. "I was ready to go back to Earth."

"There's no hope of a cure," Rawlins told him.

He slowly rose to his feet and ran his hand through his long golden hair. He arranged his disarrayed clothing. He picked up the flask, went to the liqueur fountain and filled it. Returning, he handed the flask to Muller, who drank from it. Rawlins finished the flask. Something small and voracious-looking ran past them and slipped through the gate leading to Zone D.

Finally Muller said, "Do you want to explain some of this?"

"We aren't archaeologists."

"Go on."

"We came here looking especially for you. It wasn't any accident. We knew all along where you were. You were tracked from the time you left Earth nine years ago."

"I took precautions."

"They weren't any use. Boardman knew where you were going, and he had you tracked. He left you in peace because he had no use for you. But when a need developed he had to come after you. He was holding you in reserve, so to speak."

"Charles Boardman sent you to fetch me?" Muller asked.

"That's why we're here, yes. That's the whole purpose of this expedition," Rawlins replied tonelessly. "I was picked to make contact with you because you once knew my father and might trust me. And because I have an innocent face. All the time Boardman was directing me, telling me what to say, coaching me, even telling me what mistakes to make, how to blunder successfully. He told me to get into that cage, for instance. He thought it would help win your sympathy."

"Boardman is *here*? Here on Lemnos?"

"In Zone F. He's got a camp there."

"*Charles* Boardman?"

"He's here, yes. Yes."

Muller's face was stony. Within, all was turmoil. "Why did he do all this? What does he want with me?"

Rawlins said, "You know that there's a third intelligent race in the universe, beside us and the Hydrans."

"Yes. They had just been discovered when I left. That was why I went to visit the Hydrans. I was supposed to arrange a defensive alliance with them, before these other people, these extragalactics, came in contact with us. It didn't work. But what does this have to—"

"How much do you know about these extragalactics?"

"Very little," Muller admitted. "Essentially, nothing but what I've just told you. The day I agreed to go to Beta Hydri IV was the first time I had heard about them. Boardman told me, but he wouldn't say anything else. All he said was that they were extremely intelligent—a superior species, he said—and that they lived in a neighboring cluster. And that they had a galactic drive and might visit us some day."

"We know more about them now," Rawlins said.

"First tell me what Boardman wants with me."

"Everything in order, and it'll be easier." Rawlins grinned, perhaps a bit tipsily. He leaned against the stone tub and stretched his legs far out in front of himself. He said, "We don't actually know a great deal about the extragalactics. What we did was send out a ramjet, throw it into warp, and bring it out a few thousand light-years away. Or a few million light-years. I don't know the details. Anyway, it was a drone ship with all sorts of eyes. The place it went to was one of the X-ray galaxies, classified information, but I've heard it was either in Cygnus A or Scorpius II. We found that one planet of the galactic system was inhabited by an advanced race of very alien aliens."

"How alien?"

"They can see all up and down the spectrum," Rawlins said. "Their basic visual range is in the high frequencies. They see by the light of X-rays. They also seem to be able to make use of the radio frequencies to see, or at least to get some kind of sensory information. And they pick up most wavelengths in between, except that they don't have a great deal of interest in the stuff between infrared and ultraviolet. What we like to call the visible spectrum."

"Wait a minute. Radio senses? Do you have any idea how long radio waves are? If they're going to get any information out of a single wave, they'll need eyes or receptors or whatever of gigantic size. How big are these beings supposed to be?"

"They could eat elephants for breakfast," said Rawlins.

"Intelligent life doesn't come that big."

"What's the limitation? This is a gas giant planet, all ocean, no gravity to speak of. They float. They have no square-cube problems."

"And a bunch of superwhales has developed a technological culture?" Muller asked. "You won't get me to believe—"

"They have," said Rawlins. "I've told you, these are very alien aliens. They can't build machinery themselves. But they have slaves."

"Oh," said Muller quietly.

"We're only beginning to understand this, and of course I don't have much of the inside information myself, but as I piece it together it seems that these beings make use of lower life-forms, turning them essentially into radio-controlled robots. They'll use anything with limbs and mobility. They started with certain animals of their own planet, a small dolphin-like form perhaps on the threshold of intelligence, and worked through them to achieve a space drive. Then they got to neighboring planets—land planets—and took control of pseudoprimates, protochimps of some kind. They look for fingers. Manual dexterity counts a great deal with them. At present their sphere of influence covers some eighty light-years and appears to be spreading at an exponential rate."

Muller shook his head. "This is worse nonsense than the stuff you were handing me about a cure. Look, there's a limiting velocity for radio transmission, right? If they're controlling flunkeys from eighty light-years away, it'll take eighty years for any command to reach its destination. Every twitch of a muscle, every trifling movement—"

"They can leave their home world," said Rawlins.

"But if they're so big—"

"They've used their slave beings to build gravity tanks. They also have a star drive. All their colonies are run by overseers in orbit a few thousand kilometers up, floating in a simulated home-world environment. It takes one overseer to run one planet. I suppose they rotate tours of duty."

Muller closed his eyes a moment. The image came to him of these colossal, unimaginable beasts spreading through their distant galaxy, impressing animals of all sorts into service, forging a captive society, vicariously technological, and drifting in orbit like spaceborne whales to direct and coordinate the grandiose improbable enterprise while themselves remaining incapable of the smallest physical act. Monstrous masses of glossy pink protoplasm, fresh from the sea, bristling with perceptors functioning at both ends of the spectrum. Whispering to one another in pulses of X-rays. Sending out orders via radio. No, he thought. No.

"Well," he said at length, "what of it? They're in another galaxy."

"Not any longer. They've impinged on a few of our outlying colonies. Do you know what they do when they find a human world? They station an orbiting overseer above it and take control of the colonists. They find that humans make outstanding slaves, which isn't very surprising. At the moment they have six of our worlds. They had a seventh, but we shot up their overseer. Now they make it much harder to do that. They just take control of our missiles as they home in, and throw them back."

"If you're inventing this," said Muller, "I'll kill you!"

"It's true. I swear."

"When did this begin?"

"Within the past year."

"And what happens? Do they just march right through our galaxy and turn us all into zombies?"

"Boardman thinks we have one chance to prevent that."

"Which is?"

Rawlins said, "The aliens don't appear to realize that we're intelligent beings. We can't communicate with them, you see. They function on a completely nonverbal level, some kind of telepathic system. We've tried all sorts of ways to reach them, bombarding them with messages at every wavelength, without any flicker of a sign that they're receiving us. Boardman believes that if we could persuade them that we have—well, souls—they might leave us alone. God knows why he thinks so. It's some kind of computer prediction. He feels that these aliens work on a consistent moral scheme, that they're willing to grab any animals which look useful, but that they wouldn't touch a species that's on the same side of the intelligence boundary as they are. And if we could show them somehow—"

"They see that we have cities. That we have a star drive. Doesn't that prove intelligence?"

"Beavers make dams," said Rawlins. "But we don't make treaties with beavers. We don't pay reparations when we drain their marshes. We know that in some way a beaver's feelings don't count."

"Do we? Or have we simply decided arbitrarily that beavers are expendable? And what's this talk of an intelligence boundary? There's a continuous spectrum of intelligence, from the protozoa up through the primates. We're a little smarter than the chimps, sure, but is it a *qualitative* difference? Does the mere fact that we can record our knowledge and use it again make that much of a change?"

"I don't want to argue philosophy with you," Rawlins said hoarsely. "I'm trying to tell you what the situation is—and how it affects you."

"Yes. How it affects me."

"Boardman thinks that we really can get the radio beasts to leave our galaxy alone if we show them that we're closer to them in intelligence than we are to their other slaves. If we get across to them that we have emotions, needs, ambitions, dreams."

Muller spat. "Hath not a Jew eyes? Hath not a Jew hands, organs, dimensions, senses, affections, passions? If you prick us, do we not bleed?"

"Like that, yes."

"How do we get this across to them if they don't speak a verbal language?"

"Don't you see?" Rawlins asked.

"No, I—*yes*. Yes. God, yes!"

"We have one man, out of all our billions, who doesn't need words to communicate. He broadcasts his inner feelings. His soul. We don't know what frequency he uses, but *they* might."

"Yes. Yes."

"And so Boardman wanted to ask you to do one more thing for mankind. To go to these aliens. To allow them to pick up your broadcast. To show them what we are, that we're something more than beasts."

"Why the talk of taking me to Earth to be cured, then?"

"A trick. A trap. We had to get you out of the maze somehow. Once you were out, we could tell you the story and ask you to help."

"Admitting that there was no cure?"

"Yes."

"What makes you think I would lift a finger to keep all of man's worlds from being swallowed up?"

"Your help wouldn't have to be voluntary," Rawlins said.

7

Now it came flooding forth, the hatred, the anguish, the fear, the jealousy, the torment, the bitterness, the mockery, the loathing, the contempt, the despair, the viciousness, the fury, the desperation, the vehemence, the agitation, the grief, the pangs, the agony, the furor, the fire. Rawlins pulled back as though singed. Now Muller cruised the depths of desolation. A trick, a trick, all a trick! Used again. Boardman's tool. Muller blazed. He spoke only a few words aloud; the rest came from within, pouring out, the gates wide, nothing penned back, a torrent of anger.

When the wild spasm passed Muller said, standing braced between two jutting façades, "Boardman would dump me onto the aliens whether I was willing to go or not?"

"Yes. He said this was too important to allow you free choice. Your wishes are irrelevant. The many against the one."

With deadly calm Muller said, "You're part of this conspiracy. Why have you been telling me all this?"

"I resigned."

"Of course."

"No, I mean it. Oh, I was part of it. I was going along with Boardman, yes, I was lying in everything I said to you. But I didn't know the last part—that you wouldn't be given any choice. I had to pull out there. I couldn't let them do this to you. I had to tell you the truth."

"Very thoughtful. I now have two options, eh, Ned? I can let myself be dragged out of here to play catspaw for Boardman again—or I can kill myself a minute from now and let mankind go to hell. Yes?"

"Don't talk like that," Rawlins said edgily.

"Why not? Those are my options. You were kind enough to tell me the real situation, and now I can react as I choose. You've handed me a death sentence, Ned."

"No."

"What else is there? Let myself be used again?"

"You could—cooperate with Boardman," Rawlins said. He licked his lips. "I know it sounds crazy. But you could show him what you're made of. Forget all this bitterness. Turn the other cheek. Remember that Boardman isn't all of humanity. There are billions of innocent people—"

"Father, forgive them, for they know not what they do."

"Yes!"

"Every one of those billions would run from me if I came near."

"What of it? They can't help that! But they're your own people!"

"And I'm one of theirs. They didn't think of that when they cast me out."

"You aren't being rational."

"No I'm not. And I don't intend to start now. Assuming that it could affect humanity's destiny in the slightest if I became ambassador to these radio people—and I don't buy that idea at all—it would give me great pleasure to shirk my duty. I'm grateful to you for your warning. Now that at last I know what's going on here, I have the excuse I've been looking for all along. I know a thousand places here where death is quick and probably not painful. Then let Charles Boardman talk to the aliens himself. I—"

"Please don't move, Dick," said Boardman from a point about thirty meters behind him.

twelve

Boardman found all this distasteful. But it was also necessary, and he was not surprised that events had taken this turn. In his original analysis he had forecast two events of equal probability: that Rawlins would succeed in winning Muller out of the maze, and that Rawlins would ultimately rebel and blurt out the truth. He was prepared for either.

Now Boardman had advanced into the center of the maze, coming from Zone F to follow Rawlins before the damage became irreparable. He could predict one of Muller's likely responses: suicide. Muller would never commit suicide out of despair, but he might do it by way of vengeance. With Boardman were Ottavio, Davis, Reynolds, and Greenfield. Hosteen and the others were monitoring from outer zones. All were armed.

Muller turned. The look on his face was not easy to behold.

"I'm sorry, Dick," Boardman said. "We had to do this."

"You have no shame at all, do you?" Muller asked.

"Not where Earth is concerned."

"I realized that a long time ago. But I thought you were human, Charles. I didn't comprehend your depths."

"I wish we didn't have to do any of this, Dick. But we do. Come with us."

"No."

"You can't refuse. The boy's told you what's at stake. We already owe you more than we can ever repay, Dick, but run the debt a little higher. Please."

"I'm not leaving Lemnos. I feel no sense of obligation to humanity. I won't do your work."

"Dick—"

Muller said, "Fifty meters to the northwest of where I stand is a flame pit. I'm going to walk over and step into it. Within ten seconds there will be no more Richard

Muller. One unfortunate calamity will cancel out another, and Earth will be no worse off than it was before I acquired my special ability. Since you people didn't appreciate that ability before, I can't see any reason for letting you make use of it now."

"If you want to kill yourself," Boardman said, "why not wait a few months?"

"Because I don't care to be of service."

"That's childish. The last sin I'd ever imagine *you* committing."

"It was childish of me to dream of stars," Muller said. "I'm simply being consistent. The galactics can eat you alive, Charles. I don't care if they do. Won't you fancy being a slave? Somewhere under your skull you'll still be there, screaming to be released, and the radio messages will tell you which arm to lift, which leg to move. I wish I could last long enough to see that. But I'm going to walk into that flame pit. Do you want to wish me a good journey? Come close, let me touch your arm. Get a good dose of me first. Your last. I'll cease to give offense." Muller was trembling. His face was sweaty. His upper lip quivered.

Boardman said, "At least come out to Zone F with me. Let's sit down quietly and discuss this over brandy."

"Side by side?" Muller laughed. "You'd vomit. You couldn't bear it."

"I'm willing to talk."

"I'm not," Muller said. He took a shaky step toward the northwest. His big powerful body seemed shrunken and withered, nothing but sinews stretching tighter over a yielding armature. He took another step. Boardman watched. Ottavio and Davis stood beside him to the left; Reynolds and Greenfield on the other side, between Muller and the flame pit. Rawlins, like an afterthought, was alone at the far side of the group.

Boardman felt a throbbing in his larynx, a stirring and a tickle of tension in his loins. A great weariness possessed him, and at the same time a fierce soaring excitement of a kind he had not known since he had been a young man. He allowed Muller to take a third step toward self-destruction. Then, casually, Boardman gestured with two flicking fingers.

Greenfield and Reynolds pounced.

Catlike they darted forth, ready for this, and caught Muller by the inner forearms. Boardman saw the grayness sweep over their faces as the impact of Muller's field got to them. Muller struggled, heaved, tried to break loose. Davis and Ottavio were upon him now too. In the gathering darkness the group formed a surging Laocoon, Muller only half visible as the smaller men coiled and wound about his flexed battling body. A stungun would have been easier, Boardman reflected. But stunguns were risky, sometimes, on humans. They had been known to send hearts into wild runaways. They had no defibrillator here.

A moment more, and Muller was forced to his knees.

"Disarm him," Boardman said.

Ottavio and Davis held him. Reynolds and Greenfield searched him. From a pocket Greenfield pulled forth the deadly little windowed globe. "That's all he seems to be carrying," Greenfield said.

"Check carefully."

They checked. Meanwhile Muller remained motionless, his face frozen, his eyes stony. It was the posture and the expression of a man at the headsman's block. At length Greenfield looked up again. "Nothing," he said.

Muller said, "One of my left upper molars contains a secret compartment full of carniphage. I'll count to ten and bite hard, and I'll melt away before your eyes."

Greenfield swung around and grabbed for Muller's jaws.

Boardman said, "Leave him alone. He's joking."

"But how do we know—" Greenfield began.

"Let him be. Step back." Boardman gestured. "Stand five meters away from him. Don't go near him unless he moves."

They stepped away, obviously grateful to get back from the full thrust of Muller's field. Boardman, fifteen meters from him, could feel faint strands of pain. He went no closer.

"You can stand up now," Boardman said. "But please don't try to move. I regret this, Dick."

Muller got to his feet. His face was black with hatred. But he said nothing, nor did he move.

"If we have to," Boardman said, "we'll tape you in a

webfoam cradle and carry you out of the maze to the ship. We'll keep you in foam from then on. You'll be in foam when you meet the aliens. You'll be absolutely helpless. I would hate to do that to you, Dick. The other choice is willing cooperation. Go with us of your own free will to the ship. Do what we ask of you. Help us this last time."

"May your intestines rust," said Muller almost casually. "May you live a thousand years with worms eating you. May you choke on your own smugness and never die."

"Help us. Willingly."

"Put me in the webfoam, Charles. Otherwise I'll kill myself the first chance I get."

"What a villain I must seem, eh?" Boardman said. "But I don't want to do it this way. Come willingly, Dick."

Muller's reply was close to a snarl.

Boardman sighed. This was an embarrassment. He looked toward Ottavio.

"The webfoam," he said.

Rawlins, who had been standing as though in a trance, burst into sudden activity. He darted forward, seized Reynolds' gun from its holster, ran toward Muller and pressed the weapon into his hand. "There," he said thickly. "Now you're in charge!"

2

Muller studied the gun as though he had never seen one before, but his surprise lasted only a fraction of a second. He slipped his hand around its comfortable butt and fingered the firing stud. It was a familiar model, only slightly changed from those he had known. In a quick flaring burst he could kill them all. Or himself. He stepped back so they could not come upon him from the rear. Probing with his kickstaff, he checked the wall, found it trustworthy, and planted his shoulderblades against it. Then he moved the gun in an arc of some 270°, taking them all in.

"Stand close together," he said. "The six of you. Stand one meter apart in a straight row, and keep your hands out where I can see them at all times."

He enjoyed the black, glowering look that Boardman threw at Ned Rawlins. The boy seemed dazed, flushed, confused, a figure in a dream. Muller waited patiently as the six men arranged themselves according to his orders. He was surprised at his own calmness.

"You look unhappy, Charles," he said. "How old are you now, eighty years? You'd like to live that other seventy, eighty, ninety, I guess. You have your career planned, and the plan doesn't include dying on Lemnos. Stand still, Charles. And stand straight. You won't win any pity from me by trying to look old and sagging. I know that dodge. You're as healthy as I am, beneath the phony flab. Healthier. Straight, Charles!"

Boardman said raggedly, "If it'll make you feel better, Dick, kill me. And then go aboard the ship and do what we want you to do. I'm expendable."

"Do you mean that?"

"Yes."

"I almost think you do," Muller said wonderingly. "You crafty old bastard, you're offering a trade! Your life for my cooperation! But where's the *quid pro quo?* I don't enjoy killing. It won't soothe me at all to burn you down. I'll still have my curse."

"The offer stands."

"Rejected," Muller said. "If I kill you, it won't be as part of any deal. But I'm much more likely to kill myself. You know, I'm a decent man at heart. Somewhat unstable, yes, and who's to blame me for that? But decent. I'd rather use this gun on me than on you. I'm the one who's suffering. I can end it."

"You could have ended it at any time in the past nine years," Boardman pointed out. "But you survived. You devoted all your ingenuity to staying alive in this murderous place."

"Ah. Yes. But that was different! An abstract challenge, man against the maze. A test of my skills. Ingenuity. But if I kill myself now, I thwart you. I put the thumb to the nose, with all of mankind watching. I'm the indispensable man, you say? What better way then, to pay mankind back for my pain?"

"We regretted your suffering," said Boardman.

"I'm sure you wept bitterly for me. But that was all you did. You let me go creeping away, diseased, corrupt, unclean. Now comes the release. Not really suicide, but revenge." Muller smiled. He turned the gun to finest beam and let its muzzle rest against his chest. A touch of the finger, now. His eyes raked their faces. The four soldiers did not seem to care. Rawlins appeared deep in shock. Only Boardman was animated with concern and fright. "I could kill you first, I suppose, Charles. As a lesson to our young friend—the wages of deceit is death. But no. That would spoil everything. You have to live, Charles. To go back to Earth and admit that you let the indispensable man slip through your grasp. What a blotch on your career! To fail your most important assignment! Yes. Yes. My pleasure. Falling dead here, leaving you to pick up the pieces."

His finger tightened on the stud.

"Now," he said. "Quickly."

"*No!*" Boardman screamed. "For the love of—"

"Man," said Muller, and laughed, and did not fire. His arm relaxed. He tossed the weapon contemptuously toward Boardman. It landed almost at his feet.

"Foam!" Boardman cried. "Quick!"

"Don't bother," said Muller. "I'm yours."

3

Rawlins took a long while to understand it. First they had the problem of getting out of the maze. Even with Muller as their leader, it was a taxing job. As they had suspected, coming upon the traps from the inner side was not the same as working through them from without. Warily Muller took them through Zone E; they could manage F well enough by now; and after they had dismantled their camp, they pressed on into G. Rawlins kept expecting Muller to bolt suddenly and hurl himself into some fearful snare. But he seemed as eager to come alive out of the maze as any of them. Boardman, oddly, appeared to recognize that. Though he watched Muller closely, he left him unconfined.

Feeling that he was in disgrace, Rawlins kept away from the others on the nearly silent outward march. He considered his career in ruins. He had jeopardized the lives of his companions and the success of the mission. Yet it had been worth it, he felt. A time comes when a man takes his stand against what he believes to be wrong.

The simple moral pleasure that he took in that was balanced and overbalanced by the knowledge that he had acted naively, romantically, foolishly. He could not bear to face Boardman now. He thought more than once of letting one of the deadly traps of these outer zones have him; but that too, he decided, would be naive, romantic, and foolish.

He watched Muller striding ahead—tall, proud, all tensions resolved, all doubts crystallized. And he wondered a thousand times why Muller had given back the gun.

Boardman finally explained it to him when they camped for the night in a precarious plaza near the outward side of Zone G.

"Look at me," Boardman said. "What's the matter? Why can't you look at me?"

"Don't toy with me, Charles. Get it over with."

"Get what over with?"

"The tonguelashing. The sentence."

"It's all right, Ned. You helped us get what we wanted. Why should I be angry?"

"But the gun—I gave him the gun—"

"Confusion of ends and means again. He's coming with us. He's doing what we wanted him to do. That's what counts."

Floundering, Rawlins asked, "And if he had killed himself—or us?"

"He wouldn't have done either."

"You can say that, now. But for the first moment, when he held the gun—"

"No," Boardman said. "I told you earlier, we'd work on his sense of honor. Which we had to reawaken. You did that. Look, here I am, the brutal agent of a brutal and amoral society, right? And I confirm all of Muller's worst thoughts about mankind. Why should he help a tribe of wolves? And here you are, young and innocent, full of hope and dreams. You remind him of the mankind he once served, before the cynicism corroded him. In your blundering way you try to be moral in a world that shows no trace of morality or meaning. You demonstrate sympathy, love for a fellow man, the willingness to make a dramatic gesture for the sake of righteousness. You show Muller that there's still hope in humanity. See? You defy me, and give him a gun and make him master of the situation. He could do the obvious, and burn us down. He could do the slightly less obvious, and burn himself. Or he could match your gesture with one of his own, top it, commit a deliberate act of renunciation, express his revived sense of moral superiority. He does it. He tosses away the gun. You were vital, Ned. You were the instrument through which we won him."

"You make it sound so ugly when you spell it out that way, Charles. As if you had planned even this. Pushing me so far that I'd give him the gun, knowing that he—"

Boardman smiled.

"Did you?" Rawlins demanded suddenly. "No. You couldn't have calculated all those twists and turns. Now, after the fact, you're trying to claim credit for having engineered it all. But I saw you in the moment I handed him the gun. There was fear on your face, and anger. You weren't at all sure what he was going to do. Only when everything worked out could you claim it went according to plan. I see through you, Charles!"

"How delightful to be transparent," Boardman said gaily.

4

The maze seemed uninterested in holding them. Carefully they traced their outward path, but they met few challenges and no serious dangers. Quickly they went toward the ship.

They gave Muller a forward cabin, well apart from the quarters of the crew. He seemed to accept that as a necessity of his condition, and showed no offense. He was withdrawn, subdued, self-contained; an ironic smile often played on his lips, and much of the time his eyes displayed a glint of contempt. But he was willing to do as they directed. He had had his moment of supremacy; now he was theirs.

Hosteen and his men bustled through the liftoff preparations. Muller remained in his cabin. Boardman went to him, alone, unarmed. He could make noble gestures too.

They faced each other across a low table. Muller waited, silent, his face cleansed of emotion. Boardman said after a long moment, "I'm grateful to you, Dick."

"Save it."

"I don't mind if you despise me. I did what I had to do. So did the boy. And now so will you. You couldn't forget that you were an Earthman, after all."

"I wish I could."

"Don't say that. It's easy, glib, cheap bitterness, Dick. We're both too old for glibness. The universe is a perilous place. We do our best. Everything else is unimportant."

He sat quite close to Muller. The emanation hit him broadside, but he deliberately remained in place. That wave of despair welling out to him made him feel a thousand years old. The decay of the body, the crumbling of the soul, the heat-death of the galaxy ... the coming of winter ... emptiness ... ashes. ...

"When we reach Earth," said Boardman crisply, "I'll put you through a detailed briefing. You'll come out of it knowing as much about the radio people as we do, which isn't saying a great deal. After that you'll be on your own. But I'm sure you'll realize, Dick, that the hearts and souls of billions of Earthmen will be praying for your success and safety."

"Who's being glib now?" Muller asked.

"Is there anyone you'd like me to have waiting for you when we dock Earthside?"

"No."

"I can send word ahead. There are people who've never stopped loving you, Dick. They'll be there if I ask them."

Muller said slowly, "I see the strain in your eyes, Charles. You feel the nearness of me, and it's ripping you apart. You feel it in your gut. In your forehead. Back of your breastbone. Your face is going gray. Your cheeks are sagging. You'll sit here if it kills you, yes, because that's your style. But it's hell for you. If there's anyone on Earth who never stopped loving me, Charles, the least I can do is spare her from hell. I don't want to meet anyone. I don't want to see anyone. I don't want to talk to anyone."

"As you wish," said Boardman. Beads of sweat hung

from his bushy brows and dropped to his cheeks. "Perhaps you'll change your mind when you're close to Earth."

"I'll never be close to Earth again," Muller said.

thirteen

He spent three weeks absorbing all that was known of the giant extragalactic beings. At his insistence he did not set foot on Earth during that time, nor was his return from Lemnos made known to the public. They gave him quarters in a bunker on Luna and he lived quietly beneath Copernicus, moving like a robot through steely gray corridors lit by warm glowing torches. They showed him all the cubes. They ran off a variety of reconstructs in every sensory mode. Muller listened. He absorbed. He said very little.

They kept well away from him, as they had on the voyage from Lemnos. Whole days passed in which he saw no human being. When they came to him they remained at a distance of ten meters and more.

He did not object.

The exception was Boardman, who visited him three times a week and made a point always of coming well within the pain range. Muller found that contemptible. Boardman seemed to be patronizing him with this voluntary and wholly unnecessary submission to discomfort. "I wish you'd keep away," Muller told him on the fifth visit. "We can talk by screen. Or you could stay by the door."

"I don't mind the close contact."

"I do," said Muller. "Has it ever occurred to you that I've begun to find mankind as odious as mankind finds me? The reek of your meaty body, Charles—it goes into my nostrils like a spike. Not just you; all the others too. Sickening. Hideous. Even the look of your faces. The pores. The stupid gaping mouths. The ears. Look at a human ear closely some time, Charles. Have you ever seen anything more repulsive than that pink wrinkled cup? You all disgust me!"

"I'm sorry you feel that way," Boardman said.

The briefing went on and on. Muller was ready after

the first week to undertake his assignment, but no, first they had to feed him all the data in the bank. He absorbed the information with twitchy impatience. A shadow of his old self remained to find it fascinating, a challenge worth accepting. He would go. He would serve as before. He would honor his obligation.

At last they said he could depart.

From Luna they took him by iondrive to a point outside the orbit of Mars, where they transferred him to a warp-drive ship already programmed to kick him to the edge of the galaxy. Alone. He would not, on this voyage, have to take care not to distress the crew by his presence. There were several reasons for this, the most important being that the mission was officially considered close to suicidal; and, since a ship could make the voyage without the use of a crew, it would have been rash to risk lives— other than his, of course. But he was a volunteer. Besides, Muller had requested a solo flight.

He did not see Boardman during the five days prior to his departure, nor had he seen Ned Rawlins at all since their return from Lemnos. Muller did not regret the absence of Boardman, but he sometimes wished he could have another hour with Rawlins. There was promise in that boy. Behind all the confusion and the foggy innocence, Muller thought, lay the seeds of manhood.

From the cabin of his small sleek ship he watched the technicians drifting in space, getting ready to sever the transfer line. Then they were returning to their own ship. Now he heard from Boardman, a final message, a Boardman special, inspirational, go forth and do your duty for mankind, et cetera, et cetera. Muller thanked him graciously for his words.

The communications channel was cut.

Moments later Muller entered warp.

2

The aliens had taken possession of three solar systems on the fringes of the galactic lens, each star having two Earth-settled planets. Muller's ship was aimed at a greenish-gold star whose worlds had been colonized only forty years before. The fifth planet, dry as iron, belonged to a

Central Asian colonization society which was trying to establish a series of pastoral cultures where nomad virtues could be practiced. The sixth, with a more typically Earth-like mixture of climates and environments, was occupied by representatives of half a dozen colonization societies, each on its own continent. The relations between these groups, often intricate and touchy, had ceased to matter within the past twelve months, for both planets now were under control of extragalactic overseers.

Muller emerged from warp twenty light-seconds from the sixth planet. His ship automatically went into an observation orbit, and the scanners began to report. Screens showed him the surface picture; via template overlay he was able to compare the configurations of the outposts below with the pattern as it had been prior to alien conquest. The amplified images were quite interesting. The original settlements appeared on his screen in violet, and the recent extensions in red. Muller observed that about each of the colonies, regardless of its original ground plan, there had sprouted a network of angular streets and jagged avenues. Instinctively he recognized the geometries as alien. There sprang to mind the vivid memory of the maze; and though the patterns here bore no resemblance to those of the maze, they were alike in their lack of recognizable symmetries. He rejected the possibility that the labyrinth of Lemnos had been built long ago by direction of the radio beings. What he saw here was only the similarity of total difference. Aliens built in alien ways.

In orbit, seven thousand kilometers above the sixth planet, was a glistening capsule, slightly longer on one axis than on the other, which had about the mass of a large interstellar transport ship. Muller found a similar capsule in orbit about the fifth world. The overseers.

It was impossible for him to open communications with either of these capsules or with the planets beyond. All channels were blocked. He twisted dials fitfully for more than an hour, ignoring the irritable responses of the ship's brain which kept telling him to give up the idea. At last he conceded.

He brought his ship close to the nearer orbiting capsule. To his surprise the ship remained under his control.

Destructive missiles that had come this close to alien over-seers had been commandeered, but he was able to navigate. A hopeful sign? Was he under scan, and was the alien able to distinguish him from a hostile weapon? Or was he being ignored?

At a distance of one million kilometers he matched velocities with the alien satellite and put his ship in a parking orbit around it. He entered his drop-capsule. He ejected himself and slid from his ship into darkness.

3

Now the alien seized him. There was no doubt. The drop-capsule was programmed for a minimum-expenditure orbit that would bring it skimming past the alien in due time, but Muller swiftly discovered that he was deviating from that orbit. Deviations are never accidental. His capsule was accelerating beyond the program, which meant that it had been grasped and was being drawn forward. He accepted that. He was icily calm, expecting nothing and prepared for everything. The drop-capsule eased down. He saw the gleaming bulk of the alien satellite now.

Skin to metal skin, the vehicles met and touched and joined.

A hatch slid open.

He drifted within.

His capsule came to rest on a board platform in an immense cavernous room hundreds of meters long, high, and broad. Fully suited, Muller stepped from it. He activated his gravity pads; for, as he had anticipated, gravity in here was so close to null that the pull was imperceptible. In the blackness he saw only a faint purplish glow. Against a backdrop of utter silence he heard a resonant booming sound, like an enormously amplified sigh, shuddering through the struts and trusses of the satellite. Despite his gravity pads he felt dizzy; beneath him the floor rolled. Through his mind went a sensation like the throbbing of the sea; great waves slammed against ragged beaches; a mass of water stirred and groaned in its global cavity; the world shivered beneath the burden. Muller felt a chill that his suit could not counteract. An irresistible force drew him. Hesitantly he moved, relieved and surprised to see that his limbs still obeyed his commands though he was not entirely their master. The awareness of something vast nearby, something heaving and pulsating and sighing, remained with him.

He walked down a night-drowned boulevard. He came to a low railing—a dull red line against the deep darkness —and pressed his leg against it, keeping contact with it as he moved forward. At one point he slipped and as he hit the railing with his elbow he heard the clang of metal traveling through the entire structure. Blurred echoes drifted back to him. As though walking the maze he passed through corridors and hatches, across interlocking compartments, over bridges that spanned dark abysses, down sloping ramplike debouchments into lofty chambers whose ceilings were dimly visible. Here he moved in blind confidence, fearing nothing. He could barely see. He had no vision of the total structure of this satellite. He could scarcely imagine the purpose of these inner partitions.

From that hidden giant presence came silent waves, an ever-intensifying pressure. He trembled in its grip. Still he moved on, until now he was in some central gallery, and by a thin blue glow he was able to discern levels dwindling below him, and far beneath his balcony a broad tank, and within the tank something sparkling, something huge.

"Here I am," he said. "Richard Muller. Earthman."

He gripped the railing and peered downward, expecting anything. Did the great beast stir and shift? Did it grunt? Did it call to him in a language he understood? He heard nothing. But he felt a great deal: slowly, subtly, he became aware of a contact, of a mingling, of an engulfment.

He felt his soul escaping through his pores.

The drain was unrelenting. Yet Muller chose not to resist; he yielded, he welcomed, he gave freely. Down in the pit the monster tapped his spirit, opened petcocks of neural energy, drew forth from him, demanded more, drew that too.

"Go on," Muller said, and the echoes of his voice danced around him, chiming, reverberating. "Drink! What's it like? A bitter brew, eh? Drink! Drink!" His knees buckled, and he sagged forward, and he pressed his forehead to the cold railing as his last reservoirs were plumbed.

He surrendered himself gladly, in glittering droplets. He gave up first love and first disappointment, April rain, fever and ache. Pride and hope, warmth and cold, sweet and sour. The scent of sweat and the touch of flesh, the thunder of music, the music of thunder, silken hair knotted between his fingers, lines scratched in spongy soil. Snorting stallions; glittering schools of tiny fish; the towers of Newer Chicago; the brothels of Under New Orleans. Snow. Milk. Wine. Hunger. Fire. Pain. Sleep. Sorrow. Apples. Dawn. Tears. Bach. Sizzling grease. The laughter of old men. The sun on the horizon, the moon on the sea, the light of other stars, the fumes of rocket fuel, summer flowers on a glacier's flank. Father. Mother. Jesus. Mornings. Sadness. Joy. He gave it all, and much more, and he waited for an answer. None came to him. And when he was wholly empty he lay face downward, drained, hollow, staring blindly into the abyss.

4

When he was able to leave, he left. The hatch opened to pass his drop-capsule, and it rose toward his ship. Shortly he was in warp. He slept most of the way. In the vicinity of Antares he cut in the override, took command of the ship, and filed for a change of course. There was no need to return to Earth. The monitor station recorded his request, checked routinely to see that the channel was clear, and allowed him to proceed at once to Lemnos. Muller entered warp again instantly.

When he emerged, not far from Lemnos, he found another ship already in orbit and waiting for him. He started to go about his business anyway, but the other ship insisted on making contact. Muller accepted the communication.

"This is Ned Rawlins," a strangely quiet voice said. "Why have you changed your flight plan?"

"Does it matter? I've done my job."

"You haven't filed a report."

"I'm reporting now, then. I visited the alien. We had a pleasant, friendly chat. Then it let me go home. Now I'm almost home. I don't know what effect my visit will have on the future of human history. End of report."

"What are you going to do now?"

"Go home, I said. This is home."

"Lemnos?"

"Lemnos."

"Dick, let me come aboard. Give me ten minutes with you—in person. Please don't say no."

"I don't say no," Muller replied.

Soon a small craft detached itself from the other ship and matched velocities with his. Patiently, Muller allowed the rendezvous to take place. Rawlins stepped into his ship and shed his helmet. He looked pale, drawn, older. His eyes held a different expression. They faced one another for a long silent moment. Rawlins advanced and took Muller's wrist in greeting.

"I never thought I'd see you again, Dick," he began. "And I wanted to tell you—"

He stopped abruptly.

"Yes?" Muller asked.

"I don't feel it," said Rawlins. *"I don't feel it!"*

"What?"

"You. Your field. Look, I'm right next to you. I don't feel a thing. All that nastiness, the pain, the despair—it isn't coming through!"

"The alien drank it all," said Muller calmly. "I'm not surprised. My soul left my body. Not all of it was put back."

"What are you talking about?"

"I could feel it soaking up everything that was within me. I knew it was changing me. Not deliberately. It was just an incidental alteration. A byproduct."

Rawlins said slowly, "You knew it, then. Even before I came on board."

"This confirms it, though."

"And yet you want to return to the maze. Why?"

"It's home."

"Earth's your home, Dick. There's no reason why you shouldn't go back. You've been cured."

"Yes," said Muller. "A happy ending to my doleful story. I'm fit to consort with humanity again. My reward for nobly risking my life a second time among aliens. How neatly done! But is humanity fit to consort with me?"

"Don't go down there, Dick. You're being irrational now. Charles sent me to get you. He's terribly proud of you. We all are. It would be a big mistake to lock yourself away in the maze now."

"Go back to your own ship, Ned," Muller said.

"If you go into the maze, so will I."

"I'll kill you if you do. I want to be left alone, Ned, do you understand that? I've done my job. My last job. Now I retire, purged of my nightmares." Muller forced a thin smile. "Don't come after me, Ned. I trusted you, and you would have betrayed me. Everything else is incidental. Leave my ship now. We've said all that we need to say to each other, I think, except goodbye."

"Dick—"

"Goodbye, Ned. Remember me to Charles. And to all the others."

"Don't do this!"

"There's something down there I don't want to lose," Muller said. "I'm going to claim it now. Stay away. All of you. Stay away. I've learned the truth about Earthmen. Will you go now?"

Silently Rawlins suited up. He moved toward the hatch. As he stepped through it, Muller said, "Say goodbye to all of them for me, Ned. I'm glad you were the last one I saw. Somehow it was easier that way."

Rawlins vanished through the hatch.

A short while later Muller programmed his ship for a hyperbolic orbit on a twenty-minute delay, got into his drop-capsule, and readied himself for the descent to Lemnos. It was a quick drop and a good landing. He came down right in the impact area, two kilometers from the gateway to the maze. The sun was high and bright. Muller walked briskly toward the maze.

He had done what they wanted him to do.

Now he was going home.

5

"He's still making gestures," Boardman said. "He'll come out of there."

"I don't think so," replied Rawlins. "He meant that."

"You stood next to him, and you felt nothing?"

"Nothing. He doesn't have it any more."

"Which he realizes?"

"Yes."

"He'll come out, then," Boardman said. "We'll watch him, and when he asks to be taken off Lemnos, we'll take him off. Sooner or later he'll need other people again. He's been through so much that he needs to think everything through, and I guess he sees the maze as the best place for that. He isn't ready to plunge back into normal life again. Give him two years, three, four. He'll come out. The two sets of aliens have cancelled each other's work on him, and he's fit to rejoin society."

"I don't think so," Rawlins said quietly. "I don't think it cancelled out so evenly. Charles, I don't think he's human at all—any more."

Boardman laughed. "Shall we bet? I'll offer five to one that Muller comes out of the maze voluntarily within five years."

"Well—"

"It's a bet, then."

Rawlins left the older man's office. Night had fallen. He crossed the bridge outside the building. In an hour he'd be dining with someone warm and soft and willing, who was awed beyond measure by her liaison with the famous Ned Rawlins. She was a good listener, who coaxed him for tales of daring deeds and nodded gravely as he spoke of the challenges ahead. She was also good in bed.

He paused on the bridge to look upward at the stars.

A million million blazing points of light shimmered in the sky. Out there lay Lemnos, and Beta Hydri IV, and the worlds occupied by the radio beings, and all man's dominion, and even, invisible but real, the home galaxy of the others. Out there lay a labyrinth in a broad plain, and a forest of spongy trees hundreds of meters high, and a thousand planets planted with the young cities of Earthmen, and a tank of strangeness orbiting a conquered world. In the tank lay something unbearably alien. On the thousand planets lived worried men fearing the future. Under the spongy trees walked graceful silent creatures with many arms. In the maze dwelled a . . . man.

Perhaps, Rawlins thought, I'll visit Muller in a year or two.

It was too early to tell how the patterns would form. No one yet knew how the radio people were reacting, if at all, to the things they had learned from Richard Muller. The role of the Hydrans, the efforts of men in their own defense, the coming forth of Muller from the maze, these were mysteries—shifting, variable. It was exciting and a little frightening to think that he would live through the time of testing that lay ahead.

He crossed the bridge. He watched starships shattering the darkness overhead. He stood motionless, feeling the pull of the stars. All the universe tugged at him, each star exerting its finite power. The glow of the heavens dazzled him. Beckoning pathways lay open. He thought of the man in the maze. He thought too of the girl, lithe and passionate, dark-eyed, her eyes mirrors of silver, her body awaiting him.

Suddenly he was Dick Muller, once also twenty-four years old, with the galaxy his for the asking. Was it any different for you, he wondered? What did you feel when you looked up at the stars? Where did it hit you? Here. Here. Just where it hits me. And you went out there. And found. And lost. And found something else. Do you remember, Dick, the way you once felt? Tonight in your windy maze, what will you think about? Will you remember?

Why did you turn away from us, Dick?

What have you become?

He hurried to the girl who waited for him. They sipped young wine, tart, electric. They smiled through a candle's flickering glow. Later her softness yielded to him, and still later they stood close together on a balcony looking out over the greatest of all man's cities. Lights stretched toward infinity, rising to meet those other lights above. He slipped his arm around her, put his hand on her bare flank, held her against him.

She said, "How long do you stay this time?"

"Four more days."

"And when will you come back?"

"When the job's done."

"Ned, will you ever rest? Will you ever say you've had enough, that you won't go out any longer, that you'll take one planet and stick to it?"

"Yes," he said vaguely. "I suppose. After a while."

"You don't mean it. You're just saying it. None of you ever settle down."

"We can't," he murmured. "We keep going. There are always more worlds ... new suns. ..."

"You want too much. You want the whole universe. It's a sin, Ned. You have to accept limits."

"Yes," he said. "You're right. I know you're right." His fingers traveled over satin-smooth flesh. She trembled. He said, "We do what we have to do. We try to learn from the mistakes of others. We serve our cause. We attempt to be honest with ourselves. How else can it be?"

"The man who went back into the maze—"

"—is happy," Rawlins said. "He's following his chosen course."

"How can that be?"

"I can't explain."

"He must hate us all terribly to turn his back on the whole universe like that."

"He's beyond hate," Rawlins said. "Somehow. He's at peace. Whatever he is."

"Whatever?"

"Yes," he said gently. He felt the midnight chill and led her inside. They stood by the bed. The candle was nearly out. He kissed her solemnly, and thought of Dick Muller again, and wondered what maze was waiting for him at the end of his own path. He drew her into his arms and felt the impress of hardening flesh against his own cool skin. They lowered themselves. His hands sought, grasped, caressed. Her breath grew ragged.

When I see you again, Dick, I have much to tell you, he thought.

She said, "Why did he lock himself into the maze again, Ned?"

"For the same reason that he went among aliens in the first place. For the reason that it all happened."

"And that reason was?"

"He loved mankind," Rawlins said. It was as good an epitaph as any. He held the girl tightly. But he left before dawn.

NIGHTWINGS

For Harlan,
to remind him of open windows,
the currents of the Delaware River,
quarters with two heads,
and other pitfalls.

Part I

NIGHTWINGS

Roum is a city built on seven hills. They say it was a capital of man in one of the earlier cycles. I did not know of that, for my guild was Watching, not Remembering; but yet as I had my first glimpse of Roum, coming upon it from the south at twilight, I could see that in former days it must have been of great significance. Even now it was a mighty city of many thousands of souls.

Its bony towers stood out sharply against the dusk. Lights glimmered appealingly. On my left hand the sky was ablaze with splendor as the sun relinquished possession; streaming bands of azure and violet and crimson folded and writhed about one another in the nightly dance that brings the darkness. To my right, blackness had already come. I attempted to find the seven hills, and failed, and still I knew that this was that Roum of majesty toward which all roads are bent, and I felt awe and deep respect for the works of our bygone fathers.

We rested by the long straight road, looking up at Roum. I said, "It is a goodly city. We will find employment there."

Beside me, Avluela fluttered her lacy wings. "And food?" she asked in her high, fluty voice. "And shelter? And wine?"

"Those too," I said. "All of those."

"How long have we been walking, Watcher?" she asked.

"Two days. Three nights."

"If I had been flying, it would have been more swift."

"For you," I said. "You would have left us far behind and never seen us again. Is that your desire?"

She came close to me and rubbed the rough fabric of my sleeve, and then she pressed herself at me the way a flirting cat might do. Her wings unfolded into two broad sheets of gossamer through which I could still see the sunset and the evening lights, blurred, distorted, magical. I sensed the fragrance of her midnight hair. I put my arms to her and embraced her slender, boyish body.

She said, "You know it is my desire to remain with you always, Watcher. Always!"

"Yes, Avluela."

"Will we be happy in Roum?"

"We will be happy," I said, and released her.

"Shall we go into Roum now?"

"I think we should wait for Gormon," I said, shaking my head. "He'll be back soon from his explorations." I did not want to tell her of my weariness. She was only a child, seventeen summers old; what did she know of weariness or of age? And I was old. Not as old as Roum, but old enough.

"While we wait," she said, "may I fly?"

"Fly, yes."

I squatted beside our cart and warmed my hands at the throbbing generator while Avluela prepared to fly. First she removed her garments, for her wings have little strength and she cannot lift such extra baggage. Lithely, deftly, she peeled the glassy bubbles from her tiny feet and wriggled free of her crimson jacket and of her soft, furry leggings. The vanishing light in the west sparkled over her slim form. Like all Fliers, she carried no surplus body tissue: her breasts were mere bumps, her buttocks flat, her thighs so spindly that there was a span of inches between them when she stood. Could she have weighed more than a quintal? I doubt it. Looking at her, I felt, as always, gross and earthbound, a thing of loathsome flesh, and yet I am not a heavy man.

By the roadside she genuflected, knuckles to the ground, head bowed to knees, as she said whatever ritual it is that the Fliers say. Her back was to me. Her delicate wings fluttered, filled with life, rose about her like a cloak whipped up by the breeze. I could not comprehend how such wings could possibly lift even so slight a form as Avluela's. They were not hawk-wings but butterfly-wings, veined and transparent, marked here and there with blotches of pigment, ebony and turquoise and scarlet. A sturdy ligament joined them to the two flat pads of muscle beneath her sharp shoulderblades; but what she did not have was the massive breastbone of a flying creature, the bands of corded muscle needed for flight. Oh, I know that the Fliers use more than muscle to get aloft, that there are mystical disciplines in their mystery. Even so, I, who was of the Watchers, remained skeptical of the more fantastic guilds.

Avluela finished her words. She rose; she caught the breeze with her wings; she ascended several feet. There she remained, suspended between earth and sky, while her wings beat frantically. It was not yet night, and Avluela's wings were merely nightwings. By day she could not fly, for the terrible pressure of the solar wind would hurl her to the ground. Now, midway between dusk and dark, it was still not the best time for her to go up. I saw her thrust toward the east by the remnant of light in the sky. Her arms as well as her wings thrashed; her small pointed face was grim with concentration; on her thin lips were the words of her guild. She doubled her body and shot it out, head going one way, rump the other; and abruptly she hovered horizontally, looking groundward, her wings thrashing against the air. *Up, Avluela! Up!*

Up it was, as by will alone she conquered the vestige of light that still glowed.

With pleasure I surveyed her naked form against the darkness. I could see her clearly, for a Watcher's eyes are keen. She was five times her own height in the air, now, and her wings spread to their full expanse, so that the towers of Roum were in partial eclipse for me. She waved. I threw her a kiss and offered words of love. Watchers do not marry, nor do they engender children, but yet Avluela was as a daughter to me, and I took pride in her flight. We had traveled together a year, now, since we had first met in Agupt, and it was as though I had known her all my long life. From her I drew a renewal of strength. I do not know what it was she drew from me: security, knowledge, a continuity with the days before her birth. I hoped only that she loved me as I loved her.

Now she was far aloft. She wheeled, soared, dived, pirouetted, danced. Her long black hair streamed from her scalp. Her body seemed only an incidental appendage to those two great wings which glistened and throbbed and gleamed in the night. Up she rose, glorying in her freedom from gravity, making me feel all the more leaden-footed; and like some slender rocket she shot abruptly away in the direction of Roum. I saw the soles of her feet, the tips of her wings; then I saw her no more.

I sighed. I thrust my hands into the pits of my arms to keep them warm. How is it that I felt a winter chill while the girl Avluela could soar joyously bare through the sky?

It was now the twelfth of the twenty hours, and time once again for me to do the Watching. I went to the cart, opened my cases, prepared the instruments. Some of the dial covers were yellowed and faded; the indicator needles had lost their luminous coating; sea stains defaced the instrument housings, a relic of the time that pirates had assailed me in Earth Ocean. The worn and cracked levers and nodes responded easily to my touch as I entered the preliminaries. First one prays for a pure and perceptive mind; then one creates the affinity with one's instruments; then one does the actual Watching, searching the starry heavens for the enemies of man. Such was my skill and my craft. I grasped handles and knobs, thrust things from my mind, prepared myself to become an extension of my cabinet of devices.

I was only just past my threshold and into the first phase of Watchfulness when a deep and resonant voice behind me said, "Well, Watcher, how goes it?"

I sagged against the cart. There is a physical pain in being wrenched so unexpectedly from one's work. For a moment I felt claws clutching at my heart. My face grew hot; my eyes would not focus; the saliva drained from my throat. As soon as I could, I took the proper protective measures to ease the metabolic drain, and severed myself from my instruments. Hiding my trembling as much as possible, I turned around.

Gormon, the other member of our little band, had appeared and stood jauntily beside me. He was grinning, amused at my distress, but I could not feel angry with him. One does not show anger at a guildless person no matter what the provocation.

Tightly, with effort, I said, "Did you spend your time rewardingly?"

"Very. Where's Avluela?"

I pointed heavenward. Gormon nodded.

"What have you found?" I asked.

"That this city is definitely Roum."

"There never was doubt of that."

"For me there was. But now I have proof."

"Yes?"

"In the overpocket. Look!"

From his tunic he drew his overpocket, set it on the pavement beside me, and expanded it so that he could insert his hands into its mouth. Grunting a little, he began to pull something heavy from the pouch—something of white stone—a long marble column, I now saw, fluted, pocked with age.

"From a temple of Imperial Roum!" Gormon exulted.

"You shouldn't have taken that."

"Wait!" he cried, and reached into the overpocket once more. He took from it a handful of circular metal plaques and scattered them jingling at my feet. "Coins! Money! Look at them, Watcher! The faces of the Caesars!"

"Of whom?"

"The ancient rulers. Don't you know your history of past cycles?"

I peered at him curiously. "You claim to have no guild, Gormon. Could it be you are a Rememberer and are concealing it from me?"

"Look at my face, Watcher. Could I belong to any guild? Would a Changeling be taken?"

"True enough," I said, eyeing the golden hue of him, the thick waxen skin, the red-pupiled eyes, the jagged mouth. Gormon had been weaned on teratogenetic drugs; he was a monster, handsome in his way, but a monster nevertheless, a Changeling, outside the laws and customs of man as they are practiced in the Third Cycle of civilization. And there is no guild of Changelings.

"There's more," Gormon said. The overpocket was infinitely capacious; the contents of a world, if need be, could be stuffed into its shriveled gray maw, and still it would be no longer than a man's hand. Gormon took from it bits of machinery, reading spools, an angular thing of brown metal that might have been an ancient tool, three squares of shining glass, five slips of paper—*paper!*—and a host of other relics of antiquity. "See?" he said. "A fruitful stroll, Watcher! And not just random booty. Everything recorded, everything labeled, stratum, estimated age, position when *in situ*. Here we have many thousands of years of Roum."

"Should you have taken these things?" I asked doubtfully.

"Why not? Who is to miss them? Who of this cycle cares for the past?"

"The Rememberers."

"They don't need solid objects to help them do their work."

"Why do you want these things, though?"

"The past interests me, Watcher. In my guildless way I have my scholarly pursuits. Is that wrong? May not even a monstrosity seek knowledge?"

"Certainly, certainly. Seek what you wish. Fulfill yourself in your own way. This is Roum. At dawn we enter. I hope to find employment here."

"You may have difficulties."

"How so?"

"There are many Watchers already in Roum, no doubt. There will be little need for your services."

"I'll seek the favor of the Prince of Roum," I said.

"The Prince of Roum is a hard and cold and cruel man."

"You know of him?"

Gormon shrugged. "Somewhat." He began to stuff his artifacts back in the overpocket. "Take your chances with him, Watcher. What other choice do you have?"

"None," I said, and Gormon laughed, and I did not.

He busied himself with his ransacked loot of the past. I found myself deeply depressed by his words. He seemed so sure of himself in an uncertain world, this guildless one, this mutated monster, this man of inhuman look; how could he be so cool, so casual? He lived without concern for calamity and mocked those who admitted to fear. Gormon had been traveling with us for nine days, now, since we had met him in the ancient city beneath the volcano to the south by the edge of the sea. I had not suggested that he join us; he had invited himself along, and at Avluela's bidding I accepted. The roads are dark and cold at this time of year, and dangerous beasts of many species abound, and an old man journeying with a girl might well consider taking with him a brawny one like Gormon. Yet there were times I wished he had not come with us, and this was one.

Slowly I walked back to my equipment.

Gormon said, as though first realizing it, "Did I interrupt you at your Watching?"

I said mildly, "You did."

"Sorry. Go and start again. I'll leave you in peace." And he gave me his dazzling lopsided smile, so full of charm that it took the curse off the easy arrogance of his words.

I touched the knobs, made contact with the nodes, monitored the dials. But I did not enter Watchfulness, for I remained aware of Gormon's presence and fearful that he would break into my concentration once again at a painful moment, despite his promise. At length I looked away from the apparatus. Gormon stood at the far side of the road, craning his neck for some sight of Avluela. The moment I turned to him he became aware of me.

"Something wrong, Watcher?"

"No. The moment's not propitious for my work. I'll wait."

"Tell me," he said. "When Earth's enemies really do come from the stars, will your machines let you know it?"

"I trust they will."

"And then?"

"Then I notify the Defenders."

"After which your life's work is over?"

"Perhaps," I said.

"Why a whole guild of you, though? Why not one master center where the Watch is kept? Why a bunch of itinerant Watchers drifting from place to place?"

"The more vectors of detection," I said, "the greater the chance of early awareness of the invasion."

"Then an individual Watcher might well turn his machines on and not see anything, with an invader already here."

"It could happen. And so we practice redundancy."

"You carry it to an extreme, I sometimes think." Gormon laughed. "Do you actually believe an invasion is coming?"

"I do," I said stiffly. "Else my life was a waste."

"And why should the star people want Earth? What do we have here besides the remnants of old empires? What would they do with miserable Roum? With Perris? With Jorslem? Rotting cities! Idiot princes! Come, Watcher, admit it: the invasion's a myth, and you go through meaningless motions four times a day. Eh?"

"It is my craft and my science to Watch. It is yours to jeer. Each of us to our speciality, Gormon."

"Forgive me," he said with mock humility. "Go, then, and Watch."

"I shall."

Angrily I turned back to my cabinet of instruments, determined now to ignore any interruption, no matter how brutal. The stars were out; I gazed at the glowing constellations, and automatically my mind registered the many worlds. Let us Watch, I thought. Let us keep our vigil despite the mockers.

I entered full Watchfulness.

I clung to the grips and permitted the surge of power to rush through me. I cast my mind to the heavens and searched for hostile entities. What ecstasy! What incredible splendor! I who had never left this small planet roved the black spaces of the void, glided from star to burning star, saw the planets spinning like tops. Faces stared back at me as I journeyed, some without eyes, some with many eyes, all the complexity of the many-peopled galaxy accessible to me. I spied out possible concentrations of inimicable force. I inspected drilling-grounds and military encampments. I sought, as I had sought four times daily for all my adult life, for the invaders who had been promised us, the conquerors who at the end of days were destined to seize our tattered world.

I found nothing, and when I came up from my trance, sweaty and drained, I saw Avluela descending.

Feather-light she landed. Gormon called to her, and she ran, bare, her little breasts quivering, and he enfolded her smallness in his powerful arms, and they embraced, not passionately but joyously. When he released her she turned to me.

"Roum," she gasped. "*Roum!*"

"You saw it?"

"Everything! Thousands of people! Lights! Boulevards! A market! Broken buildings many cycles old! Oh, Watcher, how wonderful Roum is!"

"Your flight was a good one, then," I said.

"A miracle!"

"Tomorrow we go to dwell in Roum."

"No, Watcher, tonight, tonight!" She was girlishly eager, her face bright with excitement. "It's just a short journey more! Look, it's just over there!"

"We should rest first," I said. "We do not want to arrive weary in Roum."

"We can rest when we get there," Avluela answered. "Come! Pack everything! You've done your Watching, haven't you?"

"Yes. Yes."

"Then let's go. To Roum! To Roum!"

I looked in appeal at Gormon. Night had come; it was time to make camp, to have our few hours of sleep.

For once Gormon sided with me. He said to Avluela, "The Watcher's right. We can all use some rest. We'll go on into Roum at dawn."

Avluela pouted. She looked more like a child than ever. Her wings drooped; her underdeveloped body slumped. Petulantly she closed her wings until they were mere fist-sized humps on her back, and picked up the garments she had scattered on the road. She dressed while we made camp. I distributed food tablets; we entered our receptacles; I fell into troubled sleep and dreamed of Avluela limned against the crumbling moon, and Gormon flying beside her. Two hours before dawn I arose and performed my first Watch of the new day, while they still slept. Then I aroused them, and we went onward toward the fabled imperial city, onward toward Roum.

2

THE morning's light was bright and harsh, as though this were some young world newly created. The road was all but empty; people do not travel much in these latter days unless, like me, they are wanderers by habit and profession. Occasionally we stepped aside to let a chariot of some member of the guild of Masters go by, drawn by a dozen expressionless neuters harnessed in series. Four such vehicles went by in the first two hours of the day, each shuttered and sealed to hide the Master's proud features from the gaze of such common folk as we. Several rollerwagons laden with produce passed us, and a number of floaters soared overhead. Generally we had the road to ourselves, however.

The environs of Roum showed vestiges of antiquity: isolated columns, the fragments of an aqueduct transporting nothing from nowhere to nowhere, the portals of a vanished temple. That was the oldest Roum we saw, but there were accretions of the later Roums of subsequent cycles: the huts of peasants, the domes of power drains, the hulls of dwelling-towers. Infrequently we met with the burned-out shell of some ancient airship. Gormon examined everything, taking samples from time to time. Avluela looked, wide-eyed, saying nothing. We walked on, until the walls of the city loomed before us.

They were of a blue glossy stone, neatly joined, rising to a height of perhaps eight men. Our road pierced the wall through a corbeled arch; the gate stood open. As we approached the gate, a figure came toward us; he was hooded, masked, a man of extraordinary height wearing the somber garb of the guild of Pilgrims. One does not approach such a person oneself, but one heeds him if he beckons. The Pilgrim beckoned.

Through his speaking grille he said, "Where from?"

"The south. I lived in Agupt awhile, then crossed Land Bridge to Talya," I replied.

"Where bound?"

"Roum, awhile."

"How goes the Watch?"

"As customary."

"You have a place to stay in Roum?" the Pilgrim asked.

I shook my head. "We trust to the kindness of the Will."

"The Will is not always kind," said the Pilgrim absently. "Nor is there much need of Watchers in Roum. Why do you travel with a Flier?"

"For company's sake. And because she is young and needs protection."

"Who is the other one?"

"He is guildless, a Changeling."

"So I can see. But why is he with you?"

"He is strong and I am old, and so we travel together. Where are you bound, Pilgrim?"

"Jorslem. Is there another destination for my guild?"

I conceded the point with a shrug.

The Pilgrim said, "Why do you not come to Jorslem with me?"

"My road lies north now. Jorslem is in the south, close by Agupt."

"You have been to Agupt and not to Jorslem?" he said, puzzled.

"Yes. The time was not ready for me to see Jorslem."

"Come now. We will walk together on the road, Watcher, and we will talk of the old times and of the times to come, and I will assist you in your Watching, and you will assist me in my communions with the Will. Is it agreed?"

It was a temptation. Before my eyes flashed the image of Jorslem the Golden, its holy buildings and shrines, its places of renewal where the old are made young, its spires, its tabernacles. Even though I am a man set in his ways, I was willing at the moment to abandon Roum and go with the Pilgrim to Jorslem.

I said, "And my companions—"

"Leave them. It is forbidden for me to travel with the guildless, and I do not wish to travel with a female. You and I, Watcher, will go to Jorslem together."

Avluela, who had been standing to one side frowning through all this colloquy, shot me a look of sudden terror.

"I will not abandon them," I said.

"Then I go to Jorslem alone," said the Pilgrim. Out of his robe stretched a bony hand, the fingers long and white and steady. I touched my fingers reverently to the tips of his, and the Pilgrim said, "Let the Will give you mercy, friend Watcher. And when you reach Jorslem, search for me."

He moved on down the road without further conversation.

Gormon said to me, "You would have gone with him, wouldn't you?"

"I considered it."

"What could you find in Jorslem that isn't here? That's a holy city and so is this. Here you can rest awhile. You're in no shape for more walking now."

"You may be right," I conceded, and with the last of my energy I strode toward the gate of Roum.

Watchful eyes scanned us from slots in the wall. When we were at midpoint in the gate, a fat, pockmarked Sentinel with sagging jowls halted us and asked our business in Roum. I stated my guild and purpose, and he gave a snort of disgust.

"Go elsewhere, Watcher! We need only useful men here."

"Watching has its uses," I said mildly.

"No doubt. No doubt." He squinted at Avluela. "Who's this? Watchers are celibates, no?"

"She is nothing more than a traveling companion."

The Sentinel guffawed coarsely. "It's a route you travel often, I wager! Not that there's much to her. What is she, thirteen, fourteen? Come here, child. Let me check you for contraband." He ran his hands quickly over her, scowling as he felt her breasts, then raising an eyebrow as he encountered the mounds of her wings below her shoulders. "What's this? What's this? More in back than in front! A Flier, are you? Very dirty business, Fliers consorting with foul old Watchers." He chuckled and put his hand on Avluela's body in a way that sent Gormon starting forward in fury, murder in his fire-circled eyes. I caught him in time and grasped his wrist with all my strength, holding him back lest he ruin the three of us by an attack on the Sentinel. He tugged at me, nearly pulling me over; then he grew calm and subsided, icily watching as the fat one finished checking Avluela for "contraband."

At length the Sentinel turned in distaste to Gormon and said, "What kind of thing are you?"

"Guildless, your mercy," Gormon said in sharp tones. "The humble and worthless product of teratogenesis, and yet nevertheless a free man who desires entry to Roum."

"Do we need more monsters here?"

"I eat little and work hard."

"You'd work harder still, if you were neutered," said the Sentinel.

Gormon glowered. I said, "May we have entry?"

"A moment." The Sentinel donned his thinking cap and narrowed his eyes as he transmitted a message to the memory tanks. His face tensed with the effort; then it went slack, and moments later came the reply. We could not hear the transaction at all; but from his disappointed look, it appeared evident that no reason had been found to refuse us admission to Roum.

"Go on in," he said. "The three of you. Quickly!"

We passed beyond the gate.

Gormon said, "I could have split him open with a blow."

"And be neutered by nightfall. A little patience, and we've come into Roum."

"The way he handled her—!"

"You take a very possessive attitude toward Avluela," I said. "Remember that she's a Flier, and not sexually available to the guildless."

Gormon ignored my thrust. "She arouses me no more than you do, Watcher. But it pains me to see her treated that way. I would have killed him if you hadn't held me back."

Avluela said, "Where shall we stay, now that we're in Roum?"

"First let me find the headquarters of my guild," I said. "I'll register at the Watchers' Inn. After that, perhaps we'll hunt up the Fliers' Lodge for a meal."

"And then," said Gormon drily, "we'll go to the Guildless Gutter and beg for coppers."

"I pity you because you are a Changeling," I told him, "but I find it ungraceful of you to pity yourself. Come."

We walked up a cobbled, winding street away from the gate and into Roum itself. We were in the outer ring of the city, a residential section of low, squat houses topped by the unwieldy bulk of defense installations. Within lay the shining towers we had seen from the fields the night before; the remnant of ancient Roum carefully preserved across ten thousand years or more; the market, the factory zone, the communications hump, the temples of the Will, the memory tanks, the sleepers' refuges, the outworlders' brothels, the government buildings, the headquarters of the various guilds.

At the corner, beside a Second Cycle building with walls of rubbery texture, I found a public thinking cap and slipped it on my forehead. At once my thoughts raced down the conduit until they came to the interface that gave them access to one of the storage brains of a memory tank. I pierced the interface and saw the wrinkled brain itself, pale gray against the deep green of its housing. A Rememberer once told me that, in cycles past, men built machines to do their thinking for them, although these machines were hellishly expensive and required vast amounts of space and drank power gluttonously. That was not the worst of our forefathers' follies; but why build artificial brains when death each day liberates scores of splendid natural ones to hook into the memory tanks? Was it that they lacked the knowledge to use them? I find that hard to believe.

I gave the brain my guild identification and asked the coordinates of our inn. Instantly I received them, and we set out, Avluela on one side of me, Gormon on the other, myself wheeling, as always, the cart in which my instruments resided.

The city was crowded. I had not seen such throngs in sleepy, heat-fevered Agupt, nor at any other point on my northward journey. The streets were full of Pilgrims, secretive and masked. Jostling through them went busy Rememberers and glum Merchants and now and then the litter of a Master. Avluela saw a number of Fliers, but was barred by the tenets of her guild from greeting them until she had undergone her ritual purification. I regret to say that I spied many Watchers, all of whom looked upon me disdainfully and without welcome. I noted a good many Defenders and ample representation of such lesser guilds as Vendors, Servitors, Manufactories, Scribes, Communicants, and Transporters. Naturally, a host of neuters went silently about their humble business, and numerous outworlders of all descriptions flocked the streets, most of them probably tourists, some here to do what business could be done with the sullen, poverty-blighted people of Earth. I noticed many Changelings limping furtively through the crowd, not one of them as proud of bearing as Gormon beside me. He was unique among his kind; the others, dappled and piebald and asymmetrical, limbless or overlimbed, deformed in a thousand imaginative and artistic ways, were slinkers, squinters, shufflers, hissers, creepers; they were cutpurses, brain-drainers, organ-peddlers, repentance-mongers, gleam-buyers, but none held himself upright as though he thought he were a man.

The guidance of the brain was exact, and in less than an hour of walking we arrived at the Watchers' Inn. I left Gormon and Avluela outside and wheeled my cart within.

Perhaps a dozen members of my guild lounged in the main hall. I gave them the customary sign, and they returned it languidly. Were these the guardians on whom Earth's safety depended? Simpletons and weaklings!

"Where may I register?" I asked.

"New? Where from?"

"Agupt was my last place of registry."

"Should have stayed there. No need of Watchers here."

"Where may I register?" I asked again.

A foppish youngster indicated a screen in the rear of the great room. I went to it, pressed my fingertips against it, was interrogated, and gave my name, which a Watcher may utter only to another Watcher and only within the precincts of an inn. A panel shot open, and a puffy-eyed man who wore the Watcher emblem on his right cheek and not on the left, signifying his high rank in the guild, spoke my name and said, "You should have known better than to come to Roum. We're over our quota."

"I claim lodging and employment nonetheless."

"A man with your sense of humor should have been born into the guild of Clowns," he said.

"I see no joke."

"Under laws promulgated by our guild in the most recent session, an inn is under no obligation to take new lodgers once it has reached its assigned capacity. We are at our assigned capacity. Farewell, my friend."

I was aghast. "I know of no such regulation! This is incredible! For a guild to turn away a member from its own inn—when he arrives footsore and numb! A man of my age, having crossed Land Bridge out of Agupt, here as a stranger and hungry in Roum—"

"Why did you not check with us first?"

"I had no idea it would be necessary."

"The new regulations—"

"May the Will shrivel the new regulations!" I shouted. "I demand lodging! To turn away one who has Watched since before you were born—"

"Easy, brother, easy."

"Surely you have some corner where I can sleep—some crumbs to let me eat—"

Even as my tone had changed from bluster to supplication, his expression softened from indifference to mere disdain. "We have no room. We have no food. These are hard times for our guild, you know. There is talk that we will be disbanded altogether, as a useless luxury, a drain upon the Will's resources. We are very limited in our abilities. Because Roum has a surplus of Watchers, we all are on short rations as it is, and if we admit you our rations will be all the shorter."

"But where will I go? What shall I do?"

"I advise you," he said blandly, "to throw yourself upon the mercy of the Prince of Roum."

3

OUTSIDE, I told that to Gormon, and he doubled with laughter, guffawing so furiously that the striations on his lean cheeks blazed like bloody stripes. "The mercy of the Prince of Roum!" he repeated. "The mercy—of the Prince of Roum—"

"It is customary for the unfortunate to seek the aid of the local ruler," I said coldly.

"The Prince of Roum knows no mercy," Gormon told me. "The Prince of Roum will feed you your own limbs to ease your hunger!"

"Perhaps," Avluela put in, "we should try to find the Fliers' Lodge. They'll feed us there."

"Not Gormon," I observed. "We have obligations to one another."

"We could bring food out to him," she said.

"I prefer to visit the court first," I insisted. "Let us make sure of our status. Afterward we can improvise living arrangements, if we must."

She yielded, and we made our way to the palace of the Prince of Roum, a massive building fronted by a colossal column-ringed plaza, on the far side of the river that splits the city. In the plaza we were accosted by mendicants of many sorts, some not even Earthborn; something with ropy tendrils and a corrugated, noseless face thrust itself at me and jabbered for alms until Gormon pushed it away, and moments later a second creature, equally strange, its skin pocked with luminescent craters and its limbs studded with eyes, embraced my knees and pleaded in the name of the Will for my mercy. "I am only a poor Watcher," I said, indicating my cart, "and am here to gain mercy myself." But the being persisted, sobbing out its misfortunes in a blurred, feathery voice, and in the end, to Gormon's immense disgust, I dropped a few food tablets into the shelf-like pouch on its chest. Then we muscled on toward the doors of the palace. At the portico a more horrid sight presented itself: a maimed Flier, fragile limbs bent and twisted, one wing half-unfolded and severely cropped, the other missing altogether. The Flier rushed upon Avluela, called her by a name not hers, moistened her leggings with tears so copious that the fur of them matted and stained. "Sponsor me to the lodge," he appealed. "They have turned me away because I am crippled, but if you sponsor me—" Avluela explained that she could do nothing, that she was a stranger to this lodge. The broken Flier would not release her, and Gormon with great delicacy lifted him like the bundle of dry bones that he was and set him aside. We stepped up onto the portico and at once were confronted by a trio of soft-faced neuters, who asked our business and admitted us quickly to the next line of barrier, which was manned by a pair of wizened Indexers. Speaking in unison, they queried us.

"We seek audience," I said. "A matter of mercy."

"The day of audience is four days hence," said the Indexer on the right. "We will enter your request on the rolls."

"We have no place to sleep!" Avluela burst out. "We are hungry! We—"

I hushed her. Gormon, meanwhile, was groping in the mouth of his overpocket. Bright things glimmered in his hand: pieces of gold, the eternal metal, stamped with hawk-nosed, bearded faces. He had found them grubbing in the ruins. He tossed one coin to the Indexer who had refused us. The man snapped it from the air, rubbed his thumb roughly across its shining obverse, and dropped it instantly into a fold of his garment. The second Indexer waited expectantly. Smiling, Gormon gave him his coin.

"Perhaps," I said, "we can arrange for a special audience within."

"Perhaps you can," said one of the Indexers. "Go through."

And so we passed into the nave of the palace itself and stood in the great, echoing space, looking down the central aisle toward the shielded throne-chamber at the apse.

There were more beggars in here—licensed ones holding hereditary concessions—and also throngs of Pilgrims, Communicants, Rememberers, Musicians, Scribes, and Indexers. I heard muttered prayers; I smelled the scent of spicy incense; I felt the vibration of subterranean gongs. In cycles past, this building had been a shrine of one of the old religions—the Christers, Gormon told me, making me suspect once more that he was a Rememberer masquerading as a Changeling—and it still maintained something of its holy character even though it served as Roum's seat of secular government. But how were we to get to see the Prince? To my left I saw a small ornate chapel which a line of prosperous-looking Merchants and Landholders was slowly entering. Peering past them, I noted three skulls mounted on an interrogation fixture—a memory-tank input—and beside them, a burly Scribe. Telling Gormon and Avluela to wait for me in the aisle, I joined the line.

It moved infrequently, and nearly an hour passed before I reached the interrogation fixture. The skulls glared sightlessly at me; within their sealed crania, nutrient fluids bubbled and gurgled, caring for the dead, yet still functional, brains whose billion billion synaptic units now served as incomparable mnemonic devices. The Scribe seemed aghast to find a Watcher in this line, but before he could challenge me I blurted, "I come as a stranger to claim the Prince's mercy. I and my companions are without lodging. My own guild has turned me away. What shall I do? How may I gain an audience?"

"Come back in four days."

"I've slept on the road for more days than that. Now I must rest more easily."

"A public inn—"

"But I am guilded!" I protested. "The public inns would not admit me while my guild maintains an inn here, and my guild refuses me because of some new regulation, and—you see my predicament?"

In a wearied voice the Scribe said, "You may have application for a special audience. It will be denied, but you may apply."

"Where?"

"Here. State your purpose."

I identified myself to the skulls by my public designation, listed the names and status of my two companions, and explained my case. All this was absorbed and transmitted to the ranks of brains mounted somewhere in the depths of the city, and when I was done the Scribe said, "If the application is approved, you will be notified."

"Meanwhile where shall I stay?"

"Close to the palace, I would suggest."

I understood. I could join that legion of unfortunates packing the plaza. How many of them had requested some special favor of the Prince and were still there, months or years later, waiting to be summoned to the Presence? Sleeping on stone, begging for crusts, living in foolish hope!

But I had exhausted my avenues. I returned to Gormon and Avluela, told them of the situation, and suggested that we now attempt to hunt whatever accommodations we could. Gormon, guildless, was welcome at any of the squalid public inns maintained for his kind; Avluela could probably find residence at her own guild's lodge; only I would have to sleep in the streets—and not for the first time. But I hoped that we would not have to separate. I had come to think of us as a family, strange thought though that was for a Watcher.

As we moved toward the exit, my timepiece told me softly that the hour of Watching had come round again. It was my obligaton and my privilege to tend to my Watching wherever I might be, regardless of the circumstances, whenever my hour came round; and so I halted, opened the cart, activated the equipment. Gormon and Avluela stood beside me. I saw smirks and open mockery on the faces of those who passed in and out of the palace; Watching was not held in very high repute, for we had Watched so long, and the promised enemy had never come. Yet one has one's duties, comic though they may seem to others. What is a hollow ritual to some is a life's work to others. Doggedly I forced myself into a state of Watchfulness. The world melted away from me, and I plunged into the heavens. The familiar joy engulfed me; and I searched the familiar places, and some that were not so familiar, my amplified mind leaping through the galaxies in wild swoops. Was an armada massing? Were troops drilling for the conquest of Earth? Four times a day I Watched, and the other members of my guild did the same, each at slightly different hours, so that no moment went by without some vigilant mind on guard. I do not believe that that was a foolish calling.

When I came up from my trance, a brazen voice was crying, "—for the Prince of Roum! Make way for the Prince of Roum!"

I blinked and caught my breath and fought to shake off the last strands of my concentration. A gilded palanquin borne by a phalanx of neuters had emerged from the rear of the palace and was proceeding down the nave toward me. Four men in the elegant costumes and brilliant masks of the guild of Masters flanked the litter, and it was preceded by a trio of Changelings, squat and broad, whose throats were so modified to imitate the sounding-boxes of bullfrogs; they emitted a trumpetlike boom of majestic sound as they advanced. It struck me as most strange that a prince would admit Changelings to his service, even ones as gifted as these.

My cart was blocking the progress of this magnificent procession, and hastily I struggled to close it and move it aside before the parade swept down upon me. Age and fear made my fingers tremble, and I could not make the sealings properly; while I fumbled in increasing clumsiness, the strutting Changelings drew so close that the blare of their throats was deafening, and Gormon attempted to aid me, forcing me to hiss at him that it is forbidden for anyone not of my guild to touch the equipment. I pushed him away; and an instant later a vanguard of neuters descended on me and prepared to scourge me from the spot with sparkling whips. "In the Will's name," I cried, "I am a Watcher!"

And in antiphonal response came the deep, calm, enormous reply, "Let him be. He is a watcher."

All motion ceased. The Prince of Roum had spoken.

The neuters drew back. The Changelings halted their music. The bearers of the Palanquin eased it to the floor. All those in the nave of the palace had pulled back, save only Gormon and Avluela and myself. The shimmering chain-curtains of the palanquin parted. Two of the Masters hurried forward and thrust their hands through the sonic barrier within, offering aid to their monarch. The barrier died away with a whimpering buzz.

The Prince of Roum appeared.

He was so young! He was nothing more than a boy, his hair full and dark, his face unlined. But he had been born to rule, and for all his youth he was as commanding as anyone I had ever seen. His lips were thin and tightly compressed; his aquiline nose was sharp and aggressive; his eyes, deep and cold, were infinite pools. He wore the jeweled garments of the guild of Dominators, but incised on his cheek was the double-barred cross of the Defenders, and around his neck he carried the dark shawl of the Rememberers. A Dominator may enroll in as many guilds as he pleases, and it would be a strange thing for a Dominator not also to be a Defender; but it startled me to find this prince a Rememberer as well. That is not normally a guild for the fierce.

He looked at me with little interest and said, "You choose an odd place to do your Watching, old man."

"The hour chose the place, sire," I replied. "I was here, and my duty compelled me. I had no way of knowing that you were about to come forth."

"Your Watching found no enemies?"

"None, sire."

I was about to press my luck, to take advantage of the unexpected appearance of the Prince to beg for his aid; but his interest in me died like a guttering candle as I stood there, and I did not dare call to him when his head had turned. He eyed Gormon a long moment, frowning and tugging at his chin. Then his gaze fell on Avluela. His eyes brightened. His jaw muscles flickered. His delicate nostrils widened. "Come up here, little Flier," he said, beckoning. "Are you this Watcher's friend?"

She nodded, terrified.

The Prince held out a hand to her and grasped; she floated up onto the palanquin, and with a grin so evil it seemed a parody of wickedness, the young Dominator drew her through the curtain. Instantly a pair of Masters restored the sonic barrier, but the procession did not move on. I stood mute. Gormon beside me was frozen, his powerful body rigid as a rod. I wheeled my cart to a less conspicuous place. Long moments passed. The courtiers remained silent, discreetly looking away from the palanquin.

At length the curtain parted once more. Avluela came stumbling out, her face pale, her eyes blinking rapidly. She seemed dazed. Streaks of sweat gleamed on her cheeks. She nearly fell, and a neuter caught her and swung her down to floor level. Beneath her jacket her wings were partly erect, giving her a hunchbacked look and telling me that she was in great emotional distress. In ragged, sliding steps she came to us, quivering, wordless; she darted a glance at me and flung herself against Gormon's broad chest.

The bearers lifted the palanquin. The Prince of Roum went out from his palace.

When he was gone, Avluela stammered hoarsely, "The Prince has granted us lodging in the royal hostelry!"

4

THE hostelkeepers, of course, would not believe us.

Guests of the Prince were housed in the royal hostelry, which was to the rear of the palace in a small garden of frostflowers and blossoming ferns. The usual inhabitants of such a hostelry were Masters and an occasional Dominator; sometimes a particularly important Rememberer on an errand of research would win a niche there, or some highly placed Defender visiting for purposes of strategic planning. To house a Flier in a royal hostelry was distinctly odd; to admit a Watcher was unlikely; to take in a Changeling or some other guildless person was improbable beyond comprehension. When we presented ourselves, therefore, we were met by Servitors whose attitude was at first one of high good humor at our joke, then of irritation, finally of scorn. "Get away," they told us ultimately. "Scum! Rabble!"

Avluela said in a grave voice, "The Prince has granted us lodging here, and you may not refuse us."

"Away! Away!"

One snaggle-toothed Servitor produced a neural truncheon and brandished it in Gormon's face, passing a foul remark about his guildlessness. Gormon slapped the truncheon from the man's grasp, oblivious to the painful sting, and kicked him in the gut, so that he coiled and fell over, puking. Instantly a throng of neuters came rushing from within the hostelry. Gormon seized another of the Servitors and hurled him into the midst of them, turning them into a muddled mob. Wild shouts and angry cursing cries attracted the attention of a venerable Scribe who waddled to the door, bellowed for silence, and interrogated us. "That's easily checked," he said, when Avluela had told the story. To a Servitor he said contemptuously, "Send a think to the Indexers, fast!"

In time the confusion was untangled and we were admitted. We were given separate but adjoining rooms. I had never known such luxury before, and perhaps never shall again. The rooms were long, high, and deep. One entered them through telescopic pits keyed to one's own thermal output, to assure privacy. Lights glowed at the resident's merest nod, for hanging from ceiling globes and nestling in cupolas on the walls were spicules of slave-light from one of the Brightstar worlds, trained through suffering to obey such commands. The windows came and went at the dweller's whim; when not in use, they were concealed by streamers of quasi-sentient outworld gauzes, which not only were decorative in their own right, but which functioned as monitors to produce delightful scents according to requisitioned patterns. The rooms were equipped with individual thinking caps connected to the main memory banks. They likewise had conduits that summoned Servitors, Scribes, Indexers, or Musicians as required. Of course, a man of my own humble guild would not deign to make use of other human beings that way, out of fear of their glowering resentment; but in any case I had little need of them.

I did not ask of Avluela what had occurred in the Prince's palanquin to bring us such bounty. I could well imagine, as could Gormon, whose barely suppressed inner rage was eloquent of his never-admitted love for my pale, slender little Flier.

We settled in. I placed my cart beside the window, draped it with gauzes, and left it in readiness for my next period of Watching. I cleaned my body of grime while entities mounted in the wall sang me to peace. Later I ate. Afterwards Avluela came to me, refreshed and relaxed, and sat beside me in my room as we talked of our experiences. Gormon did not appear for hours. I thought that perhaps he had left this hostelry altogether, finding the atmosphere too rarefied for him, and had sought company among his own guildless kind. But at twilight, Avluela and I walked in the cloistered courtyard of the hostelry and mounted a ramp to watch the stars emerge in Roum's sky, and Gormon was there. With him was a lanky and emaciated man in a Rememberer's shawl; they were talking in low tones.

Gormon nodded to me and said, "Watcher, meet my new friend."

The emaciated one fingered his shawl. "I am the Rememberer Basil," he intoned, in a voice as thin as a fresco that has been peeled from its wall. "I have come from Perris to delve into the mysteries of Roum. I shall be here many years."

"The Rememberer has fine stories to tell," said Gormon. "He is among the foremost of his guild. As you approached, he was describing to me the techniques by which the past is revealed. They drive a trench through the strata of Third Cycle deposits, you see, and with vacuum cores they lift the molecules of earth to lay bare the ancient layers."

"We have found," Basil said, "the catacombs of Imperial Roum, and the rubble of the Time of Sweeping, the books inscribed on slivers of white metal, written toward the close of the Second Cycle. All these go to Perris for examination and classification and decipherment; then they return. Does the past interest you, Watcher?"

"To some extent." I smiled. "This Changeling here shows much more fascination for it. I sometimes suspect his authenticity. Would you recognize a Rememberer in disguise?"

Basil scrutinized Gormon; he lingered over the bizarre features, the excessively muscular frame. "He is no Rememberer," he said at length. "But I agree that he has antiquarian interests. He has asked me many profound questions."

"Such as?"

"He wishes to know the origin of guilds. He asks the name of the genetic surgeon who crafted the first true-breeding Fliers. He wonders why there are Changelings, and if they are truly under the curse of the Will."

"And do you have answers for these?" I asked.

"For some," said Basil. "For some."

"The origin of guilds?"

"To give structure and meaning to a society that has suffered defeat and destruction," said the Rememberer. "At the end of the Second Cycle all was in flux. No man knew his rank nor his purpose. Through our world strode haughty outworlders who looked upon us all as worthless. It was necessary to establish fixed frames of reference by which one man might know his value beside another. So the first guilds appeared: Dominators, Masters, Merchants, Landholders, Vendors and Servitors. Then came Scribes, Musicians, Clowns and Transporters. Afterwards Indexers became necessary, and then Watchers and Defenders. When the Years of Magic gave us Fliers and Changelings, those guilds were added, and then the guildless ones, the neuters, were produced, so that—"

"But surely the Changelings are guildless too!" said Avluela.

The Rememberer looked at her for the first time. "Who are you, child?"

"Avluela of the Fliers. I travel with this Watcher and this Changeling."

Basil said, "As I have been telling the Changeling here, in the early days his kind was guilded. The guild was dissolved a thousand years ago by the order of the Council of Dominators after an attempt by a disreputable Changeling faction to seize control of the holy places of Jorslem, and since that time Changelings have been guildless, ranking only above neuters."

"I never knew that," I said.

"You are no Rememberer," said Basil smugly. "It is our craft to uncover the past."

"True. True."

Gormon said, "And today, how many guilds are there?"

Discomfited, Basil replied vaguely, "At least a hundred, my friend. Some are quite small; some are local. I am concerned only with the original guilds and their immediate successors; what has happened in the past few hundred years is in the province of others. Shall I requisition an information for you?"

"Never mind," Gormon said. "It was only an idle question."

"Your curiosity is well developed," said the Rememberer.

"I find the world and all it contains extremely fascinating. Is this sinful?"

"It is strange," said Basil. "The guildless rarely look beyond their own horizons."

A Servitor appeared. With a mixture of awe and contempt he genuflected before Avluela and said, "The Prince has returned. He desires your company in the palace at this time."

Terror glimmered in Avluela's eyes. But to refuse was inconceivable. "Shall I come with you?" she asked.

"Please. You must be robed and perfumed. He wishes you to come to him with your wings open, as well."

Avluela nodded. The Servitor led her away.

We remained on the ramp a while longer; the Rememberer Basil talked of the old days of Roum, and I listened, and Gormon peered into the gathering darkness. Eventually, his throat dry, the Rememberer excused himself and moved solemnly away. A few moments later, in the courtyard below us, a door opened and Avluela emerged, walking as though she were of the guild of Somnambulists, not of Fliers. She was nude under transparent draperies, and her fragile body gleamed ghostly white in the starbeams. Her wings were spread and fluttered slowly in a somber systole and diastole. One Servitor grasped each of her elbows: they seemed to be propelling her toward the palace as though she were but a dreamed facsimile of herself and not a real woman.

"Fly, Avluela, fly," Gormon growled. "Escape while you can!"

She disappeared into a side entrance of the palace.

The Changeling looked at me. "She has sold herself to the Prince to provide lodging for us."

"So it seems."

"I could smash down that palace!"

"You love her?"

"It should be obvious."

"Cure yourself," I advised. "You are an unusual man, but still a Flier is not for you. Particularly a Flier who has shared the bed of the Prince of Roum."

"She goes from my arms to his."

I was staggered. "You've known her?"

"More than once," he said, smiling sadly. "At the moment of ecstasy her wings thrash like leaves in a storm."

I gripped the railing of the ramp so that I would not tumble into the courtyard. The stars whirled overhead; the old moon and its two blank-faced consorts leaped and bobbed. I was shaken without fully understanding the cause of my emotion. Was it wrath that Gormon had dared to violate a canon of the law? Was it a manifestation of those pseudo-parental feelings I had toward Avluela? Or was it mere envy of Gormon for daring to commit a sin beyond my capacity, though not beyond my desires?

I said, "They could burn your brain for that. They could mince your soul. And now you make me an accessory."

"What of it? That Prince commands, and he gets—but others have been there before him. I had to tell someone."

"Enough. Enough."

"Will we see her again?"

"Princes tire quickly of their women. A few days, perhaps a single night—then he will throw her back to us. And perhaps then we shall have to leave this hostelry." I sighed. "At least we'll have known it a few nights more than we deserved."

"Where will you go then?" Gorman asked.

"I will stay in Roum awhile."

"Even if you sleep in the streets? There does not seem to be much demand for Watchers here."

"I'll manage," I said. "Then I may go toward Perris."

"To learn from the Rememberers?"

"To see Perris. What of you? What do you want in Roum?"

"Avluela."

"Stop that talk!"

"Very well," he said, and his smile was bitter. "But I will stay here until the Prince is through with her. Then she will be mine, and we'll find ways to survive. The guildless are resourceful. They have to be. Maybe we'll scrounge lodgings in Roum awhile, and then follow you to Perris. If you're willing to travel with monsters and faithless Fliers."

I shrugged. "We'll see about that when the time comes."

"Have you ever been in the company of a Changeling before?"

"Not often. Not for long."

"I'm honored." He drummed on the parapet. "Don't cast me off, Watcher. I have a reason for wanting to stay with you."

"Which is?"

"To see your face on the day your machines tell you that the invasion of Earth has begun."

I let myself sag forward, shoulders drooping. "You'll stay with me a long time, then."

"Don't you believe the invasion is coming?"

"Some day. Not soon."

Gormon chuckled. "You're wrong. It's almost here."

"You don't amuse me."

"What is it, Watcher? Have you lost your faith? It's been known for a thousand years: another race covets Earth and owns it by treaty, and will some day come to collect. That much was decided at the end of the Second Cycle."

"I know all that, and I am no Rememberer." Then I turned to him and spoke words I never thought I would say aloud. "For twice your lifetime, Changeling, I've listened to the stars and done my Watching. Something done that often loses meaning. Say your own name ten thousand times and it will be an empty sound. I have Watched, and Watched well, and in the dark hours of the night I sometimes think I Watch for nothing, that I have wasted my life. There is a pleasure in Watching, but perhaps there is no real purpose."

His hand encircled my wrist. "Your confession is as shocking as mine. Keep your faith, Watcher. The invasion comes!"

"How could you possibly know?"

"The guildless also have their skills."

The conversation troubled me. I said, "Is it painful to be guildless?"

"One grows reconciled. And there are certain freedoms to compensate for the lack of status. I may speak freely to all."

"I notice."

"I move freely. I am always sure of food and lodging, though the food may be rotten and the lodging poor. Women are attracted to me despite all prohibitions. Because of them, perhaps. I am untroubled by ambitions."

"Never desire to rise above your rank?"

"Never."

"You might have been happier as a Rememberer."

"I am happy now. I can have a Rememberer's pleasures without his responsibility."

"How smug you are!" I cried. "To make a virtue of guildlessness!"

"How else does one endure the weight of the Will?" He looked toward the palace. "The humble rise. The mighty fall. Take this as prophecy, Watcher: that lusty Prince in there will know more of life before summer comes. I'll rip out his eyes for taking Avluela!"

"Strong words. You bubble with treason tonight."

"Take it as prophecy."

"You can't get close to him," I said. Then, irritated for taking his foolishness seriously, I added, "And why blame him? He only does as princes do. Blame the girl for going to him. She might have refused."

"And lost her wings. Or died. No, she had no choice. I do!" In a sudden, terrible gesture the Changeling held out thumb and forefinger, double-jointed, long-nailed, and plunged them forward into imagined eyes. "Wait," he said. "You'll see!"

In the courtyard two Chronomancers appeared, set up the apparatus of their guild, and lit tapers by which to read the shape of tomorrow. A sickly odor of pallid smoke rose to my nostrils. I had now lost further desire to speak with the Changeling.

"It grows late," I said. "I need rest, and soon I must do my Watching."

"Watch carefully," Gormon told me.

5

At night in my chamber I performed my fourth and last Watch of that long day, and for the first time in my life I detected an anomaly. I could not interpret it. It was an obscure sensation, a mingling of tastes and sounds, a feeling of being in contact with some colossal mass. Worried, I clung to my instruments far longer than usual, but perceived no more clearly at the end of my seance than at its commencement.

Afterward I wondered about my obligations.

Watchers are trained from childhood to be swift to sound the alarm; and the alarm must be sounded when the Watcher judges the world in peril. Was I now obliged to notify the Defenders? Four times in my life the alarm had been given, on each occasion in error; and each Watcher who had thus touched off a false mobilization had suffered a fearful loss of status. One had contributed his brain to the memory banks; one had become a neuter out of shame; one had smashed his instruments and gone to live among the guildless; and one, vainly attempting to continue in his profession, had discovered himself mocked by all his comrades. I saw no virtue in scorning one who had delivered a false alarm, for was it not preferable for a Watcher to cry out too soon than not at all? But those were the customs of our guild, and I was constrained by them.

I evaluated my position and decided that I did not have valid grounds for an alarm.

I reflected that Gormon had placed suggestive ideas in my mind that evening. I might possibly be reacting only to his jeering talk of imminent invasion.

I could not act. I dared not jeopardize my standing by hasty outcry. I mistrusted my own emotional state.

I gave no alarm.

Seething, confused, my soul roiling, I closed my cart and let myself sink into a drugged sleep.

At dawn I woke and rushed to the window, expecting to find invaders in the streets. But all was still; a winter grayness hung over the courtyard, and sleepy Servitors pushed passive neuters about. Uneasily I did my first Watching of the day, and to my relief the strangenesses of the night before did not return, although I had it in mind that my sensitivity is always greater at night than upon arising.

I ate and went to the courtyard. Gormon and Avluela were already there. She looked fatigued and downcast, depleted by her night with the Prince of Roum, but I said nothing to her about it. Gormon, slouching disdainfully against a wall embellished with the shells of radiant mollusks, said to me, "Did your Watching go well?"

"Well enough."

"What of the day?"

"Out to roam Roum," I said. "Will you come? Avluela? Gormon?"

"Surely," he said, and she gave a faint nod; and, like the tourists we were, we set off to inspect the splendid city of Roum.

Gormon acted as our guide to the jumbled pasts of Roum, belying his claim never to have been here before. As well as any Rememberer he described the things we saw as we walked the winding streets. All the scattered levels of thousands of years were exposed. We saw the power domes of the Second Cycle, and the Colosseum where at an unimaginably early date man and beast contended like jungle creatures. In the broken hull of that building of horrors Gormon told us of the savagery of that unimaginably ancient time. "They fought," he said, "naked before huge throngs. With bare hands men challenged beasts called lions, great hairy cats with swollen heads; and when the lion lay in its gore, the victor turned to the Prince of Roum and asked to be pardoned for whatever crime it was that had cast him into the arena. And if he had fought well, the Prince made a gesture with his hand, and the man was freed." Gormon made the gesture for us: a thumb upraised and jerked backward over the right shoulder several times. "But if the man had shown cowardice, or if the lion had distinguished itself in the manner of its dying, the Prince made another gesture, and the man was condemned to be slain by a second beast." Gormon showed us that gesture too: the middle finger jutting upward from a clenched fist and lifted in a short sharp thrust.

"How are these things known?" Avluela asked, but Gormon pretended not to hear her.

We saw the line of fusion-pylons built early in the Third Cycle to draw energy from the world's core; they were still functioning, although stained and corroded. We saw the shattered stump of a Second Cycle weather machine, still a mighty column at least twenty men high. We saw a hill on which white marble relics of First Cycle Roum sprouted like pale clumps of winter deathflowers. Penetrating toward the inner part of the city, we came upon the embankment of defensive amplifiers waiting in readiness to hurl the full impact of the Will against invaders. We viewed a market where visitors from the stars haggled with peasants for excavated fragments of antiquity. Gormon strode into the crowd and made several purchases. We came to a flesh-house for travelers from afar, where one could buy anything from quasi-life to mounds of passion-ice. We ate at a small restaurant by the edge of the River Tver, where guildless ones were served without ceremony, and at Gormon's insistence we dined on mounds of a soft doughy substance and drank a tart yellow wine, local specialties.

Afterward we passed through a covered arcade in whose many aisles plump Vendors peddled star-goods, costly trinkets from Afreek, and the flimsy constructs of the local Manufactories. Just beyond we emerged in a plaza that contained a fountain in the shape of a boat, and to the rear of this rose a flight of cracked and battered stone-stairs ascending to a zone of rubble and weeds. Gormon beckoned, and we scrambled into this dismal area, then passed rapidly through it to a place where a sumptuous palace, by its looks early Second Cycle or even First, brooded over a sloping vegetated hill.

"They say this is the center of the world," Gormon declared. "In Jorslem one finds another place that also claims the honor. They mark the spot here by a map."

"How can the world have one center," Avluela asked, "when it is round?"

Gormon laughed. We went in. Within, in wintry darkness, there stood a colossal jeweled globe lit by some inner glow.

"Here is your world," said Gormon, gesturing grandly.

"Oh!" Avluela gasped. "Everything! Everything is here!"

The map was a masterpiece of craftsmanship. It showed natural contours and elevations, its seas seemed deep liquid pools, its deserts were so parched as to make thirst spring in one's mouth, its cities swirled with vigor and life. I beheld the continents, Eyrop, Afreek, Ais, Stralya. I saw the vastness of Earth Ocean. I traversed the golden span of Land Bridge, which I had crossed so toilfully on foot not long before. Avluela rushed forward and pointed to Roum, to Agupt, to Jorslem, to Perris. She tapped the globe at the high mountains north of Hind and said softly, "This is where I was born, where the ice lives, where the mountains touch the moons. Here is where the Fliers have their kingdom." She ran a finger westward toward Fars and beyond it into the terrible Arban Desert, and on to Agupt. "This is where I flew. By night, when I left my girlhood. We all must fly, and I flew here. A hundred times I thought I would die. Here, here in the desert, sand in my throat as I flew, sand beating against my wings—I was forced down, I lay naked on the hot sand for days, and another Flier saw me, he came down to me and pitied me, and lifted me up, and when I was aloft my strength returned, and we flew on toward Agupt. And he died over the sea, his life stopped though he was young and strong, and he fell down into the sea, and I flew down to be with him, and the water was hot even at night. I drifted, and morning came, and I saw the living stones growing like trees in the water, and the fish of many colors, and they came to him and pecked at his flesh as he floated with his wings outspread on the water, and I left him, I thrust him down to rest there, and I rose, and I flew on to Agupt, alone, frightened, and there I met you, Watcher." Timidly she smiled to me. "Show us the place where you were young, Watcher."

Painfully, for I was suddenly stiff at the knees, I hobbled to the far side of the globe. Avluela followed me; Gormon hung back, as though not interested at all. I pointed to the scattered islands rising in two long strips from Earth Ocean—the remnants of the Lost Continents.

"Here," I said, indicating my native island in the west. "I was born here."

"So far away!" Avluela cried.

"And so long ago," I said. "In the middle of the Second Cycle, it sometimes seems to me."

"No! That is not possible!" But she looked at me as though it might just be true that I was thousands of years old.

I smiled and touched her satiny cheek. "It only seems that way to me," I said.

"When did you leave your home?"

"When I was twice your age," I said. "I came first to here—" I indicated the eastern group of islands. "I spent a dozen years as a Watcher on Palash. Then the Will moved me to cross Earth Ocean to Afreek. I came. I lived awhile in the hot countries. I went on to Agupt. I met a certain small Flier." Falling silent, I looked a long while at the islands that had been my home, and within my mind my image changed from the gaunt and eroded thing I now had become, and I saw myself young and well-fleshed, climbing the green mountains and swimming in the chill sea, doing my Watching at the rim of a white beach hammered by surf.

While I brooded Avluela turned away from me to Gormon and said, "Now you. Show us where you came from, Changeling!"

Gormon shrugged. "The place does not appear to be on this globe."

"But that's *impossible!*"

"Is it?" he asked.

She pressed him, but he evaded her, and we passed through a side exit and into the streets of Roum.

I was growing tired, but Avluela hungered for this city and wished to devour it all in an afternoon, and so we went on through a maze of interlocking streets, through a zone of sparkling mansions of Masters and Merchants, and through a foul den of Servitors and Vendors that extended into subterranean catacombs, and to a place where Clowns and Musicians resorted, and to another where the guild of Somnambulists offered its doubtful wares. A bloated female Somnambulist begged us to come inside and buy the truth that comes with trances, and Avluela urged us to go, but Gormon shook his head and I smiled, and we moved on. Now we were at the edge of a park close to the city's core. Here the citizens of Roum promenaded with an energy rarely seen in hot Agupt, and we joined the parade.

"Look there!" Avluela said. "How bright it is!"

She pointed toward the shining arc of a dimensional sphere enclosing some relic of the ancient city; shading my eyes, I could make out a weathered stone wall within, and a knot of people. Gormon said, "It is the Mouth of Truth."

"What is that?" Avluela asked.

"Come. See."

A line progressed into the sphere. We joined it and soon were at the lip of the interior, peering at the timeless region just across the threshold. Why this relic and so few others had been accorded such special protection I did not know, and I asked Gormon, whose knowledge was so unaccountably as profound as any Rememberer's, and he replied, "Because this is the realm of certainty, where what one says is absolutely congruent with what actually is the case."

"I don't understand," said Avluela.

"It is impossible to lie in this place," Gormon told her. "Can you imagine any relic more worthy of protection?" He stepped across the entry duct, blurring as he did so, and I followed him quickly within. Avluela hesitated. It was a long moment before she entered; pausing a moment on the very threshold, she seemed buffeted by the wind that blew along the line of demarcation between the outer world and the pocket universe in which we stood.

An inner compartment held the Mouth of Truth itself. The line extended toward it, and a solemn Indexer was controlling the flow of entry to the tabernacle. It was a while before we three were permitted to go in. We found ourselves before the ferocious head of a monster in high relief, affixed to an ancient wall pockmarked by time. The monster's jaws gaped; the open mouth was a dark and sinister hole. Gormon nodded, inspecting it, as though he seemed pleased to find it exactly as he had thought it would be.

"What do we do?" Avluela asked.

Gormon said, "Watcher, put your right hand into the Mouth of Truth."

Frowning, I complied.

"Now," said Gormon, "one of us asks a question. You must answer it. If you speak anything but the truth, the mouth with close and sever your hand."

"No!" Avluela cried.

I stared uneasily at the stone jaws rimming my wrist. A Watcher without both his hands is a man without a craft; in Second Cycle days one might have obtained a prosthesis more artful than one's original hand, but the Second Cycle had long ago been concluded, and such niceties were not to be purchased on Earth nowadays.

"How is such a thing possible?" I asked.

"The Will is unusually strong in these precincts," Gormon replied. "It distinguishes sternly between truth and untruth. To the rear of this wall sleeps a trio of Somnambulists through whom the Will speaks, and they control the Mouth. Do you fear the Will, Watcher?"

"I fear my own tongue."

"Be brave. Never has a lie been told before this wall. Never has a hand been lost."

"Go ahead, then," I said. "Who will ask me a question?"

"I," said Gormon. "Tell me, Watcher: all pretense aside, would you say that a life spent in Watching has been a life spent wisely?"

I was silent a long moment, rotating my thoughts, eyeing the jaws.

At length I said, "To devote oneself to vigilance on behalf of one's fellow man is perhaps the noblest purpose one can serve."

"Careful!" Gormon cried in alarm.

"I am not finished," I said.

"Go on."

"But to devote oneself to vigilance when the enemy is an imaginary one is idle, and to congratulate oneself for looking long and well for a foe that is not coming is foolish and sinful. My life has been a waste."

The jaws of the Mouth of Truth did not quiver.

I removed my hand. I stared at it as though it had newly sprouted from my wrist. I felt suddenly several cycles old. Avluela, her eyes wide, her hands to her lips, seemed shocked by what I had said. My own words appeared to hang congealed in the air before the hideous idol.

"Spoken honestly," said Gormon, "although without much mercy for yourself. You judge yourself too harshly, Watcher."

"I spoke to save my hand," I said. "Would you have had me lie?"

He smiled. To Avluela the Changeling said, "Now it's your turn."

Visibly frightened, the little Flier approached the Mouth. Her dainty hand trembled as she inserted it between the slabs of cold stone. I fought back an urge to rush toward her and pull her free of that devilish grimacing head.

"Who will question her?" I asked.

"I," said Gormon.

Avluela's wings stirred faintly beneath her garments. Her face grew pale; her nostrils flickered; her upper lip slid over the lower one. She stood slouched against the wall and stared in horror at the termination of her arm. Outside the chamber vague faces peered at us; lips moved in what no doubt were expressions of impatience over our lengthy visit to the Mouth; but we heard nothing. The atmosphere around us was warm and clammy, with a musty tang like that which would come from a well that was driven through the structure of Time.

Gormon said slowly, "This night past you allowed your body to be possessed by the Prince of Roum. Before that, you granted yourself to the Changeling Gormon, although such liaisons are forbidden by custom and law. Much prior to that you were the mate of a Flier, now deceased. You may have had other men, but I know nothing of them, and for the purposes of my question they are not relevant. Tell me this, Avluela: which of the three gave you the most intense physical pleasure, which of the three aroused your deepest emotions, and which of the three would you choose as a mate, if you were choosing a mate?"

I wanted to protest that the Changeling had asked her three questions, not one, and so had taken unfair advantage. But I had no chance to speak, because Avluela replied unfalteringly, hand wedged deep into the Mouth of Truth, "The Prince of Roum gave me greater pleasure of the body than I had ever known before, but he is cold and cruel, and I despise him. My dead Flier I loved more deeply than any person before or since, but he was weak, and I would not have wanted a weakling as a mate. You, Gormon, seem almost a stranger to me even now, and I feel that I know neither your body nor your soul, and yet, though the gulf between us is so wide, it is you with whom I would spend my days to come."

She drew her hand from the Mouth of Truth.

"Well spoken!" said Gormon, though the accuracy of her words had clearly wounded as well as pleased him. "Suddenly you find eloquence, eh, when the circumstances demand it. And now the turn is mine to risk my hand."

He neared the Mouth. I said, "You have asked the first two questions. Do you wish to finish the job and ask the third as well?"

"Hardly," he said. He made a negligent gesture with his free hand. "Put your heads together and agree on a joint question."

Avluela and I conferred. With uncharacteristic forwardness she proposed a question; and since it was the one I would have asked, I accepted it and told her to ask it.

She said, "When we stood before the globe of the world, Gormon, I asked you to show me the place where you were born, and you said you were unable to find it on the map. That seemed most strange. Tell me now: are you what you say you are, a Changeling who wanders the world?"

He replied, "I am not."

In a sense he had satisfied the question as Avluela had phrased it; but it went without saying that his reply was inadequate, and he kept his hand in the Mouth of Truth as he continued, "I did not show my birthplace to you on the globe because I was born nowhere on this globe, but on a world of a star I must not name. I am no Changeling in your meaning of the word, though by some definitions I am, for my body is somewhat disguised, and on my own world I wear a different flesh. I have lived here ten years."

"What was your purpose in coming to Earth?" I asked.

"I am obliged only to answer one question," said Gormon. Then he smiled. "But I give you an answer anyway: I was sent to Earth in the capacity of a military observer, to prepare the way for the invasion for which you have Watched so long and in which you have ceased to believe, and which will be upon you in a matter now of some hours."

"Lies!" I bellowed. "*Lies!*"

Gormon laughed. And drew his hand from the Mouth of Truth, intact, unharmed.

6

NUMB with confusion, I fled with my cart of instruments from that gleaming sphere and emerged into a street suddenly cold and dark. Night had come with winter's swiftness; it was almost the ninth hour, and almost the time for me to Watch once more.

Gormon's mockery thundered in my brain. He had arranged everything: he had maneuvered us in to the Mouth of Truth; he had wrung a confession of lost faith from me and a confession of a different sort from Avluela; he had mercilessly volunteered information he need not have revealed, spoken words calculated to split me to the core.

Was the Mouth of Truth a fraud? Could Gormon lie and emerge unscathed?

Never since I first took up my tasks had I Watched at anything but my appointed hours. This was a time of crumbling realities; I could not wait for the ninth hour to come round; crouching in the windy street, I opened my cart, readied my equipment, and sank like a diver into Watchfulness.

My amplified consciousness roared toward the stars.

Godlike I roamed infinity. I felt the rush of the solar wind, but I was no Flier to be hurled to destruction by that pressure, and I soared past it, beyond the reach of those angry particles of light, into the blackness at the edge of the sun's dominion. Down upon me there beat a different pressure.

Starships coming near.

Not the tourist lines bringing sightseers to gape at our diminished world. Not the registered mercantile transport vessels, nor the scoopships that collect the interstellar vapors, nor the resort craft on their hyperbolic orbits.

These were military craft, dark, alien, menacing. I could not tell their number; I knew only that they sped Earthward at many lights, nudging a cone of deflected energies before them; and it was that cone that I had sensed, that I had felt also the night before, booming into my mind through my instruments, engulfing me like a cube of crystal through which stress patterns play and shine.

All my life I had watched for this.

I had been trained to sense it. I had prayed that I never would sense it, and then in my emptiness I had prayed that I *would* sense it, and then I had ceased to believe in it. And then by grace of the Changeling Gormon, I had sensed it after all, Watching ahead of my hour, crouching in a cold Roumish street just outside the Mouth of Truth.

In his training, a Watcher is instructed to break from his Watchfulness as soon as his observations are confirmed by a careful check, so that he can sound the alarm. Obediently I made my check by shifting from one channel to another to another, triangulating and still picking up that foreboding sensation of titanic force rushing upon Earth at unimaginable speed.

Either I was deceived, or the invasion was come. But I could not shake from my trance to give the alarm.

Lingeringly, lovingly, I drank in the sensory data for what seemed like hours. I fondled my equipment; I drained from it the total affirmation of faith that my readings gave me. Dimly I warned myself that I was wasting vital time, that it was my duty to leave this lewd caressing of destiny to summon the Defenders.

And at last I burst free of Watchfulness and returned to the world I was guarding.

Avluela was beside me; she was dazed, terrified, her knuckles to her teeth, her eyes blank.

"Watcher! Watcher, do you hear me? What's happening? What's going to happen?"

"The invasion," I said. "How long was I under?"

"About half a minute. I don't know. Your eyes were closed. I thought you were dead."

"Gormon was speaking the truth! The *invasion* is almost here. Where is he? Where did he go?"

"He vanished as we came away from that place with the Mouth," Avluela whispered. "Watcher, I'm frightened. I feel everything collapsing. I have to fly—I can't stay down here now!"

"Wait," I said, clutching at her and missing her arm. "Don't go now. First I have to give the alarm, and then—"

But she was already stripping off her clothing. Bare to the waist, her pale body gleamed in the evening light, while about us people were rushing to and fro in ignorance of all that was about to occur. I wanted to keep Avluela beside me, but I could delay no longer in giving the alarm, and I turned away from her, back to my cart.

As though caught up in a dream born of overripe longings I reached for the node that I had never used, the one that would send forth a planetwide alert to the Defenders.

Had the alarm already been given? Had some other Watcher sensed what I had sensed, and, less paralyzed by bewilderment and doubt, performed a Watcher's final task?

No. No. For then I would be hearing the sirens' shriek reverberating from the orbiting loudspeakers above the city.

I touched the node. From the corner of my eye I saw Avluela, free of her encumbrances now, kneeling to say her words, filling her tender wings with strength. In a moment she would be in the air, beyond my grasp.

With a single swift tug I activated the alarm.

In that instant I became aware of a burly figure striding toward us. Gormon, I thought; and as I rose from my equipment I reached out to him; I wanted to seize him and hold him fast. But he who approached was not Gormon but some officious dough-faced Servitor who said to Avluela, "Go easy, Flier, let your wings drop. The Prince of Roum sends me to bring you to his presence."

He grappled with her. Her little breasts heaved; her eyes flashed anger at him.

"Let go of me! I'm going to fly!"

"The Prince of Roum summons you," the Servitor said, enclosing her in his heavy arms.

"The Prince of Roum will have other distractions tonight," I said. "He'll have no need of her."

As I spoke, the sirens began to sing from the skies.

The Servitor released her. His mouth worked noiselessly for an instant; he made one of the protective gestures of the Will; he looked skyward and grunted, "The alarm! Who gave the alarm? You, old Watcher?"

Figures rushed about insanely in the streets.

Avluela, freed, sped past me—on foot, her wings but half-furled—and was swallowed up in the surging throng. Over the terrifying sound of the sirens came booming messages from the public annunciators, giving instructions for defense and safety. A lanky man with the mark of the guild of Defenders upon his cheek rushed up to me, shouted words too incoherent to be understood, and sped on down the street. The world seemed to have gone mad.

Only I remained calm. I looked to the skies, half-expecting to see the invaders' black ships already hovering above the towers of Roum. But I saw nothing except the hovering nightlights and the other objects one might expect overhead.

"Gormon?" I called. "Avluela?"

I was alone.

A strange emptiness swept over me. I had given the alarm; the invaders were on their way; I had lost my occupation. There was no need of Watchers now. Almost lovingly I touched the worn cart that had been my companion for so many years. I ran my fingers over its stained and pitted instruments; and then I looked away, abandoning it, and went down the dark streets cartless, burdenless, a man whose life had found and lost meaning in the same instant. And about me raged chaos.

7

IT was understood that when the moment of Earth's final battle arrived, all guilds would be mobilized, the Watchers alone exempted. We who had manned the perimeter of defense for so long had no part in the strategy of combat; we were discharged by the giving of a true alarm. Now it was the time of the guild of Defenders to show its capabilities. They had planned for half a cycle what they would do in time of war. What plans would they call forth now? What deeds would they direct?

My only concern was to return to the royal hostelry and wait out the crisis. It was hopeless to think of finding Avluela, and I pummeled myself savagely for having let her slip away, naked and without a protector, in that confused moment. Where would she go? Who would shield her?

A fellow Watcher, pulling his cart madly along, nearly collided with me. "Careful!" I snapped. He looked up, breathless, stunned. "Is it true?" he asked. "The alarm?"

"Can't you hear?"

"But is it real?"

I pointed to his cart. "You know how to find that out."

"They say the man who gave the alarm was drunk, an old fool who was turned away from the inn yesterday."

"It could be so," I admitted.

"But if the alarm is real—!"

Smiling, I said, "If it is, now we all may rest. Good day to you, Watcher."

"Your cart! Where's your cart?" he shouted at me.

But I had moved past him, toward the mighty carven stone pillar of some relic of Imperial Roum.

Ancient images were carved on that pillar: battles and victories, foreign monarchs marched in the chains of disgrace through the streets of Roum, triumphant eagles celebrating imperial grandeur. In my strange new calmness I stood awhile before the column of stone and admired its elegant engravings. Toward me rushed a frenzied figure whom I recognized as the Rememberer Basil; I hailed him, saying, "How timely you come! Do me the kindness of explaining these images, Rememberer. They fascinate me, and my curiosity is aroused."

"Are you insane? Can't you hear the alarm?"

"I gave the alarm, Rememberer."

"Flee, then! Invaders come! We must fight!"

"Not I, Basil. Now my time is over. Tell me of these images. These beaten kings, these broken emperors. Surely a man of your years will not be doing battle."

"All are mobilized now!"

"All but Watchers," I said. "Take a moment. Yearning for the past is born in me. Gormon has vanished; be my guide to these lost cycles."

The Rememberer shook his head wildly, circled around me, and tried to get away. Hoping to seize his skinny arm and pin him to the spot, I made a lunge at him; but he eluded me and I caught only his dark shawl, which pulled free and came loose in my hands. Then he was gone, his spindly limbs pumping madly as he fled down the street and left my view. I shrugged and examined the shawl I had so unexpectedly acquired. It was shot through with glimmering threads of metal arranged in intricate patterns that teased the eye: it seemed to me that each strand disappeared into the weave of the fabric, only to reappear at some improbable point, like the lineage of dynasties unexpectedly revived in distant cities. The workmanship was superb. Idly I draped the shawl about my shoulders.

I walked on.

My legs, which had been on the verge of failing me earlier in the day, now served me well. With renewed youthfulness I made my way through the chaotic city, finding no difficulties in choosing my route. I headed for the river, then crossed it and, on the Tver's far side, sought the palace of the Prince. The night had deepened, for most lights were extinguished under the mobilization orders; and from time to time a dull boom signaled the explosion of a screening bomb overhead, liberating clouds of murk that shielded the city from most forms of long-range scrutiny. There were fewer pedestrians in the streets. The sirens still cried out. Atop the buildings the defensive installations were going into action; I heard the bleeping sounds of repellors warming up, and I saw long spidery arms of amplification booms swinging from tower to tower as they linked for maximum output. I had no doubt now that the invasion actually was coming. My own instruments might have been fouled by inner confusion, but they would not have proceeded thus far with the mobilization if the initial report had not been confirmed by the findings of hundreds of other members of my guild.

As I neared the palace a pair of breathless Rememberers sped toward me, their shawls flapping behind them. They called to me in words I did not comprehend—some code of their guild, I realized, recollecting that I wore Basil's shawl. I could not reply, and they rushed upon me, still gabbling; and switching to the language of ordinary men they said, "What is the matter with you? To your post! We must record! We must comment! We must observe!"

"You mistake me," I said mildly. "I keep this shawl only for your brother Basil, who left it in my care. I have no post to guard at this time."

"A Watcher," they cried in unison, and cursed me separately, and ran on. I laughed and went to the palace.

Its gates stood open. The neuters who had guarded the outer portal were gone, as were the two Indexers who had stood just within the door. The beggars that had thronged the vast plaza had jostled their way into the building itself to seek shelter; this had awakened the anger of the licensed hereditary mendicants whose customary stations were in that part of the building, and they had fallen upon the inflowing refugees with fury and unexpected strength. I saw cripples lashing out with their crutches held as clubs; I saw blind men landing blows with suspicious accuracy; meek penitents were wielding a variety of weapons ranging from stilettos to sonic pistols. Holding myself aloof from this shameless spectacle, I penetrated to the inner recesses of the palace and peered into chapels where I saw Pilgrims beseeching the blessings of the Will, and Communicants desperately seeking spiritual guidance as to the outcome of the coming conflict.

Abruptly I heard the blare of trumpets and cries of, "Make way! Make way!"

A file of sturdy Servitors marched into the palace, striding toward the Prince's chambers in the apse. Several of them held a struggling, kicking, frantic figure with half-unfolded wings: Avluela! I called out to her, but my voice died in the din, nor could I reach her. The Servitors shoved me aside. The procession vanished into the princely chambers. I caught a final glimpse of the little Flier, pale and small in the grip of her captors, and then she was gone once more.

I seized a bumbling neuter who had been moving uncertainly in the wake of the Servitors.

"That Flier! Why was she brought here?"

"Ha—he—they—"

"Tell me!"

"The Prince—his woman—in his chariot—he—he—they—the invaders—"

I pushed the flabby creature aside and rushed toward the apse. A brazen wall ten times my own height confronted me. I pounded on it. "Avluela!" I shouted hoarsely. "Av . . . lu . . . ela . . . !"

I was neither thrust away nor admitted. I was ignored. The bedlam at the western doors of the palace had extended itself now to the nave and aisles, and as the ragged beggars boiled toward me I executed a quick turn and found myself passing through one of the side doors of the palace.

Suspended and passive, I stood in the courtyard that led to the royal hostelry. A strange electricity crackled in the air. I assumed it was an emanation from one of Roum's defense installations, some kind of beam designed to screen the city from attack. But an instant later I realized that it presaged the actual arrival of the invaders.

Starships blazed in the heavens.

When I had perceived them in my Watching they had appeared black against the infinite blackness, but now they burned with the radiance of suns. A stream of bright, hard, jewel-like globes bedecked the sky; they were ranged side by side, stretching from east to west in a continuous band, filling all the celestial arch, and as they erupted simultaneously into being it seemed to me that I heard the crash and throb of an invisible symphony heralding the arrival of the conquerors of Earth.

I do not know how far above me the starships were, nor how many of them hovered there, nor any of the details of their design. I know only that in sudden massive majesty they were there, and that if I had been a Defender my soul would have withered instantly at the sight.

Across the heavens shot light of many hues. The battle had been joined. I could not comprehend the actions of our warriors, and I was equally baffled by the maneuvers of those who had come to take possession of our history-crusted but time-diminished planet. To my shame I felt not only out of the struggle but above the struggle, as though this were no quarrel of mine. I wanted Avluela beside me, and she was somewhere within the depths of the palace of the Prince of Roum. Even Gormon would have been a comfort now, Gormon the Changeling, Gormon the spy, Gormon the monstrous betrayer of our world.

Gigantic amplified voices bellowed, "Make way for the Prince of Roum! The Prince of Roum leads the Defenders in the battle for the fatherworld!"

From the palace emerged a shining vehicle the shape of a teardrop, in whose bright-metaled roof a transparent sheet had been mounted so that all the populace could see and take heart in the presence of the ruler. At the controls of the vehicle sat the Prince of Roum, proudly erect, his cruel, youthful features fixed in harsh determination; and beside him, robed like an empress, I beheld the slight figure of the Flier Avluela. She seemed in a trance.

The royal chariot soared upward and was lost in the darkness.

It seemed to me that a second vehicle appeared and followed its path, and that the Prince's reappeared, and that the two flew in tight circles, apparently locked in combat. Clouds of blue sparks wrapped both chariots now; and then they swung high and far and were lost to me behind one of the hills of Roum.

Was the battle now raging all over the planet? Was Perris in jeopardy, and holy Jorslem, and even the sleepy isles of the Lost Continents? Did starships hover everywhere? I did not know. I perceived events in only one small segment of the sky over Roum, and even there my awareness of what was taking place was dim, uncertain, and ill-informed. There were momentary flashes of light in which I saw battalions of Fliers streaming across the sky; and then darkness returned as though a velvet shroud had been hurled over the city. I saw the great machines of our defense firing in fitful bursts from the tops of our towers; and yet I saw the starships untouched, un-harmed, unmoved above. The courtyard in which I stood was deserted, but in the distance I heard voices, full of fear and foreboding, shouting in tinny tones that might have been the screeching of birds. Occasionally there came a booming sound that rocked all the city. Once a platoon of Somnambulists was driven past where I was; in the plaza fronting the palace I observed what appeared to be an array of Clowns unfolding some sort of sparkling netting of a military look; by one flash of lightning I was able to see a trio of Rememberers making copious notes of all that elapsed as they soared aloft on the gravity plate. It seemed—I was not sure—that the vehicle of the Prince of Roum returned, speeding across the sky with its pursuer clinging close. "Avluela," I whispered, as the twin dots of lights left my sight. Were the starships disgorging troops? Did colossal pylons of force spiral down from those orbiting brightnesses to touch the surface of the Earth? Why had the Prince seized Avluela? Where was Gormon? What were our Defenders doing? Why were the enemy ships not blasted from the sky?

Rooted to the ancient cobbles of the courtyard, I ob-served the cosmic battle in total lack of understanding throughout the long night.

Dawn came. Strands of pale light looped from tower to tower. I touched fingers to my eyes, realizing that I must have slept while standing. Perhaps I should apply for membership in the guild of Somnambulists, I told myself lightly. I put my hands to the Rememberer's shawl about my shoulders and wondered how I managed to acquire it, and the answer came.

I looked toward the sky.

The alien starships were gone. I saw only the ordinary morning sky, gray with pinkness breaking through. I felt the jolt of compulsion and looked about for my cart, and reminded myself that I need do no more Watching, and I felt more empty than one would ordinarily feel at such an hour.

Was the battle over?

Had the enemy been vanquished?

Were the ships of the invaders blasted from the sky and lying in charred ruin outside Roum?

All was silent. I heard no more celestial symphonies. Then out of the eerie stillness there came a new sound, a rumbling noise as of wheeled vehicles passing through the streets of the city. And the invisible Musicians played one final note, deep and resonant, which trailed away jaggedly as though every string had been broken at once.

Over the speakers used for public announcements came quiet words.

"Roum is fallen. Roum is fallen."

8

THE royal hostelry was untended. Neuters and members of the servant guilds all had fled. Defenders, Masters, and Dominators must have perished honorably in combat. Basil the Rememberer was nowhere about; likewise none of his brethren. I went to my room, cleansed and refreshed and fed myself, gathered my few possessions, and bade farewell to the luxuries I had known so briefly. I regretted that I had had such a short time to visit Roum; but at least Gormon had been a most excellent guide, and I had seen a great deal.

Now I proposed to move on.

It did not seem prudent to remain in a conquered city. My room's thinking cap did not respond to my queries, and so I did not know what the extent of the defeat was, here or in other regions, but it was evident to me that Roum at least had passed from human control, and I wished to depart quickly. I weighed the thought of going to Jorslem, as that tall pilgrim had suggested upon my entry into Roum; but then I reflected and chose a westward route, toward Perris, which not only was closer but held the headquarters of the Rememberers. My own occupation had been destroyed; but on this first morning of Earth's conquest I felt a sudden powerful and strange yearning to offer myself humbly to the Rememberers and seek with them knowledge of our more glittering yesterdays.

At midday I left the hostelry. I walked first to the palace, which still stood open. The beggars lay strewn about, some drugged, some sleeping, most dead; from the crude manner of their death I saw that they must have slain one another in their panic and frenzy. A despondent-looking Indexer squatted beside the three skulls of the interrogation fixture in the chapel. As I entered he said, "No use. The brains do not reply."

"How goes it with the Prince of Roum?"

"Dead. The invaders shot him from the sky."

"A young Flier rode beside him. What do you know of her?"

"Nothing. Dead, I suppose."

"And the city?"

"Fallen. Invaders are everywhere."

"Killing?"

"Not even looting," the Indexer said. "They are most gentle. They have *collected* us."

"In Roum alone, or everywhere?"

The man shrugged. He began to rock rhythmically back and forth. I let him be, and walked deeper into the palace. To my surprise, the imperial chambers of the Prince were unsealed. I went within; I was awed by the sumptuous luxury of the hangings, the draperies, the lights, the furnishings. I passed from room to room, coming at last to the royal bed, whose coverlet was the flesh of a colossal bivalve of the planet of another star, and as the shell yawned for me I touched the infinitely soft fabric under which the Prince of Roum had lain, and I recalled that Avluela too had lain here, and if I had been a younger man I would have wept.

I left the palace and slowly crossed the plaza to begin my journey toward Perris.

As I departed I had my first glimpse of our conquerors. A vehicle of alien design drew up at the plaza's rim and perhaps a dozen figures emerged. They might almost have been human. They were tall and broad, deep-chested, as Gormon had been, and only the extreme length of their arms marked them instantly as alien. Their skins were of strange texture, and if I had been closer I suspect I would have seen eyes and lips and nostrils that were not of a human design. Taking no notice of me, they crossed the plaza, walking in a curiously loose-jointed loping way that reminded me irresistibly of Gormon's stride, and entered the palace. They seemed neither swaggering nor belligerent.

Sightseers. Majestic Roum once more exerted its magnetism upon strangers.

Leaving our new masters to their amusement, I walked off, toward the outskirts of the city. The bleakness of eternal winter crept into my soul. I wondered: did I feel sorrow that Roum had fallen? Or did I mourn the loss of Avluela? Or was it only that I now had missed three successive Watchings, and like an addict I was experiencing the pangs of withdrawal?

It was all of these that pained me, I decided. But mostly the last.

No one was abroad in the city as I made for the gates. Fear of the new masters kept the Roumish in hiding, I supposed. From time to time one of the alien vehicles hummed past, but I was unmolested. I came to the city's western gate late in the afternoon. It was open, revealing to me a gently rising hill on whose breast rose trees with dark green crowns. I passed through and saw, a short distance beyond the gate, the figure of a Pilgrim who was shuffling slowly away from the city.

I overtook him easily.

His faltering, uncertain walk seemed strange to me, for not even his thick brown robes could hide the strength and youth of his body; he stood erect, his shoulders square and his back straight, and yet he walked with the hesitating, trembling step of an old man. When I drew abreast of him and peered under his hood I understood, for affixed to the bronze mask all Pilgrims wear was a reverberator, such as is used by blind men to warn them of obstacles and hazards. He became aware of me and said, "I am a sightless Pilgrim. I pray you do not molest me."

It was not a Pilgrim's voice. It was a strong and harsh and imperious voice.

I replied, "I molest no one. I am a Watcher who has lost his occupation this night past."

"Many occupations were lost this night past, Watcher."

"Surely not a Pilgrim's."

"No," he said. "Not a Pilgrim's."

"Where are you bound?"

"Away from Roum."

"No particular destination?"

"No," the Pilgrim said. "None. I will wander."

"Perhaps we should wander together," I said, for it is accounted good luck to travel with a Pilgrim, and, shorn of my Flier and my Changeling, I would otherwise have traveled alone. "My destination is Perris. Will you come?"

"There as well as anywhere else," he said bitterly. "Yes. We will go to Perris together. But what business does a Watcher have there?"

"A Watcher has no business anywhere. I go to Perris to offer myself in service to the Rememberers."

"Ah," he said. "I was of that guild too, but it was only honorary."

"With Earth fallen, I wish to learn more of Earth in its pride."

"Is all Earth fallen, then, and not only Roum?"

"I think it is so," I said.

"Ah," replied the Pilgrim. "Ah!"

He fell silent and we went onward. I gave him my arm, and now he shuffled no longer, but moved with a young man's brisk stride. From time to time he uttered what might have been a sigh or a smothered sob. When I asked him details of his Pilgrimage, he answered obliquely or not at all. When we were an hour's journey outside Roum, and already amid forests, he said suddenly, "This mask gives me pain. Will you help me adjust it?"

To my amazement he began to remove it. I gasped, for it is forbidden for a Pilgrim to reveal his face. Had he forgotten that I was not sightless too?

As the mask came away he said, "You will not welcome this sight."

The bronze grillwork slipped down from his forehead, and I saw first eyes that had been newly blinded, gaping holes where no surgeon's knife, but possibly thrusting fin-

the Second Cycle, and we have been unable thus far to determine how long, in previous eras, it took for our world to circle its sun. Somewhat longer than at present, perhaps.

The First Cycle was the time of Imperial Roum and of the first flowering of Jorslem. Eyrop remained savage long after Ais and parts of Afreek were civilized. In the west, two great continents occupied much of Earth Ocean, and these too were held by savages.

It is understood that in this cycle mankind had no contact with other worlds or stars. Such solitude is difficult to comprehend; but yet so it occurred. Mankind had no way of creating light except through fire; he could not cure his ills; life was not susceptible to renewal. It was a time without comforts, a gray time, harsh in its simplicity. Death came early; one barely had time to scatter a few sons about, and one was carried off. One lived with fear, but mostly not fear of real things.

The soul recoils from such an era. But yet it is true that in the First Cycle magnificent cities were founded— Roum, Perris, Atin, Jorslem—and splendid deeds were accomplished. One stands in awe of those ancestors, foul-smelling (no doubt), illiterate, without machines, and still capable of coming to terms with their universe and to some extent of mastering it.

War and grief were constant throughout the First Cycle. Destruction and creation were nearly simultaneous. Flames ate man's most glorious cities. Chaos threatened always to engulf order. How could men have endured such conditions for thousands of years?

Towards the close of the First Cycle much of the primitivism was outgrown. At last sources of power were accessible to man; there was the beginning of true transportation; communication over distances became possible; many inventions transformed the world in a short time. Methods of making war kept pace with the technological growth in other directions; but total catastrophe was averted, although several times it appeared to have arrived. It was during this final phase of the cycle that the Lost Continents were colonized, also Stralya, and that first contact was made with the adjoining planets of our solar system.

The transition from First Cycle to Second is arbitrarily fixed at the point when man first encountered intelligent beings from distant worlds. This, the Rememberers now believe, took place less than fifty generations after the First Cycle folk had mastered electronic and nuclear energy. Thus we may rightly say that the early people of Earth stumbled headlong from savagery to galactic contact—or, perhaps, that they crossed that gap in a few quick strides.

This too is cause for pride. For if the First Cycle was great despite its handicaps, the Second Cycle knew of no handicaps and achieved miracles.

In this epoch mankind spread out to the stars, and the stars came to mankind. Earth was a market for goods of all worlds. Wonders were commonplace. One might hope to live for hundreds of years; eyes, hearts, lungs, kidneys were replaced as easily as shoes; the air was pure, no man went hungry, war was forgotten. Machines of every sort served man. But the machines were not enough, and so the Second Cycle folk bred men who were machines, or machines who were men: creatures that were genetically human, but were born artificially, and were treated with drugs that prevented the permanent storing of memories. These creatures, analogous to our neuters, were capable of performing an efficient day's work, but were unable to build up that permanent body of experiences, memories, expectations, and abilities that is the mark of a human soul. Millions of such not-quite-humans handled the duller tasks of the day, freeing others for lives of glistening fulfillment. After the creation of the subhumans came the creation of the superanimals who, through biochemical manipulation of the brain, were able to carry out tasks once beyond the capacity of their species: dogs, cats, mice, and cattle were enrolled in the labor force, while certain high primates received functions formerly reserved for humans. Through this exploitation of the environment to the fullest, man created a paradise on Earth.

The spirit of man soared to the loftiest peak it had known. Poets, scholars, and scientists made splendid contributions. Shining cities sprawled across the land. The population was enormous, and even so, there was ample room for all, with no shortage of resources. One could indulge one's whims to any extent; there was much experimentation with genetic surgery and with mutagenetic and teratogenetic drugs, so that the human species adopted many new forms. There was, however, nothing yet like the variant forms of our cycle.

Across the sky in stately procession moved space stations serving every imaginable need. It was at this time that the two new moons were built, although the Rememberers have not yet determined whether their purpose was functional or esthetic. The auroras that now appear each night in the sky may have been installed at this time, although some factions of Rememberers argue that the presence of temperate-zone auroras began with the geophysical upheavals that heralded the close of the cycle.

It was, at any rate, the finest of times to be alive.

"See earth and die," was the watchword of the outworlders. No one making the galactic grand tour dared pass up this planet of miracles. We welcomed the strangers, accepted their compliments and their money, made them comfortable in the ways they preferred, and proudly displayed our greatnesses.

The Prince of Roum can testify that it is the fate of the mighty eventually to be humbled, and also that the higher one reaches for splendor, the more catastrophic one's downfall is apt to be. After some thousands of years of glories beyond my capacity to comprehend, the fortunate ones of the Second Cycle overreached themselves and committed two misdeeds, one born of foolish arrogance, the other born of excessive confidence. Earth is paying yet for those overreachings.

The effects of the first were slow to be felt. It was a function of Earth's attitude toward the other species of the galaxy, which had shifted during the Second Cycle from awe to matter-of-fact acceptance to contempt. At the beginning of the cycle, brash and naive Earth had erupted into a galaxy already peopled by advanced races that long had been in contact with one another. This could well have produced a soul-crushing trauma, but instead it generated an aggressive urge to excel and surpass. And so it happened that Earthmen quickly came to look upon most of the galactics as equals, and then, as progress continued on Earth, as inferiors. This bred the easy habit of contempt for the backward.

Thus it was proposed to establish "study compounds" on Earth for specimens of inferior races. These compounds would reproduce the natural habitat of the races and would be accessible to scholars wishing to observe the life-processes of these races. However, the expense of collecting and maintaining the specimens was such that it quickly became necessary to open the compounds to the public at large, for purposes of amusement. These supposedly scientific compounds were, in fact, zoos for other intelligent species.

At the outset only the truly alien beings were collected, those so remote from human biological or psychological norms that there was little danger of regarding them as "people." A many-limbed thing that dwells in a tank of methane under high pressure does not strike a sympathetic response from those likely to object to the captivity of intelligent creatures. If that methane-dweller happens to have a complex civilization of a sort uniquely fitted to its environment, it can be argued that it is all the more important to duplicate that environment on Earth so that one can study so strange a civilization. Therefore the early compounds contained only the bizarre. The collectors were limited, also, to taking creatures who had not attained the stage of galactic travel themselves. It would not have been good form to kidnap life-forms whose relatives were among the interstellar tourists on whom our world's economy had come so heavily to depend.

The success of the first compounds led to the demand for the formation of others. Less critical standards were imposed; not merely the utterly alien and grotesque were collected, but samplings of any sort of galactic life not in a position to register diplomatic protests. And, as the audacity of our ancestors increased, so did the restrictions on collection loosen, until there were samplings from a thousand worlds on Earth, including some whose civilizations were older and more intricate than our own.

The archives of the Rememberers show that the expansion of our compounds stirred some agitation in many parts of the universe. We were denounced as marauders, kidnapers, and pirates; committees were formed to criticize our wanton disregard for the rights of sentient beings; Earthmen traveling to other planets were occasionally beset by mobs of hostile life-forms demanding that we free the prisoners of the compounds at once. However, these protesters were only a minority—most galactics kept an uncomfortable silence about our compounds. They regretted the barbarity of them, and nevertheless made a point of touring them when they visited Earth. Where else, after all, could one see hundreds of life-forms, culled from every part of the universe, in a few days? Our compounds were a major attraction, one of the wonders of the cosmos. By silent conspiracy our neighbors in the galaxy winked at the amorality of the basic concept in order to share the pleasure of inspecting the prisoners.

There is in the archives of the Rememberers a memory-tank entry of a visit to a compound area. It is one of the oldest visual records possessed by the guild, and I obtained a look at it only with great difficulty and upon the direct intercession of the Rememberer Olmayne. Despite the use of a double filter in the cap, one sees the scene only blurredly; but yet it is clear enough. Behind a curved shield of a transparent material are fifty or more beings of an unnamed world. Their bodies are pyramidal, with dark blue surfaces and pink visual areas at each vertex; they walk upon short, thick legs; they have one pair of grasping limbs on each face. Though it is risky to attempt to interpret the inner feelings of extraterrestrial beings, one can clearly sense a mood of utter despair in these creatures. Through the murky green gases of their environment they move slowly, numbly, without animation. Several have joined tips in what must be communication. One appears newly dead. Two are bowed to the ground like tumbled toys, but their limbs move in what perhaps is prayer. It is a dismal scene. Later, I discovered other such records in neglected corners of the building. They taught me much.

For more than a thousand Second Cycle years the growth of these compounds continued unchecked, until it came to seem logical and natural to all except the victims that Earth should practice these cruelties in the name of science. Then, upon a distant world not previously visited by Earthmen, there were discovered certain beings of a primitive kind, comparable perhaps to Earthmen in early First Cycle days. These beings were roughly humanoid in form, undeniably intelligent, and fiercely savage. At the loss of several Earthborn lives, a collecting team acquired a breeding colony of these people and transported them to Earth to be placed in a compound.

This was the first of the Second Cycle's two fatal errors.

At the time of the kidnaping, the beings of this other world—which is never named in the records, but known only by the code designation H362—were in no position to protest or to take punitive steps. But shortly they were visited by emissaries from certain other worlds aligned politically against Earth. Under the guidance of these emissaries, the beings of H362 requested the return of their people. Earth refused, citing the long precedent of interstellar condonement of the compounds. Lengthy diplomatic representations followed, in the course of which Earth simply reaffirmed its right to have acted in such a fashion.

The people of H362 responded with threats. "One day," they said, "we will cause you to regret this. We will invade and conquer your planet, set free all the inhabitants of the compounds, and turn Earth itself into a gigantic compound for its own people."

Under the circumstances this appeared quite amusing.

Little more was heard of the outraged inhabitants of H362 over the next few millennia. They were progressing rapidly, in their distant part of the universe, but since by all calculations it would take them a cosmic period to pose any menace to Earth, they were ignored. How could one fear spear-wielding savages?

Earth addressed itself to a new challenge: full control of the planetary climate.

Weather modification had been practiced on a small scale since late First Cycle. Clouds holding potential rain could be induced to release it; fogs could be dispelled; hail could be made less destructive. Certain steps were taken toward reducing the polar ice packs and toward making deserts more fruitful. However, these measures were strictly local and, with few exceptions, had no lasting effects on environment.

The Second Cycle endeavor involved the erection of enormous columns at more than one hundred locations around the globe. We do not know the heights of these columns, since none has survived intact and the specifications are lost, but it is thought that they equaled or exceeded the highest buildings previously constructed, and perhaps attained altitudes of two miles or more. Within these columns was equipment which was designed, among other things, to effect displacements of the poles of Earth's magnetic field.

As we understand the aim of the weather machines, it was to modify the planet's geography according to a carefully conceived plan arising from the division of what we call Earth Ocean into a number of large bodies. Although interconnected, these suboceans were considered to have individual existences, since along most of their boundary region they were cut off from the rest of Earth Ocean by land masses. In the north polar region, for example, the joining of Ais to the northern Lost Continent (known as Usa-amrik) in the west and the proximity of Usa-amrik to Eyrop in the east left only narrow straits through which the polar waters could mingle with those of the warmer oceans flanking the Lost Continents.

Manipulation of magnetic forces produced a libration of Earth on its orbit, calculated to break up the north polar ice pack and permit the cold water trapped by this pack to come in contact with warmer water from elsewhere. By removing the northern ice pack and thus exposing the northern ocean to evaporation, precipitation would be greatly increased there. To prevent this precipitation from falling in the north as snow, additional manipulations were to be induced to change the pattern of the prevailing westerly winds which carried precipitation over temperate areas. A natural conduit was to be established that would bring the precipitation of the polar region to areas in lower latitudes lacking in proper moisture.

There was much more to the plan than this. Our knowledge of the details is hazy. We are aware of schemes to shift ocean currents by causing land subsidence or emergence, of proposals to deflect solar heat from the tropics to the poles, and of other rearrangements. The details are unimportant. What is significant to us are the consequences of this grandiose plan.

After a period of preparation lasting centuries and after absorbing more effort and wealth than any other project in human history, the weather machines were put into operation.

The result was devastation.

The disastrous experiment in planetary alteration resulted in a shifting of the geographical poles, a lengthy period of glacial conditions throughout most of the northern hemisphere, the unexpected submergence of Usa-amrik and Sud-amrik, its neighbor, the creation of Land Bridge joining Afreek and Eyrop, and the near destruction of human civilization. These upheavals did not take place with great speed. Evidently the project went smoothly for the first several centuries; the polar ice thawed, and the corresponding rise in sea levels was dealt with by constructing fusion evaporators—small suns, in effect—at selected oceanic points. Only slowly did it become clear that the weather machines were bringing about architectonic changes in the crust of Earth. These, unlike the climatic changes, proved irreversible.

It was a time of furious storms followed by unending droughts; of the loss of hundreds of millions of lives; of the disruption on all communications; of panicky mass migrations out of the doomed continents. Chaos triumphed. The splendid civilization of the Second Cycle was shattered. The compounds of alien life were destroyed.

For the sake of saving what remained of its population, several of the most powerful galactic races took command of our planet. They established energy pylons to stabilize Earth's axial wobble; they dismantled those weather machines that had not been destroyed by the planetary convulsions; they fed the hungry, clothed the naked, and offered reconstruction loans. For us it was a Time of Sweeping, when all the structures and conventions of society were expunged. No longer masters in our own world, we accepted the charity of strangers and crept pitifully about.

Yet, because we were still the same race we had been, we recovered to some extent. We had squandered our planet's capital and so could never again be anything but bankrupts and paupers, but in a humbler way we entered into our Third Cycle. Certain scientific techniques of earlier days still remained to us. Others were devised, working generally on different principles. Our guilds were formed to give order to society: Dominators, Master, Merchants, and the rest. The Rememberers strove to salvage what could be pulled from the wreck of the past.

Our debts to our rescuers were enormous. As bankrupts, we had no way of repaying those debts; we hoped instead for a quitclaim, a statement of absolution. Negotiations to that effect were already under way when an unexpected intervention occurred. The inhabitants of H362 approached the committee of Earth's receivers and offered to reimburse them for their expenses—in return for an assignment of all rights and claims in Earth to H362.

It was done.

H362 now regarded itself the owner by treaty of our world. It served notice to the universe at large that it reserved the right to take possession at any future date. As well it might, since at that time H362 was still incapable of interstellar travel. Thereafter, though, H362 was deemed legal possessor of the assets of Earth, as purchaser in bankruptcy.

No one failed to realize that this was H362's way of fulfilling its threat to "turn Earth itself into a gigantic compound," as revenge for the injury inflicted by our collecting team long before.

On Earth, Third Cycle society constituted itself along the lines it now holds, with its rigid stratification of guilds. The threat of H362 was taken seriously, for ours was a chastened world that sneered at no menace, however slight; and a guild of Watchers was devised to scan the skies for attackers. Defenders and all the rest followed. In some small ways we demonstrated our old flair for imagination, particularly in the Years of Magic, when a fanciful impulse created the self-perpetuating mutant guild of Fliers, a parallel guild of Swimmers, of whom little is heard nowadays, and several other varieties, including a troublesome and unpredictable guild of Changelings whose genetic characteristics were highly erratic.

The Watchers watched. The Dominators ruled. The Fliers soared. Life went on, year after year, in Eyrop and in Ais, in Stralya, in Afreek, in the scattered islands that were the only remnants of the Lost Continents of Usa-amrik and Sud-amrik. The vow of H362 receded into mythology, but yet we remained vigilant. And far across the cosmos our enemies gathered strength, attaining some measure of the power that had been ours in our Second Cycle. They never forgot the day when their kinsmen had been held captive in our compounds.

In a night of terror they came to us. Now they are our masters, and their vow is fulfilled, their claim asserted.

All this, and much more, I learned as I burrowed in the accumulated knowledge of the guild of Rememberers.

5

Meanwhile the former Prince of Roum was wantonly abusing the hospitality of our co-sponsorer, the Rememberer Elegro. I should have been aware of what was going on, for I knew the Prince and his ways better than any other man in Perris. But I was too busy in the archives, learning of the past. While I explored the details of the Second Cycle's protoplasm files and regeneration nodules, its time-wind blowers and its photonic-flux fixers, Prince Enric was seducing the Rememberer Olmayne.

Like most seductions, I imagine that this was no great contest of wills. Olmayne was a woman of sensuality, whose attitude toward her husband was affectionate but patronizing. She regarded Elegro openly as ineffectual, a bumbler; and Elegro, whose haughtiness and stern mien did not conceal his underlying weakness of purpose, seemed to merit her disdain. What kind of marriage they had was not my business to observe, but clearly she was the stronger, and just as clearly he could not meet her needs.

Then, too, why had Olmayne agreed to sponsor us into her guild?

Surely not out of any desire for a tattered old Watcher. It must have been the wish to know more of the strange and oddly commanding blind Pilgrim who was that Watcher's companion. From the very first, then, Olmayne must have been drawn to Prince Enric; and he, naturally, would need little encouragement to accept the gift she offered.

Possibly they were lovers almost from the moment of our arrival in the Hall of Rememberers.

I went my way, and Elegro went his, and Olmayne and Prince Enric went theirs, and summer gave way to autumn and autumn to winter. I excavated the records with passionate impatience. Never before had I known such involvement, such intensity of curiosity. Without benefit of a visit to Jorslem I felt renewed. I saw the Prince infrequently, and our meetings were generally silent; it was not my place to question him about his doings, and he felt no wish to volunteer information to me.

Occasionally I thought of my former life, and of my travels from place to place, and of the Flier Avluela who was now, I supposed, the consort of one of our conquerors. How did the false Changeling Gormon style himself, now that he had emerged from his disguise and owned himself to be one of those from H362? Earthking Nine? Oceanlord Five? Overman Three? Wherever he was, he must feel satisfaction, I thought, at the total success of the conquest of Earth.

Toward winter's end I learned of the affair between the Rememberer Olmayne and Prince Enric of Roum. I picked up whispered gossip in the apprentice quarters first; then I noticed the smiles on the faces of other Rememberers when Elegro and Olmayne were about; lastly, I observed the behavior of the Prince and Olmayne toward one another. It was obvious. Those touchings of hand to hand, those sly exchanges of catchwords and private phrases—what else could they mean?

Among the Rememberers the marriage vow is regarded solemnly. As with the Fliers, mating is for life, and one is not supposed to betray one's partner as Olmayne was doing. When one is married to a fellow Rememberer—a custom in the guild, but not universal—the union is all the more sacred.

What revenge would Elegro take when in time he learned the truth?

It happened that I was present when the situation at last crystallized into conflict. It was a night in earliest spring. I had worked long and hard in the deepest pits of the memory tanks, prying forth data that no one had bothered with since it had first been stored; and, with my head aswim with images of chaos, I walked through the glow of the Perris night, seeking fresh air. I strolled along the Senn and was accosted by an agent for a Somnambulist, who offered to sell me insight into the world of dreams. I came upon a lone Pilgrim at his devotions before a temple of flesh. I watched a pair of young Fliers in passage overhead, and shed a self-pitying tear or two. I was halted by a starborn tourist in breathing mask and jeweled tunic; he put his cratered red face close to mine and vented hallucinations in my nostrils. At length I returned to the Hall of Rememberers and went to the suite of my sponsors to pay my respects before retiring.

Olmayne and Elegro were there. So, too, was Prince Enric. Olmayne admitted me with a quick gesture of one fingertip, but took no further notice of me, nor did the others. Elegro was tensely pacing the floor, stomping about so vehemently that the delicate life-forms of the carpet folded and unfolded their petals in wild agitation. "A Pilgrim!" Elegro cried. "If it had been some trash of a Vendor, it would only be humiliating. But a Pilgrim? That makes it monstrous!"

Prince Enric stood with arms folded, body motionless.

It was impossible to detect the expression beneath his mask of Pilgrimage, but he appeared wholly calm.

Elegro said, "Will you deny that you have been tampering with the sanctity of my pairing?"

"I deny nothing. I assert nothing."

"And you?" Elegro demanded, whirling on his lady. "Speak truth, Olmayne! For once, speak truth! What of the stories they tell of you and this Pilgrim?"

"I have heard no stories," said Olmayne sweetly.

"That he shares your bed! That you taste potions together! That you travel to ecstasy together!"

Olmayne's smile did not waver. Her broad face was tranquil. To me she looked more beautiful than ever.

Elegro tugged in anguish at the strands of his shawl. His dour, bearded face darkened in wrath and exasperation. His hand slipped within his tunic and emerged with the tiny glossy bead of a vision capsule, which he thrust forth toward the guilty pair on the palm of his hand.

"Why should I waste breath?" he asked. "Everything is here. The full record in the photonic flux. You have been under surveillance. Did either of you think anything could be hidden here, of all places? You, Olmayne, a Rememberer, how could you think so?"

Olmayne examined the capsule from a distance, as though it were a primed implosion bomb. With distaste she said, "How like you to spy on us, Elegro. Did it give you great pleasure to watch us in our joy?"

"Beast!" he cried.

Pocketing the capsule, he advanced toward the motionless Prince. Elegro's face now was contorted with righteous wrath. Standing an arm's length from the Prince he declared icily, "You will be punished to the fullest for this impiety. You will be stripped of your Pilgrim's robes and delivered up to the fate reserved for monsters. The Will shall consume your soul!"

Prince Enric replied, "Curb your tongue."

"Curb my tongue? Who are you to speak that way? A Pilgrim who lusts for the wife of his host—who doubly violates holiness—who drips lies and sanctimony at the same moment?" Elegro frothed. His iciness was gone.

Now he ranted in nearly incoherent frenzy, displaying his interior weakness by his lack of self-control. We three stood frozen, astounded by his torrent of words, and at last the stasis broke when the Rememberer, carried away by the tide of his own indignation, seized the Prince by the shoulders and began violently to shake him.

"Filth," Enric bellowed, "you may not put your hands to me!"

With a double thrust of his fists against Elegro's chest he hurled the Rememberer reeling backward across the room. Elegro crashed into a suspension cradle and sent a flank of watery artifacts tumbling; three flasks of scintillating fluids shivered and spilled their contents; the carpet set up a shrill cry of pained protest. Gasping, stunned, Elegro pressed a hand to his breast and looked to us for assistance.

"Physical assault—" Elegro wheezed. "A shameful crime!"

"The first assault was your doing," Olmayne reminded her husband.

Pointing trembling fingers, Elegro muttered, "For this there can be no forgiveness, Pilgrim!"

"Call me Pilgrim no longer," Enric said. His hands went to the grillwork of his mask. Olmayne cried out, trying to prevent him; but in his anger the Prince knew no check. He hurled the mask to the floor and stood with his harsh face terribly exposed, the cruel features hawk-lean, the gray mechanical spheres in his eyesockets masking the depths of his fury. "I am the Prince of Roum," he announced in a voice of thunder. "Down and abase! Down and abase! Quick, Rememberer, the three prostrations and the five abasements!"

Elegro appeared to crumble. He peered in disbelief; then he sagged, and in a kind of reflex of amazement he performed a ritual obeisance before his wife's seducer. It was the first time since the fall of Roum that the Prince had asserted his former status, and the pleasure of it was so evident on his ravaged face that even the blank eyeballs appeared to glow in regal pride.

"Out," the Prince ordered. "Leave us."

Elegro fled.

I remained, astounded, staggered. The Prince nodded courteously to me. "Would you pardon us, old friend, and grant us some moments of privacy?"

6

A weak man can be put to rout by a surprise attack, but afterward he pauses, reconsiders, and hatches schemes. So was it with the Rememberer Elegro. Driven from his own suite by the unmasking of the Prince of Roum, he grew calm and crafty once he was out of that terrifying presence. Later that same night, as I settled into my sleeping cradle and debated aiding slumber with a drug, Elegro summoned me to his research cell on a lower level of the building.

There he sat amid the paraphernalia of his guild: reels and spools, data-flakes, capsules, caps, a quartet of series-linked skulls, a row of output screens, a small ornamental helix, all the symbology of the gatherers of information. In his hands he grasped a tension-draining crystal from one of the Cloud-worlds; its milky interior was rapidly tingeing with sepia as it pulled anxieties from his spirit. He pretended a look of stern authority, as if forgetting that I had seen him exposed in his spinelessness.

He said, "Were you aware of this man's identity when you came with him to Perris?"

"Yes."

"You said nothing about it."

"I was never asked."

"Do you know what a risk you have exposed all of us to, by causing us unknowingly to harbor a Dominator?"

"We are Earthmen," I said. "Do we not still acknowledge the authority of the Dominators?"

"Not since the conquest. By decree of the invaders all former governments are dissolved and their leaders subject to arrest."

"But surely we should resist such an order!"

The Rememberer Elegro regarded me quizzically. "Is it a Rememberer's function to meddle in politics? Tomis, we obey the government in power, whichever it may be and however it may have taken control. We conduct no resistance activities here."

"I see."

"Therefore we must rid ourselves at once of this dangerous fugitive. Tomis, I instruct you to go at once to occupation headquarters and inform Manrule Seven that we have captured the Prince of Roum and hold him here for pickup."

"*I* should go?" I blurted. "Why send an old man as a messenger in the night? An ordinary thinking-cap transmission would be enough!"

"Too risky. Strangers may intercept cap communications. It would not go well for our guild if this were spread about. This has to be a personal communication."

"But to choose an unimportant apprentice to carry it—it seems strange."

"There are only two of us who know," said Elegro. "I will not go. Therefore you must."

"With no introduction to Manrule Seven I will never be admitted."

"Inform his aides that you have information leading to the apprehension of the Prince of Roum. You'll be heard."

"Am I to mention your name?"

"If necessary. You may say that the Prince is being held prisoner in my quarters with the cooperation of my wife."

I nearly laughed at that. But I held a straight face before this cowardly Rememberer, who did not even dare to go himself to denounce the man who had cuckolded him.

"Ultimately," I said, "the Prince will become aware of what we have done. Is it right of you to ask me to betray a man who was my companion for so many months?"

"It is not a matter of betrayal. It is a matter of obligations to the government."

"I feel no obligation to this government. My loyalties are to the guild of Dominators. Which is why I gave assistance to the Prince of Roum in his moment of peril."

"For that," said Elegro, "your own life could be forfeit to our conquerors. Your only expiation is to admit your error and cooperate in bringing about his arrest. Go. Now."

In a long and tolerant life I have never despised anyone so vehemently as I did the Rememberer Elegro at that moment.

Yet I saw that I was faced with few choices, none of them palatable. Elegro wished his undoer punished, but lacked the courage to report him himself; therefore I must give over to the conquering authorities one whom I had sheltered and assisted, and for whom I felt a responsibility. If I refused, Elegro would perhaps hand me to the invaders for punishment myself, as an accessory to the Prince's escape from Roum; or he might take vengeance against me within the machinery of the guild of Rememberers. If I obliged Elegro, though, I would have a stain on my conscience forever, and in the event of a restoration of the power of the Dominators I would have much to answer for.

As I weighed the possibilities, I triply cursed the Rememberer Elegro's faithless wife and her invertebrate husband.

I hesitated a bit. Elegro offered more persuasion, threatening to arraign me before the guild on such charges as unlawfully gaining access to secret files and improperly introducing into guild precincts a proscribed fugitive. He threatened to cut me off forever from the information pool. He spoke vaguely of vengeance.

In the end I told him I would go to the invaders' headquarters and do his bidding. I had by then conceived a betrayal that would—I hoped—cancel the betrayal Elegro was enforcing on me.

Dawn was near when I left the building. The air was mild and sweet; a low mist hung over the streets of Perris, giving them a gentle shimmer. No moons were in sight. In the deserted streets I felt uneasy, although I told myself that no one would care to do harm to an aged Rememberer; but I was armed only with a small blade, and I feared bandits.

My route lay on one of the pedestrian ramps. I panted a bit at the steep incline, but when I had attained the proper level I was more secure, since here there were patrol nodes at frequent intervals, and here, too, were some other late-night strollers. I passed a spectral figure garbed in white satin through which alien features peered: a revenant, a ghostly inhabitant of a planet of the Bull, where reincarnation is the custom and no man goes about installed in his own original body. I passed three female beings of a Swan planet who giggled at me and asked if I had seen males of their species, since the time of conjugation was upon them. I passed a pair of Changelings who eyed me speculatively, decided I had nothing on me worth robbing, and moved on, their piebald dewlaps jiggling and their radiant skins flashing like beacons.

At last I came to the squat octagonal building occupied by the Procurator of Perris.

It was indifferently guarded. The invaders appeared confident that we were incapable of mounting a counterassault against them, and quite likely they were right; a planet which can be conquered between darkness and dawn is not going to launch a plausible resistance afterwards. Around the building rose the pale glow of a protective scanner. There was a tingle of ozone in the air. In the wide plaza across the way, Merchants were setting up their market for the morning; I saw barrels of spices being unloaded by brawny Servitors, and dark sausages carried by files of neuters. I stepped through the scanner beam and an invader emerged to challenge me.

I explained that I carried urgent news for Manrule Seven, and in short order, with amazingly little consultation of intermediaries, I was ushered into the Procurator's presence.

The invader had furnished his office simply but in good style. It was decked entirely with Earthmade objects: a drapery of Afreek weave, two alabaster pots from ancient Agupt, a marble statuette that might have been early Roumish, and a dark Talyan vase in which a few wilting deathflowers languished. When I entered, he seemed preoccupied with several message-cubes; as I had heard, the invaders did most of their work in the dark hours, and it did not surprise me to find him so busy now. After a moment he looked up and said, "What is it, old man? What's this about a fugitive Dominator?"

"The Prince of Roum," I said. "I know of his location."

At once his cold eyes sparkled with interest. He ran his many-fingered hands across his desk, on which were mounted the emblems of several of our guilds, Transporters and Rememberers and Defenders and Clowns, among others. "Go on," he said.

"The Prince is in this city. He is in a specific place and has no way of escaping from it."

"And you are here to inform me of his location?"

"No," I said. "I'm here to buy his liberty."

Manrule Seven seemed perplexed. "There are times when you humans baffle me. You say you've captured this runaway Dominator, and I assume that you want to sell him to us, but you say you want to *buy* him. Why bother coming to us? Is this a joke?"

"Will you permit an explanation?"

He brooded into the mirrored top of his desk while I told him in a compressed way of my journey from Roum with the blinded Prince, of our arrival at the Hall of Rememberers, of Prince Enric's seduction of Olmayne, and of Elegro's petty, fuming desire for vengeance. I made it clear that I had come to the invaders only under duress and that it was not my intention to betray the Prince into their hands. Then I said, "I realize that all Dominators are forfeit to you. Yet this one has already paid a high price for his freedom. I ask you to notify the Rememberers that the Prince of Roum is under amnesty, and to permit him to continue on as a Pilgrim to Jorslem. In that way Elegro will lose power over him."

"What is it that you offer us," asked Manrule Seven, "in return for this amnesty for your Prince?"

"I have done research in the memory tanks of the Rememberers."

"And?"

"I have found that for which you people have been seeking."

Manrule Seven studied me with care. "How would you have any idea of what we seek?"

"There is in the deepest part of the Hall of Rememberers," I said quietly, "an image recording of the compound in which your kidnaped ancestors lived while they were prisoners on Earth. It shows their sufferings in poignant detail. It is a superb justification for the conquest of Earth by H362."

"Impossible! There's no such document!"

From the intensity of the invader's reaction, I knew that I had stung him in the vulnerable place.

He went on, "We've searched your files thoroughly. There's only one recording of compound life, and it doesn't show our people. It shows a nonhumanoid pyramid-shaped race, probably from one of the Anchor worlds."

"I have seen that one," I told him. "There are others. I spent many hours searching for them, out of hunger to know of our past injustices."

"The indexes—"

"—are sometimes incomplete. I found this recording only by accident. The Rememberers themselves have no idea it's there. I'll lead you to it—if you agree to leave the Prince of Roum unmolested."

The Procurator was silent a moment. At length he said, "You puzzle me. I am unable to make out if you are a scoundrel or a man of the highest virtue."

"I know where true loyalty lies."

"To betray the secrets of your guild, though—"

"I am no Rememberer, only an apprentice, formerly a Watcher. I would not have you harm the Prince at the wish of a cuckolded fool. The Prince is in his hands; only you can obtain his release now. And so I must offer you this document."

"Which the Rememberers have carefully deleted from their indexes, so it will not fall into our hands."

"Which the Rememberers have carelessly misplaced and forgotten."

"I doubt it," said Manrule Seven. "They are not careless folk. They hid that recording; and by giving it to us, are you not betraying all your world? Making yourself a collaborator with the hated enemy?"

I shrugged. "I am interested in having the Prince of Roum made free. Other means and ends are of no concern to me. The location of the document is yours in exchange for the grant of amnesty."

The invader displayed what might have been his equivalent of a smile. "It is not in our best interests to allow members of the former guild of Dominators to remain at large. Your position is precarious, do you see? I could extract the document's location from you by force—and still have the Prince as well."

"So you could," I agreed. "I take that risk. I assume a certain basic honor among people who came to avenge an ancient crime. I am in your power, and the whereabouts of the document is in my mind, yours for the picking."

Now he laughed in an unmistakable show of good humor.

"Wait one moment," he said. He spoke a few words of his own language into an amber communication device, and shortly a second member of his species entered the office. I recognized him instantly, although he was shorn of some of the flamboyant disguise he had worn when he traveled with me as Gormon, the supposed Changeling. He offered the ambivalent smile of his kind and said, "I greet you, Watcher."

"And I greet you, Gormon."

"My name now is Victorious Thirteen."

"I now am called Tomis of the Rememberers," I said.

Manrule Seven remarked, "When did you two become such fast friends?"

"In the time of the conquest," said Victorious Thirteen. "While performing my duties as an advance scout, I encountered this man in Talya and journeyed with him to Roum. But we were companions, in truth, and not friends."

I trembled. "Where is the Flier Avluela?"

"In Pars, I believe," he said offhandedly. "She spoke of returning to Hind, to the place of her people."

"You loved her only a short while, then?"

"We were more companions than lovers," said the invader. "It was a passing thing for us."

"For you, maybe," I said.

"For us."

"And for this passing thing you stole a man's eyes?"

He who had been Gormon shrugged. "I did that to teach a proud creature a lesson in pride."

"You said at the time that your motive was jealousy," I reminded him. "You claimed to act out of love."

Victorious Thirteen appeared to lose interest in me. To Manrule Seven he said, "Why is this man here? Why have you summoned me?"

"The Prince of Roum is in Perris," said Manrule Seven.

Victorious Thirteen registered sudden surprise.

Manrule Seven went on, "He is a prisoner of the Rememberers. This man offers a strange bargain. You know the Prince better than any of us; I ask your advice."

The Procurator sketched the outlines of the situation. He who had been Gormon listened thoughtfully, saying nothing. At the end, Manrule Seven said, "The problem is this: shall we give amnesty to a proscribed Dominator?"

"He is blind," said Victorious Thirteen. "His power is gone. His followers are scattered. His spirit may be unbroken, but he presents no danger to us. I say accept the bargain."

"There are administrative risks in exempting a Dominator from arrest," Manrule Seven pointed out. "Nevertheless, I agree. We undertake the deal." To me he said, "Tell us the location of the document we desire."

"Arrange the liberation of the Prince of Roum first," I said calmly.

Both invaders displayed amusement. "Fair enough," said Manrule Seven. "But look: how can we be certain that you'll keep your word? Anything might happen to you in the next hour while we're freeing the Prince."

"A suggestion," put in Victorious Thirteen. "This is not so much a matter of mutual mistrust as it is one of timing. Tomis, why not record the document's location on a six-hour delay cube? We'll prime the cube so that it will release its information only if within that six hours the Prince of Roum himself, and no one else, commands it to do so. If we haven't found and freed the Prince in that time, the cube will destruct. If we do release the Prince, the cube will give us the information, even if—ah—something should have happened to you in the interval."

"You cover all contingencies," I said.

"Are we agreed?" Manrule Seven asked.

"We are agreed," I said.

They brought me a cube and placed me under a privacy screen while I inscribed on its glossy surface the rack number and sequence equations of the document I had discovered. Moments passed; the cube everted itself and the information vanished into its opaque depths. I offered it to them.

Thus did I betray my Earthborn heritage and perform a service for our conquerors, out of loyalty to a blinded wife-stealing Prince.

7

Dawn had come by this time. I did not accompany the invaders to the Hall of Rememberers; it was no business of mine to oversee the intricate events that must ensue, and I preferred to be elsewhere. A fine drizzle was falling as I turned down the gray streets that bordered the dark Senn. The timeless river, its surface stippled by the drops, swept unwearyingly against stone arches of First Cycle antiquity, bridges spanning uncountable millennia, survivors from an era when the only problems of mankind were of his own making. Morning engulfed the city. Through an old and ineradicable reflex I searched for my instruments so that I could do my Watching, and had to remind myself that that was far behind me now. The Watchers were disbanded, the enemy had come, and old Wuellig, now Tomis of the Rememberers, had sold himself to mankind's foes.

In the shadow of a twin-steepled religious house of the ancient Christers I let myself be enticed into the booth of a Somnambulist. This guild is not one with which I have often had dealings; in my way I am wary of charlatans, and charlatans are abundant in our time. The Somnambulist, in a state of trance, claims to see what has been, what is, and what will be. I know something of trances myself, for as a Watcher I entered such a state four times each day; but a Watcher with pride in his craft must necessarily despise the tawdry ethics of those who use second sight for gain, as Somnambulists do.

However, while among the Rememberers I had
learned, to my surprise, that Somnambulists frequently
were consulted to aid in unearthing some site of ancient
times, and that they had served the Rememberers well.
Though still skeptical, I was willing to be instructed. And,
at the moment, I needed a shelter from the storm that
was breaking over the Hall of Rememberers.

A dainty, mincing figure garbed in black greeted me
with a mocking bow as I entered the low-roofed booth.

"I am Samit of the Somnambulists," he said in a high,
whining voice. "I offer you welcome and good tidings. Behold my companion, the Somnambulist Murta."

The Somnambulist Murta was a robust woman in lacy
robes. Her face was heavy with flesh, deep rings of darkness surrounded her eyes, a trace of mustache lined her
upper lip. Somnambulists work their trade in teams, one
to do the huckstering, one to perform; most teams were
man and wife, as was this. My mind rebelled at the
thought of the embrace of the flesh-mountain Murta and
the miniature-man Samit, but it was no concern of mine.
I took my seat as Samit indicated. On a table nearby I
saw some food tablets of several colors; I had interrupted
this family's breakfast. Murta, deep in trance, wandered
the room with ponderous strides, now and again grazing
some article of furniture in a gentle way. Some Somnambulists, it is said, waken only two or three hours of the
twenty, simply to take meals and relieve bodily needs;
there are some who ostensibly live in continuous trance
and are fed and cared for by acolytes.

I scarcely listened as Samit of the Somnambulists delivered his sales-talk in rapid, feverish bursts of ritualized
word-clusters. It was pitched to the ignorant; Somnambulists do much of their trade with Servitors and Clowns
and other menials. At length, seemingly sensing my impatience, he cut short his extolling of the Somnambulist
Murta's abilities and asked me what it was I wished to
know.

"Surely the Somnambulist already is aware of that," I
said.

"You wish a general analysis?"

"I want to know of the fate of those about me. I wish

particularly for the Somnambulist's concentration to center on events now occurring in the Hall of Rememberers."

Samit tapped long fingernails against the smooth table and shot a glaring look at the cowlike Murta. "Are you in contact with the truth?" he asked her.

Her reply was a long feathery sigh wrenched from the core of all the quivering meat of her.

"What do you see?" he asked her.

She began to mutter thickly. Somnambulists speak in a language not otherwise used by mankind; it is a harsh thing of edgy sounds, which some claim is descended from an ancient tongue of Agupt. I know nothing of that. To me it sounded incoherent, fragmentary, impossible to hold meaning. Samit listened a while, then nodded in satisfaction and extended his palm to me.

"There is a great deal," he said.

We discussed the fee, bargained briefly, came to a settlement. "Go on," I told him. "Interpret the truth."

Cautiously he began, "There are outworlders involved in this, and also several members of the guild of Rememberers." I was silent, giving him no encouragement. "They are drawn together in a difficult quarrel. A man without eyes is at the heart of it."

I sat upright with a jolt.

Samit smiled in cool triumph. "The man without eyes has fallen from greatness. He is Earth, shall we say, broken by conquerors? Now he is near the end of his time. He seeks to restore his former condition, but he knows it is impossible. He has caused a Rememberer to violate an oath. To their guildhall have come several of the conquerors to—to chastise him? No. No. To free him from captivity. Shall I continue?"

"Quickly!"

"You have received all that you have paid for."

I scowled. This was extortion; but yet the Somnambulist had clearly seen the truth. I had learned nothing here than I did not already know, but that was sufficient to tell me I might learn more. I added to my fee.

Samit closed his fist on my coins and conferred once more with Murta. She spoke at length, in some agitation, whirling several times, colliding violently with a musty divan.

Samit said, "The man without eyes has come between a man and his wife. The outraged husband seeks punishment; the outworlders will thwart that. The outworlders seek hidden truths; they will find them, with a traitor's help. The man without eyes seeks freedom and power; he will find peace. The stained wife seeks amusement; she will find hardship."

"And I?" I said into an obstinate and expensive silence. "You say nothing of me!"

"You will leave Perris soon, in the same manner as you entered it. You will not leave alone. You will not leave in your present guild."

"What will be my destination?"

"You know that as well as we do, so why waste your money to tell you?"

He fell silent again.

"Tell me what will befall me as I journey to Jorslem," I said.

"You could not afford such information. Futures become costly. I advise you to settle for what you now know."

"I have some questions about what has already been said."

"We do not clarify at any price."

He grinned. I felt the force of his contempt. The Somnambulist Murta, still bumbling about the room, groaned and belched. The powers with whom she was in contact appeared to impart new information to her; she whimpered, shivered, made a blurred chuckling sound. Samit spoke to her in their language. She replied at length. He peered at me. "At no cost," he said, "a final information. Your life is in no danger, but your spirit is. It would be well if you made your peace with the Will as quickly as possible. Recover your moral orientation. Remember your true loyalties. Atone for well-intentioned sins. I can say no more."

Indeed, Murta stirred and seemed to wake. Great slabs of flesh jiggled in her face and body as the convulsion of leaving the trance came over her. Her eyes opened, but I saw only whites, a terrible sight. Her thick lips twitched to reveal crumbling teeth. Samit beckoned me out with quick brushing gestures of his tiny hands. I fled into a dark, rain-drenched morning.

Hurriedly I returned to the Hall of Rememberers, arriving there out of breath, with a red spike of pain behind my breastbone. I paused a while outside the superb building to recover my strength. Floaters passed overhead, leaving the guildhall from an upper level. My courage nearly failed me. But in the end I entered the hall and ascended to the level of the suite of Elegro and Olmayne.

A knot of agitated Rememberers filled the hall. A buzz of whispered comment drifted toward me. I pressed forward; and a man whom I recognized as high in the councils of the guild held up a hand and said, "What business do you have here, apprentice?"

"I am Tomis, who was sponsored by the Rememberer Olmayne. My chamber is close to here."

"Tomis!" a voice cried.

I was seized and thrust ahead into the familiar suite, now a scene of devastation.

A dozen Rememberers stood about, fingering their shawls in distress. I recognized among them the taut and elegant figure of Chancellor Kenishal, his gray eyes now dull with despair. Beneath a coverlet to the left of the entrance lay a crumpled figure in the robes of a Pilgrim: the Prince of Roum, dead in his own pooled blood. His gleaming mask, now stained, lay beside him. At the opposite side of the room, slumped against an ornate credenza containing Second Cycle artifacts of great beauty, was the Rememberer Elegro, seemingly asleep, looking furious and surprised both at once. His throat was transfixed by a single slender dart. To the rear, with burly Rememberers flanking her, stood the Rememberer Olmayne looking wild and disheveled. Her scarlet robe was torn in front and revealed high white breasts; her black hair tumbled in disorder; her satiny skin glistened with perspiration. She appeared lost in a dream, far from these present surroundings.

"What has happened here?" I asked.

"Murder twice over," said Chancellor Kenishal in a broken voice. He advanced toward me: a tall, haggard man, white-haired, an uncontrollable tic working in the lid of one eye. "When did you last see these people alive, apprentice?"

"In the night."

"How did you come to be here?"

"A visit, no more."

"Was there a disturbance?"

"A quarrel between the Rememberer Elegro and the Pilgrim, yes," I admitted.

"Over what?" asked the Chancellor thinly.

I looked uneasily at Olmayne, but she saw nothing and heard less.

"Over her," I said.

I heard snickerings from the other Rememberers. They nudged each other, nodded, even smiled; I had confirmed the scandal. The Chancellor grew more solemn.

He indicated the body of the Prince.

"This was your companion when you entered Perris," he said. "Did you know of his true identity?"

I moistened my lips. "I had suspicions."

"That he was—"

"The fugitive Prince of Roum," I said. I did not dare attempt subterfuges now; my status was precarious.

More nods, more nudges. Chancellor Kenishal said, "This man was subject to arrest. It was not your place to conceal your knowledge of his identity."

I remained mute.

The Chancellor went on, "You have been absent from this hall for some hours. Tell us of your activities after leaving the suite of Elegro and Olmayne."

"I called upon the Procurator Manrule Seven," I said.

Sensation.

"For what purpose?"

"To inform the Procurator," I said, "that the Prince of Roum had been apprehended and was now in the suite of a Rememberer. I did this at the instruction of the Rememberer Elegro. After delivering my information I walked the streets several hours for no particular end, and returned here to find—to find—"

"To find everything in chaos," said Chancellor Kenishal.

"The Procurator was here at dawn. He visited this suite; both Elegro and the Prince must still have been alive at that time. Then he went into our archives and removed—and removed—material of the highest sensitivity—the highest sensitivity—removed—material not believed to be accessible to—the highest sensitivity—" The Chancellor faltered. Like some intricate machine smitten with instant rust, he slowed his motions, emitted rasping sounds, appeared to be on the verge of systematic breakdown. Several high Rememberers rushed to his aid; one thrust a drug against his arm. In moments the Chancellor appeared to recover. "These murders occurred after the Procurator departed from the building," he said. "The Rememberer Olmayne has been unable to give us information concerning them. Perhaps you, apprentice, know something of value."

"I was not present. Two Somnambulists near the Senn will testify that I was with them at the time the crimes were committed."

Someone guffawed at my mention of Somnambulists. Let them; I was not seeking to retrieve dignity at a time like this. I knew that I was in peril.

The Chancellor said slowly, "You will go to your chamber, apprentice, and you will remain there to await full interrogation. Afterwards you will leave the building and be gone from Perris within twenty hours. By virtue of my authority I declare you expelled from the guild of Rememberers."

Forewarned as I had been by Samit, I was nevertheless stunned.

"*Expelled?* Why?"

"We can no longer trust you. Too many mysteries surround you. You bring us a Prince and conceal your suspicions; you are present at murderous quarrels; you visit a Procurator in the middle of the night. You may even have helped to bring about the calamitous loss suffered by our archive this morning. We have no desire for men of enigmas here. We sever our relationship with you." The Chancellor waved his hand in a grand sweep. "To your chamber now, to await interrogation, and then go!"

I was rushed from the room. As the entrance pit closed

behind me, I looked back and saw the Chancellor, his face ashen, topple into the arms of his associates, while in the same instant the Rememberer Olmayne broke from her freeze and fell to the floor, screaming.

8

Alone in my chamber, I spent a long while gathering together my possessions, though I owned little. The morning was well along before a Rememberer whom I did not know came to me; he carried interrogation equipment. I eyed it uneasily, thinking that all would be up with me if the Rememberers found proof that it was I who had betrayed the location of that compound record to the invaders. Already they suspected me of it; the Chancellor had hesitated to make the accusation only because it must have seemed odd to him that an apprentice such as myself would have cared to make a private search of the guild archive.

Fortune rode with me. My interrogator was concerned only with the details of the slaying; and once he had determined that I knew nothing on that subject, he let me be, warning me to depart from the hall within the allotted time. I told him I would do so.

But first I needed rest. I had had none that night; and so I drank a three-hour draught and settled into soothing sleep. When I awakened a figure stood beside me: the Rememberer Olmayne.

She appeared to have aged greatly since the previous evening. She was dressed in a single chaste tunic of a somber color, and she wore neither ornament nor decoration. Her features were rigidly set. I mastered my surprise at finding her there, and sat up, mumbling an apology for my delay in acknowledging her presence.

"Be at ease," she said gently. "Have I broken your sleep?"

"I had my full hours."

"I have had none. But there will be time for sleep later. We owe each other explanations, Tomis."

"Yes." I rose uncertainly. "Are you well? I saw you earlier, and you seemed lost in trance."

"They have given me medicines," she replied.

"Tell me what you can tell me about last night."

Her eyelids slid momentarily closed. "You were there when Elegro challenged us and was cast out by the Prince. Some hours later, Elegro returned. With him were the Procurator of Perris and several other invaders. Elegro appeared to be in a mood of great jubilation. The Procurator produced a cube and commanded the Prince to put his hand to it. The Prince balked, but Manrule Seven persuaded him finally to cooperate. When he had touched the cube, the Procurator and Elegro departed, leaving the Prince and myself together again, neither of us comprehending what had happened. Guards were posted to prevent the Prince from leaving. Not long afterward the Procurator and Elegro returned. Now Elegro seemed subdued and even confused, while the Procurator was clearly exhilarated. In our room the Procurator announced that amnesty had been granted to the former Prince of Roum, and that no man was to harm him. Thereupon all of the invaders departed."

"Proceed."

Olmayne spoke as though a Somnambulist. "Elegro did not appear to comprehend what had occurred. He cried out that treason had been done; he screamed that he had been betrayed. An angry scene followed. Elegro was womanish in his fury; the Prince grew more haughty; each ordered the other to leave the suite. The quarrel became so violent that the carpet itself began to die. The petals drooped; the little mouths gaped. The climax came swiftly. Elegro seized a weapon and threatened to use it if the Prince did not leave at once. The Prince misjudged Elegro's temper, thought he was bluffing, and came forward as if to throw Elegro out. Elegro slew the Prince. An instant later I grasped a dart from our rack of artifacts and hurled it into Elegro's throat. The dart bore poison; he died at once. I summoned others, and I remember no more."

"A strange night," I said.

"Too strange. Tell me now, Tomis: why did the Procurator come, and why did he not take the Prince into custody?"

I said, "The Procurator came because I asked him to, under the orders of your late husband. The Procurator did not arrest the Prince because the Prince's liberty had been purchased."

"At what price?"

"The price of a man's shame," I said.

"You speak a riddle."

"The truth dishonors me. I beg you not to press me for it."

"The Chancellor spoke of a document that had been taken by the Procurator—"

"It has to do with that," I confessed, and Olmayne looked toward the floor and asked no further questions.

I said ultimately, "You have committed a murder, then. What will your punishment be?"

"The crime was committed in passion and fear," she replied. "There will be no penalty of the civil administration. But I am expelled from my guild for my adultery and my act of violence."

"I offer my regrets."

"And I am commanded to undertake the Pilgrimage to Jorslem to purify my soul. I must leave within the day, or my life is forfeit to the guild."

"I too am expelled," I told her. "And I too am bound at last for Jorslem, though of my own choosing."

"May we travel together?"

My hesitation betrayed me. I had journeyed here with a blind Prince; I cared very little to depart with a murderous and guildless woman. Perhaps the time had come to travel alone. Yet the Somnambulist had said I would have a companion.

Olmayne said smoothly, "You lack enthusiasm. Perhaps I can create some in you." She opened her tunic. I saw mounted between the snowy hills of her breasts a gray pouch. She was tempting me not with her flesh but with an overpocket. "In this," she said, "is all that the Prince of Roum carried in his thigh. He showed me those treasures, and I removed them from his body as he lay dead in my room. Also there are certain objects of my own. I am not without resources. We will travel comfortably. Well?"

"I find it hard to refuse."

"Be ready in two hours."

"I am ready now," I said.

"Wait, then."

She left me to myself. Nearly two hours later she returned, clad now in the mask and robes of a Pilgrim. Over her arm she held a second set of Pilgrim's gear, which she offered to me. Yes: I was guildless now, and it was an unsafe way to travel. I would go, then, as a Pilgrim to Jorslem. I donned the unfamiliar gear. We gathered our possessions.

"I have notified the guild of Pilgrims," she declared as we left the Hall of Rememberers. "We are fully registered. Later today we may hope to receive our starstones. How does the mask feel, Tomis?"

"Snug."

"As it should be."

Our route out of Perris took us across the great plaza before the ancient gray holy building of the old creed. A crowd had gathered; I saw invaders at the center of the group. Beggars made the profitable orbit about it. They ignored us, for no one begs from a Pilgrim; but I collared one rascal with a gouged face and said, "What ceremony is taking place here?"

"Funeral of the Prince of Roum," he said "By order of the Procurator. State funeral with all the trimmings. They're making a real festival out of it."

"Why hold such an event in Perris?" I asked. "How did the Prince die?"

"Look, ask somebody else. I got work to do."

He wriggled free and scrambled on to work the crowd.

"Shall we attend the funeral?" I asked Olmayne.

"Best not to."

"As you wish."

We moved toward the massive stone bridge that spanned the Senn. Behind us, a brilliant blue glow arose as the pyre of the dead Prince was kindled. That pyre lit the way for us as we made our slow way through the night, eastward to Jorslem.

PART III

THE ROAD TO JORSLEM

OUR WORLD was now truly theirs. All the way across Eyrop I could see that the invaders had taken everything, and we belonged to them as beasts in a barnyard belong to the farmer.

They were everywhere, like fleshy weeds taking root after a strange storm. They walked with cool confidence, as if telling us by the sleekness of their movements that the Will had withdrawn favor from us and conferred it upon them. They were not cruel to us, and yet they drained us of vitality by their mere presence among us. Our sun, our moons, our museums of ancient relics, our ruins of former cycles, our cities, our palaces, our future, our present, and our past had all undergone a transfer of title. Our lives now lacked meaning.

At night the blaze of the stars mocked us. All the universe looked down on our shame.

The cold wind of winter told us that for our sins our freedom had been lost. The bright heat of summer told us that for our pride we had been humbled.

Through a changed world we moved, stripped of our past selves. I, who had roved the stars each day now had lost that pleasure. Now, bound for Jorslem, I found cool comfort in the hope that as a Pilgrim I might gain redemption and renewal in that holy city. Olmayne and I repeated each night the rituals of our Pilgrimage toward that end:

"We yield to the Will."

"We yield to the Will."
"In all things great and small."
"In all things great and small."
"And ask forgiveness."
"And ask forgiveness."
"For sins actual and potential."
"For sins actual and potential."
"And pray for understanding and repose."
"And pray for understanding and repose."
"Through all our days until redemption comes."
"Through all our days until redemption comes."

Thus we spoke the words. Saying them, we clutched the cool polished spheres of starstone, icy as frostflowers, and made communion with the Will. And so we journeyed Jorslemward in this world that no longer was owned by man.

2

It was at the Talyan approach to Land Bridge that Olmayne first used her cruelty on me. Olmayne was cruel by first nature; I had had ample proof of that in Perris; and yet we had been Pilgrims together for many months, traveling from Perris eastward over the mountains and down the length of Talya to the Bridge, and she had kept her claws sheathed. Until this place.

The occasion was our halting by a company of invaders coming north from Afreek. There were perhaps twenty of them, tall and harsh-faced, proud of being masters of conquered Earth. They rode in a gleaming covered vehicle of their own manufacture, long and narrow, with thick sand-colored treads and small windows. We could see the vehicle from far away, raising a cloud of dust as it neared us.

This was a hot time of year. The sky itself was the color of sand, and it was streaked with folded sheets of heat-radiation—glowing and terrible energy streams of turquoise and gold.

Perhaps fifty of us stood beside the road, with the land

of Talya at our backs and the continent of Afreek before us. We were a varied group: some Pilgrims, like Olmayne and myself, making the trek toward the holy city of Jorslem, but also a random mix of the rootless, men and women who floated from continent to continent for lack of other purpose. I counted in the band five former Watchers, and also several Indexers, a Sentinel, a pair of Communicants, a Scribe, and even a few Changelings. We gathered into a straggling assembly awarding the road by default to the invaders.

Land Bridge is not wide, and the road will not allow many to use it at any time. Yet in normal times the flow of traffic had always gone in both directions at once. Here, today, we feared to go forward while invaders were this close, and so we remained clustered timidly, watching our conquerors approach.

One of the Changelings detached himself from the others of his kind and moved toward me. He was small of stature for that breed, but wide through the shoulders; his skin seemed much too tight for his frame; his eyes were large and green-rimmed; his hair grew in thick widely spaced pedestal-like clumps, and his nose was barely perceptible, so that his nostrils appeared to sprout from his upper lip. Despite this he was less grotesque than most Changelings appear. His expression was solemn, but had a hint of bizarre playfulness lurking somewhere.

He said in a voice that was little more than a feathery whisper, "Do you think we'll be delayed long, Pilgrims?"

In former times one did not address a Pilgrim unsolicited—especially if one happened to be a Changeling. Such customs meant nothing to me, but Olmayne drew back with a hiss of distaste.

I said, "We will wait here until our masters allow us to pass. Is there any choice?"

"None, friend, none."

At that *friend,* Olmayne hissed again and glowered at the little Changeling. He turned to her, and his anger showed, for suddenly six parallel bands of scarlet pigment blazed brightly beneath the glossy skin of his cheeks. But his only overt response to her was a courteous bow. He said, "I introduce myself. I am Bernalt, naturally guildless, a native of Nayrub in Deeper Afreek. I do not inquire after your names, Pilgrims. Are you bound for Jorslem?"

"Yes," I said, as Olmayne swung about to present her back. "And you? Home to Nayrub after travels?"

"No," said Bernalt. "I go to Jorslem also."

Instantly I felt cold and hostile, my initial response to the Changeling's suave charm fading at once. I had had a Changeling, false though he turned out to be, as a traveling companion before; he too had been charming, but I wanted no more like him. Edgily, distantly, I said, "May I ask what business a Changeling might have in Jorslem?"

He detected the chill in my tone, and his huge eyes registered sorrow. "We too are permitted to visit the holy city, I remind you. Even our kind. Do you fear that Changelings will once again seize the shrine of renewal, as we did a thousand years ago before we were cast down into guildlessness?" He laughed harshly. "I threaten no one, Pilgrim. I am hideous of face, but not dangerous. May the Will grant you what you seek, Pilgrim." He made a gesture of respect and went back to the other Changelings.

Furious, Olmayne spun round on me.

"Why do you talk to such beastly creatures?"

"The man approached me. He was merely being friendly. We are all cast together here, Olmayne, and—"

"*Man. Man!* You call a Changeling a man?"

"They *are* human, Olmayne."

"Just barely. Tomis, I loathe such monsters. My flesh creeps to have them near me. If I could, I'd banish them from this world!"

"Where is the serene tolerance a Rememberer must cultivate?"

She flamed at the mockery in my voice. "We are not required to love Changelings, Tomis. They are one of the curses laid upon our planet—parodies of humanity, enemies of truth and beauty. I despise them!"

It was not a unique attitude. But I had no time to reproach Olmayne for her intolerance; the vehicle of the invaders was drawing near. I hoped we might resume our journey once it went by. It slowed and halted, however, and several of the invaders came out. They walked unhurriedly toward us, their long arms dangling like slack ropes.

"Who is the leader here?" asked one of them.

No one replied, for we were independent of one another in our travel.

The invader said impatiently, after a moment, "No leader? No leader? Very well, all of you, listen. The road must be cleared. A convoy is coming through. Go back to Palerm and wait until tomorrow."

"But I must be in Agupt by—" the Scribe began.

"Land Bridge is closed today," said the invader. "Go back to Palerm."

His voice was calm. The invaders are never peremptory, never overbearing. They have the poise and assurance of those who are secure possessors.

The Scribe shivered, his jowls swinging, and said no more.

Several of the others by the side of the road looked as if they wished to protest. The Sentinel turned away and spat. A man who boldly wore the mark of the shattered guild of Defenders in his cheek clenched his fists and plainly fought back a surge of fury. The Changelings whispered to one another. Bernalt smiled bitterly at me and shrugged.

Go back to Palerm? Waste a day's march in this heat? For what? For what?

The invader gestured casually, telling us to disperse.

Now it was that Olmayne was unkind to me. In a low voice she said, "Explain to them, Tomis, that you are in the pay of the Procurator of Perris, and they will let the two of us pass."

Her dark eyes glittered with mockery and contempt.

My shoulders sagged as if she had loaded ten years on me. "Why did you say such a thing?" I asked.

"It's hot. I'm tired. It's idiotic of them to send us back to Palerm."

"I agree. But I can do nothing. Why try to hurt me?"

"Does the truth hurt that much?"

"I am no collaborator, Olmayne."

She laughed. "You say that so well! But you are, Tomis, you are! You sold them the documents."

"To save the Prince, your lover," I reminded her.

"You dealt with the invaders, though. No matter what your motive was, that fact remains."

"Stop it, Olmayne."

"Now you give me orders?"

"Olmayne—"

"Go up to them, Tomis. Tell them who you are, make them let us go ahead."

"The convoys would run us down on the road. In any case I have no influence with invaders. I am not the Procurator's man."

"I'll die before I go back to Palerm!"

"Die, then," I said wearily, and turned my back on her.

"Traitor! Treacherous old fool! Coward!"

I pretended to ignore her, but I felt the fire of her words. There was no falsehood in them, only malice. I *had* dealt with the conquerors, I *had* betrayed the guild that sheltered me, I *had* violated the code that calls for sullen passivity as our only way of protest for Earth's defeat. All true; yet it was unfair for her to reproach me with it. I had given no thought to higher matters of patriotism when I broke my trust; I was trying only to save a man to whom I felt bound, a man moreover with whom she was in love. It was loathsome of Olmayne to tax me with treason now, to torment my conscience, merely because of a petty rage at the heat and dust of the road.

But this woman had coldly slain her own husband. Why should she not be malicious in trifles as well?

The invaders had their way; we abandoned the road and straggled back to Palerm, a dismal, sizzling, sleepy town. That evening, as if to console us, five Fliers passing in formation overhead took a fancy to the town, and in the moonless night they came again and again through the sky, three men and two women, ghostly and slender and beautiful. I stood watching them for more than an hour, until my soul itself seemed lifted from me and into the air to join them. Their great shimmering wings scarcely hid the starlight; their pale angular bodies moved in graceful arcs, arms held pressed close to sides, legs together, backs gently curved. The sight of these five stirred my memories of Avluela and left me tingling with troublesome emotions.

The Fliers made their last pass and were gone. The false moons entered the sky soon afterward. I went into our hostelry then, and shortly Olmayne asked admittance to my room.

She looked contrite. She carried a squat octagonal flask of green wine, not a Talyan brew but something from an outworld, no doubt purchased at great price.

"Will you forgive me, Tomis?" she asked. "Here. I know you like these wines."

"I would rather not have had those words before, and not have the wine now," I told her.

"My temper grows short in the heat. I'm sorry, Tomis. I said a stupid and tactless thing."

I forgave her, in hope of a smoother journey thereafter, and we drank most of the wine, and then she went to her own room nearby to sleep. Pilgrims must live chaste lives —not that Olmayne would ever have bedded with such a withered old fossil as I, but the commandments of our adopted guild prevented the question from arising.

For a long while I lay awake beneath a lash of guilt. In her impatience and wrath Olmayne had stung me at my vulnerable place: I was a betrayer of mankind. I wrestled with the issue almost to dawn.

—What had I done?

I had revealed to our conquerors a certain document.

—Did the invaders have a moral right to the document?

It told of the shameful treatment they had had at the hands of our ancestors.

—What, then, was wrong about giving it to them?

One does not aid one's conquerors even when they are morally superior to one.

—Is a small treason a serious thing?

There are no small treasons.

—Perhaps the complexity of the matter should be investigated. I did not act out of love of the enemy, but to aid a friend.

Nevertheless I collaborated with our foes.

—This obstinate self-laceration smacks of sinful pride.

But I feel my guilt. I drown in shame.

In this unprofitable way I consumed the night. When the day brightened, I rose and looked skyward and begged the Will to help me find redemption in the waters of the house of renewal in Jorslem, at the end of my Pilgrimage. Then I went to awaken Olmayne.

3

Land Bridge was open on this day, and we joined the throng that was crossing over out of Talya into Afreek. It was the second time I had traveled Land Bridge, for the year before—it seemed so much farther in the past—I had come the other way, out of Agupt and bound for Roum.

There are two main routes for Pilgrims from Eyrop to Jorslem. The northern route involves going through the Dark Lands east of Talya, taking the ferry at Stanbool, and skirting the western coast of the continent of Ais to Jorslem. It was the route I would have preferred since, of all the world's great cities, old Stanbool is the one I have never visited. But Olmayne had been there to do research in the days when she was a Rememberer, and disliked the place; and so we took the southern route—across Land Bridge into Afreek and along the shore of the great Lake Medit, through Agupt and the fringes of the Arban Desert and up to Jorslem.

A true Pilgrim travels only by foot. It was not an idea that had much appeal to Olmayne, and though we walked a great deal, we rode whenever we could. She was shameless in commandeering transportation. On only the second day of our journey she had gotten us a ride from a rich Merchant bound for the coast; the man had no intention of sharing his sumptuous vehicle with anyone, but he could not resist the sensuality of Olmayne's deep, musical voice, even though it issued from the sexless grillwork of a Pilgrim's mask.

The Merchant traveled in style. For him the conquest of Earth might never have happened, nor even all the long centuries of Third Cycle decline. His self-primed landcar was four times the length of a man and wide enough to house five people in comfort; and it shielded its riders against the outer world as effectively as a womb. There was no direct vision, only a series of screens revealing upon command what lay outside. The temperature never varied from a chosen norm. Spigots supplied liqueurs and stronger things; food tablets were available; pressure couches insulated travelers against the irregularities of the road. For illumination, there was slavelight keyed to the Merchant's whims. Beside the main couch sat a thinking cap, but I never learned whether the Merchant carried a pickled brain for his private use in the depths of the landcar, or enjoyed some sort of remote contact with the memory tanks of the cities through which he passed.

He was a man of pomp and bulk, clearly a savorer of his own flesh. Deep olive of skin, with a thick pompadour of well-oiled black hair and somber, scrutinizing eyes, he rejoiced in his solidity and in his control of an uncertain environment. He dealt, we learned, in foodstuffs of other worlds; he bartered our poor manufactures for the delicacies of the starborn ones. Now he was en route to Marsay to examine a cargo of hallucinatory insects newly come in from one of the Belt planets.

"You like the car?" he asked, seeing our awe. Olmayne, no stranger to ease herself, was peering at the dense inner mantle of diamonded brocade in obvious amazement. "It was owned by the Comt of Perris," he went on. "Yes, I mean it, the Comt himself. They turned his palace into a museum, you know."

"I know," Olmayne said softly.

"This was his chariot. It was supposed to be part of the museum, but I bought it off a crooked invader. You didn't know they had crooked ones too, eh?" The Merchant's robust laughter caused the sensitive mantle on the walls of the car to recoil in disdain. "This one was the Procurator's boy friend. Yes, they've got *those*, too. He was looking for a certain fancy root that grows on a planet of the Fishes, something to give his virility a little boost, you know, and he learned that I controlled the whole supply here, and so we were able to work out a little deal. Of course, I had to have the car adapted, a little. The Comt kept four neuters up front and powered the engine right off their metabolisms, you understand, running the thing on thermal differentials. Well, that's a fine way to power a car, if you're a Comt, but it uses up a lot of neuters through the year, and I felt I'd be overreaching my status if I tried anything like that. It might get me into trouble with the invaders, too. So I had the drive compartment stripped down and replaced with a standard heavy-duty rollerwagon engine—a really subtle job—and there you are. You're lucky to be in here. It's only that you're Pilgrims. Ordinarily I don't let folks come inside, on account of them feeling envy, and envious folks are dangerous to a man who's made something out of his life. Yet the Will brought you two to me. Heading for Jorslem, eh?"

"Yes," Olmayne said.

"Me too, but not yet! Not just yet, thank you!" He patted his middle. "I'll be there, you can bet on it, when I feel ready for renewal, but that's a good way off, the Will willing! You two been Pilgriming long?"

"No," Olmayne said.

"A lot of folks went Pilgrim after the conquest, I guess. Well, I won't blame 'em. We each adapt in our own ways to changing times. Say, you carrying those little stones the Pilgrims carry?"

"Yes," Olmayne said.

"Mind if I see one? Always been fascinated by the things. There was this trader from one of the Darkstar worlds—little skinny bastard with skin like oozing tar—he offered me ten quintals of the things. Said they were genuine, gave you the real communion, just like the Pilgrims had. I told him no, I wasn't going to fool with the Will. Some things you don't do, even for profit. But afterward I wished I'd kept one as a souvenir. I never even touched one." He stretched a hand toward Olmayne. "Can I see?"

"We may not let others handle the starstone," I said.

"I wouldn't tell anybody you let me!"

"It is forbidden."

"Look, it's private in here, the most private place on Earth, and—"

"Please. What you ask is impossible."

His face darkened, and I thought for a moment he would halt the car and order us out, which would have caused me no grief. My hand slipped into my pouch to finger the frigid starstone sphere that I had been given at the outset of my Pilgrimage. The touch of my fingertips brought faint resonances of the communion-trance to me, and I shivered in pleasure. He must not have it, I swore. But the crisis passed without incident. The Merchant, having tested us and found resistance, did not choose to press the matter.

We sped onward toward Marsay.

He was not a likable man, but he had a certain gross charm, and we were rarely offended by his words. Olmayne, who after all was a fastidious woman and had lived most of her years in the glossy seclusion of the Hall of Rememberers, found him harder to take than I; my intolerances have been well blunted by a lifetime of wandering. But even Olmayne seemed to find him amusing when he boasted of his wealth and influence, when he told of the women who waited for him on many worlds, when he catalogued his homes and his trophies and the guildmasters who sought his counsel, when he bragged of his friendships with former Masters and Dominators. He talked almost wholly of himself and rarely of us, for which we were thankful; once he asked how it was that a male Pilgrim and a female Pilgrim were traveling together, implying that we must be lovers; we admitted that the arrangement was slightly irregular and went on to another theme, and I think he remained persuaded of our unchastity. His bawdy guesses mattered not at all to me nor, I believe, to Olmayne. We had more serious guilts as our burdens.

Our Merchant's life seemed enviably undisrupted by the fall of our planet: he was as rich as ever, as comfortable, as free to move about. But even he felt occasionally irked by the presence of the invaders, as we found out by night not far from Marsay, when we were stopped at a checkpoint on the road.

Spy-eye scanners saw us coming, gave a signal to the spinnerets, and a golden spiderweb spurted into being from one shoulder of the highway to the other. The landcar's sensors detected it and instantly signaled us to a halt. The screens showed a dozen pale human figures clustered outside.

"Bandits?" Olmayne asked.

"Worse," said the Merchant. "Traitors." He scowled and turned to his communicator horn. "What is it?" he demanded.

"Get out for inspection."

"By whose writ?"

"The Procurator of Marsay," came the reply.

It was an ugly thing to behold: human beings acting as road-agents for the invaders. But it was inevitable that we should have begun to drift into their civil service, since work was scarce, especially for those who had been in the defensive guilds. The Merchant began the complicated process of unsealing his car. He was stormy-faced with rage, but he was stymied, unable to pass the checkpoint's web. "I go armed," he whispered to us. "Wait inside and fear nothing."

He got out and engaged in a lengthy discussion, of which we could hear nothing, with the highway guards. At length some impasse must have forced recourse to higher authority, for three invaders abruptly appeared, waved their hired collaborators away, and surrounded the Merchant. His demeanor changed; his face grew oily and sly, his hands moved rapidly in eloquent gestures, his eyes glistened. He led the three interrogators to the car, opened it, and showed them his two passengers, ourselves. The invaders appeared puzzled by the sight of Pilgrims amid such opulence, but they did not ask us to step out. After some further conversation the Merchant rejoined us and sealed the car; the web was dissolved; we sped onward toward Marsay.

As we gained velocity he muttered curses and said, "Do you know how I'd handle that long-armed filth? All we need is a coordinated plan. A night of knives: every ten Earthmen make themselves responsible for taking out one invader. We'd get them all."

"Why has no one organized such a movement?" I asked.

"It's the job of the Defenders, and half of them are

dead, and the other half's in the pay of *them*. It's not my place to set up a resistance movement. But that's how it should be done. Guerrilla action: sneak up behind 'em, give 'em the knife. Quick. Good old First Cycle methods; they've never lost their value."

"More invaders would come," Olmayne said morosely.

"Treat 'em the same way!"

"They would retaliate with fire. They would destroy our world," she said.

"These invaders pretend to be civilized, more civilized than ourselves," the Merchant replied. "Such barbarity would give them a bad name on a million worlds. No, they wouldn't come with fire. They'd just get tired of having to conquer us over and over, of losing so many men. And they'd go away, and we'd be free again."

"Without having won redemption for our ancient sins," I said.

"What's that, old man? What's that?"

"Never mind."

"I suppose you wouldn't join in, either of you, if we struck back at them?"

I said, "In former life I was a Watcher, and I devoted myself to the protection of this planet against them. I am no more fond of our masters than you are, and no less eager to see them depart. But your plan is not only impractical: it is also morally valueless. Mere bloody resistance would thwart the scheme the Will has devised for us. We must earn our freedom in a nobler way. We were not given this ordeal simply so that we might have practice in slitting throats."

He looked at me with contempt and snorted. "I should have remembered. I'm talking to Pilgrims. All right. Forget it all. I wasn't serious, anyway. Maybe you like the world the way it is, for all I know."

"I do not," I said.

He glanced at Olmayne. So did I, for I half-expected her to tell the Merchant that I had already done my bit of collaborating with our conquerors. But Olmayne fortunately was silent on that topic, as she would be for some months more, until that unhappy day by the approach to

Land Bridge when, in her impatience, she taunted me with my sole fall from grace.

We left our benefactor in Marsay, spent the night in a Pilgrim hostelry, and set out on foot along the coast the next morning. And so we traveled, Olmayne and I, through pleasant lands swarming with invaders; now we walked, now we rode some peasant's rollerwagon, once even we were the guests of touring conquerors. We gave Roum a wide berth when we entered Talya, and turned south. And so we came to Land Bridge, and met delay, and had our frosty moment of bickering, and then were permitted to go on across that narrow tongue of sandy ground that links the lake-sundered continents. And so we crossed into Afreek, at last.

4

Our first night on the other side, after our long and dusty crossing, we tumbled into a grimy inn near the lake's edge. It was a square whitewashed stone building, practically windowless and arranged around a cool inner courtyard. Most of its clientele appeared to be Pilgrims, but there were some members of other guilds, chiefly Vendors and Transporters. At a room near the turning of the building there stayed a Rememberer, whom Olmayne avoided even though she did not know him; she simply did not wish to be reminded of her former guild.

Among those who took lodging there was the Changeling Bernalt. Under the new laws of the invaders, Changelings might stay at any public inn, not merely those set aside for their special use; yet it seemed a little strange to see him here. We passed in the corridor. Bernalt gave me a tentative smile, as though about to speak again, but the smile died and the glow left his eyes. He appeared to realize I was not ready to accept his friendship. Or perhaps he merely recalled that Pilgrims, by the laws of their guild, were not supposed to have much to do with guild-less ones. That law still stood.

Olmayne and I had a greasy meal of soups and stews.

Afterward I saw her to her room and began to wish her good night when she said, "Wait. We'll do our communion together."

"I've been seen coming into your room," I pointed out. "There will be whispering if I stay long."

"We'll go to yours, then!"

Olmayne peered into the hall. All clear: she seized my wrist, and we rushed toward my chamber, across the way. Closing and sealing the warped door, she said, "Your starstone, now!"

I took the stone from its hiding place in my robe, and she produced hers, and our hands closed upon them.

During this time of Pilgrimage I had found the starstone a great comfort. Many seasons now had passed since I had last entered a Watcher's trance, but I was not yet reconciled entirely to the breaking of my old habit; the starstone provided a kind of substitute for the swooping ecstasy I had known in Watching.

Starstones come from one of the outer worlds—I could not tell you which—and may be had only by application to the guild. The stone itself determines whether one may be a Pilgrim, for it will burn the hand of one whom it considers unworthy to don the robe. They say that without exception every person who has enrolled in the guild of Pilgrims has shown uneasiness as the stone was offered to him for the first time.

"When they gave you yours," Olmayne asked, "were you worried?"

"Of course."

"So was I."

We waited for the stones to overwhelm us. I gripped mine tightly. Dark, shining, more smooth than glass, it glowed in my grasp like a pellet of ice, and I felt myself becoming attuned to the power of the Will.

First came a heightened perception of my surroundings. Every crack in the walls of this ancient inn seemed now a valley. The soft wail of the wind outside rose to a keen pitch. In the dim glow of the room's lamp I saw colors beyond the spectrum.

The quality of the experience the starstone offered was altogether different from that given by my instruments of

Watching. That, too, was a transcending of self. When in a state of Watchfulness I was capable of leaving my Earthbound identity and soaring at infinite speed over infinite range, perceiving all, and this is as close to godhood as a man is likely to come. The starstone provided none of the highly specific data that a Watcher's trance yielded. In the full spell I could see nothing, nor could I identify my surroundings. I knew only that when I let myself be drawn into the stone's effect, I was engulfed by something far larger than myself, that I was in direct contact with the matrix of the universe.

Call it communion with the Will.

From a great distance I heard Olmayne say, "Do you believe what some people say of these stones? That there is no communion, that it's all an electrical deception?"

"I have no theory about that," I said. "I am less interested in causes than in effects."

Skeptics say that the starstones are nothing more than amplifying loops which bounce a man's own brain-waves back into his mind; the awesome oceanic entity with which one comes in contact, these scoffers hold, is merely the thunderous recycling oscillation of a single shuttling electrical pulse beneath the roof of the Pilgrim's own skull. Perhaps. Perhaps.

Olmayne extended the hand that gripped her stone. She said, "When you were among the Rememberers, Tomis, did you study the history of early religion? All through time, man has sought union with the infinite. Many religions—not all!—have held forth the hope of such a divine merging."

"And there were drugs, too," I murmured.

"Certain drugs, yes, cherished for their ability to bring the taker momentarily to a sensation of oneness with the universe. These starstones, Tomis, are only the latest in a long sequence of devices for overcoming the greatest of human curses, that is, the confinement of each individual soul within a single body. Our terrible isolation from one another and from the Will itself is more than most races of the universe would be able to bear. It seems unique to humanity."

Her voice grew feathery and vague. She said much

more, speaking to me out of the wisdom she had learned with the Rememberers, but her meaning eluded me; I was always quicker to enter communion than she, because of my training as a Watcher, and often her final words did not register.

That night as on other nights I seized my stone and felt the chill and closed my eyes, and heard the distant tolling of a mighty gong, the lapping of .waves on an unknown beach, the whisper of the wind in an alien forest. And felt a summons. And yielded. And entered the state of communion. And gave myself up to the Will.

And slipped down through the layers of my life, through my youth and middle years, my wanderings, my old loves, my torments, my joys, my troubled later years, my treasons, my insufficiencies, my griefs, my imperfections.

And freed myself of myself. And shed my selfness. And merged. And became one of thousands of Pilgrims, not merely Olmayne nearby, but others trekking the mountains of Hind and the sands of Arba, Pilgrims at their devotions in Ais and Palash and Stralya, Pilgrims moving toward Jorslem on the journey that some complete in months, some in years, and some never at all. And shared with all of them the instant of submergence into the Will. And saw in the darkness a deep purple glow on the horizon—which grew in intensity until it became an all-encompassing red brilliance. And went into it, though unworthy, unclean, flesh-trapped, accepting fully the communion offered and wishing no other state of being than this divorce from self.

And was purified.

And awakened alone.

5

I knew Afreek well. When still a young man I had settled in the continent's dark heart for many years. Out of restlessness I had left, finally, going as far north as Agupt, where the antique relics of First Cycle days have survived better than anywhere else. In those days antiquity held no interest for me, however. I did my Watching and went about from place to place, since a Watcher does not need to have a fixed station; and chance brought me in contact with Avluela just as I was ready to roam again, and so I left Agupt for Roum and then Perris.

Now I had come back with Olmayne. We kept close to the coast and avoided the sandy inland wastes. As Pilgrims we were immune from most of the hazards of travel: we would never go hungry or without shelter, even in a place where no lodge for our guild existed, and all owed us respect. Olmayne's great beauty might have been a hazard to her, traveling as she was with no escort other than a shriveled old man, but behind the mask and robe of a Pilgrim she was safe. We unmasked only rarely, and never where we might be seen.

I had no illusions about my importance to Olmayne. To her I was merely part of the equipment of a journey—someone to help her in her communions and rituals, to arrange for lodgings, to smooth her way for her. That role suited me. She was, I knew, a dangerous woman, given to strange whims and unpredictable fancies. I wanted no entanglements with her.

She lacked a Pilgrim's purity. Even though she had passed the test of the starstone, she had not triumphed—as a Pilgrim must—over her own flesh. She slipped off, sometimes, for half a night or longer, and I pictured her lying maskless in some alley gasping in a Servitor's arms. That was her affair entirely; I never spoke of her absences upon her return.

Within our lodgings, too, she was careless of her virtue. We never shared a room—no Pilgrim hostelry would permit it—but we usually had adjoining ones, and she summoned me to hers or came to mine whenever the mood took her. Often as not she was unclothed; she attained the height of the grotesque one night in Agupt when I found her wearing only her mask, all her gleaming white flesh belying the intent of the bronze grillwork that hid her face. Only once did it seem to occur to her that I might ever have been young enough to feel desire. She looked my scrawny, shrunken body over and said, "How will you look, I wonder, when you've been renewed in Jorslem? I'm trying to picture you young, Tomis. Will you give me pleasure then?"

"I gave pleasure in my time," I said obliquely.

Olmayne disliked the heat and dryness of Agupt. We traveled mainly by night and clung to our hostelries by day. The roads were crowded at all hours. The press of Pilgrims towards Jorslem was extraordinarily heavy, it appeared. Olmayne and I speculated on how long it might take us to gain access to the waters of renewal at such a time.

"You've never been renewed before?" she asked.

"Never."

"Nor I. They say they don't admit all who come."

"Renewal is a privilege, not a right," I said. "Many are turned away."

"I understand also," said Olmayne, "that not all who enter the waters are successfully renewed."

"I know little of this."

"Some grow older instead of younger. Some grow young too fast, and perish. There are risks."

"Would you not take those risks?"

She laughed. "Only a fool would hesitate."

"You are in no need of renewal at this time," I pointed out. "You were sent to Jorslem for the good of your soul, not that of your body, as I recall."

"I'll tend to my soul as well, when I'm in Jorslem."

"But you talk as if the house of renewal is the only shrine you mean to visit."

"It's the important one," she said. She rose, flexing her supple body voluptuously. "True, I have atoning to do. But do you think I've come all the way to Jorslem just for the sake of my spirit?"

"I have," I pointed out.

"You! You're old and withered! You'd better look after your spirit—and your flesh as well. I wouldn't mind shedding some age, though. I won't have them take off much. Eight, ten years, that's all. The years I wasted with that fool Elegro. I don't need a full renewal. You're right: I'm still in my prime." Her face clouded. "If the city is full of Pilgrims, maybe they won't let me into the house of renewal at all! They'll say I'm too young—tell me to come back in forty or fifty years—Tomis, would they do that to me?"

"It is hard for me to say."

She trembled. "They'll let *you* in. You're a walking corpse already—they have to renew you! But me—Tomis, I won't let them turn me away! If I have to pull Jorslem down stone by stone, I'll get in somehow!"

I wondered privately if her soul were in fit condition for one who poses as a candidate for renewal. Humility is recommended when one becomes a Pilgrim. But I had no wish to feel Olmayne's fury, and I kept my silence. Perhaps they would admit her to renewal despite her flaws. I had concerns of my own. It was vanity that drove Olmayne; my goals were different. I had wandered long and done much, not all of it virtuous; I needed a cleansing of my conscience in the holy city more, perhaps, than I did a lessening of my years.

Or was it only vanity for me to think so?

6

Several days eastward of that place, as Olmayne and I walked through a parched countryside, village children chattering in fear and excitement rushed upon us.

"Please, come, come!" they cried. "Pilgrims, come!"

Olmayne looked bewildered and irritated as they plucked at her robes. "What are they saying, Tomis? I can't get through their damnable Aguptan accents!"

"They want us to help," I said. I listened to their shouts. "In their village," I told Olmayne, "there is an outbreak of the crystallization disease. They wish us to seek the mercies of the Will upon the sufferers."

Olmayne drew back. I imagined the disdainful wince behind her mask. She flicked out her hands, trying to keep the children from touching her. To me she said, "We can't go there!"

"We must."

"We're in a hurry! Jorslem's crowded; I don't want to waste time in some dreary village."

"They need us, Olmayne."

"Are we Surgeons?"

"We are Pilgrims," I said quietly. "The benefits we gain from that carry certain obligations. If we are entitled to the hospitality of all we meet, we must also place our souls at the free disposal of the humble. Come."

"I won't go!"

"How will that sound in Jorslem, when you give an accounting of yourself, Olmayne?"

"It's a hideous disease. What if we get it?"

"Is that what troubles you? Trust in the Will! How can you expect renewal if your soul is so deficient in grace?"

"May you rot, Tomis," she said in a low voice. "When did you become so pious? You're doing this deliberately, because of what I said to you by Land Bridge. In a stupid moment I taunted you, and now you're willing to expose us both to a ghastly affliction for your revenge. Don't do it, Tomis!"

I ignored her accusation. "The children are growing agitated, Olmayne. Will you wait here for me, or will you go on to the next village and wait in the hostelry there?"

"Don't leave me alone in the middle of nowhere!"

"I have to go to the sick ones," I said.

In the end she accompanied me—I think not out of any suddenly conceived desire to be of help, but rather out of fear that her selfish refusal might somehow be held against her in Jorslem. We came shortly to the village, which was small and decayed, for Agupt lies in a terrible hot sleep and changes little with the millennia. The contrast with the busy cities farther to the south in Afreek— cities that prosper on the output of luxuries from their great Manufactories—is vast.

Shivering with heat, we followed the children to the houses of sickness.

The crystallization disease is an unlovely gift from the stars. Not many afflictions of outworlders affect the Earthborn; but from the worlds of the Spear came this ailment, carried by alien tourists, and the disease has settled among us. If it had come during the glorious days of the

Second Cycle we might have eradicated it in a day; but our skills are dulled now, and no year has been without its outbreak. Olmayne was plainly terrified as we entered the first of the clay huts where the victims were kept.

There is no hope for one who has contracted this disease. One merely hopes that the healthy will be spared; and fortunately it is not a highly contagious disease. It works insidiously, transmitted in an unknown way, often failing to pass from husband to wife and leaping instead to the far side of a city, to another land entirely, perhaps. The first symptom is a scaliness of the skin; itch, flakes upon the clothing, inflammation. There follows a weakness in the bones as the calcium is dissolved. One grows limp and rubbery, but this is still an early phase. Soon the outer tissues harden. Thick, opaque membranes form on the surface of the eyes; the nostrils may close and seal; the skin grows coarse and pebbled. In this phase prophecy is common. The sufferer partakes of the skills of a Somnambulist, and utters oracles. The soul may wander, separating from the body for hours at a time, although the life-processes continue. Next, within twenty days after the onset of the disease, the crystallization occurs. While the skeletal structure dissolves, the skin splits and cracks, forming shining crystals in rigid geometrical patterns. The victim is quite beautiful at this time and takes on the appearance of a replica of himself in precious gems. The crystals glow with rich inner lights, violet and green and red; their sharp facets adopt new alignments from hour to hour; the slightest illumination in the room causes the sufferer to give off brilliant glittering reflections that dazzle and delight the eye. All this time the internal body is changing, as if some strange chrysalis is forming. Miraculously the organs sustain life throughout every transformation, although in the crystalline phase the victim is no longer able to communicate with others and possibly is unaware of the changes in himself. Ultimately the metamorphosis reaches the vital organs, and the process fails. The alien infestation is unable to reshape those organs without killing its host. The crisis is swift: a brief convulsion, a final discharge of energy along the nervous system of the crystallized one, and there is a quick arching of the body, accompanied by the delicate tinkling sounds of shivering glass, and then all is over. On the planet to which this is native, crystallization is not a disease but an actual metamorphosis, the result of thousands of years of evolution toward a symbiotic relationship. Unfortunately, among the Earthborn, the evolutionary preparation did not take place, and the agent of change invariably brings its subject to a fatal outcome.

Since the process is irreversible, Olmayne and I could do nothing of real value here except offer consolation to these ignorant and frightened people. I saw at once that the disease had seized this village some time ago. There were people in all stages, from the first rash to the ultimate crystallization. They were arranged in the hut according to the intensity of their infestation. To my left was a somber row of new victims, fully conscious and morbidly scratching their arms as they contemplated the horrors that awaited them. Along the rear wall were five pallets on which lay villagers in the coarse-skinned and prophetic phase. To my right were those in varying degrees of crystallization, and up front, the diadem of the lot, was one who clearly was in his last hours of life. His body, encrusted with false emeralds and rubies and opals, shimmered in almost painful beauty; he scarcely moved; within that shell of wondrous color he was lost in some dream of ecstasy, finding at the end of his days more passion, more delight, than he could ever have known in all his harsh peasant years.

Olmayne shied back from the door.

"It's horrible," she whispered. "I won't go in!"

"We must. We are under an obligation."

"I never wanted to be a Pilgrim!"

"You wanted atonement," I reminded her. "It must be earned."

"We'll catch the disease!"

"The Will can reach us anywhere to infect us with this, Olmayne. It strikes at random. The danger is no greater for us inside this building than it is in Perris."

"Why, then, are so many in this one village smitten?"

"This village has earned the displeasure of the Will."

"How neatly you serve up the mysticism, Tomis," she

said bitterly. "I misjudged you. I thought you were a sensible man. This fatalism of yours is ugly."

"I watched my world conquered," I said. "I beheld the Prince of Roum destroyed. Calamities breed such attitudes as I now have. Let us go in, Olmayne."

We entered, Olmayne still reluctant. Now fear assailed me, but I concealed it. I had been almost smug in my piety while arguing with the lovely Rememberer woman who was my companion, but I could not deny the sudden seething of fright.

I forced myself to be tranquil.

There are redemptions and redemptions, I told myself. If this disease is to be the source of mine, I will abide by the Will.

Perhaps Olmayne came to some such decision too, as we went in, or maybe her own sense of the dramatic forced her into the unwanted role of the lady of mercy. She made the rounds with me. We passed from pallet to pallet, heads bowed, starstones in our hands. We said words. We smiled when the newly sick begged for reassurance. We offered prayers. Olmayne paused before one girl in the secondary phase, whose eyes already were filming over with horny tissue, and knelt and touched her starstone to the girl's scaly cheek. The girl spoke in oracles, but unhappily not in any language we understood.

At last we came to the terminal case, he who had grown his own superb sarcophagus. Somehow I felt purged of fear, and so too was Olmayne, for we stood a long while before this grotesque sight, silent, and then she whispered, "How terrible! How wonderful! How beautiful!"

Three more huts similar to this one awaited us.

The villagers clustered at the doorways. As we emerged from each building in turn, the healthy ones fell down about us, clutching at the hems of our robes, stridently demanding that we intercede for them with the Will. We spoke such words as seemed appropriate and not too insincere. Those within the huts received our words blankly, as if they already realized there was no chance for them; those outside, still untouched by the disease, clung to every syllable. The headman of the village—only an act-

ing headman; the true chief lay crystallized—thanked us
again and again, as though we had done something real.
At least we had given comfort, which is not to be despised.

When we came forth from the last of the sickhouses,
we saw a slight figure watching us from a distance: the
Changeling Bernalt. Olmayne nudged me.

"That creature has been following us, Tomis. All the
way from Land Bridge!"

"He travels to Jorslem also."

"Yes, but why should he stop here? Why in this awful
place?"

"Hush, Olmayne. Be civil to him now."

"To a *Changéling?*"

Bernalt approached. The mutated one was clad in a soft
white robe that blunted the strangeness of his appearance. He nodded sadly toward the village and said, "A
great tragedy. The Will lies heavy on this place."

He explained that he had arrived here several days ago
and had met a friend from his native city of Nayrub. I
assumed he meant a Changeling, but no, Bernalt's friend
was a Surgeon, he said, who had halted here to do what
he could for the afflicted villagers. The idea of a friendship between a Changeling and a Surgeon seemed a bit
odd to me, and positively contemptible to Olmayne, who
did not trouble to hide her loathing of Bernalt.

A partly crystallized figure staggered from one of the
huts, gnarled hands clutching. Bernalt went forward and
gently guided it back within. Returning to us, he said,
"There are times one is actually glad one is a Changeling.
That disease does not affect us, you know." His eyes acquired a sudden glitter. "Am I forcing myself on you, Pilgrims? You seem like stone behind your masks. I mean no
harm; shall I withdraw?"

"Of course not," I said, meaning the opposite. His company disturbed me; perhaps the ordinary disdain for
Changelings was a contagion that had at last reached me.
"Stay awhile. I would ask you to travel with us to Jorslem, but you know it is forbidden for us."

"Certainly. I quite understand." He was coolly polite,
but the seething bitterness in him was close to the sur-

face. Most Changelings are such degraded bestial things that they are incapable of knowing how detested they are by normal guilded men and women; but Bernalt clearly was gifted with the torment of comprehension. He smiled, and then he pointed. "My friend is here."

Three figures approached. One was Bernalt's Surgeon, a slender man, dark-skinned, soft-voiced, with weary eyes and sparce yellow hair. With him were an official of the invaders and another outworlder from a different planet. "I had heard that two Pilgrims were summoned to this place," said the invader. "I am grateful for the comfort you may have brought these sufferers. I am Earthclaim Nineteen; this district is under my administration. Will you be my guests at dinner this night?"

I was doubtful of taking an invader's hospitality, and Olmayne's sudden clenching of her fist over her starstone told me that she also hesitated. Earthclaim Nineteen seemed eager for our acceptance. He was not as tall as most of his kind, and his malproportioned arms reached below his knees. Under the blazing Aguptan sun his thick waxy skin acquired a high gloss, although he did not perspire.

Into a long, tense, and awkward silence the Surgeon inserted: "No need to hold back. In this village we all are brothers. Join us tonight, will you?"

We did. Earthclaim Nineteen occupied a villa by the shore of Lake Medit; in the clear light of late afternoon I thought I could detect Land Bridge jutting forward to my left, and even Eyrop at the far side of the lake. We were waited upon by members of the guild of Servitors who brought us cool drinks on the patio. The invader had a large staff, all Earthborn; to me it was another sign that our conquest had become institutionalized and was wholly accepted by the bulk of the populace. Until long after dusk we talked, lingering over drinks even as the writhing auroras danced into view to herald the night. Bernalt the Changeling remained apart, though, perhaps ill at ease in our presence. Olmayne too was moody and withdrawn; a mingled depression and exaltation had settled over her in the stricken village, and the presence of Bernalt at the dinner party had reinforced her silence, for she had no idea how to be polite in the presence of a Changeling. The invader, our host, was charming and attentive, and tried to bring her forth from her bleakness. I had seen charming conquerors before. I had traveled with one who had posed as the Earthborn Changeling Gormon in the days just before the conquest. This one, Earthclaim Nineteen, had been a poet on his native world in those days. I said, "It seems unlikely that one of your inclinations would care to be part of a military occupation."

"All experiences strengthen the art," said Earthclaim Nineteen. "I seek to expand myself. In any case I am not a warrior but an administrator. Is it so strange that a poet can be an administrator, or an administrator a poet?" He laughed. "Among your many guilds, there is no guild of Poets. Why?"

"There are Communicants," I said. "They serve your muse."

"But in a religious way. They are interpreters of the Will, not of their own souls."

"The two are indistinguishable. The verses they make are divinely inspired, but rise from the hearts of their makers," I said.

Earthclaim Nineteen looked unconvinced. "You may argue that all poetry is at bottom religious, I suppose. But this stuff of your Communicants is too limited in scope. It deals only with acquiescence to the Will."

"A paradox," said Olmayne. "The Will encompasses everything, and yet you say that our Communicants' scope is limited."

"There are other themes for poetry besides immersion in the Will, my friends. The love of person for person, the joy of defending one's home, the wonder of standing naked beneath the fiery stars—" The invader laughed. "Can it be that Earth fell so swiftly because its only poets were poets of acquiescence to destiny?"

"Earth fell," said the Surgeon, "because the Will required us to atone for the sin our ancestors committed when they treated your ancestors like beasts. The quality of our poetry had nothing to do with it."

"The Will decreed that you would lose to us by way of punishment, eh? But if the Will is omnipotent, it must have decreed the sin of your ancestors that made the punishment necessary. Eh? Eh? The Will playing games with itself? You see the difficulty of believing in a divine force that determines all events? Where is the element of choice that makes suffering meaningful? To force you into a sin, and then to require you to endure defeat as atonement, seems to me an empty exercise. Forgive my blasphemy."

The Surgeon said, "You misunderstand. All that has happened on this planet is part of a process of moral instruction. The Will does not shape every event great or small; it provides the raw material of events, and allows us to follow such patterns as we desire."

"Example?"

"The Will imbued the Earthborn with skills and knowledge. During the First Cycle we rose from savagery in little time; in the Second Cycle we attained greatness. In our moment of greatness we grew swollen with pride, choosing to exceed our limitations. We imprisoned intelligent creatures of other worlds under the pretense of 'study,' when we acted really out of an arrogant desire for amusement; and we toyed with our world's climate until oceans joined and continents sank and our old civilization was destroyed. Thus the Will instructed us in the boundaries of human ambition."

"I dislike that dark philosphy even more," said Earthclaim Nineteen. "I—"

"Let me finish," said the Surgeon. "The collapse of Second Cycle Earth was our punishment. The defeat of Third Cycle Earth by you folk from the stars is a completion of that earlier punishment, but also the beginning of a new phase. You are the instruments of our redemption. By inflicting on us the final humiliation of conquest, you bring us to the bottom of our trough; now we renew our souls, now we begin to rise, tested by adversities."

I stared in sudden amazement at this Surgeon, who was uttering ideas that had been stirring in me all along the road to Jorslem, ideas of redemption both personal and planetary. I had paid little attention to the Surgeon before.

"Permit me a statement," Bernalt said suddenly, his first words in hours.

We looked at him. The pigmented bands in his face were ablaze, marking his emotion.

He said, nodding to the Surgeon, "My friend, you speak of redemption for the Earthborn. Do you mean *all* Earthborn, or only the guilded ones?"

"All Earthborn, of course," said the Surgeon mildly. "Are we not all equally conquered?"

"We are not equal in other things, though. Can there be redemption for a planet that keeps millions of its people thrust into guildlessness? I speak of my own folk, of course. We sinned long ago when we thought we were striking out against those who had created us as monsters. We strove to take Jorslem from you; and for this we were punished, and our punishment has lasted for a thousand years. We are still outcasts, are we not? Where has our hope of redemption been? Can you guilded ones consider yourself purified and made virtuous by your recent suffering, when you still step on us?"

The Surgeon looked dismayed. "You speak rashly, Bernalt. I know the Changelings have a grievance. But you know as well as I that your time of deliverance is at hand. In the days to come no Earthborn one will scorn you, and you will stand beside us when we regain our freedom."

Bernalt peered at the floor. "Forgive me, my friend. Of course, of course, you speak the truth. I was carried away. The heat—this splendid wine—how foolishly I spoke!"

Earthclaim Nineteen said, "Are you telling me that a resistance movement is forming that will shortly drive us from your planet?"

"I speak only in abstract terms," said the Surgeon.

"I think your resistance movement will be purely abstract, too," the invader replied easily. "Forgive me, but I see little strength in a planet that could be conquered in a single night. We expect our occupation of Earth to be a long one and to meet little opposition. In the months that we have been here there has been no sign of increasing hostility to us. Quite the contrary: we are increasingly accepted among you."

"It is part of a process," said the Surgeon. "As a poet, you should understand that words carry meanings of many kinds. We do not need to overthrow our alien masters in order to be free of them. Is that poetic enough for you?"

"Splendid," said Earthclaim Nineteen, getting to his feet. "Shall we go to dinner now?"

6

THERE was no way to return to the subject. A philosophical discussion at the dinner table is difficult to sustain; and our host did not seem comfortable with this analysis of Earth's destinies. Swiftly he discovered that Olmayne had been a Rememberer before turning Pilgrim, and thereafter directed his words to her, questioning her on our history and on our early poetry. Like most invaders he had a fierce curiosity concerning our past. Olmayne gradually came out of the silence that gripped her, and spoke at length about her researches in Perris. She talked with great familiarity of our hidden past, with Earthclaim Nineteen occasionally inserting an intelligent and informed question; meanwhile we dined on delicacies of a number of worlds, perhaps imported by that same fat, insensitive Merchant who had driven us from Perris to Marsay; the villa was cool and the Servitors attentive; that miserable plague-stricken peasant village half an hour's walk away might well have been in some other galaxy, so remote was it from our discourse now.

When we left the villa in the morning, the Surgeon asked permission to join our Pilgrimage. "There is nothing further I can do here," he explained. "At the outbreak of the disease I came up from my home in Nayrub, and I've been here many days, more to console than to cure, of course. Now I am called to Jorslem. However, if it violates your vows to have company on the road—"

"By all means come with us," I said.

"There will be one other companion," the Surgeon told us.

He meant the third person who had met us at the village: the outworlder, an enigma, yet to say a word in our presence. This being was a flattened spike-shaped creature somewhat taller than a man and mounted on a jointed tripod of angular legs; its place of origin was in the Golden Spiral; its skin was rough and bright red in hue, and vertical rows of glassy oval eyes descended on three sides from the top of its tapered head. I had never seen such a creature before. It had come to Earth, according to the Surgeon, on a data-gathering mission, and had already roamed much of Ais and Stralya. Now it was touring the lands on the margin of Lake Medit; and after seeing Jorslem it would depart for the great cities of Eyrop. Solemn, unsettling in its perpetual watchfulness, never blinking its many eyes nor offering a comment on what those eyes beheld, it seemed more like some odd machine, some information-intake for a memory tank, than a living creature. But it was harmless enough to let it come with us to the holy city.

The Surgeon bade farewell to his Changeling friend, who went on alone ahead of us, and paid a final call on the crystallized village. We stayed back, since there was no point in our going. When he returned, his face was somber. "Four new cases," he said. "This entire village will perish. There has never been an outbreak of this kind before on Earth—so concentrated an epidemic."

"Something new, then?" I asked. "Will it spread everywhere?"

"Who knows? No one in the adjoining villages has caught it. The pattern is unfamiliar: a single village wholly devastated, and nowhere else besides. These people see it as divine retribution for unknown sins."

"What could peasants have done," I asked, "that would bring the wrath of the Will so harshly upon them?"

"They are asking that too," said the Surgeon.

Olmayne said, "If there are new cases, our visit yesterday was useless. We risked ourselves and did them no good."

"Wrong," the Surgeon told her. "These cases were already incubating when you arrived. We may hope that the disease will not spread to those who still were in full health."

He did not seem confident of that.

Olmayne examined herself from day to day for symptoms of the disease, but none appeared. She gave the Surgeon much trouble on that score, bothering him for opinions concerning real or fancied blemishes of her skin, embarrassing him by removing her mask in his presence so that he could determine that some speck on her cheek was not the first trace of crystallization.

The Surgeon took all this in good grace, for, while the outworld being was merely a cipher plodding alongside us, the Surgeon was a man of depth, patience, and sophistication. He was native to Afreek, and had been dedicated to his guild at birth by his father, since healing was the family tradition. Traveling widely, he had seen most of our world and had forgotten little of what he had seen. He spoke to us of Roum and Perris, of the frostflower fields of Stralya, of my own birthplace in the western island group of the Lost Continents. He questioned us tactfully about our starstones and the effects they produced—I could see he hungered to try the stone himself, but that of course was forbidden to one who had not declared himself a Pilgrim—and when he learned that in former life I had been a Watcher, he asked me a great deal concerning the instruments by which I had scanned the heavens, wishing to know what it was I perceived and how I imagined the perception was accomplished. I spoke to him as fully as I could on these matters, though in truth I knew little.

Usually we kept to the green strip of fertile land bordering the lake, but once, at the Surgeon's insistence, we detoured into the choking desert to see something that he promised would be of interest. He would not tell us what it was. We were at this point traveling in hired rollerwagons, open on top, and sharp winds blew gusts of sand in our faces. Sand adhered briefly to the outworlder's eyes, I saw; and I saw how efficiently it flushed each eye with a flood of blue tears every few moments. The rest of us huddled in our garments, heads down, whenever the wind arose.

"We are here," the Surgeon announced finally. "When I traveled with my father I first visited this place long ago. We will go inside—and then you, the former Rememberer, will tell us where we are."

It was a building two stories high made of bricks of white glass. The doors appeared sealed, but they gave at the slightest pressure. Lights glowed into life the moment we entered.

In long aisles, lightly strewn with sand, were tables on which instruments were mounted. Nothing was comprehensible to me. There were devices shaped like hands, into which one's own hands could be inserted; conduits led from the strange metal gloves to shining closed cabinets, and arrangements of mirrors transmitted images from the interiors of those cabinets to giant screens overhead. The Surgeon placed his hands in the gloves and moved his fingers; the screens brightened, and I saw images of tiny needles moving through shallow arcs. He went to other machines that released dribbles of unknown fluids; he touched small buttons that produced musical sounds; he moved freely through a laboratory of wonders, clearly ancient, which seemed still in order and awaiting the return of its users.

Olmayne was ecstatic. She followed the Surgeon from aisle to aisle, handling everything.

"Well, Rememberer?" he asked finally. "What is this?"

"A Surgery," she said in lowered voice. "A Surgery of the Years of Magic!"

"Exactly! Splendid!" He seemed in an oddly excited state. "We could make dazzling monsters here! We could work miracles! Fliers, Swimmers, Changelings, Twiners, Burners, Climbers—invent your own guilds, shape men to your whims! This was the place!"

Olmayne said, "These Surgeries have been described to me. There are six of them left, are there not, one in northern Eyrop, one on Palash, one here, one far to the south in Deeper Afreek, one in western Ais—" She faltered.

"And one in Hind, the greatest of all!" said the Surgeon.

"Yes, of course, Hind! The home of the Fliers!"

Their awe was contagious. I said, "This was where the shapes of men were changed? How was it done?"

The Surgeon shrugged. "The art is lost. The Years of Magic were long ago, old man."

"Yes, yes, I know. But surely if the equipment survives, we could guess how—"

"With these knives," said the Surgeon, "we cut into the fabric of the unborn, editing the human seed. The Surgeon placed his hands here—he manipulated—and within that incubator the knives did their work. Out of this came Fliers and all the rest. The forms bred true. Some are extinct today, but our Fliers and our Changelings owe their heritage to some such building as this. The Changelings, of course, were the Surgeons' mistakes. They should not have been permitted to live."

"I thought that these monsters were the products of teratogenic drugs given to them when they still were within the womb," I said. "You tell me now that Changelings were made by Surgeons. Which is so?"

"Both," he replied. "All Changelings today are descended from the flaws and errors committed by the Surgeons of the Years of Magic. Yet mothers in that unhappy group often enhance the monstrousness of their children with drugs, so that they will be more marketable. It is an ugly tribe not merely in looks. Small wonder that their guild was dissolved and they were thrust outside society. We—"

Something bright flew through the air, missing his face by less than a hand's breadth. He dropped to the floor and shouted to us to take cover. As I fell I saw a second missile fly toward us. The outworld being, still observing all phenomena, studied it impassively in the moment of life that remained to it. Then the weapon struck two thirds of the way up the outworlder's body and severed it instantly. Other missiles followed, clattering against the wall behind us. I saw our attackers: a band of Changelings, fierce, hideous. We were unarmed. They moved toward us. I readied myself to die.

From the doorway a voice cried out: a familiar voice, using the thick and unfamiliar words of the language

Changelings speak among themselves. Instantly the assault ceased. Those who menaced us turned toward the door. The Changeling Bernalt entered.

"I saw your vehicle," he said. "I thought you might be here, and perhaps in trouble. It seems I came in time."

"Not altogether," said the Surgeon. He indicated the fallen outworlder, which was beyond all aid. "But why this attack?"

Bernalt gestured. "*They* will tell you."

We looked at the five Changelings who had ambushed us. They were not of the educated, civilized sort such as Bernalt, nor were any two of them of the same styles; each was a twisted, hunched mockery of the human form, one with ropy tendrils descending from his chin, one with a face that was a featureless void, another whose ears were giant cups, and so forth. From the one closest to us, a creature with small platforms jutting from his skin in a thousand places, we learned why we had been assaulted. In a brutal Aguptan dialect he told us that we had profaned a temple sacred to Changelings. "We keep out of Jorslem,'" he told us. "Why must you come here?"

Of course he was right. We asked forgiveness as sincerely as we could, and the Surgeon explained that he had visited this place long ago and it had not been a temple then. That seemed to soothe the Changeling, who admitted that only in recent years had his kind used it as a shrine. He was soothed even more when Olmayne opened the overpocket fastened between her breasts and offered a few glittering gold coins, part of the treasure she had brought with her from Perris. The bizarre and deformed beings were satisfied at that and allowed us to leave the building. We would have taken the dead outworlder with us, but during our parley with the Changelings the body had nearly vanished, nothing but a faint gray streak remaining on the sandy floor to tell us where it had fallen. "A mortuary enzyme," the Surgeon explained. "Triggered by interruption of the life processes."

Others of this community of desert-dwelling Changelings were lurking about outside the building as we came forth. They were a tribe of nightmares, with skin of every texture and color, facial features arranged at random, all kinds of genetic improvisations of organs and bodily accessories. Bernalt himself, although their brother, seemed appalled by their monstrousness. They looked to him with awe. At the sight of us some of them fondled the throwing weapons at their hips, but a sharp command from Bernalt prevented any trouble.

He said, "I regret the treatment you received and the death of the outworlder. But of course it is risky to enter a place that is sacred to backward and violent people."

"We had no idea," the Surgeon said. "We never would have gone in if we had realized—"

"Of course. Of course." Was there something patronizing about Bernalt's soft, civilized tones? "Well, again I bid you farewell."

I blurted suddenly, "No. Travel with us to Jorslem! It's ridiculous for us to go separately to the same place."

Olmayne gasped. Even the Surgeon seemed amazed. Only Bernalt remained calm. He said, "You forget, friend, that it is improper for Pilgrims to journey with the guildless. Besides, I am here to worship at this shrine, and it will take me a while. I would not wish to delay you." His hand reached out to mine. Then he moved away, entering the ancient Surgery. Scores of his fellow Changelings rushed in after him. I was grateful to Bernalt for his tact; my impulsive offer of companionship, though sincerely meant, had been impossible for him to accept.

We boarded our rollerwagons. In a moment we heard a dreadful sound: a discordant Changeling hymn in praise of I dare not think what deity, a scraping, grinding, screeching song as misshapen as those who uttered it.

"The beasts," Olmayne muttered. "A sacred shrine! A Changeling temple! How loathsome! They might have killed us all, Tomis. How can such monsters have a religion?"

I made no reply. The Surgeon looked at Olmayne sadly and shook his head as though distressed by so little charity on the part of one who claimed to be a Pilgrim.

"They also are human," he said.

At the next town along our route we reported the starborn being's death to the occupying authorities. Then, saddened and silent, we three survivors continued onward, to the place where the coastline trends north rather than east. We were leaving sleepy Agupt behind and entering now into the borders of the land in which holy Jorslem lies.

7

THE city of Jorslem sits some good distance inland from Lake Medit on a cool plateau guarded by a ring of low, barren, rock-strewn mountains. All my life, it seemed, had been but a preparation for my first glimpse of this golden city, whose image I knew so well. Hence when I saw its spires and parapets rising in the east, I felt not so much awe as a sense of a homecoming.

A winding road took us down through the encircling hills to the city, whose wall was made of squared blocks of a fine stone, dark pink-gold in color. The houses and shrines, too, were of this stone. Groves of trees bordered the road, nor were they star-trees, but native products of Earth, as was fitting to this, the oldest of man's cities, older than Roum, older than Perris, its roots deep in the First Cycle.

The invaders, shrewdly, had not meddled with Jorslem's administration. The city remained under the governorship of the Guildmaster of Pilgrims, and even an invader was required to seek the Guildmaster's permission to enter. Of course, this was strictly a matter of form; the Pilgrim Guildmaster, like the Chancellor of the Rememberers and other such officials, was in truth a puppet subject to our conquerors' wishes. But that harsh fact was kept concealed. The invaders had left our holy city as a city apart, and we would not see them swaggering in armed teams through Jorslem's streets.

At the outer wall we formally requested entry from the Sentinel guarding the gate. Though elsewhere most Sentinels now were unemployed—since cities stood open by command of our masters—this man was in full guild array and calmly insisted on thorough procedure. Olmayne and I, as Pilgrims, were entitled to automatic access to Jorslem; yet he made us produce our starstones as evidence that we came by our robes and masks honestly, and then donned a thinking cap to check our names with the archives of our guild. In time we met approval. The Surgeon our companion had an easier time; he had applied in advance for entry while in Afreek, and after a moment to check his identity he was admitted.

Within the walls everything had the aspect of great antiquity. Jorslem alone of the world's cities still preserves much of its First Cycle architecture: not merely broken columns and ruined aqueducts, as in Roum, but whole streets, covered arcades, towers, boulevards, that have lasted through every upheaval our world has seen. And so once we passed into the city we wandered in wonder through its strangeness, down streets paved with cobbled stones, into narrow alleys cluttered with children and beggars, across markets fragrant with spices. After an hour of this we felt it was time to seek lodgings, and here it was necessary for us to part company with the Surgeon, since he was ineligible to stay at a Pilgrim hostelry, and it would have been costly and foolish for us to stay anywhere else. We saw him to the inn where he had previously booked a room. I thanked him for his good companionship on our journey, and he thanked us just as gravely and expressed the hope that he would see us again in Jorslem in the days to come. Then Olmayne and I took leave of him and rented quarters in one of the numerous places catering to the Pilgrim trade.

The city exists solely to serve Pilgrims and casual tourists, and so it is really one vast hostelry; robed Pilgrims are as common in Jorslem's streets as Fliers in Hind. We settled and rested awhile; then we dined and afterward walked along a broad street from which we could see, to the east, Jorslem's inner and most sacred district. There is a city within a city here. The most ancient part, so small it can be traversed in less than an hour on foot, is wrapped in a high wall of its own. Therein lie shrines revered by Earth's former religions: the Christers, the Hebers, the Mislams. The place where the god of the Christers died is said to be there, but this may be a distortion wrought by time, since what kind of god is it that dies?

On a high place in one corner of the Old City stands a gilded dome sacred to the Mislams, which is carefully tended by the common folk of Jorslem. And to the fore part of that high place are the huge gray blocks of a stone wall worshiped by the Hebers. These things remain, but the ideas behind them are lost; never while I was among the Rememberers did I meet any scholar who could explain the merit of worshiping a wall or a gilded dome. Yet the old records assure us that these three First Cycle creeds were of great depth and richness.

In the Old City, also, is a Second Cycle place that was of much more immediate interest to Olmayne and myself. As we stared through the darkness at the holy precincts Olmayne said, "We should make application tomorrow at the house of renewal."

"I agree. I long now to give up some of my years."

"Will they accept me, Tomis?"

"Speculating on it is idle," I told her. "We will go, and we will apply, and your question will be answered."

She said something further, but I did not hear her words, for at that moment three Fliers passed above me, heading east. One was male, two female; they flew naked, according to the custom of their guild; and the Flier in the center of the group was a slim, fragile girl, mere bones and wings, moving with a grace that was exceptional even for her airy kind.

"*Avluela!*" I gasped.

The trio of Fliers disappeared beyond the parapets of the Old City. Stunned, shaken, I clung to a tree for support and struggled for breath.

"Tomis?" Olmayne said. "Tomis, are you ill?"

"I know it was Avluela. They said she had gone back to Hind, but no, that was Avluela! How could I mistake her?"

"You've said that about every Flier you've seen since leaving Perris," said Olmayne coldly.

"But this time I'm certain! Where is a thinking cap? I must check with the Fliers' Lodge at once!"

Olmayne's hand rested on my arm. "It's late, Tomis. You act feverish. Why this excitement over your skinny Flier, anyway? What did she mean to you?"

"She—"

I halted, unable to put my meaning in words. Olmayne knew the story of my journey up out of Agupt with the girl, how as a celebate old Watcher I had conceived a kind of paternal fondness for her, how I had perhaps felt something more powerful than that, how I had lost her to the false Changeling Gormon, and how *he* in turn had lost her to the Prince of Roum. But yet what was Avluela to me? Why did a glimpse of someone who merely might have been Avluela send me into this paroxysm of confusion? I chased symbols in my turbulent mind and found no answers.

"Come back to the inn and rest," Olmayne said. "Tomorrow we must seek renewal."

First, though, I donned a cap and made contact with the Fliers' Lodge. My thoughts slipped through the shielding interface to the storage brain of the guild registry; I asked and received the answer I had sought. Avluela of the Fliers was indeed now a resident in Jorslem. "Take this message for her," I said. "The Watcher she knew in Roum now is here as a Pilgrim, and wishes to meet her outside the house of renewal at midday tomorrow."

With that done, I accompanied Olmayne to our lodgings. She seemed sullen and aloof; and when she unmasked in my room her face appeared rigid with—jealousy? Yes. To Olmayne all men were vassals, even one so shriveled and worn as I; and she loathed it that another woman could kindle such a flame in me. When I drew forth my starstone, Olmayne at first would not join me in communion. Only when I began the rituals did she submit. But I was so tense that night that I was unable to make the merging with the Will, nor could she achieve it; and thus we faced one another glumly for half an hour, and abandoned the attempt, and parted for the night.

ONE must go by one's self to the house of renewal. At dawn I awoke, made a brief and more successful communion, and set out unbreakfasted, without Olmayne. In half an hour I stood before the golden wall of the Old City; in half an hour more I had finished my crossing of the inner city's tangled lanes. Passing before that gray wall so dear to the ancient Hebers, I went up onto the high place; I passed near the gilded dome of the vanished Mislams and, turning to the left, followed the stream of Pilgrims which already at this early hour was proceeding to the house of renewal.

This house is a Second Cycle building, for it was then that the renewal process was conceived; and of all that era's science, only renewal has come down to us approximately as it must have been practiced in that time. Like those other few Second Cycle structures that survive, the house of renewal is supple and sleek, architecturally understated, with deft curves and smooth textures; it is without windows; it bears no external ornament whatever. There are many doors. I placed myself before the easternmost entrance, and in an hour's time I was admitted.

Just inside the entrance I was greeted by a green-robed member of the guild of Renewers—the first member of this guild I had ever seen. Renewers are recruited entirely from Pilgrims who are willing to make it their life's work to remain in Jorslem and aid others toward renewal. Their guild is under the same administration as the Pilgrims; a single guildmaster directs the destinies of both; even the garb is the same except for color. In effect Pilgrims and Renewers are of one guild and represent different phases of the same affiliation. But a distinction is always drawn.

The Renewer's voice was light and cheerful. "Welcome to this house, Pilgrim. Who are you, where are you from?"

"I am the Pilgrim Tomis, formerly Tomis of the Rememberers, and prior to that a Watcher, born to the name Wuellig. I am native to the Lost Continents and have traveled widely both before and after beginning my Pilgrimage."

"What do you seek here?"

"Renewal. Redemption."

"May the Will grant your wishes," said the Renewer. "Come with me."

I was led through a close, dimly lit passage into a small stone cell. The Renewer instructed me to remove my mask, enter into a state of communion, and wait. I freed myself from the bronze grillwork and clasped my starstone tightly. The familiar sensations of communion stole over me, but no union with the Will took place; rather, I felt a specific link forming with the mind of another human being. Although mystified, I offered no resistance.

Something probed my soul. Everything was drawn forth and laid out as if for inspection on the floor of the cell: my acts of selfishness and of cowardice, my flaws and failings, my doubts, my despairs, above all the most shameful of my acts, the selling of the Rememberer document to the invader overlord. I beheld these things and knew that I was unworthy of renewal. In this house one might extend one's lifetime two or three times over; but why should the Renewers offer such benefits to anyone as lacking in merit as I?

I remained a long while in contemplation of my faults. Then the contact broke, and a different Renewer, a man of remarkable stature, entered the cell.

"The mercy of the Will is upon you, friend," he said, reaching forth fingers of extraordinary length to touch the tips of mine.

When I heard that deep voice and saw those white fingers, I knew that I was in the presence of a man I had met briefly before, as I stood outside the gates of Roum in the season before the conquest of Earth. He had been a Pilgrim then, and he had invited me to join him on his journey to Jorslem, but I had declined, for Roum had beckoned to me.

"Was your Pilgrimage an easy one?" I asked.

"It was a valuable one," he replied. "And you? You are a Watcher no longer, I see."

"I am in my third guild this year."

"With one more yet to come," he said.

"Am I to join you in the Renewers, then?"

"I did not mean that guild, friend Tomis. But we can talk more of that when your years are fewer. You have been approved for renewal, I rejoice to tell you."

"Despite my sins?"

"Because of your sins, such that they are. At dawn tomorrow you enter the first of the renewal tanks. I will be your guide through your second birth. I am the Renewer Talmit. Go, now, and ask for me when you return."

"One question—"

"Yes?"

"I made my Pilgrimage together with a woman, Olmayne, formerly a Rememberer of Perris. Can you tell me if she has been approved for renewal as well?"

"I know nothing of this Olmayne."

"She's not a good woman," I said. "She is vain, imperious, and cruel. But yet I think she is not beyond saving. Can you do anything to help her?"

"I have no influence in such things," Talmit said. "She must face interrogation like everyone else. I can tell you this, though: virtue is not the only criterion for renewal."

He showed me from the building. Cold sunlight illuminated the city. I was drained and depleted, too empty even to feel cheered that I had qualified for renewal. It was midday; I remembered my appointment with Avluela; I circled the house of renewal in rising anxiety. Would she come?

She was waiting by the front of the building, beside a glittering monument from Second Cycle days. Crimson jacket, furry leggings, glassy bubbles on her feet, telltale humps on her back: from afar I could make her out to be a Flier. "Avluela!" I called.

She whirled. She looked pale, thin, even younger than when I had last seen her. Her eyes searched my face, once again masked, and for a moment she was bewildered.

"Watcher?" she said. "Watcher, is that you?"

"Call me Tomis now," I told her. "But I am the same man you knew in Agupt and Roum."

"Watcher! Oh, Watcher! *Tomis*." She clung to me. "How long it's been! So much has happened!" She sparkled now, and the paleness fled her cheeks. "Come, let's find an inn, a place to sit and talk! How did you discover me here?"

"Through your guild. I saw you overhead last night."

"I came here in the winter. I was in Fars for a while, halfway back to Hind, and then I changed my mind. There could be no going home. Now I live near Jorslem, and I help with—" She cut her sentence sharply off. "Have you won renewal, Tomis?"

We descended from the high place into a humbler part of the inner city. "Yes," I said, "I am to be made younger. My guide is the Renewer Talmit—we met him as a Pilgrim outside Roum, do you remember?"

She had forgotten that. We seated ourselves at an open-air patio adjoining an inn, and Servitors brought us food and wine. Her gaiety was infectious; I felt renewed just to be with her. She spoke of those final cataclysmic days in Roum, when she had been taken into the palace of the Prince as a concubine; and she told me of that terrible moment when Gormon the Changeling defeated the Prince of Roum on the evening of conquest—announcing himself as no Changeling but an invader in disguise, and taking from the Prince at once his throne, his concubine, and his vision.

"Did the Prince die?" she asked.

"Yes, but not of his blinding." I told her how that proud man had fled Roum disguised as a Pilgrim, and how I had accompanied him to Perris, and how, while we were among the Rememberers, he had involved himself with Olmayne, and had been slain by Olmayne's husband, whose life was thereupon taken by his wife. "I also saw Gormon in Perris," I said. "He goes by the name of Victorious Thirteen now. He is high in the councils of the invaders."

Avleula smiled. "Gormon and I were together only a short while after the conquest. He wanted to tour Eyrop; I flew with him to Donsk and Sved, and there he lost interest in me. It was then that I felt I must go home to Hind, but later I changed my mind. When does your renewal begin?"

"At dawn."

"Oh, Tomis, how will it be when you are a young man? Did you know that I loved you? All the time we traveled, all while I was sharing Gormon's bed and consorting with the Prince, you were the one I wanted! But of course you were a Watcher, and it was impossible. Besides, you were so old. Now you no longer Watch, and soon you will no longer be old, and—" Her hand rested on mine. "I should never have left your side. We both would have been spared much suffering."

"We learn, from suffering," I said.

"Yes. Yes. I see that. How long will your renewal take?"

"The usual time, whatever that may be."

"After that, what will you do? What guild will you choose? You can't be a Watcher, not now."

"No, nor a Rememberer either. My guide Talmit spoke of some other guild, which he would not name, and assumed that I would enroll in it when I was done with renewal. I supposed he thought I'd stay here and join the Renewers, but he said it was another guild."

"Not the Renewers," said Avluela. She leaned close. "The Redeemers," she whispered.

"Redeemers? That is a guild I do not know."

"It is newly founded."

"No new guild has been established in more than a—"

"This is the guild Talmit meant. You would be a desirable member. The skills you developed when you were a Watcher make you exceptionally useful."

"Redeemers," I said, probing the mystery. "*Redeemers*. What does this guild do?"

Avluela smiled jauntily. "It rescues troubled souls and saves unhappy worlds. But this is no time to talk of it. Finish your business in Jorslem, and everything will become clear." We rose. Her lips brushed mine. "This is the last time I'll see you as an old man. It will be strange, Tomis, when you're renewed!"

She left me then.

Toward evening I returned to my lodging. Olmayne was not in her room. A Servitor told me that she had been out all day. I waited until it was late; then I made my communion and slept, and at dawn I paused outside her door. It was sealed. I hurried to the house of renewal.

9

THE Renewer Talmit met me within the entrance and conducted me down a corridor of green tile to the first renewal tank. "The Pilgrim Olmayne," he informed me, "has been accepted for renewal and will come here later this day." This was the last reference to the affairs of another human being that I was to hear for some time. Talmit showed me into a small low room, close and humid, lit by dim blobs of slavelight and smelling faintly of crushed deathflower blossoms. My robe and my mask were taken from me, and the Renewer covered my head with a fine golden-green mesh of some flimsy metal, through which he sent a current; and when he removed the mesh, my hair was gone, my head was as glossy as the tiled walls. "It makes insertion of the electrodes simpler," Talmit explained. "You may enter the tank, now."

A gentle ramp led me down into the tank, which was a tub of no great size. I felt the warm soft slipperiness of mud beneath my feet, and Talmit nodded and told me it was irradiated regenerative mud, which would stimulate the increase of cell division that was to bring about my renewal, and I accepted it. I stretched out on the floor of the tank with only my head above the shimmering dark violet fluid that it contained. The mud cradled and caressed my tired body. Talmit loomed above me, holding what seemed to be a mass of entangled copper wires, but as he pressed the wires to my bare scalp they opened as of their own accord and their tips sought my skull and burrowed down through skin and bone into the hidden wrinkled grayness. I felt nothing more than tiny prickling sensations. "The electrodes," Talmit explained, "seek out the centers of aging within your brain; we transmit signals that will induce a reversal of the normal processes of decay, and your brain will lose its perception of the direction of the flow of time. Your body thus will become more receptive to the stimulation it receives from the environment of the renewal tank. Close your eyes." Over my face he placed a breathing mask. He gave me a gentle shove, and the back of my head slipped from the edge of the tank, so that I floated out into the middle. The warmth increased. I dimly heard bubbling sounds. I imagined black sulfurous bubbles coming up from the mud and through the fluid in which I floated; I imagined that the fluid had turned the color of mud. Adrift in a tideless sea I lay, distantly aware that a current was passing over the electrodes, that something was tickling my brain, that I was engulfed in mud and in what could well have been an amniotic fluid. From far away came the deep voice of the Renewer Talmit summoning me to youth, drawing me back across the decades, unreeling time for me. There was a taste of salt in my mouth. Again I was crossing Earth Ocean, beset by pirates, defending my Watching equipment against their jeers and thrusts. Again I stood beneath the hot Aguptan sun meeting Avluela for the first time. I lived once more on Palash. I returned to the place of my birth in the western isles of the Lost Continents, in what formerly had been Usa-amrik. I watched Roum fall a second time. Fragments of memories swam through my softening brain. There was no sequence, no rational unrolling of events. I was a child. I was a weary ancient. I was among the Rememberers. I visited the Somnambulists. I saw the Prince of Roum attempt to purchase eyes from an Artificer in Dijon. I bargained with the Procurator of Perris. I gripped the handles of my instruments and entered Watchfulness. I ate sweet things from a far-off world; I drew into my nostrils the perfume of springtime on Palash; I shivered in an old man's private winter; I swam in a surging sea, buoyant and happy; I sang; I wept; I resisted temptation; I yielded to temptations; I quarreled with Olmayne; I embraced Avluela; I experienced a flickering succession of nights and days as my biological clock moved in strange rhythms of reversal and acceleration. Illusions beset me. It rained fire from the sky; time rushed in several directions; I grew small and then enormous. I heard voices speaking in shades of scarlet and turquoise. Jagged music sparkled on the mountains. The sound of my drumming heartbeats was rough and fiery. I was trapped between strokes of my brain-piston, arms pressed to my sides so that I would occupy as little space as possible as it rammed itself home again and again and again. The stars throbbed, contracted, melted. Avluela said gently, "We earn a second youthtime through the indulgent, benevolent impulses of the Will and not through the performance of individual good works." Olmayne said, "How sleek I get!" Talmit said, "These oscillations of perception signify only the dissolution of the wish toward self-destruction that lies at the heart of the aging process." Gormon said, "These perceptions of oscillation signify only the self-destruction of the wish toward dissolution that lies at the aging process of the heart." The Procurator Manrule Seven said, "We have been sent to this world as the devices of your purgation. We are instruments of the Will." Earthclaim Nineteen said, "On the other hand, permit me to disagree. The intersection of Earth's destinies and ours is purely accidental." My eyelids turned to stone. The small creatures comprising my lungs began to flower. My skin sloughed off, revealing strands of muscle clinging to bone. Olmayne said, "My pores grow smaller. My flesh grows tight. My breasts grow small." Avluela said, "Afterwards you will fly with us, Tomis." The Prince of Roum covered his eyes with his hands. The towers of Roum swayed in the winds of the sun. I snatched a shawl from a passing Rememberer. Clowns wept in the streets of Perris. Talmit said, "Awaken, now, Tomis, come up from it, open your eyes."

"I am young again," I said.

"Your renewal has only begun," he said.

I could no longer move. Attendants seized me and swathed me in porous wrappings, and placed me on a rolling car, and took me to a second tank, much larger, in which dozens of people floated, each in a dreamy seclusion from the others. Their naked skulls were festooned with electrodes; their eyes were covered with pink tape; their hands were peacefully joined on their chests. Into this tank I went, and there were no illusions here, only a long slumber unbroken by dreams. This time I awakened to the sounds of a rushing tide, and found myself passing feet first through a constricted conduit into a sealed tank, where I breathed only fluid, and where I remained something more than a minute and something less than a century, while layers of sin were peeled from my soul. It was slow, taxing work. The Surgeons worked at a distance, their hands thrust into gloves that controlled the tiny flaying-knives, and they flensed me of evil with flick after flick after flick of the little blades, cutting out guilt and sorrow, jealousy and rage, greed, lust, and impatience.

When they were done with me they opened the lid of the tank and lifted me out. I was unable to stand unaided. They attached instruments to my limbs that kneaded and massaged my muscles, restoring the tone. I walked again. I looked down at my bare body, strong and taut-fleshed and vigorous. Talmit came to me and threw a handful of mirror-dust into the air so that I could see myself; and as the tiny particles cohered, I peered at my gleaming reflection.

"No," I said. "You have the face wrong. I didn't look like that. The nose was sharper—the lips weren't so full—the hair not such a deep black—"

"We have worked from the records of the guild of Watchers, Tomis. You are more exactly a replica of your early self than your own memory realizes."

"Can that be?"

"If you prefer, we can shape you to fit your self-conceptions and not reality. But it would be a frivolous thing to do, and it would take much time."

"No," I said. "It hardly matters."

He agreed. He informed me then that I would have to remain in the house of renewal a while longer, until I was fully adapted to my new self. I was given the neutral clothes of a guildless one to wear, for I was without affiliation now; my status as Pilgrim had ended with my renewal, and I might now opt for any guild that would admit me once I left the house. "How long did my renewal last?" I asked Talmit as I dressed. He replied, "You came here in summer. Now it is winter. We do not work swiftly."

"And how fares my companion Olmayne?"

"We failed with her."

"I don't understand."

"Would you like to see her?" Talmit asked.

"Yes," I said, thinking that he would bring me to Olmayne's room. Instead he conveyed me to Olmayne's tank. I stood on a ramp looking down into a sealed container; Talmit indicated a fiber telescope, and I peered into its staring eye and beheld Olmayne. Or rather, what I was asked to believe was Olmayne. A naked girl-child of about eleven, smooth-skinned and breastless, lay curled up in the tank, knees drawn close to the flat chest, thumb thrust in mouth. At first I did not understand. Then the child stirred, and I recognized the embryonic features of the regal Olmayne I had known: the wide mouth, the strong chin, the sharp, strong cheekbones. A dull shock of horror rippled through me, and I said to Talmit, "What is this?"

"When the soul is too badly stained, Tomis, we must dig deep to cleanse it. Your Olmayne was a difficult case. We should not have attempted her; but she was insistent, and there were some indications that we might succeed with her. Those indications were in error, as you can see."

"But what happened to her?"

"The renewal entered the irreversible stage before we could achieve a purging of her poisons," Talmit said.

"You went too far? You made her too young?"

"As you can see. Yes."

"What will you do? Why don't you get her out of there and let her grow up again?"

"You should listen more carefully, Tomis. I said the renewal is irreversible."

"*Irreversible?*"

"She is lost in childhood's dreams. Each day she grows years younger. The inner clock whirls uncontrollably. Her body shrinks; her brain grows smooth. She enters babyhood shortly. She will never awaken."

"And at the end—" I looked away. "What then? A sperm and an egg, separating in the tank?"

"The retrogression will not go that far. She will die in infancy. Many are lost this way."

"She spoke of the risks of renewal," I said.

"Yet she insisted on our taking her. Her soul was dark, Tomis. She lived only for herself. She came to Jorslem to be cleansed, and now she has been cleansed, and she is at peace with the Will. Did you love her?"

"Never. Not for an instant."

"Then what have you lost?"

"A segment of my past, perhaps." I put my eye to the telescope again and beheld Olmayne, innocent now, restored to virginity, sexless, cleansed. At peace with the Will. I searched her oddly altered yet familiar face for insight into her dreams. Had she known what was befalling her, as she tumbled helplessly into youthfulness? Had she cried out in anguish and frustration when she felt her life slipping away? Had there been a final flare of the old imperious Olmayne, before she sank into this unwanted purity? The child in the tank was smiling. The supple little body uncoiled, then drew more tightly into a huddled ball. Olmayne was at peace with the Will. Suddenly, as though Talmit had spread another mirror in the air, I looked into my own new self, and saw what had been done for me, and knew that I had been granted another life with the proviso that I make something more of it than I had of my first one, and I felt humbled, and pledged myself to serve the Will, and I was engulfed in joy that came in mighty waves, like the surging tides of Earth Ocean, and I said farewell to Olmayne, and asked Talmit to take me to another place.

10

AND Avluela came to me in my room in the house of renewal, and we both were frightened when we met. The jacket she wore left her bunched-up wings bare; they seemed hardly under her control at all, but fluttered nervously, starting to open a short way, their gossamer tips expanding in little quivering flickers. Her eyes were large and solemn; her face looked more lean and pointed than ever. We stared in silence at one another a long while; my skin grew warm, my vision hazy; I felt the churning of inner forces that had not pulled at me in decades, and I feared them even as I welcomed them.

"Tomis?" she said finally, and I nodded.

She touched my shoulders, my arms, my lips. And I put my fingers to her wrists, her flanks, and then, hesitantly, to the shallow bowls of her breasts. Like two who had lost their sight we learned each other by touch. We were strangers. That withered old Watcher she had known and perhaps loved was gone, banished for the next fifty years or more, and in his place stood someone mysteriously transformed, unknown, unmet. The old Watcher had been a sort of father to her; what was this guildless young Tomis supposed to be? And what was she to me, a daughter no longer? I did not know myself of myself. I was alien to my sleek, taut skin. I was perplexed and delighted by the juices that now flowed, by the throbbings and swellings that I had nearly forgotten.

"Your eyes are the same," she said. "I would always know you by your eyes."

"What have you done these many months, Avluela?"

"I have been flying every night. I flew to Agupt and deep into Afreek. Then I returned and flew to Stanbool. When it gets dark, I go aloft. Do you know, Tomis, I feel truly alive only when I'm up there?"

"You are of the Fliers. It is in the nature of your guild to feel that way."

"One day we'll fly side by side, Tomis."

I laughed at that. "The old Surgeries are closed, Avluela. They work wonders here, but they can't transform me into a Flier. One must be born with wings."

"One doesn't need wings to fly."

"I know. The invaders lift themselves without the help of wings. I saw you, one day soon after Roum fell—you and Gormon in the sky together—" I shook my head. "But I am no invader either."

"You will fly with me, Tomis. We'll go aloft, and not only by night, even though my wings are merely nightwings. In bright sunlight we'll soar together."

Her fantasy pleased me. I gathered her into my arms, and she was cool and fragile against me, and my own body pulsed with new heat. For a while we talked no more of flying, though I drew back from taking what she offered at that moment, and was content merely to caress her. One does not awaken in a single lunge.

Later we walked through the corridors, passing others who were newly renewed, and we went into the great central room whose ceiling admitted the winter sunlight, and studied each other by that changing pale light, and walked, and talked again. I leaned a bit on her arm, for I did not have all my strength yet, and so in a sense it was as it had been for us in the past, the girl helping the old dodderer along. When she saw me back to my room, I said, "Before I was renewed, you told me of a new guild of Redeemers. I—"

"There is time for that later," she said, displeased.

In my room we embraced, and abruptly I felt the full fire of the renewed leap up within me, so that I feared I might consume her cool, slim body. But it is a fire that does not consume—it only kindles its counterpart in others. In her ecstasy her wings unfolded until I was wrapped in their silken softness. And as I gave myself to the violence of joy, I knew I would not need again to lean on her arm.

We ceased to be strangers; we ceased to feel fear with one another. She came to me each day at my exercise time, and I walked with her, matching her stride for stride. And the fire burned even higher and more brightly for us.

Talmit was with me frequently too. He showed me the arts of using my renewed body, and helped me successfully grow youthful. I declined his invitation to view Olmayne once more. One day he told me that her retrogression had come to its end. I felt no sorrow over that, just a curious brief emptiness that soon passed.

"You will leave here soon," the Renewer said. "Are you ready?"

"I think so."

"Have you given much thought to your destination after this house?"

"I must seek a new guild, I know."

"Many guilds would have you, Tomis. But which do you want?"

"The guild in which I would be most useful to mankind," I said. "I owe the Will a life."

Talmit said, "Has the Flier girl spoken to you of the possibilities before you?"

"She mentioned a newly founded guild."

"Did she give it a name?"

"The guild of Redeemers."

"What do you know of it?"

"Very little," I said.

"Do you wish to know more?"

"If there is more to know."

"I am of the guild of Redeemers," Talmit said. "So is the Flier Avluela."

"You both are already guilded! How can you belong to more than one guild? Only the Dominators were permitted such freedom; and they—"

"Tomis, the guild of Redeemers accepts members from all other guilds. It is the supreme guild, as the guild of Dominators once was. In its ranks are Rememberers and Scribes, Indexers, Servitors, Fliers, Landholders, Somnambulists, Surgeons, Clowns, Merchants, Vendors. There are Changelings as well, and—"

"Changelings?" I gasped. "They are outside all guilds, by law! How can a guild embrace Changelings?"

"This is the guild of Redeemers. Even Changelings may win redemption, Tomis."

Chastened, I said, "Even Changelings, yes. But how strange it is to think of such a guild!"

"Would you despise a guild that embraces Changelings?"

"I find this guild difficult to comprehend."

"Understanding will come at the proper time."

"When is the proper time?"

"The day you leave this place," said Talmit.

That day arrived shortly. Avluela came to fetch me. I stepped forth uncertainly into Jorslem's springtime to complete the ritual of renewal. Talmit had instructed her on how to guide me. She took me through the city to the holy places, so that I could worship at each of the shrines. I knelt at the wall of the Hebers and at the gilded dome of the Mislams; then I went down into the lower part of the city, through the marketplace, to the gray, dark, ill-fashioned building covering the place where the god of the Christers is said to have died; then I went to the spring of knowledge and the fountain of the Will, and from there to the guildhouse of the guild of Pilgrims to surrender my mask and robes and starstone, and thence to the wall of the Old City. At each of these places I offered myself to the Will with words I had waited long to speak. Pilgrims and ordinary citizens of Jorslem gathered at a respectful distance; they knew that I had been lately renewed and hoped that some emanation from my new youthful body would bring them good fortune. At last my obligations were fulfilled. I was a free man in full health, able now to choose the quality of the life I wished to lead.

Avluela said, "Will you come with me to the Redeemers now?"

"Where will we find them? In Jorslem?"

"In Jorslem, yes. A meeting will convene in an hour's time for the purpose of welcoming you into membership."

From her tunic she drew something small and gleaming, which I recognized in bewilderment as a starstone. "What are you doing with that?" I asked. "Only Pilgrims—"

"Put your hand over mine," she said, extending a fist in which the starstone was clenched.

I obeyed. Her small pinched face grew rigid with concentration for a moment. Then she relaxed. She put the starstone away.

"Avluela, what—?"

"A signal to the guild," she said gently. "A notice to them to gather now that you are on your way."

"How did you get that stone?"

"Come with me," she said. "Oh, Tomis, if only we could fly there! But it is not far. We meet almost in the shadow of the house of renewal. Come, Tomis. Come!"

11

THERE was no light in the room. Avluela led me into the subterranean blackness, and told me that I had reached the guildhall of the Redeemers, and left me standing by myself. "Don't move," she cautioned.

I sensed the presence of others in the room about me. But I heard nothing and saw nothing.

Something was thrust toward me.

Avluela said, "Put out your hands. What do you feel?"

I touched a small square cabinet resting, perhaps, on a metal framework. Along its face were familiar dials and levers. My groping hands found handles rising from the cabinet's upper surface. At once it was as though all my renewal had been undone, and the conquest of Earth canceled as well: I was a Watcher again, for surely this was a Watcher's equipment!

I said, "It is not the same cabinet I once had. But it is not greatly different."

"Have you forgotten your skills, Tomis?"

"I think they remain with me even now."

"Use the machine, then," said Avluela. "Do your Watching once more, and tell me what you see."

Easily and happily I slipped into the old attitudes. I performed the preliminary rituals quickly, clearing my mind of doubts and frictions. It was surprisingly simple to bring myself into a spirit of Watchfulness; I had not attempted it since the night Earth fell, and yet it seemed to me that I was able to enter the state more rapidly than in the old days.

Now I grasped the handles. How strange they were! They did not terminate in the grips to which I was accustomed: rather, something cool and hard was mounted at the tip of each handle. A gem of some kind, perhaps. Possibly even a starstone, I realized. My hands closed over the twin coolnesses. I felt a moment of apprehension, even of raw fear. Then I regained the necessary tranquillity, and my soul flooded into the device before me, and I began to Watch.

In my Watchfulness I did not soar to the stars, as I had in the old days. Although I perceived, my perception was limited to the immediate surroundings of my room. Eyes closed, body hunched in trance, I reached out and came first to Avluela; she was near me, almost upon me. I saw her plainly. She smiled; she nodded; her eyes were aglow.

—I love you.

—Yes, Tomis. And we will be together always.

—I have never felt so close to another person.

—In this guild we are all close, all the time. We are the Redeemers, Tomis. We are new. Nothing like this has been on Earth before.

—How am I speaking to you, Avluela?

—Your mind speaks to mine through the machine. And some day the machine will not be needed.

—And then we will fly together?

—Long before then, Tomis.

The starstones grew warm in my hands. I clearly perceived the instrument, now: a Watcher's cabinet, but with certain modifications, among them the starstones mounted on the handles. And I looked beyond Avluela and saw other faces, ones that I knew. The austere figure of the Renewer Talmit was to my left. Beside him stood the Surgeon with whom I had journeyed to Jorslem, with the Changeling Bernalt at his elbow, and now at last I knew what business it was that had brought these men of Nayrub to the holy city. The others I did not recognize; but there were two Fliers, and a Rememberer grasping his shawl, and a woman Servitor, and others. And I saw them all by an inner light for the room was as dark as it had been when I entered it. Not only did I see them, but I touched them, mind to mind.

The mind I touched first was Bernalt's. I met it easily though fearfully, drew back, met it again. He greeted me and welcomed me. I realized then that only if I could look upon a Changeling as my brother could I, and Earth itself, win the sought-for redemption. For until we were truly one people, how could we earn an end to our punishment?

I tried to enter Bernalt's mind. But I was afraid. How could I hide those prejudices, those petty contempts, those conditioned reflexes with which we unavoidably think of Changelings?

"Hide nothing," he counseled. "Those things are no secret to me. Give them up now and join me."

I struggled. I cast out demons. I summoned up the memory of the moment outside the Changeling shrine, after Bernalt had saved us, when I had invited him to journey with us. How had I felt then toward him? Had I regarded him, at least for a moment, as a brother?

I amplified that moment of gratitude and companionship. I let it swell, and blaze, and it obliterated the encrustations of scorn and empty disdain; and I saw the human soul beneath the strange Changeling surface, and I broke through that surface and found the path to redemption. He drew me toward his mind.

I joined Bernalt, and he enrolled me in his guild. I was of the Redeemers now.

Through my mind rolled a voice, and I did not know whether I heard the resonant boom of Talmit, or the dry ironic tone of the Surgeon, or Bernalt's controlled murmur, or Avluela's soft whisper, for it was all these voices at once, and others, and they said:

"When all mankind is enrolled in our guild, we will be conquered no longer. When each of us is part of every other one of us, our sufferings will end. There is no need for us to struggle against our conquerors, for we will absorb them, once we are all Redeemed. Enter us, Tomis who was the Watcher Wuellig."

And I entered.

And I became the Surgeon and the Flier and the Renewer and the Changeling and the Servitor and the rest. And they became me. And so long as my hands gripped the starstones we were of one soul and one mind. This was not the merging of communion, in which a Pilgrim sinks anonymously into the Will, but rather a union of self and self, maintaining independence within a larger dependence. It was the keen perception one gets from Watching coupled with the submergence in a larger entity that one gets from communion, and I knew this was something wholly new on Earth, not merely the founding of a new guild but the initiation of a new cycle of human existence, the birth of the Fourth Cycle upon this defeated planet.

The voice said, "Tomis, we will Redeem those in greatest need first. We will go into Agupt, into the desert where miserable Changelings huddle in an ancient building that they worship, and we will take them into us and make them clean again. We will go on, to the west, to a pitiful village smitten by the crystallization disease, and we will reach the souls of the villagers and free them from taint, and the crystallization will cease and their bodies will be healed. And we will go on beyond Agupt, to all the lands of the world, and find those who are without guilds, and those who are without hope, and those who are without tomorrows, and we will give them life and purpose again. And a time will come when all Earth is Redeemed."

They put a vision before me of a transformed planet, and of the harsh-faced invaders yielding peacefully to us and begging to be incorporated into that new thing that had germinated in the midst of their conquest. They showed me an Earth that had been purged of its ancient sins.

Then I felt it was time to withdraw my hands from the machine I grasped, and I withdrew my hands.

The vision ebbed. The glow faded. But yet I was no longer alone in my skull, for some contact lingered, and the room ceased to be dark.

"How did this happen?" I asked. "When did this begin?"

"In the days after the conquest," said Talmit, "we asked ourselves why we had fallen so easily, and how we could lift ourselves above what we had been. We saw that our guilds had not provided enough of a structure for our lives, that some closer union was our way to redemption. We had the starstones; we had the instruments of Watching; all that remained was to fuse them."

The Surgeon said, "You will be important to us, Tomis, because you understand how to throw your mind forth. We seek former Watchers. They are the nucleus of our guild. Once your soul roved the stars to search out mankind's enemies; now it will roam the Earth to bring mankind together."

Avluela said, "You will help me to fly, Tomis, even by day. And you will fly beside me."

"When do you leave?" I asked.

"Now," she said. "I go to Agupt, to the temple of the Changelings, to offer them what we have to offer. And all of us will join to give me strength, and that strength will be focused through you, Tomis." Her hands touched mine. Her lips brushed mine. "The life of Earth begins again, now, this year, this new cycle. Oh, Tomis, we are all reborn!"

12

I remained alone in the room. The others scattered. Avluela went above, into the street. I put my hands to the mounted starstones, and I saw her as clearly as though she stood beside me. She was preparing herself for flight. First she put off her clothing, and her bare body glistened in the afternoon sun. Her little body seemed impossibly delicate; a strong wind would shatter her, I thought. Then she knelt, bowed, made her ritual. She spoke to herself, yet I heard her words, the words Fliers say as they ready themselves to leave the ground. All guilds are one in this new guild; we have no secrets from one another; there are no mysteries. And as she beseeched the favor of the Will and the support of all her kind, my prayers joined with hers.

She rose and let her wings unfold. Some passers-by looked oddly at her, not because there was anything unusual about the sight of a naked Flier in the streets of Jorslem, but because the sunlight was so strong and her transparent wings, so lightly stained with pigment, were evidently nightwings incapable of withstanding the pressure of the solar wind.

"I love you," we said to her, and our hands ran lightly over her satiny skin in a brief caress.

Her nostrils flickered in delight. Her small girl-child's breasts became agitated. Her wings now were fully spread, and they gleamed wondrously in the sunlight.

"Now we fly to Agupt," she murmured, "to Redeem the Changelings and make them one with us. Tomis, will you come with me?"

"I will be with you," we said, and I gripped the star-stones tightly and crouched over my cabinet of instruments in the dark room beneath the place where she stood. "We will fly together, Avluela."

"Up, then," she said, and we said, "Up."

Her wings beat, curving to take the wind, and we felt her struggling in the first moment, and we gave her the strength she needed, and she took it as it poured from us through me to her, and we rose high. The spires and parapets of Jorslem the golden grew small, and the city became a pink dot in the green hills, and Avluela's throbbing wings thrust her swiftly westward, toward the setting sun, toward the land of Agupt. Her ecstasy swept through us all. "See, Tomis, how wonderful it is, far above everything? Do you feel it?"

"I feel it," I whispered. "The cool wind against bare flesh—the wind in my hair—we drift on the currents, we coast, we soar, Avluela, we soar!"

To Agupt. To the sunset.

We looked down at sparkling Lake Medit. In the distance somewhere was Land Bridge. To the north, Eyrop. To the south, Afreek. Far ahead, beyond Earth Ocean, lay my homeland. Later I would return there, flying westward with Avluela, bringing the good news of Earth's transformation.

From this height one could not tell that our world had ever been conquered. One saw only the beauty of the colors of the land and the sea, not the checkpoints of the invaders.

Those checkpoints would not long endure. We would conquer our conquerors, not with weapons but with love; and as the Redemption of Earth became universal we would welcome into our new self even the beings who had seized our planet.

"I knew that some day you would fly beside me, Tomis," said Avluela.

In my dark room I sent new surges of power through her wings.

She hovered over the desert. The old Surgery, the Changeling shrine, would soon be in sight. I grieved that we would have to come down. I wished we could stay aloft forever, Avluela and I.

"We will, Tomis, we will!" she told me. "Nothing can separate us now! You believe that, don't you, Tomis?"

"Yes," we said, "I believe that." And we guided her down through the darkening sky.

DOWNWARD TO THE EARTH

Who knoweth the spirit of man that goeth upward, and the spirit of the beast that goeth downward to the earth?

Ecclesiastes 3:21

ONE

He had come back to Holman's World after all. He was not sure why. Call it irresistible attraction; call it sentimentality; call it foolishness. Gundersen had never planned to revisit this place. Yet here he was, waiting for the landing, and there it was in the vision screen, close enough to grasp and squeeze in one hand, a world slightly larger than Earth, a world that had claimed the prime decade of his life, a world where he had learned things about himself that he had not really wanted to know. Now the signal light in the lounge was flashing red. The ship would shortly land. Despite everything, he was coming back.

He saw the shroud of mist that covered the temperate zones, and the great sprawling icecaps, and the girdling blue-black band of the scorched tropics. He remembered riding through the Sea of Dust at blazing twilight, and he remembered a silent, bleak river-journey beneath bowers of twittering dagger-pointed leaves, and he remembered golden cocktails on the veranda of a jungle station on the Night of Five Moons, with Seena close by his side and a herd of nildoror mooing in the bush. That was a long time ago. Now the nildoror were masters of Holman's World again. Gundersen had a hard time accepting that. Perhaps that was the real reason why he had come back: to see what sort of job the nildoror could do.

"Attention, passengers in lounge," came a voice over the speaker. "We enter landing orbit for Belzagor in fifteen minutes. Please prepare to return to cradles."

Belzagor. That was what they called the planet now.

The native name, the nildoror's own word. To Gundersen it seemed like something out of Assyrian mythology. Of course, it was a romanticized pronunciation; coming from a nildor it would really sound more like *Bllls'grr*. Belzagor it was, though. He would try to call the planet by the name it now wore, if that was what he was supposed to do. He attempted never to give needless offense to alien beings.

"Belzagor," he said. "It's a voluptuous sound, isn't it? Rolls nicely off the tongue."

The tourist couple beside him in the ship's lounge nodded. They agreed readily with whatever Gundersen said. The husband, plump, pale, overdressed, said, "They were still calling it Holman's World when you were last out here, weren't they?"

"Oh, yes," Gundersen said. "But that was back in the good old imperialist days, when an Earthman could call a planet whatever he damn pleased. That's all over now."

The tourist wife's lips tightened in that thin, pinched, dysmenorrheal way of hers. Gundersen drew a somber pleasure from annoying her. All during the voyage he had deliberately played a role out of Kipling for these tourists—posing as the former colonial administrator going out to see what a beastly botch the natives must be making out of the task of governing themselves. It was an exaggeration, a distortion, of his real attitude, but sometimes it pleased him to wear masks. The tourists—there were eight of them—looked upon him in mingled awe and contempt as he swaggered among them, a big fair-skinned man with the mark of outworld experience stamped on his features. They disapproved of him, of the image of himself that he gave them; and yet they knew he had suffered and labored and striven under a foreign sun, and there was romance in that.

"Will you be staying at the hotel?" the tourist husband asked.

"Oh, no. I'm going right out into the bush, toward the mist country. Look—there, you see? In the northern hemisphere, that band of clouds midway up. The temperature gradient's very steep: tropic and arctic practically side by side. Mist. Fog. They'll take you on a tour of it. I have some business in there."

"Business? I thought these new independent worlds were outside the zone of economic penetration that—"

"Not commercial business," Gundersen said. "Personal business. Unfinished business. Something I didn't manage to discover during my tour of duty here." The signal light flashed again, more insistently. "Will you excuse me? We really should cradle up now."

He went to his cabin and readied himself for landing. Webfoam spurted from the spinnerets and enfolded him. He closed his eyes. He felt deceleration thrust, that curiously archaic sensation hearkening back to space travel's earliest days. The ship dropped planetward as Gundersen swayed, suspended, insulated from the worst of the velocity change.

Belzagor's only spaceport was the one that Earthmen had built more than a hundred years before. It was in the tropics, at the mouth of the great river flowing into Belzagor's single ocean. Madden's River, Benjamini Ocean —Gundersen didn't know the nildoror names at all. The spaceport was self-maintaining, fortunately. Automatic high-redundancy devices operated the landing beacon; homeostatic surveillance kept the pad repaved and the bordering jungle cropped back. All, all by machine; it was unrealistic to expect the nildoror to operate a spaceport, and impossible to keep a crew of Earthmen stationed here to do it. Gundersen understood that there were still perhaps a hundred Earthmen living on Belzagor, even after the general withdrawal, but they were not such as would operate a spaceport. And there was a treaty, in any case. Administrative functions were to be performed by nildoror, or not at all.

They landed. The webfoam cradle dissolved upon signal. They went out of the ship.

The air had the tropical reek: rich loam, rotting leaves, the droppings of jungle beasts, the aroma of creamy flowers. It was early evening. A couple of the moons were out. As always, the threat of rain was in the air; the humidity was 99%, probably. But that threat almost never materialized. Rainstorms were rare in this tropical belt. The water simply precipitated out of the air in droplets all the time, imperceptibly, coating you with fine wet beads. Gundersen saw lightning flicker beyond the tops of the hullygully trees at the edge of the pad. A stewardess marshaled the nine debarkees. "This way, please," she said crisply, and led them toward the one building.

On the left, three nildoror emerged from the bush and solemnly gazed at the newcomers. Tourists gasped and pointed. "Look! Do you see them? Like elephants, they are! Are those nili—nildoror?"

"Nildoror, yes," Gundersen said. The tang of the big beasts drifted across the clearing. A bull and two cows, he guessed, judging by the size of the tusks. They were all about the same height, three meters plus, with the deep green skins that marked them as western-hemisphere nildoror. Eyes as big as platters peered back at him in dim curiosity. The short-tusked cow in front lifted her tail and placidly dropped an avalanche of steaming purple dung. Gundersen heard deep blurred sounds, but at this distance he could not make out what the nildoror were saying. Imagine them running a spaceport, he thought. Imagine them running a planet. But they do. But they do.

There was no one in the spaceport building. Some robots, part of the homeostasis net, were repairing the wall at the far side, where the gray plastic sheeting had apparently succumbed to spore implantation; sooner or later the jungle rot got everything in this part of the planet. But that was the only visible activity. There was no customs desk. The nildoror did not have a bureaucracy of that sort. They did not care what you brought with you to their world. The nine passengers had undergone a customs inspection on Earth, just before setting out; Earth did care, very much, what was taken to undeveloped planets. There was also no spaceline office here, nor were there money-changing booths, nor newsstands, nor any of the other concessions one normally finds in a spaceport. There was only a big bare shed, which once had been the nexus of a bustling colonial outpost, in the days when Holman's World had been the property of Earth. It seemed to Gundersen that he saw ghosts of those days all about him: figures in tropical khaki carrying messages, supercargoes waving inventory sheets, computer technicians draped in festoons of memory beads, nildoror bearers laden with outgoing produce. Now all was still. The scrapings of the repair robots echoed across the emptiness.

The spaceline stewardess was telling the eight passengers, "Your guide should be here any minute. He'll take you to the hotel, and—"

Gundersen was supposed to go to the hotel too, just for tonight. In the morning he hoped to arrange for transport. He had no formal plans for his northward journey; it was going to be largely an improvisation, a reconnaissance into his own pockmarked past.

He said to the stewardess, "Is the guide a nildor?"

"You mean, native? Oh, no, he's an Earthman, Mr. Gundersen." She rummaged in a sheaf of printout slips. "His name's Van Beneker, and he was supposed to be here at least half an hour before the ship landed, so I don't understand why—"

"Van Beneker was never strong on punctuality," Gundersen said. "But there he is."

A beetle, much rusted and stained by the climate, had pulled up at the open entrance to the building, and from it now was coming a short red-haired man, also much rusted and stained by the climate. He wore rumpled fatigues and a pair of knee-high jungle boots. His hair was thinning and his tanned bald skull showed through the slicked-down strands. He entered the building and peered around, blinking. His eyes were light blue and faintly hyperthyroid-looking.

"Van?" Gundersen said. "Over here, Van."

The little man came over. In a hurried, perfunctory way he said, while he was still far from them, "I want to welcome all you people to Belzagor, as Holman's World is now known. My name's Van Beneker, and I'm going to show you as much of this fascinating planet as is legally permissible to show you, and—"

"Hello, Van," Gundersen cut in.

The guide halted, obviously irritated, in mid-spiel. He blinked again and looked closely at Gundersen. Finally he said, clearly not believing it, "Mr. Gundersen?"

"Just Gundersen. I'm not your boss any more."

"Jesus, Mr. Gundersen. Jesus, are you here for the tour?"

"Not exactly. I'm here to take my own tour."

Van Beneker said to the others, "I want you to excuse me. Just for a minute." To the spaceline stewardess he said, "It's okay. You can officially convey them to me. I take responsibility. They all here? One, two, three—eight. That's right. Okay, the luggage goes out there, next to the beetle. Tell them all to wait. I'll be right with them." He tugged at Gundersen's elbow. "Come on over here,

Mr. Gundersen. You don't know how amazed I am. Jesus!"

"How have you been, Van?"

"Lousy. How else, on this planet? When did you leave, exactly?"

"2240. The year after relinquishment. Eight years ago."

"Eight years. And what have you been doing?"

"The home office found work for me," Gundersen said. "I keep busy. Now I've got a year's accumulated leave."

"To spend it *here?*"

"Why not?"

"What for?"

"I'm going up mist country," Gundersen said. "I want to visit the sulidoror."

"You don't want to do that," said Van Beneker. "What do you want to do that for?"

"To satisfy a curiosity."

"There's only trouble when a man goes up there. You know the stories, Mr. Gundersen. I don't need to remind you, how many guys went up there, how many didn't come back." Van Beneker laughed. "You didn't come all the way to this place just to rub noses with the sulidoror. I bet you got some other reason."

Gundersen let the point pass. "What do you do here now, Van?"

"Tourist guide, mostly. We get nine, ten batches a year. I take them up along the ocean, then show them a bit of the mist country, then we hop across the Sea of Dust. It's a nice little tour."

"Yes."

"The rest of the time I relax. I talk to the nildoror a lot, and sometimes I visit friends at the bush stations. You'll know everyone, Mr. Gundersen. It's all the old people, still out there."

"What about Seena Royce?" Gundersen asked.

"She's up by Shangri-la Falls."

"Still have her looks?"

"She thinks so," Van Beneker said. "You figure you'll go up that way?"

"Of course," Gundersen said. "I'm making a sentimental pilgrimage. I'll tour all the bush stations. See the old friends. Seena. Cullen. Kurtz. Salamone. Whoever's still there."

"Some of them are dead."

"Whoever's still there," Gundersen said. He looked down

at the little man and smiled. "You'd better take care of your tourists, now. We can talk at the hotel tonight. I want you to fill me in on everything that's happened while I've been gone."

"Easy, Mr. Gundersen. I can do it right now in one word. Rot. Everything's rotting. Look at the spaceport wall over there."

"I see."

"Look at the repair robots, now. They don't shine much, do they? They're giving out too. If you get close, you can see the spots on their hulls."

"But homeostasis—"

"Sure. Everything gets repaired, even the repair robots. But the system's going to break down. Sooner or later, the rot will get into the basic programs, and then there won't be any more repairs, and this world will go straight back into the stone age. I mean *all* the way back. And then the nildoror will finally be happy. I understand those big bastards as much as anybody does. I know they can't wait to see the last trace of Earthmen rot right off this planet. They pretend they're friendly, but the hate's there all the time, real sick hate, and—"

"You ought to look after your tourists, Van," Gundersen said. "They're getting restless."

TWO

A caravan of nildoror was going to transport them
from the spaceport to the hotel—two Earthmen per alien,
with Gundersen riding alone, and Van Beneker, with the
luggage, leading the way in his beetle. The three nildoror
grazing at the edge of the field ambled over to enroll
in the caravan, and two others emerged from the bush.
Gundersen was surprised that nildoror were still willing
to act as beasts of burden for Earthmen. "They don't
mind," Van Beneker explained. "They like to do us favors.
It makes them feel superior. They can't hardly tell there's
weight on them, anyhow. And they don't think there's
anything shameful about letting people ride them."

"When I was here I had the impression they resented
it," Gundersen said.

"Since relinquishment they take things like that easier.
Anyway, how could you be sure what they thought? I
mean, what they *really* thought."

The tourists were a little alarmed at riding nildoror.
Van Beneker tried to calm them by telling them it was
an important part of the Belzagor experience. Besides,
he added, machinery did not thrive on this planet and
there were hardly any functioning beetles left. Gundersen
demonstrated how to mount, for the benefit of the ap-
prehensive newcomers. He tapped his nildor's left-hand
tusk, and the alien knelt in its elephantine way, ponderously coming down on its front knees, then its back ones. The
nildor wriggled its shoulders, in effect dislocating them to
create the deep swayback valley in which a man could
ride so comfortably, and Gundersen climbed aboard, seizing the short backward-thrusting horns as his pommels.

The spiny crest down the middle of the alien's broad skull began to twitch. Gundersen recognized it as a gesture of welcome; the nildoror had a rich language of gesture, employing not only the spines but also their long ropy trunks and their many-pleated ears. *"Sssukh!"* Gundersen said, and the nildor arose. "Do you sit well?" it asked him in its own language. "Very well indeed," Gundersen said, feeling a surge of delight as the unforgotten vocabulary came to his lips.

In their clumsy, hesitant way, the eight tourists did as he had done, and the caravan set out down the river road toward the hotel. Nightflies cast a dim glow under the canopy of trees. A third moon was in the sky, and the mingled lights came through the leaves, revealing the oily fast-moving river just to their left. Gundersen stationed himself at the rear of the procession in case one of the tourists had a mishap. There was only one uneasy moment, though, when a nildor paused and left the rank. It rammed the triple prongs of its tusks into the riverbank to grub up some morsel, and then resumed its place in line. In the old days, Gundersen knew, that would never have happened. Nildoror were not permitted then to have whims.

He enjoyed the ride. The jouncing strides were agreeable, and the pace was swift without being strenuous for the passengers. What good beasts these nildoror are, Gundersen thought. Strong, docile, intelligent. He almost reached forward to stroke his mount's spines, deciding at the last moment that it would seem patronizing. The nildoror are something other than funny-looking elephants, he reminded himself. They are intelligent beings, the dominant life-forms of their planet, *people,* and don't you forget it.

Soon Gundersen could hear the crashing of the surf. They were nearing the hotel.

The path widened to become a clearing. Up ahead, one of the tourist women pointed into the bush; her husband shrugged and shook his head. When Gundersen reached that place he saw what was bothering them. Black shapes crouched between the trees, and dark figures were moving slowly to and fro. They were barely visible in the shadows. As Gundersen's nildor went past, two of the dim forms emerged and stood by the edge of the path. They were husky bipeds, close to three meters tall, covered with thick coats of dark red hair. Massive tails swished slowly through the greenish gloom. Hooded eyes, slit-wide even in this scant light, appraised the procession. Drooping rubbery snouts, tapir-long, sniffed audibly.

A woman turned gingerly and said to Gundersen, "What are they?"

"Sulidoror. The secondary species. They come from up mist country. These are northern ones."

"Are they dangerous?"

"I wouldn't call them that."

"If they're northern animals, why are they down here?" her husband wanted to know.

"I'm not sure," Gundersen said. He questioned his mount and received an answer. "They work at the hotel," Gundersen called ahead. "Bellhops. Kitchen hands." It seemed strange to him that the nildoror would have turned the sulidoror into domestic servants at an Earthman's hotel. Not even before relinquishment had sulidoror been used as servants. But of course there had been plenty of robots here then.

The hotel lay just ahead. It was on the coast, a glistening geodesic dome that showed no external signs of decay. Before relinquishment, it had been a posh resort run exclusively for the benefit of the top-level administrators of the Company. Gundersen had spent many happy hours in it. Now he dismounted, and he and Van Beneker helped the tourists down. Three sulidoror stood at the hotel entrance. Van Beneker gestured fiercely at them and they began to take the luggage from the beetle's storage hold.

Inside, Gundersen quickly detected symptoms of decline. A carpet of tiger-moss had begun to edge out of an ornamental garden strip along the lobby wall, and was starting to reach onto the fine black slabs of the main hall's floor; he saw the toothy little mouths hopefully snapping as he walked in. No doubt the hotel's maintenance robots once had been programmed to cut the ornamental moss back to the border of the garden bed, but the program must have subtly altered with the years so that now the moss was allowed to intrude on the interior of the building as well. Possibly the robots were gone altogether, and the sulidoror who had replaced them were lax in their pruning duties. And there were other hints that control was slipping away.

"The boys will show you to your rooms," Van Beneker said. "You can come down for cocktails whenever you're ready. Dinner will be served in about an hour and a half."

A towering sulidor conducted Gundersen to a third-floor room overlooking the sea. Reflex led him to offer the huge creature a coin; but the sulidor merely looked blankly at him and did not venture to take it. It seemed to Gundersen that there was a suppressed tension about the sulidor, an inward seething, but perhaps it existed only in his own imagination. In the old days sulidoror had rarely been seen outside the zone of mist, and Gundersen did not feel at ease with them.

In nildoror words he said, "How long have you been at the hotel?" But the sulidor did not respond. Gundersen did not know the language of the sulidoror, but he was aware that every sulidor was supposed to speak fluent nildororu as well as sulidororu. Enunciating more clearly, he repeated his question. The sulidor scratched its pelt with gleaming claws and said nothing. Moving past Gundersen, it deopaqued the window-wall, adjusted the atmospheric filters, and stalked solemnly out.

Gundersen frowned. Quickly he stripped and got under the cleanser. A quick whirr of vibration took from him the grime of his day's journey. He unpacked and donned evening clothes, a close gray tunic, polished boots, a mirror for his brow. He toned the color of his hair down the spectrum a short distance, dimming it from yellow almost to auburn.

Suddenly he felt very tired.

He was just into early middle years, only forty-eight, and travel ordinarily did not affect him. Why this fatigue, then? He realized that he had been holding himself unusually stiff these few hours he had been back on this planet. Rigid, inflexible, tense—uncertain of his motives in returning, unsure of his welcome, perhaps touched a bit by curdled guilts, and now the strain was telling. He touched a switch and made the wall a mirror. Yes, his face was drawn; the cheekbones, always prominent, now jutted like blades, and the lips were clamped and the forehead was furrowed. The thin slab of his nose was distended by tension-flared nostrils. Gundersen shut his eyes and went through one of the drills of a relaxation mode. He looked better thirty seconds later; but a drink might help, he decided. He went down to the lounge.

None of the tourists were there yet. The louvers were

open, and he heard the roar and crash of the sea, smelled its saltiness. A white curdled line of accumulated salt had been allowed to form along the margin of the beach. The tide was in; only the tips of the jagged rocks that framed the bathing area were visible. Gundersen looked out over the moonslight-streaked water, staring into the blackness of the eastern horizon. Three moons had also been up on his last night here, when they gave the farewell party for him. And after the revelry was over, he and Seena had gone for a midnight swim, out to the tide-hidden shoal where they could barely stand, and when they returned to shore, naked and salt-encrusted, he had made love to her behind the rocks, embracing her for what he was sure would be the last time. And now he was back.

He felt a stab of nostalgia so powerful that he winced.

Gundersen had been thirty years old when he came out to Holman's World as an assistant station agent. He had been forty, and a sector administrator, when he left. In a sense the first thirty years of his life had been a pale prelude to that decade, and the last eight years of it had been a hollow epilogue. He had lived his life on this silent continent, bounded by mist and ice to the north, mist and ice to the south, the Benjamini Ocean to the east, the Sea of Dust to the west. For a while he had ruled half a world, at least in the absence of the chief resident; and this planet had shrugged him off as though he had never been. Gundersen turned away from the louvers and sat down.

Van Beneker appeared, still in his sweaty, rumpled fatigues. He winked cordially at Gundersen and began rummaging in a cabinet. "I'm the bartender too, Mr. G. What can I get you?"

"Alcohol," Gundersen said. "Any form you recommend."

"Snout or flask?"

"Flask. I like the taste."

"As you say. But snout for me. It's the effect, sir, the *effect*." He set an empty glass before Gundersen and handed him a flask containing three ounces of a dark red fluid. Highland rum, local product. Gundersen hadn't tasted it in eight years. The flask was equipped with its own condensation chiller; Gundersen thumbed it with a quick short push and quietly watched the flakes of ice beginning to form along the inside. When his drink was properly chilled he poured it and put it quickly to his lips.

"That's pre-relinquishment stock," Van Beneker said. "Not much of it left, but I knew you'd appreciate it." He was holding an ultrasonic tube to his left forearm. *Zzz!* and the snout spurted alcohol straight into his vein. Van Beneker grinned. "Works faster this way. The working-class man's boozer. Eh? Eh? Get you another rum, Mr. G?"

"Not just yet. Better look after your tourists, Van."

The tourist couples were beginning to enter the bar: first the Watsons, then the Mirafloreses, the Steins, finally the Christophers. Evidently they had expected to find the bar throbbing with life, full of other tourists giddily hailing one another from distant parts of the room, and red-jacketed waiters ferrying drinks. Instead there were peeling plastic walls, a sonic sculpture that no longer worked and was deeply cobwebbed, empty tables, and that unpleasant Mr. Gundersen moodily peering into a glass. The tourists exchanged cheated glances. Was this what they had spanned the light-years to see? Van Beneker went to them, offering drinks, weeds, whatever else the limited resources of the hotel might be able to supply. They settled in two groups near the windows and began to talk in low voices, plainly self-conscious in front of Gundersen. Surely they felt the foolishness of their roles, these soft well-to-do people whose boredom had driven them to peer at the remote reaches of the galaxy. Stein ran a helix parlor in California, Miraflores a chain of lunar casinos, Watson was a doctor, and Christopher— Gundersen could not remember what Christopher did. Something in the financial world.

Mrs. Stein said, "There are some of those animals on the beach. The green elephants."

Everyone looked. Gundersen signaled for another drink, and got it. Van Beneker, flushed, sweating, winked again and put a second snout to his arm. The tourists began to titter. Mrs. Christopher said, "Don't they have any shame at all?"

"Maybe they're simply playing, Ethel," Watson said.

"Playing? Well, if you call that playing—"

Gundersen leaned forward, glancing out the window without getting up. On the beach a pair of nildoror were coupling, the cow kneeling where the salt was thickest, the bull mounting her, gripping her shoulders, pressing his central tusk down firmly against the spiny crest of her skull, jockeying his hindquarters about as he made ready for the consummating thrust. The tourists, giggling, making heavy-handed comments of appreciation, seemed both shocked and titillated. To his considerable surprise, Gundersen realized he was shocked, too, although coupling nildoror were nothing new to him; and when a ferocious orgasmic bellowing rose from below he glanced away, embarrassed and not understanding why.

"You look upset," Van Beneker said.

"They didn't have to do that *here.*"

"Why not? They do it all over the place. You know how it is."

"They deliberately went out there," Gundersen muttered. "To show off for the tourists? Or to annoy the tourists? They shouldn't be reacting to the tourists at all. What are they trying to prove? That they're just animals, I suppose."

"You don't understand the nildoror, Gundy."

Gundersen looked up, startled as much by Van Beneker's words as by the sudden descent from "Mr. Gundersen" to "Gundy." Van Beneker seemed startled, too, blinking rapidly and tugging at a stray sparse lock of fading hair.

"I don't?" Gundersen asked. "After spending ten years here?"

"Begging pardon, but I never did think you understood them, even when you were here. I used to go around with you a lot to the villages when I was clerking for you. I watched you."

"In what way do you think I failed to understand them, Van?"

"You despised them. You thought of them as animals."

"That isn't so!"

"Sure it is, Gundy. You never once admitted they had any intelligence at all."

"That's absolutely untrue," Gundersen said. He got up and took a new flask of rum from the cabinet, and returned to the table.

"I would have gotten that for you," Van Beneker said. "You just had to ask me."

"It's all right." Gundersen chilled the drink and downed it fast. "You're talking a load of nonsense, Van. I did everything possible for those people. To improve them, to lift them toward civilization. I requisitioned tapes for them, sound pods, culture by the ton. I put through new regulations about maximum labor. I insisted that my men respect their rights as the dominant indigenous culture. I—"

"You treated them like very intelligent animals. Not like intelligent alien *people*. Maybe you didn't even realize it yourself, Gundy, but I did, and God knows they did. You talked down to them. You were kind to them in the wrong way. All your interest in uplifting them, in improving them—crap, Gundy, they have their own culture. They didn't want yours!"

"It was my duty to guide them," Gundersen said stiffly. "Futile though it was to think that a bunch of animals who don't have a written language, who don't—" He stopped, horrified.

"Animals," Van Beneker said.

"I'm tired. Maybe I've had too much to drink. It just slipped out."

"Animals."

"Stop pushing me, Van. I did the best I could, and if what I was doing was wrong, I'm sorry. I tried to do what was right." Gundersen pushed his empty glass forward. "Get me another, will you?"

Van Beneker fetched the drink, and one more snout for himself. Gundersen welcomed the break in the conversation, and apparently Van Beneker did, too, for they both remained silent a long moment, avoiding each other's eyes. A sulidor entered the bar and began to gather the empties, crouching to keep from grazing the Earthman-scaled ceiling. The chatter of the tourists died away as the fierce-looking creature moved through the room. Gundersen looked toward the beach. The nildoror were gone. One of the moons was setting in the east, leaving a fiery track across the surging water. He realized that he had forgotten the names of the moons. No matter; the old Earthman-given names were dead history now. He said finally to Van Beneker, "How come you decided to stay here after relinquishment?"

"I felt at home here. I've been here twenty-five years. Why should I go anywhere else?"

"No family ties elsewhere?"

"No. And it's comfortable here. I get a company pension. I get tips from the tourists. There's a salary from the hotel. That's enough to keep me supplied with what I need. What I need, mostly, is snouts. Why should I leave?"

"Who owns the hotel?" Gundersen asked.

"The confederation of western-continent nildoror. The Company gave it to them."

"And the nildoror pay you a salary? I thought they were outside the galactic money economy."

"They are. They arranged something with the Company."

"What you're saying is the Company still runs this hotel."

"If anybody can be said to run it, the Company does, yes," Van Beneker agreed. "But that isn't much of a violation of the relinquishment law. There's only one employee. Me. I pocket my salary from what the tourists pay for accommodations. The rest I spend on imports from the money sphere. Don't you see, Gundy, it's all just a big joke? It's a routine designed to allow me to bring in liquor, that's all. This hotel isn't a commercial proposition. The Company is really out of this planet. Completely."

"All right. All right. I believe you."

Van Beneker said, "What are you looking for up mist country?"

"You really want to know?"

"It passes the time to ask things."

"I want to watch the rebirth ceremony. I never saw it, all the time I was here."

The bulging blue eyes seemed to bulge even more. "Why can't you be serious, Gundy?"

"I am."

"It's dangerous to fool with the rebirth thing."

"I'm prepared for the risks."

"You ought to talk to some people here about it, first. It's not a thing for us to meddle in."

Gundersen sighed. "Have you seen it?"

"No. Never. Never even been interested in seeing it. Whatever the hell the sulidoror do in the mountains, let them do it without me. I'll tell you who to talk to, though. Seena."

"She's watched the rebirth?"

"Her husband has."

Gundersen felt a spasm of dismay. "Who's her husband?"

"Jeff Kurtz. You didn't know?"

"I'll be damned," Gundersen murmured.

"You wonder what she saw in him, eh?"

"I wonder that she could bring herself to live with a man like that. You talk about *my* attitude toward the natives! There's someone who treated them like his own property, and—"

"Talk to Seena, up at Shangri-la Falls. About the rebirth." Van Beneker laughed. "You're playing games with me, aren't you? You know I'm drunk and you're having a little fun."

"No. Not at all." Gundersen rose uneasily. "I ought to get some sleep now."

Van Beneker followed him to the door. Just as Gundersen went out, the little man leaned close to him and said, "You know, Gundy, what the nildoror were doing on the beach before—they weren't doing that for the tourists. They were doing it for you. It's the kind of sense of humor they have. Good night, Gundy."

THREE

Gundersen woke early. His head was surprisingly clear. It was just a little after dawn, and the green-tinged sun was low in the sky. The eastern sky, out over the ocean: a welcome touch of Earthliness. He went down to the beach for a swim. A soft south wind was blowing, pushing a few clouds into view. The hullygully trees were heavy with fruit; the humidity was as high as ever; thunder boomed back from the mountains that ran in an arc paralleling the coast a day's drive inland. Mounds of nildoror dung were all over the beach. Gundersen stepped warily, zigzagging over the crunching sand and hurling himself flat into the surf. He went under the first curling row of breakers and with quick powerful strokes headed toward the shoals. The tide was low. He crossed the exposed sandbar and swam beyond it until he felt himself tiring. When he returned to the shore area, he found two of the tourist men had also come out for a swim, Christopher and Miraflores. They smiled tentatively at him. "Bracing," he said. "Nothing like salt water."

"Why can't they keep the beach clean, though?" Miraflores asked.

A sullen sulidor served breakfast. Native fruits, native fish. Gundersen's appetite was immense. He bolted down three golden-green bitterfruits for a start, then expertly boned a whole spiderfish and forked the sweet pink flesh into himself as though engaged in a speed contest. The sulidor brought him another fish and a bowl of phallic-looking forest candles. Gundersen still was working on these when Van Beneker entered, wearing clean though frayed clothes. He looked bloodshot and chastened. Instead of joining Gundersen at the table he merely smiled a perfunctory greeting and sailed past.

"Sit with me, Van," Gundersen said.

Uncomfortably, Van Beneker complied. "About last night—"

"Forget it."

"I was insufferable, Mr. Gundersen."

"You were in your cups. Forgiven. In vino veritas. You were calling me Gundy last night, too. You may as well do it this morning. Who catches the fish?"

"There's an automatic weir just north of the hotel. Catches them and pipes them right into the kitchen. God knows who'd prepare food here if we didn't have the machines."

"And who picks the fruit? Machines?"

"The sulidoror do that," Van Beneker said.

"When did sulidoror start working as menials on this planet?"

"About five years ago. Six, maybe. The nildoror got the idea from us, I suppose. If we could turn them into bearers and living bulldozers, they could turn the sulidoror into bellhops. After all, the sulidoror *are* the inferior species."

"But always their own masters. Why did they agree to serve? What's in it for them?"

"I don't know," Van Beneker said. "When did anybody ever understand the sulidoror?"

True enough, Gundersen thought. No one yet had succeeded in making sense out of the relationship between this planet's two intelligent species. The presence of two intelligent species, in the first place, went against the general evolutionary logic of the universe. Both nildoror and sulidoror qualified for autonomous ranking, with perception levels beyond those of the higher hominoid primates; a sulidor was considerably smarter than a chimpanzee, and a nildor was a good deal more clever than that. If there had been no nildoror here at all, the presence of the sulidoror alone would have been enough to force the Company to relinquish possession of the planet when the decolonization movement reached its peak. But why two species, and why the strange unspoken accommodation between them, the bipedal carnivorous sulidoror ruling over the mist country, the quadrupedal herbivorous nildoror dominating the tropics? How had they carved this world up so neatly? And why was the division of authority breaking down, if breaking down was really what was happening? Gundersen knew that there were ancient treaties between these creatures, that a system of claims and prerogatives existed, that every nildor went back to the mist country when the time for its rebirth arrived. But he did not know what role the sulidoror really played in the life and the rebirth of the nildoror. No one did. The pull of that mystery was, he admitted, one of the things that had brought him back to Holman's World, to Belzagor, now that he had shed his administrative responsibilities and was free to risk his life indulging private curiosities. The shift in the nildoror-sulidoror relationship that seemed to be taking place around this hotel troubled him, though; it had been hard enough to comprehend that relationship when it was static. Of course, the habits of alien beings were none of his business, really. Nothing was his business, these days. When a man had no business, he had to appoint himself to some. So he was here to do research, ostensibly, which is to say to snoop and spy. Putting it that way made his return to this planet seem more like an act of will, and less like the yielding to irresistible compulsion that he feared it had been.

"—more complicated than anybody ever thought," Van Beneker was saying.

"I'm sorry. I must have missed most of what you said."

"It isn't important. We theorize a lot, here. The last hundred of us. How soon do you start north?"

"In a hurry to be rid of me, Van?"

"Only trying to make plans, sir," the little man said, hurt. "If you're staying, we need provisions for you, and—"

"I'm leaving after breakfast. If you'll tell me how to get to the nearest nildoror encampment so I can apply for my travel permit."

"Twenty kilometers, southeast. I'd run you down there in the beetle, but you understand—the tourists—"

"Can you get me a ride with a nildor?" Gundersen suggested. "If it's too much bother, I suppose I can hike it, but—"

"I'll arrange things," Van Beneker said.

A young male nildor appeared an hour after breakfast to take Gundersen down to the encampment. In the old days Gundersen would simply have climbed on his back, but now he felt the necessity of making introductions. One does not ask an autonomous intelligent being to carry you twenty kilometers through the jungle, he thought, without attempting to enter into elementary courtesies. "I am Edmund Gundersen of the first birth," he said, "and I wish you joy of many rebirths, friend of my journey."

"I am Srin'gahar of the first birth," replied the nildor evenly, "and I thank you for your wish, friend of my journey. I serve you of free choice and await your commands."

"I must speak with a many-born one and gain permission to travel north. The man here says you will take me to such a one."

"So it can be done. Now?"

"Now."

Gundersen had one suitcase. He rested it on the nildor's broad rump and Srin'gahar instantly curved his tail up and back to clamp the bag in place. Then the nildor knelt and Gundersen went through the ritual of mounting. Tons of powerful flesh rose and moved obediently toward the rim of the forest. It was almost as though nothing had ever changed.

They traveled the first kilometer in silence, through an ever-thickening series of bitterfruit glades. Gradually it occurred to Gundersen that the nildor was not going to speak unless spoken to, and he opened the conversation by remarking that he had lived for ten years on Belzagor. Srin'gahar said that he knew that; he remembered Gundersen from the era of Company rule. The nature of the nildoror vocal system drained all overtones and implications from the statement. It came out flat, a mooing nasal grunt that did not reveal whether the nildor remembered Gundersen fondly, bitterly, or indifferently. Gundersen might have drawn a hint from the movements of Srin'gahar's cranial crest, but it was impossible for someone seated on a nildor's back to detect any but the broadest such movements. The intricate nildoror system of nonverbal supplementary communication had not evolved for the convenience of passengers. In any event Gundersen had known only a few of the almost infinite number of supplementary gestures, and he had forgotten most of those. But the nildor seemed courteous enough.

Gundersen took advantage of the ride to practice his nildororu. So far he had done well, but in an interview with a many-born one he would need all the verbal skill he could muster. Again and again he said, "I spoke that the right way, didn't I? Correct me if I didn't."

"You speak very well," Srin'gahar insisted.

Actually the language was not difficult. It was narrow in range, simple in grammar. Nildororu words did not inflect; they agglutinated, piling syllable atop syllable so that a complex concept like "the former grazing-ground of my mate's clan" emerged as a long grumbled growl of sound unbroken even by a brief pause. Nildoror speech was slow and stolid, requiring broad rolling tones that an Earthman had to launch from the roots of his nostrils; when Gundersen shifted from nildororu to any Earth language, he felt sudden exhilaration, like a circus acrobat transported instantaneously from Jupiter to Mercury.

Srin'gahar was taking a nildoror path, not one of the old Company roads. Gundersen had to duck low-hanging branches now and then, and once a quivering nicalanga vine descended to catch him around the throat in a gentle, cool, quickly broken, and yet frightening embrace. When he looked back, he saw the vine tumescent with excitement, red and swollen from the thrill of caressing an Earthman's skin. Shortly the jungle humidity reached the top of the scale and the level of condensation became something close to that of rain; the air was so wet that Gundersen had trouble breathing, and streams of sweat poured down his body. The sticky moment passed. Minutes later they intersected a Company road. It was a narrow fading track in the jungle, nearly overgrown. In another year it would be gone.

The nildor's vast body demanded frequent feedings. Every half hour they halted and Gundersen dismounted while Srin'gahar munched shrubbery. The sight fed Gundersen's latent prejudices, troubling him so much that he tried not to look. In a wholly elephantine way the nildor uncoiled his trunk and ripped leafy branches from low trees; then the great mouth sagged open and in the bundle went. With his triple tusks Srin'gahar shredded slabs of bark for dessert. The big jaws moved back and forth tirelessly, grinding, milling. We are no prettier when we eat, Gundersen told himself, and the demon within him counterpointed his tolerance with a shrill insistence that his companion was a beast.

Srin'gahar was not an outgoing type. When Gundersen

said nothing, the nildor said nothing; when Gundersen asked a question, the nildor replied politely but minimally. The strain of sustaining such a broken-backed conversation drained Gundersen, and he allowed long minutes to pass in silence. Caught up in the rhythm of the big creature's steady stride, he was content to be carried effortlessly along through the steamy jungle. He had no idea where he was and could not even tell if they were going in the right direction, for the trees far overhead met in a closed canopy, screening the sun. After the nildor had stopped for his third meal of the morning, though, he gave Gundersen an unexpected clue to their location. Cutting away from the path in a sudden diagonal, the nildor trotted a short distance into the most dense part of the forest, battering down the vegetation, and came to a halt in front of what once had been a Company building—a glassy dome now dimmed by time and swathed in vines.

"Do you know this house, Edmund of the first birth?" Srin'gahar asked.

"What was it?"

"The serpent station. Where you gathered the juices."

The past abruptly loomed like a toppling cliff above Gundersen. Jagged hallucinatory images plucked at his mind. Ancient scandals, long forgotten or suppressed, sprang to new life. This the serpent station, this ruin? This the place of private sins, the scene of so many falls from grace? Gundersen felt his cheeks reddening. He slipped from the nildor's back and walked haltingly toward the building. He stood at the door a moment, looking in. Yes, there were the hanging tubes and pipes, the runnels through which the extracted venom had flowed, all the processing equipment still in place, half devoured by warmth and moisture and neglect. There was the entrance for the jungle serpents, drawn by alien music they could not resist, and there they were milked of their venom, and there—and there—

Gundersen glanced back at Srin'gahar. The spines of the nildor's crest were distended: a mark of tension, a mark perhaps of shared shame. The nildoror, too, had memories of this building. Gundersen stepped into the station, pushing back the half-open door. It split loose from its moorings as he did so, and a musical tremor ran *whang whang whang* through the whole of the spherical building, dying away to a blurred feeble tinkle. *Whang* and Gundersen heard Jeff Kurtz's guitar again, and the years fell away and he was thirty-one years old once more, a newcomer on Holman's World and about to begin his first stint at the serpent station, finally assigned to that place that was the focus of so much gossip. Yes. Out of the shroud of memory came the image of Kurtz. There he was, standing just inside the station door, impossibly tall, the tallest man Gundersen had ever seen, with a great pale domed hairless head and enormous dark eyes socketed in prehistoric-looking bony ridges, and a bright-toothed smile that ran at least a kilometer's span from cheek to cheek. The guitar went *whang* and Kurtz said, "You'll find it interesting here, Gundy. This station is a unique experience. We buried your predecessor last week." *Whang.* "Of course, you must learn to establish a distance between yourself and what happens here. That's the secret of maintaining your identity on an alien world, Gundy. Comprehend the esthetics of distance: draw a boundary line about yourself and say to the planet, thus far you can go in consuming me, and no farther. Otherwise the planet will eventually absorb you and make you part of it. Am I being clear?"

"Not at all," said Gundersen.

"The meaning will manifest itself eventually." *Whang.* "Come see our serpents."

Kurtz was five years older than Gundersen and had been on Holman's World three years longer. Gundersen had known him by reputation long before meeting him. Everyone seemed to feel awe of Kurtz, and yet he was only an assistant station agent, who had never been promoted beyond that lowly rank. After five minutes of exposure to him, Gundersen thought he knew why. Kurtz gave an impression of instability—not quite a fallen angel but certainly a falling one, Lucifer on his way down, descending from morn to noon, noon to dewy eve, but now only in the morning of his drop. One could not trust a man like that with serious responsibilities until he had finished his transit and had settled into his ultimate state.

They went into the serpent station together. Kurtz reached up as he passed the distilling apparatus, lightly caressing tubing and petcocks. His fingers were like a spider's legs, and the caress was astonishingly obscene. At the far end of the room stood a short, stocky man, dark-haired, black-browed, the station supervisor, Gio' Sala-mone. Kurtz made the introductions. Salamone grinned. "Lucky you," he said. "How did you manage to get assigned here?"

"They just sent me," Gundersen said.

"As somebody's practical joke," Kurtz suggested.

"I believe it," said Gundersen. "Everyone thought I was fibbing when I said I was sent here without applying."

"A test of innocence," Kurtz murmured.

Salamone said, "Well, now that you're here, you'd better learn our basic rule. The basic rule is that when you leave this station, you never discuss what happens here with anybody else. *Capisce?* Now say to me, 'I swear by the Father, Son, and Holy Ghost, and also by Abraham, Isaac, Jacob, and Moses—' "

Kurtz choked with laughter.

Bewildered, Gundersen said, "That's an oath I've never heard before."

"Salamone's an Italian Jew," said Kurtz. "He's trying to cover all possibilities. Don't bother swearing, but he's right: what happens here isn't anybody else's business. Whatever you may have heard about the serpent station is probably true, but nevertheless tell no tales when you leave here." *Whang. Whang.* "Watch us carefully, now. We're going to call up our demons. Loose the amplifiers, Gio'."

Salamone seized a plastic sack of what looked like golden flour and hauled it toward the station's rear door. He scooped out a handful. With a quick upward heave he sent it into the air; the breeze instantly caught the tiny glittering grains and carried them aloft. Kurtz said, "He's just scattered a thousand microamplifiers into the jungle. In ten minutes they'll cover a radius of ten kilometers. They're tuned to pick up the frequencies of my guitar and Gio's flute, and the resonances go bouncing back and forth all over the place." Kurtz began to play, picking up a melody in mid-course. Salamone produced a short transverse flute and wove a melody of his own through the spaces in Kurtz's tune. Their playing became a stately sarabande, delicate, hypnotic, two or three figures repeated endlessly without variations in volume or pitch. For ten minutes nothing unusual occurred. Then Kurtz nodded toward the edge of the jungle. "They're coming," he whispered. "We're the original and authentic snake charmers."

Gundersen watched the serpents emerging from the forest. They were four times as long as a man, and as thick as a big man's arm. Undulating fins ran down their backs from end to end. Their skins were glossy, pale green, and evidently sticky, for the detritus of the forest floor stuck to them in places, bits of leaves and soil and crumpled petals. Instead of eyes, they had rows of platter-sized sensor spots flanking their rippling dorsal fins. Their heads were blunt; their mouths only slits, suitable merely for nibbling on gobbets of soil. Where nostrils might be, there protruded two slender quills as long as a man's thumb; these extended to five times that length in moments of stress or when the serpent was under attack, and yielded a blue fluid, a venom. Despite the size of the creatures, despite the arrival of perhaps thirty of them at once, Gundersen did not find them frightening, although he would certainly have been uneasy at the arrival of a platoon of pythons. These were not pythons. They were not even reptiles at all, but low-phylum creatures, actually giant worms. They were sluggish and of no apparent intelligence. But clearly they responded powerfully to the music. It had drawn them to the station, and now they writhed in a ghastly ballet, seeking the source of the sound. The first few were already entering the building.

"Do you play the guitar?" Kurtz asked. "Here—just keep the sound going. The tune's not important now." He thrust the instrument at Gundersen, who struggled with the fingerings a moment, then brought forth a lame, stumbling imitation of Kurtz's melody. Kurtz, meanwhile, was slipping a tubular pink cap over the head of the nearest serpent. When it was in place, the cap began rhythmic contractions; the serpent's writhings became momentarily more intense, its fin moved convulsively, its tail lashed the ground. Then it grew calm. Kurtz removed the cap and slid it over the head of another serpent, and another, and another.

He was milking them of venom. These creatures were deadly to native metabolic systems, so it was said; they never attacked, but when provoked they struck, and their poison was universally effective. But what was poison on Holman's World was a blessing on Earth. The venom of the jungle serpents was one of the Company's most profitable exports. Properly distilled, diluted, crystallized, purified, the juice served as a catalyst in limb-regeneration work. A dose of it softened the resistance of the human cell to change, insidiously corrupting the cytoplasm, leading it to induce the nucleus to switch on its genetic material. And so it greatly encouraged the reawakening of cell division, the replication of bodily parts, when a new arm or leg or face had to be grown. How or why it worked, Gundersen knew not, but he had seen the stuff in action during his training period, when a fellow trainee had lost both legs below the knee in a soarer accident. The drug made the flesh flow. It liberated the guardians of the body's coded pattern, easing the task of the genetic surgeons tenfold by sensitizing and stimulating the zone of regeneration. Those legs had grown back in six months.

Gundersen continued to strum the guitar, Salamone to play his flute, Kurtz to collect the venom. Mooing sounds came suddenly from the bush: a herd of nildoror evidently had been drawn by the music as well. Gundersen saw them lumber out of the underbrush and stand almost shyly by the border of the clearing, nine of them. After a moment they entered into a clumsy, lurching, ponderous dance. Their trunks waved in time to the music; their tails swung, their spiny crests revolved. "All done," Kurtz announced. "Five liters—a good haul." The serpents, milked, drifted off into the forest as soon as the music ceased. The nildoror stayed a while longer, peering intently at the men inside the station, but finally they left also. Kurtz and Salamone instructed Gundersen in the techniques of distilling the precious fluid, making it ready for shipment to Earth.

And that was all. He could see nothing scandalous in what had happened, and did not understand why there had been so much sly talk at headquarters about this place, nor why Salamone had tried to wring an oath of silence from him. He dared not ask. Three days later they again summoned the serpents, again collected their venom, and again the whole process seemed unexceptionable to Gundersen. But soon he came to realize that Kurtz and Salamone were testing his reliability before initiating him into their mysteries.

In the third week of his stint at the serpent station they finally admitted him to the inner knowledge. The collection was done; the serpents had gone; a few nil-doror, out of more than a dozen that had been attracted by that day's concert, still lingered outside the building. Gundersen realized that something unusual was about to happen when he saw Kurtz, after darting a sharp glance at Salamone, unhook a container of venom before it started on its route through the distilling apparatus. He poured it into a broad bowl that held at least a liter of fluid. On Earth, that much of the drug would be worth a year of Gundersen's salary as an assistant station agent.

"Come with us," Kurtz said.

The three men stepped outside. At once three nildoror approached, behaving oddly, their spines upraised, their ears trembling. They seemed skittish and eager. Kurtz handed the bowl of raw venom to Salamone, who sipped from it and handed it back. Kurtz also drank. He gave the bowl to Gundersen, saying, "Take communion with us?"

Gundersen hesitated. Salamone said, "It's safe. It can't work on your nuclei when you take it internally."

Putting the bowl to his lips, Gundersen took a cautious swig. The venom was sweet but watery.

"—only on your brain," Salamone added.

Kurtz gently took the bowl from him and set it down on the ground. Now the largest nildor advanced and delicately dipped his trunk into it. Then the second nildor drank, and the third. The bowl now was empty.

Gundersen said, "If it's poisonous to native life—"

"Not when they drink it. Just when it's shot directly into the bloodstream," Salamone said.

"What happens now?"

"Wait," Kurtz said, "and make your soul receptive to any suggestions that arise."

Gundersen did not have to wait long. He felt a thickening at the base of his neck and a roughness about his face, and his arms seemed impossibly heavy. It seemed best to drop to his knees as the effect intensified. He turned toward Kurtz, seeking reassurance from those dark shining eyes, but Kurtz's eyes had already begun to flatten and expand, and his green and prehensile trunk nearly reached the ground. Salamone, too, had entered the metamorphosis, capering comically, jabbing the soil with his tusks. The thickening continued. Now Gundersen knew that he weighed several tons, and he tested his body's coordination, striding back and forth, learning how to move on four limbs. He went to the spring and sucked up water in his trunk. He rubbed his leathery hide against trees. He trumpeted bellowing sounds of joy in his hugeness. He joined with Kurtz and Salamone in a wild dance, making the ground quiver. The nildoror too were transformed; one had become Kurtz, one had become Salamone, one had become Gundersen, and the three former beasts moved in wild pirouettes, tumbling and toppling in their unfamiliarity with human ways. But Gundersen lost interest in what the nildoror were doing. He concentrated solely on his own experience. Somewhere at the core of his soul it terrified him to know that this change had come over him and he was doomed forever to live as a massive animal of the jungle, shredding bark and ripping branches; yet it was rewarding to have shifted bodies this way and to have access to an entirely new range of sensory data. His eyesight now was dimmed, and everything that he saw was engulfed in a furry halo, but there were compensations: he was able to sort odors by their directions and by their textures, and his hearing was immensely more sensitive. It was the equivalent of being able to see into the ultraviolet and the infrared. A dingy forest flower sent dizzying waves of sleek moist sweetness at him; the click of insect-claws in underground tunnels was like a symphony for percussion. And the bigness of him! The ecstasy of carrying such a body! His transformed consciousness soared, swooped, rose high again. He trampled trees and praised himself for it in booming tones. He grazed and gorged. Then he sat for a while, perfectly still, and meditated on the existence of evil in the universe, asking himself why there should be such a thing, and indeed whether evil in fact existed as an objective phenomenon. His answers surprised and delighted him, and he turned to Kurtz to communicate his insights, but just then the effect of the venom began to fade with quite startling suddenness, and in a short while Gundersen felt altogether normal again. He was weeping, though, and he felt an anguish of shame, as though he had been flagrantly detected molesting a child. The three nildoror were nowhere in sight. Salamone picked up the bowl and went into the station. "Come," Kurtz said. "Let's go in too."

They would not discuss any of it with him. They had

let him share in it, but they would not explain a thing, cutting him off sternly when he asked. The rite was hermetically private. Gundersen was wholly unable to evaluate the experience. Had his body actually turned into that of a nildor for an hour? Hardly. Well, then, had his mind, his soul, somehow migrated into the nildor's body? And had the nildor's soul, if nildoror had souls, gone into his? What kind of sharing, what sort of union of innernesses, had occurred in that clearing?

Three days afterward, Gundersen applied for a transfer out of the serpent station. In those days he was easily upset by the unknown. Kurtz's only reaction, when Gundersen announced he was leaving, was a short brutal chuckle. The normal tour of duty at the station was eight weeks, of which Gundersen had done less than half. He never again served a stint there.

Later, he gathered what gossip he could about the doings at the serpent station. He was told vague tales of sexual abominations in the grove, of couplings between Earthman and nildor, between Earthman and Earthman; he heard murmurs that those who habitually drank the venom underwent strange and terrible and permanent changes of the body; he heard stories of how the nildoror elders in their private councils bitterly condemned the morbid practice of going to the serpent station to drink the stuff the Earthmen offered. But Gundersen did not know if any of these whispers were true. He found it difficult, in later years, to look Kurtz in the eye on the rare occasions when they met. Sometimes he found it difficult even to live with himself. In some peripheral way he had been tainted by his single hour of metamorphosis. He felt like a virgin who had stumbled into an orgy, and who had come away deflowered but yet ignorant of what had befallen her.

The phantoms faded. The sound of Kurtz's guitar diminished and was gone.

Srin'gahar said, "Shall we leave now?"

Gundersen slowly emerged from the ruined station. "Does anyone gather the juices of the serpents today?"

"Not here," said the nildor. He knelt. The Earthman mounted him, and in silence Srin'gahar carried him away, back to the path they had followed earlier.

FOUR

In early afternoon they neared the nildoror encampment that was Gundersen's immediate goal. For most of the day they had been traveling across the broad coastal plain, but now the back of the land dipped sharply, for this far inland there was a long, narrow depression running from north to south, a deep rift between the central plateau and the coast. At the approach to this rift Gundersen saw the immense devastation of foliage that signaled the presence of a large nildoror herd within a few kilometers. A jagged scar ran through the forest from ground level to a point about twice a man's height.

Even the lunatic tropical fertility of this region could not keep up with the nildoror appetite; it took a year or more for such zones of defoliation to restore themselves after the herd had moved on. Yet despite the impact of the herd, the forest on all sides of the scar was even more close-knit here than on the coastal plain to the east. This was a jungle raised to the next higher power, damp, steamy, dark. The temperature was considerably higher in the valley than at the coast, and though the atmosphere could not possibly have been any more humid here, there was an almost tangible wetness about the air. The vegetation was different, too. On the plain the trees tended to have sharp, sometimes dangerously sharp, leaves. Here the foliage was rounded and fleshy, heavy sagging disks of dark blue that glistened voluptuously whenever stray shafts of sunlight pierced the forest canopy overhead.

Gundersen and his mount continued to descend, following the line of the grazing scar. Now they made their way along the route of a stream that flowed perversely inland; the soil was spongy and soft, and more often than not Srin'gahar walked knee-deep in mud. They were entering a wide circular basin at what seemed to be the lowest point in the entire region. Streams flowed into it on three or four sides, feeding a dark weed-covered lake at the center; and around the margin of the lake was Srin'gahar's herd. Gundersen saw several hundred nildoror grazing, sleeping, coupling, strolling.

"Put me down," he said, taking himself by surprise. "I'll walk beside you."

Wordlessly Srin'gahar allowed him to dismount.

Gundersen regretted his egalitarian impulse the moment he stepped down. The nildor's broad-padded feet were able to cope with the muddy floor; but Gundersen discovered that he had a tendency to begin to sink in if he remained in one place more than a moment. But he would not remount now. Every step was a struggle, but he struggled. He was tense and uncertain, too, of the reception he would get here, and he was hungry as well, having eaten nothing on the long journey but a few bitterfruits plucked from passing trees. The closeness of the climate made each breath a battle for him. He was greatly relieved when the footing became easier a short distance down the slope. Here, a webwork of spongy plants spreading out from the lake underwove the mud to form a firm, if not altogether reassuring, platform a few centimeters down.

Srin'gahar raised his trunk and sounded a trumpetblast of greeting to the encampment. A few of the nildoror replied in kind. To Gundersen, Srin'gahar said, "The many-born one stands at the edge of the lake, friend of my journey. You see him, yes, in that group? Shall I lead you now to him?"

"Please," said Gundersen.

The lake was congested with drifting vegetation. Humped masses of it broke the surface everywhere: leaves like horns of plenty, cup-shaped spore-bodies, ropy tangled stems, everything dark blue against the lighter blue-green of the water. Through this maze of tight-packed flora there slowly moved huge semiaquatic mammals, half a dozen malidaror, whose tubular yellowish bodies were almost totally submerged. Only the rounded bulges of their backs and the jutting periscopes of their stalked eyes were in view, and now and then a pair of cavernous snorting nostrils. Gundersen could see the immense swaths that the malidaror had cut through the vegetation in this day's feeding, but at the far side of the lake the wounds were beginning to close as new growth hastened to fill the fresh gaps.

Gundersen and Srin'gahar went down toward the water. Suddenly the wind shifted, and Gundersen had a whiff of the lake's fragrance. He coughed; it was like breathing the fumes of a distillery vat. The lake was in ferment. Alcohol was a by-product of the respiration of these water-plants, and, having no outlet, the lake became one large tub of brandy. Both water and alcohol evaporated from it at a rapid pace, making the surrounding air not only steamy but potent; and during centuries when evaporation of water had exceeded the inflow from the streams, the proof of the residue had steadily risen. When the Company ruled this planet, such lakes had been the undoing of more than one agent, Gundersen knew.

The nildoror appeared to pay little heed to him as he came near them. Gundersen was aware that every member of the encampment was actually watching him closely, but they pretended to casualness and went about their business. He was puzzled to see a dozen brush shelters flanking one of the streams. Nildoror did not live in dwellings of any sort; the climate made it unnecessary, and besides they were incapable of constructing anything, having no organs of manipulation other than the three "fingers" at the tips of their trunks. He studied the crude lean-tos in bewilderment, and after a moment it dawned on him that he had seen structures of this sort before: they were the huts of sulidoror. The puzzle deepened. Such close association between the nildoror and the carnivorous bipeds of the mist country was unknown to him. Now he saw the sulidoror themselves, perhaps twenty of them, sitting crosslegged inside their huts. Slaves? Captives? Friends of the tribe? None of those ideas made sense.

"That is our many-born," Srin'gahar said, indicating with a wave of his trunk a seamed and venerable nildor in the midst of a group by the lakeshore.

Gundersen felt a surge of awe, inspired not only by the great age of the creature, but by the knowledge that this ancient beast, blue-gray with years, must have taken part several times in the unimaginable rites of the rebirth ceremony. The many-born one had journeyed beyond the barrier of spirit that held Earthmen back. Whatever nirvana the rebirth ceremony offered, this being had tasted it, and Gundersen had not, and that crucial distinction of experience made Gundersen's courage shrivel as he approached the leader of the herd.

A ring of courtiers surrounded the old one. They were gray-skinned and wrinkled, too: a congregation of seniors. Younger nildoror, of the generation of Srin'gahar, kept a respectful distance. There were no immature nildoror in the encampment at all. No Earthman had ever seen a young nildor. Gundersen had been told that the nildoror were always born in the mist country, in the home country of the sulidoror, and apparently they remained in close seclusion there until they had reached the nildoror equivalent of adolescence, when they migrated to the jungles of the tropics. He also had heard that every nildor hoped to go back to the mist country when its time had come to die. But he did not know if such things were true. No one did.

The ring opened, and Gundersen found himself facing the many-born one. Protocol demanded that Gundersen speak first; but he faltered, dizzied by tension perhaps, or perhaps by the fumes of the lake, and it was an endless moment before he pulled himself together.

He said at last, "I am Edmund Gundersen of the first birth, and I wish you joy of many rebirths, O wisest one."

Unhurriedly the nildor swung his vast head to one side, sucked up a snort of water from the lake, and squirted it into his mouth. Then he rumbled, "You are known to us, Edmundgundersen, from days past. You kept the big house of the Company at Fire Point in the Sea of Dust."

The nildor's sharpness of memory astonished and distressed him. If they remembered him so well, what chance did he have to win favors from these people? They owed him no kindnesses.

"I was there, yes, a long time ago," he said tightly.

"Not so long ago. Ten turnings is not a long time." The nildor's heavy-lidded eyes closed, and it appeared for some moments as though the many-born one had fallen asleep. Then the nildor said, eyes still closed, "I am Vol'himyor of the seventh birth. Will you come into the water with me? I grow tired easily on the land in this present birth of mine."

Without waiting, Vol'himyor strode into the lake, swimming slowly to a point some forty meters from shore and floating there, submerged up to the shoulders. A malidar that had been browsing on the weeds in that part of the lake went under with a bubbling murmur of discontent and reappeared far away. Gundersen knew that he had no choice but to follow the many-born one. He stripped off his clothing and walked forward.

The tepid water rose about him. Not far out, the spongy matting of fibrous stems below ground level gave way to soft warm mud beneath Gundersen's bare feet. He felt the occasional movement of small many-legged things under his soles. The roots of the water-plants swirled whiplike about his legs, and the black bubbles of alcohol that came up from the depths and burst on the surface almost stifled him with their release of vapor. He pushed plants aside, forcing his way through them with the greatest difficulty, and feeling a great relief when his feet lost contact with the mud. Quickly he paddled himself out to Vol'himyor. The surface of the water was clear there, thanks to the malidar. In the dark depths of the lake, though, unknown creatures moved to and fro, and every few moments something slippery and quick slithered along Gundersen's body. He forced himself to ignore such things.

Vol'himyor, still seemingly asleep, murmured, "You have been gone from this world for many turnings, have you not?"

"After the Company relinquished its rights here, I returned to my own world," said Gundersen.

Even before the nildor's eyelids parted, even before the round yellow eyes fixed coldly on him, Gundersen was aware that he had blundered.

"Your Company never had rights here to relinquish," said the nildor in the customary flat, neutral way. "Is this not so?"

"It is so," Gundersen conceded. He searched for a graceful correction and finally said, "After the Company relinquished possession of this planet, I returned to my own world."

"Those words are more nearly true. Why, then, have you come back here?"

"Because I love this place and wish to see it again."

"Is it possible for an Earthman to feel love for Belzagor?"

"An Earthman can, yes."

"An Earthman can become *captured* by Belzagor," Vol'himyor said with more than usual slowness. "An Earthman may find that his soul has been seized by the forces of this planet and is held in thrall. But I doubt that an Earthman can feel love for this planet, as I understand your understanding of love."

"I yield the point, many-born one. My soul has become captured by Belzagor. I could not help but return."

"You are quick to yield such points."

"I have no wish to give offense."

"Commendable tact. And what will you do here on this world that has seized your soul?"

"Travel to many parts of your world," said Gundersen. "I wish particularly to go to the mist country."

"Why there?"

"It is the place that captures me most deeply."

"That is not an informative answer," the nildor said.

"I can give no other."

"What thing has captured you there?"

"The beauty of the mountains rising out of the mist. The sparkle of sunlight on a clear, cold, bright day. The splendor of the moons against a field of glittering snow."

"You are quite poetic," said Vol'himyor.

Gundersen could not tell if he were being praised or mocked.

He said, "Under the present law, I must have the permission of a many-born one to enter the mist country. So I come to make application to you for such permission."

"You are fastidious in your respect for our law, my once-born friend. Once it was different with you."

Gundersen bit his lip. He felt something crawling up his calf, down in the depths of the lake, but he compelled himself to stare serenely at the many-born one. Choosing his words with care, he said, "Sometimes we are slow to understand the nature of others, and we give offense without knowing that we do so."

"It is so."

"But then understanding comes," Gundersen said, "and one feels remorse for the deeds of the past, and one hopes that one may be forgiven for his sins."

"Forgiveness depends on the quality of the remorse," said Vol'himyor, "and also on the quality of the sins."

"I believe my failings are known to you."

"They are not forgotten," said the nildor.

"I believe also that in your creed the possibility of personal redemption is not unknown."

"True. True."

"Will you allow me to make amends for my sins of the past against your people, both known and unknown?"

"Making amends for unknown sins is meaningless," said the nildor. "But in any case we seek no apologies. Your redemption from sin is your own concern, not ours. Perhaps you will find that redemption here, as you hope. I sense already a welcome change in your soul, and it will count heavily in your favor."

"I have your permission to go north, then?" Gundersen asked.

"Not so fast. Stay with us a while as our guest. We must think about this. You may go to shore, now."

The dismissal was clear. Gundersen thanked the many-born one for his patience, not without some self-satisfaction at the way he had handled the interview. He had always displayed proper deference toward many-born ones—even a really Kiplingesque imperialist knew enough to show respect for venerable tribal leaders—but in Company days it had never been more than a charade for him, a put-on show of humility, since ultimate power resided with the Company's sector agent, not with any nildor no matter how holy. Now, of course, the old nildor really did have the power to keep him out of the mist country, and might even see some poetic justice in banning him from it. But Gundersen felt that his deferential and apologetic attitude had been reasonably sincere just now, and that some of that sincerity had been communicated to Vol'himyor. He knew that he could not deceive the many-born one into thinking that an old Company hand like himself was suddenly eager to grovel before the former victims of Earth's expansionism; but unless some show of earnestness did come through, he stood no chance at all of gaining the permission he needed.

Abruptly, when Gundersen was still a good distance from shore, something hit him a tremendous blow between the shoulders and flung him, stunned and gasping, face forward into the water.

As he went under, the thought crossed his mind that Vol'himyor had treacherously come up behind him and lashed him with his trunk. Such a blow could easily be fatal if aimed with real malice. Spluttering, his mouth full of the lake's liquor, his arms half numbed by the impact of the blow, Gundersen warily surfaced, expecting to find the old nildor looming above him ready to deliver the coup de grace.

He opened his eyes, with some momentary trouble focusing them. No, there was the many-born one far away across the water, looking in another direction. And then Gundersen felt a curious prickly premonition and got his head down just in time to avoid being decapitated by whatever it was that had hit him before. Huddling nose-deep in the water, he saw it swing by overhead, a thick yellowish rod like a boom out of control. Now he heard thunderous shrieks of pain and felt widening ripples sweeping across the lake. He glanced around.

A dozen sulidoror had entered the water and were killing a malidar. They had harpooned the colossal beast with sharpened sticks; now the malidar thrashed and coiled in its final agonies, and it was the mighty tail of the animal that had knocked Gundersen over. The hunters had fanned out in the shallows, waist-deep, their thick fur bedraggled and matted. Each group grasped the line of one harpoon, and they were gradually drawing the malidar toward shore. Gundersen was no longer in danger, but he continued to stay low in the water, catching his breath, rotating his shoulders to assure himself that no bones were broken. The malidar's tail must have given him the merest tip-flick the first time; he would surely have been destroyed the second time that tail came by, if he had not ducked. He was beginning to ache, and he felt half drowned by the water he had gulped. He wondered when he would start to get drunk.

Now the sulidoror had beached their prey. Only the malidar's tail and thick web-footed hind legs lay in the water, moving fitfully. The rest of the animal, tons of it, stretching five times the length of a man, was up on shore, and the sulidoror were methodically driving long stakes into it, one through each of the forelimbs and several into the broad wedge-shaped head. A few nildoror were watching the operation in mild curiosity. Most ignored it. The remaining malidaror continued to browse in the woods as though nothing had happened.

A final thrust of a stake severed the malidar's spinal column. The beast quivered and lay still.

Gundersen hurried from the water, swimming quickly, then wading through the unpleasantly voluptuous mud, at last stumbling out onto the beach. His knees suddenly failed him and he toppled forward, trembling, choking, puking. A thin stream of fluid burst from his lips. Afterward he rolled to one side and watched the sulidoror cutting gigantic blocks of pale pink meat from the malidar's sides and passing them around. Other sulidoror were coming from the huts to share the feast. Gundersen shivered. He was in a kind of shock, and a few minutes passed before he realized that the cause of his shock was not only the blow he had received and the water he had swallowed, but also the knowledge that an act of violence had been committed in front of a herd of nildoror, and the nildoror did not seem at all disturbed. He had imagined that these peaceful, nonbelligerent creatures would react in horror to the slaughter of a malidar. But they simply did not care. The shock Gundersen felt was the shock of disillusionment.

A sulidor approached him and stood over him. Gundersen stared up uneasily at the towering shaggy figure. The sulidor held in its forepaws a gobbet of malidar meat the size of Gundersen's head.

"For you," said the sulidor in the nildoror language. "You eat with us?"

It did not wait for a reply. It tossed the slab of flesh to the ground next to Gundersen and rejoined its fellows. Gundersen's stomach writhed. He had no lust for raw meat just now.

The beach was suddenly very silent.

They were all watching him, sulidoror and nildoror both.

FIVE

Shakily Gundersen got to his feet. He sucked warm air into his lungs and bought a little time by crouching at the lake's edge to wash his face. He found his discarded clothing and consumed a few minutes by getting it on. Now he felt a little better; but the problem of the raw meat remained. The sulidoror, enjoying their feast, rending and tearing flesh and gnawing on bones, nevertheless frequently looked his way to see whether he would accept their hospitality. The nildoror, who of course had not touched the meat themselves, also seemed curious about his decision. If he refused the meat, would he offend the sulidoror? If he ate it, would he stamp himself as bestial in the eyes of the nildoror? He concluded that it was best to force some of the meat into him, as a gesture of good will toward the menacing-looking bipeds. The nildoror, after all, did not seem troubled that the sulidoror were eating meat; why should it bother them if an Earthman, a known carnivore, did the same?

He would eat the meat. But he would eat it as an Earthman would.

He ripped some leaves from the water-plant and spread them out to form a mat; he placed the meat on this. From his tunic he took his fusion torch, which he adjusted for wide aperture, low intensity, and played on the meat until its outer surface was charred and bubbling. With a narrower beam he cut the cooked meat into chunks he could manage. Then, squatting cross-legged, he picked up a chunk and bit into it.

The meat was soft and cheesy, interlaced by tough string-like masses forming an intricate grid. By will alone Gundersen succeeded in getting three pieces down. When he decided he had had enough, he rose, called out his thanks to the sulidoror, and knelt by the side of the lake to scoop up some of the water. He needed a chaser.

During all this time no one spoke to him or approached him.

The nildoror had all left the water, for night was approaching. They had settled down in several groups well back from the shore. The feast of the sulidoror continued noisily, but was nearing its end; already several small scavenger-beasts had joined the party, and were at work at the lower half of the malidar's body while the sulidoror finished the other part.

Gundersen looked about for Srin'gahar. There were things he wished to ask.

It still troubled him that the nildoror had accepted the killing in the lake so coolly. He realized that he had somehow always regarded the nildoror as more noble than the other big beasts of this planet because they did not take life except under supreme provocation, and sometimes not even then. Here was an intelligent race exempt from the sin of Cain. And Gundersen saw in that a corollary: that the nildoror, because they did not kill, would look upon killing as a detestable act. Now he knew that his reasoning was faulty and even naïve. The nildoror did not kill simply because they were not eaters of meat; but the moral superiority that he had attributed to them on that score must in fact be a product of his own guilty imagination.

The night came on with tropic swiftness. A single moon glimmered. Gundersen saw a nildor he took to be Srin'gahar, and went to him.

"I have a question, Srin'gahar, friend of my journey," Gundersen began. "When the sulidoror entered the water—"

The nildor said gravely, "You make a mistake. I am Thali'vanoom of the third birth."

Gundersen mumbled an apology and turned away, aghast. What a typically Earthman blunder, he thought. He remembered his old sector chief making the same blunder a dozen dozen times, hopelessly confusing one nildor with another and muttering angrily, "Can't tell one of these big bastards from the next! Why don't they wear badges?" The ultimate insult, the failure to recognize the natives as individuals. Gundersen had always made it a point of honor to avoid such gratuitous insults. And so, here, at this delicate time when he depended wholly on winning the favor of the nildoror—

He approached a second nildor, and saw just at the last moment that this one too was not Srin'gahar. He backed off as gracefully as he could. On the third attempt he finally found his traveling companion. Srin'gahar sat placidly against a narrow tree, his thick legs folded beneath his body. Gundersen put his question to him and Srin'gahar said, "Why should the sight of violent death shock us? Malidaror have no *g'rakh*, after all. And it is obvious that sulidoror must eat."

"No *g'rakh?*" Gundersen said. "This is a word I do not know."

"The quality that separates the souled from the unsouled," Srin'gahar explained. "Without *g'rakh* a creature is but a beast."

"Do sulidoror have *g'rakh?*"

"Of course."

"And nildoror also, naturally. But malidaror don't. What about Earthmen?"

"It is amply clear that Earthmen have *g'rakh.*"

"And one may freely kill a creature which lacks that quality?"

"If one has the need to do so, yes," said Srin'gahar. "These are elementary matters. Have you no such concepts on your own world?"

"On my world," said Gundersen, "there is only one species that has been granted *g'rakh,* and so perhaps we give such matters too little thought. We know that whatever is not of our own kind must be lacking in *g'rakh.*"

"And so, when you come to another world, you have difficulty in accepting the presence of *g'rakh* in other beings?" Srin'gahar asked. "You need not answer. I understand."

"May I ask another question?" said Gundersen. "Why are there sulidoror here?"

"We allow them to be here."

"In the past, in the days when the Company ruled Belzagor, the sulidoror never went outside the mist country."

"We did not allow them to come here then."

"But now you do. Why?"

"Because now it is easier for us to do so. Difficulties stood in the way at earlier times."

"What kind of difficulties?" Gundersen persisted.

Softly Srin'gahar said, "You will have to ask that of someone who has been born more often than I. I am once-born, and many things are as strange to me as they are to you. Look, another moon is in the sky! At the third moon we shall dance."

Gundersen looked up and saw the tiny white disk moving rapidly, low in the sky, seemingly skimming the fringe of the treetops. Belzagor's five moons were a random assortment, the closest one just outside Roche's Limit, the farthest so distant it was visible only to sharp eyes on a clear night. At any given time two or three moons were in the night sky, but the fourth and fifth moons had such eccentric orbits that they could never be seen at all from vast regions of the planet, and passed over most other zones no more than three or four times a year. One night each year all five moons could be seen at once, just along a band ten kilometers wide running at an angle of about forty degrees to the equator from northeast to southwest. Gundersen had experienced the Night of Five Moons only a single time.

The nildoror were starting to move toward the lakeshore now.

The third moon appeared, spinning retrograde into view from the south.

So he was going to see them dance again. He had witnessed their ceremonies once before, early in his career, when he was stationed at Shangri-la Falls in the northern tropics. That night the nildoror had massed just upstream of the falls, on both banks of Madden's River, and for hours after dark their blurred cries could be heard even above the roar of the water. And finally Kurtz, who was also stationed at Shangri-la then, said, "Come, let's watch the show!" and led Gundersen out into the night. This was six months before the episode at the serpent station, and Gundersen did not then realize how strange Kurtz was. But he realized it quickly enough after Kurtz joined the nildoror in their dance. The huge beasts were clustered in loose semicircles, stamping back and forth, trumpeting piercingly, shaking the ground, and suddenly there was Kurtz out there among them, arms upflung, bare chest beaded with sweat and shining in the moonlight, dancing as intensely as any of them, crying out in great booming roars, stamping his feet, tossing his head. And the nildoror were forming a group around him, giving him plenty of space, letting him enter fully into the frenzy, now running toward him, now backing away, a systole and diastole of ferocious power. Gundersen stood awed, and did not move when Kurtz called to him to join the dance. He watched for what seemed like hours, hypnotized by the boom boom *boom* boom of the dancing nildoror, until in the end he broke somehow from his trance, and searched for Kurtz and found him still in ceaseless motion, a gaunt bony skeletonic figure jerking puppet-like on invisible strings, looking fragile despite his extreme height as he moved within the circle of colossal nildoror. Kurtz could neither hear Gundersen's words nor take note of his presence, and finally Gundersen went back to the station alone. In the morning he found Kurtz, looking spent and worn, slumped on the bench overlooking the waterfall. Kurtz merely said, "You should have stayed. You should have danced."

Anthropologists had studied these rites. Gundersen had looked up the literature, learning what little there was to learn. Evidently the dance was preceded and surrounded by drama, a spoken episode akin to Earth's medieval mystery plays, a theatrical reenactment of some supremely important nildoror myth, serving both as mode of entertainment and as ecstatic religious experience. Unfortunately the language of the drama was an obsolete liturgical tongue, not a word of which could be understood by an Earthman, and the nildoror, who had not hesitated to instruct their first Earthborn visitors in their relatively simple modern language, had never offered any clue to the nature of the other one. The anthropological observers had noted one point which Gundersen now found cheering: invariably, within a few days after the performance of this particular rite, groups of nildoror from the herd performing it would set out for the mist country, presumably to undergo rebirth.

He wondered if the rite might be some ceremony of purification, some means of entering a state of grace before undergoing rebirth.

The nildoror all had gathered, now, beside the lake. Srin'gahar was one of the last to go. Gundersen sat alone on the slope above the basin, watching the massive forms assembling. The contrary motions of the moons fragmented the shadows of the nildoror, and the cold light from above turned their smooth green hides into furrowed black cloaks. Looking over to his left, Gundersen saw the sulidoror squatting before their huts, excluded from the ceremony but apparently not forbidden to view it.

In the silence came a low, clear, forceful flow of words. He strained to hear, hoping to catch some clue to the meaning, seeking a magical gateway that would let him burst through into an understanding of that secret language. But no understanding came. Vol'himyor was the speaker, the old many-born one, reciting words clearly familiar to everyone at the lake, an invocation, an introit. Then came a long interval of silence, and then came a response from a second nildor at the opposite end of the group, who exactly duplicated the rhythms and sinuosities of Vol'himyor's utterance. Silence again; and then a reply from Vol'himyor, spoken more crisply. Back and forth the center of the service moved, and the interplay between the two celebrants became what was for nildoror a surprisingly quick exchange of dialogue. About every tenth line the herd at large repeated what a celebrant had said, sending dark reverberations through the night.

After perhaps ten minutes of this the voice of a third solo nildor was heard. Vol'himyor made reply. A fourth speaker took up the recitation. Now isolated lines were coming in rapid bursts from many members of the congregation. No cue was missed; no nildor trampled on another's lines. Each seemed intuitively to know when to speak, when to stay silent. The tempo accelerated. The ceremony had become a mosaic of brief utterances blared forth from every part of the group in a random rotation. A few of the nildoror were up and moving slowly in place, lifting their feet, putting them down.

Lightning speared through the sky. Despite the closeness of the atmosphere, Gundersen felt a chill. He saw himself as a wanderer on a prehistoric Earth, spying on some grotesque conclave of mastodons. All the things of man seemed infinitely far away now. The drama was reaching some sort of climax. The nildoror were bellowing, stamping, calling to one another with tremendous snorts. They were taking up formations, assembling in aisled rows. Still there came utterances and responses, antiphonal amplifications of words heavy with strange significance. The air

grew more steamy. Gundersen could no longer hear individual words, only rich deep chords of massed grunts,
ah ah *ah* ah, ah ah *ah* ah, the old rhythm that he remembered from the night at Shangri-la Falls. It was a
breathy, gasping sound now, ecstatic, an endless chuffing
pattern of exhalations, ah ah *ah* ah, ah ah *ah* ah, ah ah
ah ah, with scarcely a break between each group of four
beats, and the whole jungle seemed to echo with it. The
nildoror had no musical instruments whatever, yet to Gundersen it appeared that vast drums were pounding out that
hypnotically intense rhythm. Ah ah *ah* ah. Ah ah *ah* ah.
AH AH *AH* AH! AH AH *AH* AH!

And the nildoror were dancing.

Down below on the margin of the lake moved scores of
great shadowy shapes, prancing like gazelles, two running
steps forward, stamp down hard on the third step, regain
the balance on the fourth. The universe trembled. Boom
boom *boom* boom, boom boom *boom* boom. The earlier
phase of the ceremony, the dramatic dialogue, which
might have been some sort of subtle philosophical disquisi-
tion, had given way totally to this primeval pounding,
this terrifying shuffling of gigantic elephantine bodies.
Boom boom *boom* boom. Gundersen looked to his left and
saw the sulidoror entranced, hairy heads switching back
and forth in the rhythm of the dance; but not one of the
bipeds had risen from the crosslegged posture. They were
content to rock and nod, and now and then to pound their
elbows on the ground.

Gundersen was cut off from his own past, even from a
sense of his own kinship to his species. Disjointed memories
floated up. Again he was at the serpent station, a prisoner
of the hallucinatory venom, feeling himself transformed into a nildor and capering thickly in the grove. Again he
stood by the bank of the great river, seeing another
performance of this very dance. And also he remembered
nights spent in the safety of Company stations deep in
the forest, among his own kind, when they had listened
to the sound of stamping feet in the distance. All those
other times Gundersen had drawn back from whatever
strangeness this planet was offering him; he had transferred
out of the serpent station rather than taste the venom a
second time, he had refused Kurtz's invitation to join the
dance, he had remained within the stations when the rhythmic poundings began in the forest. But tonight he felt

little allegiance to mankind. He found himself longing to join that black and incomprehensible frenzy at the lakeshore. Something monstrous was running free within him, liberated by the incessant repetition of that boom boom *boom* boom. But what right had he to caper Kurtzlike in an alien ceremony? He did not dare intrude on their ritual.

Yet he discovered that he was walking down the spongy slope toward the place where the massed nildoror cavorted.

If he could think of them only as leaping, snorting elephants it would be all right. If he could think of them even as savages kicking up a row it would be all right. But the suspicion was unavoidable that this ceremony of words and dancing held intricate meanings for these people, and that was the worst of it. They might have thick legs and short necks and long dangling trunks, but that did not make them elephants, for their triple tusks and spiny crests and alien anatomies said otherwise; and they might be lacking in all technology, lacking even in a written language, but that did not make them savages, for the complexity of their minds said otherwise. They were creatures who possessed *g'rakh*. Gundersen remembered how he had innocently attempted to instruct the nildoror in the arts of terrestrial culture, in an effort to help them "improve" themselves; he had wanted to humanize them, to lift their spirits upward, but nothing had come of that, and now he found his own spirit being drawn—downward?—certainly to their level, wherever that might lie. Boom boom *boom* boom. His feet hesitantly traced out the four-step as he continued down the slope toward the lake. Did he dare? Would they crush him as blasphemous?

They had let Kurtz dance. They had let Kurtz dance.

It had been in a different latitude, a long time ago, and other nildoror had been involved, but they had let Kurtz dance.

"Yes," a nildor called to him. "Come, dance with us!"

Was it Vol'himyor? Was it Srin'gahar? Was it Thali'vanoom of the third birth? Gundersen did not know which of them had spoken. In the darkness, in the sweaty haze, he could not see clearly, and all these giant shapes looked identical. He reached the bottom of the slope. Nildoror were everywhere about him, tracing out passages in their private journeys from point to point on the lakeshore. Their bodies emitted acrid odors, which, mixing with the fumes of the lake, choked and dizzied him. He heard several of them say to him, "Yes, yes, dance with us!"

And he danced.

He found an open patch of marshy soil and laid claim to it, moving forward, then backward, covering and recovering his one little tract in his fervor. No nildoror trespassed on him. His head tossed; his eyes rolled; his arms dangled; his body swayed and rocked; his feet carried him untiringly. Now he sucked in the thick air. Now he cried out in strange tongues. His skin was on fire; he stripped away his clothing, but it made no difference. Boom boom *boom* boom. Even now, a shred of his old detachment was left, enough so that he could marvel at the spectacle of himself dancing naked amid a herd of giant alien beasts. Would they, in their ultimate transports of passion, sweep in over his plot and crush him into the muck? Surely it was dangerous to stay here in the heart of the herd. But he stayed. Boom boom *boom* boom, again, again, yet again. As he whirled he looked out over the lake, and by sparkling refracted moonlight he saw the malidaror placidly munching the weeds, heedless of the frenzy on land. They are without *g'rakh*, he thought. They are beasts, and when they die their leaden spirits go downward to the earth. Boom. Boom. BOOM. Boom.

He became aware that glossy shapes were moving along the ground, weaving warily between the rows of dancing nildoror. The serpents! This music of pounding feet had summoned them from the dense glades where they lived.

The nildoror seemed wholly unperturbed that these deadly worms moved among them. A single stabbing thrust of the two spiny quills would bring even a mighty nildor toppling down; but no matter. The serpents were welcome, it appeared. They glided toward Gundersen, who knew he was in no mortal danger from their venom, but who did not seek another encounter with it. He did not break the stride of his dance, though, as five of the thick pink creatures wriggled past him. They did not touch him.

The serpents passed through, and were gone. And still the uproar continued. And still the ground shook. Gundersen's heart hammered, but he did not pause. He gave himself up fully, blending with those about him, sharing as deeply as he was able to share it the intensity of the experience.

The moons set. Early streaks of dawn stained the sky.

Gundersen became aware that he no longer could hear the thunder of stamping feet. He danced alone. About him, the nildoror had settled down, and their voices again could be heard, in that strange unintelligible litany. They spoke quietly but with great passion. He could no longer follow the patterns of their words; everything merged into an echoing rumble of tones, without definition, without shape. Unable to halt, he jerked and twisted through his obsessive gyration until the moment that he felt the first heat of the morning sun.

Then he fell exhausted, and lay still, and slipped down easily into sleep.

SIX

When he woke it was some time after midday. The normal life of the encampment had resumed; a good many of the nildoror were in the lake, a few were munching on the vegetation at the top of the slope, and most were resting in the shade. The only sign of last night's frenzy was in the spongy turf near the lakeshore, which was terribly scuffed and torn.

Gundersen felt stiff and numb. Also he was abashed, with the embarrassment of one who has thrown himself too eagerly into someone else's special amusement. He could hardly believe that he had done what he knew himself to have done. In his shame he felt an immediate impulse to leave the encampment at once, before the nildoror could show him their contempt for an Earthman capable of making himself a thrall to their festivity, capable of allowing himself to be beguiled by their incantations. But he shackled the thought, remembering that he had a purpose in coming here.

He limped down to the lake and waded out until its water came up to his breast. He soaked a while, and washed away the sweat of the night before. Emerging, he found his clothing and put it on.

A nildor came to him and said, "Vol'himyor will speak to you now."

The many-born one was halfway up the slope. Coming before him, Gundersen could not find the words of any of the greetings formulas, and simply stared raggedly at the old nildor until Vol'himyor said, "You dance well, my once-born friend. You dance with joy. You dance with love. You dance like a nildor, do you know that?"

"It is not easy for me to understand what happened to me last night," said Gundersen.

"You proved to us that our world has captured your spirit."

"Was it offensive to you that an Earthman danced among you?"

"If it had been offensive," said Vol'himyor slowly, "you would not have danced among us." There was a long silence. Then the nildor said, "We will make a treaty, we two. I will give you permission to go into the mist country. Stay there until you are ready to come out. But when you return, bring with you the Earthman known as Cullen, and offer him to the northernmost encampment of nildoror, the first of my people that you find. Is this agreed?"

"Cullen?" Gundersen asked. Across his mind flared the image of a short broad-faced man with fine golden hair and mild green eyes. "Cedric Cullen, who was here when I was here?"

"The same man."

"He worked with me when I was at the station in the Sea of Dust."

"He lives now in the mist country," Vol'himyor said, "having gone there without permission. We want him."

"What has he done?"

"He is guilty of a grave crime. Now he has taken sanctuary among the sulidoror, where we are unable to gain access to him. It would be a violation of our covenant with them if we removed this man ourselves. But we may ask you to do it."

Gundersen frowned. "You won't tell me the nature of his crime?"

"Does it matter? We want him. Our reasons are not trifling ones. We request you to bring him to us."

"You're asking one Earthman to seize another and turn him in for punishment," said Gundersen. "How am I to know where justice lies in this affair?"

"Under the treaty of relinquishment, are we not the arbiters of justice on this world?" asked the nildor.

Gundersen admitted that this was so.

"Then we hold the right to deal with Cullen as he deserves," Vol'himyor said.

That did not, of course, make it proper for Gundersen to act as catspaw in handing his old comrade over to the nildoror. But Vol'himyor's implied threat was clear: do as we wish, or we grant you no favors.

Gundersen said, "What punishment will Cullen get if he falls into your custody?"

"Punishment? Punishment? Who speaks of punishment?"

"If the man's a criminal—"

"We wish to purify him," said the many-born one. "We desire to cleanse his spirit. We do not regard that as punishment."

"Will you injure him physically in any way?"

"It is not to be thought."

"Will you end his life?"

"Can you mean such a thing? Of course not."

"Will you imprison him?"

"We will keep him in custody," said Vol'himyor, "for however long the rite of purification takes. I do not think it will be long. He will swiftly be freed, and he will be grateful to us."

"I ask you once more to tell me the nature of his crime."

"He will tell you that himself," the nildor said. "It is not necessary for me to make his confession for him."

Gundersen considered all aspects of the matter. Shortly he said, "I agree to our treaty, many-born one, but only if I may add several clauses."

"Go on."

"If Cullen will not tell me the nature of his crime, I am released from my obligation to hand him over."

"Agreed."

"If the sulidoror object to my taking Cullen out of the mist country, I am released from my obligation also."

"They will not object. But agreed."

"If Cullen must be subdued by violence in order to bring him forth, I am released."

The nildor hesitated a moment. "Agreed," he said finally.

"I have no other conditions to add."

"Then our treaty is made," Vol'himyor said. "You may begin your northward journey today. Five of our once-born ones must also travel to the mist country, for their time of rebirth has come, and if you wish they will accompany you and safeguard you along the way. Among them is Srin'gahar, whom you already know."

"Will it be troublesome for them to have me with them?"

"Srin'gahar has particularly requested the privilege of serving as your guardian," said Vol'himyor. "But we would not compel you to accept his aid, if you would rather make your journey alone."

"It would be an honor to have his company," Gundersen said.

"So be it, then."

A senior nildor summoned Srin'gahar and the four others who would be going toward rebirth. Gundersen was gratified at this confirmation of the existing data: once more the frenzied dance of the nildoror had preceded the departure of a group bound for rebirth.

It pleased him, too, to know that he would have a nildoror escort on the way north. There was only one dark aspect to the treaty, that which involved Cedric Cullen. He wished he had not sworn to barter another Earthman's freedom for his own safe-conduct pass. But perhaps Cullen had done something really loathsome, something that merited punishment—or purification, as Vol'himyor put it. Gundersen did not understand how that normally sunny man could have become a criminal and a fugitive, but Cullen had lived on this world a long time, and the strangeness of alien worlds ultimately corroded even the brightest souls. In any case, Gundersen felt that he had opened enough honorable exits for himself if he needed to escape from his treaty with Vol'himyor.

Srin'gahar and Gundersen went aside to plan their route. "Where in the mist country do you intend to go?" the nildor asked.

"It does not matter. I just want to enter it. I suppose I'll have to go wherever Cullen is."

"Yes. But we do not know exactly where he is, so we will have to wait until we are there to learn it. Do you have special places to visit on the way north?"

"I want to stop at the Earthman stations," Gundersen said. "Particularly at Shangri-la Falls. So my idea is that we'll follow Madden's River northwestward, and—"

"These names are unknown to me."

"Sorry. I guess they've all reverted back to nildororu names. And I don't know those. But wait—" Seizing a stick, Gundersen scratched a hasty but serviceable map of Belzagor's western hemisphere in the mud. Across the waist of the disk he drew the thick swath of the tropics. At the right side he gouged out a curving bite to indicate the ocean; on the left he outlined the Sea of Dust. Above and below the band of the tropics he drew the thinner lines representing the northern and southern mist zones, and beyond them he indicated the gigantic icecaps. He marked the spaceport and the hotel at the coast with an X, and cut a wiggly line up from there, clear across the tropics into the northern mist country, to show Madden's River. At the midway point of the river he placed a dot to mark Shangri-la Falls. "Now," said Gundersen, "if you follow the tip of my stick—"

"What are those marks on the ground?" asked Srin'gahar.

A map of your planet, Gundersen wanted to say. But there was no nildororu word in his mind for "map." He found that he also lacked words for "image," "picture," and similar concepts. He said lamely, "This is your world. This is Belzagor, or at least half of it. See, this is the ocean, and the sun rises here, and—"

"How can this be my world, these marks, when my world is so large?"

"This is *like* your world. Each of these lines, here, stands for a place on your world. You see, here, the big river that runs out of the mist country and comes down to the coast, where the hotel is, yes? And this mark is the spaceport. These two lines are the top and the bottom of the northern mist country. The—"

"It takes a strong sulidor a march of many days to cross the northern mist country," said Srin'gahar. "I do not understand how you can point to such a small space and tell me it is the northern mist country. Forgive me, friend of my journey. I am very stupid."

Gundersen tried again, attempting to communicate the nature of the marks on the ground. But Srin'gahar simply could not comprehend the idea of a map, nor could he see how scratched lines could represent places. Gundersen considered asking Vol'himyor to help him, but rejected that plan when he realized that Vol'himyor, too, might not understand; it would be tactless to expose the many-born one's ignorance in any area. The map was a metaphor of place, an abstraction from reality. Evidently even beings possessing *g'rakh* might not have the capacity to grasp such abstractions.

He apologized to Srin'gahar for his own inability to express concepts clearly, and rubbed out the map with his boot. Without it, planning the route was somewhat more difficult, but they found ways to communicate. Gundersen learned that the great river at whose mouth the hotel was situated was called the Seran'nee in nildororu, and that the place where the river plunged out of the mountains into the coastal plain, which Earthmen knew as Shangri-la Falls, was Du'jayukh to nildoror. Then it was simple for them to agree to follow the Seran'nee to its source, with a stop at Du'jayukh and at any other settlement of Earthmen that happened to lie conveniently on the path north.

While this was being decided, several of the sulidoror brought a late breakfast of fruit and lake fish to Gundersen, exactly as though they recognized his authority under the Company. It was a curiously anachronistic gesture, almost servile, not at all like the way in which they had tossed him a raw slab of malidar meat the day before. Then they had been testing him, even taunting him; now they were waiting upon him. He was uncomfortable about that, but he was also quite hungry, and he made a point of asking Srin'gahar to tell him the sulidororu words of thanks. There was no sign that the powerful bipeds were pleased or flattered or amused by his use of their language, though.

They began their journey in late afternoon. The five nildoror moved in single file, Srin'gahar at the back of the group with Gundersen perched on his back; the Earthman did not appear to be the slightest burden for him. Their path led due north along the rim of the great rift, with the mountains that guarded the central plateau rising on their left. By the light of the sinking sun Gundersen stared toward that plateau. Down here in the valley, his surroundings had a certain familiarity; making the necessary allowances for the native plants and animals, he might almost be in some steamy jungle of South America. But the plateau appeared truly alien. Gundersen eyed the thick tangles of spiky purplish moss that festooned and nearly choked the trees along the top of the rift wall. The way the parasitic growth drowned its hosts the trees seemed grisly to him. The wall itself, of some soapy gray-green rock, dotted with angry blotches of crimson lichen and punctuated every few hundred meters by long ropy strands of a swollen blue fungus, cried out its otherworldliness: the soft mineral had never felt the impact of raindrops, but had been gently carved and shaped by the humidity alone, taking on weird knobbinesses and hollows over the millennia. Nowhere on Earth could one see a rock wall like that, serpentine and involute and greasy.

The forest beyond the wall looked impenetrable and vaguely sinister. The silence, the heavy and sluggish air, the sense of dark strangeness, the flexible limbs of the glossy trees bowed almost to the ground by moss, the occasional distant snort of some giant beast, made the central plateau seem forbidding and hostile. Few Earthmen had ever entered it, and it had never been surveyed in detail. The Company once had had some plans for stripping away large patches of jungle up there and putting in agricultural settlements, but nothing had come of the scheme, because of relinquishment. Gundersen had been in the plateau country only once, by accident, when his pilot had had to make a forced landing en route from coastal headquarters to the Sea of Dust. Seena had been with him. They spent a night and a day in that forest, Seena terrified from the moment of landing, Gundersen comforting her in a standard manly way but finding that her terror was somehow contagious. The girl trembled as one alien happening after another presented itself, and shortly Gundersen was on the verge of trembling too. They watched, fascinated and repelled, while an army of innumerable insects with iridescent hexagonal bodies and long hairy legs strode with maniacal persistence into a sprawling glade of tiger-moss; for hours the savage mouths of the carnivorous plants bit the shining insects into pieces and devoured them, and still the horde marched on to destruction. At last the moss was so glutted that it went into sporulation, puffing up cancerously and sending milky clouds of reproductive bodies spewing into the air. By morning the whole field of moss lay deflated and helpless, and tiny green reptiles with broad rasping tongues moved in to devour every strand, laying bare the soil for a new generation of flora. And then there were the feathery jelly-like things, streaked with blue and red, that hung in billowing cascades from the tallest trees, trapping unwary flying creatures. And bulky rough-skinned beasts as big as rhinos, bearing mazes of blue antlers with interlocking tines, grubbed for roots a dozen meters from their camp, glaring sourly at the strangers from Earth. And long-necked browsers with eyes like beacons munched on high leaves, squirting barrelfuls of purple urine from openings at the bases of their taut throats. And dark fat otter-like beings ran chattering past the stranded Earthmen, stealing anything within quick grasp. Other animals visited them also. This planet, which had never known the hunter's hand, abounded in big mammals. He and Seena and the pilot had seen more grotesqueness in a day and a night than they had bargained for when they signed up for outworld service.

"Have you ever been in there?" Gundersen asked Srin'gahar, as night began to conceal the rift wall.

"Never. My people seldom enter that land."

"Occasionally, flying low over the plateau, I used to see nildoror encampments in it. Not often, but sometimes. Do you mean that your people no longer go there?"

"No," said Srin'gahar. "A few of us have need to go to the plateau, but most do not. Sometimes the soul grows stale, and one must change one's surroundings. If one is not ready for rebirth, one goes to the plateau. It is easier to confront one's own soul in there, and to examine it for flaws. Can you understand what I say?"

"I think so," Gundersen said. "It's like a place of pilgrimage, then—a place of purification?"

"In a way."

"But why have the nildoror never settled permanently up there? There's plenty of food—the climate is warm—"

"It is not a place where *g'rakh* rules," the nildor replied.

"Is it dangerous to nildoror? Wild animals, poisonous plants, anything like that?"

"No, I would not say that. We have no fear of the plateau, and there is no place on this world that is dangerous to us. But the plateau does not interest us, except those who have the special need of which I spoke. As I say, *g'rakh* is foreign to it. Why should we go there? There is room enough for us in the lowlands."

The plateau is too alien even for them, Gundersen thought. They prefer their nice little jungle. How curious!

He was not sorry when darkness hid the plateau from view.

They made camp that night beside a hissing-hot stream. Evidently its waters issued from one of the underground cauldrons that were common in this sector of the continent; Srin'gahar said that the source lay not far to the north. Clouds of steam rose from the swift flow; the water, pink with high-temperature microorganisms, bubbled and boiled. Gundersen wondered if Srin'gahar had chosen this stopping place especially for his benefit, since nildoror had no use for hot water, but Earthmen notoriously did.

He scrubbed his face, taking extraordinary pleasure in it, and supplemented a dinner of food capsules and fresh fruit with a stew of greenberry roots—delectable when boiled, poisonous otherwise. For shelter while sleeping Gundersen used a monomolecular jungle blanket that he had stowed in his backpack, his one meager article of luggage on this journey. He draped the blanket over a tripod of boughs to keep away nightflies and other noxious insects, and crawled under it. The ground, thickly grassed, was a good enough mattress for him.

The nildoror did not seem disposed toward conversation. They left him alone. All but Srin'gahar moved several hundred meters upstream for the night. Srin'gahar settled down protectively a short distance from Gundersen and wished him a good sleep.

Gundersen said, "Do you mind talking a while? I want to know something about the process of rebirth. How do you know, for instance, that your time is upon you? Is it something you feel within yourself, or is it just a matter of reaching a certain age? Do you—" He became aware that Srin'gahar was paying no attention. The nildor had fallen into what might have been a deep trance, and lay perfectly still.

Shrugging, Gundersen rolled over and waited for sleep, but sleep was a long time coming.

He thought a good deal about the terms under which he had been permitted to make this northward journey. Perhaps another many-born one would have allowed him to go into the mist country without attaching the condition that he bring back Cedric Cullen; perhaps he would not have been granted safe-conduct at all. Gundersen suspected that the results would have been the same no matter which encampment of nildoror he had happened to go to for his travel permission. Though the nildoror had no means of long-distance communication, no governmental structure in an Earthly sense, no more coherence as a race than a population of jungle beasts, they nevertheless were remarkably well able to keep in touch with one another and to strike common policies.

What was it that Cullen had done, Gundersen wondered, to make him so eagerly sought?

In the old days Cullen had seemed overwhelmingly normal: a cheerful, amiable ruddy man who collected insects, spoke no harsh words, and held his liquor well. When Gundersen had been the chief agent out at Fire Point, in the Sea of Dust, a dozen years before, Cullen had been his assistant. Months on end there were only the two of them in the place, and Gundersen had come to know him quite well, he imagined. Cullen had no plans for making a career with the Company; he said he had signed a six-year contract, would not renew, and intended to take up a university appointment when he had done his time on Holman's World. He was here only for seasoning, and for the prestige that accrues to anyone who has a record of outworld service. But then the political situation on Earth grew complex, and the Company was forced to agree to relinquish a great many planets that it had colonized. Gundersen, like most of the fifteen thousand Company people here, had accepted a transfer to another assignment. Cullen, to Gundersen's amazement, was among the handful who opted to stay, even though that meant severing his ties with the home world. Gundersen had not asked him why; one did not discuss such things. But it seemed odd.

He saw Cullen clearly in memory, chasing bugs through the Sea of Dust, killing bottle jouncing against his hip as he ran from one rock outcropping to the next—an overgrown boy, really. The beauty of the Sea of Dust was altogether lost on him. No sector of the planet was more truly alien, nor more spectacular: a dry ocean bed, greater in size than the Atlantic, coated with a thick layer of fine crystalline mineral fragments as bright as mirrors when the sun was on them. From the station at Fire Point one could see the morning light advancing out of the east like a river of flame, spilling forth until the whole desert blazed. The crystals swallowed energy all day, and gave it forth all night, so that even at twilight the eerie radiance rose brightly, and after dark a throbbing purplish glow lingered for hours. In this almost lifeless but wondrously beautiful desert the Company had mined a dozen precious metals and thirty precious and semiprecious stones. The mining machines set forth from the station on far-ranging rounds, grinding up loveliness and returning with treasure; there was not much for an agent to do there except keep inventory of the mounting wealth and play host to the tourist parties that came to see the splendor of the countryside. Gundersen had grown terribly bored, and even the glories of the scenery had become tiresome to him, but Cullen, to whom the incandescent desert was merely a flashy nuisance, fell back on his hobby for entertainment, and filled bottle after bottle with his insects. Were the mining machines still standing in the Sea of Dust, Gundersen wondered, waiting for the command to resume operations? If the Company had not taken them away after relinquishment, they would surely stand there throughout all eternity, unrusting, useless, amidst the hideous gouges they had cut. The machines had scooped down through the crystalline layer to the dull basalt below, and had spewed out vast heaps of tailings and debris as they gnawed for wealth. Probably the Company had left the things behind, too, as monuments to commerce. Machinery was cheap, interstellar transport was costly; why bother removing them? "In another thousand years," Gundersen once had said, "the Sea of Dust will all be destroyed and there'll be nothing but rubble here, if these machines continue to chew up the rock at the present rate." Cullen had shrugged and smiled. "Well, one won't need to wear these dark glasses, then, once the infernal glare is gone," he had said. "Eh?" And now the rape of the desert was over and the machines were still; and now Cullen was a fugitive in the mist country, wanted for some crime so terrible the nildoror would not even give it a name.

SEVEN

When they took to the road in the morning it was Srin'gahar, uncharacteristically, who opened the conversation.

"Tell me of elephants, friend of my journey. What do they look like, and how do they live?"

"Where did you hear of elephants?"

"The Earthpeople at the hotel spoke of them. And also in the past, I have heard the word said. They are beings of Earth that look like nildoror, are they not?"

"There is a certain resemblance," Gundersen conceded.

"A close one?"

"There are many similarities." He wished Srin'gahar were able to comprehend a sketch. "They are long and high in the body, like you, and they have four legs, and tails, and trunks. They have tusks, but only two, one here, one here. Their eyes are smaller and placed in a poor position, here, here. And here—" He indicated Srin'gahar's skull-crest. "Here they have nothing. Also their bones do not move as your bones do."

"It sounds to me," said Srin'gahar, "as though these elephants look very much like nildoror."

"I suppose they do."

"Why is this, can you say? Do you believe that we and the elephants can be of the same race?"

"It isn't possible," said Gundersen. "It's simply a—a—" He groped for words; the nildororu vocabulary did not include the technical terms of genetics. "Simply a pattern in the development of life that occurs on many worlds. Certain basic designs of living creatures recur everywhere. The elephant design—the nildoror design—is one of them.

The large body, the huge head, the short neck, the long trunk enabling the being to pick up objects and handle them without having to bend—these things will develop wherever the proper conditions are found."

"You have seen elephants, then, on many other worlds?"

"On some," Gundersen said. "Following the same general pattern of construction, or at least some aspects of it, although the closest resemblance of all is between elephants and nildoror. I could tell you of half a dozen other creatures that seem to belong to the same group. And this is also true of many other life-forms—insects, reptiles, small mammals, and so on. There are certain niches to be filled on every world. The thoughts of the Shaping Force travel the same path everywhere."

"Where, then, are Belzagor's equivalents of men?"

Gundersen faltered. "I didn't say that there were exact equivalents everywhere. The closest thing to the human pattern on your planet, I guess, is the sulidoror. And they aren't very close."

"On Earth, the men rule. Here the sulidoror are the secondary race."

"An accident of development. Your *g'rakh* is superior to that of the sulidoror; on our world we have no other species that possesses *g'rakh* at all. But the physical resemblances between men and sulidoror are many. They walk on two legs; so do we. They eat both flesh and fruit; so do we. They have hands which can grasp things; so do we. Their eyes are in front of their heads; so are ours. I know, they're bigger, stronger, hairier, and less intelligent than human beings, but I'm trying to show you how patterns can be similar on different planets, even though there's no real blood relationship between—"

Srin'gahar said quietly, "How do you know that elephants are without *g'rakh*?"

"We—they—it's clear that—" Gundersen stopped, uneasy. After a pause for thought he said carefully, "They've never demonstrated any of the qualities of *g'rakh*. They have no village life, no tribal structure, no technology, no religion, no continuing culture."

"We have no village life and no technology," the nildor said. "We wander through the jungles, stuffing ourselves with leaves and branches. I have heard this said of us, and it is true."

"But you're different. You—"

"How are we different? Elephants also wander through jungles, stuffing themselves with leaves and branches, do they not? They wear no skins over their own skins. They make no machines. They have no books. Yet you admit that we have *g'rakh,* and you insist that they do not."

"They can't communicate ideas," said Gundersen desperately. "They can tell each other simple things, I guess, about food and mating and danger, but that's all. If they have a true language, we can't detect it. We're aware of only a few basic sounds."

"Perhaps their language is so complex that you are *unable* to detect it," Srin'gahar suggested.

"I doubt that. We were able to tell as soon as we got here that the nildoror speak a language; and we were able to learn it. But in all the thousands of years that men and elephants have been sharing the same planet, we've never been able to see a sign that they can accumulate and transmit abstract concepts. And that's the essence of having *g'rakh,* isn't it?"

"I repeat my statement. What if you are so inferior to your elephants that you cannot comprehend their true depths?"

"A cleverly put point, Srin'gahar. But I won't accept it as any sort of description of the real world. If elephants have *g'rakh,* why haven't they managed to get anywhere in their whole time on Earth? Why does mankind dominate the planet, with the elephants crowded into a couple of small corners and practically wiped out?"

"You kill your elephants?"

"Not any more. But there was a time when men killed elephants for pleasure, or for food, or to use their tusks for ornaments. And there was a time when men used elephants for beasts of burden. If the elephants had *g'rakh,* they—"

He realized that he had fallen into Srin'gahar's trap.

The nildor said, "On this planet, too, the 'elephants' let themselves be exploited by mankind. You did not eat us and you rarely killed us, but often you made us work for you. And yet you admit we are beings of *g'rakh.*"

"What we did here," said Gundersen, "was a gigantic mistake, and when we came to realize it, we relinquished your world and got off it. But that still doesn't mean that elephants are rational and sentient beings. They're animals, Srin'gahar, big simple animals, and nothing more."

"Cities and machines are not the only achievements of *g'rakh.*"

"Where are their spiritual achievements, then? What does an elephant believe about the nature of the universe? What does he think about the Shaping Force? How does he regard his own place in his society?"

"I do not know," said Srin'gahar. "And neither do you, friend of my journey, because the language of the elephants is closed to you. But it is an error to assume the absence of *g'rakh* where you are incapable of seeing it."

"In that case, maybe the malidaror have *g'rakh* too. And the venom-serpents. And the trees, and the vines, and—"

"No," said Srin'gahar. "On this planet, only nildoror and sulidoror possess *g'rakh.* This we know beyond doubt. On your world it is not necessarily the case that humans alone have the quality of reason."

Gundersen saw the futility of pursuing the point. Was Srin'gahar a chauvinist defending the spiritual supremacy of elephants throughout the universe, or was he deliberately adopting an extreme position to expose the arrogances and moral vulnerabilities of Earth's imperialism? Gundersen did not know, but it hardly mattered. He thought of Gulliver discussing the intelligence of horses with the Houyhnhnms.

"I yield the point," he said curtly. "Perhaps someday I'll bring an elephant to Belzagor, and let you tell me whether or not it has *g'rakh.*"

"I would greet it as a brother."

"You might be unhappy over the emptiness of your brother's mind," Gundersen said. "You would see a being fashioned in your shape, but you wouldn't succeed in reaching its soul."

"Bring me an elephant, friend of my journey, and I will be the judge of its emptiness," said Srin'gahar. "But tell me one last thing, and then I will not trouble you: when your people call us elephants, it is because they think of us as mere beasts, yes? Elephants are 'big simple animals,' those are your words. Is this how the visitors from Earth see us?"

"They're referring only to the resemblance in form between nildoror and elephants. It's a superficial thing. They say you are *like* elephants."

"I wish I could believe that," the nildor said, and fell silent, leaving Gundersen alone with his shame and guilt. In the old days it had never been his habit to argue the nature of intelligence with his mounts. It had not even occurred to him then that such a debate might be possible. Now he sensed the extent of Srin'gahar's suppressed resentment. Elephants—yes, that was how he too had seen the nildoror. Intelligent elephants, perhaps. But still elephants.

In silence they followed the boiling stream northward. Shortly before noon they came to its source, a broad bow-shaped lake pinched between a double chain of steeply rising hills. Clouds of oily steam rose from the lake's surface. Thermophilic algae streaked its waters, the pink ones forming a thin scum on top and nearly screening the meshed tangles of the larger, thicker blue-gray plants a short distance underneath.

Gundersen felt some interest in stopping to examine the lake and its unusual life-forms. But he was strangely reluctant to ask Srin'gahar to halt. Srin'gahar was not only his carrier, he was his companion on a journey; and to say, tourist-fashion, "Let's stop here a while," might reinforce the nildor's belief that Earthmen still thought of his people merely as beasts of burden. So he resigned himself to passing up this bit of sightseeing. It was not right, he told himself, that he should delay Srin'gahar's journey toward rebirth merely to gratify a whim of idle curiosity.

But as they were nearing the lake's farther curve, there came such a crashing and smashing in the underbrush to the east that the entire procession of nildoror paused to see what was going on. To Gundersen it sounded as if some prowling dinosaur were about to come lurching out of the jungle, some huge clumsy tyrannosaur inexplicably displaced in time and space. Then, emerging from a break in the row of hills, there came slowly across the bare soil flanking the lake a little snub-snouted vehicle, which Gundersen recognized as the hotel's beetle, towing a crazy primitive-looking appendage of a trailer, fashioned from raw planks and large wheels. Atop this jouncing, clattering trailer four small tents had been pitched, covering most of its area; alongside the tents, over the wheels, luggage was mounted in several racks; and at the rear, clinging to a railing and peering nervously about, were the eight tourists whom Gundersen had last seen some days earlier in the hotel by the coast.

Srin'gahar said, "Here are some of your people. You will want to talk with them."

The tourists were, in fact, the last species whatever that Gundersen wanted to see at this point. He would have preferred locusts, scorpions, fanged serpents, tyrannosaurs, toads, anything at all. Here he was coming from some sort of mystical experience among the nildoror, the nature of which he barely understood; here, insulated from his own kind, he rode toward the land of rebirth struggling with basic questions of right and wrong, of the nature of intelligence, of the relationship of human to nonhuman and of himself to his own past; only a few moments before he had been forced into an uncomfortable, even painful confrontation with that past by Srin'gahar's casual, artful questions about the souls of elephants; and abruptly Gundersen found himself once more among these empty, trivial human beings, these archetypes of the ignorant and blind tourist, and whatever individuality he had earned in the eyes of his nildor companion vanished instantly as he dropped back into the undifferentiated class of Earthmen. These tourists, some part of his mind knew, were not nearly as vulgar and hollow as he saw them; they were merely ordinary people, friendly, a bit foolish, overprivileged, probably quite satisfactory human beings within the context of their lives on Earth, and only seeming to be cardboard figurines here because they were essentially irrelevant to the planet they had chosen to visit. But he was not yet ready to have Srin'gahar lose sight of him as a person separate from all the other Earthmen who came to Belzagor, and he feared that the tide of bland chatter welling out of these people would engulf him and make him one of them.

The beetle, obviously straining to haul the trailer, came to rest a dozen meters from the edge of the lake. Out of it came Van Beneker, looking sweatier and seedier than usual. "All right," he called to the tourists. "Everyone down! We're going to have a look at one of the famous hot lakes!" Gundersen, high atop Srin'gahar's broad back, considered telling the nildor to move along. The other four nildoror, having satisfied themselves about the cause of the commotion, had already done that and were nearly out of view at the far end of the lake. But he decided to stay a while; he knew that a display of snobbery toward his own species would win him no credit with Srin'gahar.

Van Beneker turned to Gundersen and called out, "Morning, sir! Glad to see you! Having a good trip?"

The four Earth couples clambered down from their trailer. They were fully in character, behaving exactly as Gundersen's harsh image of them would have them behave: they seemed bored and glazed, surfeited with the alien wonders they had already seen. Stein, the helix-parlor proprietor, dutifully checked the aperture of his camera, mounted it in his cap, and routinely took a 360-degree hologram of the scene; but when the printout emerged from the camera's output slot a moment later he did not even bother to glance at it. The act of picture-taking, not the picture itself, was significant. Watson, the doctor, muttered a joyless joke of some sort to Christopher, the financier, who responded with a mechanical chuckle. The women, bedraggled and jungle-stained, paid no attention to the lake. Two simply leaned against the beetle and waited to be told what it was they were being shown, while the other two, as they became aware of Gundersen's presence, pulled facial masks from their backpacks and hurriedly slipped the thin plastic films over their heads so that they could present at least the illusion of properly groomed features before the handsome stranger.

"I won't stay here long," Gundersen heard himself promising Srin'gahar, as he dismounted.

Van Beneker came up to him. "What a trip!" the little man blurted. "What a stinking trip! Well, I ought to be used to it by now. How's everything been going for you, Mr. G?"

"No complaints." Gundersen nodded at the trailer. "Where'd you get that noisy contraption?"

"We built it a couple of years ago when one of the old cargo haulers broke down. Now we use it to take tourists around when we can't get any nildoror bearers."

"It looks like something out of the eighteenth century."

"Well, you know, sir, out here we don't have much left in the way of modern equipment. We're short of servos and hydraulic walkers and all that. But you can always find wheels and some planks around. We make do."

"What happened to the nildoror we were riding coming from the spaceport to the hotel? I thought they were willing to work for you."

"Sometimes yes, sometimes no," Van Beneker said. "They're unpredictable. We can't force them to work, and we can't hire them to work. We can only ask them politely, and if they say they're not available, that's it.

Couple of days back, they decided they weren't going to be available for a while, so we had to get out the trailer." He lowered his voice. "If you ask me, it's on account of these eight baboons here. They think the nildoror don't understand any English, and they keep telling each other how terrible it is that we had to hand a planet as valuable as this over to a bunch of elephants."

"On the voyage out here," said Gundersen, "some of them were voicing quite strong liberal views. At least two of them were big pro-relinquishment people."

"Sure. Back on Earth they bought relinquishment as a political theory. 'Give the colonized worlds back to their long-oppressed natives,' and all that. Now they're out here and suddenly they've decided that the nildoror aren't 'natives,' just animals, just funny-looking elephants, and maybe we should have kept the place after all." Van Beneker spat. "And the nildoror take it all in. They pretend they don't understand the language, but they do, they do. You think they feel like hauling people like that on their backs?"

"I see," said Gundersen. He glanced at the tourists. They were eyeing Srin'gahar, who had wandered off toward the bush and was energetically ripping soft boughs loose for his midday meal. Watson nudged Miraflores, who quirked his lips and shook his head as if in disapproval. Gundersen could not hear what they were saying, but he imagined that they were expressing scorn for Srin'gahar's enthusiastic foraging. Evidently civilized beings were not supposed to pull their meals off trees with their trunks.

Van Beneker said, "You'll stay and have lunch with us, won't you, Mr. G?"

"That's very kind of you," Gundersen said.

He squatted in the shade while Van Beneker rounded up his charges and led them down to the rim of the steaming lake. When they were all there Gundersen rose and quietly affiliated himself with the group. He listened to the guide's spiel, but managed to train only half his attention on what was being said. "High-temperature life-zone . . . better than 70°C . . . more in some places, even above boiling, yet things live in it . . . special genetic adaptation . . . thermophilic, we call it, that is, heat-loving . . . the DNA doesn't get cooked, no, but the rate of spontaneous mutation is pretty damned high, and the species change so fast you wouldn't believe it . . . enzymes resist the heat . . .

put the lake organisms in cool water and they'll freeze in about a minute . . . life processes extraordinarily fast . . . unfolded and denatured proteins can also function when circumstances are such that . . . you get quite a range up to middle-phylum level . . . a pocket environment, no interaction with the rest of the planet . . . thermal gradients . . . quantitative studies . . . the famous kinetic biologist, Dr. Brock . . . continuous thermal destruction of sensitive molecules . . . unending resynthesis. . . ."

Srin'gahar was still stuffing himself with branches. It seemed to Gundersen that he was eating far more than he normally did at this time of day. The sounds of rending and chewing clashed with the jerky drone of Van Beneker's memorized scientific patter.

Now, unhooking a biosensitive net from his belt, Van Beneker began to dredge up samples of the lake's fauna for the edification of his group. He gripped the net's handle and made vernier. adjustments governing the mass and length of the desired prey; the net, mounted at the end of an almost infinitely expandable length of fine flexible metal coil, swept back and forth beneath the surface of the lake, hunting for organisms of the programmed dimensions. When its sensors told it that it was in the presence of living matter, its mouth snapped open and quickly shut again. Van Beneker retracted it, bringing to shore some unhappy prisoner trapped within a sample of its own scalding environment.

Out came one lake creature after another, red-skinned, boiled-looking, but live and angry and flapping. An armored fish emerged, concealed in shining plates, embellished with fantastic excrescences and ornaments. A lobster-like thing came forth, lashing a long spiked tail, waving ferocious eye-stalks. Up from the lake came something that was a single immense claw with a tiny vestigial body. No two of Van Beneker's grotesque catches were alike. The heat of the lake, he repeated, induces frequent mutations. He rattled off the whole genetic explanation a second time, while dumping one little monster back into the hot bath and probing for the next.

The genetic aspects of the thermophilic creatures seemed to catch the interest of only one of the tourists—Stein, who, as a helix-parlor owner specializing in the cosmetic editing of human genes, would know more than a little about mutation himself. He asked a few intelligent-sounding questions, which Van Beneker naturally was unable to answer; the others simply stared, patiently waiting for their guide to finish showing them funny animals and take them somewhere else. Gundersen, who had never had a chance before to examine the contents of one of these high-temperature pockets, was grateful for the exhibition, although the sight of writhing captive lake-dwellers quickly palled on him. He became eager to move on.

He glanced around and discovered that Srin'gahar was nowhere in sight.

"What we've got this time," Van Beneker was saying, "is the most dangerous animal of the lake, what we call a razor shark. Only I've never seen one like this before. You see those little horns? Absolutely new. And that lantern sort of thing on top of the head, blinking on and off?" Squirming in the net was a slender crimson creature about a meter in length. Its entire underbelly, from snout to gut, was hinged, forming what amounted to one gigantic mouth rimmed by hundreds of needle-like teeth. As the mouth opened and closed, it seemed as if the whole animal were splitting apart and healing itself. "This beast feeds on anything up to three times its own size," Van Beneker said. "As you can see, it's fierce and savage, and—"

Uneasy, Gundersen drifted away from the lake to look for Srin'gahar. He found the place where the nildor had been eating, where the lower branches of several trees were stripped bare. He saw what seemed to be the nildor's trail, leading away into the jungle. A painful white light of desolation flared in his skull at the awareness that Srin'-gahar must quietly have abandoned him.

In that case his journey would have to be interrupted. He did not dare go alone and on foot into that pathless wilderness ahead. He would have to ask Van Beneker to take him back to some nildoror encampment where he might find another means of getting to the mist country.

The tour group was coming up from the lake now. Van Beneker's net was slung over his shoulder; Gundersen saw some lake creatures moving slowly about in it.

"Lunch," he said. "I got us some jelly-crabs. You hungry?"

Gundersen managed a thin smile. He watched, not at all hungry, as Van Beneker opened the net; a gush of hot water rushed from it, carrying along eight or ten oval purplish creatures, each different from the others in the number of legs, shell markings, and size of claws. They crawled in stumbling circles, obviously annoyed by the relative coolness of the air. Steam rose from their backs. Expertly Van Beneker pithed them with sharpened sticks, and cooked them with his fusion torch, and split open their shells to reveal the pale quivering jelly-like metabolic regulators within. Three of the women grimaced and turned away, but Mrs. Miraflores took her crab and ate it with delight. The men seemed to enjoy it. Gundersen, merely nibbling at the jelly, eyed the forest and worried about Srin'gahar.

Scraps of conversation drifted toward him.

"—enormous profit potential, just wasted, altogether wasted—"

"—even so, our obligation is to encourage self-determination on every planet that—"

"—but are they *people?*"

"—look for the soul, it's the only way to tell that—"

"—elephants, and nothing but elephants. Did you see him ripping up the trees and—"

"—relinquishment was the fault of a highly vocal minority of bleeding hearts who—"

"—no soul, no relinquishment—"

"—you're being too harsh, dear. There were definite abuses on some of the planets, and—"

"—stupid political expediency, I call it. The blind leading the blind—"

"—can they write? Can they think? Even in Africa we were dealing with human beings, and even there—"

"—the soul, the inner spirit—"

"—I don't need to tell you how much I favored relinquishment. You remember, I took the petitions around and everything. But even so, I have to admit that after seeing—"

"—piles of purple crap on the beach—"

"—victims of sentimental overreaction—"

"— I understand the annual profit was on the order of—"

"—no doubt that they have souls. No doubt at all." Gundersen realized that his own voice had entered the conversation. The others turned to him; there was a sudden vacuum to fill. He said, "They have a religion, and that implies the awareness of the existence of a spirit, a soul, doesn't it?"

"What kind of religion?" Miraflores asked.

"I'm not sure. One important part of it is ecstatic dancing—a kind of frenzied prancing around that leads to some sort of mystic experience. I know. I've danced with them. I've felt at least the edges of that experience. And they've got a thing called rebirth, which I suppose is central to their rituals. I don't understand it. They go north, into the mist country, and something happens to them there. They've always kept the details a secret. I think the sulidoror give them something, some drug, maybe, and it rejuvenates them in some inner way, and leads to a kind of illumination—am I at all clear?" Gundersen, as he spoke, was working his way almost unconsciously through the pile of uneaten jelly-crabs. "All I can tell you is that rebirth is vitally important to them, and they seem to derive their tribal status from the number of rebirths they've undergone. So you see they're not just animals. They have a society, they have a cultural structure—complex, difficult for us to grasp."

Watson asked, "Why don't they have a civilization, then?"

"I've just told you that they do."

"I mean cities, machines, books—"

"They're not physically equipped for writing, for building things, for any small manipulations," Gundersen said. "Don't you see, they have no *hands*? A race with hands makes one kind of society. A race built like elephants makes another." He was drenched in sweat and his appetite was suddenly insatiable. The women, he noticed, were staring at him strangely. He realized why: he was cleaning up all the food in sight, compulsively stuffing it into his mouth. Abruptly his patience shattered and he felt that his skull would explode if he did not instantly drop all barriers and admit the one great guilt that by stabbing his soul had spurred him into strange odysseys. It did not matter that these were not the right people from whom to seek absolution. The words rushed uncontrollably upward to his lips and he said, "When I came here I was just like you. I underestimated the nildoror. Which led me into a grievous sin that I have to explain to you. You know, I was a sector administrator for a while, and one of my jobs was arranging the efficient deployment of native labor. Since we didn't fully understand that the nildoror were intelligent autonomous beings, we *used* them, we put them to work on heavy construction jobs, lifting girders with their trunks, anything we thought they were capable of handling on sheer muscle alone. We just ordered them around as if they were machines." Gundersen closed his eyes and felt the past roaring toward him, inexorably, a black cloud of memory that enveloped and overwhelmed him, "The nildoror let us use them, God knows why. I guess we were the crucible in which their race had to be purged. Well, one day a dam broke, out in Monroe District up in the north, not far from where the mist country begins, and a whole thornbush plantation was in danger of flooding, at a loss to the Company of who knows how many millions. And the main power plant of the district was endangered too, along with our station headquarters and—let's just say that if we didn't react fast, we'd lose our entire investment in the north. My responsibility. I began conscripting nildoror to build a secondary line of dikes. We threw every robot we had into the job, but we didn't have enough, so we got the nildoror too, long lines of them plodding in from every part of the jungle, and we worked day and night until we were all ready to fall down dead. We were beating the flood, but I couldn't be sure of it. And on the sixth morning I drove out to the dike site to see if the next crest would break through, and there were seven nildoror I hadn't ever seen before, marching along a path going north. I told them to follow me. They refused, very gently. They said, no, they were on their way to the mist country for the rebirth ceremony, and they couldn't stop. Rebirth? What did I care about rebirth? I wasn't going to take that excuse from them, not when it looked like I might lose my whole district. Without thinking I ordered them to report for dike duty or I'd execute them on the spot. Rebirth can wait, I said. Get reborn some other time. This is serious business. They put their heads down and pushed the tips of their tusks into the ground. That's a sign of great sadness among them. Their spines drooped. Sad. Sad. We pity you, one of them said to me, and I got angry and told him what he could do with his pity. Where did he get the right to pity me? Then I pulled my fusion torch. Go on, get moving, there's a work crew that needs you. Sad. Big eyes looking pity at me. Tusks in the ground. Two or three of the nildoror said they were very sorry, they couldn't do any work for me now, it was impossible for them to break their journey. But they were ready to die right there, if I insisted on it. They didn't want to hurt my prestige by defying me, but they *had* to defy me, and so they were willing to pay the price. I was about to fry one, as an example to the others, and then I stopped and said to myself, what the hell am I doing, and the nildoror waited, and my aides were watching and so were some of our other nildoror, and I lifted the fusion torch again, telling myself that I'd kill one of them, the one who said he pitied me, and hoping that then the others would come to their senses. They just waited. Calling my bluff. How could I fry seven pilgrims even if they were defying a sector chief's direct order? But my authority was at stake. So I pushed the trigger. I just gave him a slow burn, not deep, enough to scar the hide, that was all, but the nildor stood there taking it, and in another few minutes I would have burned right through to a vital organ. And so I soiled myself in front of them by using force. It was what they had been waiting for. Then a couple of the nildoror who looked older than the others said, stop it, we wish to reconsider, and I turned off the torch, and they went aside for a conference. The one I had burned was hobbling a little, and looked hurt, but he wasn't badly wounded, not nearly as badly as I was. The one who pushes the trigger can get hurt worse than his target, do you know that? And in the end the nildoror all agreed to do as I asked. So instead of going north for rebirth they went to work on the dike, even the burned one, and nine days later the flood crest subsided and the plantation and the power plant and all the rest were saved and we lived happily ever after." Gundersen's voice trailed off. He had made his confession, and now he could not face these people any longer. He picked up the shell of the one remaining crab and explored it for some scrap of jelly, feeling depleted and drained. There was an endless span of silence.

Then Mrs. Christopher said, "So what happened then?"

Gundersen looked up, blinking. He thought he had told it all.

"Nothing happened then," he said. "The flood crest subsided."

"But what was the point of the story?"

He wanted to hurl the empty crab in her tensely smiling face. "The point?" he said. "The point? Why—" He was dizzy, now. He said, "Seven intelligent beings were journeying toward the holiest rite of their religion, and at gunpoint I requisitioned their services on a construction job to save property that meant nothing to them, and they came and hauled logs for me. Isn't the point obvious enough? Who was spiritually superior there? When you treat a rational autonomous creature as though he's a mere beast, what does that make you?"

"But it was an emergency," said Watson. "You needed all the help you could get. Surely other considerations could be laid aside at a time like that. So they were nine days late getting to their rebirth. Is that so bad?"

Gundersen said hollowly, "A nildor goes to rebirth only when the time is ripe, and I can't tell you how they know the time is ripe, but perhaps it's astrological, something to do with the conjunction of the moons. A nildor has to get to the place of rebirth at the propitious time, and if he doesn't make it in time, he isn't reborn just then. Those seven nildoror were already late, because the heavy rains had washed out the roads in the south. The nine days more that I tacked on made them *too* late. When they were finished building dikes for me, they simply went back south to rejoin their tribe. I didn't understand why. It wasn't until much later that I found out that I had cost them their chance at rebirth and they might have to wait ten or twenty years until they could go again. Or maybe never get another chance." Gundersen did not feel like talking any more. His throat was dry. His temples throbbed. How cleansing it would be, he thought, to dive into the steaming lake. He got stiffly to his feet, and as he did so he noticed that Srin'gahar had returned and was standing motionless a few hundred meters away, beneath a mighty swordflower tree.

He said to the tourists, "The point is that the nildoror have religion and souls, and that they are people, and that if you can buy the concept of relinquishment at all, you can't object to relinquishing this planet. The point is also that when Earthmen collide with an alien species they usually do so with maximum misunderstanding. The point is furthermore that I'm not surprised you think of the nildoror the way you do, because I did too, and learned a little better when it was too late to matter, and even so I didn't learn enough to do me any real good, which is one of the reasons why I came back to this planet. And I'd like you to excuse me now, because this is the propitious time for me to move on, and I have to go." He walked quickly away from them.

Approaching Srin'gahar, he said, "I'm ready to leave now."

The nildor knelt. Gundersen remounted.

"Where did you go?" the Earthman asked. "I was worried when you disappeared."

"I felt that I should leave you alone with your friends," said Srin'gahar. "Why did you worry? There is an obligation on me to bring you safely to the country of the mist."

EIGHT

The quality of the land was undoubtedly changing. They were leaving the heart of the equatorial jungle behind, and starting to enter the highlands that led into the mist zone. The climate here was still tropical, but the humidity was not so intense; the atmosphere, instead of holding everything in a constant clammy embrace, released its moisture periodically in rain, and after the rain the texture of the air was clear and light until its wetness was renewed. There was different vegetation in this region: harsh-looking angular stuff, with stiff leaves sharp as blades. Many of the trees had luminous foliage that cast a cold light over the forest by night. There were fewer vines here, and the treetops no longer formed a continuous canopy shutting out most of the sunlight; splashes of brightness dappled the forest floor, in some places extending across broad open plazas and meadows. The soil, leached by the frequent rains, was a pale yellowish hue, not the rich black of the jungle. Small animals frequently sped through the underbrush. At a slower pace moved solemn slug-like creatures, blue-green with ebony mantles, which Gundersen recognized as the mobile fungoids of the highlands—plants that crawled from place to place in quest of fallen boughs or a lightning-shattered tree-trunk. Both nildoror and men considered their taste a great delicacy.

On the evening of the third day northward from the place of the boiling lake Srin'gahar and Gundersen came upon the other four nildoror, who had marched on ahead. They were camped at the foot of a jagged crescent-shaped hill, and evidently had been there at least a day, judging by the destruction they had worked upon the foliage all around their resting-place. Their trunks and faces, smeared and stained with luminous juices, glowed brightly. With them was a sulidor, by far the largest one Gundersen had ever seen, almost twice Gundersen's own height, with a pendulous snout the length of a man's forearm. The sulidor stood erect beside a boulder encrusted with blue moss, his legs spread wide and his tail, tripod fashion, bracing his mighty weight. Narrowed eyes surveyed Gundersen from beneath shadowy hoods. His long arms, tipped with terrifying curved claws, hung at rest. The fur of the sulidor was the color of old bronze, and unusually thick.

One of the candidates for rebirth, a female nildor called Luu'khamin, said to Gundersen, "The sulidor's name is Na-sinisul. He wishes to speak with you."

"Let him speak, then."

"He prefers that you know, first, that he is not a sulidor of the ordinary kind. He is one of those who administers the ceremony of rebirth, and we will see him again when we approach the mist country. He is a sulidor of rank and merit, and his words are not to be taken lightly. Will you bear that in mind as you listen to him?"

"I will. I take no one's words lightly on this world, but I will give him a careful hearing beyond any doubt. Let him speak."

The sulidor strode a short distance forward and once again planted himself firmly, digging his great spurred feet deep into the resilient soil. When he spoke, it was in a nildororu stamped with the accent of the north: thick-tongued, slow, positive.

"I have been on a journey," said Na-sinisul, "to the Sea of Dust, and now I am returning to my own land to aid in the preparations for the event of rebirth in which these five travelers are to take part. My presence here is purely accidental. Do you understand that I am not in this place for any particular purpose involving you or your companions?"

"I understand," said Gundersen, astounded by the precise and emphatic manner of the sulidor's speech. He had known the sulidoror only as dark, savage, ferocious-looking figures lurking in mysterious glades.

Na-sinisul continued, "As I passed near here yesterday, I came by chance to the site of a former station of your Company. Again by chance, I chose to look within, though it was no business of mine to enter that place. Within I found two Earthmen whose bodies had ceased to serve them. They were unable to move and could barely talk. They requested me to send them from this world, but I could not do such a thing on my own authority. Therefore I ask you to follow me to this station and to give me instructions. My time is short here, so it must be done at once."

"How far is it?"

"We could be there before the rising of the third moon."

Gundersen said to Srin'gahar, "I don't remember a Company station here. There should be one a couple of days north of here, but—"

"This is the place where the food that crawls was collected and shipped downriver," said the nildor.

"Here?" Gundersen shrugged. "I guess I've lost my bearings again. All right, I'll go there." To Na-sinisul he said, "Lead and I'll follow."

The sulidor moved swiftly through the glowing forest, and Gundersen, atop Srin'gahar, rode just to his rear. They seemed to be descending, and the air grew warm and murky. The landscape also changed, for the trees here had aerial roots that looped up like immense scraggy elbows, and the fine tendrils sprouting from the roots emitted a harsh green radiance. The soil was loose and rocky; Gundersen could hear it crunching under Srin'-gahar's tread. Bird-like things were perched on many of the roots. They were owlish creatures that appeared to lack all color; some were black, some white, some a mottled black and white. He could not tell if that was their true hue or if the luminosity of the vegetation simply robbed them of color. A sickly fragrance came from vast, pallid parasitic flowers sprouting from the trunks of the trees.

By an outcropping of naked, weathered yellow rock lay the remains of the Company station. It seemed even more thoroughly ruined than the serpent station far to the south; the dome of its roof had collapsed and coils of wiry-stemmed saprophytes were clinging to its sides, perhaps feeding on the decomposition products that the rain eroded from the abrasions in the plastic walls. Srin'gahar allowed Gundersen to dismount. The Earthman hesitated outside the building, waiting for the sulidor to take the lead. A fine warm rain began to fall; the tang of the forest changed at once, becoming sweet where it had been sour. But it was the sweetness of decay.

"The Earthmen are inside," said Na-sinisul. "You may go in. I await your instructions."

Gundersen entered the building. The reek of rot was far more intense here, concentrated, perhaps, by the curve of the shattered dome. The dampness was all-pervasive. He wondered what sort of virulent spores he sucked into his nostrils with every breath. Something dripped in the darkness, making a loud tocking sound against the lighter patter of the rain coming through the gaping roof. To give himself light, Gundersen drew his fusion torch and kindled it at the lowest beam. The warm white glow spread through the station. At once he felt a flapping about his face as some thermotropic creature, aroused and attracted by the heat of the torch, rose up toward it. Gundersen brushed it away; there was slime on his fingertips afterward.

Where were the Earthmen?

Cautiously he made a circuit of the building. He remembered it vaguely, now—one of the innumerable bush stations the Company once had scattered across Holman's World. The floor was split and warped, requiring him to climb over the buckled, sundered sections. The mobile fungoids crawled everywhere, devouring the scum that covered all interior surfaces of the building and leaving narrow glistening tracks behind. Gundersen had to step carefully to avoid putting his feet on the creatures, and he was not always successful. Now he came to a place where the building widened, puckering outward; he flashed his torch around and caught sight of a blackened wharf, overlooking the bank of a swift river. Yes, he remembered. The fungoids were wrapped and baled here and sent downriver on their voyage toward the market. But the Company's barges no longer stopped here, and the tasty pale slugs now wandered unmolested over the mossy relics of furniture and equipment.

"Hello?" Gundersen called. "Hello, hello, hello?"

He received a moan by way of answer. Stumbling and slipping in the dimness, fighting a swelling nausea, he forced his way onward through a maze of unseen obstacles. He came to the source of the loud dripping sound. Something bright red and basket-shaped and about the size of a man's chest had established itself high on the wall, perpendicular to the floor. Through large pores in its spongy surface a thick black fluid exuded, falling in a continuous greasy splash. As the light of Gundersen's torch probed it, the exudation increased, becoming almost a cataract of tallowy liquid. When he moved the light away the flow became less copious, though still heavy.

The floor sloped here so that whatever dripped from the spongy basket flowed quickly down, collecting at the far side of the room in the angle between the floor and the wall. Here Gundersen found the Earthmen. They lay side by side on a low mattress; fluid from the dripping thing had formed a dark pool around them, completely covering the mattress and welling up over their bodies. One of the Earthmen, head lolling to the side, had his face totally immersed in the stuff. From the other one came the moans.

They both were naked. One was a man, one a woman, though Gundersen had some difficulty telling that at first; both were so shrunken and emaciated that the sexual characteristics were obscured. They had no hair, not even eyebrows. Bones protruded through parchment-like skin. The eyes of both were open, but were fixed in a rigid, seemingly sightless stare, unblinking, glassy. Lips were drawn back from teeth. Grayish algae sprouted in the furrows of their skins, and the mobile fungoids roamed their bodies, feeding on this growth. With a quick automatic gesture of revulsion Gundersen plucked two of the slug-like creatures from the woman's empty breasts. She stirred; she moaned again. In the language of the nildoror she murmured, "Is it over yet?" Her voice was like a flute played by a sullen desert breeze.

Speaking English, Gundersen said, "Who are you? How did this happen?"

He got no response from her. A fungoid crept across her mouth, and he flicked it aside. He touched her cheek. There was a rasping sound as his hand ran across her skin; it was like caressing stiff paper. Struggling to remember her, Gundersen imagined dark hair on her bare skull, gave her light arching brows, saw her cheeks full and her lips smiling. But nothing registered; either he had forgotten her, or he had never known her, or she was unrecognizable in her present condition.

"Is it over soon?" she asked, again in nildororu.

He turned to her companion. Gently, half afraid the fragile neck would snap, Gundersen lifted the man's head out of the pool of fluid. It appeared that he had been breathing it; it trickled from his nose and lips, and after a moment he showed signs of being unable to cope with ordinary air. Gundersen let his face slip back into the pool. In that brief moment he had recognized the man as a certain Harold—or was it Henry?—Dykstra, whom he had known distantly in the old days.

The unknown woman was trying to move one arm. She lacked the strength to lift it. These two were like living ghosts, like death-in-life, mired in their sticky fluid and totally helpless. In the language of the nildoror he said, "How long have you been this way?"

"Forever," she whispered.

"Who are you?"

"I don't . . . remember. I'm . . . waiting."

"For what?"

"For the end."

"Listen," he said, "I'm Edmund Gundersen, who used to be sector chief. I want to help you."

"Kill me first. Then him."

"We'll get you out of here and back to the spaceport. We can have you on the way to Earth in a week or ten days, and then—"

"No . . . please. . . ."

"What's wrong?" he asked.

"Finish it. Finish it." She found enough strength to arch her back, lifting her body halfway out of the fluid that nearly concealed her lower half. Something rippled and briefly bulged beneath her skin. Gundersen touched the taut belly and felt movement within, and that quick inward quiver was the most frightening sensation he had ever known. He touched the body of Dykstra, too: it also rippled inwardly.

Appalled, Gundersen scrambled to his feet and backed away from them. By faint torchlight he studied their shriveled bodies, naked but sexless, bone and ligament, shorn of flesh and spirit yet still alive. A terrible fear came over him. "Na-sinisul!" he called. "Come in here! Come in!"

The sulidor shortly was at his side. Gundersen said, "Something's inside their bodies. Some kind of parasite? It moves. What is it?"

"Look there," said Na-sinisul, indicating the spongy basket from which the dark fluid trickled. "They carry its young. They have become hosts. A year, two years, perhaps three, and the larvae will emerge."

"Why aren't they both dead?"

"They draw nourishment from this," said the sulidor, swishing his tail through the black flow. "It seeps into their skins. It feeds them, and it feeds that which is within them."

"If we took them out of here and sent them down to the hotel on rafts—?"

"They would die," Na-sinisul said, "moments after they were removed from the wetness about them. There is no hope of saving them."

"When does it end?" the woman asked.

Gundersen trembled. All his training told him never to accept the finality of death; any human in whom some shred of life remained could be saved, rebuilt from a few scraps of cells into a reasonable facsimile of the original. But there were no facilities for such things on this world. He confronted a swirl of choices. Leave them here to let alien things feed upon their guts; try to bring them back to the spaceport for shipment to the nearest tectogenetic hospital; put them out of their misery at once; seek to free their bodies himself of whatever held them in thrall. He knelt again. He forced himself to experience that inner quivering again. He touched the woman's stomach, her thighs, her bony haunches. Beneath the skin she was a mass of strangeness. Yet her mind still ticked, though she had forgotten her name and her native language. The man was luckier; though he was infested too, at least Dykstra did not have to lie here in the dark waiting for the death that could come only when the harbored larvae erupted from the enslaved human flesh. Was this what they had desired, when they refused repatriation from this world that they loved? An Earthman can become captured by Belzagor, the many-born nildor Vol'himyor had said. But this was too literal a capture.

The stink of bodily corruption made him retch.

"Kill them both," he said to Na-sinisul. "And be quick about it."

"This is what you instruct me to do?"

"Kill them. And rip down that thing on the wall and kill it too."

"It has given no offense," said the sulidor. "It has done only what is natural to its kind. By killing these two,

I will deprive it of its young, but I am not willing to deprive it of life as well."

"All right," Gundersen said. "Just the Earthmen, then. Fast."

"I do this as an act of mercy, under your direct orders," said Na-sinisul. He leaned forward and lifted one powerful arm. The savage curved claws emerged fully from their sheath. The claw descended twice.

Gundersen compelled himself to watch. The bodies split like dried husks; the things within came spilling out, unformed, raw. Even now, in some inconceivable reflex, the two corpses twitched and jerked. Gundersen stared into their eroded depths. "Do you hear me?" he asked. "Are you alive or dead?" The woman's mouth gaped but no sound came forth, and he did not know whether this was an attempt to speak or merely a last convulsion of the ravaged nerves. He stepped his fusion torch up to high power and trained it on the dark pool. I am the resurrection and the life, he thought, reducing Dykstra to ashes, and the woman beside him, and the squirming unfinished larvae. Acrid, choking fumes rose; not even the torch could destroy the building's dampness. He turned the torch back to illumination level. "Come," he said to the sulidor, and they went out together.

"I feel like burning the entire building and purifying this place," Gundersen said to Na-sinisul.

"I know."

"But you would prevent me."

"You are wrong. No one on this world will prevent you from doing anything."

But what good would it do . . . Gundersen asked himself. The purification had already been accomplished. He had removed the only beings in this place that were foreign to it.

The rain had stopped. To the waiting Srin'gahar, Gundersen said, "Will you take me away from here?"

They rejoined the other four nildoror. Then, because they had lingered too long here and the land of rebirth was still far away, they resumed the march, even though it was night. By morning Gundersen could hear the thunder of Shangri-la Falls, which the nildoror called Du'jayukh.

NINE

It was as though a white wall of water descended from the sky. Nothing on Earth could match the triple plunge of this cataract, by which Madden's River, or the Seran'nee, dropped five hundred meters, and then six hundred, and then five hundred more, falling from ledge to ledge in its tumble toward the sea. Gundersen and the five nildoror stood at the foot of the falls, where the entire violent cascade crashed into a broad rock-flanged basin out of which the serpentine river continued its southeasterly course; the sulidor had taken his leave in the night and was proceeding northward by his own route. To Gundersen's rear lay the coastal plain, behind his right shoulder, and the central plateau, behind his left. Before him, up by the head of the falls, the northern plateau began, the highlands that controlled the approach to the mist country. Just as a titanic north-south rift cut the coastal plain off from the central plateau, so did another rift running east-west separate both the central plateau and the coastal plain from the highlands ahead.

He bathed in a crystalline pool just beyond the tumult of the cataract, and then they began their ascent. The Shangri-la Station, one of the Company's most important outposts, was invisible from below; it was set back a short way from the head of the falls. Once there had been way-stations at the foot of the falls and at the head of the middle cataract, but no trace of these structures remained; the jungle had swallowed them utterly in only eight years. A winding road, with an infinity of switchbacks, led to the top. When he first had seen it, Gundersen had imagined it was the work of Company engineers, but he had learned that it was a natural ridge in the face of the plateau, which the nildoror themselves had enlarged and deepened to make their journeys toward rebirth more easy.

The swaying rhythm of his mount lulled him into a doze; he held tight to Srin'gahar's pommel-like horns and prayed that in his grogginess he would not fall off. Once he woke suddenly and found himself clinging only by his left hand, with his body half slung out over a sheer drop of at least two hundred meters. Another time, drowsy again, he felt cold spray and snapped to attention to see the entire cascade of the falling river rushing past him no more than a dozen meters away. At the head of the lowest cataract the nildoror paused to eat, and Gundersen dashed icy water in his face to shatter his sluggishness. They went on. He had less difficulty keeping awake now; the air was thinner, and the afternoon breeze was cool. In the hour before twilight they reached the head of the falls.

Shangri-la Station, seemingly unchanged, lay before him: three rectangular unequal blocks of dark shimmering plastic, a somber ziggurat rising on the western bank of the narrow gorge through which the river sped. The formal gardens of tropical plants, established by a forgotten sector chief at least forty years before, looked as though they were being carefully maintained. At each of the building's setbacks there was an outdoor veranda overlooking the river, and these, too, were bedecked with plants. Gundersen felt a dryness in his throat and a tightness in his loins. He said to Srin'gahar, "How long may we stay here?"

"How long do you wish to stay?"

"One day, two—I don't know yet. It depends on the welcome I get."

"We are not yet in a great hurry," said the nildor. "My friends and I will make camp in the bush. When it is time for you to go on, come to us."

The nildoror moved slowly into the shadows. Gundersen approached the station. At the entrance to the garden he paused. The trees here were gnarled and bowed, with long feathery gray fronds dangling down; highland flora was different from that to the south, although perpetual summer ruled here even as in the true tropics behind him. Lights glimmered within the station. Everything out here seemed surprisingly orderly; the contrast with the shambles of the serpent station and the nightmare decay of the fungoid station was sharp. Not even the hotel garden was this well tended. Four neat rows of fleshy, obscene-looking pink forest candles bordered the walkway that ran toward the building. Slender, stately globe-flower trees, heavy with gigantic fruit, formed little groves to left and right. There were hullygully trees and bitterfruits—exotics here, imported from the steaming equatorial tropics—and mighty swordflower trees in full bloom, lifting their long shiny stamens to the sky. Elegant glitterivy and spiceburr vines writhed along the ground, but not in any random way. Gundersen took a few steps farther in, and heard the soft sad sigh of a sensifrons bush, whose gentle hairy leaves coiled and shrank as he went by, opening warily when he had gone past, shutting again when he whirled to steal a quick glance. Two more steps, and he came to a low tree whose name he could not recall, with glossy red winged leaves that took flight, breaking free of their delicate stems and soaring away; instantly their replacements began to sprout. The garden was magical. Yet there were surprises here. Beyond the glitterivy he discovered a crescent patch of tiger-moss, the carnivorous ground cover native to the unfriendly central plateau. The moss had been transplanted to other parts of the planet—there was a patch of it growing out of control at the seacoast hotel—but Gundersen remembered that Seena abhorred it, as she abhorred all the productions of that forbidding plateau. Worse yet, looking upward so that he could follow the path of the gracefully gliding leaves, Gundersen saw great masses of quivering jelly, streaked with blue and red neural fibers, hanging from several of the biggest trees: more carnivores, also natives of the central plateau. What were those sinister things doing in this enchanted garden? A moment later he had a third proof that Seena's terror of the plateau had faded: across his path there ran one of the plump, thieving otter-like animals that had bedeviled them the time they had been marooned there. It halted a moment, nose twitching, cunning paws upraised, looking for something to seize. Gundersen hissed at it and it scuttled into the shrubbery.

Now a massive two-legged figure emerged from a shadowed corner and blocked his way. Gundersen thought at first it was a sulidor, but he realized it was merely a robot, probably a gardener. It said resonantly, "Man, why are you here?"

"As a visitor I'm a traveler seeking lodging for the night."

"Does the woman expect you?"

"I'm sure she doesn't. But she'll be willing to see me. Tell her Edmund Gundersen is here."

The robot scanned him carefully. "I will tell her. Remain where you are and touch nothing."

Gundersen waited. What seemed like an unhealthily long span of time went by. The twilight deepened, and one moon appeared. Some of the trees in the garden became luminous. A serpent, of the sort once used as a source of venom, slid silently across the path just in front of Gundersen and vanished. The wind shifted, stirring the trees and bringing him the faint sounds of a conversation of nildoror somewhere not far inland from the riverbank.

Then the robot returned and said, "The woman will see you. Follow the path and enter the station."

Gundersen went up the steps. On the porch he noticed unfamiliar-looking potted plants, scattered casually as though awaiting transplantation to the garden. Several of them waved tendrils at him or wistfully flashed lights intended to bring curious prey fatally close. He went in, and, seeing no one on the ground floor, caught hold of a dangling laddercoil and let himself be spun up to the first veranda. He observed that the station was as flawlessly maintained within as without, every surface clean and bright, the decorative murals unfaded, the artifacts from many worlds still mounted properly in their niches. This station had always been a showplace, but he was surprised to see it so attractive in these years of the decay of Earth's presence on Belzagor.

"Seena?" he called.

He found her alone on the veranda, leaning over the rail. By the light of two moons he saw the deep cleft of her buttocks and thought she had chosen to greet him in the nude; but as she turned toward him he realized that a strange garment covered the front of her body. It was a pale, gelatinous sprawl, shapeless, purple-tinged, with the texture and sheen that he imagined an immense amoeba might have. The central mass of it embraced her belly and loins, leaving her hips and haunches bare; her left breast also was bare, but one broad pseudopod extended upward over the right one. The stuff was translucent, and Gundersen plainly could see the red eye of her covered nipple, and the narrow socket of her navel. It was also alive, to some degree, for it began to flow, apparently of its own will, sending out slow new strands that encircled her left thigh and right hip.

The eeriness of this clinging garment left him taken aback. Except for it, she appeared to be the Seena of old; she had gained some weight, and her breasts were heavier, her hips broader, yet she was still a handsome woman in the last bloom of youth. But the Seena of old would never have allowed such a bizarreness to touch her skin.

She regarded him steadily. Her lustrous black hair tumbled to her shoulders, as in the past. Her face was unlined. She faced him squarely and without shame, her feet firmly planted, her arms at ease, her head held high. "I thought you were never coming back here, Edmund," she said. Her voice had deepened, indicating some inner deepening as well. When he had last known her she had tended to speak too quickly, nervously pitching her tone too high, but now, calm and perfectly poised, she spoke with the resonance of a fine cello. "Why are you back?" she asked.

"It's a long story, Seena. I can't even understand all of it myself. May I stay here tonight?"

"Of course. How needless to ask!"

"You look so good, Seena. Somehow I expected—after eight years—"

"A hag?"

"Well, not exactly." His eyes met hers, and he was shaken abruptly by the rigidity he found there, a fixed and inflexible gaze, a beadiness that reminded him terrifyingly of the expression in the eyes of Dykstra and his woman at the last jungle station. "I—I don't know what I expected," he said.

"Time's been good to you also, Edmund. You have that stern, disciplined look, now—all the weakness burned away by years, only the core of manhood left. You've never looked better."

"Thank you."

"Won't you kiss me?" she asked.

"I understand you're a married woman."

She winced and tightened one fist. The thing she was wearing reacted also, deepening in color and shooting a pseudopod up to encircle, though not to conceal, her bare breast. "Where did you hear that?" she asked.

"At the coast. Van Beneker told me you married Jeff Kurtz."

"Yes. Not long after you left, as a matter of fact."

"I see. Is he here?"

She ignored his question. "Don't you *want* to kiss me? Or do you have a policy about kissing other men's wives?"

He forced a laugh. Awkwardly, self-consciously, he reached for her, taking her lightly by the shoulders and drawing her toward him. She was a tall woman. He inclined his head, trying to put his lips to hers without having any part of his body come in contact with the amoeba. She pulled back before the kiss.

"What are you afraid of?" she asked.

"What you're wearing makes me nervous."

"The slider?"

"If that's what it's called."

"It's what the sulidoror call it," Seena said. "It comes from the central plateau. It clings to one of the big mammals there and lives by metabolizing perspiration. Isn't it splendid?"

"I thought you hated the plateau."

"Oh, that was a long time ago. I've been there many times. I brought the slider back on the last trip. It's as much of a pet as it is something to wear. Look." She touched it lightly and it went through a series of color changes, expanding as it approached the blue end of the spectrum, contracting toward the red. At its greatest extension it formed a complete tunic covering Seena from throat to thighs. Gundersen became aware of something dark and pulsing at the heart of it, resting just above her loins, hiding the pubic triangle: its nerve-center, perhaps. "Why do you dislike it?" she asked. "Here. Put your hand on it." He made no move. She took his hand in hers and touched it to her side; he felt the slider's cool dry surface and was surprised that it was not slimy. Easily Seena moved his hand upward until it came to the heavy globe of a breast, and instantly the slider contracted, leaving the firm warm flesh bare to his fingers. He cupped it a moment, and, uneasy, withdrew his hand. Her nipples had hardened; her nostrils had flared.

He said, "The slider's very interesting. But I don't like it on you."

"Very well." She touched herself at the base of her belly, just above the organism's core. It shrank inward and flowed down her leg in one swift rippling movement, gliding away and collecting itself at the far side of the veranda. "Is that better?" Seena asked, naked, now, sweat-shiny, moist-lipped.

The coarseness of her approach startled him. Neither he nor she had ever worried much about nudity, but there was a deliberate sexual aggressiveness about this kind of self-display that seemed out of keeping with what he regarded as her character. They were old friends, yes; they had once been lovers for several years; they had been married in all but the name for many months of that time; but even so the ambiguity of their parting should have destroyed whatever intimacy once existed. And, leaving the question of her marriage to Kurtz out of it, the fact that they had not seen one another for eight years seemed to him to dictate the necessity of a more gradual return to physical closeness. He felt that by making herself pantingly available to him within minutes of his unexpected arrival she was committing a breach not of morals but of esthetics.

"Put something on," he said quietly. "And not the slider. I can't have a serious conversation with you while you're waving all those jiggling temptations in my face."

"Poor conventional Edmund. All right. Have you had dinner?"

"No."

"I'll have it served out here. And drinks. I'll be right back."

She entered the building. The slider remained behind on the veranda; it rolled tentatively toward Gundersen, as though offering to climb up and be worn by him for a while, but he glared at it and enough feeling got through to make the plateau creature move hurriedly away. A minute later a robot emerged, bearing a tray on which two golden cocktails sat. It offered one drink to Gundersen, set the other on the railing, and noiselessly departed. Then Seena returned, chastely clad in a soft gray shift that descended from her shoulders to her shins.

"Better?" she asked.

"For now." They touched glasses; she smiled; they put their drink to their lips. "You remembered that I don't like sonic snouts," he said.

"I forget very little, Edmund."

"What's it like, living up here?"

"Serene. I never imagined that my life could be so calm. I read a good deal; I help the robots tend the garden; occasionally there are guests; sometimes I travel. Weeks often go by without my seeing another human being."

"What about your husband?"

"Weeks often go by without my seeing another human being," she said.

"You're alone here? You and the robots?"

"Quite alone."

"But the other Company people must come here fairly frequently."

"Some do. There aren't many of us left now," Seena said. "Less than a hundred, I imagine. About six at the Sea of Dust. Van Beneker down by the hotel. Four or five at the old rift station. And so on—little islands of Earthmen widely scattered. There's a sort of a social circuit, but it's a sparse one."

"Is this what you wanted when you chose to stay here?" Gundersen asked.

"I didn't know what I wanted, except that I wanted to stay. But I'd do it again. Knowing everything I know, I'd do it just the same way."

He said, "At the station just south of here, below the falls, I saw Harold Dykstra—"

"Henry Dykstra."

"Henry. And a woman I didn't know."

"Pauleen Mazor. She was one of the customs girls, in the time of the Company. Henry and Pauleen are my closest neighbors, I guess. But I haven't seen them in years. I never go south of the falls any more, and they haven't come here."

"They're dead, Seena."

"Oh?"

"It was like stepping into a nightmare. A sulidor led me to them. The station was a wreck, mold and fungoids everywhere, and something was hatching inside them, the larvae of some kind of basket-shaped red sponge that hung on a wall and dripped black oil—"

"Things like that happen," Seena said, not sounding disturbed. "Sooner or later this planet catches everyone, though always in a different way."

"Dykstra was unconscious, and the woman was begging to be put out of her misery, and—"

"You said they were dead."

"Not when I got there. I told the sulidor to kill them. There was no hope of saving them. He split them open, and then I used my torch on them."

"We had to do that for Gio' Salamone, too," Seena said. "He was staying at Fire Point, and went out into the Sea of Dust and got some kind of crystalline parasite into a cut. When Kurtz and Ced Cullen found him, he was all cubes and prisms, outcroppings of the most beautiful iridescent minerals breaking through his skin everywhere. And he was still alive. For a while. Another drink?"

"Please. Yes."

She summoned the robot. It was quite dark, now. A third moon had appeared.

In a low voice Seena said, "I'm so happy you came tonight, Edmund. It was such a wonderful surprise."

"Kurtz isn't here now?"

"No," she said. "He's away, and I don't know when he'll be back."

"How has it been for him, living here?"

"I think he's been quite happy, generally speaking. Of course, he's a very strange man."

"He is," Gundersen said.

"He's got a quality of sainthood about him, I think."

"He would have been a dark and chilling saint, Seena."

"Some saints are. They don't all have to be St. Francis of Assisi."

"Is cruelty one of the desirable traits of a saint?"

"Kurtz saw cruelty as a dynamic force. He made himself an artist of cruelty."

"So did the Marquis de Sade. Nobody's canonized *him*."

"You know what I mean," she said. "You once spoke of Kurtz to me, and you called him a fallen angel. That's exactly right. I saw him out among the nildoror, dancing with hundreds of them, and they came to him and practically worshipped him. There he was, talking to them, caressing them. And yet also doing the most destructive things to them as well, but they loved it."

"What kind of destructive things?"

"They don't matter. I doubt that you'd approve. He— gave them drugs, sometimes."

"The serpent venom?"

"Sometimes."

"Where is he now? Out playing with the nildoror?"

"He's been ill for a while." The robot now was serving dinner. Gundersen frowned at the strange vegetables on his plate. "They're perfectly safe," Seena said. "I grow them myself, in back. I'm quite the farmer."

"I don't remember any of these."

"They're from the plateau."

Gundersen shook his head. "When I think of how disgusted you were by the plateau, how strange and frightening it seemed to you that time we had to crash-land there—"

"I was a child then. When was it, eleven years ago? Soon after I met you. I was only twenty years old. But on Belzagor you must defeat what frightens you, or you will be defeated. I went back to the plateau. Again and again. It ceased to be strange to me, and so it ceased to frighten me, and so I came to love it. And brought many of its plants and animals back here to live with me. It's so very different from the rest of Belzagor—cut off from everything else, almost alien."

"You went there with Kurtz?"

"Sometimes. And sometimes with Ced Cullen. And most often alone."

"Cullen," Gundersen said. "Do you see him often?"

"Oh, yes. He and Kurtz and I have been a kind of triumvirate. My other husband, almost. I mean, in a spiritual way. Physical too, at times, but that's not as important."

"Where is Cullen now?" he asked, looking intently into her harsh and glossy eyes.

Her expression darkened. "In the north. The mist country."

"What's he doing there?"

"Why don't you go ask him?" she suggested.

"I'd like to do just that," Gundersen said. "I'm on my way up mist country, actually, and this is just a sentimental stop on the way. I'm traveling with five nildoror going for rebirth. They're camped in the bush out there somewhere."

She opened a flask of a musky gray-green wine and gave him some. "Why do you want to go to the mist country?" she asked tautly.

"Curiosity. The same motive that sent Cullen up there, I guess."

"I don't think his motive was curiosity."

"Will you amplify that?"

"I'd rather not," she said.

The conversation sputtered into silence. Talking to her led only in circles, he thought. This new serenity of hers could be maddening. She told him only what she cared to tell him, playing with him, seemingly relishing the touch of her sweet contralto voice on the night air, communicating no information at all. This was not a Seena he had ever known. The girl he had loved had been resilient and strong, but not crafty or secretive; there had been an innocence about her that seemed totally lost now. Kurtz might not be the only fallen angel on this planet.

He said suddenly, "The fourth moon has risen!"

"Yes. Of course. Is that so amazing?"

"One rarely sees four, even in this latitude."

"It happens at least ten times a year. Why waste your awe? In a little while the fifth one will be up, and—"

Gundersen gasped. "Is that what tonight is?"

"The Night of Five Moons, yes."

"No one told me!"

"Perhaps you never asked."

"Twice I missed it because I was at Fire Point. One year I was at sea, and once I was in the southern mist country, the time that the copter went down. And so on and on. I managed to see it only once, Seena, right here, ten years ago, with you. When things were at their best for us. And now, to come in by accident and have it happen!"

"I thought you had arranged to be here deliberately. To commemorate that other time."

"No. No. Pure coincidence."

"Happy coincidence, then."

"When does it rise?"

"Perhaps an hour."

He watched the four bright dots swimming through the sky. It was so long ago that he had forgotten where the fifth moon should be coming from. Its orbit was retrograde, he thought. It was the most brilliant of the moons, too, with a high-albedo surface of ice, smooth as a mirror.

Seena filled his glass again. They had finished eating. "Excuse me," she said. "I'll be back soon."

Alone, he studied the sky and tried to comprehend this strangely altered Seena, this mysterious woman whose body had grown more voluptuous and whose soul, it seemed, had turned to stone. He saw now that the stone had been in her all along: at their breakup, for example, when he had put in for transfer to Earth, and she had absolutely refused to leave Holman's World. I love you, she had said, and I'll always love you, but this is where I stay. Why? Why? Because I want to stay, she told him. And she stayed; and he was just as stubborn, and left without her; and they slept together on the beach beneath the hotel on his last night, so that the warmth of her body was still on his skin when he boarded the ship that took him away. She loved him and he loved her, but they broke apart, for he saw no future on this world, and she saw all her future on it. And she had married Kurtz. And she had explored the unknown plateau. And she spoke in a rich deep new voice, and let alien amoebas clasp her loins, and shrugged at the news that two nearby Earthmen had died a horrible death. Was she still Seena, or some subtle counterfeit?

Nildoror sounds drifted out of the darkness. Gundersen heard another sound, too, closer by, a kind of stifled snorting grunt that was wholly unfamiliar to him. It seemed like a cry of pain, though perhaps that was his imagination. Probably it was one of Seena's plateau beasts, snuffling around searching for tasty roots in the garden. He heard it twice more, and then not again.

Time went by and Seena did not return.

Then he saw the fifth moon float placidly into the sky, the size of a large silver coin, and so bright that it dazzled the eye. About it the other four danced, two of them mere tiny dots, two of them more imposing, and the shadows of the moonslight shattered and shattered again as planes of brilliance intersected. The heavens poured light upon the land in icy cascades. He gripped the rail of the veranda and silently begged the moons to hold their pattern; like Faust he longed to cry out to the fleeting moment, stay, stay forever, stay, you are beautiful! But the moons shifted, driven by the unseen Newtonian machinery; he knew that in another hour two of them would be gone and the magic would ebb. Where was Seena?

"Edmund?" she said, from behind him.

She was bare, again, and once more the slider was on

her body, covering her loins, sending a long thin projection up to encompass only the nipple of each ripe breast. The light of the five moons made her tawny skin glitter and shine. Now she did not seem coarse to him, nor overly aggressive; she was perfect in her nudity, and the moment was perfect, and unhesitatingly he went to her. Quickly he dropped his clothing. He put his hands to her hips, touching the slider, and the strange creature understood, flowing obediently from her body, a chastity belt faithless to its task. She leaned toward him, her breasts swaying like fleshy bells, and he kissed her, here, here, there, and they sank to the veranda floor, to the cold smooth stone.

Her eyes remained open, and colder than the floor, colder than the shifting light of the moons, even at the moment when he entered her.

But there was nothing cold about her embrace. Their bodies thrashed and tangled, and her skin was soft and her kiss was hungry, and the years rolled away until it was the old time again, the happy time. At the highest moment he was dimly aware of that strange grunting sound once more. He clasped her fiercely and let his eyes close.

Afterward they lay side by síde, wordless in the moonslight, until the brilliant fifth moon had completed its voyage across the sky and the Night of the Five Moons had become as any other night.

TEN

He slept by himself in one of the guest rooms on the topmost level of the station. Awakening unexpectedly early, he watched the sunrise coming over the gorge, and went down to walk through the gardens, which still were glistening with dew. He strolled as far as the edge of the river, looking for his nildoror companions; but they were not to be seen. For a long time he stood beside the river watching the irresistible downward sweep of that immense volume of water. Were there fish in the river here, he wondered? How did they avoid being carried over the brink? Surely anything once caught up in that mighty flow would have no choice but to follow the route dictated for it, and be swept toward the terrible drop.

He went back finally to the station. By the light of morning Seena's garden seemed less sinister to him. Even the plants and animals of the plateau appeared merely strange, not menacing; each geographical district of this world had its own typical fauna and flora, that was all, and it was not the fault of the plateau's creatures that man had not chosen to make himself at ease among them.

A robot met him on the first veranda and offered him breakfast.

"I'll wait for the woman," Gundersen said.

"She will not appear until much later in the morning."

"That's odd. She never used to sleep that much."

"She is with the man," the robot volunteered. "She stays with him and comforts him at this hour."

"What man?"

"The man Kurtz, her husband."

Gundersen said, amazed, "Kurtz is here at the station?"

"He lies ill in his room."

She said he was away somewhere, Gundersen thought. She didn't know when he'd be coming back.

Gundersen said, "Was he in his room last night?"

"He was."

"How long has he been back from his last journey away from here?"

"One year at the solstice," the robot said. "Perhaps you should consult the woman on these matters. She will be with you after a while. Shall I bring breakfast?"

"Yes," Gundersen said.

But Seena was not long in arriving. Ten minutes after he had finished the juices, fruits, and fried fish that the robot had brought him, she appeared on the veranda, wearing a filmy white wrap though which the contours of her body were evident. She seemed to have slept well. Her skin was clear and glowing, her stride was vigorous, her dark hair streamed buoyantly in the morning breeze; but yet the curiously rigid and haunted expression of her eyes was unchanged, and clashed with the innocence of the new day.

He said, "The robot told me not to wait breakfast for you. It said you wouldn't be down for a long while."

"That's all right. I'm not usually down this early, it's true. Come for a swim?"

"In the river?"

"No, silly!" She stripped away her wrap and ran down the steps into the garden. He sat frozen a moment, caught up in the rhythms of her swinging arms, her jouncing buttocks; then he followed her. At a twist in the path that he had not noticed before she turned to the left and halted at a circular pool that appeared to have been punched out of the living rock on the river's flank. As he reached it, she launched herself in a fine arching dive, and appeared to hang suspended a moment, floating above the dark water, her breasts drawn into a startling roundness by gravity's pull. Then she went under. Before she came up for breath, Gundersen was naked and in the pool beside her. Even in this mild climate the water was bitterly cold.

"It comes from an underground spring," she told him. "Isn't it wonderful? Like a rite of purification."

A gray tendril rose from the water behind her, tipped with rubbery claws. Gundersen could find no words to warn her. He pointed with short stabbing motions of two fingers and made hollow chittering noises of horror. A second tendril spiraled out of the depths and hovered over her. Smiling, Seena turned, and seemed to fondle some large creature; there was a thrashing in the water and then the tendrils slipped out of view.

"What was *that?*"

"The monster of the pool," she said. "Ced Cullen brought it for me as a birthday present two years ago. It's a plateau medusa. They live in lakes and sting things."

"How big is it?"

"Oh, the size of a big octopus, I'd say. Very affectionate. I wanted Ced to catch me a mate for it, but he didn't get around to it before he went north, and I suppose I'll have to do it myself before long. The monster's lonely." She pulled herself out of the pool and sprawled out on a slab of smooth black rock to dry in the sun. Gundersen followed her. From this side of the pool, with the light penetrating the water at just the right angle, he was able to see a massive many-limbed shape far below. Seena's birthday present.

He said, "Can you tell me where I can find Ced now?"

"In the mist country."

"I know. That's a big place. Any particular part?"

She rolled over onto her back and flexed her knees. Sunlight made prisms of the droplets of water on her breasts. After a long silence she said, "Why do you want to find him so badly?"

"I'm making a sentimental journey to see old friends. Ced and I were very close, once. Isn't that reason enough for me to go looking for him?"

"It's no reason to betray him, is it?"

He stared at her. The fierce eyes now were closed; the heavy mounds of her breasts rose and fell slowly, serenely. "What do you mean by that?" he asked.

"Didn't the nildoror put you up to going after him?"

"What kind of crazy talk is that?" he blurted, not sounding convincingly indignant even to himself.

"Why must you pretend?" she said, still speaking from within that impregnable core of total assurance. "The nildoror want him brought back from there. By treaty they're prevented from going up there and getting him themselves. The sulidoror don't feel like extraditing him. Certainly none of the Earthmen living on this planet will fetch him.

Now, as an outsider you need nildoror permission to enter the mist country, and since you're a stickler for the rules you probably applied for such permission, and there's no special reason why the nildoror should grant favors to you unless you agree to do something for them in return. Eh? Q.E.D."

"Who told you all this?"

"Believe me, I worked it all out for myself."

He propped his head on his hand and reached out admiringly with the other hand to touch her thigh. Her skin was dry and warm now. He let his hand rest lightly, and then not so lightly, on the firm flesh. Seena showed no reaction. Softly he said, "Is it too late for us to make a treaty?"

"What kind?"

"A nonaggression pact. We've been fencing since I got here. Let's end the hostilities. I've been hiding things from you, and you've been hiding things from me, and what good is it? Why can't we simply help one another? We're two human beings on a world that's much stranger and more dangerous than most people suspect, and if we can't supply a little mutual aid and comfort, what are the ties of humanity worth?"

She said quietly,

"Ah, love, let us be true
    To one another: for the world, which seems
    To lie before us like a land of dreams,
    So various, so beautiful, so new—"

The words of the old poem flowed up from the well of his memory. His voice cut in:

"—Hath really neither joy, nor love, nor light,
    Nor certitude, nor peace, nor help for pain;
    And we are here as on a darkling plain
    Swept with confused alarms of struggle and flight
    Where—where—"

" 'Where ignorant armies clash by night,' " she finished for him. "Yes. How like you it is, Edmund, to fumble your lines just at the crucial moment, just at the final climax."

"Then there's to be no nonaggression pact?"

"I'm sorry. I shouldn't have said that." She turned toward him, took his hand from her thigh, pressed it tenderly between her breasts, brushed her lips against it. "All right, we've been playing little games. They're over, and now we'll speak only truth, but you go first. Did the nildoror ask you to bring Ced Cullen out of the mist country?"

"Yes," Gundersen said. "It was the condition of my entry."

"And you promised you'd do it?"

"I made certain reservations and qualifications, Seena. If he won't go willingly, I'm not bound by honor to force him. But I do have to find him, at least. That much I've pledged. So I ask you again to tell me where I should look."

"I don't know," she said. "I have no idea. He could be anywhere at all up there."

"Is this the truth?"

"The truth," she said, and for a moment the harshness was gone from her eyes, and her voice was the voice of a woman and not that of a cello.

"Can you tell me, at least, why he fled, why they want him so eagerly?"

She was slow in replying. Finally she said, "About a year ago, he went down into the central plateau on one of his regular collecting trips. He was planning to get me another medusa, he said. Most of the time I went with him into the plateau, but this time Kurtz was ill and I had to stay behind. Ced went to a part of the plateau we had never visited before, and there he found a group of nildoror taking part in some kind of religious ceremony. He stumbled right into them and evidently he profaned the ritual."

"Rebirth?" Gundersen asked.

"No, they do rebirth only in the mist country. This was something else, something almost as serious, it seems. The nildoror were furious. Ced barely escaped alive. He came back here and said he was in great trouble, that the nildoror wanted him, that he had committed some sort of sacrilege and had to take sanctuary. Then he went north, with a posse of nildoror chasing him right to the border. I haven't heard anything since. I have no contact with the mist country. And that's all I can tell you."

"You haven't told me what sort of sacrilege he committed," Gundersen pointed out.

"I don't know it. I don't know what kind of ritual it was, or what he did to interrupt it. I've told you only as much as he told me. Will you believe that?"

"I'll believe it," he said. He smiled. "Now let's play

another game, and this time I'll take the lead. Last night you told me that Kurtz was off on a trip, that you hadn't seen him for a long time and didn't know when he'd be back. You also said he'd been sick, but you brushed over that pretty quickly. This morning, the robot who brought me breakfast said that you'd be late coming down, because Kurtz was ill and you were with him in his room, as you were every morning at this time. Robots don't ordinarily lie."

"The robot wasn't lying. I was."

"Why?"

"To shield him from you," Seena said. "He's in very bad shape, and I don't want him to be disturbed. And I knew that if I told you he was here, you'd want to see him. He isn't strong enough for visitors. It was an innocent lie, Edmund."

"What's wrong with him?"

"We aren't sure. You know, there isn't much of a medical service left on this planet. I've got a diagnostat, but it gave me no useful data when I put him through it. I suppose I could describe his disease as a kind of cancer. Only cancer isn't what he has."

"Can you describe the symptoms?"

"What's the use? His body began to change. He became something strange and ugly and frightening, and you don't need to know the details. If you thought that what had happened to Dykstra and Pauleen was horrible, you'd be rocked to your roots by Kurtz. But I won't let you see him. It's as much to shield you from him as the other way around. You'll be better off not seeing him." Seena sat up, cross-legged on the rock, and began to untangle the wet snarled strands of her hair. Gundersen thought he had never seen her looking as beautiful as she looked right at this moment, clothed only in alien sunlight, her flesh taut and ripe and glowing, her body supple, full-blown, mature. And the fierceness of her eyes, the one jarring discordancy? Had that come from viewing, each morning, the horror that Kurtz now was? She said after a long while, "Kurtz is being punished for his sins."

"Do you really believe that?"

"I do," she said. "I believe that there are such things as sins, and that there is retribution for sin."

"And that an old man with a white beard is up there in the sky, keeping score on everyone, running the show, tallying up an adultery here, a lie there, a spot of gluttony, a little pride?"

"I have no idea who runs the show," said Seena. "I'm not even sure that anyone does. Don't mislead yourself, Edmund: I'm not trying to import medieval theology to Belzagor. I won't give you the Father, the Son, and the Holy Ghost, and say that all over the universe certain fundamental principles hold true. I simply say that here on Belzagor we live in the presence of certain moral absolutes, native to this planet, and if a stranger comes to Belzagor and transgresses against those absolutes, he'll regret it. This world is not ours, never was, never will be, and we who live here are in a constant state of peril, because we don't understand the basic rules."

"What sins did Kurtz commit?"

"It would take me all morning to name them," she said. "Some were sins against the nildoror, and some were sins against his own spirit."

"We all committed sins against the nildoror," Gundersen said.

"In a sense, yes. We were proud and foolish, and we failed to see them for what they were, and we used them unkindly. That's a sin, yes, of course, a sin that our ancestors committed all over Earth long before we went into space. But Kurtz had a greater capacity for sin than the rest of us, because he was a greater man. Angels have farther to fall, once they fall."

"What did Kurtz do to the nildoror? Kill them? Dissect them? Whip them?"

"Those are sins against their bodies," said Seena. "He did worse."

"Tell me."

"Do you know what used to go on at the serpent station, south of the spaceport?"

"I was there for a few weeks with Kurtz and Salamone," Gundersen said. "Long ago, when I was very new here, when you were still a child on Earth. I watched the two of them call serpents out of the jungle, and milk the raw venom from them, and give the venom to nildoror to drink. And drink the venom themselves."

"And what happened then?"

He shook his head. "I've never been able to understand it. When I tried it with them, I had the illusion that the three of us were turning into nildoror. And that three nildoror had turned into *us*. I had a trunk, four legs, tusks, spines. Everything looked different; I was seeing through nildoror eyes. Then it ended, and I was in my own body again, and I felt a terrible rush of guilt, of shame. I had no way of knowing whether it had been a real bodily metamorphosis or just hallucination."

"It was hallucination," Seena told him. "The venom opened your mind, your soul, and enabled you to enter the nildor consciousness, at the same time that the nildor was entering yours. For a little while that nildor thought he was Edmund Gundersen. Such a dream is great ecstasy to a nildor."

"Is this Kurtz's sin, then? To give ecstasy to nildoror?"

"The serpent venom," Seena said, "is also used in the rebirth ceremony. What you and Kurtz and Salamone were doing down there in the jungle was going through a very mild—*very* mild—version of rebirth. And so were the nildoror. But it was blasphemous rebirth for them, for many reasons. First, because it was held in the wrong place. Second, because it was done without the proper rituals. Third, because the celebrants who guided the nildoror were men, not sulidoror, and so the entire thing became a wicked parody of the most sacred act this planet has. By giving those nildoror the venom, Kurtz was tempting them to dabble in something diabolical, literally diabolical. Few nildoror can resist that temptation. He found pleasure in the act—both in the hallucinations that the venom gave him, and in the tempting of the nildoror. I think that he enjoyed the tempting even more than the hallucinations, and that was his worst sin, for through it he led innocent nildoror into what passes for damnation on this planet. In twenty years on Belzagor he inveigled hundreds, perhaps thousands, of nildoror into sharing a bowl of venom with him. Finally his presence became intolerable, and his own hunger for evil became the source of his destruction. And now he lies upstairs, neither living nor dead, no longer a danger to anything on Belzagor."

"You think that staging the local equivalent of a Black Mass is what brought Kurtz to whatever destiny it is that you're hiding from me?"

"I know it," Seena replied. She got to her feet, stretched voluptuously, and beckoned to him. "Let's go back to the station now."

As though this were time's first dawn they walked naked

through the garden, close together, the warmth of the sun and the warmth of her body stirring him and raising a fever in him. Twice he considered pulling her to the ground and taking her amidst these alien shrubs, and twice he held back, not knowing why. When they were a dozen meters from the house he felt desire climb again, and he turned to her and put his hand on her breast. But she said, "Tell me one more thing, first."

"If I can."

"Why have you come back to Belzagor? Really. What draws you to the mist country?"

He said, "If you believe in sin, you must believe in the possibility of redemption from sin."

"Yes."

"Well, then, I have a sin on my conscience, too. Perhaps not as grave a sin as the sins of Kurtz, but enough to trouble me, and I've come back here as an act of expiation."

"How have you sinned?" she asked.

"I sinned against the nildoror in the ordinary Earthman way, by collaborating in their enslavement, by patronizing them, by failing to credit their intelligence and their complexity. In particular I sinned by preventing seven nildoror from reaching rebirth on time. Do you remember, when the Monroe dam broke, and I commandeered those pilgrims for a labor detail? I used a fusion torch to make them obey, and on my account they missed rebirth. I didn't know that if they were late for rebirth they'd lose their turn, and if I had known I wouldn't have thought it mattered. Sin within sin within sin. I left here feeling stained. Those seven nildoror bothered me in my dreams. I realized that I had to come back and try to cleanse my soul."

"What kind of expiation do you have in mind?" she asked.

His eyes had difficulty meeting hers. He lowered them, but that was worse, for the nakedness of her unnerved him even more, as they stood together in the sunlight outside the station. He forced his glance upward again.

He said, "I've determined to find out what rebirth is, and to take part in it. I'm going to offer myself to the sulidoror as a candidate."

"No."

"Seena, what's wrong? You—"

She trembled. Her cheeks were blazing, and the rush of scarlet spread even to her breasts. She bit her lip, spun away from him, and turned back. "It's insanity," she said. "Rebirth isn't something for Earthmen. Why do you think you can possibly expiate anything by getting yourself mixed up in an alien religion, by surrendering yourself to a process none of us knows anything about, by—"

"I have to, Seena."

"Don't be crazy."

"It's an obsession. You're the first person I've ever spoken to about it. The nildoror I'm traveling with aren't aware of it. I can't stop. I owe this planet a life, and I'm here to pay. I have to go, regardless of the consequences."

She said, "Come inside the station with me." Her voice was flat, mechanical, empty.

"Why?"

"Come inside."

He followed her silently in. She led him to the middle level of the building, and into a corridor blocked by one of her robot guardians. At a nod from her the robot stepped aside. Outside a room at the rear she paused and put her hand to the door's scanner. The door rolled back. Seena gestured to him to walk in with her.

He heard the grunting, snorting sound that he had heard the night before, and now there was no doubt in his mind that it had been a cry of terrible throttled pain.

"This is the room where Kurtz spends his time," Seena said. She drew a curtain that had divided the room. "And this is Kurtz," she said.

"It isn't possible," Gundersen murmured. "How— how—"

"How did he get that way?"

"Yes."

"As he grew older he began to feel remorse for the crimes he had committed. He suffered greatly in his guilt, and last year he resolved to undertake an act of expiation. He decided to travel to the mist country and undergo rebirth. This is what they brought back to me. This is what a human being looks like, Edmund, when he's undergone rebirth."

ELEVEN

What Gundersen beheld was apparently human, and probably it had once even been Jeff Kurtz. The absurd length of the body was surely Kurtzlike, for the figure in the bed seemed to be a man and a half long, as if an extra section of vertebrae and perhaps a second pair of femurs had been spliced in. The skull was plainly Kurtz's too: mighty white dome, jutting brow-ridges. The ridges were even more prominent than Gundersen remembered. They rose above Kurtz's closed eyes like barricades guarding against some invasion from the north. But the thick black brows that had covered those ridges were gone. So were the lush, almost feminine eyelashes.

Below the forehead the face was unrecognizable.

It was as if everything had been heated in a crucible and allowed to melt and run. Kurtz's fine high-bridged nose was now a rubbery smear, so snoutlike that Gundersen was jolted by its resemblance to a sulidor's. His wide mouth now had slack, pendulous lips that drooped open, revealing toothless gums. His chin sloped backward in pithecanthropoid style. Kurtz's cheekbones were flat and broad, wholly altering the planes of his face.

Seena drew the coverlet down to display the rest. The body in the bed was utterly hairless, a long boiled-looking pink thing like a giant slug. All superfluous flesh was gone, and the skin lay like a shroud over plainly visible ribs and muscles. The proportions of the body were wrong. Kurtz's waist was an impossibly great distance from his chest, and his legs, though long, were not nearly as long as they should have been; his ankles seemed to crowd his knees. His toes had fused, so that his feet terminated in bestial pads. Perhaps by compensation, his fingers had added extra joints and were great spidery things that flexed and clenched in irregular rhythms. The attachment of his arms to his torso appeared strange, though it was not until Gundersen saw Kurtz slowly rotate his left arm through a 360-degree twist that he realized the armpit must have been reconstructed into some kind of versatile ball-and-socket arrangement.

Kurtz struggled desperately to speak, blurting words in a language Gundersen had never heard. His eyeballs visibly stirred beneath his lids. His tongue slipped forth to moisten his lips. Something like a three-lobed Adam's apple bobbed in his throat. Briefly he humped his body, drawing the skin tight over curiously broadened bones. He continued to speak. Occasionally an intelligible word in English or nil-dororu emerged, embedded in a flow of gibberish: "River . . . death . . . lost . . . horror . . . river . . . cave . . . warm . . . lost . . . warm . . . smash . . . black . . . go . . . god . . . horror . . . born . . . lost . . . born. . . ."

"What is he saying?" Gundersen asked.

"No one knows. Even when we can understand the words, he doesn't make sense. And mostly we can't even understand the words. He speaks the language of the world where he must live now. It's a very private language."

"Has he been conscious at all since he's been here?"

"Not really," Seena said. "Sometimes his eyes are open, but he never responds to anything around him. Come. Look." She went to the bed and drew Kurtz's eyelids open. Gundersen saw eyes that had no whites at all. From rim to rim their shining surfaces were a deep, lustrous black, dappled by random spots of light blue. He held three fingers up before those eyes and waved his hand from side to side. Kurtz took no notice. Seena released the lids, and the eyes remained open, even when the tips of Gundersen's fingers approached quite closely. But as Gundersen withdrew his hand, Kurtz lifted his right hand and seized Gundersen's wrist. The grotesquely elongated fingers encircled the wrist completely, met, and coiled halfway around it again. Slowly and with tremendous strength Kurtz pulled Gundersen down until he was kneeling beside the bed.

Now Kurtz spoke only in English. As before he seemed to be in desperate anguish, forcing the words out of some nightmare recess, with no perceptible accenting or punctuation: "Water sleep death save sleep sleep fire love water dream cold sleep plan rise fall rise fall rise rise rise." After a moment he added, "Fall." Then the flow of nonsense syllables returned and the fingers relinquished their fierce grip on Gundersen's wrist.

Seena said, "He seemed to be telling us something. I never heard him speak so many consecutive intelligible words."

"But what was he saying?"

"I can't tell you that. But a meaning was there."

Gundersen nodded. The tormented Kurtz had delivered his testament, his blessing: *Sleep plan rise fall rise fall rise rise rise. Fall.* Perhaps it even made sense.

"And he reacted to your presence," Seena went on. "He saw you, he took your arm! Say something to him. See if you can get his attention again."

"Jeff?" Gundersen whispered, kneeling. "Jeff, do you remember me? Edmund Gundersen. I've come back, Jeff. Can you hear anything I'm saying? If you understand me, Jeff, raise your right hand again."

Kurtz did not raise his hand. He uttered a strangled moan, low and appalling; then his eyes slowly closed and he lapsed into a rigid silence. Muscles rippled beneath his altered skin. Beads of acrid sweat broke from his pores. Gundersen got to his feet shortly and walked away.

"How long was he up there?" he asked.

"Close to half a year. I thought he was dead. Then two sulidoror brought him back, on a kind of stretcher."

"Changed like this?"

"Changed. And here he lies. He's changed much more than you imagine," Seena said. "Inside, everything's new and different. He's got almost no digestive tract at all. Solid food is impossible for him; I give him fruit juices. His heart has extra chambers. His lungs are twice as big as they should be. The diagnostat couldn't tell me a thing, because he didn't correspond to any of the parameters for a human body."

"And this happened to him in rebirth?"

"In rebirth, yes. They take a drug, and it changes them. And it works on humans too. It's the same drug they use on Earth for organ regeneration, the venom, but here they use a stronger dose and the body runs wild. If you go up there, Edmund, this is what'll happen to you."

"How do you *know* it was rebirth that did this to him?"

"I know."

"How?"

"That's what he said he was going up there for. And the sulidoror who brought him back said he had undergone rebirth."

"Maybe they were lying. Maybe rebirth is one thing, a beneficial thing, and there's another thing, a harmful thing, which they gave to Kurtz because he had been so evil."

"You're deceiving yourself," Seena said. "There's only one process, and this is its result."

"Possibly different people respond differently to the process, then. If there is only one process. But I still say you can't be sure that it was rebirth that actually did this to him."

"Don't talk nonsense!"

"I mean it. Maybe something within Kurtz made him turn out like this, and I'd turn out another way. A better way."

"Do you *want* to be changed, Edmund?"

"I'd risk it."

"You'd cease to be human!"

"I've tried being human for quite a while. Maybe it's time to try something else."

"I won't let you go," Seena said.

"You won't? What claim do you have on me?"

"I've already lost Jeff to them. If you go up there too—"

"Yes?"

She faltered. "All right. I've got no way to threaten you. But don't go."

"I have to."

"You're just like him! Puffed up with the importance of your own supposed sins. Imagining the need for some kind of ghastly redemption. It's sick, don't you see? You just want to hurt yourself, in the worst possible way." Her eyes glittered even more brightly. "Listen to me. If you need to suffer, I'll help you. You want me to whip you? Stamp on you? If you've got to play masochist, I'll play sadist for you. I'll give you all the torment you want. You can wallow in it. But don't go up mist country. That's carrying a game too far, Edmund."

"You don't understand, Seena."

"Do you?"

"Perhaps I will, when I come back from there."

"You'll come back like *him!*" she screamed. She rushed

toward Kurtz's bed. "Look at him! Look at those feet! Look at his eyes! His mouth, his nose, his fingers, his everything! He isn't human any more. Do you want to lie there like him—muttering nonsense, living in some weird dream all day and all night?"

Gundersen wavered. Kurtz *was* appalling; was the obsession so strong on him that he wanted to undergo the same transformation?

"I have to go," he said, less firmly than before.

"He's living in hell," Seena said. "You'll be there too."

She came to Gundersen and pressed herself against him. He felt the hot tips of her breasts grazing his skin; her hands clawed his back desperately; her thighs touched his. A great sadness came over him, for all that Seena once had meant to him, for all that she had been, for what she had become, for what her life must be like with this monster to care for. He was shaken by a vision of the lost and irrecoverable past, of the dark and uncertain present, of the bleak, frightening future. Again he wavered. Then he gently pushed her away from him. "I'm sorry," he said. "I'm going."

"Why? Why? What a *waste!*" Tears trickled down her cheeks. "If you need a religion," she said, "pick an Earth religion. There's no reason why you have to—"

"There is a reason," Gundersen said. He drew her close to him again and very lightly kissed her eyelids, and then her lips. Then he kissed her between the breasts and released her. He walked over to Kurtz and stood for a moment looking down, trying to come to terms with the man's bizarre metamorphosis. Now he noticed something he had not observed earlier: the thickened texture of the skin of Kurtz's back, as if dark little plaques were sprouting on both sides of his spine. No doubt there were many other changes as well, apparent only on a close inspection. Kurtz's eyes opened once again, and the black glossy orbs moved, as if seeking to meet Gundersen's eyes. He stared down at them, at the pattern of blue speckles against the shining solid background. Kurtz said, amidst many sounds Gundersen could not comprehend, "Dance . . . live . . . seek . . . die . . . die."

It was time to leave.

Walking past the motionless, rigid Seena, Gundersen went out of the room. He stepped onto the veranda and saw that his five nildoror were gathered outside the station, in the garden, with a robot uneasily watching lest they begin ripping up the rarities for fodder. Gundersen called out, and Srin'gahar looked up.

"I'm ready," Gundersen said. "We can leave as soon as I have my things."

He found his clothes and prepared to depart. Seena came to him again: she was dressed in a clinging black robe, and her slider was wound around her left arm. Her face was bleak. He said, "Do you have any messages for Ced Cullen, if I find him?"

"I have no messages for anyone."

"All right. Thanks for the hospitality, Seena. It was good to see you again."

"The next time I see you," she said, "you won't know who I am. Or who you are."

"Perhaps."

He left her and went to the nildoror. Srin'gahar silently accepted the burden of him. Seena stood on the veranda of the station, watching them move away. She did not wave, nor did he. In a little while he could no longer see her. The procession moved out along the bank of the river, past the place where Kurtz had danced all night with the nildoror so many years ago.

Kurtz. Closing his eyes, Gundersen saw the glassy blind stare, the lofty forehead, the flattened face, the wasted flesh, the twisted legs, the deformed feet. Against that he placed his memories of the old Kurtz, that graceful and extraordinary-looking man, so tall and slender, so self-contained. What demons had driven Kurtz, in the end, to surrender his body and his soul to the priests of rebirth? How long had the reshaping of Kurtz taken, and had he felt any pain during the process, and how much awareness did he now have of his own condition? What had Kurtz said? I am Kurtz who toyed with your souls, and now I offer you my own? Gundersen had never heard Kurtz speak in any tone but that of sardonic detachment; how could Kurtz have displayed real emotion, fear, remorse, guilt? I am Kurtz the sinner, take me and deal with me as you wish. I am Kurtz the fallen. I am Kurtz the damned. I am Kurtz, and I am yours. Gundersen imagined Kurtz lying in some misty northern valley, his bones softened by the elixirs of the sulidoror, his body dissolving, becoming a pink jellied lump which now was free to seek a new form, to strive toward an altered kurtzness that would be cleansed of its old satanic impurities. Was it presumptuous to place himself in the same class as Kurtz, to claim the same spiritual shortcomings, to go forward to meet that same terrible destiny? Was Seena not right, that this was a game, that he was merely playing at masochistic self-dramatization, electing himself the hero of a tragic myth, burdened by the obsession to undertake an alien pilgrimage? But the compulsion seemed real enough to him, and not at all a pretense. I will go, Gundersen told himself. I am not Kurtz, but I will go, because I must go. In the distance, receding but yet powerful, the roar and throb of the waterfall still sounded, and as the rushing water hurtled down the face of the cliff it seemed to drum forth the words of Kurtz, the warning, the blessing, the threat, the prophecy, the curse: *water sleep death save sleep sleep fire love water dream cold sleep plan rise fall rise fall rise rise rise.*

Fall.

TWELVE

For administrative purposes, the Earthmen during their years of occupation of Holman's World had marked off boundaries arbitrarily here and here and here, choosing this parallel of latitude, that meridian of longitude, to encompass a district or sector. Since Belzagor itself knew nothing of parallels of latitude nor of other human measures and boundaries, those demarcations by now existed only in the archives of the Company and in the memories of the dwindling human population of the planet. But one boundary was far from arbitrary, and its power still held: the natural line dividing the tropics from the mist country. On one side of that line lay the tropical highlands, sunbathed, fertile, forming the upper limit of the central band of lush vegetation that stretched down to the torrid equatorial jungle. On the other side of that line, only a few kilometers away, the clouds of the north came rolling in, creating the white world of the mists. The transition was sharp and, for a newcomer, even terrifying. One could explain it prosaically enough in terms of Belzagor's axial tilt and the effect that had on the melting of polar snows; one could speak learnedly of the huge icecaps in which so much moisture was locked, icecaps that extended so far into the temperate zones of the planet that the warmth of the tropics was able to nibble at them, liberating great masses of water-vapor that swirled upward, curved poleward, and returned to the icecaps as regenerating snow; one could talk of the clash of climates and of the resulting marginal zones that were neither hot nor cold, and forever shrouded in the dense clouds born of that clash. But even these explanations did not prepare one for the initial shock of crossing the divide. One had a few hints: stray tufts of fog that drifted across the boundary and blotted out broad patches of the tropical highlands until the midday sun burned them away. Yet the actual change, when it came, was so profound, so absolute, that it stunned the spirit. On other worlds one grew accustomed to an easy transition from climate to climate, or else to an unvarying global climate; one could not easily accept the swiftness of the descent from warmth and ease to chill and bleakness that came here.

Gundersen and his nildoror companions were still some kilometers short of that point of change when a party of sulidoror came out of the bush and stopped them. They were border guards, he knew. There was no formal guard system, nor any other kind of governmental or quasigovernmental organization; but sulidoror nevertheless patrolled the border and interrogated those who wished to cross it. Even in the time of the Company the jurisdiction of the sulidoror had been respected, after a fashion: it might have cost too much effort to override it, and so the few Earthmen bound for the mist-country stations obligingly halted and stated their destinations before going on.

Gundersen took no part in the discussion. The nildoror and the sulidoror drew to one side, leaving him alone to contemplate the lofty banks of white mist on the northern horizon. There seemed to be trouble. One tall, sleek young sulidor pointed several times at Gundersen and spoke at length; Srin'gahar replied in a few syllables, and the sulidor appeared to grow angry, striding back and forth and vehemently knocking bark from trees with swipes of his huge claws. Srin'gahar spoke again, and then some agreement was reached; the angry sulidor stalked off into the forest and Srin'gahar beckoned to Gundersen to remount. Guided by the two sulidoror who remained, they resumed the northward march.

"What was the argument about?" Gundersen asked.

"Nothing."

"But he seemed very angry."

"It did not matter," said Srin'gahar.

"Was he trying to keep me from crossing the boundary?"

"He felt you should not go across," Srin'gahar admitted.

"Why? I have a many-born's permission."

"This was a personal grudge, friend of my journey. The

sulidor claimed that you had offended him in time past. He knew you from the old days."

"That's impossible," Gundersen said. "I had hardly any contact at all with sulidoror back then. They never came out of the mist country and I scarcely ever went into it. I doubt that I spoke a dozen words to sulidoror in eight years on this world."

"The sulidor was not wrong in remembering that he had had contact with you," said Srin'gahar gently. "I must tell you that there are reliable witnesses to the event."

"When? Where?"

"It was a long time ago," Srin'gahar said. The nildor appeared content with that vague answer, for he offered no other details. After a few moments of silence he added, "The sulidor had good reason to be unhappy with you, I think. But we told him that you meant to atone for all of your past deeds, and in the end he yielded. The sulidoror often are a stubborn and vindictive race."

"What did I *do* to him?" Gundersen demanded.

"We do not need to talk of such things," replied Srin'gahar.

Since the nildor then retreated into impermeable silence, Gundersen had ample time to ponder the grammatical ambiguities of that last sentence. On the basis of its verbal content alone, it might have meant "It is useless to talk of such things," or "It would be embarrassing to me to talk of such things," or "It is improper to talk of such things," or "It is tasteless to talk of such things." Only with the aid of the supplementary gestures, the movements of the crest-spines, the trunk, the ears, could the precise meaning be fathomed, and Gundersen had neither the skill nor the right position for detecting those gestures. He was puzzled, for he had no recollection of ever having given offense to a sulidor, and could not comprehend how he might have done it even indirectly or unknowingly; but after a while he concluded that Srin'gahar was deliberately being cryptic, and might be speaking in parables too subtle or too alien for an Earthman's mind to catch. In any case the sulidor had withdrawn his mysterious objections to Gundersen's journey, and the mist country was only a short distance away. Already the foliage of the jungle trees was more sparse than it had been a kilometer or two back, and the trees themselves were smaller and more widely spaced. Pockets of heavy fog now were more frequent. In many places the sandy yellow soil was wholly exposed. Yet the air was warm and clear and the underbrush profuse, and the bright golden sun was reassuringly visible; this was still unmistakably a place of benign and even commonplace climate.

Abruptly Gundersen felt a cold wind out of the north, signaling change. The path wound down a slight incline, and when it rose on the far side he looked over a hummock into a broad field of complete desolation, a nothing's-land between the jungle and the mist country. No tree, no shrub, no moss grew here; there was only the yellow soil, covered with a sprinkling of pebbles. Beyond this sterile zone Gundersen was confronted by a white palisade fiercely glittering with reflected sunlight; seemingly it was a cliff of ice hundreds of meters high that barred the way as far as he could see. In the extreme distance, behind and above this white wall, soared the tip of a high-looming mountain, pale red in color, whose rugged spires and peaks and parapets stood forth sharply and strangely against an iron-gray sky. Everything appeared larger than life, massive, monstrous, excessive.

"Here you must walk by yourself," said Srin'gahar. "I regret this, but it is the custom. I can carry you no farther."

Gundersen clambered down. He was not unhappy about the change; he felt that he should go to rebirth under his own power, and he had grown abashed at sitting astride Srin'gahar for so many hundreds of kilometers. But unexpectedly he found himself panting after no more than fifty meters of walking beside the five nildoror. Their pace was slow and stately, but the air here, evidently, was thinner than he knew. He forced himself to hide his distress. He would go on. He felt light-headed, oddly buoyant, and he would master the pounding in his chest and the throbbing in his temples. The new chill in the air was invigorating in its austerity. They were halfway across the zone of emptiness, and Gundersen now could clearly tell that what had appeared to be a solid white barrier stretching across the world was in fact a dense wall of mist at ground level. Outlying strands of that mist kissed his face. At its clammy touch images of death stirred in his mind, skulls and tombs and coffins and veils, but they did not dismay him. He looked toward the rose-red mountain dominating the land far to the north, and as he did so the clouds that lay over the mist country parted, permitting the sun to strike the mountain's highest peak, a snowy dome of great expanse, and it seemed to him then that the face of Kurtz, transfigured, serene, looked down at him out of that smooth rounded peak.

From the whiteness ahead emerged the figure of a giant old sulidor: Na-sinisul, keeping the promise he had made to be their guide. The sulidoror who had accompanied them this far exchanged a few words with Na-sinisul and trudged off back toward the jungle belt. Na-sinisul gestured. Walking alongside Srin'gahar, Gundersen went forward.

In a few minutes the procession entered the mist.

He did not find the mist so solid once he was within it. Much of the time he could see for twenty or thirty or even fifty meters in any direction. There were occasional inexplicable vortices of fog that were much thicker in texture, and in which he could barely make out the green bulk of Srin'gahar beside him, but these were few and quickly traversed. The sky was gray and sunless; at moments the solar ball could be discerned as a vague glow behind the clouds. The landscape was one of raw rock, bare soil, and low trees—practically a tundra, although the air was merely chilly and not really cold. Many of the trees were of species also found in the south, but here they were dwarfed and distorted, sometimes not having the form of trees at all, but running along the ground like woody vines. Those trees that stood upright were no taller than Gundersen, and gray moss draped every branch. Beads of moisture dotted their leaves, their stems, the outcroppings of rock, and everything else.

No one spoke. They marched for perhaps an hour, until Gundersen's back was bowed and his feet were numb. The ground sloped imperceptibly upward; the air seemed to grow steadily thinner; the temperature dropped quite sharply as the day neared its end. The dreary envelope of low-lying fog, endless and all-engulfing, exacted a toll on Gundersen's spirit. When he had seen that band of mist from outside, glittering brilliantly in the sunlight, it had stirred and excited him, but now that he was inside it he felt small cheer. All color and warmth had drained from the universe. He could not even see the glorious rose-red mountain from here.

Like a mechanical man, he went onward, sometimes even forcing himself into a trot to keep up with the others.

Na-sinisul set a formidable pace, which the nildoror had no difficulty in meeting, but which pushed Gundersen to his limits. He was shamed by the loudness of his own gasps and grunts, though no one else took notice of them. His breath hung before his face, fog within fog. He wanted desperately to rest. He could not bring himself to ask the others to halt a while and wait for him, though. This was their pilgrimage; he was merely the self-invited guest.

A dismal dusk began to descend. The grayness grew more gray, and the faint hint of sunlight that had been evident now diminished. Visibility lessened immensely. The air became quite cold. Gundersen, dressed for jungle country, shivered. Something that had never seemed important to him before now suddenly perturbed him: the alienness of the atmosphere. Belzagor's air, not only in the mist country but in all regions, was not quite the Earthnorm mix, for there was a trifle too much nitrogen and just a slight deficiency in oxygen; and the residual impurities were different as well. But only a highly sensitive olfactory system would notice anything amiss. Gundersen, conditioned to Belzagor's air by his years of service here, had had no awareness of a difference. Now he did. His nostrils reported a sinister metallic tang; the back of his throat, he believed, was coated with some dark grime. He knew it was a foolish illusion born of fatigue. Yet for a few minutes he found himself trying to reduce his intake of breath, as though it was safest to let as little of the dangerous stuff as possible into his lungs.

He did not stop fretting over the atmosphere and other discomforts until the moment when he realized he was alone.

The nildoror were nowhere to be seen. Neither was Na-sinisul. Mist engulfed everything. Stunned, Gundersen rolled back the screen of his memory and saw that he must have been separated from his companions for several minutes, without regarding it as in any way remarkable. By now they might be far ahead of him on some other road.

He did not call out.

He yielded first to the irresistible and dropped to his knees to rest. Squatting, he pressed his hands to his face, then put his knuckles to the cold ground and let his head loll forward while he sucked in air. It would have been easy to sprawl forward altogether and lose consciousness.

They might find him sleeping in the morning. Or frozen in the morning. He struggled to rise, and succeeded on the third attempt.

"Srin'gahar?" he said. He whispered it, making only a private appeal for help.

Dizzy with exhaustion, he rushed forward, stumbling, sliding, colliding with trees, catching his feet in the undergrowth. He saw what was surely a nildor to his left and ran toward it, but when he clutched its flank he found it wet and icy, and he realized that he was grasping a boulder. He flung himself away from it. Just beyond, a file of massive shapes presented themselves: the nildoror marching past him? "Wait?" he called, and ran, and felt the shock at his ankles as he plunged blindly into a shallow frigid rivulet. He fell, landing on hands and knees in the water. Grimly he crawled to the far bank and lay there, recognizing the dark blurred shapes now as those of low, broad trees whipped by a rising wind. All right, he thought. I'm lost. I'll wait right here until morning. He huddled into himself, trying to wring the cold water from his clothes.

The night came, blackness in place of grayness. He sought moons overhead and found none. A terrible thirst consumed him, and he tried to creep back to the brook, but he could not even find that. His fingers were numb; his lips were cracking. But he discovered an island of calm within his discomfort and fear, and clung to it, telling himself that none of what was happening was truly perilous and that all of it was somehow necessary.

Unknown hours later, Srin'gahar and Na-sinisul came to him.

First Gundersen felt the soft probing touch of Srin'gahar's trunk against his cheek. He recoiled and flattened himself on the ground, relaxing slowly as he realized what it was that had brushed his skin. Far above, the nildor said, "Here he is."

"Alive?" Na-sinisul asked, dark voice coming from worlds away, swaddled in layers of fog.

"Alive. Wet and cold. Edmundgundersen, can you stand up?"

"Yes. I'm all right, I think." Shame flooded his spirit. "Have you been looking for me all this time?"

"No," said Na-sinisul blandly. "We continued on to the village. There we discussed your absence. We could not be sure if you were lost or had separated yourself from us with a purpose. And then Srin'gahar and I returned. Did you intend to leave us?"

"I got lost," Gundersen said miserably.

Even now he was not permitted to ride the nildor. He staggered along between Srin'gahar and Na-sinisul, now and then clutching the sulidor's thick fur or grasping the nildor's smooth haunch, steadying himself whenever he felt his strength leaving him or whenever the unseen footing grew difficult. In time lights glimmered in the dark, a pale lantern glow coming milkily through the fogbound blackness. Dimly Gundersen saw the shabby huts of a sulidor village. Without waiting for an invitation he lurched into the nearest of the ramshackle log structures. It was steep-walled, musty-smelling, with strings of dried flowers and the bunched skins of animals suspended from the rafters. Several seated sulidoror looked at him with no show of interest. Gundersen warmed himself and dried his clothing; someone brought him a bowl of sweet, thick broth, and a little while afterward he was offered some strips of dried meat, which were difficult to bite and chew but extraordinarily well flavored. Dozens of sulidoror came and went. Once, when the flap of hide covering the door was left open, he caught sight of his nildoror sitting just outside the hut. A tiny fierce-faced animal, fog-white and wizened, skittered up to him and inspected him with disdain: some northern beast, he supposed, that the sulidoror favored as pets. The creature plucked at Gundersen's still soggy clothing and made a cackling sound. Its tufted ears twitched; its sharp little fingers probed his sleeve; its long prehensile tail curled and uncurled. Then it leaped into Gundersen's lap, seized his arm with quick claws, and nipped his flesh. The bite was no more painful than the pricking of a mosquito, but Gundersen wondered what hideous alien infection he would now contract. He made no move to push the little animal away, however. Suddenly a great sulidor paw descended, claws retracted, and knocked the beast across the room with a sweeping swing. The massive form of Na-sinisul lowered itself into a crouch next to Gundersen; the ejected animal chattered its rage from a far corner.

Na-sinisul said, "Did the munzor bite you?"

"Not deeply. Is it dangerous?"

"No harm will come to you," said the sulidor. "We will punish the animal."

"I hope you won't. It was only playing."

"It must learn that guests are sacred," said Na-sinisul firmly. He leaned close. Gundersen was aware of the sulidor's fishy breath. Huge fangs gaped in the deep-muzzled mouth. Quietly Na-sinisul said, "This village will house you until you are ready to go on. I must leave with the nildoror, and continue to the mountain of rebirth."

"Is that the big red mountain north of here?"

"Yes. Their time is very close, and so is mine. I will see them through their rebirths, and then my turn will come."

"Sulidoror undergo rebirth too, then?"

Na-sinisul seemed surprised. "How else could it be?"

"I don't know. I know so little about all of this."

"If sulidoror were not reborn," said Na-sinisul, "then nildoror could not be reborn. One is inseparable from the other."

"In what way?"

"If there were no day, could there be night?"

That was too cryptic. Gundersen attempted to press for an explanation, but Na-sinisul had come to speak of other matters. Avoiding the Earthman's questions, the sulidor said, "They tell me that you have come to our country to speak with a man of your own people, the man Cullen. Is that so?"

"It is. It's one of the reasons I'm here, anyway."

"The man Cullen lives three villages north of here, and one village to the west. He has been informed that you have arrived, and he summons you. Sulidoror of this village will conduct you to him when you wish to leave."

"I'll leave in the morning," Gundersen said.

"I must declare one thing to you first. The man Cullen has taken refuge among us, and so he is sacred. There can be no hope of removing him from our country and delivering him to the nildoror."

"I ask only to speak with him."

"That may be done. But your treaty with the nildoror is known to us. You must remember that you can fulfill that treaty only by a breach of our hospitality."

Gundersen made no reply. He did not see how he could promise anything of this nature to Na-sinisul without at the same time forswearing his promise to the many-born Vol'himyor. So he clung to his original inner treaty: he would speak with Cedric Cullen, and then he would decide how to act. But it disturbed him that the sulidoror were already aware of his true purpose in seeking Cullen.

Na-sinisul left him. Gundersen attempted to sleep, and for a while he achieved an uneasy doze. But the lamps flickered all night in the sulidor hut, and lofty sulidoror strode back and forth noisily around and about him, and the nildoror just outside the building engaged in a long debate of which Gundersen could catch only a few meaningless syllables. Once Gundersen awoke to find the little long-eared munzor sitting on his chest and cackling. Later in the night three sulidoror hacked up a bloody carcass just next to the place where Gundersen huddled. The sounds of the rending of flesh awakened him briefly, but he slipped back into his troubled sleep, only to wake again when a savage quarrel erupted over the division of the meat. When the bleak gray dawn came, Gundersen felt more tired than if he had not slept at all.

He was given breakfast. Two young sulidoror, Se-holomir and Yi-gartigok, announced that they had been chosen to escort him to the village where Cullen was staying. Na-sinisul and the five nildoror prepared to leave for the mountain of rebirth. Gundersen made his farewells to his traveling companions.

"I wish you joy of your rebirth," he said, and watched as the huge shapes moved off into the mist.

Not long afterward he resumed his own journey. His new guides were taciturn and aloof: just as well, for he wanted no conversation as he struggled through this hostile country. He needed to think. He was not sure at all what he would do after he had seen Cullen; his original plan of undergoing rebirth, which had seemed so noble in the abstract, now struck him as the highest folly—not only because of what Kurtz had become, but because he saw it as a trespass, an unspontaneous and self-conscious venture into the rites of an alien species. Go to the rebirth mountain, yes. Satisfy your curiosity. But submit to rebirth? For the first time he was genuinely unsure whether he would, and more than half suspicious that in the end he would draw back, unreborn.

The tundra of the border zone was giving way now to forest country which seemed a curious inversion to him: trees growing larger here in higher latitudes. But these were different trees. The dwarfed and twisted shrubs to his rear were natives of the jungle, making an unhappy adaptation to the mist; here, deeper in the mist country, true northern trees grew. They were thick-boled and lofty, with dark corrugated bark and tiny sprays of needle-like leaves. Fog shrouded their upper branches. Through this cold and misty forest too there ran lean, straggly animals, long-nosed and bony, which erupted from holes in the ground and sped up the sides of trees, evidently in quest of bough-dwelling rodents and birds. Broad patches of ground were covered with snow here, although summer was supposedly approaching in this hemisphere. On the second night northward there came a hailstorm when a dense and tossing cloud of ice rode toward them on a thin whining wind. Mute and glum, Gundersen's companions marched on through it, and so did he, not enjoying it.

Generally now the mist was light at ground level, and often there was none at all for an hour or more, but it congealed far overhead as an unbroken veil, hiding the sky. Gundersen became accustomed to the barren soil, the angular branches of so many bare trees, the chilly penetrating dampness that was so different from the jungle's humidity. He came to find beauty in the starkness. When fleecy coils of mist drifted like ghosts across a wide gray stream, when furry beasts sprinted over glazed fields of ice, when some hoarse ragged cry broke the incredible stillness, when the marchers turned an angle in the path and came upon a white tableau of harsh wintry emptiness, Gundersen responded with a strange kind of delight. In the mist country, he thought, the hour is always the hour just after dawn, when everything is clean and new.

On the fourth day Se-holomir said, "The village you seek lies behind the next hill."

THIRTEEN

It was a substantial settlement, forty huts or more arranged in two rows, flanked on one side by a grove of soaring trees and on the other by a broad silvery-surfaced lake. Gundersen approached the village through the trees, with the lake shining beyond. A light fall of snowflakes wandered through the quiet air. The mists were high just now, thickening to an impenetrable ceiling perhaps five hundred meters overhead.

"The man Cullen—?" Gundersen asked.

Cullen lay in a hut beside the lake. Two sulidoror guarded the entrance, stepping aside at a word from Yigartigok; two sulidoror more stood at the foot of the pallet of twigs and hides on which Cullen rested. They too stepped aside, revealing a burned-out husk of a man, a remnant, a cinder.

"Are you here to fetch me?" Cullen asked. "Well, Gundy, you're too late."

Cullen's golden hair had turned white and gone coarse; it was a tangled snowy mat through which patches of pale blotched scalp showed. His eyes, once a gentle liquid green, now were muddy and dull, with angry bloodshot streaks in the yellowed whites. His face was a mask of skin over bones, and the skin was flaky and rough. A blanket covered him from the chest down, but the severe emaciation of his arms indicated that the rest of his body probably was similarly eroded. Of the old Cullen little seemed to remain except the mild, pleasant voice and the cheerful smile, now grotesque emerging from the ravaged face. He looked like a man of a hundred years.

"How long have you been this way?" Gundersen demanded.

"Two months. Three, I don't know. Time melts here, Gundy. But there's no going back for me now. This is where I stop. Terminal. Terminal."

Gundersen knelt by the sick man's pallet. "Are you in pain? Can I give you something?"

"No pain," Cullen said. "No drugs. Terminal."

"What do you have?" Gundersen asked, thinking of Dykstra and his woman lying gnawed by alien larvae in a pool of muck, thinking of Kurtz anguished and transformed at Shangri-la Falls, thinking of Seena's tale of Gio' Salamone turned to crystal. "A native disease? Something you picked up around here?"

"Nothing exotic," said Cullen. "I'd guess it's the old inward rot, the ancient enemy. The crab, Gundy. The crab. In the gut. The crab's pincers are in my gut."

"Then you *are* in pain?"

"No," Cullen said. "The crab moves slowly. A nip here, a nip there. Each day there's a little less of me. Some days I feel that there's nothing left of me at all. This is one of the better days."

"Listen," Gundersen said, "I could get you downriver to Seena's place in a week. She's bound to have a medical kit, a spare tube of anticarcin for you. You aren't so far gone that we couldn't manage a remission if we act fast, and then we could ship you to Earth for template renewal, and—"

"No. Forget it."

"Don't be absurd! We aren't living in the Middle Ages, Ced. A case of cancer is no reason for a man to lie down in a filthy hut and wait to die. The sulidoror will set up a litter for you. I can arrange it in five minutes. And then—"

"I wouldn't ever reach Seena's, and you know it," Cullen said softly. "The nildoror would pick me up the moment I came out of the mist country. You know that, Gundy. You *have* to know that."

"Well—"

"I don't have the energy to play these games. You're aware, aren't you, that I'm the most wanted man on this planet?"

"I suppose so."

"Were you sent here to fetch me?"

"The nildoror asked me to bring you back," Gundersen

admitted. "I had to agree to it in order to get permission to come up here."

"Of course." Bitterly.

"But I stipulated that I wouldn't bring you out unless you'd come willingly," Gundersen said. "Along with certain other stipulations. Look, Ced, I'm not here as Judas. I'm traveling for reasons of my own, and seeing you is strictly a side-venture. But I want to help you. Let me bring you down to Seena's so you can get the treatment that you have to—"

"I told you," Cullen said, "the nildoror would grab me as soon as they had a chance."

"Even if they knew you were mortally ill and being taken down to the falls for medical care?"

"Especially so. They'd love to save my soul as I lay dying. I won't give them the satisfaction, Gundy. I'm going to stay here, safe, beyond their reach, and wait for the crab to finish with me. It won't be long now. Two days, three, a week, perhaps even tonight. I appreciate your desire to rescue me. But I won't go."

"If I got a promise from the nildoror to let you alone until you were able to undergo treat—"

"I won't go. You'd have to force me. And that's outside the scope of your promise to the nildoror, isn't it?" Cullen smiled for the first time in some minutes. "There's a flask of wine in the corner there. Be a good fellow."

Gundersen went to get it. He had to walk around several sulidoror. His colloquy with Cullen had been so intense, so private, that he had quite forgotten that the hut was full of sulidoror: his two guides, Cullen's guards, and at least half a dozen others. He picked up the wine and carried it to the pallet. Cullen, his hand trembling, nevertheless managed not to spill any. When he had had his fill, he offered the flask to Gundersen, asking him so insistently to drink that Gundersen could not help but accept. The wine was warm and sweet.

"Is it agreed," Cullen said, "that you won't make any attempt to take me out of this village? I know you wouldn't seriously consider handing me over to the nildoror. But you might decide to get me out of here for the sake of saving my life. Don't do that either, because the effect would be the same: the nildoror would get me. I stay here. Agreed?"

Gundersen was silent a while. "Agreed," he said finally.

Cullen looked relieved. He lay back, face toward the wall, and said, "I wish you hadn't wasted so much of my energy on that one point. We have so much more to talk about. And now I don't have the strength."

"I'll come back later. Rest, now."

"No. Stay here. Talk to me. Tell me where you've been all these years, why you came back here, who you've seen, what you've done. Give me the whole story. I'll rest while I'm listening. And afterward—and afterward—"

Cullen's voice faded. It seemed to Gundersen that he had slipped into unconsciousness, or perhaps merely sleep. Cullen's eyes were closed; his breath was slow and labored. Gundersen remained silent. He paced the hut uneasily, studying the hides tacked to the walls, the crude furniture, the debris of old meals. The sulidoror ignored him. Now there were eight in the hut, keeping their distance from the dying man and yet focusing all their attention on him. Momentarily Gundersen was unnerved by the presence of these giant two-legged beasts, these nightmare creatures with fangs and claws and thick tails and drooping snouts, who came and went and moved about as though he were less than nothing to them. He gulped more wine, though he found the texture and flavor of it unpleasant.

Cullen said, eyes still shut, "I'm waiting. Tell me things."

Gundersen began to speak. He spoke of his eight years on Earth, collapsing them into six curt sentences. He spoke of the restlessness that had come over him on Earth, of his cloudy and mystifying compulsion to return to Belzagor, of the sense of a need to find a new structure for his life now that he had lost the scaffolding that the Company had been for him. He spoke of his journey through the forest to the lakeside encampment, and of how he had danced among the nildoror, and how they had wrung from him the qualified promise to bring them Cullen. He spoke of Dykstra and his woman in their forest ruin, editing the tale somewhat in respect for Cullen's own condition, though he suspected that such charity was unnecessary. He spoke of being with Seena again on the Night of Five Moons. He spoke of Kurtz and how he had been changed through rebirth. He spoke of his pilgrimage into the mist country.

He was certain at least three times that Cullen had fallen asleep, and once he thought that the sick man's breathing had ceased altogether. Each time Gundersen paused, though, Cullen gave some faint indication—a twitch of the mouth, a flick of the fingertips—that he should go on. At the end, when Gundersen had nothing left to say, he stood in silence a long while waiting for some new sign from Cullen, and at last, faintly, Cullen said, "Then?"

"Then I came here."

"And where do you go after here?"

"To the mountain of rebirth," said Gundersen quietly.

Cullen's eyes opened. With a nod he asked that his pillows be propped up, and he sat forward, locking his fingers into his coverlet. "Why do you want to go there?" he asked.

"To find out what kind of thing rebirth is."

"You saw Kurtz?"

"Yes."

"He also wanted to learn more about rebirth," Cullen said. "He already understood the mechanics of it, but he had to know its inwardness as well. To try it for himself. It wasn't just curiosity, of course. Kurtz had spiritual troubles. He was courting self-immolation because he'd persuaded himself he needed to atone for his whole life. Quite true, too. Quite true. So he went for rebirth. The sulidoror obliged him. Well, behold the man. I saw him just before I came north."

"For a while I thought I might try rebirth also," said Gundersen, caught unawares by the words surfacing in his mind. "For the same reasons. The mixture of curiosity and guilt. But I think I've given the idea up now. I'll go to the mountain to see what they do, but I doubt that I'll ask them to do it to me."

"Because of the way Kurtz looks?"

"Partly. And also because my original plan looks too— well, too *willed*. Too unspontaneous. An intellectual choice, not an act of faith. You can't just go up there and volunteer for rebirth in a coldly scientific way. You have to be driven to it."

"As Kurtz was?" Cullen asked.

"Exactly."

"And as you aren't?"

"I don't know any longer," Gundersen said. "I thought I was driven, too. I told Seena I was. But somehow, now that I'm so close to the mountain, the whole quest has started to seem artificial to me."

"You're sure you aren't just afraid to go through with it?"

Gundersen shrugged. "Kurtz wasn't a pretty sight."

"There are good rebirths and bad rebirths," Cullen said. "He had a bad rebirth. How it turns out depends on the quality of one's soul, I gather, and on a lot of other things. Give us some more wine, will you?"

Gundersen extended the flask. Cullen, who appeared to be gaining strength, drank deeply.

"Have you been through rebirth?" Gundersen asked.

"Me? Never. Never even tempted. But I know a good deal about it. Kurtz wasn't the first of us to try it, of course. At least a dozen went before him."

"Who?"

Cullen mentioned some names. They were Company men, all of them from the list of those who had died while on field duty. Gundersen had known some of them; others were figures out of the far past, before he or Cullen had ever come to Holman's World.

Cullen said, "And there were others. Kurtz looked them up in the records, and the nildoror gave him the rest of the story. None of them ever returned from the mist country. Four or five of them turned out like Kurtz— transformed into monsters."

"And the others?"

"Into archangels, I suppose. The nildoror were vague about it. Some sort of transcendental merging with the universe, an evolution to the next bodily level, a sublime ascent—that kind of thing. All that's certain is that they never came back to Company territory. Kurtz was hoping on an outcome like that. But unfortunately Kurtz was Kurtz, half angel and half demon, and that's how he was reborn. And that's what Seena nurses. In a way it's a pity you've lost your urge, Gundy. You might just turn out to have one of the good rebirths. Can you call Hor-tenebor over? I think I should have some fresh air, if we're going to talk so much. He's the sulidor leaning against the wall there. The one who looks after me, who hauls my old bones around. He'll carry me outside."

"It was snowing a little while ago, Ced."

"So much the better. Shouldn't a dying man see some snow? This is the most beautiful place in the universe," Cullen said. "Right here, in front of this hut. I want to see it. Get me Hor-tenebor."

Gundersen summoned the sulidor. At a word from Cullen, Hor-tenebor scooped the fragile, shrunken invalid into his immense arms and bore him through the door-flap of the hut, setting him down on a cradle-like framework overlooking the lake. Gundersen followed. A heavy mist had descended on the village, concealing even the huts closest at hand, but the lake itself was clearly visible under the gray sky. Fugitive wisps of mist hung just above the lake's dull surface. A bitter chill was in the air, but Cullen, wrapped only in a thin hide, showed no discomfort. He held forth his hand, palm upraised, and watched with the wonder of a child as snowflakes struck it.

At length Gundersen said, "Will you answer a question?"

"If I can."

"What was it you did that got the nildoror so upset?"

"They didn't tell you when they sent you after me?"

"No," Gundersen said. "They said that you would, and that in any case it didn't really matter to them whether I knew or not. Seena didn't know either. And I can't begin to guess. You were never the kind who went in for killing or torturing intelligent species. You couldn't have been playing around with the serpent venom the way Kurtz was—he was doing that for years and they never tried to grab him. So what could you possibly have done that caused so much—"

"The sin of Actaeon," said Cullen.

"Pardon?"

"The sin of Actaeon, which was no sin at all, but really just an accident. In Greek myth he was a huntsman who blundered upon Diana bathing, and saw what he shouldn't have seen. She changed him into a stag and he was torn to pieces by his own hounds."

"I don't understand what that has to do with—"

Cullen drew a long breath. "Did you ever go up on the central plateau?" he asked, his voice low but firm. "Yes. Yes, of course you did. I remember, you crash-landed there, you and Seena, on your way back to Fire Point after a holiday on the coast, and you were stranded a little while and weird animals bothered you and that was when Seena first started to hate the plateau. Right? Then you know what a strange and somehow mysterious place it is, a place apart from the rest of this planet, where not even the nildoror like to go. All right. I started to go there, a year or two after relinquishment. It became my private retreat. The animals of the plateau interested me, the insects, the plants, everything. Even the air had a special taste—sweet, clean. Before relinquishment, you know, it would have been considered a little eccentric for anybody to visit the plateau on his free time, or at any other time. Afterward nothing mattered to anyone. The world was mine. I made a few plateau trips. I collected specimens. I brought some little oddities to Seena, and she got to be fond of them before she realized they were from the plateau, and little by little I helped her overcome her irrational fear of the plateau. Seena and I went there often together, sometimes with Kurtz also. There's a lot of flora and fauna from the plateau at Shangri-la Station; maybe you noticed it. Right? We collected all that. The plateau came to seem like any other place to me, nothing supernatural, nothing eerie, merely a neglected backwoods region. And it was my special place, where I went whenever I felt myself growing empty or bored or stale. A year ago, maybe a little less than a year, I went into the plateau. Kurtz had just come back from his rebirth, and Seena was terribly depressed by what had happened to him, and I wanted to get her a gift, some animal, to cheer her up. This time I came down a little to the southwest of my usual landing zone, over in a part of the plateau I had never seen before, where two rivers meet. One of the first things I noticed was how ripped up the shrubbery was. Nildoror! Plenty nildoror! An immense area had been grazed, and you know how nildoror graze. It made me curious. Once in a while I had seen an isolated nildor on the plateau, always at a distance, but never a whole herd. So I followed the line of devastation. On and on it went, this scar through the forest, with broken branches and trampled underbrush, all the usual signs. Night came, and I camped, and it seemed to me I heard drums in the night. Which was foolish, since nildoror don't use drums; I realized after a while that I heard them dancing, pounding the ground, and these were reverberations carried through the soil. There were other sounds, too: screams, bellows, the cries of frightened animals. I had to know what was happening. So I broke camp in the middle of the night and crept through the jungle, hearing the noise grow louder and louder, until finally I reached the edge of the trees, where the jungle gave way to a kind of broad savanna running down to the river, and there in the open were maybe five hundred nildoror. Three moons were up, and I had no trouble seeing. Gundy, would you believe that they had *painted* themselves? Like savages, like something out of a nightmare. There were three deep pits in the middle of the clearing. One of the pits was filled with a kind of wet red mud, and the other two contained branches and berries and leaves that the nildoror had trampled to release dark pigments, one black, one blue. And I watched the nildoror going down to these pits, and first they'd roll in the pit of red mud and come up plastered with it, absolutely scarlet; and then they'd go to the adjoining pits and give each other dark stripes over the red, hosing it on with their trunks. A barbaric sight: all that color, all that flesh. When they were properly decorated, they'd go running—not strolling, *running*—across the field to the place of dancing, and they'd begin that four-step routine. You know it: boom boom *boom* boom. But infinitely more fierce and frightening now, on account of the war-paint. An army of wild-looking nildoror, stamping their feet, nodding their tremendous heads, lifting their trunks, bellowing, stabbing their tusks into the ground, capering, singing, flapping their ears. Frightening, Gundy, frightening. And the moonslight on their painted bodies—

"Keeping well back in the forest, I circled around to the west to get a better view. And saw something on the far side of the dancers that was even stranger than the paint. I saw a corral with log walls, huge, three or four times the size of this village. The nildoror couldn't have built it alone; they might have uprooted trees and hauled them with their trunks, but they must have needed sulidoror to help pile them up and shape them. Inside the corral were plateau animals, hundreds of them, all sizes and shapes. The big leaf-eating ones with giraffe necks, and the kind like rhinos with antlers, and timid ones like gazelles, and dozens that I'd never even seen before, all crowded together as if in a stockyard. There must have been sulidoror hunters out beating the bush for days, driving that menagerie together. The animals were restless and scared. So was I. I crouched in the darkness, waiting, and finally all the nildoror were properly painted, and then a ritual started in the midst of the dancing group. They began to cry out, mostly in their ancient language, the one we can't understand, but also they were talking in ordinary nildororu, and eventually I understood what was going on. Do you know who these painted beasts were? They were sinning nildoror, nildoror who were in disgrace! This was the place of atonement and the festival of purification. Any nildor who had been tinged with corruption in the past year had to come here and be cleansed. Gundy, do you know what sin they had committed? They had taken the venom from Kurtz. The old game, the one everybody used to play down at the serpent station, give the nildoror a swig, take one yourself, let the hallucinations come? These painted prancing nildoror here had all been led astray by Kurtz. Their souls were stained. The Earthman-devil had found their one vulnerable place, the one area of temptation they couldn't resist. So here they were, trying to cleanse themselves. The central plateau is the nildoror purgatory. They don't live there because they need it for their rites, and obviously you don't set up an ordinary encampment in a holy place.

"They danced, Gundy, for hours. But that wasn't the rite of atonement. It was only the prelude to the rite. They danced until I was dizzy from watching them, the red bodies, the dark stripes, the boom of their feet, and then, when no moons were left in the sky, when dawn was near, the real ceremony started. I watched it, and I looked right down into the darkness of the race, into the real nildoror soul. Two old nildoror approached the corral and started kicking down the gate. They broke an opening maybe ten meters wide, and stepped back, and the penned-up animals came rushing out onto the plain. The animals were terrified from all the noise and dancing, and from being imprisoned, and they ran in circles, not knowing what to do or where to go. And the rest of the nildoror charged into them. The peaceful, noble, nonviolent nildoror, you know? Snorting. Trampling. Spearing with their tusks. Lifting animals with their trunks and hurling them into trees. An orgy of slaughter. I became sick, just watching. A nildor can be a terrible machine of death. All that weight, those tusks, the trunk, the big feet—everything berserk, all restraints off. Some of the animals escaped, of course. But most were trapped right in the middle of the chaos. Crushed bodies everywhere, rivers of blood, scavengers coming out of the forest to have dinner while the killing was still going on. That's how the nildoror atone: sin for sin. That's how they purge themselves. The plateau is where they loose their violence, Gundy. They put aside all their restraints and let out the beast that's within them. I've never felt such horror as when I watched how they cleansed their souls. You know how much respect I had for the nildoror. Still have. But to see a thing like that, a massacre, a vision of hell—Gundy, I was numb with despair. The nildoror didn't seem to enjoy the killing, but they weren't hesitant about it, either; they just went on and on, because it had to be done, because this was the form of the ceremony, and they thought nothing more of it than Socrates would think of sacrificing a lamb to Zeus, a cock to Aesculapius. That was the real horror, I think. I watched the nildoror destroying life for the sake of their souls, and it was like dropping through a trapdoor, entering a new world whose existence I had never even suspected, a dark new world beneath the old. Then dawn came. The sun rose, lovely, golden, light glistening on the trampled corpses, and the nildoror were sitting calmly in the midst of the devastation, resting, calm, purged, all their inner storms over. It was amazingly peaceful. They had wrestled with their demons, and they had won. They had come through all the night's horror, all the ghastliness, and—I don't know how—they really *were* purged and purified. I can't tell you how to find salvation through violence and destruction. It's alien to me and probably to you. Kurtz knew, though. He took the same road as the nildoror. He fell and fell and fell, through level after level of evil, enjoying his corruption, glorying in depravity, and then in the end he was still able to judge himself and find himself wanting, and recoil at the darkness he found inside himself, and so he went and sought rebirth, and showed that the angel within him wasn't altogether dead. This finding of purity by passing through evil—you'll have to come to terms with it by yourself, Gundy. I can't help you. All I can do is tell you of the vision I had at sunrise that morning beside the field of blood. I looked into an abyss. I peered over the edge, and saw where Kurtz had gone, where these nildoror had gone. Where perhaps you'll go. I couldn't follow.

"And then they almost caught me.

"They picked up my scent. While the frenzy was on them, I guess they hadn't noticed—especially with hundreds of animals giving off fear-smells in the corral. But they began to sniff. Trunks started to rise and move around like periscopes. The odor of sacrilege was on the air. The reek of a blaspheming spying Earthman. Five, ten minutes they sniffed, and I stood in the bushes still wrapped in my vision, not even remotely realizing they were sniffing *me,* and suddenly it dawned on me that they knew I was there, and I turned and began to slip away through the forest, and they came after me. Dozens. Can you imagine what it's like to be chased through the jungle by a herd of angry nildoror? But I could fit through places too small for them. I gave them the slip. I ran and ran and ran, until I fell down dizzy in a thicket and vomited, and I rested, and then I heard them bashing along on my trail, and I ran some more. And came to a swamp, and jumped in, hoping they'd lose my scent. And hid in the reeds and marshes, while things I couldn't see nipped at me from below. And the nildoror ringed the entire region. We know you're in there, they called to me. Come out. Come out. We forgive you and we wish to purify you. They explained it all quite reasonably to me. I had inadvertently—oh, of course, inadvertently, they were diplomatic!—seen a ceremony that no one but a nildor was allowed to see, and now it would be necessary to wipe what I had seen from my mind, which could be managed by means of a simple technique that they didn't bother to describe to me. A drug, I guess. They invited me to come have part of my mind blotted out. I didn't accept. I didn't say anything. They went right on talking, telling me that they held no malice, that they realized it obviously hadn't been my intention to watch their secret ceremony, but nevertheless since I had seen it they must now take steps, et cetera, et cetera. I began to crawl downstream, breathing through a hollow reed. When I surfaced the nildoror were still calling to me, and now they sounded more angry, as far as it's possible to tell such a thing. They seemed annoyed that I had refused to come out. They didn't blame me for spying on them, but they did object that I wouldn't let them purify me. That was my real crime: not that I hid in the bushes and watched them, but declining afterward to undergo the treatment. That's what they still want me for. I stayed in the creek all day, and when it got dark I slithered out and picked up the vector-beep of my beetle, which turned out to be about half a kilometer away. I expected to find it guarded by nildoror, but it wasn't, and I got in and cleared out fast and landed at Seena's place by midnight. I knew I didn't have much time. The nildoror would be after me from one side of the continent to the other. I told her what had happened, more or less, and I collected some supplies, and I took off for the mist country. The sulidoror would give me sanctuary. They're jealous of their sovereignty; blasphemy or not, I'd be safe here. I came to this village. I explored the mist country a good bit. Then one day I felt the crab in my gut and I knew it was all over. Since then I've been waiting for the end, and the end isn't far away."

He fell silent.

Gundersen, after a pause, said, "But why not risk going back? Whatever the nildoror want to do to you can't be as bad as sitting on the porch of a sulidor hut and dying of cancer."

Cullen made no reply.

"What if they give you a memory-wiping drug?" Gundersen asked. "Isn't it better to lose a bit of your past than to lose your whole future? If you'll only come back, Ced, and let us treat your disease—"

"The trouble with you, Gundy, is that you're too logical," Cullen said. "Such a sensible, reasonable, rational chap! There's another flask of wine inside. Would you bring it out?"

Gundersen walked past the crouching sulidoror into the hut, and prowled the musty darkness a few moments, looking for the wine. As he searched, the solution to the Cullen situation presented itself: instead of bringing Cullen to the medicine, he would bring the medicine to Cullen. He would abandon his journey toward the rebirth mountain at least temporarily and go down to Shangri-la Falls to get a dose of anticarcin for him. It might not be too late to check the cancer. Afterward, restored to health, Cullen could face the nildoror or not, as he pleased. What happens between him and the nildoror, Gundersen told himself, will not be a matter that concerns me. I regard my treaty with Vol'himyor as nullified. I said I would bring Cullen forth only with his consent, and clearly he won't go willingly. So my task now is just to save his life. Then I can go to the mountain.

He located the wine and went outside with it.

Cullen leaned backward on the cradle, his chin on his chest, his eyes closed, his breath slow, as if his lengthy monologue had exhausted him. Gundersen did not disturb him. He put the wine down and walked away, strolling for more than an hour, thinking, reaching no conclusion. Then he returned. Cullen had not moved. "Still asleep?" Gundersen asked the sulidoror.

"It is the long sleep," one of them replied.

FOURTEEN

The mist came in close, bringing jewels of frost that hung from every tree, every hut; and by the brink of the leaden lake Gundersen cremated Cullen's wasted body with one long fiery burst of the fusion torch, while sulidoror looked on, silent, solemn. The soil sizzled a while when he was done, and the mist whirled wildly as cold air rushed in to fill the zone of warmth his torch had made. Within the hut were a few unimportant possessions. Gundersen searched through them, hoping to find a journal, a memoir, anything with the imprint of Cedric Cullen's soul and personality. But he found only some rusted tools, and a box of dried insects and lizards, and faded clothing. He left these things where he found them.

The sulidoror brought him a cold dinner. They let him eat undisturbed, sitting on the wooden cradle outside Cullen's hut. Darkness came, and he retreated into the hut to sleep. Se-holomir and Yi-gartigok posted themselves as guards before the entrance, although he had not asked them to stay there. He said nothing to them. Early in the evening he fell asleep.

He dreamed, oddly, not of the newly dead Cullen but of the still living Kurtz. He saw Kurtz trekking through the mist country, the old Kurtz, not yet metamorphosed to his present state: infinitely tall, pale, eyes burning in the domed skull, glowing with strange intelligence. Kurtz carried a pilgrim's staff and strode tirelessly forward into the mist. Accompanying him, yet not really with him, was a procession of nildoror, their green bodies stained bright red by pigmented mud; they halted whenever Kurtz halted, and knelt beside him, and from time to time he let them drink from a tubular canteen he was carrying. Whenever Kurtz offered his canteen to the nildoror, he and not they underwent a transformation. His lips joined in a smooth sealing; his nose lengthened; his eyes, his fingers, his toes, his legs changed and changed again. Fluid, mobile, Kurtz kept no form for long. At one stage in the journey he became a sulidor in all respects but one: his own high-vaulted bald head surmounted the massive hairy body. Then the fur melted from him, the claws shrank, and he took on another form, a lean loping thing, rapacious and swift with double-jointed elbows and long spindly legs. More changes followed. The nildoror sang hymns of adoration, chanting in thick monotonous skeins of gray sound. Kurtz was gracious. He bowed, he smiled, he waved. He passed around his canteen, which never needed replenishing. He rippled through cycle upon cycle of dizzy metamorphosis. From his backpack he drew gifts that he distributed among the nildoror: torches, knives, books, message cubes, computers, statues, color organs, butterflies, flasks of wine, sensors, transport modules, musical instruments, beads, old etchings, holy medallions, baskets of flowers, bombs, flares, shoes, keys, toys, spears. Each gift fetched ecstatic sighs and snorts and moos of gratitude from the nildoror; they frolicked about him, lifting their new treasures in their trunks, excitedly displaying them to one another. "You see?" Kurtz cried. "I am your benefactor. I am your friend. I am the resurrection and the life." They came now to the place of rebirth, not a mountain in Gundersen's dream but rather an abyss, dark and deep, at the rim of which the nildoror gathered and waited. And Kurtz, undergoing so many transformations that his body flickered and shifted from moment to moment, now wearing horns, now covered with scales, now clad in shimmering flame, walked forward while the nildoror cheered him, saying to him, "This is the place, rebirth will be yours," and he stepped into the abyss, which enfolded him in absolute night. And then from the depths of the pit came a single prolonged cry, a shrill wail of terror and dismay so awful that it awakened Gundersen, who lay sweating and shivering for hours waiting for dawn.

In the morning he shouldered his pack and made signs of departing. Se-holomir and Yi-gartigok came to him; and one of the sulidoror said, "Where will you go now?"

"North."

"Shall we go with you?"

"I'll go alone," Gundersen said.

It would be a difficult journey, perhaps a dangerous one, but not impossible. He had direction-finding equipment, food concentrates, a power supply, and other such things. He had the necessary stamina. He knew that the sulidoror villages along the way would extend hospitality to him if he needed it. But he hoped not to need it. He had been escorted long enough, first by Srin'gahar, then by various sulidoror; he felt he should finish this pilgrimage without a guide.

Two hours after sunrise he set out.

It was a good day for beginning such an endeavor. The air was crisp and cool and clear and the mist was high; he could see surprisingly far in all directions. He went through the forest back of the village and emerged on a fair-sized hill from the top of which he was able to gauge the landscape ahead. He saw rugged, heavily forested country, much broken by rivers and streams and lakes; and he succeeded in glimpsing the tip of the mountain of rebirth, a jagged sentinel in the north. That rosy peak on the horizon seemed close enough to grasp. Just reach out; just extend the fingers. And the fissures and hillocks and slopes that separated him from his goal were no challenge; they could be traversed in a few quick bounds. His body was eager for the attempt: heartbeat steady, vision exceptionally keen, legs moving smoothly and tirelessly. He sensed an inward soaring of the soul, a restrained but ecstatic upsweep toward life and power; the phantoms that had veiled him for so many years were dropping away; in this chill zone of mist and snow he felt annealed, purified, tempered, ready to accept whatever must be accepted. A strange energy surged through him. He did not mind the thinness of the air, nor the cold, nor the bleakness of the land. It was a morning of unusual clarity, with bright sunlight cascading through the lofty covering of fog and imparting a dreamlike brilliance to the trees and the bare soil. He walked steadily onward.

The mist closed in at midday. Visibility dwindled until Gundersen could see only eight or ten meters ahead. The giant trees became serious obstacles; their gnarled roots and writhing buttresses now were traps for unwary feet. He picked his way with care. Then he entered a region where large flat-topped boulders jutted at shallow angles from the ground, one after another, slick mist-slippery slabs forming stepping-stones to the land beyond. He had to crawl over them, blindly feeling along, not knowing how much of a drop he was likely to encounter at the far end of each boulder. Jumping off was an act of faith; one of the drops turned out to be about four meters, and he landed hard, so that his ankles tingled for fifteen minutes afterward. Now he felt the first fatigue of the day spreading through his thighs and knees. But yet the mood of controlled ecstasy, sober and nevertheless jubilant, remained with him.

He made a late lunch beside a small, flawlessly circular pond, mirror-bright, rimmed by tall narrow-trunked trees and hemmed in by a tight band of mist. He relished the privacy, the solitude of the place; it was like a spherical room with walls of cotton, within which he was perfectly isolated from a perplexing universe. Here he could shed the tensions of his journey, after so many weeks of traveling with nildoror and sulidoror, worrying all the while that he would give offense in some unknown but unforgivable way. He was reluctant to leave.

As he was gathering his belongings, an unwelcome sound punctured his seclusion: the drone of an engine not far overhead. Shading his eyes against the glare of the mist, he looked up, and after a moment caught a glimpse of an airborne beetle flying just below the cloud-ceiling. The little snubnosed vehicle moved in a tight circle, as if looking for something. For me, he wondered? Automatically he shrank back against a tree to hide, though he knew it was impossible for the pilot to see him here even in the open. A moment later the beetle was gone, vanishing in a bank of fog just to the west. But the magic of the afternoon was shattered. That ugly mechanical droning noise in the sky still reverberated in Gundersen's mind, shattering his newfound peace.

An hour's march onward, passing through a forest of slender trees with red gummy-looking bark, Gundersen encountered three sulidoror, the first he had seen since parting from Yi-gartigok and Se-holomir that morning. Gundersen was uneasy about the meeting. Would they permit him free access here? These three evidently were a hunting party returning to a nearby village; two of them carried, lashed to a pole slung from shoulder to shoulder, the trussed-up carcass of some large four-legged grazing animal with velvety black skin and long recurved horns. He felt a quick instinctive jolt of fear at the sight of the three gigantic creatures coming toward him among the trees; but to his surprise the fear faded almost as rapidly as it came. The sulidoror, for all their ferocious mien, simply did not hold a threat. True, they could kill him with a slap, but what of that? They had no more reason to attack him than he did to burn them with his torch. And here in their natural surroundings, they did not even seem bestial or savage. Large, yes. Powerful. Mighty of fang and claw. But natural, fitting, proper, and so not terrifying.

"Does the traveler journey well?" asked the lead sulidor, the one who bore no part of the burden of the kill. He spoke in a soft and civil tone, using the language of the nildoror.

"The traveler journeys well," said Gundersen. He improvised a return salutation: "Is the forest kind to the huntsmen?"

"As you see, the huntsmen have fared well. If your path goes toward our village, you are welcome to share our kill this night."

"I go toward the mountain of rebirth."

"Our village lies in that direction. Will you come?"

He accepted the offer, for night was coming on, and a harsh wind was slicing through the trees now. The sulidoror village was a small one, at the foot of a sheer cliff half an hour's walk to the northeast. Gundersen passed a pleasant night there. The villagers were courteous though aloof, in a manner wholly free of any hostility; they gave him a corner of a hut, supplied him with food and drink, and left him alone. He had no sense of being a member of a despised race of ejected conquerors, alien and unwanted. They appeared to look upon him merely as a wayfarer in need of shelter, and showed no concern over his species. He found that refreshing. Of course, the sulidoror did not have the same reasons for resentment as the nildoror, since these forest folk had never actually been turned into slaves by the Company; but he had always imagined a seething, sizzling rage within the sulidoror, and their easygoing kindness now was an agreeable departure from that image, which Gundersen now suspected might merely have been a projection of his own guilts. In the morning they brought him fruits and fish, and then he took his leave.

The second day of his journey alone was not as rewarding as the first. The weather was bad, cold and damp and frequently snowy, with dense mist hanging low nearly all the time. He wasted much of the morning by trapping himself in a cul-de-sac, with a long ridge of hills to his right, another to his left, and, unexpectedly, a broad and uncrossable lake appearing in front of him. Swimming it was unthinkable; he might have to pass several hours in its frigid water, and he would not survive the exposure. So he had to go on a wearying eastward detour over the lesser ridge of hills, which swung him about so that by midday he was in no higher a latitude than he had been the night before. The sight of the fog-wreathed rebirth mountain drew him on, though, and for two hours of the afternoon he had the illusion that he was making up for the morning's delay, only to discover that he was cut off by a swift and vast river flowing from west to east, evidently the one that fed the lake that had blocked him earlier. He did not dare to swim this, either; the current would sweep him into the distant deeps before he had reached the farther bank. Instead he consumed more than an hour following the river upstream, until he came to a place where he might ford it. It was even wider here than below, but its bed looked much more shallow, and some geological upheaval had strewn a line of boulders across it like a necklace, from bank to bank. A dozen of the boulders jutted up, with white water swirling around them; the others, though submerged, were visible just below the surface. Gundersen started across. He was able to hop from the top of one boulder to the next, keeping dry until he had gone nearly a third of the way. Then he had to scramble in the water, wading shin-deep, slipping and groping. The mist enveloped him. He might have been alone in the universe, with nothing ahead but billows of whiteness, nothing to the rear but the same. He could see no trees, no shore, not even the boulders awaiting him. He concentrated rigidly on keeping his footing and staying to his path. Putting one foot down awry, he slid and toppled, landing in a half-crouch in the river, drenched to the armpits, buffeted by the current, and so dizzied for a moment that he could not rise. All his energy was devoted to clinging to the angular mass of rock beneath him. After a few minutes he found the strength to get to his feet again, and tottered forward, gasping, until he reached a boulder whose upper face stood half a meter above the water; he knelt on it, chilled, soaked, shivering, trying to shake himself dry. Perhaps five minutes passed. With the mist clinging close, he got no drier, but at least he had his breath again, and he resumed his crossing. Experimentally reaching out the tip of a boot, he found another dry-topped boulder just ahead. He went to it. There was still another beyond it. Then came another. It was easy, now: he would make it to the far side without another soaking. His pace quickened, and he traversed another pair of boulders. Then, through a rift in the mist, he was granted a glimpse of the shore.

Something seemed wrong.

The mist sealed itself; but Gundersen hesitated to go on without some assurance that all was as it should be. Carefully he bent low and dipped his left hand in the water. He felt the thrust of the current coming from the right and striking his open palm. Wearily, wondering if cold and fatigue had affected his mind, he worked out the topography of his situation several times and each time came to the same dismaying conclusion: if I am making a northward crossing of a river that flows from west to east, I should feel the current coming from my *left*. Somehow, he realized, he had turned himself around while scrambling for purchase in the water, and since then he had with great diligence been heading back toward the southern bank of the river.

His faith in his own judgment was destroyed. He was tempted to wait here, huddled on this rock, for the mist to clear before going on; but then it occurred to him that he might have to wait through the night, or even longer. He also realized belatedly that he was carrying gear designed to cope with just such problems. Fumbling in his backpack, he pulled out the small cool shaft of his compass and aimed it at the horizon, sweeping his arm in an arc that terminated where the compass emitted its north-indicating beep. It confirmed his conclusions about the current, and he started across the river again, shortly coming to the place of the submerged stepping-stones where he had fallen. This time he had no difficulties.

On the far shore he stripped and dried his clothing and himself with the lowest-power beam of his fusion torch. Night now was upon him. He would not have regretted another invitation to a sulidoror village, but today no hospitable sulidoror appeared. He spent an uncomfortable night huddled under a bush.

The next day was warmer and less misty. Gundersen went warily forward, forever fearing that his hours of hard hiking might be wasted when he came up against some unforeseen new obstacle, but all went well, and he was able to cope with the occasional streams or rivulets that crossed his path. The land here was ridged and folded as though giant hands, one to the north and one to the south, had pushed the globe together; but as Gundersen was going down one slope and up the next, he was also gaining altitude constantly, for the entire continent sloped upward toward the mighty plateau upon which the rebirth mountain was reared.

In early afternoon the prevailing pattern of east-west folds in the land subsided; here the landscape was skewed around so that he found himself walking parallel to a series of gentle north-south furrows, which opened into a wide circular meadow, grassy but treeless. The large animals of the north, whose names Gundersen did not know, grazed here in great numbers, nuzzling in the lightly snow-covered ground. There seemed to be only four or five species—something heavy-legged and humpbacked, like a badly designed cow, and something in the style of an oversized gazelle, and several others—but there were hundreds or even thousands of each kind. Far to the east, at the very border of the plain, Gundersen saw what appeared to be a small sulidoror hunting-party rounding up some of the animals.

He heard the drone of the engine again.

The beetle he had seen the other day now returned, passing quite low overhead. Instinctively Gundersen threw himself to the ground, hoping to go unnoticed. About him the animals milled uneasily, perplexed at the noise, but they did not bolt. The beetle drifted to a landing about a thousand meters north of him. He decided that Seena must have come after him, hoping to intercept him before he could submit himself to the sulidoror of the mountain of rebirth. But he was wrong. The hatch of the beetle opened, and Van Beneker and his tourists began to emerge.

Gundersen wriggled forward until he was concealed behind a tall stand of thistle-like plants on a low hummock. He could not abide the thought of meeting that crew again, not at this stage in his pilgrimage, when he had been purged of so many vestiges of the Gundersen who had been.

He watched them.

They were walking up to the animals, photographing them, even daring to touch some of the more sluggish beasts. Gundersen heard their voices and their laughter cracking the congealed silence; isolated words drifted randomly toward him, as meaningless as Kurtz's flow of dream-fogged gibberish. He heard, too, Van Beneker's voice cutting through the chatter, describing and explaining and expounding. These nine humans before him on the meadow seemed as alien to Gundersen as the sulidoror. More so, perhaps. He was aware that these last few days of mist and chill, this solitary odyssey through a world of whiteness and quiet, had worked a change in him that he barely comprehended. He felt lean of soul, stripped of the excess baggage of the spirit, a simpler man in all respects, and yet more complex.

He waited an hour or more, still hidden, while the tourist party finished touring the meadow. Then everyone returned to the beetle. Where now? Would Van take them north to spy on the mountain of rebirth? No. No. It wasn't possible. Van Beneker himself dreaded the whole business of rebirth, like any good Earthman; he wouldn't dare to trespass on that mysterious precinct.

When the beetle took off, though, it headed toward the north.

Gundersen, in his distress, shouted to it to turn back. As though heeding him, the gleaming little vehicle veered round as it gained altitude. Van Beneker must have been trying to catch a tailwind, nothing more. Now the beetle made for the south. The tour was over, then. Gundersen saw it pass directly above him and disappear into a lofty bank of fog. Choking with relief, he rushed forward, scattering the puzzled herds with wild loud whoops.

Now all obstacles seemed to be behind him. Gundersen crossed the valley, negotiated a snowy divide without effort, forded a shallow brook, pushed his way through a forest of short, thick, tightly packed trees with narrow pointed crowns. He slipped into an easy rhythm of travel, paying no heed any longer to cold, mist, damp, altitude, or fatigue. He was tuned to his task. When he slept, he slept soundly and well; when he foraged for food to supplement his concentrates, he found that which was good;

when he sought to cover distance, he covered it. The peace of the misty forest inspired him to do prodigies. He tested himself, searching for the limits of his endurance, finding them, exceeding them at the next opportunity.

Through this phase of the journey he was wholly alone. Sometimes he saw sulidoror tracks in the thin crust of snow that covered much of the land, but he met no one. The beetle did not return. Even his dreams were empty; the Kurtz phantom that had plagued him earlier was absent now, and he dreamed only blank abstractions, forgotten by the time of awakening.

He did not know how many days had elapsed since the death of Cedric Cullen. Time had flowed and melted in upon itself. He felt no impatience, no weariness, no sense of wanting it all to be over. And so it came as a mild surprise to him when, as he began to ascend a wide, smooth, shelving ledge of stone, about thirty meters wide, bordered by a wall of icicles and decorated in places by tufts of grass and scraggly trees, he looked up and realized that he had commenced the scaling of the mountain of rebirth.

FIFTEEN

From afar, the mountain had seemed to rise dramatically from the misty plain in a single sweeping thrust. But now that Gundersen was actually upon its lower slopes, he saw that at close range the mountain dissolved into a series of ramps of pink stone, one atop another. The totality of the mountain was the sum of that series, yet from here he had no sense of a unified bulk. He could not even see the lofty peaks and turrets and domes that he knew must hover thousands of meters above him. A layer of clinging mist severed the mountain less than halfway up, allowing him to see only the broad, incomprehensible base. The rest, which had guided him across hundreds of kilometers, might well have never been.

The ascent was easy. To the right and to the left Gundersen saw sheer faces, impossible spires, fragile bridges of stone linking ledge to ledge; but there was also a switchback path, evidently of natural origin, that gave the patient climber access to the higher reaches. The dung of innumerable nildoror littered this long stone ramp, telling him that he must be on the right route. He could not imagine the huge creatures going up the mountain any other way. Even a sulidor would be taxed by those precipices and gullies.

Chattering munzoror leaped from ledge to ledge, or walked with soft, shuffling steps across terrifying abysses spanned by strands of vines. Goat-like beasts, white with diamond-shaped black markings, capered in graveled pockets of unreachable slopes, and launched booming halloos that echoed through the afternoon. Gundersen climbed steadily. The air was cold but invigorating; the mists were wispy at this level, giving him a clear view before and behind. He looked back and saw the fog-shrouded lowlands suddenly quite far below him. He imagined that he was able to see all the way to the open meadow where the beetle had landed.

He wondered when some sulidor would intercept him. This was, after all, the most sacred spot on this planet. Were there no guardians? No one to stop him, to question him, to turn him back?

He came to a place about two hours' climb up the mountainside where the upward slope diminished and the ramp became a long horizontal promenade, curving off to the right and vanishing beyond the mass of the mountain. As Gundersen followed it, three sulidoror appeared, coming around the bend. They glanced briefly at him and went past, taking no other notice, as though it were quite ordinary that an Earthman should be going up the mountain of rebirth.

Or, Gundersen thought strangely, as though he were *expected.*

After a while the ramp turned upward again. Now an overhanging stone ledge formed a partial roof for the path, but it was no shelter, for the little cackling wizen-faced munzoror nested up there, dropping pebbles and bits of chaff and worse things down. Monkeys? Rodents? Whatever they were, they introduced a sacrilegious note to the solemnity of this great peak, mocking those who went up. They dangled by their prehensile tails; they twitched their long tufted ears; they spat; they laughed. What were they saying? "Go away, Earthman, this is no shrine of yours!" Was that it? How about, "Abandon hope, all ye who enter here!"

He camped for the night beneath that ledge. Munzoror several times scrambled across his face. Once he woke to what sounded like the sobbing of a woman, deep and intense, in the abyss below. He went to the edge and found a bitter snowstorm raging. Soaring through the storm, rising and sinking, rising and sinking, were sleek bat-like things of the upper reaches, with tubular black bodies and great rubbery yellow wings; they went down until they were lost to his sight, and sped upward again toward their eyries clasping chunks of raw meat in their sharp red beaks. He did not hear the sobbing again. When sleep returned, he lay as if drugged until a brillant dawn crashed like thunder against the side of the mountain.

He bathed in an ice-rimmed stream that sped down a smooth gully and intersected the path. Then he went upward, and in the third hour of his morning's stint he overtook a party of nildoror plodding toward rebirth. They were not green but pinkish-gray, marking them as members of the kindred race, the nildoror of the eastern hemisphere. Gundersen had never known whether these nildoror enjoyed rebirth facilities in their own continent, or came to undergo the process here. That was answered now. There were five of them, moving slowly and with extreme effort. Their hides were cracked and ridged, and their trunks—thicker and longer than those of western nildoror—drooped limply. It wearied him just to look at them. They had good reason to be tired, though: since nildoror had no way of crossing the ocean, they must have taken the land route, the terrible northeastward journey across the dry bed of the Sea of Dust. Occasionally, during his tour of duty there, Gundersen had seen eastern nildoror dragging themselves through that crystalline wasteland, and at last he understood what their destination had been.

"Joy of your rebirth!" he called to them as he passed, using the terse eastern inflection.

"Peace be on your journey," one of the nildoror replied calmly.

They, too, saw nothing amiss in his presence here. But he did. He could not avoid thinking of himself as an intruder, an interloper. Instinctively he began to lurk and skulk, keeping to the inside of the path as though that made him less conspicuous. He anticipated his rejection at any moment by some custodian of the mountain, stepping forth suddenly to block his climb.

Above him, another two or three spirals of the path overhead, he spied a scene of activity.

Two nildoror and perhaps a dozen sulidoror were in view up there, standing at the entrance to some dark chasm in the mountainside. He could see them only by taking up a precarious position at the rim of the path. A third nildor emerged from the cavern; several sulidoror went in. Some way-station, maybe, on the road to rebirth? He craned his neck to see, but as he continued along his path he reached a point from which that upper level was no longer visible.

It took him longer than he expected to reach it. The switchback path looped out far to one side in order to encircle a narrow jutting spiky tower of rock sprouting from the great mountain's flank, and the detour proved to be lengthy. It carried Gundersen well around to the northeastern face. By the time he was able to see the level of the chasm again, a sullen twilight was falling, and the place he sought was still somewhere above him.

Full darkness came before he was on its level. A heavy blanket of fog sat close upon things now. He was perhaps midway up the peak. Here the path spread into the mountain's face, creating a wide plaza covered with brittle flakes of pale stone, and against the vaulting wall of the mountain Gundersen saw a black slash, a huge inverted V, the opening of what must be a mighty cavern. Three nildoror lay sleeping to the left of this entrance, and five sulidoror, to its right, seemed to be conferring.

He hung back, posting himself behind a convenient boulder and allowing himself wary peeps at the mouth of the cavern. The sulidoror went within, and for more than an hour nothing happened. Then he saw them emerge, awaken one of the nildoror, and lead it inside. Another hour passed before they came back for the second. After a while they fetched the third. Now the night was well advanced. The mist, the constant companion here, approached and clung. The big-beaked bat-creatures, like marionettes on strings, swooped down from higher zones of the mountain, shrieking past and vanishing in the drifting fog below, returning moments later in equally swift ascent. Gundersen was alone. This was his moment to peer into the cavern, but he could not bring himself to make the inspection. He hesitated, shivering, unable to go forward. His lungs were choked with mist. He could see nothing in any direction now; even the bat-beasts were invisible, mere dopplering blurts of sound as they rose and fell. He struggled to recapture some of the jauntiness he had felt on that first day after Cullen's death, setting out unaccompanied through this wintry land. With a conscious effort he found a shred of that vigor at last.

He went to the mouth of the cavern.

He saw only darkness within. Neither sulidoror nor nildoror were evident at the entrance. He took a cautious step inward. The cavern was cool, but it was a dry coolness far more agreeable than the mist-sodden chill outside. Drawing his fusion torch, he risked a quick flash of light and discovered that he stood in the center of an immense chamber, the lofty ceiling of which was lost in the shadows overhead. The walls of the chamber were a baroque fantasy of folds and billows and buttresses and fringes and towers, all of stone, polished and translucent, gleaming like convoluted glass during the instant that the light was upon them. Straight ahead, flanked by two rippling wings of stone that were parted like frozen curtains, lay a passageway, wide enough for Gundersen but probably something of a trial for the bulky nildoror who had earlier come this way.

He went toward it.

Two more brief flashes from the torch got him to it. Then he proceeded by touch, gripping one side of the opening and feeling his way into its depths. The corridor bent sharply to the left and, about twenty paces farther on, angled just as sharply the other way. As Gundersen came around the second bend a dim light greeted him. Here a pale green fungoid growth lining the ceiling afforded a minimal sort of illumination. He felt relieved and yet suddenly vulnerable, for, while he now could see, he could also be seen.

The corridor was about twice a nildor's width and three times a nildor's height, rising to the peaked vault in which the fungoids dwelled. It stretched for what seemed an infinite distance into the mountain. Branching off it on both sides, Gundersen saw, were secondary chambers and passages.

He advanced and peered into the nearest of these chambers.

It held something that was large and strange and apparently alive. On the floor of a bare stone cell lay a mass of pink flesh, shapeless and still. Gundersen made out short thick limbs and a tail curled tightly over broad flanks; he could not see its head, nor any distinguishing marks by which he could associate it with a species he knew. It might have been a nildor, but it did not seem quite large enough. As he watched, it swelled with the intake of a breath, and slowly subsided. Many minutes passed before it took another breath. Gundersen moved on.

In the next cell he found a similar sleeping mound of unidentifiable flesh. In the third cell lay another. The fourth cell, on the opposite side of the corridor, contained a nildor of the western species, also in deep slumber. The cell beside it was occupied by a sulidor lying oddly on its back with its limbs poking rigidly upward. The next cell held a sulidor in the same position, but otherwise quite startlingly different, for it had shed its whole thick coat of fur and lay naked, revealing awesome muscles beneath a gray, slick-looking skin. Continuing, Gundersen came to a chamber that housed something even more bizarre: a figure that had a nildor's spines and tusks and trunk but a sulidor's powerful arms and legs and a sulidor's frame. What nightmare composite was this? Gundersen stood awed before it for a long while, trying to comprehend how the head of a nildor might have been joined to the body of a sulidor. He realized that no such joining could have occurred; the sleeper here simply partook of the characteristics of both races in a single body. A hybrid? A genetic mingling?

He did not know. But he knew now that this was no mere way-station on the road toward rebirth. This was the place of rebirth itself.

Far ahead, figures emerged from one of the subsidiary corridors and crossed the main chamber: two sulidoror and a nildor. Gundersen pressed himself against the wall and remained motionless until they were out of sight, disappearing into some distant room. Then he continued inward.

He saw nothing but miracles. He was in a garden of fantasies where no natural barriers held.

Here was a round spongy mass of soft pink flesh with just one recognizable feature sprouting from it: a sulidor's huge tail.

Here was a sulidor, bereft of fur, whose arms were foreshortened and pillar-like, like the limbs of a nildor, and whose body had grown round and heavy and thick.

Here was a sulidor in full fur with a nildor's trunk and ears.

Here was raw meat that was neither nildor nor sulidor, but alive and passive, a mere thing awaiting a sculptor's shaping hand.

Here was another thing that resembled a sulidor whose bones had melted.

Here was still another thing that resembled a nildor who had never had bones.

Here were trunks, spines, tusks, fangs, claws, tails, paws. Here was fur, and here was smooth hide. Here was flesh flowing at will and seeking new shapes. Here were dark chambers, lit only by flickering fungoid-glow, in which no firm distinction of species existed.

Biology's laws seemed suspended here. This was no trifling gene-tickling that he saw, Gundersen knew. On Earth, any skilled helix-parlor technician could redesign an organism's gene-plasm with some cunning thrusts of a needle and a few short spurts of drugs; he could make a camel bring forth a hippopotamus, a cat bring forth a chipmunk, or, for that matter, a woman bring forth a sulidor. One merely enhanced the desired characteristics within sperm and ovum, and suppressed other characteristics, until one had a reasonable facsimile of the creature to be reproduced. The basic genetic building-blocks were the same for every life-form; by rearranging them, one could create any kind of strange and monstrous progeny. But that was not what was being done here.

On Earth, Gundersen knew, it was also possible to persuade any living cell to play the part of a fertilized egg, and divide, and grow, and yield a full organism. The venom from Belzagor was one catalyst for that process; there were others. And so one could induce the stump of a man's arm to regrow that arm; one could scrape a bit of skin from a frog and generate an army of frogs with it; one could even rebuild an entire human being from the shards of his own ruined body. But that was not what was being done here.

What was being done here, Gundersen realized, was a transmutation of species, a change worked not upon ova but upon adult organisms. Now he understood Na-sinisul's remark, when asked if sulidoror also underwent rebirth: "If there were no day, could there be night?" Yes. Nildor into sulidor. Sulidor into nildor. Gundersen shivered in shock. He reeled, clutching at a wall. He was plunged into a universe without fixed points. What was real? What was enduring?

He comprehended now what had happened to Kurtz in this mountain.

Gundersen stumbled into a cell in which a creature lay midway in its metamorphosis. Smaller than a nildor, larger than a sulidor; fangs, not tusks; trunk, not snout; fur, not hide; flat footpads, not claws; body shaped for walking upright.

"Who are you?" Gundersen whispered. "What are you? What were you? Which way are you heading?"

Rebirth. Cycle upon cycle upon cycle. Nildoror bound upon a northward pilgrimage, entering these caves, becoming . . . sulidoror? Was it possible?

If this is true, Gundersen thought, then we have never really known anything about this planet. And this is true.

He ran wildly from cell to cell, no longer caring whether he might be discovered. Each cell confirmed his guess. He saw nildoror and sulidoror in every stage of metamorphosis, some almost wholly nildoror, some unmistakably sulidoror, but most of them occupying intermediate positions along that journey from pole to pole; more than half were so deep in transformation that it was impossible for him to tell which way they were heading. All slept. Before his eyes flesh flowed, but nothing moved. In these cool shadowy chambers change came as a dream.

Gundersen reached the end of the corridor. He pressed his palms against cold, unyielding stone. Breathless, sweat-drenched, he turned toward the last chamber in the series and plunged into it.

Within was a sulidor not yet asleep, standing over three of the sluggish serpents of the tropics, which moved in gentle coils about him. The sulidor was huge, age-grizzled, a being of unusual presence and dignity.

"Na-sinisul?" Gundersen asked.

"We knew that in time you must come here, Edmund-gundersen."

"I never imagined—I didn't understand—" Gundersen paused, struggling to regain control. More quietly he said, "Forgive me if I have intruded. Have I interrupted your rebirth's beginning?"

"I have several days yet," the sulidor said. "I merely prepare the chamber now."

"And you'll come forth from it as a nildor."

"Yes," said Na-sinisul.

"Life goes in a cycle here, then? Sulidor to nildor to sulidor to nildor to—"

"Yes. Over and over, rebirth after rebirth."

"All nildoror spend part of their lives as sulidoror? All sulidoror spend part of their lives as nildoror?"

"Yes. All."

How had it begun, Gundersen wondered? How had the destinies of these two so different races become entangled? How had an entire species consented to undergo such a metamorphosis? He could not begin to understand it. But he knew now why he had never seen an infant nildor or sulidor. He said, "Are young ones of either race ever born on this world?"

"Only when needed as replacements for those who can be reborn no more. It is not often. Our population is stable."

"Stable, yet constantly changing."

"Through a predictable pattern of change," said Na-sinisul. "When I emerge, I will be Fi'gontor of the ninth birth. My people have waited for thirty turnings for me to rejoin them; but circumstances required me to remain this long in the forest of the mists."

"Is nine rebirths unusual?"

"There are those among us who have been here fifteen times. There are some who wait a hundred turnings to be called once. The summons comes when the summons comes; and for those who merit it, life will have no end."

"No—end—"

"Why should it?" Na-sinisul asked. "In this mountain we are purged of the poisons of age, and elsewhere we purge ourselves of the poisons of sin."

"On the central plateau, that is."

"I see you have spoken with the man Cullen."

"Yes," Gundersen said. "Just before his—death."

"I knew also that his life was over," said Na-sinisul. "We learn things swiftly here."

Gundersen said, "Where are Srin'gahar and Luu'khamin and the others I traveled with?"

"They are here, in cells not far away."

"Already in rebirth?"

"For some days now. They will be sulidoror soon, and will live in the north until they are summoned to assume the nildor form again. Thus we refresh our souls by undertaking new lives."

"During the sulidor phase, you keep a memory of your past life as a nildor?"

"Certainly. How can experience be valuable if it is not retained? We accumulate wisdom. Our grasp of truth is heightened by seeing the universe now through a nildor's eyes, now through a sulidor's. Not in body alone are the two forms different. To undergo rebirth is to enter a new world, not merely a new life."

Hesitantly Gundersen said, "And when someone who is not of this planet undergoes rebirth? What effect is there? What kind of changes happen?"

"You saw Kurtz?"

"I saw Kurtz," said Gundersen. "But I have no idea what Kurtz has become."

"Kurtz has become Kurtz," the sulidor said. "For your kind there can be no true transformation, because you have no complementary species. You change, yes, but you become only what you have the potential to become. You liberate such forces as already exist within you. While he slept, Kurtz chose his new form himself. No one else designed it for him. It is not easy to explain this with words, Edmundgundersen."

"If I underwent rebirth, then, I wouldn't necessarily turn into something like Kurtz?"

"Not unless your soul is as Kurtz's soul, and that is not possible."

"What *would* I become?"

"No one may know these things before the fact. If you wish to discover what rebirth will do to you, you must accept rebirth."

"If I asked for rebirth, would I be permitted to have it?"

"I told you when we first met," said Na-sinisul, "that no one on this world will prevent you from doing anything. You were not stopped as you ascended the mountain of rebirth. You were not stopped when you explored these chambers. Rebirth will not be denied you if you feel you need to experience it."

Easily, serenely, instantly, Gundersen said, "Then I ask for rebirth."

SIXTEEN

Silently, unsurprised, Na-sinisul leads him to a vacant cell and gestures to him to remove his clothing. Gundersen strips. His fingers fumble only slightly with the snaps and catches. At the sulidor's direction, Gundersen lies on the floor, as all other candidates for rebirth have done. The stone is so cold that he hisses when his bare skin touches it. Na-sinisul goes out. Gundersen looks up at the glowing fungoids in the distant vault of the ceiling. The chamber is large enough to hold a nildor comfortably; to Gundersen, on the floor, it seems immense.

Na-sinisul returns, bearing a bowl made from a hollow log. He offers it to Gundersen. The bowl contains a pale blue fluid. "Drink," says the sulidor softly.

Gundersen drinks.

The taste is sweet, like sugar-water. This is something he has tasted before, and he knows when it was: at the serpent station, years ago. It is the forbidden venom. He drains the bowl, and Na-sinisul leaves him.

Two sulidoror whom Gundersen does not know enter the cell. They kneel on either side of him and begin a low, mumbling chant, some sort of ritual. He cannot understand any of it. They knead and stroke his body; their hands, with the fearful claws retracted, are strangely soft, like the pads of a cat. He is tense, but the tension ebbs. He feels the drug taking effect now: a thickness at the back of his head, a tightness in his chest, a blurring of his vision. Na-sinisul is in the room again, although Gundersen did not see him enter. He carries a bowl.

"Drink," he says, and Gundersen drinks.

It is another fluid entirely, or perhaps a different distillate of the venom. Its flavor is bitter, with undertastes of smoke and ash. He has to force himself to get to the bottom of the bowl, but Na-sinisul waits, silently insistent, for him to finish it. Again the old sulidor leaves. At the mouth of the cell he turns and says something to Gundersen, but the words are overgrown with heavy blue fur, and will not enter Gundersen's ears. "What did you say?" the Earthman asks. "What? What?" His own words sprout leaden weights, teardrop-shaped, somber. They fall at once to the floor and shatter. One of the chanting sulidoror sweeps the broken words into a corner with a quick motion of his tail.

Gundersen hears a trickling sound, a glittering spiral of noise, as of water running into his cell. His eyes are closed, but he feels the wetness swirling about him. It is not water, though. It has a more solid texture. A sort of gelatin, perhaps. Lying on his back, he is several centimeters deep in it, and the level is rising. It is cool but not cold, and it insulates him nicely from the chill rock of the floor. He is aware of the faint pink odor of the inflowing gelatin, and of its firm consistency, like the tones of a bassoon in its deepest register. The sulidoror continue to chant. He feels a tube sliding into his mouth, a sleek piccolo-shriek of a tube, and through its narrow core there drips yet another substance, thick, oily, emitting the sound of muted kettledrums as it hits his palate. Now the gelatin has reached the lower curve of his jaw. He welcomes its advance. It laps gently at his chin. The tube is withdrawn from his mouth just as the flow of gelatin covers his lips. "Will I be able to breathe?" he asks. A sulidor answers him in cryptic Sumerian phrases, and Gundersen is reassured.

He is wholly sealed in the gelatin. It covers the floor of the chamber to a depth of one meter. Light dimly penetrates it. Gundersen knows that its upper surface is smooth and flawless, forming a perfect seal where it touches the walls of the cell. Now he has become a chrysalis. He will be given nothing more to drink. He will lie here, and he will be reborn.

One must die in order that one may be reborn, he knows.

Death comes to him and enfolds him. Gently he slides into a dark abyss. The embrace of death is tender. Gundersen floats through a realm of trembling emptiness. He hovers suspended in the black void. Bands of scarlet and purple light transfix him, buffeting him like bars of metal. He tumbles. He spins. He soars.

He encounters death once more, and they wrestle, and he is defeated by death, and his body is shivered into splinters, and a shower of bright Gundersen-fragments scatters through space.

The fragments seek one another. They solemnly circle one another. They dance. They unite. They take on the form of Edmund Gundersen, but this new Gundersen glows like pure, transparent glass. He is glistening, a transparent man through whom the light of the great sun at the core of the universe passes without resistance. A spectrum spreads forth from his chest. The brilliance of his body illuminates the galaxies.

Strands of color emanate from him and link him to all who possess g'rakh in the universe.

He partakes of the biological wisdom of the cosmos.

He tunes his soul to the essence of what is and what must be.

He is without limits. He can reach out and touch any soul. He reaches toward the soul of Na-sinisul, and the sulidor greets him and admits him. He reaches toward Srin'gahar, toward Vol'himyor the many-born, toward Luu'khamin, Se-holomir, Yi-gartigok, toward the nildoror and sulidoror who lie in the caves of metamorphosis, and toward the dwellers in the misty forests, and toward the dwellers in the steaming jungles, and toward those who dance and rage in the forlorn plateau, and to all others of Belzagor who share in g'rakh.

And he comes now to one that is neither nildor nor sulidor, a sleeping soul, a veiled soul, a soul of a color and a timbre and a texture unlike the others. It is an Earthborn soul, the soul of Seena, and he calls softly to her, saying, Awaken, awaken, I love you, I have come for you. She does not awaken. He calls to her, I am new, I am reborn, I overflow with love. Join me. Become part of me. Seena? Seena? Seena? And she does not respond.

He sees the souls of the other Earthmen now. They have g'rakh, but rationality is not enough; their souls are blind and silent. Here is Van Beneker; here are the tourists; here are the lonely keepers of solitary outposts in the jungle. Here is the charred gray emptiness where the soul of Cedric Cullen belongs.

He cannot reach any of them.

He moves on, and a new soul gleams beyond the mist. It is the soul of Kurtz. Kurtz comes to him, or he to Kurtz, and Kurtz is not asleep.

Now you are among us, Kurtz says, and Gundersen says, Yes, here I am at last. Soul opens to soul and Gundersen looks down into the darkness that is Kurtz, past the pearl-gray curtain that shrouds his spirit, into a place of terror where black figures shuttle with many legs along ridged webs. Chaotic forms cohere, expand, dissolve within Kurtz. Gundersen looks beyond this dark and dismal zone, and beyond it he finds a cold hard bright light shining whitely out of the deepest place, and then Kurtz says, See? Do you see? Am I a monster? I have goodness within me.

You are not a monster, Gundersen says.

But I have suffered, says Kurtz.

For your sins, Gundersen says.

I have paid for my sins with my suffering, and I should now be released.

You have suffered, Gundersen agrees.

When will my suffering end, then?

Gundersen replies that he does not know, that it is not he who sets the limits of such things.

Kurtz says, I knew you. Nice young fellow, a little slow. Seena speaks highly of you. Sometimes she wishes things had worked out better for you and her. Instead she got me. Here I lie. Here lie we. Why won't you release me?

What can I do, asks Gundersen?

Let me come back to the mountain. Let me finish my rebirth.

Gundersen does not know how to respond, and he seeks along the circuit of g'rakh, consulting Na-sinisul, consulting Vol'himyor, consulting all the many-born ones, and they join, they join, they speak with one voice, they tell Gundersen in a voice of thunder that Kurtz is finished, his rebirth is over, he may not come back to the mountain.

Gundersen repeats this to Kurtz, but Kurtz has already heard. Kurtz shrivels. Kurtz shrinks back into darkness. He becomes enmeshed in his own webs.

Pity me, he calls out to Gundersen across a vast gulf. Pity me, for this is hell, and I am in it.

Gundersen says, I pity you. I pity you. I pity you. I pity you.

The echo of his own voice diminishes to infinity. All is silent. Out of the void, suddenly, comes Kurtz's wordless reply, a shrill and deafening crescendo blast of rage and hatred and malevolence, the scream of a flawed Prometheus flailing at the beak that pierces him. The shriek reaches a climax of shattering intensity. It dies away. The shivering fabric of the universe grows still again. A soft violet light appears, absorbing the lingering disharmonies of that one terrible outcry.

Gundersen weeps for Kurtz.

The cosmos streams with shining tears, and on that salty river Gundersen floats, traveling without will, visiting this world and that, drifting among the nebulae, passing through clouds of cosmic dust, soaring over strange suns.

He is not alone. Na-sinisul is with him, and Srin'gahar, and Vol'himyor, and all the others.

He becomes aware of the harmony of all things g'rakh. He sees, for the first time, the bonds that bind g'rakh to g'rakh. He, who lies in rebirth, is in contact with them all, but also they are each in contact with one another, at any time, at every time, every soul on the planet joined in wordless communication.

He sees the unity of all g'rakh, and it awes and humbles him.

He perceives the complexity of this double people, the rhythm of its existence, the unending and infinite swing of cycle upon cycle of rebirth and new creation, above all the union, the oneness. He perceives his own monstrous isolation, the walls that cut him off from other men, that cut off man from man, each a prisoner in his own skull. He sees what it is like to live among people who have learned to liberate the prisoner in the skull.

That knowledge dwindles and crushes him. He thinks, We made them slaves, we called them beasts, and all the time they were linked, they spoke in their minds without words, they transmitted the music of the soul one to one to one. We were alone, and they were not, and instead of kneeling before them and begging to share the miracle, we gave them work to do.

Gundersen weeps for Gundersen.

Na-sinisul says, This is no time for sorrow, and Srin'-

gahar says, The past is past, and Vol'himyor says, Through remorse you are redeemed, and all of them speak with one voice and at one time, and he understands. He understands.

Now Gundersen understands all.

He knows that nildor and sulidor are not two separate species but merely forms of the same creature, no more different than caterpillar and butterfly, though he cannot tell which is the caterpillar, which the butterfly. He is aware of how it was for the nildoror when they were still in their primeval state, when they were born as nildoror and died helplessly as nildoror, perishing when the inevitable decay of their souls came upon them. And he knows the fear and the ecstasy of those first few nildoror who accepted the serpent's temptation and drank the drug of liberation, and became things with fur and claws, misshapen, malformed, transmuted. And he knows their pain as they were driven out, even into the plateau where no being possessing g'rakh would venture.

And he knows their sufferings in that plateau.

And he knows the triumph of those first sulidoror, who, surmounting their isolation, returned from the wilderness bearing a new creed. Come and be changed, come and be changed! Give up this flesh for another! Graze no more, but hunt and eat flesh! Be reborn, and live again, and conquer the brooding body that drags the spirit to destruction!

And he sees the nildoror accepting their destiny and giving themselves up joyfully to rebirth, a few, and then more, and then more, and then whole encampments, entire populations, going forth, not to hide in the plateau of purification, but to live in the new way, in the land where mist rules. They cannot resist, because with the change of body comes the blessed liberation of soul, the unity, the bond of g'rakh to g'rakh.

He understands now how it was for these people when the Earthmen came, the eager, busy, ignorant, pitiful, short-lived Earthmen, who were beings of g'rakh yet who could not or would not enter into the oneness, who dabbled with the drug of liberation and did not taste it to the fullest, whose minds were sealed one against the other, whose roads and buildings and pavements spread like pockmarks over the tender land. He sees how little the Earthmen knew, and how little they were capable of learning, and how much was kept from them since they would misunderstand it, and why it was necessary for the sulidoror to hide in the mists all these years of occupation, giving no clue to the strangers that they might be related to the nildoror, that they were the sons of the nildoror and the fathers of the nildoror as well. For if the Earthmen had known even half the truth they would have recoiled in fright, since their minds are sealed one against the other, and they would not have it any other way, except for the few who dared to learn, and too many of those were dark and demon-ridden, like Kurtz.

He feels vast relief that the time of pretending is over on this world and that nothing need be hidden any longer, that sulidoror may go down into the lands of the nildoror and move freely about, without fear that the secret and the mystery of rebirth may accidentally be revealed to those who could not withstand such knowledge.

He knows joy that he has come here and survived the test and endured his liberation. His mind is open now, and he has been reborn.

He descends, rejoining his body. He is aware once more that he lies embedded in congealed gelatin on the cold floor of a dark cell abutting a lengthy corridor within a rose-red mountain wreathed in white mist on a strange world. He does not rise. His time is not yet come.

He yields to the tones and colors and odors and textures that flood the universe. He allows them to carry him back, and he floats easily along the time-line, so that now he is a child peering at the shield of night and trying to count the stars, and now he is timidly sipping raw venom with Kurtz and Salamone, and now he enrolls in the Company and tells a personnel computer that his strongest wish is to foster the expansion of the human empire, and now he grasps Seena on a tropic beach under the light of several moons, and now he meets her for the first time, and now he sifts crystals in the Sea of Dust, and now he mounts a nildor, and now he runs laughing down a childhood street, and now he turns his torch on Cedric Cullen, and now he climbs the rebirth mountain, and now he trembles as Kurtz walks into a room, and now he takes the wafer on his tongue, and now he stares at the wonder of a white breast filling his cupped hand, and now he steps forth into mottled alien sunlight, and now he crouches over Henry Dykstra's swollen body, and now, and now, and now, and now. . . .

He hears the tolling of mighty bells.

He feels the planet shuddering and shifting on its axis.

He smells dancing tongues of flame.

He touches the roots of the rebirth mountain.

He feels the souls of nildoror and sulidoror all about him.

He recognizes the words of the hymn the sulidoror sing, and he sings with them.

He grows. He shrinks. He burns. He shivers. He changes. He awakens.

"Yes," says a thick, low voice. "Come out of it now. The time is here. Sit up. Sit up."

Gundersen's eyes open. Colors surge through his dazzled brain. It is a moment before he is able to see.

A sulidor stands at the entrance to his cell.

"I am Ti-munilee," the sulidor says. "You are born again."

"I know you," Gundersen says. "But not by that name. Who are you?"

"Reach out to me and see," says the sulidor.

Gundersen reaches out.

"I knew you as the nildor Srin'gahar," Gundersen says.

SEVENTEEN

Leaning on the sulidor's arm, Gundersen walked unsteadily out of the chamber of rebirth. In the dark corridor he asked, "Have I been changed?"

"Yes, very much," Ti-munilee said.

"How? In what way?"

"You do not know?"

Gundersen held a hand before his eyes. Five fingers, yes, as before. He looked down at his naked body and saw no difference in it. Obscurely he experienced disappointment; perhaps nothing had really happened in that chamber. His legs, his feet, his loins, his belly—everything as it had been.

"I haven't changed at all," he said.

"You have changed greatly," the sulidor replied.

"I see myself, and I see the same body as before."

"Look again," advised Ti-munilee.

In the main corridor Gundersen caught sight of himself dimly reflected in the sleek glassy walls by the light of the glowing fungoids. He drew back, startled. He had changed, yes; he had outkurtzed Kurtz in his rebirth. What peered back at him from the rippling sheen of the walls was scarcely human. Gundersen stared at the mask-like face with hooded slots for eyes, at the slitted nose, the gill-pouches trailing to his shoulders, the many-jointed arms, the row of sensors on the chest, the grasping organs at the hips, the cratered skin, the glow-organs in the cheeks. He looked down again at himself and saw none of those things. Which was the illusion?

He hurried toward daylight.

"Have I changed, or have I not changed?" he asked the sulidor.

"You have changed."

"Where?"

"The changes are within," said the former Srin'gahar.

"And the reflection?"

"Reflections sometimes lie. Look at yourself through my eyes, and see what you are."

Gundersen reached forth again. He saw himself, and it was his old body he saw, and then he flickered and underwent a phase shift and he beheld the being with sensors and slots, and then he was himself again.

"Are you satisfied?" Ti-munilee asked.

"Yes," said Gundersen. He walked slowly toward the lip of the plaza outside the mouth of the cavern. The seasons had changed since he had entered that cavern; now an iron winter was on the land, and the mist was piled deep in the valley, and where it broke he saw the heavy mounds of snow and ice. He felt the presence of nildoror and sulidoror about him, though he saw only Ti-munilee. He was aware of the soul of old Na-sinisul within the mountain, passing through the final phases of a rebirth. He touched the soul of Vol'himyor far to the south. He brushed lightly over the soul of tortured Kurtz. He sensed suddenly, startlingly, other Earthborn souls, as free as his, open to him, hovering nearby.

"Who are you?" he asked.

And they answered, "You are not the first of your kind to come through rebirth intact."

Yes. He remembered. Cullen had said that there had been others, some transformed into monsters, others simply never heard from again.

"Where are you?" he asked them.

They told him, but he did not understand, for what they said was that they had left their bodies behind. "Have I also left my body behind?" he asked. And they said, no, he was still wearing his flesh, for so he had chosen, and they had chosen otherwise. Then they withdrew from him.

"Do you feel the changes?" Ti-munilee asked.

"The changes are within me," said Gundersen.

"Yes. Now you are at peace."

And, surprised by joy, he realized that that was so. The fears, the conflicts, the tensions, were gone. Guilt was gone. Sorrow was gone. Loneliness was gone.

Ti-munilee said, "Do you know who I was, when I was Srin'gahar? Reach toward me."

Gundersen reached. He said, in a moment, "You were one of those seven nildoror whom I would not allow to go to their rebirth, many years ago."

"Yes."

"And yet you carried me on your back all the way to the mist country."

"My time had come again," said Ti-munilee, "and I was happy. I forgave you. Do you remember, when we crossed into the mist country, there was an angry sulidor at the border?"

"Yes," Gundersen said.

"He was another of the seven. He was the one you touched with your torch. He had had his rebirth finally, and still he hated you. Now he no longer does. Tomorrow, when you are ready, reach toward him, and he will forgive you. Will you do that?"

"I will," said Gundersen. "But will he really forgive?"

"You are reborn. Why should he not forgive?" Ti-munilee said. Then the sulidor asked, "Where will you go now?"

"South. To help my people. First to help Kurtz, to guide him through a new rebirth. Then the others. Those who are willing to be opened."

"May I share your journey?"

"You know that answer."

Far off, the dark soul of Kurtz stirred and throbbed. Wait, Gundersen told it. Wait. You will not suffer much longer.

A blast of cold wind struck the mountainside. Sparkling flakes of snow whirled into Gundersen's face. He smiled. He had never felt so free, so light, so young. A vision of a mankind transformed blazed within him. I am the emissary, he thought. I am the bridge over which they shall cross. I am the resurrection and the life. I am the light of the world: he that followeth me shall not walk in darkness, but shall have the light of life. A new commandment I give unto you, that ye love one another.

He said to Ti-munilee, "Shall we go now?"

"I am ready when you are ready."

"Now."

"Now," said the sulidor, and together they began to descend the windswept mountain.